"Hey!" I snapped, trying to tug at my hand but Tate held true and kept dragging me.

"Tate!" I cried, but he kept going, right by the office, right by the storeroom to the dark, poorly lit, very back of the hall.

Then his hands were at my hips and he was pushing me against the wall.

"Tate," I snapped, but he was concentrating on studying my body, his eyes at my chest as his hands slid up my sides to stop with his thumbs right below my breasts, his fingers splayed at my sides.

"Tate," I repeated, but said no more because his head bent and he kissed me.

His lips and tongue worked wonders against my mind. As in clearing it of all thoughts of him not calling for a month and filling it with only thoughts of kissing him back as hard as I could. The beard helped. I'd never been kissed by a man with a beard. It was scratchy, but in a very sexy way.

"Sweet as I remembered," he muttered against my lips.

Acclaim for Kristen Ashley and Her Novels

"A unique, not-to-be-missed voice in romance. Kristen Ashley is a star in the making!"

—Carly Phillips, *New York Times* bestselling author

"I adore Kristen Ashley's books. She writes engaging, romantic stories with intriguing, colorful, and larger-than-life characters. Her stories grab you by the throat from page one and don't let go until well after the last page. They continue to dwell in your mind days after you finish the story and you'll find yourself anxiously awaiting the next. Ashley is an addicting read no matter which of her stories you find yourself picking up."

—Maya Banks, *New York Times* bestselling author

"There is something about them [Ashley's books] that I find crackalicious."
—Kati Brown, DearAuthor.com

"Run, don't walk...to get [the Dream Man] series. I love [Kristen Ashley's] rough, tough, hard-loving men. And I love the cosmo-girl club!"
—NocturneReads.com

"[*Law Man* is an] excellent addition to a phenomenal series!"
—ReadingBetweentheWinesBookclub.blogspot.com

"[*Law Man*] made me laugh out loud. Kristen Ashley is an amazing writer!"
—TotallyBookedblog.com

"I felt all of the rushes, the adrenaline surges, the anger spikes...my heart pumping in fury. My eyes tearing up when my heart (I mean... *her* heart) would break."
—Maryse's Book Blog (Maryse.net) on *Motorcycle Man*

sweet dreams

Also by Kristen Ashley

The Colorado Mountain Series

The Gamble
Lady Luck
Breathe
Jagged
Kaleidoscope

The Dream Man Series

Mystery Man
Wild Man
Law Man
Motorcycle Man

The Chaos Series

Own the Wind
Fire Inside
Ride Steady
Walk Through Fire

sweet dreams

KRISTEN ASHLEY

FOREVER

NEW YORK   BOSTON

Copyright © 2012 by Kristen Ashley
Cover design by Elizabeth Turner
Cover copyright © 2017 by Hachette Book Group, Inc.

Forever
Hachette Book Group
1290 Avenue of the Americas, New York, NY 10104
forever-romance.com
twitter.com/foreverromance

Originally as an ebook by Forever Yours in December 2012
First trade paperback edition: June 2017

Forever is an imprint of Grand Central Publishing. The Forever name and logo are trademarks of Hachette Book Group, Inc.

The publisher is not responsible for websites (or their content) that are not owned by the publisher.

The Hachette Speakers Bureau provides a wide range of authors for speaking events. To find out more, go to www.hachettespeakersbureau.com or call (866) 376-6591.

LCCN: 2017933246

ISBN: 978-1-5387-4435-2

Printed in the United States of America

LSC-C

10   9   8   7   6   5   4   3   2   1

Acknowledgments

A shout-out to John "Dukeboy" Wynne and Gib Moutaw for assisting with this book by advising me on all things football. Thanks for not getting impatient with my constant questions, for giving such informative answers and for reading blocks of dialogue to help me make certain Tate's voice was real. I love you both to the deepest depths of my heart and not just because you explained the NFL Draft to me.

sweet dreams

CHAPTER ONE

Bubba's

I SAT IN my parked car outside the bar.

It looked like a bar. It could be any bar anywhere, small town, big city, it didn't matter. It was just a bar. Bubba's bar, apparently, for it said "Bubba's" in blue lettering on a black background in a huge sign at the top.

I looked out the window to my left. There were two Harley-Davidson motorcycles parked there.

I looked back at the bar, which it would seem might be a bit of a biker bar.

I looked out my window to the right. There was a beat-up, old blue Chevy pickup parked at the edge of the parking lot.

I looked back at the bar, which would seem was not high-class and not highbrow. They probably didn't even have martini glasses.

I looked at the window of the bar. In it there was a sign that said "Help Wanted." In the little white space at the bottom of the sign was written, "Waitress."

I pulled breath in through my nose. Then I exhaled, got out of the car and walked right to the door, through the door, and into the bar.

I was right. Nothing special. Nothing high-class or highbrow. It could be any bar anywhere.

There was a man sitting on a corner stool at the long bar at the back of the room. He had a ball cap on. There were two other men playing pool at one of four pool tables. Two to the left, two to the right, the men were at one of the tables to the left. Evidently, bikers played pool. There was a woman behind the bar. She had a lot of platinum blonde hair. She also had a lot of flesh at her cleavage. I could see this because it was bursting out the top of her Harley tank as well as straining the material.

Her eyes came to the door the minute I walked in and didn't leave me as I walked to the bar.

"Hi," I started.

"Chantelle's about twenty miles down the road. Straight on," the blonde interrupted me. "Just turn right out the parking lot and keep goin'."

"Sorry?" I asked and felt the man with the ball cap turn to look at me.

"You lookin' for Chantelle?" the blonde asked.

"No, I'm—"

"Gnaw Bone?" she asked.

"Gnaw bone?" I repeated.

"Gnaw Bone. Not too far away from Chantelle," she told me. "That what you lookin' for?"

I didn't know what to say. Then I asked, "You mean Gnaw Bone is the name of a town?"

She didn't answer. She looked at the man with the ball cap. I looked too. When I did, I saw firstly that his ball cap had definitely seen better days and those days were about four hundred years ago. Secondly, I saw that he was staring at my breasts.

I looked back at the blonde.

"I'm here about the waitress position."

For a second there was loaded silence. Then the man with the ball cap burst into a loud guffaw.

The blonde's eyes narrowed.

"Did Bubba put you up to this?" she asked.

"Bubba?" I asked back, at this point confused.

"Bubba," she bit out, then glanced around before looking at me. "This ain't funny. I got things to do."

I glanced around too and saw that she actually didn't have much to do. The two guys were playing pool and didn't seem all that thirsty. The ball cap guy had nearly a full draft in front of him.

I looked again at the blonde.

"I'm not kidding," I told her.

"Bullshit," she replied irately, already at the end of her patience.

This was shocking. It wasn't like I'd never heard a curse word before, or used them myself, just that I didn't tend to blurt them out to strangers looking for jobs. Or strangers on the whole. And also I'd been there for about three minutes and hadn't done anything to strain anyone's patience, much less push them to the end of it.

"No, seriously. I'd like to apply for the position," I explained.

She didn't answer for a while and took the time she was silent to study me. I decided to do the same.

She'd be pretty, if she didn't tease her hair out so much and wear that much makeup and look clearly like she was in a bad mood and anyone could set her off. Though she really pulled off that tank top. I had serious cleavage too but it didn't come with a petite, slim but rounded body. It came with a big ass and a mini–Buddha belly and a hint of back fat. Not to mention somewhat flabby arms.

I decided to break the silence and announce, "I'm Lauren Grahame."

I stuck out my hand. She stared at my hand and didn't get the chance to speak because the ball cap man spoke.

"Jim-Billy," he said and I turned to him.

"Sorry?"

His hand was out to me, he was smiling and this time looking into my eyes. On the left side he'd lost the second tooth in and hadn't bothered to replace it. For some reason, instead of this making him look like a hillbilly with bad dental hygiene, it made him look a little goofy and a little sweet.

"Jim-Billy," he repeated. "That's my name."

I took his hand and shook it. "Nice to meet you, Jim-Billy."

I repeated his name because I learned a long time ago at a training seminar to do that when you met someone. It solidified their name in your mind so you wouldn't forget it. I was terrible with names and I found this worked and I figured a waitress in a small town needed to remember the names of the regulars at the bar. And Jim-Billy definitely looked like a regular.

It also worked that I chanted *Jim-Billy, Jim-Billy, Jim-Billy* in my head.

Then again, who'd forget the name Jim-Billy?

He gave me a squeeze, released my hand and his gaze swung to the blonde.

"Tate'll like her. *Big time*," he declared. "Bubba'll like her even better."

"Shut up, Jim-Billy," the blonde muttered.

"About the job...," I stated, bringing us back to the matter at hand and the blonde looked at me.

Then she leaned into me. "Girl, take this as me doin' you a favor. Boys around here"—she threw out a hand—"they'd eat you alive. Go to Chantelle. Gnaw Bone. Woman like you has got no business in Carnal."

Carnal.

That was one of the reasons I picked that town. Its name was Carnal. I thought that was funny and interesting but that was as interesting as I wanted to get.

I wanted to live in a Nowheresville town called Carnal. I wanted to work in an anywhere bar called Bubba's. There was nothing to either, except the names. Nothing memorable. Nothing special. Nothing.

"You don't understand," I told her. "I—"

She leaned back and stated, "Oh girl, I understand." Her eyes moved from the top of my head to my midriff, which was all she could see with the bar in her way then they came back to mine. "You're lookin' for a thrill. You're lookin' for adventure."

"I'm not. I'm—"

She threw her hands up. "You think I don't know it when I see it? Do I look like a woman who ain't been around? Do I look like a woman who feels like hirin' and trainin' and learnin' to put up with the new shit a new waitress is gonna feed me? Then when she realizes that she wants her old life back she ups and leaves and then I have to hire and train and learn to put up with new shit *again*?"

"I wouldn't give you...um..."

"Everyone shovels shit and I don't like the taste of it from *my kind*. I already know I *really* don't like the taste of it from *yours*."

I again didn't know what to say because it was dawning that she was discriminating against me.

"Not to be rude or anything," I said softly, "but you don't really know me. You don't know what kind I am."

"Right," she replied and there was derision heavy in her word.

"You don't," I asserted.

"Girl—" she started but I leaned forward and I did it for a reason.

I leaned forward because I needed her to hear me. I leaned forward because I'd been searching for Carnal a long time. I'd been searching for Bubba's a long time. I needed to be there and to be there I needed that job.

"Right," I repeated. "You think I'm some kind of lost woman like out of a book, traveling the globe on some idiot journey to find myself?" I asked and before she could answer, I continued, "Thinking I can go out there and find good food and experience interesting places while soul searching, wearing fabulous clothes and being gorgeous and making everyone I run into love me and, in the end, find a fantastic man who's really good at sex and adores me beyond reason?" I shook my head. "Well, I'm not. I know who I am and I know what I want and I know that isn't it because that doesn't exist. I also know what I'm looking for and I know I found it right here."

"Listen—" she began.

"No, you listen to me," I interrupted her. "All my life, or as long as I can remember, I thought something special was going to happen to me. I just had this feeling, deep in my bones. I didn't know what it was but it was going to be beautiful, spectacular, *huge*." I leaned in farther. "All...my...life." I shook my head again and put my hand on the bar. "It didn't. I waited and it didn't happen. I waited more and it didn't happen. I waited more and it *still* didn't happen. I tried to make it happen and it *still* didn't happen. Now I know it isn't going to. It's never going to happen because there isn't anything special out there *to* happen."

I sucked in breath, she opened her mouth but I kept talking.

"I had a husband. I had a home. I had a job. I had friends. Then I found out my husband was sleeping with my best friend. Not an affair, they'd been doing it *for five years*. When the cat was out of the bag, they decided to be together for real. He divorced me and I couldn't afford the house on my own so we sold it. Then, all of a sudden, after ten years of being with someone, I was alone. They got the friends who always thought behind my back they were *perfect* together. They all knew. For five years. And no one told me."

"Fuckin' shit, woman," Jim-Billy muttered.

"Yeah," I said to Jim-Billy and looked back at the blonde. "But, you know, after the shock of it wore off, I didn't care. I swear. I didn't. Because all of a sudden I realized that I had a shit marriage to a shit guy and I had a shit best friend and all sorts of other shit friends besides. And all that time I was living in a house I didn't want, it was too darned big and it was too darned *everything*. A house should be a home, not a *house*. And that house was in a town I didn't like because every house looked the same and every woman dressed the same and every man played around the same and every car was shiny and new and there was no personality *anywhere*. And in that town I had a job I didn't much care about even though it paid me good money."

My voice dropped as I went on.

"I realized I didn't have anything special. All of a sudden I realized that life didn't have anything special in store for me."

I took in a breath and finished.

"And I'm okay with that. I don't want special anymore. I waited and I tried to make it happen and it didn't. So be it. Now, I want to live someplace that is just a place. I want a job where I can do a good job while I'm doing it and then I can go home to a place that's a home and just be home. I don't *want* anything. I'm done wanting. I've been wanting and yearning for forty-two years. The only thing I want is peace."

"You think you'll find peace in a Harley bar?" Jim-Billy asked what was possibly a pertinent question and I looked at him.

"I think I can get to work on time, do a good job, feel good about myself because I worked hard and did my best and go home and not think about a Harley bar. I can think about myself or what I have a taste to eat for dinner or what might be good on TV. Then I'll go to sleep not thinking about anything and get up and get to work on time again." I turned to the blonde. "That's what I think. I'm not looking for a thrill. I'm not looking for adventure. I'm looking for nothing special because I can be content with that. That's what I'm looking for. Can you give me that?"

The blonde said nothing, just looked me in the eyes. Her face was blank and no less hard and it stayed blank and hard for a long time.

Then she said, "I'm Krystal. I'll get you an application."

*   *   *

I stood at the window of my hotel room holding the curtains back with a hand and staring at the pool.

Carnal Hotel wasn't much to write home about. A long block of building, two stories, all the doors facing the front, fourteen on top, fourteen on bottom. I was on the bottom in number thirteen. The rooms were clean, mine had a king-sized bed and a TV that had to have been purchased fifteen years ago suspended from the wall. The low four-drawer dresser and nightstands stuck out of the wall and had no legs. The closet had two extra pillows and an extra blanket. The bathtub and kitchen sink had rust stains but even so, they were clean too. The whole of it was below average but it would do.

That pool, though, that was something else. It wasn't big but it was pristine clean. The lounge chairs around it weren't top of the line but they were okay, in great repair, and obviously taken care of.

I looked from the pool to reception. It wasn't so much reception as a tiny house. A tiny well-kept house with a little upstairs. It also had big half barrels full of newly planted flowers out front. It wasn't quite summer but it was the end of spring so the flowers hadn't come close to filling out.

Carnal was in the Rocky Mountains. More precisely, it was in a small valley surrounded by hills that were surrounded by mountains. It was closing on May, there was a nip in the air, and I wondered if those flowers were hopeful.

If they were, whoever planted them had the capacity for a lot of hope. There were more flowers in window boxes in the front windows of the reception-slash-house. There were also more flowers in half barrels intermittently placed by the poles on the walk in front of the hotel rooms with more window boxes on the railing of the balcony in front of the rooms upstairs. And lastly there were more half barrels dotted around the pool area.

The parking lot was tidy and well kept and the hotel and reception/house both had a good paint job.

All of this indicated that Carnal Hotel might be below average but the people who owned it cared about it.

I had checked in with a nice lady at the front desk who said anything I needed, change for the vending machines or laundry room, Wi-Fi access, menus for restaurants and takeout in town, "just holler."

Then I'd unpacked my car. All of it. I unpacked it for the first time in four and a half months. Then I cleaned it out. All the junk food wrappers, discarded pop cans, fallen mints, lost pieces of candy, bits of paper. The flotsam and jetsam of a killer road trip. I lugged my suitcases (there were five) and boxes (there were two) into the hotel room and took a plastic bag I'd found and filled full of trash to the big outdoor bin tucked close to the side of the hotel not facing any streets.

Then I unpacked my clothes.

Over the past four and a half months, I'd been in tons of hotel rooms but I'd never unpacked. I'd never stayed beyond three days. I'd only stayed long enough to do laundry, take a breather, and decide where I'd head next in my search, zigzagging across so many states I'd lost count in my search for Nowheresville.

After I unpacked, I'd walked into town, which amounted to me walking by room number fourteen and turning the corner. Carnal Hotel was on the edge of town right before the road opened up to nothing again. I'd found a deli, bought a pastrami on rye and ate it on the sidewalk, chasing it with a diet pop. Then I'd walked the town up one side and down the other.

Bubba's was in the middle, five blocks from the hotel, and it was definitely a biker bar because Carnal was a biker town. There were two bike shops and one bike mechanic at the opposite end from Carnal Hotel and it had a sign that said "We Take Cars Too." There were also three motorcycle paraphernalia shops that I could see, looking in the windows, sold a lot of leather bike accessories and more leather biker clothing.

There was also the deli, a diner, an Italian restaurant, a pizza delivery place and a coffee house, which was strangely called La-La Land Coffee. Again looking in the windows of La-La Land, I saw it was not run by bikers but hippies that were so hippie they wore tie-dyed shirts with peace signs on front and had long hair. One of the two behind the counter had on round, blue-tinted sunglasses even though he was inside and the other had a thin braided headband wrapped around her forehead. They looked in danger of dropping cross-legged on the floor and singing "Kumbaya."

This all was intermingled with a discount tobacco store that sold all types of smoker delights for all types of things you could smoke. There were two discount liquor stores, a drugstore, and a tailor who seemed to specialize in stitching biker patches into leather (or at least that was what the sign in the window said).

The town also had two convenience stores, one opposite the hotel, one at the other end of town opposite the mechanic. It had a busy grocery store about a quarter the size of the mega–grocery stores that every other town in the nation seemed to have and it looked like it'd been there since 1967.

All this was rounded out by a bakery, a hardware store, a flower shop, a gas station, and a variety of other Nowheresville places to fill a Nowheresville town.

There were people on the street and I knew they were friendly because most of them smiled at me.

After I checked out the Main Street (called Main Street and it was also the only street with businesses, the rest was residential) of my new home, I went back to reception at the hotel. I bought a week's worth of Wi-Fi from the nice lady who took that opportunity to share with me that her name was Betty. I shared my name too and decided to go ahead and pay a week in advance on my room when I got the Wi-Fi. This decision overjoyed Betty and I knew that because she told me.

"Sweetie! A week! I'm overjoyed!" she'd shouted.

She would be. Mine was the only car in the lot and she had a flower and pool habit and those weren't exactly cheap.

Nevertheless, she was friendly and open and I decided I liked Betty.

After telling her I was glad I'd brought her joy, I went back to number thirteen and dragged out my laptop. Then I logged in.

I ignored all my e-mail and sent a message to my parents and my baby sister that all was well, I was fine, and I'd check in with more information later. I saw that they'd sent e-mails to me but I didn't read them. I didn't read them because I knew they would freak me out because I knew my mom and dad and sister Caroline were freaked out. They weren't big on me upping stakes and roaming the country looking for nothing special. They were bigger on me moving home, sorting myself out, finding a decent man and starting over (in that order).

I shut down my computer, sat on the big, soft bed, stared at the wall and thought about the next day when I was supposed to be at Bubba's at eleven to train to be a waitress and start my new life.

Then I smiled.

After that, I watched TV until it got dark and the pool beckoned me.

Now I was standing and looking outside to see the pool was clean and enticing and it was all lit up. In fact, the parking lot was all lit up. Seeing it, I knew four things about Reception Betty. She was friendly, she liked flowers, she was proud of her below-average hotel and small but clean pool, and she wanted her guests to feel safe.

That's when I saw the car pull in. It was a convertible, an old model something. It looked like a Chrysler, not great condition but also not a junker.

It parked outside reception, the door opened and a woman folded out.

I stared at the woman.

She had thick, long dark hair and long legs most of which I could see coming out the bottom of her very short, frayed-hemmed jean skirt. She had a tight tank top and more cleavage than Krystal (but as much as me). She wasn't petite or slim. She was long and *very* rounded but it was clear she didn't care. A mini–Buddha belly and a hint of back fat didn't bother her. Not in the slightest. In fact, she *worked it*.

She sashayed into reception and I saw a man was there.

He was Betty's upper-middle-age. He smiled at her like he knew her and she waved and smiled back giving the same impression. I knew this was the truth when he handed her a key without doing any of the usual checking in business.

She took the key, put both her hands on the counter, lifted herself up, booty pointed up in the air, feet in high-heeled stiletto sandals on tiptoe. She kicked back one foot and leaned toward him, giving him an across-the-counter air kiss. Then she strutted back out to her convertible, got in and drove through the parking lot to park three spots down from my Lexus. She got out, didn't grab a suitcase, and walked toward a door where I lost sight of her.

I had a feeling I was going to have to buy some tank tops to fit in in Carnal.

I dropped the curtain and went to the dresser. Most of my clothes were folded and sitting on top, there wasn't enough room for them all in the drawers and closet. But at least they'd been released from their suitcase captivity. In the drawers I'd put my underwear, socks and pajamas. I'd also put my bathing suit in there.

Seeing my clothes laid out I thought it wasn't much but it was more home than I'd had in a good long while and it made me feel weirdly settled.

It had been a warm day but it couldn't be over sixty-five degrees outside. Still, I loved pools, I loved to be in water, and for some reason I really wanted a swim so I figured it would be like any time you got in cold water. Once you were in, you'd get used to it. At least I hoped so. If not, so what? I'd just drag my carcass out and come back to my room.

I changed into my swimsuit, put on a pair of track pants, a sweatshirt and some flip-flops. Before I could chicken out, I grabbed a towel and my room key and headed to the pool.

I slipped off my shoes and sweats and decided to dive right in. Better to get it over with all at once. I moved to the side of the pool, braced for impact and dove.

The pool was heated.

Heaven.

I swam five laps of the short pool and had to stop because I couldn't breathe. This, I told myself, had to do with the fact that I was in the Rocky Mountains, at altitude, and it did *not* have to do with the fact that I was seriously out of shape.

I forced out four more laps and had to stop again.

Then I forced out one more lap and put a hand to the edge to turn back for another lap when I heard the roar of bike pipes.

Stopped at the edge of the pool, holding on and peering over the side, my eyes followed the black and chrome Harley gleaming in Reception Betty's parking lot lights as it glided along, pulled in and parked next to the convertible. Then my eyes watched the man shove the stand down with his booted foot and swing his leg off the bike.

His back was to me so all I could see was that he was tall and he had a *great* behind. He also had on faded jeans and a long-sleeved black thermal shirt and he had a head of thick dark hair that also shone in the lights, just like his Harley.

One of the hotel room doors opened and the woman in the jean miniskirt ran out and threw herself at the tall man. Her arms wrapped around his neck and I couldn't see it but I could tell her lips latched on to his.

He didn't even go back on a foot when her body impacted his. He just curved his arms around her and leaned into her kiss.

That's something special.

The thought just popped into my head and I didn't know why. I didn't know what was happening. I didn't know these two people. All I knew was that it *looked* special. So special, all I could do was stare.

They stopped kissing and she tipped her head back and laughed with pure delight, the sound ringing through the air, filling it with music.

I decided I hated her and I didn't know why. I didn't know who she was or what was happening. I just knew she had something special and I didn't and never would and that sucked. It wasn't a nice thought, which was unusual because I was normally a nice person. But it was the one I had.

She disengaged from him and came to his side, wrapping her arm around his waist and propelling him forward.

He looked down at her and I saw his profile in Reception Betty's bright parking lot lights and when I did I held my breath.

If he was that handsome in profile, so handsome he was breathtaking, he'd be sensational full-on.

That's when I decided I *really* hated her.

They got close to the door and he moved suddenly and quickly. Swinging her up in front of him, she wrapped her legs around his hips, her arms around his shoulders and tipped her head down to look at him. But he seemed to be peering in the room like he expected to see something or someone, something or someone important, something or someone he was looking forward to seeing. But before he found that something or someone, she fisted a hand in his hair, tilting his back, her mouth went down on his and they entered the room necking.

He closed the door with his booted foot.

Yes, sensational. If he could pick her up like that and carry her anywhere, he was beyond sensational.

"Like the pool?"

I jumped and pushed off the side with my foot, my head jerking around as I stared at the Reception Guy who checked in Lucky as Hell Girl that I hated. He was standing at the side of the pool and looking down at me. I was so engrossed in Handsome Harley Guy and Lucky as Hell Girl I hadn't heard him coming.

"Sorry?" I asked.

"The pool," he answered. "Like it?"

"Um…," I mumbled, staring up at him. "Yes."

"It's heated," he informed me.

"Um…," I mumbled again. "I can tell."

"Betty 'n' me got it relined last year. One or t'other of us clean it every day. Best pool in the county."

I couldn't disagree. It was a fantastic pool, clean, heated, and everything.

Therefore I said, "It's really nice."

He rocked back on his heels and took in the pool with his eyes before he looked back at me.

"Thanks. Ned," he said.

"Uh, my name is Lauren," I said back and he laughed.

"No, pretty lady. Name's Ned." He jerked a thumb at himself. "I'm Ned."

"Oh," I replied, feeling like an idiot. "Hey, Ned."

"Hey back atcha, Lauren." He grinned. "Betty tells me you're stayin' awhile."

"Yeah," I told him thinking he seemed friendly enough but not certain how much to share because, well, I didn't know him and every girl in a pool in the parking lot of a hotel on the edge of Nowheres-ville should be smart and not tell their story, current or past, to some random man who snuck up on them. In fact, girls like that should get out of the pool, get into their room, and lock the danged door.

"That's great." Ned was still grinning. "We don't get a lot of long-timers. Weekenders. Nighters. Yeah. Long-timers. No."

"Oh," I replied, my eyes going back to the long block of hotel, specifically to my room where I figured I should be at that present moment.

"That's Neeta," Ned said and I looked back at him.

"Neeta?" I asked.

Ned nodded. "Neeta and Jackson." He shook his head. "Bad news."

My gaze slid back in the direction of the hotel. He'd misinter-preted where I was looking. He thought I was looking at Harley Guy and Lucky as Hell Girl's room.

I didn't inform him of his mistake. Instead, I asked softly, "Bad news?"

"Yeah," Ned answered. "She swings into town and shoo!" My eyes went to him to see he'd put his hands up at his sides and had taken a step back. "We brace."

"Brace for what?" I asked.

He dropped his hands. "Brace for whatever Neeta's got up her sleeve."

"Is that…" I stopped and motioned toward the Harley and the convertible with my head, "Neeta with that man?"

"Jackson, yeah. He's great, a good man, smart, solid, salt of the earth. Loses his mind around Neeta, though. Then again, not many men wouldn't but I'm guessing you know all about that."

My eyes had wandered back to the Harley as I treaded water and Ned talked but I looked at Ned when I heard his comment.

"I do?"

His grin came back and it was bigger this time, brighter, trans-forming his whole face, making me think he might just be a friendly innkeeper in a biker town in the Rocky Mountains, just like he seemed.

"Sure you do. Ain't shittin' me, pretty lady."

He was right. I wasn't shitting him mostly because I had no idea what he was talking about.

"Figure, though," he went on and his eyes moved toward the Harley, "you'd be worth whatever trouble you might cause."

"What?" I whispered and he looked back at me.

"I'm a good judge of people," he informed me instead of explaining himself.

"Yes?" I asked because I didn't know what else to say.

"Yeah," he replied quietly, moved closer to the edge of the pool and squatted down. I kept treading water and staring at him. "See," he continued, still quiet, "any trouble you might cause I'm guessin' would be trouble you don't mean to cause."

"I've never caused any trouble," I told him.

This was true. I hadn't. I was a good girl. I'd always been a good girl.

I'd always made the right decisions and done the right things. I might have chosen the wrong husband and the wrong friends but they were the jerks in those scenarios, not me. I was nice. I was thoughtful. I was considerate. I looked out for my neighbors. I got up when old ladies needed a seat in a waiting room. I let people who had two or three items go in front of me at the checkout in grocery stores if I had a full cart of food. I kept secrets. I bit my lip when people I knew did stupid things I knew they would regret and then kept biting my lip when those stupid things bit them in the ass and they came to me and whined about it.

I didn't wear miniskirts, not ones with frayed hems, not any miniskirts at all. If I did, I wouldn't wear them with high-heeled sandals. Maybe flip-flops or flats but not high heels. I didn't air kiss front desk reception guys named Ned even if I knew them. I didn't drive a convertible. I didn't rush out a door and throw myself in the arms of a man.

And I'd never laughed so loud I filled the air with music.

"Betty's different than me." Ned broke into my thoughts and I focused on him.

"She is?" I asked, thinking I may have missed something.

"I'm a good judge of people. She's got the sight."

"The sight?" I repeated stupidly.

He grinned again while straightening. It was his big grin. He had all his teeth, the left eyetooth was wonky but they were all clean and white and the rest were straight. His hair was a little thin, light brown. He wasn't tall, not short either. Lean and on the thin side. And, I was beginning to believe, a genuinely nice guy, not the creepy night clerk at a hotel in Nowheresville.

"The sight." He nodded then looked toward the hotel before he turned to me as I moved my arms through the water to take me back to the side so I could stop treading. I reached out and held on to the edge as he kept going. "She told me she met you and she just knew."

"Knew what?"

"Somethin' big was gonna happen."

I blinked and it wasn't to get the water out of my eyes.

"Something big?"

"Yep."

"To me?"

"To you, through you, because of you, whatever. But whatever it is, it'll be big and it'll be good."

I didn't know what to do with this mostly because it was a little crazy.

"She said that?"

He nodded and crossed his arms on his chest, rocking back on his heels again.

"Yep. And she's never wrong. We been married twenty-five years and she gets these feelin's and, I'll repeat, she's never wrong. My Betty's always right. Always."

I didn't know what to say to that so I stayed silent.

"Anyhoots!" he exclaimed loudly. "Best leave you to your swim.

You need anythin' at all, you know where to find me. I hit the hay around midnight but you just gotta ring the buzzer outside the front door and it'll wake me up. Yeah?"

I nodded.

"Anythin' you need, pretty lady, I mean that," he said and it sounded like he meant it.

"Okay," I replied.

"Glad to have you with us, Lauren."

"Thanks, Ned."

He lifted a hand in a wave and wandered back to the reception/house.

I looked at the Harley and listened to the quiet of Carnal.

Then I forced out ten more laps (with three more rest periods), got out of the pool, toweled off, grabbed my stuff, and ran to my room.

CHAPTER TWO

A Job to Do

I spent more time wondering what to wear to work than I did training at Bubba's.

Since Krystal was in a tank top the day before, I decided that it probably wasn't work casual, more like anything goes.

So I put on a nice pair of jeans, a belt, and a peachy-pink colored T-shirt that had a crew neck and three ruffles made up the sleeves. I thought it was bright and cute. My ex, Brad, told me he thought it was a little young for me but I liked it, I thought it suited my coloring. I wore flip-flops because I usually wore flip-flops if I could but also because I figured I'd need comfortable shoes. I put in some earrings that were little dangles of peachy-pink crystals, a half-inch choker that was a net of peachy-pink beads and a bunch of brace-lets that were elasticized bands of multicolored crystal beads, peach, pink, peachy-pink, creamy peach, creamy pink, clear, and I threw in a couple of blue ones to go with my jeans.

I walked from the hotel to Bubba's thinking that I should have planned ahead last night and maybe stocked some provisions in my room. I left early so I could pop by the bakery to get a doughnut and a coffee. I hadn't even thought of dinner the night before and didn't eat any so I was starving.

My muscles also ached. It was dull but they were not used to being worked. They'd been cooped up in a car for four and a half months for one. But even before that it wasn't like I was a regular at the gym. I didn't think this was good considering I'd be on my feet all day.

Krystal was there when I got there and I knew right off she was in a bad mood. I didn't know why but I suspected it was because there were some dirty glasses and beer bottles left out "on the floor" as she called it. Though most of them were on ledges on the walls around the pool tables and not on the floor at all. Also, when we turned the chairs off the tables, most of them hadn't been wiped down.

I suspected this was why she was in a bad mood because she muttered irately, "Fuckin' Tonia and Jonelle. How many times do I gotta tell them? Wipe the tables, clear the floor of empties. Shit." She looked at me. "You got evening shift, you clear the empties off the floor and wipe down the tables real good. It ain't hard to do and Anita comes in in the mornin' to sweep and mop so it ain't like you're part cleanin' lady."

I nodded, making a mental note to clear the empties and wipe down the tables "real good." I did this because I figured that Krystal was the sort of person who didn't need a lot to tick her off and I didn't want to do anything to add to her seemingly perpetual bad mood.

She showed me around the bar but there wasn't much to it. The front, which had the bar, a mess of tables out front, and the pool tables to the sides. She explained that day shift there was only one waitress and bartender unless it was a weekend. If it was a weekend, the floor was split into two sections for two waitresses. Weeknights there were always two waitresses and one or two bartenders. Weekend nights there were three waitresses and at least two bartenders.

"We don't have no busser," she informed me, leading me out of the bar and down one of the two doorways that led off the back of the bar. It had a sign over it that said "Private Do Not Enter." "Don't need another person on payroll when you waitresses can nab your own empties."

I nodded even though she wasn't looking at me.

She took me to an office and let us in. "You stow your purse in here and you take your breaks in here. We don't give keys out to everyone so you need to come back here, you find Tate, Bubba, Dalton or me to let you in."

"Tate, Bubba and Dalton?" I asked.

"Bubba's my old man," she answered. "Tate owns the bar with us. He ain't around a lot. Then again, Bubba ain't around a lot either. Like now. He's *fishin'*." She said the word "fishin'" like it tasted bad and she had to get it out of her mouth fast or she'd have that taste forever. "Dalton's the other bartender," she finished.

"Oh. Okay," I said and she eyed me.

"Gonna say this now, gonna say it once. Bubba, Tate, and me own this place and Bubba's been in my bed goin' on a decade. That's about as much fraternization as we need. Half the time I don't *want* that jackass in my bed, half the time he ain't in my bed because he's fishin'. You get an eye for Tate or Dalton, and they all get an eye for Tate or Dalton, rethink it. You're here to work, not get laid."

"Oh," I repeated, more than a little surprised at this subject matter and the way she presented it. "Okay."

She didn't move but she spoke. "Not jokin', girl."

"Um…" I decided to give as good as I got in an effort to make her think I wasn't the fancy pants she clearly thought I was from her comments the day before. Though, in all honesty, I kind of was or at least I wasn't a biker babe like her. "I'm not exactly in the market to get laid, Krystal."

She kept staring at me. Then she moved out of the office muttering, "Yeah, you haven't seen Tate or Dalton yet."

I had to admit this worried me a little bit. I didn't need to be working alongside good-looking men, especially starting out. It'd make me anxious. Once I got used to things, got my bearings, I'd be fine mainly because I wasn't lying. I wasn't in the market to get laid. That market had closed and I was okay with that. But I didn't want to be fumbling around learning how to be a waitress in a biker bar with handsome biker men as my audience.

As if she read my mind, Krystal talked as she led me down the hall. "I'm keepin' you on day shifts for a week, maybe two, see how you do. Cut your teeth. Get the lay of the land before you go nights."

"Thanks," I said when she stopped outside a closed door.

She turned to me. "Don't thank me. Tips are shit on the day shift."

She unlocked and pushed open the door and showed me the storeroom. Then she told me that waitresses might be called on to help stock or run back and get something if the bartenders were busy. She showed me the clipboard where they kept track of stock in a complicated way that would be far easier if put on a computer spreadsheet. Even though I probably could set that up for her in about an hour, I didn't inform her of this.

"We open at noon close at three," she went on, walking back down the hall. "Shifts run eleven to seven with two fifteen-minute breaks and half-hour dinner break. Night shift is seven to three. Last call is two thirty so you get those drinks in and you get your cleanup done best you can while we got folks in the bar. You don't wanna be hangin' around 'til four clearin' and cleanin' and I don't wanna be payin' you to do it. Yeah?"

"Yes." I nodded but she wasn't looking at me. She was leading me through the bar and taking me toward the other hall. The opening had a sign over it that said "Restrooms."

"Anita cleans these in the mornin' and loads 'em up with toilet paper. We got a customer reports a bathroom problem with the toilets, you tell one of the boys. Toilet paper is in the storeroom. You might need to restock and, I'm warnin' you, you might need to do cleanup. Shit happens you would *not* believe in the bathroom of a bar." She stopped in the hall between the two bathroom doors, ladies up front, gents to the rear, and she turned to me. "You got a problem with that?"

"Are we talking vomit?" I asked because I had to admit, I was not a vomit person.

"Vomit, piss, shit, anything a body can produce, I've had to clean it up."

I felt my eyes get big and I asked, "Anything?"

"Girl, this is a biker bar. Those boys get randy, they need to get off and they don't care much where they get them some. And girls who hang with bikers care even less."

"Wow," I whispered.

"So, you got a problem with that?" she repeated.

I looked at her and straightened my spine. "You can get used to anything, right?"

She stared at me a second then mumbled, "Right."

She took me back front and showed me how to use the cash register.

She finished with, "You'll have a float in your apron and you'll figure your own way to keep tabs on what you're sellin' and what's in your apron. Me, Bubba, Dalton, or Tate will cash you out, take your float and our take and do the reconcile, leavin' you with your tips." She gave me a hard look. "It'd be in your best interest to keep on top a' that. It gets busy, you'll be bustin' your hump to earn those tips. I ain't sayin' any of us'll fuck you over. I'm just sayin' you need to look out for yourself. And you fuck up on a transaction, that's your gig. You sell what you sell, you track it, we track it. It all don't jive, it comes outta your tips. You won't use the register much but you should know your way around."

I nodded. She studied me as if thinking it wasn't sinking in due to the fact that middle-class women were incapable of selling a beer, making change, and keeping track due to their middle-class nature. Then she shrugged as if it was all the same to her.

She showed me the complicated three-sink procedure of how to wash glasses, where empty bottles went, and told me that bartenders did most of the washing but if things were busy, the waitresses were expected to pitch in where they could. She gave me a paper with a list of drinks and snacks (they sold bags of potato chips, pork rinds, and peanuts) and their prices.

"Memorize that, soon's you can," she ordered then crossed her arms under her tank top–covered bosoms (another Harley tank, this one white with very cool silver, red, and black lettering) and looked me in the eye. "We get trouble, Lauren, and it isn't infrequent-like. Boys come in here, get blitzed, act stupid. Some of 'em got knives, all of 'em got fists. You sense trouble, you tell me, Bubba, Tate, or Dalton and you stay clear."

I wasn't happy with the cleaning up of vomit and anything else a body can produce part of the job description but men with knives was taking it to a new level.

Though I also had to admit to some concern that she'd want me to tell her. She was four inches shorter than me and at least fifty pounds lighter. She had no business wading into a knife fight, or *any* fight.

I decided to focus on the latter.

"Tell *you*?" I asked.

"Me," she answered.

"But, shouldn't I get a man—?"

"I been around the block, girl, and this is my fuckin' bar. It's been my fuckin' bar for five years. You think I can't sort out trouble?"

"Um . . . you're five foot five and weigh about a hundred pounds," I informed her of a fact she likely knew (though I was being nice about the weight, considering her behind and cleavage).

"I'm smart, fast but that don't matter since I know where we keep our shotgun," she replied. "Even wasted, men stop fightin' quick when they got a loaded shotgun aimed at 'em." She pointed across the room to the wall where there were a bunch of visible pockmarks in the wood. "Buckshot. Mine. Round these parts it's not only known that I know where the shotgun is but that I know how to use it and someone messes around in my bar, I *will*."

I nodded again wondering why I was undeterred by the variety of craziness she was telling me and standing there listening to her rather than saying, "Thanks…but, um, I think I'll just be leaving."

Instead, I said, "Okay."

"All right," she replied and the door opened.

We both turned to look and when I saw who came in I stopped breathing.

It was the Harley Guy from last night at the hotel. Even though I hadn't seen his face straight on, I knew it was him. And I was right. He was sensational straight on.

He was tall, maybe taller than he seemed in the parking lot or maybe he just seemed bigger in the bar since his shoulders were so broad. But his hips were lean and his legs were long, his thighs obviously powerfully muscled—I could tell that even through his jeans.

His dark brown hair gleamed even in the dull light of the bar. It was thick and it was clear he washed it and let it fall where it lay for the part was natural and not straight. It was swept back but some of it fell around his temples and curled a bit around his ears and at the back of his neck.

His eyes looked dark, I couldn't tell the color but there were sun lines emanating from the sides that were attractive. His brow was heavy. His nose wasn't perfect but it was straight with a slight bump at the top of the bridge that made it interesting. His cheekbones were cut and his jaw was strong.

His skin was tanned in a way where I knew he didn't get that color lounging by a pool.

And he was wearing faded jeans, black motorcycle boots, and a long-sleeved, skintight heather gray–blue thermal henley.

He was beautiful.

"Hey, Tate," Krystal called and I turned woodenly to her.

Okay, maybe Krystal was right earlier. I hadn't seen "Tate" yet though I had. I just didn't know it and thought his name was Jackson.

And if this was Tate then I definitely wanted to get laid by him. Definitely.

Though a man like that who could get a girl like Neeta wouldn't even look at me, and he could get a girl like Neeta. He already had Neeta but hell, he could get anyone.

I turned back to Tate to find I was wrong. He was close, stopped at the side of the bar where there was an opening. I saw his eyes were dark brown and they were on me.

"Who's this?" he asked, his voice deep and a bit rough. He didn't take his eyes off me and, like Krystal, he looked like he was in a bad mood.

"This is Lauren, our new girl," Krystal answered.

I opened my mouth to say hello when he spoke.

"*Lauren?*" he asked and his tone was scathing. Downright scathing. And his face had gone from making him look like he was in a bad mood to sheer and utter contempt.

I felt my body automatically get tight.

"Yeah, Lauren, she's—" Krystal started but he interrupted her.

"Talk," he growled and then turned down the hall.

Krystal looked at me. "Check the fridges." She pointed to a bunch of glass-fronted, half fridges at the back of the bar. "See what we need to stock up and go to the storeroom. Put the new ones in the back, the old ones in the front." She handed me her set of keys and followed Tate down the hall.

I waited a second because I was recovering from that strange scene and wondering why all these people took an instant dislike to me. Krystal hired me, which was good but she wasn't exactly welcoming even during training. And Tate, well...

I shook this feeling off as just my inexperience with biker folk. Maybe they were a close-knit group and you had to prove yourself. I could do that. I hadn't waitressed since I was a cocktail waitress at a dinner theater during my summers in college but it couldn't be difficult to pick it up again. I was a hard worker. As far as I could remember, my entire work life I'd called in sick once when I got the flu. I hated being late and never was. In fact, usually I was early. Once they got to know me, I told myself, they'd like me.

I walked down the hall and the door was closed to the office. I nearly made it to the storeroom when I heard Tate's raised voice.

"Jesus, Krys, maybe you wanna talk to me before you hire some sorry-ass, old, fat, suburban bitch to drag around our goddamned bar?"

I stopped and had to put a hand to the wall to hold myself up.

Sorry-ass, old, fat, suburban bitch.

That beautiful man's words ricocheted around my head causing damage that was so excruciating I knew the way it was inflicted it would never, *never* heal.

Then my body jolted and I rushed to the storeroom, found the key on the fourth try and went in, flipping on the light switch and closing the door behind me.

I leaned in and put my forehead to it.

Okay, I was forty-two, not exactly a spring chicken. Okay, I wasn't svelte by a long shot and had a body that just couldn't *be* svelte and never would even if I tried (though I could stand to take off a few pounds, or more than a few). But I wasn't sorry-ass. And I'd lived in suburbia but I'd never liked it. I just told myself for Brad, because I loved him, that I did. But it wasn't me and the minute I got my chance, I left.

And forty-two wasn't eighty-five. I was over twenty years away from retirement. That was hardly *old*.

Not everyone could be gorgeous, like him. Not everyone could have fantastic bone structure, like him. Not everyone could have thick, gorgeous hair, like him. Not everyone could have a beautiful body, like him. Most of that (maybe not the body, because that would take work) he inherited from his parents! He was just lucky! Not everyone was that lucky, especially not me.

What a jerk!

"Fuck him," I whispered and pressed my lips together because I didn't like to swear. Then, out of my control, I whispered, "Fuck Krystal too."

I turned and stared at the shelves filled with bottles of liquor, crates of beer and wine, kegs lined up the walls, boxes of potato chips, and huge plastic wrapped rolls of toilet paper and I realized that I didn't take stock of what I needed before I went in there.

Whatever.

Whatever!

This was my life as I wanted to lead it. This was the place I wanted to live it. I'd been on the road driving through towns and cities looking for what I needed and after four and a half months, this was the only place that felt right. And Bubba's felt right too. Even though it wasn't much and the people weren't nice, it still felt right.

And I didn't care if they didn't like me. I didn't care if they didn't think I was one of them. I didn't care that my jeans cost twice as much as theirs and my T-shirt was designer and they saw it, knew it, and didn't like it.

Fuck them. Both of them.

I walked out of the storeroom and back into the bar. I found a sheet of paper, took stock of what was needed and went back to the storeroom to search through the shelves and find it. I was on trip three and squatted down rotating bottles of Bud and Coors Light when I heard them come back.

I sucked in breath, looked up and when I did I looked right at Tate. When my eyes caught his, I watched his face change sharply and it did this with a small head twitch and wince.

He knew I'd heard him and at least the jerk had the good grace to react.

I put in the last bottles, stood, pushed the fridge door to and walked toward them both, saying, "One more trip and restock should be done. I made notes of what I took and I'll mark it on your clipboard. Then I'll wipe down the tables."

I walked by them, down the hall and into the storeroom.

Fuck them.

Both of them.

I had a job to do.

CHAPTER THREE

Shake It Off

I walked out of my hotel room and the door closed behind me.

"Hey, hon," Betty called. "That's a pretty top."

I turned to Betty to see she had a hose and was doing her morning watering of the flowers. She had on a sundress, a light cardigan, and hot pink Crocs. Her hair was dyed a very flaming red and was pulled back in a ponytail. Her legs had a hint of tan I guessed because she was often out watering her flowers or cleaning the pool or sweeping the walkways or cleaning the cool deck around the pool with a blast from the hose. And I noticed she was always in a sundress.

I was on day four in Carnal just about to start day three of my job at Bubba's.

I hadn't been wrong. It wasn't hard to pick up, but then again the traffic in the bar was light. During the day it was mostly Jim-Billy and a few drifters. It started to get busier around five and by the time I left at seven thirty (the first day because Tonia had been late coming in) and seven twenty (the second day because Jonelle had been late) it was going on really busy.

The hardest part was remembering what everything cost and making change on the fly. I'd screwed up my float the first day and because of that went home with fifteen dollars' worth of tips. I'd learned quickly the next day and told my customers I was new and took my time and luckily they didn't seem to mind. I still went home with only twenty-three dollars' worth of tips. The day shift seriously wouldn't cut it if I actually had to make a living at this.

Luckily, I had my share of what Brad and I made off the house plus me selling everything I owned in an "everything must go" yard sale before I got the heck out of the Horizon Summit housing development where Brad and I had lived for five years (the five years he was screwing Hayley). We had a huge house with four bedrooms and three-and-a-half baths and a yard that a man named Juan-Carlos, who had seven thousand Mexican men working for him, tended. We had Juan-Carlos because all our friends used Juan-Carlos and we did what all our friends did. I also had a girl named Griselle who cleaned my house because everyone used Griselle and her sister Alicia.

That wasn't my choice, it was Brad's. He said people like us had cleaning ladies.

But I kind of liked cleaning. It was one thing I could do where I could see the results and I used to put on music and not even think about what I was doing, just fade into the music and move around my house and clean. Cleaning my house, weirdly, was the only time I liked to be in it. Then Griselle came and, well, that was that.

I wasn't loaded but I had a significant nest egg. Then again, I might want to buy a house in Carnal eventually and would need money to set that up with furniture and the like and the money I had wouldn't last forever. I couldn't make it on twenty-three dollars a day plus the terrible hourly rate I got. I was going to have to step things up somehow.

I walked to Betty and smiled.

"Thanks, I like your sundress too," I told her.

"Momma always put me in a skirt. Said, she had a girl, no girl of hers would wear pants and, as you can see, she had a girl." She grinned at the spray shooting at her flowers and kept talking. "I can count on one hand the times I been in pants. Don't know why. What Momma did just took and I never think about puttin' on pants." Betty finished sharing a random piece of her life, looked my way, then nodded to my top. "You're good with color. I notice you always pick the right ones. Perfect for you."

I looked down at myself.

I was wearing my last pair of the three pairs of jeans I owned. These were slightly more faded and beat up than the others I'd worn the previous two days to Bubba's. I'd had them a while and I actually hadn't worn them for some time because they were getting too tight. They fit now, for some reason, were even a bit loose, so I went with them.

I also had on a pale pink camisole over which I wore a nearly see-through kelly green blouse. It had a little ruffle around the rounded collar and the cuffs of the short sleeves. It also had tiny ruffles and pin tucks down the front of it and teeny pearl buttons, a lot of them. I paired this with silver stud earrings in the shapes of little daisies, a bunch of silver bangles on my wrist with dangly daisies or roses on them and a pair of kelly green suede flats with a big flower on the rounded toe.

"Thanks," I said to Betty.

"Uppin' the class at Bubba's, you are," Betty smiled at me.

I'd told her yesterday when I chatted with her before walking to the bar that I was working at Bubba's.

Thinking on it, her comment wasn't exactly welcome, albeit kind.

Thankfully, Tate had left before I got back from the storeroom on day one and hadn't been around day two. But Krystal, who had been my bartender both days, hadn't thawed (not even a little). Having briefly met both Tonia and Jonelle, I noted they were worse than Krystal on the frosty front.

The only people I figured liked me were Jim-Billy, Nadine (another regular who showed around four each day so far), and Dalton who showed at five thirty both days.

Dalton was very good-looking too. Longish, dirty blond hair that nearly hit his shoulders, lean body but without the bulk and power of Tate's. He was just a couple of inches taller than me unlike Tate, who had to be four or five inches taller than me and I was five foot nine. And Dalton wore jeans like they were invented solely for him and thus he needed to be consulted by all and sundry for his approval before they could don a pair. Last, Dalton had an easy smile that he flashed a lot and I could tell straight away it was genuine.

Even with the half-and-half mix of those who might like me and those who didn't, I didn't think me wearing a blouse that cost more than two pairs of Levi's was going to be jotted in the good column during my job evaluation. Then again, I didn't have many T-shirts and I figured Krystal's Harley tanks, being authentic Harley-Davidson gear, weren't exactly cheap.

"I should probably go to the mall. Get some stuff to fit in with everyone else," I suggested to Betty.

She stopped the spray on the hose and yanked it down to the pot in front of room fourteen with me following, all while advising, "Hon, you look sweet. Be yourself. Only thing you can be."

I filed that away but still figured I should up my T-shirt inventory even though Tonia and Jonelle didn't wear T-shirts. When I met Tonia, she was wearing a tan piece of soft triangular suede covering her breasts held in place with nothing but a thin strap around her back and another one wrapped around her neck. Jonelle was in a sparkly purple tube top. No way was I going to ever be able to wear a backless, suede halter top or a tube top. Never.

If I wanted to fit in, T-shirts were my only way to go.

"Maybe you're right," I said to Betty while she sprayed her barrel. "Gotta go get coffee and breakfast."

Betty nodded and looked at me. "You ever wanna come over for breakfast, you just come on over and ring. Ned's usually still asleep when I open at seven but I always get me a good breakfast in, the whole shebang. Eggs, bacon, toast or pancakes and sausage. Gotta set yourself up for the day right. Even if you ain't a big eater in the mornin', we always got a good pot o' joe on and you're always welcome to a mug."

I had to admit, waiting until ten thirty to get my first hit of caffeine wasn't working for me. I'd intended to ask Betty or Ned if I could put an electric kettle in my room but hadn't had the chance. The first night after work I'd been dog tired. I wasn't run off my feet until the end of the night when it got busy but I was still recovering from my swim. I'd just gone to the hotel room and crashed. Didn't even get any dinner. The second night after work I'd walked straight to the diner and had a burger, got my second wind, and went to the hotel and had a swim. Then I'd crashed.

"Do you mind if I buy an electric kettle for my room?" I asked. "It might take me a while to get myself a place and—"

I stopped talking because she stopped the spray on the hose and turned to me.

"Sure thing, Lauren, that's a great idea. And we got one a' those little minifridges. We ain't usin' it. I'll get Ned to put it in your room. You're gonna be around a while you'll need somewhere to store your milk."

"That's very kind of you, but—"

She talked over me. "In fact, I'll get Ned to go out today and get you a kettle. You're on your feet all day, you don't need to be runnin' errands at night."

"I really couldn't—"

"Maybe we'll get two or three. Offer 'em to customers with some of those little packets of instant. Rent 'em out. Nice little extra." She tipped her head to the side. "How you take your coffee?"

"Milk and sugar," I answered. "But, Betty—"

"I'll get Ned to pick some a' that up too."

"Betty—"

She waved me quiet. "I like this idea. Kettles. Little mugs. Prolly could rent 'em out for five dollars a go. Could put that in the brochure. An extra amenity. I'll get Ned to make a sign for reception." She wandered to the side of the hotel, preparing to roll the hose to where there was a holder. "Thanks, hon. Always lookin' for ways to improve service."

Weirdly, Betty thought her and Ned doing me a favor was me doing her one.

Yes, you could say I liked Betty.

"I'll give you my five dollars when I get back," I told her.

"You. Gratis seein' as you're a long-timer." She looked up from rolling the hose and grinned big at me. "And you like our pool."

I decided to let her kindness go, even though it was generous and considering there were only two other vehicles in her parking lot (one minivan, one Harley), she and Ned weren't exactly rolling in it. Then again, my father always told me if someone offers a kindness, take it. Just be the sort of person who does the same on a regular basis so you can be certain to even things out in your way.

"Who wouldn't like your pool?" I teased. "I hear it's the best in the county."

She laughed, shook her head and muttered, "My Ned. He's a bragger." She threw me another grin. "Get to work, hon."

"See you later, Betty."

"Maybe tomorrow for coffee?"

"Yeah."

Her grin got even bigger. "I'd like that."

I smiled at her, walked into town and went right to La-La Land. I'd done the bakery and their coffee and doughnuts the first day. I'd tried La-La Land the second. La-La Land's coffee was far superior and their banana bread was, if it could be believed, better than any doughnut I'd ever tasted and therefore definitely by far the best banana bread I'd had in my life.

I walked in and the man had purple-tinted, round-framed glasses on this time. The woman had a tie-dyed kerchief shielding some but not all of her frizzy ash blonde hair.

"Hey!" the man cried. "You were in here yesterday!"

He said this like it was a miracle and he was considering calling the Vatican.

I felt my face go soft as I gave him a small smile and walked to the counter. "Yes."

"She had a banana and a skinny butterscotch," the girl noted and asked me, "You like?"

"The banana bread was fantastic and you do good coffee," I told her.

"I make the bread," the guy said. "Secret's mayo."

"What?" I asked.

"I put a tablespoon of mayo in it."

I blinked at him. "You do?"

"He puts a tablespoon of mayo in everything," the girl said.

"Not pie," the guy amended.

"Not pie," the girl repeated.

"Why do you do that?" I asked.

"Moist Factor Five Hundred, babeeeeeee," the guy said with a big, goofy grin and I laughed.

"Moist Factor Five Hundred?"

"Yeah, a tablespoon of mayo ups the moist factor by five hundred. You doubt me, make your favorite cake, brownies, whatever, just not pie. A recipe you've made for ages. Put in a tablespoon of mayo and *wham!* You won't know what hit you. Moist Factor Five Hundred," he shared.

"He makes his own mayo too," the girl added.

"Make my own everything," he agreed. "Homemade...only way to go."

"Well, considering your banana bread is the best I've ever tasted, and I like banana bread so I've tried a lot, then you aren't wrong," I informed him and his goofy grin nearly split his face. "Though, I won't be able to try the Mayo Moist Factor Five Hundred because I live at the hotel and don't have a kitchen but when I get set up, I'll do it and let you know."

Both of them stared at me and then the girl asked, "Why do you live at the hotel?"

"I just moved here," I explained. "Just started waitressing at Bubba's and haven't really had time to settle in yet."

"Come over for dinner," the guy invited instantly.

"Sorry?" I asked.

"Yeah, tonight," the girl put in. "Shambala makes *unbelievable* veggie chili and it's chili night."

"Shambala?" I asked and the guy stuck his hand over the counter.

"I'm Shambala." I shook his hand. He let mine go and the girl stuck her hand over the counter so I took it and Shambala went on, "This is Sunray Goddess but I call her Sunny."

I shook her hand and said, "Well, um...hi, Shambala and Sunny. I'm—"

"Flower Petal," Sunny cut in and touched her finger to her ear-lobe and then to her wrist. "All flowery. I like!"

"And call me Shambles, everyone does," Shambala said.

I laughed softly. "All right, Shambles."

"So…dinner?" Shambles prompted.

"Well, I'm working and getting used to being on my feet all day so I won't be in any shape to socialize tonight," I declined but I did it gently because as I did, their faces fell and because they did, I went on, "But I'm off tomorrow."

"Tomorrow it is!" Shambles exclaimed.

"Tomorrow is Middle Eastern night and that's *way* better than chili. Shambala makes all his own everything. Even the hummus and pita," Sunny told me.

"Sounds great." I smiled.

"I'll write down our address and directions. You can come any time after five. We close at five and go straight on home. But we'll eat around six thirty," Sunny said while writing.

"And now, you give me the go ahead, I'll rock your world. Don't order. I'll give you the best that we got," Shambala offered.

"Okay." I was still smiling. "I'm up for that."

"Groovintude!" Shambala shouted with excitement and jumped toward the espresso machine.

"This is awesome," Sunny declared. "We're new to this burg too. Everyone thought we were nuts, us, opening a coffee place in a Harley town. But we like it. The mountains are close and we can draw down the sun anytime we like. Just close up, bike out, and do it wherever the spirit moves us." She leaned toward me. "But, you know, we haven't been exactly embraced by the populace."

I knew. I definitely knew, therefore I nodded.

"They'll come," Shambles muttered with both hope and determination in his two words.

"You give out free bites of your banana bread for a couple of days, you'll be beating them back with a stick," I told him.

"Hey!" he yelled, his head snapping back to look at me. "Great idea!"

Sunny turned to Shambles. "Why didn't we think of that?"

"Because half the time we're stoned?" Shambles asked back.

"Yeah." Sunny grinned at me. "That sometimes messes with the synapses."

I laughed and Shambles mumbled, "Mary Jane Enlightenment comes with a price," so I laughed even more.

Two minutes later I had the directions to their house in my purse. Shambles gave me a skinny vanilla-cinnamon latte and a piece of zucchini bread loaded with pecans. I took a bite, then a sip. Then I grinned at him.

"Rock your world?" he asked.

"Consider me a regular," I answered while paying.

"Right on!" Shambles shouted.

"See you tomorrow morning then," Sunny said as I headed to the door. "And tomorrow night!" she called.

"Yeah, definitely. Nice to meet you," I said in farewell.

"Heck yeah, nice to meet you too!" Shambles yelled.

"Later, Flower Petal," Sunny called.

"Later," I replied and walked out eating and sipping. I crossed the street and headed the one block to Bubba's thinking that maybe with Betty and Sunny and Shambles and great bread and coffee and a heated pool outside my front and only door, a door in a hotel that might not be five stars but at least it had personality, Carnal would be all right.

I was five minutes early for my shift but there was a Harley parked outside the door and it looked familiar. I didn't think that boded well and I was right when I walked through carrying my cardboard cup and the last bite of bread.

Tate was standing behind the bar wearing another henley, this one burgundy, not thermal but long-sleeved and skintight. I noticed instantly that burgundy suited him.

Dang.

He turned, eyed me, didn't smile, and greeted in his deep voice, "You got me today, Ace."

Great.

I nodded and headed to the bar asking, "Can I have the key to the office?"

He reached into his front pocket, pulled out his keys and tossed them on the bar. I shoved the last bite of bread into my mouth, acutely aware that he thought I was fat and I was eating in front of him, and, not looking at him, I grabbed the keys and headed to the hall.

"I got kegs to switch, you good with the restock?" I heard him ask as I kept moving.

"Sure," I replied still not looking at him.

I went to the office, stowed my purse and went back to the bar. He was working under it at a keg and I tossed his keys as close to him as I cared to get (which wasn't very close) but I did it loudly so he'd hear them hit the top of the bar. His head came up and his eyes hit me but I turned instantly and surveyed the fridges.

"Ace, you'll need the keys to get into the storeroom." I heard him say.

Dang. I was so stupid. Desperate to return his keys and not have anything that was *his* touch my flesh, I'd made a mistake that made me look like an idiot.

"Right," I muttered, turned to nab them, and went back to what I was doing.

Silently I went about my task, taking notes, sipping coffee, and going back and forth to the storeroom as Tate went about his business. If our paths crossed, I avoided his eyes and gave him as wide a berth as I could manage. After the restock I took down the chairs and inspected the tables while searching for forgotten empties. Unusually, half the tables in the bar were clean, the area devoid of empties. The other half of the tables needed a wipe down and I found two bottles of beer and a half-full mug.

When I went behind the bar to deposit the empties and get the spray cleaner and a cloth, Tate spoke.

"Wendy was on last night. Came in late when Tonia didn't show."

Forced to look at him due to my innate politeness, I did but I didn't speak. I lifted my brows in question.

"You haven't met Wendy?" he asked.

I shook my head.

"Waitress, only good one we got," he told me. "She does her cleanup."

"Unh-hunh," I mumbled and walked out from behind the bar wondering if Wendy wore halter tops or tube tops or if she had another way of exposing as much flesh as possible to the mostly male customers.

Tonia had long, sleek, black hair. She was tall, slim to the point of skinny, had obviously fake boobs and wore high heels and short-short cutoffs with her halter top. Jonelle had wild, huge, curly-wavy auburn hair, was average height, rounded like Neeta (just a little slimmer and what I figured was a lot younger), and wore a micro-mini with her tube top. Wendy probably rounded out the lineup with blonde hair and looked like a biker brand of supermodel.

I was dreading the night shift and going up against one of those girls. Not only had they, so far, proved themselves bitches, but also all the men would probably move from my station and tips would likely be even less.

I started toward the dirty tables when I heard Tate call, "Ace."

Considering this was obviously his nickname for me which I thought was weird since he'd known me less than twenty minutes and you didn't give a nickname to someone you'd known less than twenty minutes (more like ten years) and I figured it was meant to be not very nice, I looked at him even though I didn't want to. However, I couldn't ignore him. He couldn't be calling to anyone else, ignoring him would be rude, and he *was* my boss.

"Yes?" I asked when I caught his eyes.

"I know you heard," he said.

I knew he knew; I was just surprised he brought it up. I showed no response except to raise my brows again.

"I was in a shit mood, babe. Shake it off," he ordered and I stared.

He'd called me old, sorry-ass, and fat and he wanted me just to *shake it off*?

"Sure," I agreed, turned and spritzed a table with the cleaner.

"Ace," he called again when I'd bent to wipe. I sucked in a visibly annoyed breath and twisted only my neck so I could look at him. When my eyes hit his, he repeated, "I said, shake it off."

I turned fully to him. "And I said, sure."

"You said it but you didn't mean it," he returned.

No, I didn't.

"I did," I lied.

"Babe, you didn't," he replied.

"I did," I repeated, turned back to the table and started wiping.

"Ace, look at me," he demanded and he sounded like he was getting impatient.

I straightened and looked at him, again raising my brows.

"Let it go," he ordered.

"I've let it go," I lied again.

"You haven't," he shot back.

I inhaled deeply and on the exhale, I said, "Due respect, considering you're my boss, but since they don't exist, you're not a mind reader. I've let it go or I *would* if you'd quit talking about it."

"You haven't," he repeated. "You're stewin' on it."

This was true too. If I had a dollar for every time his words popped into my head and made me flinch the last two days, I could move to the Riviera. They even woke me up in the middle of the night.

Then again, I had insomnia and always did, even as a kid. I regularly thought of stuff in my life, stuff that embarrassed me or hurt me or worried me or freaked me out and I couldn't get to sleep. Then, when I did, I'd wake up three, four times a night sometimes tossing and turning for hours before finding sleep again.

This beautiful man saying those horrible words when talking about me was not only fresh, it was the worst of all my nightly demons by far and would be in a way I knew would last the rest of my life.

But it hit me just then that since not only did he feel free to shout those things about me when he barely knew me, also he knew I'd heard it and he didn't apologize but told me to shake it off and let it go because I should somehow accept he was in a shit mood and just deal with it that he obviously wasn't a very nice person. And maybe, even though I *was* a nice person, there were some people who deserved to get back what they got.

I mean really. Why did I always have to be nice? Why did I always have to do the right thing, turn the other cheek, a blind eye? Why did I always have to be the good girl?

So he could fire me. Whatever. I'd just see if they needed cashiers at the grocery store or move on. If I could find one Carnal, I could find another. It might take another four and a half months but I had money and I had time.

Fuck it.

"Yes," I said softly, staring him straight in the eyes. "I'm stewing on it. I hear you say those words again and again. So much, I can't get to sleep at night. So much, they come to me in my sleep and wake me up."

"Ace—"

"But you said them, I heard them, and those are the consequences. No taking it back, no shaking it off, no letting it go. It happened. I deal and move on and maybe you'd do me the courtesy of shutting up about it."

He walked from behind the bar and toward me and I watched him do it while forcing my body to stay where it was and not take a step back or, better yet, flee.

He stopped a foot away and looked down at me. That close to him, I saw he didn't have dark brown eyes. They were dark brown but they had tawny flecks in them that made them even more interesting.

Great, the lucky jerk was even luckier.

"I'm a silent partner," he declared.

"Sorry?" I asked.

"Me. I'm a silent partner," he repeated.

I tipped my head to the side and felt my brows draw together. "So?"

Tate threw a hand out to indicate the bar. "I look silent to you?"

Considering he was clearly my bartender that day and he was changing kegs, the answer to that would be no.

Instead I said, "And?"

"Deal was, I put in the money because Krys and Bubba didn't have the cake to take this on but I wasn't involved. I just get my piece and I do my own thing. Five years, Ace, I find more often than not I usually gotta wade in. Bubba's off fishin' and Krystal's always hirin' folk who suck. Tonia and Jonelle both make an art outta being the worst waitresses in history. They're here to socialize, when they drag their asses in that is. I got shit to do and I ain't doin' it 'cause I'm here. 'Cause I gotta keep an eye on my investment. 'Cause Bubba's a moron and Krystal's tryin' her best but she can't do it on her own. That pisses me off. Bubba's gone again and I got pissed again and you bore the brunt of that. It was an asshole remark. I said it and didn't mean it. I get pissed I say a lotta shit I don't mean. Now you know that, you need to shake it off."

Maybe for him it could be that easy. For me, it was not.

"I appreciate that but you're old enough to know better. You're old enough to know words have power and to use them wisely. You're angry at Bubba, take potshots at him, not some woman you don't know."

"Like I said, when I get pissed I say a lotta shit I don't mean and what I said about you I didn't mean," he repeated, beginning to look as impatient as he sounded.

"And like I said, you're old enough to learn you shouldn't do that," I repeated too, probably also looking impatient.

"That isn't me," he replied.

"Well, then, this obviously is eating you and that's *your* consequence because I have feelings and you walked all over them and you can't order me to shake it off so you can feel better. It's there, burned in my brain and I can't just forget it because you tell me to. So you have to live with that. You can't and want me gone, say it now because I'm beginning to like Betty and I met Shambles and Sunny and I'm having dinner with them tomorrow night and I'd rather not make ties when I'm going to need to hit the road because my boss is going to get rid of me."

"Shambles and Sunny?" he asked.

"Shambles and Sunny," I answered but didn't share more. "Now, can we just move on and do our best to work together and all other times avoid each other or do you want me to go?"

He moved forward an inch and I again fought the urge to retreat.

"Forgiveness is divine," he said softly and I'd never heard him talk softly. He had a very nice voice but when it went soft, it was beautiful.

This also sucked.

"I'm not divine," I returned. "I'm also not Ace and I'm not babe. I'm Lauren. You don't like my name, don't call me anything at all. Now can I clean the danged table?"

I had my head tipped back to look him in the eye but I could tell he was expending effort to hold his whole body still.

Then he said in that soft voice, "I'm sorry, Ace."

"Me too," I replied instantly being clear I didn't accept his apology, which wasn't a nice thing to do. Then again, I was trying out this not being nice thing and I found that what he'd said hurt so much I could do it, so I was going to go with it. "Now can I get back to work?"

He moved so he was far less than a foot away and edging into my space.

"Krys told me your story," he said quietly and I sighed but didn't speak. "You bust your husband's balls like this?"

I felt my innards seize and it didn't feel very nice.

Then I asked, "Are you pissed now? Is that the reason for the latest asshole remark?"

"Nope, just curious."

"Then no," I replied and went on to share with brutal honesty,

"I loved him. He meant everything to me. I thought we were happy, mostly. We had our crap times but most of the time I thought we were happy. Or at least I was. So I didn't need to bust his balls because I loved him, we were good together and we had a good life. That is, until I found out it was all a lie, every last nuance of it, and I *still* didn't bust his balls. I granted him a divorce, sold our house and stepped aside. I could have wrung him dry but it would only prolong my sorrow and maybe build bitterness so what's the point of that?"

Tate watched me while I spoke, his eyes riveted to mine in a strange way that made it seem like the words I spoke etched themselves on his soul the instant I said them.

When I was done he asked, "So you forgive him for bein' a cheatin' asshole and a liar and a dickhead who's so fuckin' dumb he throws away a good thing but you can't forgive me for sayin' somethin' stupid?"

"I didn't forgive him. I just didn't bust his balls. That was your question and that was my answer. *Now* can I wipe down the table?"

He was silent for several long moments before he said, "Yeah, Ace, you can wipe the table *and* we can find a way to work together but I'll tell you straight. I ain't puttin' the effort in to avoid you just because you're holdin' tight to somethin' that didn't mean shit. You can try to avoid me but it ain't a big bar, it ain't a big town. You got attitude and you're stubborn as all hell but you ain't gonna be able to avoid me. Our paths will cross."

I looked to the ceiling. "Great, more reasons to lose sleep."

"Babe," he called and I rolled my eyes back to him.

"Stop calling me babe," I demanded.

Tate ignored me. "You want sweet dreams, lose the attitude and you might find I'll give you reason to have them."

I felt my body seize at his words but he was done. I knew this because he turned and walked away, going straight down the hall until the murky darkness enveloped him and I lost sight of him.

My body stayed frozen while new words in Tate's deep, rough voice ricocheted around in my brain.

And a dickhead who's so fuckin' dumb he throws away a good thing...

And if that wasn't enough.

You want sweet dreams, lose the attitude and you might find I'll give you reason to have them.

The first one was undeniably nice. The second one I didn't get at all.

"Hey there, Lauren," I heard, jumped at the sound, and whirled to see Jim-Billy entering. "I'm early but could I have a draft?"

I looked at my watch then at Jim-Billy. "It's just past eleven thirty."

"I had a tough mornin'," Jim-Billy replied, heading to his stool.

"What happened?" I asked, abandoning the still dirty table and going to Jim-Billy.

"I woke up," Jim-Billy answered and then stopped talking.

"You woke up...," I prompted.

"Yep," he said. "Now can I have a draft?"

I couldn't help it. After that scene with Tate, what he said, what it might mean, the fact that I really didn't like him and not only had to work with him but he was my boss, what Jim-Billy said made me laugh so hard I had to throw my head back to do it. Maybe it wasn't that funny but I really needed the release of a laugh so I took it.

I put down my cloth and the spray and headed behind the bar.

"Don't know if I'm allowed but seeing as you had to wake up and all, you deserve a draft." I grabbed a mug and went to the taps. "And anyway, maybe me serving you will get me fired."

"You wanna get fired?" Jim-Billy asked.

"Right now I do," I replied.

"You been here three days, woman," Jim-Billy reminded me. "And four days ago you practically begged Krystal to take you on."

"Yes, but I got to work with Krystal those two days. Tate's in today," I told him, filling the mug with beer.

"Darlin', every other waitress in this bar and most the women in this town would think it the other way around," Jim-Billy returned.

"I'm not them," I retorted, pushed back the tap and took the beer to Jim-Billy seeing his eyebrows up and his forehead scrunched together in long lines.

"You got a problem with Tate?" he asked in disbelief.

Seeing that even though Tate wasn't nice enough to know better but I was, I didn't share by saying words I shouldn't say.

I threw a beer coaster in front of Jim-Billy and put his mug on it. "We just don't see eye to eye."

"Shit," Jim-Billy muttered and I saw he looked like he was fighting a smile.

"Shit what?" I asked.

"Nothin'," Jim-Billy mumbled into the beer mug that was at his lips.

"Shit what?" I repeated and Jim-Billy took a sip then grinned at me.

"'Nother time, Lauren, when you aren't on and you and me are shootin' the shit, drinkin' a brew, I'll tell you shit what."

"Jesus, Billy, we aren't open for twenty minutes," I heard Tate say and I jumped a mile as he walked up behind me and then stopped at my back, just to the side but then leaned a hand into the bar so he was totally in my space. So totally in my space, I felt the heat from his body and if I moved, I knew my shoulder would brush his chest.

I was forcing my body to stay still again while Jim-Billy was surveying Tate and me and continuing to fight his smile.

"You know how it is, Jackson," Jim-Billy replied and that was the second time I heard someone refer to Tate as Jackson and I wondered why. Was that his last name?

"I know how it is, Billy," Tate said in that soft voice of his. Then he said, "Ace, you gonna wipe down those tables or what?"

I twisted my neck to look at him to see he was staring down at me and he was closer than I expected and I expected him to be pretty danged close. He was also back to looking impatient and I resisted the urge to give him a sharp elbow to the ribs.

"Right away, oh Captain, my captain," I mumbled and moved away, nabbing the spray and cloth.

*   *   *

"Two Miller Lites, a vodka rocks, and a Jack and Coke," I ordered from Tate, my eyes bent to my pad of paper where I kept my notes as to what I ordered.

I learned about two hours into my shift that this was a perfect way of avoiding eye contact and pretending he didn't exist at all. If I tried hard enough, I could almost believe my drinks appeared by magic.

Now it was ten minutes from the end of my shift and I was nearly home free.

This tactic had worked beautifully and I'd been able to do it nearly my entire shift seeing as we were busy nearly all day. Ten bikers roared in at one thirty and hadn't left and with the drifters and the regulars I'd been pretty much on the go, which was an excuse to be away from Tate.

I was also attempting to ignore Tate's very existence by sliding into research mode, trying out strategies in an effort to up my tips. I was keeping track and I figured what I was doing was working.

My first strategy was to be a little more friendly and talkative, take a little more time and hang out and it appeared the boys liked that. So, since that worked, my next strategy was to find out names, memorize them, and use them. Even if you weren't at your regular bar, anyone liked to be made to feel at home. And nothing felt like home more than someone knowing you, or acting like they did. At least that's what I guessed, and from keeping tabs on my escalating tips, I was right.

In no time at all, I found when I was in my approach to see if anyone needed a fresh one, eyes slid to me, smiles lit faces, and the witty rapport would ensue. Sometimes even before I made it to them they'd call out a joke or a silly compliment I knew they didn't mean.

And sometimes they'd order drinks even though their last ones weren't close to empty.

And my tips went up and up.

Because of this, I was pretty pleased with myself and my efforts for the day, even though they came on a day I had to share with Tate.

"Babe," Tate called, taking me from my end-of-shift pleasant thoughts.

"Yeah?" I answered, pulling a pencil from behind my ear to make my additions to my pad.

"Ace," he called.

"Yeah?" I answered again, scratching on my pad.

"For fuck's sake, Lauren, look at me," Tate demanded and my head came up because he used my name for the first time ever and also because he sounded slightly angry.

"Yes?" I asked.

He was leaning into the bar with both fists on the top but out to his sides. This could be a casual stance for some but for him it seemed both aggressive and dominant.

"What's your game here?" he asked.

"Sorry?" I asked back, confused at his question and his apparent irritation.

"Your game," he repeated, then went on, shaking his head. "Fuck it, I don't care. Just stop playin' it."

My head tipped a bit to the side when I asked, "What are you talking about?"

"Don't be stupid," he answered and at his words, I edged closer to the bar as I felt my temper snag.

"Stupid?" I whispered.

"Gettin' friendly with those guys to make your point." He jerked his head to the pool tables to his right where my most generous customers, and my new best buds, the bikers from one thirty had been camped out.

"What point?" I asked.

"And don't think I'm stupid," he told me.

Now I was really confused.

"I don't think you're stupid."

"You do if you think I don't get your game."

I changed tactics. "Why's it stupid to be friendly? I thought it was my job."

"Your job is to turn drinks, not flirt and get yourself into trouble."

Now I wasn't confused and my temper wasn't snagged. It was frayed.

I leaned into the bar too, put a hand on it and my voice got quiet as I hissed, "I'm not flirting!"

"Babe, shit, seriously? Do I look dumb?"

"No, but you are if you think I'm flirting," I replied and watched his face grow hard.

Then he leaned in farther too. Taking his fists from the bar and leaning onto both of his forearms, one resting on either side of my hand so he was in my face.

"Knock it off," he ordered and the way he said those three words, I knew he wasn't irritated. He was, for some reason, angry.

"I'm not going to knock it off," I said. "My tips are awesome!"

"You think we had problems before, you keep playin' those boys, you'll see what a problem with me means."

I stared at him.

How could he have a problem? He said half his waitresses were terrible. One would think he'd leap for joy to get a friendly one who sold a lot of booze.

"Have you been sampling your wares?" I asked only half sarcastically. The other half was seriously but he didn't take this very well for he leaned in even farther so he wasn't only in my face, he was an inch away from it.

"Don't try me," he bit out.

"Don't threaten me," I shot back.

"Hey! Cool!" we heard shouted. Tate's eyes went over my shoulder and I twisted to see a very petite woman running at me. She had dark hair cut in a short pixie that looked great on her and a friendly open face with big doe eyes. She was wearing a T-shirt that said "McLeod's Gym, Burn It!" a pair of jeans, and flip-flops and her face was devoid of makeup.

And she was also cut, as in *cut*. So in shape I could see all the muscles in her arms.

She skidded to a halt in front of me, this perfect stranger, wrapped her toned arms around me and gave me a hug. Stiff in her arms, because of my nature, I still couldn't stop myself hugging her back.

"Hey!" she shouted, head tipped back to look at me when she let me go and backed up a half step. "I'm Wendy. You're Lauren! So cool!"

"Hey," I replied, deciding automatically that I liked Wendy. Back in the day, with my family especially and early on with Brad, I was a cuddler. I liked to touch. I liked to hug. I liked to snuggle and hold hands. With my mom, my dad, my sister, Caroline, Brad, anyone really, if we were close.

Those days were gone. I hadn't had a hug in a long time and it didn't matter that it came from a perfect stranger who, even petite, looked like she could snap me like a twig. I still liked it and I liked her.

"I heard about you. Jim-Billy and Nadine said you were neat and I can't *wait* to work with you! Won't that be fun?"

She was rolling up and down on her toes, filled with such energy and enthusiasm it was unnatural. It felt like she needed so much she was sucking it from the very atmosphere, including me.

"Yeah, fun," I said on a smile.

She leaned to the side and waved. "Hey, Tate."

"Wendy," Tate returned.

"I'm gonna go dump my purse. Why don't you hang out during my shift so we can chat?" she asked.

"Um…" I said, preparing to answer and that answer, due to Tate's presence and weird behavior, would sadly be no. But before I could speak, she rounded on a foot and dashed around the bar.

"You got any tabs runnin'?" I heard Tate ask and I turned back to him.

"Yeah," I answered.

"Cash 'em out. You're off," he declared and my eyes went to the big Coors Light clock over the bar.

"I've got ten minutes before Wendy's on," I reminded him. "And Jonelle's not here yet."

Nor, if yesterday was any indication, would she be for at least half an hour.

"Serve your drinks," his head nodded to my tray, "and fuckin' cash out."

"But—"

"Not big on repeatin' myself, babe."

"Not big on being called babe, *babe*."

Honestly!

I didn't know I had it in me but I must have because Tate sure drew it right out.

"You hand Krys this attitude?" he asked me.

"I like Krystal," I lied. "*And* she's never threatened me *and* she's never called me old, fat, or a sorry-ass!" I snapped, grabbed my tray, and stomped away.

I didn't know both Jim-Billy and Nadine heard every word we'd said. I also didn't know why Tate got under my skin and made me act like a bitchy raving lunatic. I also didn't dwell since I decided early he was a jerk and had given myself permission to be a bitch. So, he kept acting like a jerk, then he'd keep getting the bitch.

I served my drinks, calculated my tab, and luckily could cash it out from my apron, and I called hello to Dalton when he walked in. I also dragged my heels until Wendy hit the floor at a couple minutes to seven. Then I went behind the bar and slapped my apron down close to Dalton.

"Hey, Dalton, can you cash me out? I'm going to go freshen up," I said to him.

"Sure, Lauren, can you give me ten?" Dalton answered.

"Not a problem," I answered and turned to go to the restrooms but found my upper arm suddenly had five strong fingers wrapped around it and my body didn't move of its own accord to the restroom. It was propelled by Tate to the office.

What now?

"Take your hand off me," I hissed.

"Shut your trap," he clipped back, opened the door and pulled me in. Then he shut the door and maneuvered me so my back was to it and he was close to my front.

"Move away," I demanded, half shocked that there I was, in the office, a place I didn't want to be, dragged there by a man I didn't like and half scared because I didn't know him very well and most of my experience with him he was angry but now he looked *really* mad.

"I hurt your feelings, I get it. I apologized," he returned. "You don't have to accept it. That's your choice. But you *do* gotta fuckin' listen to me when I'm givin' you good advice. Those boys out there are in a biker gang, not a bad one but not one that shies away from trouble. You wanna be friendly enough to sell drinks and distant enough to fly under their radar. They clocked your tits, your ass, your legs, your hair, and your attitude the minute they walked in and, trust me, Ace, you want them to admire you from afar. What you don't want to do is give them the in you've been givin' them the past four hours."

"I haven't been giving them an in," I retorted.

"Babe, you crawled into one of their laps, I wouldn't have been surprised."

"That's crazy!" I snapped.

"It is? You get I'm a man?" he asked bizarrely and I stared at him a second because pretty much no one on earth could miss that.

"Yes, I get you're a man," I answered.

"So, I get that impression from you just watchin' your shit, what do you think *they're* gettin' bein' on the receivin' end?"

Uh-oh. As much as it killed me to admit, he had a point.

"Um…," I mumbled.

"Um," he mimicked and I felt my eyes narrow on him. "Damn straight, Ace. How'd you get here?"

"Sorry?" I asked.

"To the bar. You got your car?"

"I walked," I told him.

"You're on my Harley once Dalton cashes you out."

Oh no I was not.

"*What?*" I shouted. Yes, shouted.

"I'm takin' you home," he answered.

"No you aren't."

"Babe, I am."

"No. You. Aren't!" I tried to slide to the side but his hand came up and he planted his palm in the door so I stopped. "I'm staying at the hotel until I can find a place. It's only five blocks away."

"Least two of those boys been waitin' 'til you're off. You think they won't make their move now that you are?"

This surprised me. They were bikers in a gang but there were a couple of good-looking ones and all of them, I thought, were nice. I thought they were having fun with me. Enjoying their beer and pool and male camaraderie with a somewhat sassy, older, fat-assed waitress breaking in on their bonding with some witty one-liners and a cheeky grin. Though some of them I guessed were my age, others a bit older, and among that lot were the good-looking ones.

I didn't think any of them might *like* me.

My eyes slid to the wall, which was the direction of the bar, and I said quietly, "Really?"

"Jesus," he muttered. "You *want* that attention?" he asked and my eyes shot back to him.

"Of course not!" But I had to admit, just being a breathing female, it was nice to have it all the same.

"Then you're on my bike."

"No."

"You get on it or I drag you to it."

It was my turn to get in his face. "Why are you such a jerk?"

"I can live with you thinkin' that, even though I'm protectin' your ass," he returned.

"You missed a word. You meant to say my *fat* ass!"

I slid the opposite direction from his arm, went to the filing cabinet where I stowed my purse and snatched it out. When I turned to stomp back to him, he was standing in front of the door with his arms crossed on his chest and watching me.

I walked directly to the door, put my hand on the knob and stared at it when I demanded, "Out of my way."

I felt rather than saw him move, threw open the door, and stomped out.

Dalton had my tips ready by the time I got out. He handed them to me with one of his easy smiles and turned to a customer.

"Sit awhile, have a beer?" Jim-Billy asked while I shoved my tips in my purse and I looked at him to see he was smiling at me.

"Thanks, Jim-Billy, no," I replied as I felt Tate enter my vicinity. "I skipped lunch and need some dinner."

"Take you out to dinner then," Jim-Billy suggested and I felt Tate stop at the end of the bar close to me but I was looking at Jim-Billy.

"You leave that barstool?" I asked and his smile got wider.

"To take a pretty woman to dinner, yeah," he answered.

"You're on," I said to him.

"You're going?" Wendy called, practically skipping up to us before coming to a sliding halt.

"Yeah, Wendy. I need dinner," I told her.

"That's cool," she replied and looked at Tate. "Hey Tate, can you be sure Lauren and I get a shift together soon?"

"She's off tomorrow and she's days for a while," Tate answered.

Wendy looked at me. "Then I'll call Tonia and ask her to switch shifts with me on Saturday. She'll be thrilled. She hates days. She's a night owl."

"Wendy, babe, you know we need you on nights," Tate put in.

Her head tilted down so far to the side her ear nearly touched her shoulder.

"Aw, Tate, come on. I want a shift with Lauren. Just one, *please*. Don't sentence me to full-on Jonelle and Tonia for *weeks*," Wendy begged.

I turned to look at Tate thinking that perhaps Jonelle and Tonia didn't treat just me to their frosty demeanor, maybe that was just who they were and having to work with them day in and day out (or, in this case, night in and night out) would suck.

Tate's eyes stayed on Wendy. "Tonia shifts, you can have Saturday." His eyes moved to Jim-Billy. "You take Ace to dinner, you walk her to the hotel."

"Jackson, man, why you think I'm takin' her to dinner?" Jim-Billy asked and I felt my eyes widen.

"I thought it was because I was a pretty woman," I said to him and he grinned at me.

"It is, darlin'. It's also because there's four boys at the pool table lookin' hungry like a wolf and their eyes are pinned on you," Jim-Billy replied.

I didn't look at the pool tables and I didn't want to admit Tate was right so I said to Jim-Billy, "Did you just quote Duran Duran?"

"Duran who?" he asked and Tate chuckled so I bit back my laughter because I didn't intend to share even that with him.

Instead, I walked to Jim-Billy and pulled him off his stool by his arm.

"Feed me, handsome," I urged, linking my arm through his and leaning into his side.

"Okay, *now* it's just me and a pretty woman," Jim-Billy returned and that's when I allowed myself to laugh at him.

"See you Saturday, Lauren!" Wendy yelled.

"Yeah, Wendy, Saturday," I yelled back.

"Hotel," Tate called after us as we walked to the door.

Jim-Billy lifted a hand in a wave but didn't turn and I didn't respond at all. I wasn't on shift anymore, Tate Jackson, or whatever his last name was, had ceased to exist.

I turned to my buds at the pool table and shouted, "I'm off to dinner with my sugar daddy! See you guys later!"

"Bye, Laurie!"

"Bye, darlin'!"

"Bye, babe!"

"Bye, gorgeous!"

"Later!"

And so on.

I walked out smiling because all those farewells were nice and no one tried to jump me and Jim-Billy in order to wrest me from him and drag me by the hair to their cave.

So take that Tate Whatever-His-Last-Name-Was.

Okay, so he hadn't exactly ceased to exist … whatever.

CHAPTER FOUR

Nighttime Swimming

"LATER!" WENDY CALLED, hanging out the window of her blue Honda CR-V.

"Later!" I called back and inserted the key into the lock of my hotel room, twisted it, opened the door, walked in, heard the door close behind me and fell face-first onto my bed.

I'd just been to McLeod's Gym, owned by Wendy's boyfriend, Tyler, who was a six-foot blond powerhouse with biceps so huge I couldn't wrap both my hands around one. And, at Wendy's invitation and Tyler's smiling agreement, I'd tried. Tyler did boot camps three times a week where fifteen insane Carnalites showed up at seven in the morning to be tortured.

On Saturday, Wendy had talked me into trying a session and I told her I probably shouldn't unless I had a day off. Luckily (to Wendy's way of thinking) one of the boot camps was on Tuesday.

Today. My day off.

I thought during the session I was going to throw up. Then later during the session I thought I was going to die. I didn't do either. I'd survived and kept myself standing and breathing. Afterward, Wendy took me to her and Tyler's condo to make me a protein shake, which consisted of organic Greek yogurt, a banana, a tablespoon of peanut butter, a squeeze of honey, a dash of milk, a bunch of ice cubes and a scoop of protein powder.

The protein shake was delicious and the best part of my morning.

But at that moment lying facedown on my bed, I was pretty sure I was going to die.

Regardless, I was on day eight in Carnal and, notwithstanding boot camp torture, I knew I'd made the right decision.

*   *   *

After my first day working with Tate at Bubba's, Jim-Billy took me to dinner at the diner where he spent an hour entertaining me. I hadn't laughed so much or so hard in so long I forgot how good the pain felt when your belly hurt deep down just from laughing. Jim-Billy's eyes often strayed to my chest area but I could forgive that because all the rest of the time he was darned funny and definitely sweet.

After he walked me to the hotel, I entered to find my room had undergone a mini-transformation.

There was a six-drawer dresser on the wall by the door and my clothes that had been folded and stacked on the built-in dresser were gone and I found they'd been moved into the new dresser. On top of the standing dresser was a vase of fresh flowers. On top of the built-in there was an electric kettle, two huge coffee mugs with colorful swirls on them sitting next to a matching sugar bowl and a creamer with a jar of instant coffee next to that and two teaspoons. There were also two brightly striped tea towels in colors that matched the cups and the sugar bowl was filled. A minifridge sat beside the mug paraphernalia on the built-in and when I looked inside I saw there was a jug of milk, a bottle of cheap champagne, and a note that read:

Welcome home, Betty and Ned.
PS: We already had the dresser and we weren't using it.

Reading it, I walked backward, clutching the note in my hand, until my knees hit the bed.

I sat down and burst into tears.

*   *   *

The next day I got up early, got ready to face the day, and went to have coffee with Betty.

By the time I made it to her, she'd had her breakfast and opened up so I sat in reception with her while we sipped and chatted. Then I went to my car and drove it to the mechanics at the other end of town and learned very quickly what Tate was talking about the day before.

Carnal was definitely a small town and because of that, it would make it hard to avoid him.

I learned this because Tate was in the massive forecourt of the mechanics, standing by his Harley and talking to a man that was nearly as tall as him but older and softer with long gray hair pulled back in a ponytail and he sported a beer belly. The gray-haired man was wearing jeans, a black T-shirt and a black leather vest with a bunch of patches on it. Tate was wearing jeans, his boots and another tight, long-sleeved T-shirt, not a henley this time, and it was navy blue.

I ignored Tate, parked, got out and started walking to the door with a sign over it that said "Office."

I had long since had a strict personal edict that there was never a time when you were allowed to look bad.

Of course, when I was in denial that my marriage was collapsing and I was ignoring the signs, I started to put on weight but I never quit doing my hair and putting on at least light makeup and a decent outfit before going out anywhere, even if it was a quick stop at the grocery store.

Then I'd overheard two friends talking. I confronted Brad with what I heard them say, he came clean about Hayley and that he wanted out and I spent two months eating everything that was edible and dragging around town like the sorry-ass Tate thought I was.

One morning, I'd found I was out of coffeecake and since I ate half of one most mornings for breakfast, I got in my car in my pajama bottoms and a sweatshirt and went to the grocery store.

I was on a mission for coffeecake. But the minute I walked into the store I saw Brad, dressed in a suit and ready to go to the office, and Hayley, slim and perfect and wearing a fashionable, figure-skimming dress and high heels, flashing toned legs and arms and her pert bottom. They were standing and waiting for drinks at the chain coffee booth at the front of the store. They looked perfect together and they were smiling at each other about something, clearly in their own little happy world bubble.

And I was in my pajamas. I hadn't washed my hair in three days. And I knew I intended to go to work without doing my hair, putting on makeup, or ironing my clothes.

I didn't get the coffeecake. I rushed back to my car, went home and took a shower, shaved my legs for the first time in forever, did my hair, ironed my clothes, and made it to work with just seconds to spare.

I also vowed never to let myself sink that low again. Not for losing my beautiful Brad to the perfect Hayley, not for anything.

Unfortunately, I didn't stop eating but at least it was something.

That day, in Carnal, at the mechanics, even though it was my day off, I still put on a to-the-knee jean skirt that was a muted shade of red, the red just a bit off rust. I added my mushroom-colored knit top that was one of the few articles of clothing I'd bought in semirecent times (which was to say, over a year ago) that Brad had commented on. He told me I looked good in it before he led me to our bed and took it off. It fit well, was even a bit tight, had an empire seam under my breasts, a shelf bra that worked wonders against gravity, a deep V that exposed just above a hint of cleavage and it was sleeveless.

I'd parted my hair to the side, plaited it in soft French braids down both sides and secured it at the back with a big oval tortoise-shell clip. I'd put in medium-hoop silver earrings that had a row of red beads dangling from the bottom and a wide, stretchy bracelet that was also beaded in different shades of red and brown. I'd also put on my brown sandals that had a short, but cute, heel I thought did wonders for my calves. The sandals had crisscross thin straps at the toe and a matching wraparound strap at the ankle.

I was lucky in one respect. I might be carrying extra weight but my legs and calves were impervious. Even slightly heavy, they were so well formed, they always looked good. This I got from my mother's side of the family, bless her.

I started toward the office and didn't make it when three men emerged from one of the two big double bays in which there were a bunch of cars and bikes being worked on.

I stopped, waited, and two of the three men glanced at the front-runner, a close-cropped-black-haired man who had a thick goatee with a hint of gray in it, and a solid body (great arms with lots of interesting-looking tattoos). He looked to be a few inches taller than me even in my miniheels. He was wearing a white T-shirt, faded jeans, and motorcycle boots and all—except for the boots, but what did I know, they were black, they could be—were stained with black smears of grease.

"Hey," he said when he was several feet away. His hands held a cloth that was also white with black smears and he was adding to the stains as he twisted it around his fingers. "Can I help you?"

I started toward him and met him halfway with a smile.

"Hi, that's my car." I twisted and pointed at my black Lexus, seeing across the forecourt that both Tate and the man he was talking to had their eyes on me. Therefore I twisted back to the black-haired man. "I need some work done."

"What's wrong?" he asked.

"Nothing, I've just been on the road a while. I need an oil change, maybe a tuneup, the tires rotated, and it'd be cool to get it detailed. Do you do that?"

He grinned at me and I noticed he had nice white teeth that seemed whiter against his goatee and tan face.

"Yep," he answered and I smiled back at him.

"Great, how long will it take?"

"We're covered," he said, glancing over his shoulder at the mess of vehicles in the bays and then back at me. "Shop's closed on Sunday. It'll probably be late Monday."

I bit my lip since I needed my car to go to Sunny and Shambles's house that night.

He saw me biting my lip and asked, "You need a loaner?"

"You do that?"

"No," he replied and I couldn't help it, I blinked.

"Then, um…"

He interrupted my mumbling, "Find one for you, though."

I blinked again, surprised.

"Really?"

He grinned again. "Yep."

"Okay, that'd be nice. I'll, uh…pay extra if you like."

"Not necessary," he said. "You draw down the tank, just fill it up before you return it. That good?"

I smiled at him. "Yeah, that's great. Very nice of you."

"Not nice," he replied.

"Sorry?"

"I'm not nice," he repeated.

I tipped my head to the side. "You seem nice to me."

"It'd be nice, I was doin' this just to do it. I'm not doin' it just to do it. I'm doin' it so you'll owe me."

I blinked again and righted my head.

"Sorry?" I asked.

"Like the idea that you'd owe me."

"Oh," I whispered because I really didn't know what else to say to that odd and vaguely scary (but also vaguely exciting) remark.

He stuck out a big, strong, attractive hand that had black grease stains edging his fingernails. "I'm Wood."

I took his hand and his fingers closed around mine, not shaking it, just holding it strong and tight and not letting go.

"I'm Lauren," I said softly because he was kind of freaking me out.

"Pretty name," he muttered, his black eyes not leaving mine. "Suits you."

"Thanks." I was still talking soft.

"You new to town?" he asked, not dropping my hand.

"Yes," I answered, wondering if I should but not stopping myself or pulling my hand away.

"Where you from?" he asked.

"Um...Phoenix, kind of. I grew up in Indiana though."

"What're you doin' in Carnal?"

I shrugged even though he still had hold of my hand and I kept talking even though I didn't know if I should. "Found myself roaming, roamed here, liked it, and stayed."

He threw his head back and laughed, at the same time giving my hand a gentle tug so I had to take a half step toward him.

When he stopped laughing he dipped his chin and looked in my eyes again.

"Roamed to Carnal, liked it, and stayed. You crazy?"

"No," I replied.

"Think you are, you just don't know it."

"Um...can you let go of my hand?" I whispered.

"No," he whispered back and I felt my heartbeat speed up.

"Ace." I heard Tate call and I twisted my head to see him striding up to us, his long legs eating the distance, the gray-haired man he was with struggling to keep up.

"Tate, hey," I said to him, tugged at my hand and luckily Wood let it go.

"Ace?" Wood asked and I turned back to him.

"Um...Tate's nickname for me," I said and Wood's face got a little scary.

"Tate's nickname?" he asked as Tate stopped somewhat close to my side.

"She's mine," Tate announced; my body gave a little jerk at his curiously proprietary words and my head twisted fast to look up at him.

"Yours?" Wood asked and his voice was now a little scary.

"I work for him," I explained and watched Wood's face and body relax.

"Ah," he murmured, crossed his arms on his chest and his mouth twitched.

"You got car troubles?" Tate asked me, ignoring Wood.

"She needs an oil change and a detail," Wood answered for me, not ignoring Tate. Then he looked at the gray-haired man. "I'm givin' her the 'Stang as a loaner."

The gray-haired man's bushy eyebrows went straight to his hairline and I felt Tate go tense at my side.

"You're givin' her the 'Stang as a loaner for an oil change?" the gray-haired man asked, clearly surprised.

"Yep," Wood answered casually.

"Shee-it," the gray-haired man muttered.

"Um…I can walk, mostly," I informed them. "But I have to go to Shambles and Sunny's tonight so I need a car, just for tonight."

"I'll give you a ride on my bike," Tate offered and my head twisted again, and again it was fast, and I did this just so I could stare at him.

Then I said, "That isn't necessary."

"When you gotta be there?" Tate asked.

Before I could decline, Wood spoke, "She's gettin' the 'Stang."

Tate's eyes sliced to Wood and he returned, "I got her."

"We already made the deal," Wood replied.

"I got her," Tate repeated.

"Um…," I mumbled. Tate's gaze sliced to me and at the look in his eyes I clamped my mouth shut.

"You're on my bike," he growled.

"She's in the 'Stang," Wood growled back and Tate looked at him and I could swear, for some reason, if anyone moved it would set them off and they'd jump and rip each other's throats out.

"Flower Petal!" I heard.

I braced for mayhem but turned to see Shambles, his long hair flying out behind him, his round blue-tinted glasses on his nose. He was carrying a plate with a napkin on it and what looked like pieces of bread and he was running toward us.

"Hey, Shambles," I called.

He skidded to a halt at our grouping and smiled at me, oblivious to the bizarre tension curling insidiously through the air.

"You didn't come for coffee today," Shambles accused good-naturedly.

"That's my next stop," I told him.

"Groovintude!" he shouted.

"Is that your banana bread?" I motioned to the plate with my head.

"Yeah!" he yelled. "Been wanderin' the sidewalk all mornin' handin' it out. Like, *five* people took a bite and then walked right to the shop to get themselves a slice. You…are…*genius*!" Shambles answered on another yell.

"Great." I smiled at him then pulled in breath, turned to the boys and declared, "That banana bread is the best you'll ever eat and you can get it right down the street."

I saw all the men were staring at Shambles like they didn't know what to make of him but what they were coming up with they didn't like all that much.

Shambles looked around the forecourt and his eyes came to me.

"You got car troubles?" he asked.

"No," I answered quickly before anyone else could say anything. "Just need an oil change and stuff. Though, my car'll be here for a while."

"Okay, that's groovy. Sunny and I'll swing by the hotel and pick you up before we go home. You come up early, you can help me smush chickpeas for the hummus."

Thank God for Shambles, unexpected but welcome problem-solver.

"That's perfect," I told him.

"Awesome!" he cried. "Be at your place at five-ish."

"See you then," I said and he looked at the guys and stuck out his plate at them.

"Bread?" he asked.

"Pass," Tate growled, glaring at Shambles.

"No," Wood growled, also glaring at Shambles.

"I'll take a piece," the gray-haired man said and took a piece, popped it in his mouth, and chewed while Shambles watched.

"Well?" Shambles asked.

The gray-haired man looked at me and stated, "You're right, sweetheart. That shit's great."

"Right on!" Shambles yelled.

"You should taste his coffee," I said to the gray-haired man. "Heaven."

"May do that," he mumbled as Tate and Wood remained staunchly silent.

"Speakin' a' that, Flower Petal, you haven't had your fix," Shambles put in.

"Oh, right, yeah," I muttered and then turned to Wood and held out my keys. "I'll be back on Monday?"

"Need your number," Wood replied, taking my keys and Tate got tense at my side again.

"My number?" I asked, forcing my eyes to stay on Wood.

"Yeah, baby, need it if we find somethin' you need to know about," Wood replied. He wasn't tense and his voice had gone gentle and him calling me baby in that gentle voice, I had to admit, I liked.

"I don't have a number," I told him. "I'm at the hotel."

"Ace," Tate bit off quietly and I looked at him to see, for some reason, he was shaking his head.

"You don't have a cell?" Wood asked and I looked at him.

"Well, I do. It just isn't charged and has a Phoenix number. I haven't charged it in four months."

All the men stared at me, including Shambles, but it was Tate who spoke.

"Babe, what in *the fuck* are you thinking?"

I looked up at him and saw that, just like any time I was around Tate, I'd done something to piss him off.

"Sorry?" I asked.

"Jesus, honest to God, are you insane?" Tate asked.

"Why?" I snapped, because, just like any time I was around Tate, he did something to piss *me* off.

"A woman alone without a goddamned phone?" Tate went on.

"Yes, so?"

Tate turned fully to me and got closer. "So?"

"So?" I repeated.

He looked over my head and muttered, "Christ almighty." Then his eyes came back to mine. "You got a death wish?"

I put my hand to my hip and asked acidly, "Captain, tell me, how does me not having a cell phone translate into me having a death wish?"

"It ain't safe," he answered.

"I'm standing here breathing, aren't I?" I shot back.

"Way you're goin', Ace, I give you a month," he returned.

"I can take care of myself," I snapped.

"You aren't in suburbia anymore, babe," he informed me.

"Yeah, I'm not," I retorted and leaned into him. "Duh!"

Tate's face turned to stone.

It would seem, considering I continued to speak regardless of Tate's stony expression, that I *might* have a death wish.

"Jeez, Captain, it's a town filled with bikers, not Viking marauders!"

That's when I watched Tate's face turn to granite.

"Uh...Flower Petal," Shambles edged close and took my hand, "maybe we should get you some coffee."

I didn't pry my eyes away from Tate's furious ones as I spoke to Shambles, "That sounds great."

Shambles tugged at my hand and I continued glaring at Tate and he continued scowling at me as I walked two steps away. Then I looked to Wood and said, "Thanks, Wood. Lovely to meet you."

Wood was looking at Tate but when I spoke to him his eyes came to mine. He smiled slow and he muttered, "Yeah, Lauren."

"Bye," I said to the gray-haired guy I hadn't been introduced to.

"Later, sweetheart," he replied.

Then I turned away and walked with Shambles out of the forecourt and turned with him on the sidewalk.

It didn't occur to me until way later that Shambles and I held hands all the way to his shop.

*   *   *

Sunny and Shambles drove an old VW van and lived in a log cabin that was powered by two windmills. Every piece of land surrounding their cabin either had newly planted flowers or vegetables planted in it and they had a fledgling grape arbor. They told me they turned on the hot water heater half an hour before they needed hot water and turned it off when they were done. And we ate on the floor because most of their furniture was big pillows or beanbags.

They were also immensely kind, extraordinarily generous, and Shambles had a gift in the kitchen and not just with baked goods.

When I told them about my journey to Carnal, they both nodded as if in complete understanding.

Then Sunny said, "We *so* get that, Petal. That's how we both felt the minute we drove into town."

"It wasn't anything," Shambles went on. "It was just this feeling. This strong feeling. We both had it and it just screamed... *here!*"

"So we stayed here," Sunny finished on a sweet smile, leaned forward, took my hand and squeezed.

They drove me home and, full of their good food and the homemade wine they brought from Austin, Texas, where they used to live, I fell right to sleep.

But I woke up in the middle of night, as usual, but it wasn't because I heard Tate saying I was fat and old. It was hearing his deep voice saying, *She's mine.*

Tossing and turning and not able to get to sleep, I got up, booted up my laptop, and sent my parents and sister another e-mail, telling them I thought I'd found my new home and telling them a little bit about Ned and Betty, Jim-Billy, and Sunny and Shambles.

Still not sleepy after I sent my e-mail, I got up and looked out my window to the parking lot. There were two Harleys, an SUV, and an old station wagon in the lot.

It was after three in the morning but I figured most people didn't sleep light like me and swimming wasn't loud so they wouldn't hear me. I changed into my suit and went to the pool, slid in quietly and did my laps. I was getting better mostly because I was pushing myself not to take breaks, just to go slower and keep on going. I eked out fifty laps with only two rest periods and pulled myself out of the pool.

When I did, I heard a Harley idling somewhat close but that wasn't unusual in Carnal so I didn't even look. I just toweled off, pulled on my sweatpants, wrapped the towel around my hair, grabbed my flip-flops and sweatshirt and ran-walked to my room.

After my shower, I fell straight to sleep.

*   *   *

The Saturday shift with Wendy was a revelation.

Her energy didn't come from sucking it out of the atmosphere. Instead, there was so much of it, it filled the air and jazzed Dalton (our bartender that day) and me right up with her.

The three of us had a blast.

I found Dalton had a dry wit and didn't mind leaving the bar to help us collect empties.

Wendy was hilarious and didn't mind shouting across the bar any thought that came into her head and she did this often. Thus her having the idea I join her at a boot camp from which ensued our shouting back and forth and her finally talking me into it. Usually, though, these were just wild ideas that made Dalton, me, and all the patrons laugh. Not that me doing a boot camp wasn't a wild idea, I just didn't know it at the time.

Wendy also didn't have an issue with full-on making fun of Tonia and Jonelle and even did an impersonation of both of them, each lasting at least ten minutes, which again had Dalton, me, and all the customers in stitches.

Krystal showed up at four thirty looking her usual angry that the earth was still rotating but Wendy didn't change her behavior one bit and the great vibe continued regardless of Krystal imitating a wet blanket.

Jonelle showed at a quarter after seven and Wendy agreed to stay on until Tonia waltzed in so I gratefully took off. Saturdays were very different from normal days and this included there being five times as many people in the bar. I was run off my feet and, as much fun as I had, I wanted to get home.

I was walking back from the grocery store where I bought some deli meat, bread, diet pop, and fruit when I saw Tate pull his Harley into Bubba's.

His head turned my way as he rode in so my head tipped down and I studiously examined my feet as I kept going.

Thankfully, he was in the building by the time I walked past Bubba's (I peeked).

I went to the hotel, made myself a sandwich, ate an apple and then took the champagne to the reception desk where Ned was sitting.

"Betty still up?" I asked when I walked in, holding up the champagne and I saw his big grin light his face.

"I'll go get her," he said.

"And glasses!" I called after him as he walked away.

"Glasses!" he called back.

Then Betty, Ned, and I sat in reception, drinking champagne and playing Harry Potter Clue. They were both big Harry Potter fans, each had read the books and seen the movies so many times they lost count (their words) and, being a fan myself, the Clue game was *fabulous*.

Betty eventually had to hit the sack so I chatted with Ned for a while, said my good night on a smile, and headed back to my room.

*   *   *

I woke in the middle of the night and since the swimming thing worked so well the night before, I did it again and pushed myself harder, doing fifty laps with only one rest.

I was thinking about how pleased I was with my effort as I toweled off and went to my room. Therefore, I didn't notice the silent man watching me on his silent Harley that was parked on the side street abutting the hotel and couldn't have known he'd been doing it for fifteen minutes.

*   *   *

Working with Tonia on Sunday was a lot less fun than working with Wendy. Krystal was on and Tonia was an hour and a half late. When she showed, Krystal surprised me by not saying a word, just giving her a glare that should have burned two precise laser holes through her head. Tonia ignored this totally and I soon noticed she was good at ignoring a lot of things, including me, who she didn't say so much as "boo" to, and her customers, unless they were good-looking.

The good-looking ones she spent a lot of time with but not bringing them drinks. No, standing by their tables flipping her hair around or leaning into her hands and pressing her breasts together and swinging her booty this way and that. I'd seen Wendy do that the day before and now that I saw it, live and in person, I thought Wendy's impersonation was spot-on and even more hilarious.

Fortunately, Tonia ignoring her customers worked for me because all the rest of them eventually got fed up with it and moved to my section and since I wasn't a crap waitress, I was very busy but I also got great tips.

Wendy showed at ten to seven and I would have stayed until Jonelle showed at twenty past but when Tonia and I were both at the bar and Tonia said, "I'll just cash out," Krystal replied, "Yeah, you'll cash out in an hour and a half, the time you owe me." Then Krystal skewered her with a look, Tonia's mouth got tight, and Krystal finished, "Ass back out on the floor and, while you're out there, do me a favor and sell some fuckin' *booze*."

Wendy came back out while this was going on. She gave me a wide-eyed look and grabbed her apron.

After my shift, I decided to stay in order to give Wendy moral support and have a beer with Jim-Billy who, I found, showed on weekends much later.

"Like the quiet of the days," he told me as we drank beer.

"It isn't quiet now," I told him and it wasn't. The bar was jammed.

Jim-Billy grinned at me. "Also like the crazy nights." He took a sip, swallowed, then finished, "Balance."

"Right." I grinned back.

Tate showed at eight thirty and I figured that was my cue to go. Although I didn't want him to think I was leaving because of him, so I hung out for long enough to make that statement. This lasted a full twenty-five minutes all of which I avoided even looking at him.

Then I slid a bill on the bar, kissed Jim-Billy's cheek, called goodbye to Wendy and Krystal, and headed out.

*   *   *

Monday I was on days and would be for that week but Krystal told me I'd graduate to nights the week after.

Upon arrival at Bubba's with my La-La Land coffee in one hand and carrot-cinnamon muffin in the other, I saw Tate was also on.

His eyes came to me the minute I walked through the door.

Before he could say a word, I asked, "You want me to restock?"

I watched his jaw clench as I walked to the bar, sipping my coffee.

When I hit the bar, Tate asked, "You ever say hello?"

"Hello," I replied. "Now, do you want me to restock?"

He shook his head a couple of times, his eyes not leaving me and he said, "Yeah, Ace, restock."

He tossed me his keys and I waited until I was through the mouth of the hall to mutter, "Don't call me Ace."

*   *   *

Considering ten bikers didn't come in that day, I found it harder to avoid Tate because I didn't have much to do.

Therefore, I avoided him at lunch by running to the deli and buying him, Jim-Billy, and myself sandwiches and taking a detour to La-La Land on the way back to get all of us a huge oatmeal-cinnamon cookie, even Tate.

"I'm in a cinnamon mood!" Shambles had yelled when I questioned him on his cinnamon theme.

The sandwiches were good, the cookies orgasmic, and even Tate said so. Though he didn't use the word "orgasmic." He used the words "the shit" as in, "These cookies are…"

After we ate, I took the spray cleaner and wiped down all the tables *and* the chairs. That done, I braved going behind the bar with Tate and cleaning all the glass shelves the liquor sat on *and* the mirror behind it, moving bottles down and putting them back when I was done. Part of it was too high for me so I moved the bottles down then I climbed up on the back bar and, on my knees, kept going.

As I was reaching in and wiping, I heard Tate ask, "You want me to get closed down?"

"No," I answered the shelves.

"Then you wanna not commit a health and safety violation while the bar's open for business?"

"I'm perfectly fine," I told the shelves then I let out a little scream. I did this because two hands curled around my hips and I suddenly found my body in motion for two seconds before I found myself on my feet in front of Tate.

"You wanna pretend I don't exist, Ace, do it without breaking your neck. Yeah?" he asked but didn't wait for me to answer. He turned and started moving the bottles back to the high shelves, something, considering his height, that was no problem for him.

Jim-Billy chuckled. I glared at him.

Jim-Billy audibly and visibly swallowed his chuckle but didn't stop smiling.

The door opened and Nadine walked in.

"Hey, Nadine," I shouted so enthusiastically, her body jolted with surprise at my exuberant greeting.

Jim-Billy burst out laughing.

Nadine approached the bar. "Uh, hey there, Lauren."

Jim-Billy turned to her and announced, "Sam and Diane here are having a tiff."

Nadine's face registered understanding and she grinned.

"I'm not Diane," I snapped at Jim-Billy and then poked a thumb at Tate. "And he's not Sam."

"Got more hair," Tate muttered and that was funny but I didn't laugh even though both Nadine and Jim-Billy did.

I was also out of things to do to avoid Tate because Nadine sat on a barstool and Tate was already done with the liquor and pulling out Nadine's usual bottle of Bud Light. Once he popped off the cap, threw a coaster in front of her, and put it down, he moved to lean beside me where I was leaning against the back bar.

I couldn't move because I'd been made with my avoidance tactics, so I had to pretend Tate's existence didn't annoy me.

Everyone was silent.

Finally, Tate spoke. To me.

"You get a cell phone yet?" he asked.

"No," I answered.

"You gonna get one on your day off tomorrow?" he asked.

"No," I answered.

"Mm," he murmured.

This was a mysterious response and I didn't like the idea of a mysterious Tate so I asked, "What?"

"Nothin', babe."

I turned to him. "*Please,* can you stop calling me babe?"

"No," he answered.

I rolled my eyes and lifted a hand, palm up, to him. "Can I have your keys?"

"Why?"

"I'm going to go do a stock take in the back."

His eyebrows went up even as he blinked. "You're gonna do what?"

"A stock take. Count what you have and see if it's the same as what's on the stock sheet."

"Bubba and Krystal do that," Tate told me.

"Well, I'm saving them the trouble," I told him back.

"Why?" he asked.

I swung my arm out to the bar. "No one's here. There's nothing to do."

"So get a soda, take a break," Tate suggested.

"I can't not be busy," I replied.

"Why not?" he asked.

"I'm working, you're paying me. I can't drink a soda and chitchat. That's not right. I need to be doing something."

"Maybe you should get her to do a trainin' course for Tonia and Jonelle," Nadine put in and Tate's head swung in her direction in order to grin at her.

We were close but even when we weren't close I wasn't sure I'd ever seen him smile.

He looked good smiling.

I straightened my spine and lifted my hand up again.

"Captain, can you just give me your keys?" I asked, sounding as exasperated as I was.

He looked down at me, still grinning. I did my best to ignore how good that looked pointed in my direction and he dug in his front jeans pocket, came out with the keys, and dropped them in my hand.

"Knock yourself out," he said.

"Thanks," I returned and hightailed it to the hall.

*   *   *

My stock take took a while because it was a big job and I kept going out to check if there were more customers. Around five thirty, I made note of where I stopped and headed out as the after-work crowd was rolling in.

At six thirty, the after-work crowd suddenly included Wood.

As I was waiting for Dalton (who'd showed a half hour earlier) to fill my order, Wood slid onto the stool beside me. I looked at him and smiled.

"Hey there," I said.

"Hey, Lauren," he smiled back. "Car's done."

"Find anything I need to know about?" I asked.

He shook his head. "All good."

That would be the case. Brad had been obsessive about taking care of our cars even though I thought this was nuts considering he upgraded every two years. On a stringent schedule, he had the oil checks done, the tires rotated, the engine tuned, and both our cars regularly detailed. Not cleaned, *detailed*. He spent a fortune on it. Crazy.

"Wanna drink, Wood?" Dalton asked him.

"Yeah," Wood said on a chin lift. "Coors."

"Gotcha," Dalton replied and turned to the fridges.

"When're you off?" Wood asked.

"Sorry?" I was hefting up the tray that Dalton had loaded and concentrating on balancing it on my hand.

"Tonight, baby, when're you off?" he repeated and his voice had gone gentle and he'd called me baby so my eyes shot to his just as my heart started beating faster.

"Seven, depending on when one of the girls shows."

"Ridin' out tonight," he told me then went on. "You wanna be on the back of my bike?"

"Sorry?" I repeated, a thrill going through my belly at the thought of riding on a bike. I'd never done it but always wanted to. Always. I figured that thrill was a bit more thrilling because Wood would be the one in front of me on that bike.

"You get done, I'll take you to your car, follow you to the hotel and you and me can ride out."

"I need to get dinner," I said to him and he smiled.

"Then you and me'll ride out and get dinner," he amended.

"I'd like—" I started to accept but suddenly Tate was there and he had Wood's Coors.

"Need you to stay tonight," Tate said, planting the Coors in front of Wood and not looking at him because he was looking at me.

"What?" I asked Tate.

"Place is packed, babe, you need to stay until both Wendy and Tonia show," Tate answered and I looked around the bar seeing he was right. It was even more packed than it usually was with after-work drinkers.

Still, hopeful, I suggested, "Wendy can handle this crowd with two of you behind the bar."

"I'm leavin' soon, got somethin' to see to," Tate replied.

"But—"

He interrupted me, "Need you to stay."

"Um…," I started but he walked away.

I turned to Wood and saw he was watching Tate and he didn't look very happy.

"I'm sorry, Wood, I've got to stay," I said softly and his head turned to me and he still didn't look very happy.

"Yeah," he replied.

"Tonia can be pretty late. On Sunday, she was an hour and a half late. I don't know—"

I stopped speaking because I watched Wood's face gentle and it looked so good, I had to concentrate on keeping my tray aloft and not swooning.

"'Nother time, baby," Wood said softly.

"Okay," I whispered and didn't move.

When I didn't move for a while, Wood smiled at me and tipped his head to my tray. "You might wanna serve your drinks, Lauren."

"Oh!" I cried. "Right. I'll come and get my car tomorrow."

He nodded his head.

"Later," he said as I turned away.

"Later, Wood," I called over my shoulder.

*   *   *

Tonia was forty-five minutes late and by the time she showed, Wood was gone.

She sauntered in wearing a tank top cut off just below her breasts and a miniskirt that was almost nonexistent hanging on her hips. It was hanging in a way that it looked like it was valiantly trying not to give up the ghost but was about to fall off. She also had on sky-high stilettos that had crisscross straps that crissed and crossed all the way up her calves.

When she came in, I breathed a sigh of relief because I'd been on awhile and it might have been a slow day but it was a hectic night.

"Hey, Tate," she breathed, her eyes dewy as she hit the bar right next to me without even glancing in my direction.

"You're forty-five minutes late," Tate replied.

"Yeah, I—"

"You're also dressed like a whore," Tate went on and I sucked in breath and my eyes shot to Dalton who was close but edging back.

"What?" Tonia asked.

"You're forty-five minutes late, you're dressed like a whore, and when you start workin', you don't sell shit. Tell me, Tonia, why do I pay you?"

"Um..." She flipped her hair because she always flipped her hair but this time I noticed it was also to hide the fact that she was nervous. "To serve drinks."

"Your shift started nearly an hour ago. You serve any of those drinks in that hour?"

"I wasn't here, Tate. I had a situ—" Tonia began.

"Woman, you always got a situation and I don't give a fuck," Tate cut her off. "Strut your ass right back out that door. I'm done."

Wendy slid in beside me and stayed but I couldn't pull my eyes away from the scene in front of me.

"Are you firing me?" Tonia whispered, her eyes growing big and her body getting tight.

"Yeah," Tate replied.

"But Krystal—"

"Bubba's back. He never liked you. Krystal never liked you and I sure as fuck never liked you. You're always late and when you're here you act like you're in a singles club. Don't need that shit. Go."

"But—"

Tate leaned in and clipped, "Bitch, *go*."

She stared at him frozen like a deer in headlights for a second, then she turned and hurried out the door.

Tate's eyes sliced to me and I braced.

"You're off. I'll delay my shit a-fuckin'-gain and stay on."

"I'm fine to stay on, help Wendy," I offered.

He leaned in and he looked beyond his usual angry. So far beyond it I had to force my body to stay where it was rather than take a step back.

"Babe—" he started.

I threw up my hands. "Right, Captain, I'm off."

He extended a hand to me. "Give me your apron, I'll cash you out."

"I can get it on Wednesday," I offered and his eyes hit mine again and my hands immediately went behind my back to pull at the apron strings. "I'll let you cash me out."

"Good thinkin'," he muttered.

I gave him my apron. He moved to the back of the bar and I turned to Wendy who gave me wide eyes but those eyes were dancing and she was biting her lips.

"Don't laugh, that wasn't funny," I whispered.

"Sistah, you haven't worked with Tonia enough," she whispered back. "Trust me, that was hi…larry…*us*."

"Definitely," Dalton muttered and Wendy let a giggle escape. Tate turned to us, Wendy scampered and Dalton sauntered down the bar.

I waited and when Tate handed me my tips, I didn't even count them. I just mumbled, "Thanks, see you later," shoved my tips in my purse and got the heck out of there.

*   *   *

I'd had another moonlight swim that night, which, right then, lying facedown on my bed, I realized was a really stupid idea. I should have conserved my energy or maybe broke into the Italian restaurant, fixed myself a mess of spaghetti and carbed up.

I dragged myself out of the bed, took a shower, did the most minimal toilette preparations I would allow (blow-dried hair, face powder, swipe of blush, and mascara). I put on a pair of white shorts (that were strangely hanging way loose on me) and a spaghetti-strapped top made out of gauzy material that was a random pattern of muted pastels, had a thin ruffle at the material that crossed at the bodice and another tiny ruffle adorned the hem. I slid on flip-flops, grabbed my sunglasses (because it wasn't only warm, it was super sunny as only Colorado seemed to be able to be) and shoved them on top of my head. I made myself a huge coffee in one of Betty's big mugs and shuffled out to the lounge chairs by the pool.

I waved to Betty as I went. She waved back. I hit the closest lounge chair and collapsed in it.

I took two sips of coffee while staring at the twinkling water of the pool, set my mug on the cool deck and promptly passed out.

*   *   *

"Ace," I heard.

I thought that was weird. When I was asleep I heard a lot of things that Tate had said to me. Though, lately, it wasn't the first comment about me being old and fat. It was the stuff he'd said since, about Brad throwing away a good thing, about Tate giving me sweet dreams, about him calling me his, and the like. But I never heard him calling me Ace.

"Babe," I heard.

There it was again. Strange.

I shifted slightly, doing a little arched back stretch and then settled back into sleep.

"Laurie, baby, wake up," I heard Tate say gently as I felt fingers close around mine and squeeze. "You're gonna fry out here."

I opened my eyes to see Tate leaning over me and my body lurched.

"Holy crap," I breathed. "What on ...?" I stopped talking, looked around and saw I was lying on a lounge chair by Betty and Ned's pool. "Darn," I whispered. "I fell asleep."

"Yeah," Tate said and my eyes went to him to see he was moving and I watched in shock as he slid a hip onto the side of the lounge chair, pushing my hips out of the way to accommodate his. "You got sunscreen on?" he asked.

I was staring at his hip pressed to mine so I wasn't following. "Sorry?"

"Sunscreen, babe, you're closer to the sun up here, there aren't any clouds and, you don't have sunscreen, you're gonna fry."

My eyes went to his face. "I don't have sunscreen."

"Then you're gonna fry. Let's go to your room."

My body froze.

"My room?"

He stood and stretched his hand to me. "Up, Ace."

"What?"

He didn't repeat himself. He bent, grabbed hold of my hand, and hauled me out of the lounge chair. He bent again and nabbed my nearly full coffee mug. Then, his hand still in mine, he dragged me across the parking lot.

I was still kind of asleep so I didn't protest but I looked toward reception and saw Betty was watching us. When my sunglass-covered eyes caught hers, she started waving enthusiastically and I wasn't sure but it looked like she was bouncing up and down on her chair.

Tate stopped me outside room thirteen, taking me directly to my door, the location of which there was no way for him to know, something I was also still too drowsy to notice.

"You got your key?" he asked when I just stood there with him.

I fished it out of my pocket. He took it from me, opened the door, used my hand to maneuver me in front of him and push me in and he followed.

Then he dropped my hand, the door closed, and he went straight to the curtains, throwing them wide and bright sunlight hit the room. I shoved my sunglasses up my face taking my hair with them until they were on my head but I thought better of it when all that sunshine hit me.

He turned to me, tossed the key on the bed, and declared, "Quick Way probably carries aloe vera."

I blinked.

"You burn," he explained, walking toward me then beyond me to the bathroom saying, "you'll need aloe vera." Then he called from the bathroom, "Quick Way across the street."

"I know where it is," I called back, coming to myself and wondering how I allowed Tate to be in *my room*.

I heard the faucet and then he came out and went right to the kettle. He lifted it up, swished it around to check if there was water in it, put it back in its base, and flipped the on switch.

"You need coffee," he announced when he'd set the mug down and straightened.

"What are you doing here?" I asked.

"Right," he said and walked the four steps to me, his hand at his back pocket.

When he arrived, his hand came around, his other one grabbed mine, lifted it palm up, and then he planted an expensive-looking cellular phone in my hand.

"Cell," he said unnecessarily, his one hand still holding mine as his other hand went back to his pocket. It swung around again to put an envelope on top of the phone in my hand. "Your info, your number. It's charged. Got the charger and box in my bag on the Harley. Saw you fryin' and left it to wake you up."

I was still staring at the cell.

Then I looked up at him. "You bought me a cell phone?"

"You were sleepin' in the sun, babe, not goin' to the mall to get a phone. So I got you a phone."

"Why?" I asked.

"You need a phone," he answered.

"But—"

"It ain't safe, not having a phone."

"I—"

"And I'm not fuckin' squabblin' about it."

It was then I realized his fingers were still holding my hand palm up so I tugged my hand from his and took a step away.

"I'll pay you back," I said.

"Did already, did most of a stock take. Not your job. That's your bonus."

"But—"

He cut me off and he didn't do it angry. He did it sounding part frustrated but also part tired. "Lauren, seriously, just shut up, all right?"

I stared at him.

He'd worked a double shift and it was busy last night. He'd had a long day working a job he wasn't supposed to be working in the first place. He'd fired someone and even though he was really a jerk about it, with the way Wendy and Dalton reacted and the way I saw Tonia was myself, it was likely a long time coming. Someone had to do it and it probably wasn't pleasant. Now, we were a waitress down and they'd still been on the market after they hired me because, in reality, before they got me, they were *two* waitresses down. He was, as ever, stuck.

"You had a long day yesterday," I blurted.

His brows drew together. "Come again?"

"Nothing," I muttered. "Do you want coffee?" I asked and his eyes focused on me so intently, I could swear he was looking at me like he didn't know who I was.

Then he said, "No, Ace, need to get to Bubba's and make sure its fuckin' namesake has his ass behind the bar."

"So Bubba *is* back?"

"Yeah, though he's not much better than Tonia. At least it doesn't cost us money for him to take up space."

"Oh," I said softly and then jumped when a knock sounded on the door.

"Expecting company?" Tate asked and I looked at the door, then to him.

"It's probably Betty," I muttered, turning back to the door and I saw her head peek around the window to look in and then it disappeared so I smiled. "Betty," I confirmed and then I saw a uniformed policeman move to stand full in the window and look in and the smile froze on my face. "What on—?"

But Tate was on the move. He was across the room and had the door open before I could blink.

"Frank," Tate greeted, opening the door wide and the officer walked in, as did Betty.

"Been lookin' for you, saw your bike," the policeman said to Tate, then his gaze came to me.

"Hope you don't mind, Laurie, but he said he needed Tate," Betty put in.

"What's goin' on?" Tate asked. He hadn't taken his eyes off the officer.

"Tonia Payne was raped last night," the officer announced.

I gasped, tossed the stuff in my hand on the bed, and rushed to Tate's side at the same time I whispered, "Oh my God."

The officer looked at me and stated, "You got that right."

"What the fuck happened?" Tate growled. I belatedly noticed he was holding himself perfectly still and his face was rock-hard but there was a lethal energy emanating from him. It was so forceful, so strong, it was quickly filling the room and if Betty wasn't standing in the door holding it open and letting some of Tate's energy out, I fancied it would choke us all.

"Bad, man, and when I say that I mean *bad*," Frank told Tate. "She's messed up, in the hospital. Did her with a knife."

Betty cried out and, without thinking, my hand shot up. I

grabbed on to Tate's biceps and leaned my weight into it because if I didn't, I might faint.

Tate shifted so my hand disengaged but I didn't drop to the floor because he shifted so his arm was around my waist and he hauled me deep into his side.

"Jesus Christ, Frank, you got an audience," Tate ground out.

Frank glanced at Betty and me and mumbled, "Shit. Right. Sorry."

"Right, sorry," Tate repeated on an infuriated clip. "You can't say that at three in the mornin' when these women won't be able to sleep because that shit you just shared is poundin' into their brains."

"Sorry," Frank mumbled again.

"Tell me you got this guy," Tate demanded.

"Why you think I'm here?" Frank asked.

"Because you don't fuckin' got this guy," Tate bit out.

"We need you, Tate," Frank stated and there was the thin, but desperate, thread of a plea in his four words.

But I was surprised. Why would they need Tate?

I looked up at him to see a muscle leap in his jaw.

Then he clipped, "Outside."

Betty moved from the door and Frank moved out of it but Tate gave my waist a squeeze before he curled me into his front. *Right* into his front. Our hips and bellies were touching and everything!

Looking down at me, he ordered, "Close that door, make your coffee, and don't fuckin' listen. I'll be back."

He let me go and followed Frank.

"Oh dear," Betty said and I looked at her.

"Tonia," I whispered and my eyes filled with tears.

I mean, I didn't know her very well and I didn't like her but to be raped *with a knife*?

Betty nodded, grabbed my hand, and led me to the bed. Once there, she put her hands to my shoulders and pressed down.

"I'll make coffee," she whispered after I was seated and turned to the kettle.

Betty was silent while she made coffee and I got myself together.

Then she brought two mugs to the bed, sat down beside me and handed me mine.

That's when I asked, "Why would the cops come to Tate?"

"Well, he used to be one of 'em," she answered and I stared at her.

"Really?"

"Yeppo...and a good one."

"Why isn't he now?" I asked.

"Neeta," she answered.

"Sorry?"

"Neeta." She saw my face then patted my knee. "Long story and a sorry mess it was. I'll tell you later. But now isn't the time with Tate outside. Okay?"

I wanted to know then but she was right so I said, "Okay."

"Anyway, it's good they came to him," she said. "Tate'll find him."

"But, how can the cops ask him to help if he's a bartender?" I asked and she smiled.

"He isn't a bartender, sweetie. He's a bounty hunter."

"What?" I breathed.

"Good one a' those too, I hear. When Bubba isn't playin' hooky and Krystal's got a full staff, Tate gets called all over the country to find fugitives from the law."

"Really?" I was still only talking in breaths.

"Yeah, Laurie. Tatum Jackson's not the kind of man to spend his life behind a bar."

My eyes moved to the door.

"Wow," I whispered.

"Drink your coffee," Betty urged. I looked back at her and just sat there, so she prompted, "Coffee, sweetie."

"Right," I whispered and drank my coffee.

*   *   *

Five minutes later there was a knock on the door.

Betty ran to get it because I was sitting cross-legged on the bed taking a sip of coffee.

Tate nodded at Betty when he walked in but he came right to me, stopped, tossed a phone charger and a shiny box on the bed and looked down at me.

"Night swims are done, Ace," he declared in a hard voice.

I stared up at him and whispered a shocked, "Sorry?"

He bent at the waist, put a fist in the bed on either side of my hips, got in my face and I was too stunned to move.

"No more swimmin' unless it's daylight and Ned or Betty are around," he ordered.

"But, how do you—?"

"You get in your room, you put the chain on and you stay in it, got me?"

"But—"

"You don't open the door unless you know for a fact who it is and that they're alone," Tate went on.

"I—"

"I programmed my numbers into your phone. You need to go somewhere and it's night, you call me. I'll come down and you're on the back of my bike."

I swallowed but the tears still filled my eyes.

"She's bad," I whispered.

"She'll be lucky to survive," he whispered back.

"Tate," I kept whispering, calling him by his name for the first time ever.

I watched with some fascination as his eyes closed and something weird rushed into his features. It was weird because it appeared both warm and painful.

He opened them and said quietly, "I cut her loose last night."

My hand moved to wrap my fingers around his forearm. "It wasn't your fault."

"I cut her loose," he repeated.

"Tate, don't," I whispered.

"I wasn't nice about it," he went on.

"Don't—"

"Last thing she heard from my mouth was me callin' her a bitch."

"Tate—"

"She was on shift—"

My fingers squeezed and I leaned closer, "Honey, *don't*."

He was silent and we stared into each other's eyes for a while.

Then he ordered, "No more nighttime swimmin', babe."

"Okay," I replied softly.

He pushed away and walked to the door, saying to Betty, "She may need some aloe vera."

"Right, Tate," Betty replied to no one because he was out the door.

Betty turned to me and grinned in a way that, if I wasn't strung out on a variety of emotions, I would have thought, especially considering the circumstances, was bizarrely, happily hopeful.

But all I could say or think was, "How did he know about me swimming?"

"Why he was a good cop, why he's a good bounty hunter, Tate Jackson knows all," Betty answered.

I didn't think that was good news, not for me.

I just hoped it was equally bad news for the man who hurt Tonia.

CHAPTER FIVE

Exhausted You

THE NEXT DAY, it was just past two in the afternoon and it was another slow day at Bubba's when he came in.

I was on and Dalton was behind the bar.

My body ached from boot camp, all over, and I spent some time that morning trying to figure out if it was my leg muscles, arm muscles, ab muscles, or butt muscles that hurt the most but I couldn't decide since they all hurt equally bad.

When Jim-Billy had come in, Dalton and Jim-Billy spent time discussing Tonia. Dalton looked slightly strung out, like he'd had no sleep, looking this way probably because he was freaked about Tonia. They'd talked about Tonia until they saw it was distressing me. Jim-Billy gave Dalton a look and they both shut up about it.

I ran out to get Dalton, Jim-Billy, and myself sandwiches from the deli, popping by La-La Land to buy us all brownies with peanut butter morsels in them.

"Peanut butter's the theme this week, babeeee," Shambles had shouted upon my entry that morning to get my coffee and breakfast so I had to go back for treats for the boys if peanut butter was the theme. I loved peanut butter.

I was spending the day finishing up the stock take I hadn't quite finished two days before, running back and forth to the front to make sure Dalton was good. I had just finished my task and was mentally designing the spreadsheet I was going to create on my laptop that night and present to Krystal. I was walking up the hall when I saw the front door open and Tate walked in.

I took one look at his face and tripped over my feet.

"Hey, Tate. Got news?" I heard Dalton ask almost the instant Tate arrived.

"Ace," Tate called, his eyes on me, not answering Dalton's question. "Turn around. Office," he ordered.

I didn't protest. I nodded, turned, hurried down the hall and waited for him outside the office door. When he arrived, he unlocked it with his keys and pushed it open, holding it so I could precede him. I flipped on the light switch as I entered, took several steps in, and turned. Tate closed the door and put his back to it.

I opened my mouth to speak.

"She died this mornin'," Tate announced.

I closed my eyes and mouth, then opened my eyes and started to him.

"Don't," he gritted and I jerked to a halt. "Don't come near me, babe."

"Captain—"

He cut me off. "Called me my name yesterday, Ace."

I swallowed then mumbled, "Um…Tate—"

"Talked to Betty and Ned," he interrupted again. "They're movin' you to a room closer to their place. Don't want you on the end. Too far away."

"Okay," I agreed.

"You walk to work today?" he asked.

"Yes," I replied.

"I'll be here at seven, take you home," he told me.

"I'll ask Jim-Billy—"

"I'll be here, Lauren."

"Okay," I whispered.

He stopped speaking and we stared at each other.

Finally, I got brave enough to say, "You aren't responsible, Tate."

He didn't answer.

I took a step toward him and stopped when his hard face got harder.

"You aren't," I whispered.

"Why do you swim at night?" he asked and my head tilted to the side at his change in topic.

"Why do I swim at night?"

"Yeah."

"I have insomnia," I answered. "Always have, even when I was a kid."

"You can't sleep?"

I shook my head. "Sometimes I can't drop off. Sometimes I wake up, two, three times a night. Sometimes when I wake up, I can't get back to sleep."

"So you swim," he stated.

"Well, not normally, though at home I had a pool. I just never used it for some reason. But here…" I didn't finish because I didn't know why I'd rarely ever used our pool or why I so often used Ned and Betty's.

"Your man, he didn't help you sleep?" Tate asked and I drew in breath.

This wasn't any of his business, none at all.

Still, I answered, "I'm not sure he could do much about it. It kind of…" I paused, then finished, "annoyed him so in the end if I knew I was going to have a rough night, I'd move to the guest bedroom."

"He let you do that?"

"Let?" I was confused. "He asked me to."

"He asked you to leave the bed he shared with you," Tate stated like Brad asking me to move to another bed so he could get a good night's sleep was like asking me to give up our life, pack a few belongings in a big bandanna, tie it to a stick, and become hobos.

"Why are we talking about this?" I asked quietly.

"You sleep after you swam?" Tate asked back, not quietly, still shooting questions at me like this was an interrogation.

"Sorry?"

"Those nights you swam, when you got in, did you nod off?"

"Yes."

"Did you wake up again?"

"No."

"Exhausted yourself," he surmised.

"Maybe, listen—"

"So, maybe, if he'd exhausted you, you wouldn't have had trouble sleeping."

"Exhausted me?"

"Yeah, Ace, fucked you so hard you couldn't move. Couldn't do anything but sleep. Exhausted you."

I couldn't move at that moment. Couldn't do anything but stare.

"You were in my bed, couldn't sleep, that's what I'd do," he told me.

"Tate," I breathed.

"Wanna come to me now?" he asked like it was a dare.

"I…" I swallowed. "I don't think so."

"That's probably a good call."

"You're angry," I said softly, deciding that was it. That was why he was acting in this alarming way, saying these insane things. He told me he said a lot of stuff he didn't mean when he was angry. That had to be it.

"Yeah, babe, I'm angry. I was angry when I fired her ass and said shit I shouldn't say. She left, got nabbed by a goddamned psycho who tied her up and cut her up, inside and out. She was alive while he was doin' it, all the time he was doin' it. He cut all her hair off at the scalp. He even cut *into* her scalp and it didn't bleed all that much because she didn't have all that much blood left to give. Then he left her, naked, exposed to the elements and covered in blood, to be found by an old lady walkin' her fuckin' dog. So now I'm angry about that."

I hated what he just told me. Hated knowing it. Hated the images it invoked. Hated that it happened to Tonia and her beautiful body and her gorgeous hair. I hated everything about it.

But I knew he had to let it go. I didn't know why he trusted me to let it go with but he did so I also knew I had to take it.

"You aren't responsible," I repeated.

"I kicked her ass out and she was as good as dead not an hour later."

"Tate, you aren't responsible. It wasn't Tonia, it would be someone else."

"But it was Tonia."

We stared at each other a while longer.

Then I whispered, "Can I come to you now?"

"You ready for that?"

"I don't know."

"You gotta cross the room, Ace, I ain't movin'."

I didn't think. I just crossed the room.

When I made it to him, I fitted myself to his long body, wrapping my arms around his waist and pressing my cheek against his chest. When I was done, his arms came around me so tight, he squeezed the breath out of me.

I felt him rest his cheek against the top of my head.

"Now, how'd I know you'd do that?" he asked a question he didn't expect an answer to, which was good because he might have known but, until I did it, I didn't know.

"You aren't responsible, honey," I whispered to his chest.

"Keep sayin' it, baby, maybe it'll sink in."

"You aren't responsible."

He gave me a squeeze.

"Betty told me what you do," I said quietly.

Tate didn't reply.

"Are you gonna find him?" I asked.

"Yeah, I'm gonna find him. Though they think they want me to but they sure as fuck don't."

I tipped my head back to look at him and his head went up when I did.

"Why not?"

"I find him, Ace, I'm gonna rip his dick off and shove it down his throat."

I couldn't stop my face from scrunching together and my mouth muttering, "Gross."

He smiled at me, my face unscrunched, and I stared at his mouth.

He released me with one of his arms so his hand could come up to my cup jaw.

"Laurie, I'll find him," he promised.

"Okay," I whispered.

"So you don't worry," he said.

I nodded and my nod didn't disengage his hand. "Okay."

"You believe me?" he asked.

"Yes," I answered and I did.

"So you'll have sweet dreams?"

Oh.

My.

God.

My body melted into his of its own accord.

"Tate," was all I could say.

I watched and held my breath as his face dipped close to mine. He used his hand at my jaw to tip mine farther up toward his and I closed my eyes at the last second, thinking, even hoping he was going to kiss me. But I felt the side of his nose brush the side of mine and then I felt his lips against my forehead.

"Seven o'clock, babe, on my bike," he muttered there then kissed me, let me go, set me away, turned and disappeared out the door.

I stared at the empty hall for very long moments.

I stared at it for more.

Then I asked the empty hall, "What just happened?"

There was no reply.

*   *   *

At a quarter to four, the door opened, Krystal walked in, and I stared.

Her hair was no longer platinum blonde but ebony. The change was startling and it looked good on her.

When I could unglue my eyes from The New Krystal, I saw there was a man at her heels and then I stared at him.

He was huge, as in mammoth. He had to be nearly seven feet tall. He had light brown hair and a full, thick beard. His shoulders were broad, his legs like tree trunks, his arms like stout branches, and he had a big belly that worked on him because it too looked solid and it fit in with the rest of his massive physique. He was wearing a loose-fitting white T-shirt, faded jeans, and Carnal's requisite motorcycle boots.

His eyes hit me and got big, then he boomed, "Right on!" and came right at me.

I didn't have time for an evasive maneuver before his fingers curled around my shoulder, giving it a rough jerk and my body collided with his. His arms wrapped around me and he swung me side to side.

"Lauren, Super Waitress!" he shouted over my head and I tipped it back to look at him when he stopped rocking me.

"Um…hi," I said.

He looked down at me and introduced himself, "Bubba."

"I guessed that," I told him and he smiled and his smile was as huge and overwhelming as everything else about him.

"Krys told me about you. Told me you were the shit," he informed me and my eyes slid to Krystal who was standing by Jim-Billy at his end of the bar. She was watching us with an expressionless face (outside of looking mildly annoyed).

I was pretty shocked by this compliment. Krystal seemed a hard nut to crack. I couldn't imagine she was at home telling Bubba I was good at my job. I imagined when she was at home she spent her time contemplating the numerous things that annoyed her, why they did, and how they'd never stop. Or, if Bubba was home, she'd spend her time giving him stick. Not praising me.

"Thanks, that's nice," I said to Bubba and he let me go.

"Finally, a decent waitress," he declared, lumbering behind the bar and going straight to a fridge to pull out a beer. He turned around and twisted off the top. "Uh…not to speak ill of the dead."

I looked at Jim-Billy and saw him wince. Then I looked back at Bubba to see Krystal, fast as lightning, was at his side. She reached up to curl her fingers around the wrist he had raised to down some brew and yanked on it. Beer sloshed out and got in Bubba's beard and down his shirt.

"Woman!" he shouted, swiping at his beard.

"You're here to work, Bub, not tie one on," she snapped.

"What's the point of ownin' a bar if you can't have a freakin' beer?" he shot back.

"I don't know. Maybe to sell them so we can pay our mortgage?" she suggested sarcastically.

Bubba scowled at her then asked, "Again, darlin', you wanna know why I fish so goddamned much?"

"Bub—"

He looked at Jim-Billy. "Bustin' my balls in front of an audience. Shit."

"I did the stock take," I put in in an effort to defuse the situation and Bubba and Krystal looked at me. "It's finished. I finished it this morning. I wrote a report and put it on the clipboard. Everything was good, a few things here and there, nothing big except there seems to be a case of Jack Daniel's missing. I figured there was a mistake in the entry and I tried to track it but…"

I trailed off because the atmosphere got thick and I was watching Krystal's head slowly turn and tip back to look at Bubba.

Uh-oh.

"You take that case?" Krystal asked.

"Darlin'—" Bubba started.

"You take it?" she snapped.

"I'm not goin' fishin' without my Jack," he declared.

"Fuck me," she muttered, turned and stomped from behind the bar and down the hall.

I looked at Bubba to see he was watching her go. Then his eyes came to me.

"I'm so sorry," I whispered. "I didn't—"

He shook his head. "Don't worry 'bout it, gorgeous. She'd eventually find out. She's already pissed as hell at me. Might as well get it over with all in one go rather than her gettin' over her 'tude then gettin' somethin' new to have 'tude about it. Figure you did me a favor."

"Well, I'm glad you can look at it like that," I said.

"Bright side of life, Lauren. You live with a storm cloud, you learn to find the bright side," he replied and then followed Krystal.

I looked at Dalton, then at Jim-Billy.

"Um…*eek!*" I said to Jim-Billy.

"You said it," Jim-Billy muttered.

"Is it like that all the time?" I asked, moving closer to him.

"Chalk and cheese," Jim-Billy answered. "Bubba's a good ole boy, laid-back, mellow, all about havin' fun, not about havin' responsibility. Krystal's had it rough. She's worked all her life. It's made her hard and she wanted her piece of something that was just hers. Thought she'd get it with the bar, bein' the boss, not havin' to eat shit for a livin'. As you can see, she's still workin' hard and Bubba's fishin'. He sees nothin' wrong with that, not one thing. She does double shifts a lot. I don't see good things."

"Didn't she know—?" I started.

"'Bout Bubba?"

I nodded.

He nodded back. "She knew, Laurie. But he made promises to her, to Tate, he'd toe the line. He'd do his bit. He'd grow up." Jim-Billy shook his head. "Tate gets in his face, Bubba goes on the wagon but he always falls off."

I got closer and asked quietly, "Does he like fishing *that much*?"

Jim-Billy stared at me.

Then he leaned in and whispered, "Honey, he ain't fishin'." I didn't reply and must have looked confused because Jim-Billy went on whispering. "Why you think you broke through that stone around Krystal's heart and made her take a chance on you?"

"I don't—"

"He fucks around, Laurie, with anything that moves, anything that breathes. Off here, there, and everywhere, partyin' and gettin' himself laid. Folks around town call him Bender Bubba. He's on a bender and *anything goes*."

I looked to the doorway of the hall, asking, "Why does she put up with it?"

I looked back to Jim-Billy to see him shrug. "She loves 'im."

I could understand that. Many women who hadn't been cheated on didn't understand other women who put up with it. When Brad came clean, told me about Hayley, my very first thought was *I forgive you*. I couldn't see a life alone. I couldn't abide a life without him in it. I wanted him so bad and loved him so much, I would have taken him any way I could have had him.

He just didn't want me.

"Poor Krystal," I whispered.

"Don't let her hear you sayin' that," Jim-Billy whispered back.

I looked at him, bit my lip, and nodded.

The door opened and customers came in. I knew them, they'd been in before.

I grabbed my tray, headed their way and smiled, calling, "Hey Steg, Bob, what's up?"

*   *   *

"Need two Bud drafts," I said to Krystal as I hit the bar.

"Gotcha," she replied, turning to nab some mugs and turning back, her hand going to the tap.

I studied her.

There was a lot on my mind, primarily Tate, who was coming to put me on the back of his bike so he could drive me the five blocks to my hotel. Also on my mind was his rampant desire for my safety and willingness to secure it.

His words in the office, though, were flipping me out, scaring me and other, very different things besides. I didn't get it. I wasn't certain what happened in there or why it happened. All I knew was that it did.

But now, I was thinking about Krystal.

She put a mug on my tray and went for the other one.

"You okay?" I asked.

She didn't look at me when she answered, "Yeah, why?"

"Tonia," I said softly and her eyes slid to me, then back to the mug she was filling.

"Girl was a waste of space," she muttered and I felt my face flinch. Then she went on, "Still, Christ."

"Yeah," I said and she put the other mug on my tray.

Then she surprised me by asking, "You okay?"

"About Tonia?" I asked back and she nodded. "No," I answered.

"No one deserves that," she stated.

"No," I agreed. "No one deserves that."

"Folk sayin', way she dressed, way she acted, brought it on herself," Krystal told me.

"Really? People are saying that already?"

"Yep," she nodded.

"Do they know all that happened to her?" I asked.

"All that happened to her?"

"The, um...thing with her hair," I explained.

"What thing with her hair?"

I looked at her a second and then muttered, "Nothing."

She examined me and her face changed in a way I couldn't read. Then she said, "Tate."

"What?"

"Tate tell you what happened to her?"

"Um...yeah. He popped by earlier and—"

She cut me off. "No, folk don't know all that happened to her." Then she mumbled, "Fuckers."

"Got that right," I replied.

She caught my eyes and surprised me again. "Thanks for doin' the stock take, Lauren."

"Um...you're welcome."

"And Tate says you wiped down most of the bar," she went on.

"It was a slow day," I told her.

She nodded. "Speakin' a' that, with Tonia gone and Tate on the hunt, we're losin' the waitress durin' the day. I've redone the schedule. Copies of it are on the desk in the office. All the girls are nights now, even you."

I nodded back again. "Okay, that's fine with me."

"You can handle it," she said and I smiled at her.

She didn't smile back.

Instead, she informed me, "Got ads in papers all over the county and then some. Gnaw Bone, Chantelle, everywhere. Hopin' we'll get a couple of girls in soon."

"Okay," I replied.

"It'll be tough for a while—"

I interrupted her. "We'll cope."

She held my gaze a long moment.

Then I said, "Better serve these."

She turned away, muttering, "Yeah."

*   *   *

I was in the bathroom studying myself in the mirror.

I was still in research mode in order to find ways to be the best waitress I could be in an effort to make a living when the time came when I actually had to make a living. Day tips weren't great, as Krystal had warned. On Saturday and Sunday, when the bar was busy, tips were fantastic. Even fantastic, they didn't make up for the weekdays. It would be good to work nights.

In my efforts at research, I was experimenting with makeup. Today, it was slightly heavier. Not Krystal, Jonelle, and, rest her, Tonia heavy but not my normal subtle either.

I was also experimenting with footwear.

I'd dug into my clothes and pulled out a top that I bought a few years ago but it hadn't fit in a while. Seeing as I was constantly missing meals, on my feet, and swimming regularly, my clothes were fitting loose. So I'd tried it and found it fit though it was just a smidge snug at the cleavage.

A cream blouse, a bit see-through so I wore an off-white stretchy camisole under it. It also fit snug up my midriff but it was supposed to because it had two darts at both sides under my breasts and the same at both sides in the back. It had a collar and such short sleeves they couldn't really be called sleeves as they were just an inch of material.

I'd also added a layer of a bunch of silver necklaces that I usually only wore one at a time. All of them had daisies or flowers dangling from them or pendants with daisies and flowers stamped on them. I'd put on my daisy stud earrings and my flower-dangling bracelets.

I'd paired this with jeans, a tan belt, and, the new tactic of the day, stiletto high-heeled sandals. They were tan leather that almost matched the belt and they had five thin straps that led into a big rose at the toe and a wraparound ankle strap you couldn't see under the boot-cut of my jeans. This was too bad because I always thought it was sassy and Brad had agreed. He'd loved those sandals and he especially loved the sassy ankle strap.

Being on them all day, my feet were killing me so I decided to take Bubba's advice and look on the bright side. Focusing on my feet, I could stop thinking about my whole body aching. Also, when I walked up to a patron, I found they were giving me a head-to-toe and an easy smile, even if I didn't know them.

I couldn't be sure as I hadn't counted them but I thought my tips might have taken a turn for the better. Maybe not a massive one that would allow me to add a manicure to my schedule every week once I settled in, bought a house, and furnished it but I could at least maybe buy groceries.

At that moment, however, I was wondering about wearing high-heeled sandals on the back of a bike.

Was that okay?

I was also wondering if I should put on lip gloss.

I was wondering this because it was past seven and I was waiting for Tate to come and get me.

And I was wondering all of this while wondering about me wearing a little cream blouse, jeans that were not tight but a bit loose, and a pair of sandals that cost over two hundred dollars. Neeta's whole outfit probably cost half that and Tate had carried her into a hotel room, kissing her.

I was not Neeta by any stretch of the imagination. I was not the kind of woman who was bad news, who made a man change careers because of whatever, who met him at a hotel at night.

I was the kind of woman who wore cream blouses, not tank tops, and needed a ride home because her boss, who might be a jerk on occasion but who'd certainly demonstrated a fair degree of assuming responsibility, knew she was a woman alone with no one to look after her.

So he was looking after me. That was it.

Thus, I decided, no lip gloss.

But that didn't stop me from being incredibly nervous—but I was nervous in a belly-fluttering, excited way. Like I'd just made it to the top of a roller coaster and was about to take the plunge.

This, I told myself, was not because Tate informed me the way he'd cure my insomnia was by fucking me until I couldn't move. A comment, I decided, he made because he was upset about Tonia and was trying to put his mind to other things.

This, I told myself, was because I was going to ride on his bike.

The door opened and one of the female clientele walked in, dressed and made-up a lot like Krystal. I hadn't seen her before so I just smiled and moved to the door.

The minute I hit the bar, I saw Tate standing at the other end by Jim-Billy. That belly flutter escalated and I thought I might either pass out or vomit.

Then I was rocked back on a foot when a strong force hit me.

I looked down to see Wendy had her arms wrapped around me.

"Oh Lauren," she whispered.

I put one arm around her and I slid my other hand along her short hair as I tipped my head so my mouth was at her ear.

"Baby," I whispered.

"I didn't like her but this *sucks*," she whispered back, not letting go of me.

"I know."

She released me, stepped back and looked up. "Feel like a bitch, laughed when she got fired."

"Take your mind off that, Wendy," I advised.

"Right, how?" she asked.

"I don't know, honey, just…if your mind wanders there, visualize a stop sign and don't go down that path. You didn't know what would happen to her."

Her eyes slid slightly to the side before coming back to me. "I bet Tate's feelin' like an asshole."

She would win that bet.

"He'll be okay," I assured her with more confidence than I actually felt.

"Yeah, he's a tough guy. They shoulda fired her ages ago. Only could do it, really, if they had you…which they did so he did it. Still, shit timing."

"Yes," I agreed then my eyes moved to him to see he was openly watching Wendy and me. I looked back at Wendy. "I have to go, honey. He's here now because he's my ride."

Wendy blinked what could only be called a *Kapow!* blink. Her eyes squeezed together tight and quick, taking her eyebrows with them and then opening wide.

"He's your ride?"

"I walked in today and he doesn't want me walking back by myself," I explained.

"Jim-Billy, Dalton, or Bubba could take you home. Hell, half the guys here would do it," she replied.

"Um . . . well, tonight Tate's doing it."

She grinned. "He likes you."

"He doesn't like me."

"He likes you," she repeated.

"I'm a good waitress," I stated.

She shook her head. "Un-unh, that isn't why he likes you." She leaned forward. "He *likes you,* likes you."

"I'm not his type," I replied and she burst out laughing so hard she had to lean forward and shove her hands between her knees.

"What's so funny?" I asked when she straightened and swiped under her eyes.

"Sistah, you need to hang around bikers more," she told me.

"Sorry?"

"They like *ass,*" she stated and I stared at her. "And tits. Real bikers, born and bred, like their women to look like *women.* They go for curves, for hair, for attitude. You are the *queen* of all of that. That's why all the guys in here can't tear their eyes off you."

"All the guys in here can tear their eyes off me," I retorted.

"Girlfriend, wake *up.* We can get busy but we been a heckuva lot more busy weeknights and it isn't because Jonelle's testing the boundaries of indecent exposure and Tonia . . ." She trailed off.

"Wendy, it's coming on summer. People come out of hibernation when—"

"They like your ass."

"They don't."

"And your tits."

"Wendy."

"And your long-ass legs. Your legs go on for-eh-ver. Even Tyler said you had great pegs, the best."

This surprised me. "He did?"

She smiled. "Yeah. And he's not a tits-and-ass man. He likes lean and cut but he sure likes your legs."

"Shut up."

"He does!"

"Shut up!"

"Ace!" Tate shouted. Both Wendy and I jumped and twisted our necks to look his way. "You cashed out or what?" Tate asked, still shouting.

"I'm cashed out," I shouted back.

"You wanna socialize for the next hour or are we gonna go?" He was still shouting and I was acutely aware, due to the fact that the noise level declined significantly, that the entire bar was listening.

"Keep your pants on!" I yelled.

The noise level disappeared.

"Babe, get your ass over here," Tate ordered.

"Patience, Captain, I'm talking to Wendy," I shot back.

"Ass. Over. Here!" Tate commanded.

I looked at Wendy and snapped loudly, "He's so darned *bossy*!"

Two men and a woman sitting at the bar close to us burst out laughing.

"You better get your ass over there," Wendy advised.

I rolled my eyes and stomped across the bar.

Tate watched me stomp and turned his body to face me as I rounded the corner.

"I need to get my purse," I told him irritably.

"Don't take a year," he returned.

"I won't take a year!" I snapped and stomped down the hall,

stopped and stomped back to Tate. I lifted a hand and demanded, "Keys."

He dug into his pocket muttering, "Shit, you're a pain in my ass."

"I will repeat, Jim-Billy can walk me home," I informed him and looked over at Jim-Billy while I jerked a thumb at him.

Jim-Billy's neck sunk into his shoulders, his eyes stayed fixed to the back of the bar and he took a sip of his draft.

"Get your purse, Ace," was all Tate said, depositing his keys in my hand.

"Whatever," I muttered, stomped down the hall and got my purse.

When I arrived back in the bar I ignored the avid eyes of an audience that included nearly all the patrons. I could do this because Tate snatched his keys away, grabbed my hand, and dragged me to the door, so I had to concentrate on walking.

"Later guys!" I shouted over my shoulder, waving at the crew.

"See ya, Lauren!" Wendy shouted back.

"Later, gorgeous!" Bubba boomed.

Dalton lifted his chin and Krystal didn't utter a peep.

Then we were outside and Tate was dragging me toward his bike where he pulled me to a halt but didn't drop my hand.

"You know, Ace, I could do without havin' a scene with you every time I enter that fuckin' bar," he stated.

Well, at least this was familiar territory and not the confusing territory we'd been camped out in the last couple of times we were together. I'd pissed him off.

"You started it," I returned.

His brows went up. "Seriously?"

"Seriously what?"

"That's all you got?" he asked.

"Well you did!"

"Christ," he muttered. He pushed me slightly away from the bike using my hand, then he swung his leg over and started fiddling with the console. The bike roared to life and I could swear I felt wetness surge between my legs.

I was concentrating on this and biting my lip in an effort to stop a moan from escaping my throat when Tate looked at me.

"Climb on," he ordered.

I looked behind him. Then I looked at him.

"How?" I asked.

"What?" he asked back.

"How do I get on?"

He stared at me. Then he asked, "You never been on a bike?"

I shook my head.

He stared at me some more.

Then it was my turn to stare at him because a slow, sexy smile spread across his face and that wetness between my legs wasn't uncertain anymore.

"Don't got a lotta time but you're gonna get a ride," he stated.

"I know, you're taking me home."

He was still smiling when he instructed, "See that foothold?" and he jerked his head toward the back of the bike.

I looked, saw it, and nodded.

"Put your right foot on it, grab on to me, and swing your left leg over."

"Okay," I said and did as he instructed.

It was easy and I did it without incident, something I was proud of. I didn't want to topple over or make him topple over or the bike topple over. None of that happened and I settled in behind him.

"A natural," he muttered as he started walking the bike backward out of the spot.

"Sorry?" I called over the pipes.

He didn't answer. Instead he said, "Hold on."

"To what?"

He twisted his neck to catch my eyes, "To me, babe."

"Oh," I whispered, feeling like an idiot, and put my hands to his waist.

"Ace," he called and I looked to see his neck was still twisted. "Hold on."

"I am." And I was!

He leaned up. I reared back a bit but he grabbed my wrists and pulled them around in such a firm way that I had no choice but to plaster my front against his back. He let my wrists go when he had them wrapped around his flat stomach and before I could utter a noise we rocketed through the parking lot.

I was lucky his bike was so loud because I was pretty sure the moan I felt in my throat was audible.

He pulled into the street and he didn't take me to my hotel.

He drove out of Carnal.

"Where are we going?" I shouted over the wind and the pipes.

"Ride," was his response.

"Sorry?" I shouted.

"Relax, Ace, just feel it," he shouted back.

I didn't relax and just feel it. Not until he turned into the hills and then I couldn't help but relax and just feel it.

And "it" was *beautiful*. The bike, the wind, the noise, the dark vistas, Tate's solid body, my hair whipping around my face and neck.

It was phenomenal.

So phenomenal, I forgot everything but what I could see, what I could feel, and I relaxed into his back, putting my cheek to his shoulder and watching the world roar by.

I'd never been so out of mind but rooted to my body. I'd never let go that much and just let myself feel. There was something freeing about it, peaceful yet exciting. A weird combination that shouldn't work together but it really fucking did.

And I loved every second of it. So much, my mind so clear, I didn't notice we were back until Tate pulled into Carnal Hotel's parking lot. He drove straight to reception, parked out front, and turned off the bike.

I sat behind him, still holding on like we were riding and I was staring at Ned who was staring at us.

"Babe," Tate called and my body jolted.

I swung my leg off and had both feet on the ground when Tate swung off behind me.

"I'll get your new key," he said and started to reception.

I followed him.

"Jackson, hey son. Laurie," Ned greeted as we walked in.

"Ned," Tate returned.

"Hey, Ned." I smiled.

"You're in three," Ned told me, opening a drawer and taking out a key attached to a ring that also had a big red triangular piece of plastic connected to it. Ned slid the key across the counter. Tate nabbed it and Ned's eyes came to me. "We moved your stuff, hon, hope you don't mind. Betty used your suitcases and did the personal stuff. I just lugged suitcases and did the dresser and fridge," he said.

"Thanks, Ned, that's sweet of you both," I replied.

"Didn't figure you'd wanna work all day and then schlep your stuff to a new room," he explained.

"I owe you a bottle of champagne and another round of Clue," I told him.

"Lookin' forward to that, Laurie," Ned said and Tate grabbed my hand. Ned's eyes dropped to it and he quickly finished with, "'Night you two," but he said it while grinning huge.

"Later, Ned," Tate murmured as he pulled me to the door.

"'Night, Ned," I called as the door swung closed behind us.

Tate kept my hand in his as we walked to room three, which was way closer to Ned and Betty's. I had to walk double-time to keep up with his long strides. He didn't release my hand when he made it to the door. He just unlocked it, opened it, and pushed me inside.

I walked four steps in while Tate flipped the light switch.

It was an exact copy of my other room, to the letter.

I threw my purse on the bed, turned to Tate, and remarked, "Weird, it's like I didn't even move. It's the same room."

"Enjoy the ride?" Tate asked and I blinked at him.

"Sorry?"

"Did you enjoy the ride, Lauren?" he repeated and I smiled.

"Yes, Tate, it was—"

I didn't finish but I made another sound. It was a gasp because one second he was standing inside the closed door. The next he was standing right in front of me, one of his hands was sliding up my neck into my hair, the other arm was wrapped around my waist pulling my body into his.

"What are you—?" I got out before his fingers in my hair fisted, pulled down just a tad less than gentle, and his mouth was on mine.

And he kissed me.

No. He *kissed* me.

Brad was a good kisser and he was great in bed. He wasn't my first kiss though, or my first lover. I'd had a better kisser than Brad, but not a better lover.

But Tate's kiss...

There was no describing it.

It didn't start slow. It started hard and wet and so demanding I had no choice but to give back what I got. And I did. Our tongues sparred, then our teeth bit at each other's lips and our heads twisted this way and that, all of it a mindless, sexy dance that was all-consuming. There was nothing but his mouth and my mouth, what they were doing and what they were making me feel. Nothing. Not in the whole universe.

When he lifted his head a fraction of an inch I found one of my hands was up his shirt in the back and one of them was cupping the back of his head. His hand was still fisted in my hair but his other arm had moved up to curve tight just under my shoulder blades, the pads of his fingers pressed into the side of my breast.

We both were breathing deep, our breaths mingling between us. I could feel his on my sensitized lips and he had to feel mine.

Finally, he spoke. "Shit, Ace."

"Shit what?" I whispered, staring into his eyes, so close, I could count the tawny flecks.

"This isn't good," he whispered back and I swallowed and felt a sour pit forming in my belly.

"It isn't?"

"I gotta focus." He went on whispering.

"On what?" I asked, also whispering.

"On shit that doesn't include what that mouth and tongue of yours could do to my cock."

My hand at his back fisted. "Tate—"

"And if your pussy is as sweet as your mouth."

"Tate—"

"Shit," he muttered.

"Tate—"

"I gotta find this guy," he told me.

"I know."

"I get back, Lauren, you're on the back of my bike."

I blinked at what he said, mostly because I didn't understand it. Then I swayed because he let me go and without a word or looking back, the door to my room closed behind him.

Several moments later, when I could speak, I asked the door, "Get back from where?"

Like the hall earlier that day, the door didn't have an answer.

CHAPTER SIX

Trash

I WAS SITTING, cross-legged in the middle of my bed at the hotel and staring at my laptop in front of me.

It had been a month since Tate's kiss. A month where a lot had happened. A month since he'd walked out of my room and I hadn't seen or heard from him again.

I'd spent the last however many hours finally going through over six months of e-mails.

I should have checked sooner.

My mother, father, and sister all had my new location and the number to the cell phone Tate had bought me. I'd given up that information weeks ago. They had been in constant contact since then, first freaked way the heck out, then settling in because they heard I was settling in. My folks were planning to come out and visit me at the end of the summer and Caroline and her partner Mack were thinking of coming with them. I liked this idea. They'd like Carnal and Betty and Ned could always do with the business.

That was all good, the rest of my e-mails were all bad.

First were the ones from my so-called friends sending so-called concerned e-mails about my quick exit from town, selling off all my stuff and cutting off my ties to my old life. Invitations to dinner and drinks abounded, they said so they could talk to me, find out if I was okay, make sure I was doing the right thing.

What they meant was so they could find out where my head was at and then inform Hayley. She knew I had the goods on Brad and I could make the divorce uncomfortable. She knew all I had to do was tell my attorneys to nail his ass (and they were practically begging me to do it) and I could wipe the floor with him.

But I didn't. I signed the papers, took my half of our life, sold it within days of signing the papers, and got the heck out of there.

Then the e-mails changed. Instead of seeming fake concerned, they seemed more concerned. Then they seemed contrite. Then they begged me to call, check in, touch base.

Something was happening, my old, fake, two-faced friend Audrey told me, something I needed to know.

She'd sent that e-mail just two weeks before.

Which was one week before Brad sent his one and only e-mail.

"Ree," it began and just seeing his nickname for me typed on the screen sent a knife through my heart that hurt so much I almost couldn't read on. Conversely, it also pissed me off so much I almost couldn't read on.

I wished I didn't. But I did.

The rest of it said:

Where are you? I've been calling your cell and it says I can't leave a message. Your parents won't tell me. I've called Caroline a dozen times and Mack won't let me speak to her.

I can't believe you left like that. Honey, you didn't even say goodbye. We didn't get to talk. There are things that needed to be said, things that were happening you needed to know, things that had changed. We needed to talk. Didn't you get my messages before you left?

I need to speak to you, Ree, urgently, honey. When you get this, call me or tell me where you are.

I made a mistake, darling, and I need to explain.

All my love,
B

He made a mistake? What mistake?

He needed to explain? Explain what?

Things had changed? What things?

All my love? What the *fuck* was *that* about?

I stared at the e-mail.

I'd gotten his messages before I left, I'd just ignored them. He had his nose so far up my ass in an effort to make our split amicable and not do anything to make me get angry that it'd take surgery to extricate him. I didn't need his fake concern when he was not only fucking my best friend but had been for years and had left me to move in with her and had already started his new happy bubble life.

I needed to get out. So I got out.

Where in the Divorce Rulebook did it say I had to say good-bye? All the good-byes that needed to be said were said that night he told me he didn't love me anymore but he loved the woman who I'd spent two years confiding in that I was worried something was wrong in my marriage and I would rather die than lose my husband.

I hit the cross at the top of the screen and closed the e-mail. Then

I hit the cross on the viewing panel and closed the program. I shut down the machine and slapped the laptop closed.

Then my cell rang.

I picked it up and looked at the display. It said "Wood Calling."

I hit the button to take the call and put it to my ear.

"Hey," I said.

"Hey, baby," he greeted in his gentle voice and my toes curled. "What chance I got that you'll finish work tonight and drive to my place?"

I smiled into the phone. "I'm not done until after three in the morning, Wood."

"Know that, Laurie."

"I'll be dead on my feet and only want to sleep."

"I got a bed."

"Yes, and you have a job where you go to work at seven. I have a job that I sleep until noon."

"You're tellin' me this because…"

"I'll crash and three hours later you'll be gone."

"And?"

"And Ned and Betty'll worry about me."

I listened to him laugh. He had a great laugh.

"I'll swing by while you're at work. Explain to Momma Betty and Poppa Ned that Baby Laurie'll be safe with Uncle Wood."

I asked through a light giggle, "Will I be safe?"

"Fuck no," he answered and my giggle was no longer light.

Then I whispered, "I'll come over."

"That's what I wanna hear, baby," he said in his gentle voice.

I didn't know why I did this dance. For the past week, nearly every night I'd ended my shift in Wood's bed. I was not lying, all I wanted to do by the time I got there was crash, which was all I did. And he got up and went to work before seven. Half the time I didn't know he'd left me.

He didn't seem to mind about any of this. Then again, Krystal had hired two new girls and my constant work would end very soon since they both were starting in the next couple of days. I figured Wood was hanging around, waiting for his reward.

"I'll leave the door open," he said and he would. He always did.

"I'll see you later," I replied.

"Later."

Then he hung up.

I hit the button on my phone, threw it on the bed, looked at my alarm clock, and swung my tanned legs off the bed.

It was time to get ready for work.

*   *   *

My life had taken another veer the day after Tate's kiss.

I was on nights now so I had all day, which wasn't a good thing because having all day meant having all day to think about Tate's ride and then Tate's kiss and, when there was time left over, to think of all the other things about Tate.

So I went about the business of filling up my day so I wouldn't think of Tate. After coffee and a chat with Betty, I swung by La-La Land for a different kind of coffee drink, another slightly weirder chat (since I suspected both Sunny and Shambles were a wee bit high), and a sampling of more of Shambles and Sunny's wares (blueberry muffin with those crunchy bits on the top, divine; Shambles might be stoned but he still could bake). Then I walked down to the mechanics to belatedly get my car.

Wood wasn't around so I paid an older but definitely still cool and sexy lady in the office who had obviously given half of the female population of Carnal their style training. She was biker babe times a thousand and I loved her look so much I told her so.

"Dominic, darlin'," she replied. "Carnal Spa. It ain't no spa. He just does hair and manis and pedis, none of that facial or massage shit. But he's gay, as in *flamin'*, so he does *great* hair."

She was right. Her hair, dark with fabulous blonde highlights and a wicked-cool cut, was perfect on her.

"Tell him Stella sent you," she finished.

"Thanks," I replied, smiled, and waved my good-bye.

I was walking to my car when Wood pulled in on his Harley. His wasn't black, though it looked to be the same model as Tate's, it was silver.

He rounded my car and parked by it, swinging off the bike and standing there, waiting for me in the space between his bike and my car.

"Hey," I said, smiling, but he didn't smile back.

I knew why when I got close.

"Saw you ride out with Tate last night."

I pulled in a quiet breath then said, "Wood."

He looked away, running his hand along his hair, muttering, "Jesus, Lauren."

"I—"

He looked back and cut me off. "He's fuckin' my sister."

I felt my body still.

But he wasn't done. "And she's married and not to Tate."

I went back on a foot like he'd struck a blow.

He took two steps toward me, claiming my space.

"You're new in town but you'll hear about it. Everybody knows. It's better you hear about it now rather than later when he plays you and makes you look like a fuckin' moron."

"Wood—"

"Those two, fuck, it's been so long, feels like forever those two been wound up, doin' stupid shit, causin' trouble, walkin' all over people, breakin' hearts while they went their merry fuckin' way."

It hit me.

"Neeta," I whispered.

He stared at me, his face hard. "You already heard."

"I saw them together at the hotel before—"

"Bet with you there, he don't meet her there anymore."

I felt my throat close.

He got closer and wrapped his hand around my neck. "For your own good, not fuckin' mine 'cause what I'm gonna tell you ain't gonna make me your favorite person and I think you get this, baby, I want you on the back of my bike. But I want more not to see your face lookin' like I slapped you, like it does right now, so you gotta know it all."

"Wood—"

His face dipped close and his other hand curled into my waist. "Her name was Bethany, chief of police's daughter. Caught Tate's eye when he and Neeta were supposedly through, one of the many times they were off. Bethany, though, even though she knew it, lived it like the rest of us. She hoped. It was stupid, everyone knew it was. Tate hooked up with Bethany, they got tight, and Neeta blew back into town. She wasn't back a day, not even an *hour*, Laurie, before they were at each other. Bethany found out and slit her fuckin' wrists."

I sucked in a harsh breath and pulled back against his hand but it just tightened, so I stopped.

"No," I whispered.

"Yes," he returned. "Her dad found her and she survived. Moved to Colorado Springs. Neeta got a wild hair and quit Tate. Tate quit the force, started hunting. Neeta comes back, though, regular and not to see Pop. And everyone knows it 'cause you can see her car and his bike at Carnal Hotel when she does. She's livin' in Crested Butte but she comes to get her Tate fix, regular and often. And even though he knows she's legally bound to a man in CB, he gives it to her."

"I don't—" I started but stopped when both his hands gave me a squeeze.

"This is my sister I'm talkin' 'bout, baby," he said in his gentle voice. "And she's trash. I'm sayin' it, my pop'll say it. Neeta's trash. The thing you gotta know before you climb back on the back of his bike is that Tate Jackson is trash too."

After delivering that line, he let me go and stepped away. I remained silent and we stared at each other.

"Now you know." He was still talking gentle. "You let that sink in and you make up your mind. You know where I am."

With that, he walked away and I watched him do it until he

disappeared in the office. I stayed where I was until I saw Stella leave the office and stand outside, her hand lifted to her forehead to shield her eyes from the sun. I knew she was looking at me and when she looked ready to make her approach, I got in my car and drove away.

*   *   *

It took two days of no Tate and no word to ask Krystal where he was.

We were at the bar and it was raining, a lot, a downpour that followed thunder and lightning. So much rain that no one wanted to be out and business at the bar was slow.

I was on with Jonelle and Jonelle had obviously heard what Tate did to Tonia because she came in on time, she wasn't dressed one step up from streetwalker, and she was actually waiting tables.

While she was busy but Krystal wasn't, I stood beside Jim-Billy and called, "Hey, Krystal, where's Tate?"

I felt Jim-Billy straighten by my side and I saw Bubba, who was at the other end of the bar shooting the breeze with some patrons, turn to face us. Krystal looked at Jim-Billy and then she looked at me.

Then she came to me as Bubba ambled our way.

"Didn't he tell you, Lauren?" Krystal asked cautiously, her gaze sharp on my face.

"Um...," I mumbled. "No."

"He's huntin', gorgeous." Bubba entered the conversation.

"Yes, I know. Tonia's killer," I said.

Krystal looked up at Bubba but Bubba didn't take his eyes off me. He asked, "Coupla nights ago, weren't you on the back of his bike?"

"Yes," I answered. Bubba looked down at Krystal and I saw his brows go up.

"Shit," Krystal muttered.

"What?" I asked and Bubba looked back at me and they all got closer. I even fancied Jim-Billy scooted nearer.

"Guy who did Tonia is serial," Bubba said quietly so only our huddle could hear.

"Cereal?" I asked, perplexed.

"Serial, gorgeous. A serial killer. Tonia's one of seven," Bubba explained and my hand shot out so my fingers could wrap around the edge of the bar.

"Seven?" I whispered.

"Seven," Bubba said. "Seven in four years. Pisses the Feds off since they don't like nicknames but cops're callin' him the May-December Murderer. He kills in May then he kills in December."

"Oh my God," I breathed.

"They ain't all in Colorado either," Bubba went on. "But they're all in the Rockies and Colorado is a hot spot. One in Utah, one in Wyoming, two in Nevada, the rest in Colorado."

"Tonia," I whispered thinking, for some asinine reason, this made her death all the worse and it was bad enough already.

"They don't got shit," Bubba informed me. "Tonia was the one who lasted the longest. Dumped her alive, found her alive, that's a first. She never regained consciousness so they couldn't ask her questions. She was dumped away from where he hurt her, left no evidence at the scene. They don't have any witnesses, have no idea where he picked her up. Her car was outside her apartment, keys on the kitchen counter, no forced entry, no fingerprints, last anyone saw of her she was in here. They haven't found her clothes, her hair. They don't have nothin'."

My eyes stayed glued to him and I didn't look at Krystal. "You know about her hair?"

"Tate came to us before he left, Lauren," Krystal said in a voice that wasn't very Krystal. There was a soft edge to it and my eyes finally went to her. "Explained things."

He didn't explain things to me.

"So Tate's got a lot of ground to cover, he's trackin' this guy, puttin' pieces together. Four years, four states, and seven murders' worth of ground to cover," Bubba finished.

This made sense.

He still didn't explain things to me.

I changed the subject and I did it after looking Bubba right in the eye.

"Do you know Neeta?"

Bubba's upper body moved back. It was almost imperceptible but I saw it.

"Laurie," Jim-Billy said quietly and put his hand on mine on the bar.

"Don't you think about Neeta, Lauren," Krystal ordered and I looked at her.

"Why would you say that?" I asked.

"People talk, don't listen," she replied.

"That's history," Bubba said. "Way back. Not worth thinkin' about."

"It wasn't history two weeks ago when I was swimming in Ned and Betty's pool and I watched Tate carry her into a room," I returned.

I watched as Bubba closed his eyes and he did this slow. Then I felt a lump form to block my throat.

"Lauren," Krystal said and her voice was full-on soft now so I looked at her.

She looked sad and hard-as-nails Krystal looking at me like that said it all.

"Right," I whispered around the lump, the word sounding strangled, and I walked away.

*   *   *

It was closing that same night and Jim-Billy and I were getting ready to walk to the hotel when I went to get my purse.

I pulled it out of the filing cabinet, turned to the office door, and saw Krystal there.

I walked toward her saying, "Good night," but I had to stop because, when I arrived at the door, she didn't move out of my way.

I looked into her eyes.

Then she shocked me by lifting a hand and brushing the hair off one of my shoulders.

"Told you not to get an eye for Tate," she whispered.

"He got an eye for me," I whispered back.

"Same thing, honey."

I looked away and bit my lip.

"There's nothin' special in this world, we girls know that." She was still whispering and I looked back at her. "You were right, Laurie, hold tight to that peace you found. Don't look for somethin' special. It ain't out there. We know that. Just hold tight to that peace. Yeah?"

"Yeah," I said softly.

"'Night, darlin'," she replied and stepped aside.

I walked out the door.

*   *   *

It was tough, three waitresses working a biker bar that was in a town in Colorado that was shaking off a spring that, I was told, could last deep into summer. But the days were longer, almost always bright and consistently warm, then hot, so the bikes were out and the bar was buzzing, especially on the weekends.

Carnal was a hot spot for Harleys and even Ned and Betty's business picked up. There were four or more bikes in the parking lot every night. Come Friday and Saturday, there'd be far more and SUVs and minivans besides.

Unless there were kids, though, the pool was all mine. And I used it to swim and lounge nearly every day but only in the day. It wouldn't be December until Tonia's madman struck again but I wasn't taking any chances.

*   *   *

Tyler was trying out a new boot camp schedule, doing his seven o'clock one, but he started a one o'clock one that I thought he started just so Wendy could go to it. It wasn't easy for her to crawl into bed at three thirty in the morning and be ready for high-intensity interval training three and a half hours later.

I went with her three times a week mainly because I liked spending time with her and Tyler was a great trainer. He was very positive and upbeat and he made the whole thing seem like we were all a team getting prepared to compete in the Olympics, but we had to do it together. United we'd stand, divided we'd fall, so we gave it our all for Tyler and each other.

I kept going to the camps mainly because in two weeks I felt my muscles make themselves known under my flesh and not only because they ached.

And in two more weeks they made themselves known visibly and I no longer had back fat.

Tyler had started his one o'clock classes with five of us. With me and Wendy talking them up, and Wendy saying I was Tyler's success story, in a month there were twenty of us.

I still thought all of us were nuts because it was still torture.

*   *   *

On the Monday after Tate left, I went into town to hang with Sunny and Shambles and then I wandered town just because I had time on my hands.

I walked by the florist, then walked back, went in and ordered some flowers for Betty. I waited while the florist made them up, paid for them, and walked out.

I stopped on the sidewalk and walked back in.

"Everything all right?" she asked.

"Could you make up a bouquet every Monday morning? Thirty dollars' worth. I'll be in late morning to get them. If I'm not in by noon, could you deliver them to Betty at the hotel? I'll set up an account."

"Standing order?" she asked, her brows going up.

"Yes," I answered, smiling.

"Sure thing, precious."

I stuck out my hand to her. "I'm Lauren."

She shook it. "Holly."

"Nice to meet you," I said and left the shop.

From then on, Betty got a thirty-dollar bouquet for her reception desk every Monday.

Every Monday I walked up carrying the flowers, she'd watch me through the windows and I'd watch her face light up.

Sometimes, payback wasn't a bitch.

                    *   *   *

On the second Monday, after La-La Land and before picking up the flowers from Holly, I walked the length of Carnal.

I'd been careful getting ready that morning. A bit more makeup, a few more pieces of jewelry, a nice skirt that hung nicer when I had more meat on my bones but was clinging on my hips now. Nice sandals, flats but not flip-flops. And I went all out on my hair.

I turned the corner at the end of Carnal and walked into the forecourt of the mechanics.

The gray-haired man was standing in the forecourt talking to a man in coveralls. He looked at me, said something to the guy he was talking to, the man walked away, and the gray-haired man walked to me.

"Hi," I said and stopped at him.

"Hey, sweetheart," he said back.

"We never met." I stuck out my hand and saw it was kind of shaking so I was relieved when his fingers wrapped around it. "I'm Lauren."

"Pop," he replied and gave my fingers a squeeze before he let them go.

"Pop?" I asked and he grinned.

"Pop, Wood and Neeta's dad. They called me Pop and since every kid and then every kid who had kids raced through my house, wreckin' it in one way or another, I got to be known as Pop. It stuck."

Neeta's dad. Also Wood's.

"Is Wood here?" I asked and I thought it sounded like my voice was trembling. I just hoped he didn't think so too.

He examined me a minute, his eyes kind but his face blank. Then he grinned and shouted, "Wood!"

I looked beyond him to see that Wood was already halfway to us. I forced my feet to stay planted and not turn and take flight.

Pop turned and announced, "Lauren's here to see you."

Wood hit us. His eyes didn't leave me as he replied, "Take a hike, Pop."

"No respect," Pop muttered good-naturedly but walked away.

I was too busy freaking out to react to their exchange.

"Hey," Wood said.

"Um...," I replied.

His eyes narrowed. "You okay?"

"Um...," I repeated.

His eyes stayed narrowed. Then they unnarrowed and he grinned at me. He did it slow and I watched his mouth while he did it.

My heart started racing and I bit my lip.

"You work tonight?" he asked.

I found my voice. "These days it seems I work every night."

He got close, wrapped his hand around the back of my neck and he pulled me close. I put a hand on his chest.

"Then Bubba's just got itself a new regular."

I smiled up at him.

*   *   *

Wood didn't lie.

For the next week he was a regular and he always sat in my station. I took my breaks with him and we walked to the diner to have a quick bite during my dinner break.

I didn't know he worked so early because at three o'clock in the morning I was on his bike and he took me home.

He kissed me the first night, right outside my hotel room door. It wasn't a Tate kiss but it was a great kiss, far better than any of Brad's, so I felt I was still coming out on top.

He also kissed me the next night.

And the next.

I was off the night after that. Wood took me for a ride and a steak dinner at a nowhere joint, which was a nowhere joint because it was in the middle of nowhere.

The steaks were fabulous.

I told him why I was in Carnal, which meant I told him about Brad.

He told me about Maggie who got custody of their two kids and moved to Gnaw Bone. He had them every other weekend, alternating Christmas and spring breaks and four weeks in the summer. He also told me it sucked his kids were growing up essentially without him. But he said it sucked more, living with Maggie, because she was a bitch. Further, he told me she was a shit wife but a good mom and his kids needed her to be a full-time good mom and not see her being a most-of-the-time shit wife and all-of-the-time bitch.

When he took me to my hotel, I let him in and the kissing turned to fooling around.

The same the next night.

The night after that, I was wiped and so was he. He spent the night but we both slept in our clothes on top of the covers. That was when I found out he worked as early as he did and that was when the spending the night at his house verbal dance began.

I was able to resist twice.

Then he had me.

* * *

Now it was now. Carnal had become home. I was in Wood's bed more than my own even though we had yet to do the deed. And Tate was still gone.

But for me, he'd always be gone. I used to pretend he didn't exist. Now he simply didn't.

Any man who slept with a married woman he knew was married and didn't care, didn't exist.

And any man who could take me for a ride like that, kiss me like that, in less than an hour changing my world, and then walk away without looking back and not even call, not for days that turned to weeks that turned to a month definitely didn't exist.

I peeled off the new bathing suit I bought with Wendy in the shop-a-thon we had the day Dominic, the gay stylist to all Carnal biker babes, gave me a new look. Wendy had gone with me and had been so overawed by my transformation she forced me to go to the mall with her.

"I gotta admit," Dominic had said at the time, standing behind me and fluffing my hair while looking at me in the mirror. "I'm thinkin' you're my masterpiece."

I was looking at me in the mirror too and thinking he wasn't wrong.

He'd taken my dark blonde hair, which I hadn't had cut in over six months and given it bright highlights around my face, some in the back. The effect was dazzling, especially against my tan. I'd always worn my hair just past my shoulders but it was now down my back, nearly to my bra strap. He cut it to frame my face with a deep, heavy bang and the rest of it in chunky layers that flipped here and there in a glamorous and saucy way that, coupled with the highlights, made even Stella, the Premier Biker Babe's hair look dowdy.

"You're a miracle worker," I breathed as I stared into my hazel eyes that suddenly looked startling green.

"You aren't the first person who's said that, darlin'," Dominic told me without the least hint of humility.

Wendy barely let me pay him (and give him an enormous tip) before she had me out the door and in her CR-V, and we headed two towns over to the only mall in the vicinity. Luckily it was a big one and it was a good one because Wendy was determined to get me "out of those clothes that just do *not* fit you, sistah!"

And she did. We filled her little SUV with bags—skirts, jeans, shorts, T-shirts, tank tops, camisoles, blouses, shoes, boots, underwear, and pajamas.

A whole new wardrobe except two sizes smaller.

It was good I was working nights, Bubba's was busy, and I was getting great tips or that shop-a-thon would have bit huge into my nest egg.

But I had to admit, it wasn't just Wendy. It was me being tan, having fabulous hair, being a biker babe with a biker who liked me on the back of his bike and, most of all, being two sizes smaller.

It had been over five years since I was that size. Before Brad started fucking Hayley and my life disintegrated. It felt like a rebirth mainly because it was.

I tossed my new bathing suit into my new laundry hamper (wicker, I bought it at a cute little country shop that had opened in town the week before). I had five new suits. Two tankinis, the only bikini I'd ever owned—it wasn't a teeny-weeny bikini, but it was still sexy (at least I thought so) and therefore it worked for me—for laying out by the pool, and two suits for swimming.

I jumped in the shower. I got out, toweled off, lotioned, spritzed perfume, and put on a pair of my new matching undies. They were deep purple with lots of black lace.

I did my makeup. I'd settled on halfway between Krystal and the Old Me and it was working for me. I blow-dried my hair with a roller brush like Dominic showed me, pulled on a dusty lilac tank that was half tank, half camisole because the straps were thinner than a tank but not spaghetti and if I wasn't careful, my bra straps showed. The tank looked great with my tan. Not being conceited or anything but even I had to admit that.

I yanked on a new pair of jeans, a wide, thick dark brown belt and my new purple strappy, stiletto-heeled sandals. It took nearly the whole month to get used to traipsing around in high heels for hours but I didn't even feel it anymore and the effect on my tips was astounding.

I threw some fresh underwear in my purse, my deodorant, put the guard on my toothbrush and tossed that in along with a ponytail holder, slung my purse over my shoulder and left my room.

I waved to Ned. He waved back. I got in my car since I was driving to Wood's later (and Ned would know the sign, he had to be getting used to it by now) and headed to Bubba's.

CHAPTER SEVEN

All the Rest

"Jack and Coke, three Coors bottles, and a Tanqueray and tonic," I ordered from Bubba, looking down at my pad but, even with head bowed and not looking at him, I still teased (as I usually did with Bubba), "And get the lead out, big man. The last order you filled my grandma could fill faster and she's in a wheelchair."

"Fuck," Bubba muttered; my head came up because this wasn't his usual witty reply to my teasing and I saw he was pale and looking over my shoulder.

I started to turn to see what he was staring at that made him look like he'd seen a ghost. I didn't get to do so because suddenly my hair was swept from my neck, a pair of abrasive lips were there, and an arm had snaked around my belly, pulling me back into a tall, hard body.

"What—?" I started to say as my body went solid but a hand came up and yanked the pad out of mine and tossed it on the bar.

I felt the pencil yanked out of my other hand when I twisted my neck to see Tate had hold of me. Tate with a beard, a *full* beard. It looked a little straggly but it also looked *hot*.

His eyes were aimed at Bubba. "Get Wendy to serve her drinks,

Bub. Laurie's on break," he ordered and then he had my hand and he was dragging me down the hall.

"Hey!" I snapped, trying to tug at my hand but he held true and kept dragging me. "Tate!" I cried but he kept going, right by the office, right by the storeroom to the dark, poorly lit, very back of the hall.

Then his hands were at my hips and he was pushing me against the wall.

"Tate," I bit out but he was concentrating on studying my body, his eyes at my chest as his hands slid up my sides to stop with his thumbs right below my breasts, his fingers splayed at my sides.

"Jesus." His eyes came to mine and then scanned my hair. "What'd you do to yourself, baby?"

"Tate," I repeated but said no more because his head bent and he kissed me.

His lips and tongue worked wonders against my mind. As in clearing it of all thoughts of him being a cheater and not calling for a month and me being with Wood and filling it with only thoughts of kissing him back as hard as I could. The beard helped. I'd never been kissed by a man with a beard. It was scratchy but in a very sexy way.

When his lips broke from mine, they didn't actually break. They just stopped kissing me but stayed where they were so our breath mixed.

"Sweet as I remembered," he muttered against my lips.

"Tate," I whispered.

His hand left my side and came to the side of my neck and his head lifted two inches.

"I couldn't find him, babe," he said as his thumb trailed my jaw.

"Sorry?"

"That fucker who killed Tonia. Been everywhere. Asshole left nothin'. He's a ghost."

"Oh no," I breathed.

"Cops, Feds, everyone's fuckin' baffled. Includin' me."

"I'm sorry," I whispered.

"Now I gotta tell her folks that I got nothin'," he went on.

"Tate."

"That's gonna suck," he finished.

I pulled in breath and in pulling it in, life as I'd come to know it reestablished its place in my brain.

"Tate—" I began and his thumb slid across my lips.

"Sucks, but *fuck* Laurie, it's good to be home," he whispered, his thumb disappeared and his head started to come down.

"Tate!" I cried and pulled back against the wall.

His head went up.

"What?" he asked.

"Can you please step back?" I requested.

His eyes scanned my face in the dim light.

Then he answered, "No."

"We need to talk," I stated. During his kiss my hands had slid around his neck. Now they were pressing lightly against his shoulders.

"All right," he replied.

"Later. I'm working. Tomorrow, we'll, um...go to the um—"

He cut me off. "You're right here." His hand beside my breast slid around my back. "I'm right here." His hand at my neck slid up into my hair. "Talk."

"I need you to step back," I said to him.

"And I been gone a long time, Ace, I need you where you are."

My head tilted to the side. "You mean you didn't swing by Neeta's any time this past month?"

It was more than a little scary feeling his body go rock-solid against mine.

"What the fuck?" he asked in an even scarier voice.

"You might want to let me go," I suggested.

"And I might not," he shot back.

"I know about Neeta," I told him, trying not to make it sound like an accusation but pretty certain it did.

"Yeah? What do you know?"

"I know enough that that's the last kiss you'll get from me."

"Maybe you'll explain," he bit off, his voice even scarier.

"Okay, I'll explain this." I pressed on his shoulders but nothing came of it so I gave up. "My husband left me for my best friend and he'd been fucking her for five years."

"I already knew that, Ace."

"So let's just say that I'm not fired up to get involved with a man who doesn't care that he's carrying on a long-term affair with a married woman."

He let me go then, faster than I'd ever seen anyone move. So fast I wasn't ready for it and both my hands had to slam back in the wall to hold myself upright so I wouldn't tumble over.

He'd taken a step back but other than that he didn't move and he didn't speak.

So I did. "I see I've made my point."

"And I see we're back at square fuckin' one," he returned.

"What?"

He leaned in, his face all I could see and I realized the aggressive way he did it that I'd vastly misjudged the situation *and* the atmosphere. I'd seen him very angry, scary angry.

Now I realized he was enraged.

"Did you think," he growled, "for one fuckin' second, Ace, to maybe ask *me* about Neeta?"

But two could be enraged.

Because he showed me the promise of something special that night on his bike and through his kiss.

Then he walked away and didn't even *fucking* call!

"Wood explained things pretty clearly," I replied acidly.

"Wood," he whispered.

"Wood," I repeated.

"He fuck you yet?" Tate asked coarsely and I tried to step back, forgetting I was already against the wall.

"That's none of your business!" I snapped.

"He hasn't fucked you but he will," he stated. "Too bad for you there's no one helpful around like Wood to tell you a few things about *Wood*."

"Yes? Like what things?"

"Too bad, babe, with this scene, you lost out. You'll have to find out on your own." And with that he turned on his boot, walked away and I watched him, realizing I was breathing heavily. Until I stopped breathing because he stopped and turned back to me. "So all that's for Wood?" he asked bizarrely.

"All what?" I asked back.

His hand did an annoyed flick that encompassed the whole of me.

"No," I snapped.

"You looked better before, Ace. Now you just look like all the rest."

And with that highly successful parting line, he disappeared down the hall.

CHAPTER EIGHT

Martinis and Manicures

IT WAS THE day after Tate came home and the day after I drove to Wood's after work, pulled off my clothes, pulled on one of his T-shirts, crawled into his bed waking him just enough for him to roll me into his arms before he fell back asleep

But I didn't.

In Wood's arms, I didn't toss and turn because I didn't want to wake him but I couldn't get that scene with Tate out of my mind.

Or his kiss.

Or him saying, *But fuck Laurie, it's good to be home.*

Or him saying, *You looked better before, Ace. Now you just look like all the rest.*

Eventually I fell asleep and as usual Wood was gone by the time I got up.

I was lying out in the sun wearing my periwinkle blue tankini with a top made of netting that had royal blue embroidery at the hem and the top of the bodice. The shelf bra covered my breasts but the netting at my midriff hinted at the skin underneath. I had the royal blue sarong on the bottom of my lounge chair, a diet pop on the cool deck by my side next to my cell phone, sunglasses on my nose, sunscreen oil that made my body glisten, and a trashy magazine in my hands.

I was also waiting for the last load of my laundry to dry. Ned and Betty had a laundry room at the top end of the building by their house, across from the room with all the vending machines in it. The washer and dryer cost a whack, much more than the Laundromat in town (I'd checked). But I paid it because it was convenient, just two doors away. So close, I could pretend it was just inside my garage instead of two hotel rooms away.

I was reading about celebrities going to jail and viewing pictures of them in orange jumpsuits when I heard the pipes of a Harley.

It was summer. It was Carnal. Harley pipes were de rigueur so I ignored it totally.

That was, I ignored it totally until I heard the beat of motorcycle boots on the cool deck.

I looked around and up to see Tate heading my way. He was walking toward me but his head was turned to look into the parking lot so I twisted around to look over my shoulder.

Four Harley guys were outside looking like they were working on their bikes but two of them, one standing, one crouched, were looking in my direction.

My eyes moved back to Tate to find he was towering over me.

"Great show, Ace," his rough voice growled. "Word gets out you live here, Ned and Betty'll have a full house."

Why had I ever even considered the option that this man, as beautiful as he was, was *not* a jerk?

"Can I help you?" I snapped.

"Yeah, baby," he replied, his voice an insinuation and I knew that because his eyes were moving down my body. He had mirrored sunglasses on (and they looked good on him, which *sucked*) but I could tell his eyes were moving the length of me.

"Well?" I prompted irately, trying not to squirm under his stare. Tyler was a fantastic trainer but he wasn't a miracle worker.

His shaded eyes came to mine.

"Krys needs you to train the two new girls. You're on days for a while."

"And Krys couldn't tell me this because...?"

"Because she's at the bar on her own. We got some boys who rolled in and she's busy 'cause the minute Bubba saw me back, he took off. He was gone this mornin'."

I stared at him. Then I thought about Krystal.

Then I whispered, "Darn."

"So, you're on days," he finished and he looked like he was done and ready to leave.

"Tips during day shifts suck," I muttered as my phone rang. I said this not to stop him, just to whine.

"You'll survive," he muttered back as I reached for my phone, *his* phone really as he'd paid for it, saw my sister's name on the display, and hit the button to take the call. This surprised me. She should be at work and she never called when she was at work.

"Carrie, honey, what's up?" I asked.

"Laurie." Her voice broke saying my name and my body darted up, my legs separating so both my feet were on the cool deck.

She didn't say more.

"Carrie, talk to me. What?" I prompted urgently, too focused to note that Tate had stopped walking away and was moving back toward me. "Carrie!"

"It's Daddy," she whispered and then burst into tears.

I curled into a ball. It was automatic. My knees came up, my heels went in the lounge chair and my torso pressed to my thighs.

I did this because I loved my dad and the tone of my sister's voice made me lose my tenuous hold on my new biker babe and regress straight to an eight-year-old Daddy's little girl.

This was a bad trait I had. It must be said I was *not* good in a crisis. It was all Dad's fault. He had three women in his house and he was the kind of male who was all about being the man of the house so he was. He was the one who took care of everything most of my life and made me into a daddy's little girl.

"What's Dad?" I whispered but she didn't respond. "Carrie, baby, what happened to Dad?"

Tate crouched down by my side but I was still focused on the phone.

"Heart...," she hiccoughed. "Heart attack."

I closed my eyes and pressed my forehead into my knee. "Talk to me," I croaked because my throat had closed. When she didn't, I begged, "Please, honey, talk to me."

"He's...he's alive, Laurie, but they...they're worried."

My body bucked with the sob and I barely felt my cell slide out of my hand. Though my hand knew it was freed because both my arms curled around my legs as I listened vaguely to Tate speaking while I wept.

"This is Tate Jackson, who's this?" He paused. "I'm a friend of Laurie's, you're her sister?" Another pause. "All right, is there someone there with you?" Another pause. "Give him the phone." Pause. "This Mack? Tate Jackson, friend of Laurie's. What's happened?"

I felt strong fingers wrap around my hand and then it firmly, but gently, guided me up and forced me out of the lounger and to my feet.

"Hang on a second," Tate said into the phone. "Baby, put your wrap on and grab your stuff," he ordered softly.

Automatically, I did as I was told. Once I had my stuff and slid my feet into my flip-flops, he took my hand and guided me out of the pool area toward my room.

"Back," he said into the phone. "I'll get her sorted out and on a plane." Another pause. "Yeah." Another one. "Right, call back in an hour."

We were at the door. He touched the phone and slid my key out of my hand, which I held against my chest because most of my stuff was cradled in my arm.

"What'd Mack say?" I asked.

"Inside, baby," he replied gently and opened the door.

I walked in and tossed everything but the can of pop on the bed. I put the pop on the nightstand and turned to Tate.

"What'd he say?"

"He's in surgery," Tate answered and I closed my eyes. "Babe, you need to get on a plane." I opened my eyes.

"Right," I whispered.

"Get in the shower," he ordered.

"Okay," I whispered, dutifully starting toward the bathroom.

Tate headed to the door but I stopped him when I called his name. "Tate?"

He turned and looked at me.

"Did Mack say…" I swallowed. "How's Mom?"

"Hangin' in there," he lied.

"Tate," I whispered, wrapping my arms around my middle. Tate's long legs had him in front of me in what seemed less than a second.

His hands settled on my neck right where it hit my shoulders. "She's not good."

I fell forward so the top of my head was against his chest.

"He's the strong one," I whispered to the floor.

His hands gave me a squeeze. "Laurie, get in the shower."

My head tipped back and I looked at him, holding myself up with hands planted on his abs.

"Of all of us," I was still whispering.

"What?"

"He's the strong one of all of us," I explained and the tears started to fall in such great waves I didn't know where one stopped and the next began. "We…we…girls. His girls. We fall apart," I finished as a loud sob tore up my throat and it sounded only slightly less painful than it felt.

Then I was in Tate's arms.

*   *   *

"Laurie, baby, wake up," I heard Tate call and my eyes opened.

We were on a plane and I was snuggled into him, head on his chest, my arm wrapped around his stomach.

I tilted my head back and looked up at him.

"We're landing. We need to put the seatbacks up," he told me quietly.

"Right," I whispered and pulled away, brushing my hair out of my face and sitting up.

Tate was on that plane with me for reasons known only to Tate. All I knew was, he managed to get me into the bathroom at the hotel and then he disappeared. By the time I was out of the shower, Betty was in my room, my clean clothes from the laundry folded on my bed. She coaxed me through my makeup and blow-drying my hair drill and I dressed in an outfit she chose for me. She packed for me while I was doing this, grabbing my makeup and hairbrush when I was done.

Then there came a knock on the door and, like I was a celebrity, Betty shoved my sunglasses on my nose and I was whisked from my room by Ned who guided me into a big, black Ford Explorer that had Tate at the wheel.

"What're you doing here?" I asked Tate after Ned tossed my bag in the backseat.

"I'm your ride," he replied and then we were off and I barely got a chance to wave at Ned and Betty who were both standing outside my room.

"Whose SUV is this?" I asked once we were out of Carnal.

"Mine," he answered.

I looked at him. "You drive a Harley."

"Not big on puttin' bad guys on the back of my bike when I hunt them down, Ace. Fucks with my street cred."

"Oh," I mumbled, turned to face the road, black thoughts assailing my brain, and I fell silent.

I found out after the silent ride but somewhat hair-raising drive to Denver International Airport (I would understand much later that this was because my plane was leaving and Tate didn't have a lot of time to get me to it) he wasn't just my ride. This was because he didn't drop me off. He parked in short-term parking and guided me to the ticket counter. We checked my bag and got two tickets (though I didn't know that) and we both got in line to go through security. Throughout almost all this Tate had two bags, mine in one hand (my hand mostly held in his other), an overnight bag slung over his shoulder. But I was too out of it to notice it was his.

"You can't go through if you don't have a ticket," I informed him.

"I've got a ticket," he replied, looking over my head and down the line.

"To where?" I asked stupidly and his head tipped to look down at me.

"Indianapolis," he answered.

I felt my brows shoot into my hairline. "You're coming with me?"

"Gettin' you there, comin' home tomorrow."

"What?"

"Ace, you're a fuckin' mess. I'm gettin' you to your family and I fly home tomorrow."

"That's insane," I whispered.

"It's what I'm doin'," he returned.

"But—"

"Shut up, Ace."

I stared at him.

Then I said, "Okay."

Then I went through security with Tate and got on a plane with Tate.

Now I was landing in Indianapolis with Tate.

We landed. We taxied. We were let loose from our seatbelts.

Tate got up. He still had his beard and his hair had grown longer and was not only curling around his ears but also his neck. He was wearing a skintight black tee, very faded jeans, motorcycle boots, and had a very cool tattoo slithering down his biceps I'd never noticed before because he was always in long-sleeved shirts. Therefore he looked *exactly* like what you'd expect a bounty hunter to look like (but even cooler, scarier, and more handsome). So the other passengers let him have his space as he pulled his black leather overnight bag out of the overhead compartment. Then he grabbed my hand, pulled me out of the seats, and pushed me in front of him with his hand in the small of my back.

We walked through the airport and I started running when I saw my sister's partner Mack's dark blond head peering over the crowd at the end of the terminal.

I hit him straight on so hard he went back on a foot.

"Laurie, honey," he whispered as his arms went around me.

I just started crying again.

He let me cry and had a man-style, nominally syllabic conversation with Tate while he held me tight.

"You Jackson?"

"Yeah. Tate."

"Mack."

"News?"

Silence.

"Right."

Mack pushed me to his side, slid his arm around my shoulders and guided me to the escalator that would take us down to baggage claim.

"Got another situation," Mack said as we'd exited the escalator. When he said it his arm gave me a squeeze.

"Yeah?" Tate asked and my head tilted back to look at Mack.

"What?" I whispered.

"Your dad's out of surgery. He's in ICU. Only your mom's been able to see him. They're keepin' a close eye and they want him to rest," Mack told me.

"Okay," I replied.

Mack was silent and we stopped by our baggage claim.

Then he pulled in a breath. "Brad's at the hospital."

I tore out of his arm and took a step back, shouting, "*What?*"

"Laurie…," Mack said.

"Ace…," Tate said.

I looked at Tate and informed him, "That's my *ex*."

He got close to me and took my hand. "Okay, baby."

"My ex as in my *ex-husband*—who spent five years of our marriage *fucking* my best friend," I shouted, oblivious of the other travelers turning to stare.

"Yeah, babe, I know." Tate had pulled my hand up and placed it palm down on his chest with his hand over it.

"He's at the *hospital*," I screeched. "Where my father is in *I… C… U!*"

Tate's head bent so his face was close to mine. "Calm down, Laurie."

"No!" I shouted in his face. "What a *jerk*!"

"Do you want me to beat the shit outta him when we get there?" Tate asked, sounding serious and I blinked at him.

"What?"

"I will," Tate stated.

"You… you'll… beat the shit out of him?"

"Say the word, babe."

"Would… wouldn't you get arrested for something like that?" I asked.

"Probably," he answered.

"Then maybe you shouldn't," I decided.

"Your call," he muttered and turned to the baggage claim, moving my hand so it became my arm wrapped around his waist and sliding his arm along my shoulders.

"You'll yell you see the case," Mack instructed but he sounded like he found something funny.

"Yep," Tate said, his eyes on the now moving carousel.

"You're good, by the way," Mack went on.

"What?" Tate asked.

"Took me five years with Carrie to figure out how to talk her down from a drama. Laurie's been in your town for what? A month? Shit, man, you're the master."

Tate chuckled.

This conversation didn't penetrate me. I was postshouting at the Indianapolis Airport, previsit to the hospital where my father whom I adored but had left worrying about me for six months (or longer) was in the ICU and my ex-husband was hanging out for reasons that could only mean he'd gone insane.

Therefore, I collapsed into Tate's side, resting my head on his shoulder.

His arm around my shoulders got tighter.

It wouldn't be until much, *much* later that I would remember I hadn't called Wood.

*   *   *

Apparently the tear reservoir had run dry by the time we made it to St. Vincent's Hospital because when I hit the waiting room and Mom and Caroline fell on me, all I could do was hold on to both of them in our minihuddle.

"I'm so glad you're here," Mom whispered in my ear. "Missed you so much, hon."

I just held her tighter.

After a long time, we disengaged and they stepped back. Carrie looked toward Tate first. Then her mouth dropped right open.

Then she muttered, "Holy cow."

Mom heard Carrie and she stopped smiling sadly at me, looked up at Tate and then she blinked and her head reared back.

"Um…Mom, Carrie, this is Tate Jackson. He's my bo—"

"Boyfriend," Tate stated firmly, his deep, rough voice filling the waiting room and I could swear Carrie looked like she was going to faint. I could swear this because her upper body started teetering in a random pattern all the while Mom blinked again, repeatedly.

I looked up at Tate in shock but he was looking over my sister's head.

"Can I help you?" he asked and I turned to see who he was looking at.

Brad was standing there, looking pale, somewhat haggard even though he also looked like Brad. But after all these months, all that had gone on before, more than a month in Carnal with the likes of Tate and Wood, he didn't seem like my glorious, beautiful Brad anymore.

He had light brown hair he used product on to sweep back from his face and, like always, even in a hospital waiting room, his hair looked perfect. He didn't wash it and let it fall as it lay. He *styled* it and sometimes he took longer fiddling with his hair than I did blow-drying mine and this was saying something because I had a lot of hair. He was only three inches taller than me so he'd never liked me to wear very high heels. He had blue eyes that I'd used to think were piercing. Now they just seemed blue. And he had an absolutely great body but he honed this by going to the gym five times a week, never missing a scheduled visit. He even went in when he was sick, such was his aversion to the thought of losing his carefully crafted physique.

His eyes were on me.

"Ree?" he asked, staring at me like he'd never seen me before.

"What are you doing here, Brad?" I asked back.

When he heard my voice he breathed, "*Ree*."

"We couldn't get him to go away," Carrie informed me.

Brad jerked as if pulling himself together and his eyes moved to Tate briefly before they came back to me.

"This is my family," he explained.

"Sorry?" I whispered, feeling my body get tight.

"He's been sayin' that a lot," Mack muttered to Tate.

"I'm guessin' you're Brad," Tate said to Brad.

"Yes, Ree's husband," Brad said to Tate.

Tate looked down at me. "Thought you signed papers?" I nodded to him and he looked to Brad. "I think in the eyes of the law that makes you not her husband anymore."

I looked at Mom and Carrie. "Tate would probably know. He used to be a cop."

"What's he now, hon?" Mom asked.

"A bounty hunter," I answered.

Caroline's eyes shot to Tate and she repeated, "Holy cow."

Brad got even paler.

Mack chuckled.

Mom's round eyes hit Tate and she whispered, "Oh my."

Tate ignored all of us and told Brad, "So I'm thinkin' Ace's question is still pertinent."

"Ace?" Brad asked.

"Lauren," Tate answered.

Brad's eyes narrowed on me. "He calls you *Ace*?"

I threw my hands up. "What are you *doing* here, Brad?"

Brad started toward me but stopped abruptly. He stopped abruptly because Tate moved in between him and me and planted a hand on Brad's chest.

"That's about as close as I want you to her," Tate said low.

Brad took a step back and glared at Tate. "I get that you're a big guy but I'd like to talk to *my wife*."

"Then you shouldn't have thrown her away when she *was* your wife. Now she ain't. Now she's somethin' to me and I don't let men I don't like get close to her and I gotta tell you, man, I do *not* like you."

Brad's eyes came to me and he snapped, "Ree!"

I moved forward two feet until I was standing behind and beside Tate and I leaned beyond him to Brad.

"Are you telling me that you flew all the way from Phoenix to cause this drama when my father is in ICU just because you feel like a schmuck because you totally screwed me over and you didn't get to make yourself feel like a good guy and say good-bye when I left town?"

"No, I'm telling you when I heard about your dad, I knew you'd be here and I flew all the way from Phoenix so I could tell you I want you back!" Brad returned and everyone in the room got very still except Tate and me.

Tate didn't get still, as such. Instead, he got the definition of still. His body completely turned to stone, which was good because my bones turned to water and I had to grab on to Tate to remain standing.

"What?" I whispered.

Brad took a step forward, Tate moved a millimeter and Brad stopped but his eyes stayed pinned to me.

"I want you back, Ree," he said softly. "I made a huge mistake."

"Yeah, man, you did," Tate cut in and Brad's neck twisted so fast he probably gave himself a hitch when he looked up at Tate.

"Will you stay out of it?" he clipped.

"She's holdin' on to me, bud. I'd say I'm in it," Tate returned.

"Ree," Brad said when his eyes came to me.

And when they did, it hit me, like taking a bullet that ripped through me, changing my life, altering my perceptions in a way I knew there was no going back.

"Go away," I whispered.

"Him or me?" Brad asked, jerking a thumb at Tate.

"Not Tate, *you*," I was still whispering.

"Ree," Brad repeated.

"Honest to God?" I asked quietly.

Brad opened his mouth to speak but I kept talking.

"Do you know how beautiful my life is now, Brad? Can you even understand what a beautiful life is? It isn't about the perfect house and a keeping-up-with-the-Joneses new car every two years and having the right landscaper and bragging at parties that you have a housecleaner. Not when all that stuff is *shit*. It's *surface*. There's nothing underneath."

I didn't know where these words were coming from. I just knew it was someplace buried deep. Someplace that had been longing to see the light of day. Someplace that had finally broken through when that bullet tore through me.

"Ree—"

"You lied to me and all my friends, lied to me for five years. You can't do that and have a soul."

"Ree—"

"Do you know what happened to me today?" I asked and didn't wait for an answer.

I just gave it to him.

"I got a phone call from my sister that tore my world apart and I didn't have to lift a finger. Betty got me dressed and packed my bag and even got my laundry from the laundry room. Ned put me and my bag in the truck. Tate got the tickets and got me on a plane and dropped everything to come with me. These people have things to do. They have *lives.* At work Krys and Wendy will cover for me even though Tate and I are gone just because that's what you do when you're a good person. That's what you do when you have a soul. That's where I am now. That's where I live. That's my life. Do you think, for one second, I'd leave something that beautiful and come back to *you*?"

He didn't answer so I kept going.

"Even now, you're not thinking about me. My father's fighting for his life somewhere in this hospital and my family is scared out of their minds and you don't care. You don't give a *fuck.* All you care about is *you* and what *you* want. I'm standing by a man who dropped everything, and he's been on the trail of a *murderer* for a *month,* and he did it just to get me to my family. Have you ever done anything like that in your *life*?"

"You love me, Ree. You told me you did even after I explained about Hayley," Brad reminded me. "You said we'd find our way back, make it work."

"I did," I agreed. "Because I was scared and I was blind. Blinded by hope. I'd waited for something special and convinced myself you were that. Then you proved you weren't and taught me the valuable lesson that special isn't out there. Special doesn't *exist.* So the best you can do is find real. I found real, Brad, and I like it."

I let Tate go, straightened and moved to his side and kept talking.

"I guess I should thank you for being here so I can thank you to your face for teaching me that lesson. I wasted a lot of my life hoping for something special. Now I've realized I'm good with what I've got."

I watched Brad open his mouth to speak but I didn't get a chance to hear what he had to say. I didn't get that chance because Tate tagged me with an arm hooked around my neck and yanked me into him so I collided with his body. His head came down, his mouth on mine, and he kissed me hard and deep, with tongues.

Right in front of my mom!

This, at the time, didn't register on me because it was Tate and he was good with his mouth therefore that was the only thing that registered.

Then he lifted his head half an inch and stated, "You're gonna find special, Ace."

I shook my head in the minimal space allowed partially in a negative, mostly to recover from his kiss.

"Special doesn't exist, Tate," I told him. "And I'm okay with that."

His lips came back to mine and when he spoke, he did it gently. "It will for you, baby."

"I like him," Mom declared loudly.

I watched Tate's eyes smile.

"Maybe we shouldn't neck in front of my mom while my dad's in the ICU," I suggested and then watched the smile in Tate's eyes deepen.

"Don't mind us," Mack called. "They probably don't get a lot of foreplay in hospital waiting rooms. You're breakin' the monotony of tears and tantrums."

"Mack!" Carrie hissed. "Tate just kissed her, that's hardly foreplay."

"You weren't watchin' close enough, honey. That was *definitely* foreplay."

By this time Tate's head had gone up about three inches so I could see his mouth struggling against his smile, or, perhaps, out-and-out laughter.

"My family is a little crazy," I whispered.

"I get that," Tate replied.

"Perhaps I should go," Brad noted and Tate didn't release me but his head turned toward Brad.

"You think?" he asked.

I started giggling and seeing as my hands were clutching Tate's T-shirt at his waist, I just slid them along so they were loosely wrapped around his back and I could rest my weight into his body.

But Brad wasn't done. He got close and I turned my head to look at him too.

"I get this," he said. "This guy." He jerked his head at Tate. "Wild oats. But I know you, Ree. You'll want your manicures and martinis. You'll be back."

I looked at Tate and noted, "I've been meaning to talk to you about that. Can we buy some martini glasses for the bar?"

"No," Tate replied.

"All right," I muttered.

"Can we go to the hotel?" Mom asked. "I need to rest. I want to be back to check on your father first thing in the morning."

"You girls'll have to scrunch in the back. Tate and my legs are too long," Mack declared.

"It's your car, hon," Mom said and she sounded tired.

"Mom seems worn out," I whispered to Tate and he let my neck go but didn't step out of my space.

"Be with her," he whispered back.

"Okay," I agreed, then called, "Captain?"

"Yeah, Ace."

"Thanks."

His hand lifted and he trailed the backs of his fingers along my jaw.

My mind automatically committed the feel of his touch to memory right along with the look on his face when he did it.

Then I went to my mom.

*   *   *

"I'm sorry about this," I said to Tate as we entered the hotel room my mom insisted on getting us.

Us!

Our farm was only a thirty-minute drive away from Indianapolis and Carrie and Mack lived in the city. But they lived on the other side and Mom didn't want to drive back and forth so we'd all checked in and would be in (at least Mom and me) until she felt Dad was okay to leave for a while.

After having a very late dinner, we'd gone to the hotel and Mom had insisted that she pay for our room.

Tate tried to protest. Mom was losing so she looked at me, pulled out the big guns, and said, "It's what your father would do if he was here."

Tate's eyes sliced to me, his jaw clenched, then he sighed and I let Mom get *us* a room.

Now we were stuck together in a room with a king-sized bed.

Tate dumped our luggage on the built-in luggage rack while I looked around the room that was in a Marriott. It was about as far away from Ned and Betty's below-average (but now it was home) room as you could get.

"Don't worry about it," Tate muttered.

"I'll run down and get another room, try to get it on the same floor or something so they won't know and I'll sleep there."

"It's all good, Ace," Tate said. He'd sat in a chair and was pulling off his boots.

"There's only one bed," I informed him of a fact he knew.

"It's a big bed," he replied.

"Tate—" I started and his head came up.

"Babe, it's all good. Quit yappin'."

"Okay," I whispered and then just stood there, not knowing what to do.

Tate knew what to do. He went to the bed, yanked the pillows out from under the coverlet and stacked them on one side. Then he emptied his pockets, lay on the covers, back to the pillows, grabbed the remote and switched on the TV.

I stepped farther into the room.

"That was nice of you," I said to him.

"What?" he asked the TV.

"To pretend you were my boyfriend in front of Brad," I replied.

"Your ex is an asshole, babe." He was still talking to the TV.

He was right about that.

So I said, "It was also nice for you to pretend in front of my family at dinner."

"Your family's the shit, Ace." He was still watching TV.

He was right about that too.

"Mm," I mumbled and looked at the TV.

It didn't take long for the images on the screen to mesmerize me. This was because I was drained, emotionally and physically. Traveling wore me out. Brad wore me out. And I was terrified the last time I'd communicate with my dad was through an e-mail.

"Babe," Tate called.

"Mm?" I asked, eyes glued to the screen.

"Laurie, take your shoes off and lie down."

I didn't move.

"Lauren," Tate called.

I stared at the screen.

"Fuck me," Tate muttered, I heard a zip then my body was moving.

My heard jerked and I looked up at Tate as he pushed me into the bathroom.

"What?"

"Change and come to bed before you collapse on your feet," he ordered and shoved some material in my hand.

I looked at the material. "This isn't mine."

"It's mine. Not gonna waste time sortin' through your shit."

"But—"

"Put it on, Ace."

"But—"

He put a hand to my belly, shoved me fully into the bathroom, flipped on the light switch, and demanded, "Put it on." Then he closed the door.

Without any fight left in me (at all) I put it on, then I shuffled out wearing his huge navy blue T-shirt. I collapsed on top of the bedcovers on a diagonal.

Tate was right, the bed was huge. I was diagonal, he was in the bed and we weren't close to touching.

That was until his hands came to my armpits and he hauled me across the bed until my head was on his belly.

I started to lift up. "Tate—"

He pushed me back down. "Relax, watch TV."

"But Tate, this is—"

He cut me off, "I'm usin' all the pillows."

I twisted my head to look at him. "Tate!"

His fingers slid in my hair and sifted through. "Jesus, you're wound up tight. Just fuckin' *relax.*"

I couldn't *not* relax with his fingers sifting through my hair like that.

I sighed deeply, trying to sound annoyed. Then I twisted my head back and rested it on his stomach.

Tate kept sifting his fingers through my hair.

I rested my hand on his stomach just below my face, part of it tucked under my cheek.

I looked down the long length of his legs, past his bare feet crossed at the ankles and Tate and I watched TV.

Tate kept sifting his fingers through my hair.

I fell asleep.

*   *   *

But fuck Laurie, it's good to be home.

The words hit my brain, my eyes opened and I saw the room was dark.

There was a warm body pressed in behind me, its arm around me, and it wasn't Wood's.

I was in a hotel room in Indianapolis with Tate.

I shut my eyes tight.

So much for the big bed. We were only using about a quarter of it.

I knew with the way I was awake that I wasn't going to get back to sleep. So, as carefully as I could, I slipped out from under Tate's arm and out of the bed. I went to my bag, picked it up as silently as I could and took it to the bathroom. I didn't turn on the light until the door was closed. Then I opened my bag, rummaged through it, found my stuff and belatedly washed the makeup off my face, moisturized then brushed my teeth. I shoved my bag under the sink, turned out the light, and carefully made my way to the chair by the window.

If I curled up and eventually fell asleep there, I'd be okay and I wouldn't wake Tate.

So I curled up and looked out at the lights from our window, thankful Tate didn't close the curtains and I tried to clear my mind and find tired.

"Ace?" Tate called.

Darn.

"I'm so sorry, did I wake you?" I whispered.

"Come back to bed," he ordered.

"No, Captain. I can't sleep. I'm okay, this happens a lot. Just ignore me."

"Come back to bed," he repeated.

"Really, I'm…" I trailed off because I saw the covers get thrown back. Then I saw his naked chest in the city lights coming in from the window and the sight put me into a deeper stupor than the TV had. So deep, I didn't know what he was doing until I was in his arms and he was walking back to the bed. He dumped me there somewhat unceremoniously (as in he *dropped* me and I *bounced*) and he effectively shoved me deeper into the bed because I scooted away from his knee as he got in with me.

He was settling the covers over us when he repeated, "Like I said, come to bed."

"You don't want me here," I advised.

He ignored my comment and asked, "What woke you up?"

"Sorry?"

"Why do you wake up?"

"Stuff drifts through my brain, wakes me up."

"What?"

"Lots of stuff."

"What was it tonight?"

Good God, I couldn't tell him that.

"Just...I want Dad to be okay. I was pretty incommunicado while I was roaming, sorting through my head, needing to be alone and find what I was looking for. I knew Mom and him and Caroline were worried. *Really* worried. I'd reconnected lately but the last time I talked to Dad was via e-mail," I lied. "I want to hear his voice." This was not a lie.

He homed into exactly what most concerned me.

"You aren't responsible for your father's heart attack, babe."

"And *you* aren't responsible for Tonia's death, babe."

That shut him up.

We were face to face but his face was shadowed, only his shoulder and arm that was on top of the covers were visible in the lights coming from windows.

"Go back to sleep, Tate, I'll be okay," I whispered.

He ignored me again. "What keeps you up?"

"What keeps me up?"

"Yeah, if shit sifts through your brain waking you up, what *keeps* you up?"

"It keeps sifting through my brain."

"You can't shut it down?"

"No."

He fell silent.

"Tate," I said, "I've tried everything. Sleep aids. Counting sheep. Relaxation techniques. Nothing works but I'm used to it."

"The mind's a powerful thing."

"Yes," I said softly.

"Your dad's gonna be okay, Ace."

"I hope so," I whispered.

We both fell silent and this lasted a while.

Then, quietly, just in case he fell back to sleep, I said, "Everything you did today was nice."

"Babe," he muttered.

"Did I wake you again?"

"No."

Well thank goodness for that.

I kept talking. "Thank you for coming all the way out here with me."

"It's just a day."

"Still," I said. "You didn't have to do it."

"State you were in, you'd end up in Alaska."

That startled a giggle out of me.

Then I protested, "I would not."

"Babe, seriously, you were a robot without any programming."

I had to admit I kind of was.

"Told you Dad was the strong one," I reminded him.

He had no response.

"I'll pay you back for the tickets," I whispered.

"We'll talk about it later."

I ignored him this time. "Yours too."

"Lauren, we'll talk about it later."

"They had to cost a whack."

"You speak English, you just don't hear it," he stated.

"All right, we'll talk about it later," I yielded.

We fell silent again. This lasted a long time. So long, I heard Tate's breathing go even and I knew from experience with listening to Brad sleep he was out.

I rolled to my other side and the instant I did, Tate's arm came out and hooked me at the waist, pulling me back into his body.

"Tate?" I called, super quiet.

"Mm?" he replied.

"You asleep?" I was still being quiet.

"No," he replied.

If he wasn't asleep then why did he pull me into him?

"Um...," I mumbled.

"Your hair smells good."

"It does?"

"Yeah."

Wow. He thought my hair smelled good. That was nice.

I decided to ignore that and how nice it was.

"Why aren't you asleep?" I asked.

"'Cause I got a woman in bed with me who won't shut up," he answered.

"Oh," I whispered then pointed out, "I was quiet a while ago."

"This is true," he murmured.

"So why aren't you asleep?"

He was silent.

"Tate?"

He sighed then he said, "You smell good, babe."

"I do?"

"You feel good too."

Uh-oh.

"Tate—"

"Just be quiet, Lauren."

I decided to go with that.

"Okay," I whispered.

We were both quiet a long time and I was about to fall back asleep in the curve of his arm with his warm body at my back when he called my name.

"Laurie?"

"Yes," I muttered, my voice sleepy.

"I was pissed last night."

"I know."

"You look good."

"Sorry?"

"No way you can look like all the rest."

My eyes shot open.

His arm curled me deeper into his body and I felt his face burrow into my hair.

"You'd always shine through," he muttered and now he sounded sleepy but I was again wide awake. "Somethin' special," he finished.

Oh.

My.

God.

He fell asleep moments later. I knew this when I took his weight into my back, his breath evened and his strong arm curved deeper around me in a way that I'd never be able to slide out from under it. I'd never be able to move away. I'd have to stay right there, tucked tight to Tate.

I didn't sleep for a long time but I didn't care. I just lay there thinking if Brad had held me like this all those years, maybe I wouldn't have tossed and turned and driven him nuts. Maybe I would have been perfectly fine with my insomnia.

If Brad had held me like this, every night, I'd look forward to it.

CHAPTER NINE

Damn Baby

THE PHONE RANG and my eyes opened.

I was in Tate's and my hotel room, alone in our bed.

I knew I was alone (even though the bed was huge) because I

couldn't feel him, hear him or sense him. In fact, I couldn't sense him anywhere. The shower wasn't running. He was gone.

I turned toward Tate's side where the phone was and saw the note. I sat up, grabbed the receiver, and the note, putting the receiver to my ear as the words on the note registered in my brain.

Ace,
Running. Be back.

Man of few words.

"Hello?" I said into the phone.

"Hi, hon," Mom said back.

"Hi, Mom."

"I wake you?"

"That's all right."

"You sleep okay?"

"Not really. You?"

"No," she replied. "Listen, hon, we're meeting for breakfast then going over. Mack says he'll come back and get you if—"

I looked at the clock. It was six thirty. I knew two things from this. Mom didn't sleep a wink and Tate was a seriously early riser.

"Tate's running but I'll be down," I told her.

"He's running?" she asked.

"Yeah," I answered.

"In a town he doesn't know?"

"Um, he's a bounty hunter, he gets around," I guessed. "New places don't faze him," I guessed again. "He'll be okay." That wasn't a guess. I figured Tate could run through the fires of hell and emerge unscathed.

"We'll wait until he gets back. They aren't letting us in for long visits and visiting hours don't start until ten," Mom told me. "I already called the hospital and they say his status hasn't changed but it's…"

She stopped and I listened to her breathing heavily, trying to control emotion.

"Take your time, Momma," I whispered.

I listened to her inhale then she said, "They said it's good he made it through the night."

Darn but this *sucked*.

"That's good," I said softly.

"Yeah," she replied.

"I'll get a shower in, go down, and leave Tate a note. He's going back to Carnal today anyway. Maybe his flight is early and he'll need to skip breakfast and get a taxi."

"He's going back today?" Mom asked, sounding surprised.

"Um...yes."

"Why?"

"Well..."

"He should stay, at least a day, see the farm."

"He's got things to do," I told her.

"It's just a day," she replied.

I'd heard that before.

"Listen, Mom—"

"I'll talk to him," she decided.

"No! Mom, really—"

"At a time like this, you need him with you. He'll understand."

"But..." I searched desperately for something then stated, "He's got fugitives from justice to hunt down. It isn't like his job isn't important."

I didn't like lying to my mother. It was likely Tate would go home and help out at the bar and get pissed about doing it all because Bubba liked to *fish*. Still, maybe there'd be some fugitive Tate had to go round up.

"There's lots of bounty hunters, Laurie, there's even one on TV. He can delegate," she said like Tate worked in an office with a bunch of bounty hunters who got a call then said, "I'll go," or "You go," or "No, *you* go," or "Butch is up next, he'll go."

"Mom—"

"We'll talk at breakfast."

"Mom—" I repeated but there was a knock at the door and my eyes fell to Tate's nightstand. I saw his cell, wallet, and the Marriott keycard so I figured Tate went out without the keycard and he needed me to let him in. "Listen, there's a knock at the door. Tate's back. I'll talk to him. If he has to go home, then he has to go home."

"Maybe, if he has to go home, he'll come back," she suggested hopefully.

There it was. My mom thinking my life could begin again now that I found a man. Then again, she'd married my dad when he was twenty-one, she was nineteen. She'd never known a life without a good man in it so she would think that.

Another knock came at the door, this one louder. Tate was getting impatient or perhaps thought he needed to wake me.

"I've got to go," I said to Mom. "See you at breakfast."

"Yes, say eight, or whenever you're ready," Mom replied. "I just want to get there before visiting hours. See if we can talk to the doctors."

"Okay." I threw off the covers and swung my legs off the bed. "See you at eight. Love you."

"Love you too, Laurie, and glad you're here."

"Me too."

"Glad Tate's here too."

I sighed.

"Me too."

"Bye hon."

I stood up and bent over the phone saying, "Bye, Momma."

I hung up and rushed across the room to the door.

I wasn't looking because it could be no one but Tate, and pulled it open while talking, "You forgot the—"

I stopped talking because Brad stood there.

I couldn't believe my eyes so all I could do was stand there and stare, which was a bad thing. It was bad because Brad took that opportunity to move into the room and he might not have been as big as Tate but he was bigger than me and I had no choice but to move back with him. I did, walking backward, staring up at him.

"What are you doing here?" I asked when we stopped.

"I saw him running," he told me.

"Tate?"

"I knew you'd be alone."

Oh for goodness sake.

I heaved a sigh then said, "Brad—"

"We need to talk, without him here."

"No we don't."

He looked at me from top to toe, then smiled his killer Bradford Whitaker smile. "You look great, darling."

I was just awake, my dad was in the ICU, and I was not in the mood for Bradford Whitaker's killer smile or to contemplate the fact that it had, for the first time since I'd seen it, not even the slightest effect on me. Instead, I focused on forcing myself not to roll my eyes.

I hated it when he called me darling and just then I remembered that I hated it even before he screwed me over. He was from Indiana too. We'd moved to Phoenix for his work. People in Indiana didn't call people darling. They might call them darlin', without the "g." I always thought that was totally fake. Even people in Phoenix didn't say that. He wasn't an English lord of the manor for goodness sakes, even though he wanted to be or, at least, acted like he was.

Thinking this moved me to thinking about Phoenix, a place I liked. It had great shopping and excellent restaurants and out of this world Mexican food. It was also close to Sedona and Flagstaff, both of which were amazing. And the desert in bloom was not to be believed. But, even so, I never settled there. It was too hot. I never got used to the heat. I hated the summers, they were torture.

Brad loved it. He detested cold and adored golf. No matter how often I talked to him about it, he never even entertained the idea of moving anywhere else. Not even when his work offered jobs in D.C. where I really wanted to live. It was beautiful, historical and exciting. And Seattle where I'd been before and I thought it was great. So much so that it was the first place I headed after I left my old life but it didn't hit me like Carnal did when I got there. Too big, too wet, so I didn't stay.

Thinking these things made me straighten my spine, look Brad in the eye and say, "Please go."

He didn't go. He got close and put his hands to my waist.

"You look great tan, always did."

I put my hands to his and tried to remove them, repeating, "Go."

His hands slid around to my back. "And your hair…I like it like that. Sun-streaked."

"It's fake, Brad. It isn't sun streaks. It's highlights delivered from a plastic brush wielded by Dominic, the gay stylist to all biker babes." I was still pushing at his hands.

He put pressure on my back so our hips touched. "Whatever," he muttered then went on. "The length of it suits you. I wouldn't normally say a woman of your age should have long hair—"

"Brad!" I snapped, interrupting him because he was annoying me in a *variety* of ways. "Go!"

He ignored me, leaned a bit back without letting me go as I still struggled with my hands now at his wrists behind my back trying to push them away. "How much weight have you lost?"

"I don't know. Who cares? Let me go." I pushed harder.

He pulled me closer.

"What you were wearing yesterday," he murmured and I tried to remember what I was wearing yesterday. It was another tank top, this one salmon, ribbed and fitted, with jeans and a belt and flip-flops. Not exactly haute couture but even I knew they fit really well. "God, Ree." That came out as almost a groan. I noticed his eyes were locked on my mouth, I knew what that meant and I belatedly realized the situation was quickly deteriorating.

I jerked back but his arms only got tighter.

"Brad! Let! Go!"

His eyes came back to mine. "We were good together."

I stopped struggling and glared at him. "Yeah, we *were*. Then we *weren't*."

His head bent and he shoved his face in my neck. "I missed you," he whispered against my skin.

I started struggling again, squirming against his body but his arms only wrapped tighter around me and I felt his lips slide up to my ear.

"She cheated on me," he whispered and I went still.

"Sorry?" I asked.

His head came up. "Hayley. Traded up for a new model."

Oh my God.

He continued, "I made more money than Scott. Her new guy is a doctor. A *surgeon*. Obviously he makes more money than me."

I didn't know what to make of this. Though I'd always suspected Hayley was with Brad because Scott, her husband, wasn't as successful as Brad, my house was bigger than hers and she could only afford Griselle to come once every two weeks, not once a week. I also knew by things she said she wanted more. I didn't want to think ill of my best friend so I'd let her little comments slide, dozens of times. But they always made me feel weird.

Now, I knew.

I had the inappropriate desire to giggle.

Instead, I started, "Brad—"

"She's been fucking him for two years. Even while we were going through what we went through, Hayley knowing I was doing it for her, she was working her next move. He finally left his wife for her. Hayley's gone, Ree. Been gone awhile. Turned her back on me, Audrey, Janet, Colleen, all of them. She hasn't spoken to them in ages...or me. She's on hospital charity committees now. Thinks she's highbrow. Hobnobbing with society."

Well that explained the e-mails. Now they all knew just exactly what Hayley was. All of them. Even Brad.

That desire to giggle got harder to bite back.

"This isn't my problem," I reminded him.

"Honey—"

"Brad, let me go. It isn't my problem," I repeated.

He pulled me even closer and his face dipped down. "I'm here because you were right. We can work on this. We can go back to what we had."

I started struggling again. "No we can't."

"We were good together once. Then you started to let yourself go…"

I jerked back but not successfully out of his arms and my eyes narrowed on him. "I started to let myself go?"

"You know I don't like a woman to carry extra weight," he explained.

He could not be *believed*!

"I started eating because I sensed you were fucking around on me!" I shouted.

"Darling—"

"Stop calling me that!"

"You're back," he replied, his eyes going over my hair and down to my chest before coming back to mine. "Better than ever."

I stopped pushing against his wrists and pressed my hands against his chest. "Get out!"

He ignored me. "And *we* can be back and better than ever."

"Seriously, this is *not* cool."

His face got in my face. "I know what you're doing with that guy. I get it. It hurts, honey, you got yours back. We both struck our blows, learned our lessons, now we can move on."

"I wasn't striking a blow, you jerk. We're divorced," I shouted, losing it. "You fucked Hayley, carrying on with her for five years while we were *committed to each other* and *bound legally*! You wanted out and I let you out and moved on. Tate has not one thing to do with *you*!"

"Honey, you know you want me back. You practically begged to take me back even knowing what happened. You fell apart when I left."

I started pushing, squirming in earnest, rearing back and shrieking, "Fuck you!"

Finally, I was getting somewhere. He was struggling to control me.

"Ree—"

"Let me—!"

I didn't get out the word "go" because I was suddenly released but Brad wasn't the one who released me. Tate was there, drenched in sweat wearing a white T-shirt with the sleeves cut off, black sweatpants that were cut off at midthigh, and running shoes. We'd been so entrenched in our drama that we didn't hear him come in.

Tate had hold of the back of Brad's golf shirt. He pulled him back, then let fly and Brad staggered five paces before he righted himself.

He planted his feet and scowled up at Tate. "Put your hand on me again and I'll sue!" Brad shouted.

Tate advanced, not saying a word. Then he put his hand on Brad, scrunching the material of his shiny, blue golf shirt in one big fist and shoving him backward to the door. Once there, he jerked him forward making Brad lurch like a ragdoll. Brad's hands went to Tate's wrist to pull it free. Tate leaned beyond Brad, yanked open the door and then shoved him through.

Brad reeled back and righted himself halfway across the wide hall.

"You asshole!" Brad shouted.

"I see you again, it won't be pretty. I find out *she* sees you again, you'll be breathin' through a fuckin' tube. You get me?" Tate growled.

"Fuck you!" Brad yelled.

Tate shut the door. I stared at it, frozen to the spot.

Tate turned to me.

"How'd he get in here?" Tate asked.

I was still staring at the door but at his question my head jerked and I looked at him. "I opened it."

"You opened it?" Tate asked and I was too overwrought by the latest scene to let his tone penetrate.

"You"—I swung an arm out indicating in its wide sweep the nightstand—"left your keycard. I thought it was you."

Tate lifted up a hand and between two fingers was a keycard. Then he flicked his hand and the keycard went sailing. I watched it slice through the air and flutter to the floor.

"Two of us in this room, Ace, two keycards," he said and my eyes went to him. When they did, he jerked his hand, finger extended to the door. "Know what this is?"

"A door?" I asked stupidly.

"A peephole," he bit back then moved his hand to flick the security latch closed. "Know what that is?"

"Captain—"

He advanced and the aggressive way he did it made me retreat. It was dawning on me he was pissed and he wasn't pissed at Brad. He was pissed *at me*.

I stopped when my legs hit the chair to the desk. He stopped when he was in my space. I tilted my head way back to look at him.

"You got great hair, babe."

"Tate—"

"Thick."

"Tate—"

"Soft."

"Tate," I whispered.

"Shame it gets hacked off with a knife after some guy *rapes you with that knife!*" he finished on a roar.

My body jolted.

"Tate!"

"There's bad guys out there, Ace. *Bad.* Do things to you that'll make you glad you end up dead. You don't open a goddamned door not knowin' who's behind it."

"I thought it was you."

"Well it wasn't."

"Tate—"

"He fuck you?" Tate asked suddenly and my head jerked again.

"Brad?" I asked back, confused.

Tate leaned in and bellowed, "*Wood!*"

"No!" I shouted back.

Then I was flying through the air. Literally, flying through the air. I bounced once on the bed and then Tate was on top of me. He was wet, he was sweaty, and his weight felt great. His mouth on mine, his tongue in my mouth felt even better.

I didn't know what got into me. I simply ignited, all thoughts left my mind and I kissed him back, wanting, desperate, wild.

I put my hands in his shirt, shoving it up and his arms lifted, his hands going between his shoulder blades and he yanked his shirt over his head and tossed it away. I pushed off with a foot and rolled him, getting on top. I kissed him, then my mouth slid through his beard, down his jaw, his neck, all the while my hands moved on him, discovering. I saw the tattoo that painted his shoulder, going up and over, down his arm and slithering down his chest. I was too into what I was doing to see what it was but I followed it and kept going until my mouth hit his nipple. Once there, I flicked it with my tongue, then I sucked it between my lips.

Half a second later I was on my back and my T-shirt was going up. I lifted my arms and it was gone. Then Tate's hand slid into my panties, right in, and I felt one of his long fingers fill me as his mouth latched on to my nipple and pulled it deep.

That felt so good, my back left the bed, arching straight into the air. My fingers slid into his damp hair and I moaned, "Tate."

His finger slid out of me and hit the spot. His mouth sucked deeper and his finger moved and it hit me, it was coming, I knew it.

"Tate." It was a whimper.

I lost both his mouth and hand and my eyes flew open.

"Not without me," he growled and he was moving.

His hands grasped my panties at either side of my hips and tugged down. When they were gone and I felt Tate leave the bed, I got up on my elbows to see him standing at its foot. He pulled down his shorts and I saw all of him and all of it was equally beautiful in a way that knocked my ragged breath right out of me.

And *all* of him was *hard*.

He grabbed my calves and yanked them apart, then pushed them up so my knees were bent. He put a knee to the bed and moved forward, releasing one of my calves, his hand wrapped around his cock and I felt his weight begin to hit me.

"You come with me inside you, Ace," he gritted, and then he was inside me, filling me, beautiful.

At the feel of him, so hard, making me so full, my back left the bed again. "Tate."

He moved, driving deep, fast, hard. Our mouths attached, our tongues clashed. His hand went between us and he touched me and that was it. It hit me like a rocket and I combusted, my world exploding, taking me with it and I loved every nanosecond.

I tore my mouth from his and moaned, "Tate."

"That's my girl," he murmured, still moving inside me.

I came down from the orgasm he gave me to feel his hands had spanned my hips, pulling them up to meet his thrusts and I still needed him. My legs wrapped around his hips and my hands roamed, my mouth trailed, my tongue tasted. Everywhere I could touch; everything I could reach. His sweat tasted great to me, his skin even better. The muscles under his sleek, slick skin felt amazing.

His hand left my hip, came between us again, and my hips jerked.

"Honey—" I whispered against his lips.

"Hurry, baby, I'm close."

"I don't think I can—"

His finger rolled. "Hurry, Laurie."

I didn't have to hurry, he rushed me and that was that. His hips started thrusting harder, going deeper, his grunts mingling with my whimpers and then I came again. I wrapped him tight in my limbs and moaned into his mouth.

He drove deep once, twice, three times then four and five all the while he groaned into mine.

After, it felt like being with him on his bike. Out of mind but completely tuned into my body and I didn't want to be anywhere but there, in my body, attuned to every inch of my skin and every inch of Tate that was on me and in me.

His face was in my neck when he murmured an intense, *"Damn baby."*

I came back to my mind.

Oh my God. What had I just done?

I turned my head away and moved my hands from his hair to his shoulders, giving a feeble push.

I felt his head come up. "You light up like that all the time?"

"Get off," I whispered.

"Or just for me?"

"Please." I was still whispering.

"Babe," he called and I shut my eyes tight because he sounded like he was laughing. "I'm not complainin' but, later, I might wanna take things slow and, you ignite like that…"

"It's been a long time," I said quietly and with deep humiliation.

"How long? A decade?"

I righted my head and glared at him because of his joke and because I didn't think this was funny but also because when I looked at him he was smiling. "No," I snapped.

"Longer?" he teased.

"Over a year," I shared but I did it angrily and with a push on his shoulders.

He pressed his hips into mine and I quit pushing.

His brows were up and his tone was incredulous. "Not even self-induced?"

My glare turned molten.

His head dropped but I caught his smile getting bigger before it did. I felt his nose flick my ear and then he muttered there, "You've touched yourself."

"It's not the same," I informed him irritably.

His head came up, he looked at me and he whispered, "No, baby, it's not."

I decided to go on the offense. "I'll remind you that *you* threw me on the bed."

His smile got even bigger. "Yeah, Ace, a day of you cryin' in my arms, sleepin' in my arms, kissin' you, feelin' your body, smellin' your hair, your perfume, only so much a man can take. I ran for an hour, hard, didn't even fuckin' warm up, it didn't touch it. Come back, deal with that fuckwad, and you're standin' there, all legs and hair, wearin' my shirt. Seriously. Only so much a man can take."

I had to admit, all of what he said made me feel like I was sliding back out of my brain and tuning into my body, a body that felt warm and happy.

I didn't allow myself to go there.

"Will you get up? I have to take a shower and have breakfast with my family."

He didn't get up at first. Instead, his eyes moved over my face and hair.

Then he murmured, "Shower," and all of a sudden he slid out of me and we were *both* up. We were on our feet and Tate had my hand. I searched the floor frantically to find his T-shirt in order to snatch it up, put it on, and hide my nudity but he dragged me toward the bathroom.

"Tate!" I snapped, yanking at his hand to no avail.

He flipped on the switch and pulled me straight to the shower, reaching in and turning it on.

I tried to yank my hand away again but Tate responded by giving it a sharp tug so I fell forward, nearly into him.

"What are you doing?" I asked, watching him reach in to put a hand under the shower spray.

He turned to me. "In," he ordered.

"Sorry?" I breathed and then his hands were at my hips and he was shoving me in so I had no choice but to climb over the side of the tub and into the shower.

Tate came in after me and slid the curtain closed.

"Um...," I mumbled, my heart beating fast.

He had a great body, every inch of it. I didn't know how old he was but I knew how old I was and I might not have back fat anymore and my arms and shoulders were moving straight toward killer because Tyler was Mr. Decline Push-up but the rest of me...

"Tate," I said turning to face him, my forearms covering my breasts but he was examining the little bottles of stuff the hotel left for you in the shower.

He picked a bottle and moved forward so I had to step back and was fully under the spray.

Then I felt his fingers slide through my hair.

"Can we—?" I started.

"Do you first," Tate muttered. "Then you can get out and finish gettin' ready."

"Do me?"

He pulled me forward. So far forward my wet body was plastered against his.

I blinked up at him through the residual water sliding down my face and by the time I could focus his fingers were in my hair. They were strong, working at my hair and scalp.

Heaven.

I'd always loved that, someone playing with my hair, which was why, when Tate did it the night before, I could relax and fall asleep watching TV with my head on his stomach. In Phoenix, I went to a particular salon and paid extra just because they gave fifteen-minute head massages when they shampooed your hair.

I melted into him and tilted my head forward.

"That feels nice," I whispered.

He didn't reply, just kept washing my hair. Then he gently moved me under the spray, using his big hands on either side of my head to tip it back, his fingers gliding through my hair to get the soap out.

Then he moved me back out of the spray.

Not even thinking, I tipped my head back and informed him, "I wash twice, then condition."

He dipped his bearded chin, grinned at me, dipped it farther, touched his mouth to mine then he washed my hair again and, after, massaged in conditioner.

I was deep in a mellow zone, again out of mind, when Tate turned me to face the spray and I felt his soapy hands moving on me. They were everywhere and I just stood there, his front pressed to my back, and gloried in his slick, wet, soapy hands gliding along my skin.

Then one glided between my legs and stayed there while the other glided to my breast and cupped it.

My eyes opened and I blinked against the spray hitting my face.

"Tate," I whispered.

He didn't respond except his finger and thumb rolled my nipple.

My conditioner-covered head fell back and hit his shoulder.

"Tate," I breathed.

The fingers of both his hands moved and he took me there again; this time it took longer but it was no less fabulous. When I came, my hips bucked, my body jolted, my legs went weak and Tate's hand at my breast became an arm wrapped around my ribs to hold me up.

As I came down, I did it with Tate holding me close to his body, arm still wrapped around my ribs, his other hand cupping my sex. When I was steady on my legs again, he turned me and his fingers went back into my hair to rinse out the conditioner.

When done, he pulled me out of the spray, switched our positions so his back was to it and I was out of it and his arms went around me, bringing me close.

I tipped my head back to look at him.

"Get out, finish gettin' ready," he ordered softly.

I could do nothing but agree. "Okay," I whispered.

He grinned, touched his mouth to mine again, let me go, and turned to the spray.

I got out but stilled with my hand on the curtain when I saw the gigantic black ink eagle, its wingspan covering Tate's back from the bottom of his right lateral muscle sweeping up his left lat and over his shoulder with the body of the bird painted on a slant across his back, lat, and even curling around his side. The other wing, I knew, curled over his shoulder, going down his arm and partly down his chest to his pectoral. His left shoulder was covered in glorious ink, his right was naked.

It was extraordinary and somehow sexy and I felt my legs get weak at the sight.

His hands were lifted to press the water through his hair and then he reached for the dregs of the little shampoo bottle.

I resolutely shoved the curtain closed.

I grabbed a towel and ran into the bedroom. I quickly toweled off, rubbed the wet out of my hair and wrapped the towel around me. I eschewed lotioning. Indiana was a moist climate. I could get away without lotion. Colorado, even in a freak-out to get dressed before Tate got out of the shower, I'd consider it.

I went to my suitcase, which Tate had clearly moved back to the luggage rack this morning because, thankfully, it was there. I pawed through it lamenting Wendy and my shop-a-thon where, in throes of ecstasy that I was two sizes smaller, I'd bought nothing but sexy undies and threw away every piece of underwear I'd owned.

My choices were baby pink with ecru lace, fire engine red with black lace, full on black, sage green with taupe lace, it went on. But nothing unsexy.

Darn!

I grabbed the sage green, tugged the panties on under the towel and then whipped off the towel and frantically put on the bra because I heard the shower go off. I was wrapping the towel back around me when Tate walked out of the bathroom with another one wrapped around his waist.

My eyes went to him and I marveled at the fact that he looked fantastic with wet hair. Then again that wet hair came with a full on view of his bare chest and broad shoulders and that chest and those shoulders would look good with a head on top of it that had wet hair, dry hair, or no hair.

His eyes came to me and slid down the towel.

He looked back at my face. "That as far as you got?"

"I had an underwear selection to make," I explained and my voice sounded weirdly breathy.

He grinned again and before I knew what he was about, he gripped the edge of my towel and whipped it off.

I gasped and made a grab for the towel.

Tate tossed the towel on the bed, captured me with hands at my waist, tilted me back and took a long look.

Then his eyes came to mine. "Good choice, Ace."

I tried to be cool even though, with his eyes on me, I was freaking out. "I'm glad you approve. Now can I have my towel?"

His hands at my waist slid around, one arm wrapped around my waist, the fingers of the other hand sliding up into my wet and dripping hair.

I put my hands on his shoulders and exerted pressure.

"We need to get breakfast," I whispered.

His head was coming toward me. "After I kiss you."

"Tate," I was still whispering.

He kissed me. I slid out of my mind and into my body. By the time he was done I was all about my body.

So was Tate. "Don't cover up, baby," he muttered against my mouth. "I like the view."

"I'm—"

"I like it."

"But—"

His hand slid over one cheek of my bottom and he pulled my hips deeper into his.

"Babe, spent a month thinkin' about this moment, when you'd be mine and this was what I could look forward to. Don't hide it from me."

In complete shock at his words, I stared into his eyes. "You spent a month thinking about this moment?" I repeated.

"Actually, no," he answered. "Spent a month thinkin' about what I did to you in bed." He smiled. "And the shower." His smile got so sexy my fingers curled into his shoulders. "And what I'm gonna do to you later. Seein' you in sexy underwear was just bonus footage."

I had no reply to this. I couldn't even process this. All I could do was stand in his arms, my body pressed to his, and gaze in his eyes.

"You gonna stand there lookin' at me, kiss me, or get ready?" he asked.

"Get ready," I answered softly but didn't move and I didn't move mainly because I was thinking I preferred option two but option one of just staring at him had its merits.

He grinned. "Babe."

"What?"

He let me go but his hand didn't leave my ass. It stayed there so it could push me toward the bathroom.

I grabbed my stuff as I went and camped out in the bathroom, wiping the mirror and starting to get ready. I'd pulled a comb through my hair, put on a white headband, washed my face, brushed and flossed my teeth, moisturized and I was preparing for minimal makeup when Tate walked in, still in his towel, and he brushed his teeth standing next to me.

This was when I came fully back into my mind. In fact, I came speeding into it at Mach Three.

How on earth was I standing in my new sage green satin and taupe lace underwear in a bathroom in a Marriott in Indianapolis with Tatum Jackson?

My blush brush arrested in midair and I turned woodenly to him.

"How did this happen?" I asked.

He took his toothbrush out of his mouth and with a mouth full of white foam, he asked, "What?" and then kept brushing.

I swirled my blush brush in the air indicating the entirety of our situation with a flourish.

He turned to the sink, put a palm in the counter, bent his neck, and spit. Then he rinsed. He twisted, reached across the counter in front of me, grabbed a hand towel and wiped, throwing it on the counter when he was done.

"You jumped me," he answered.

"I didn't jump you! You threw me on the bed!"

"Right," he grinned. "*Then* you jumped me."

"I didn't jump you, I was on my back!"

He moved so he was behind me, his hands came to my upper hips and his head bent so he could kiss my neck, which he did. I watched him do it in the mirror and watching it made me lose my hold on my mind again.

His head came up and he looked at me in the mirror.

"Thanks for remindin' me of that," he muttered. "So, I guess I shouldn't say you jumped. It was more like you...*attacked*."

"This isn't funny," I told his reflection.

He grinned yet again and said, "Babe."

"It isn't!"

"We'll talk about it later," he declared.

"Tate—" I started.

"Get ready."

"Tate! We need to talk. This is insane."

"We'll talk."

"When?"

"Later."

"When, later?" I asked.

"Later, later," he answered with a nonanswer.

I pulled in a breath. Then with his hands still on my nearly naked hips, me in my underwear, in a bathroom, in a hotel with Tatum Jackson, I started swiping my cheeks with blush while said Tatum Jackson watched.

"That reminds me. Mom called this morning and she's going to try to talk you out of going today. She wants you to see our farm," I told him.

"She won't have to try too hard."

My blush brush arrested on the apple of my cheek and I stared into his eyes in the mirror.

His eyes moved to the brush. "Ace, you keep fuckin' around, we'll never have breakfast."

"You're staying?" I whispered.

He dropped his bearded chin to my shoulder and his arms wrapped around my belly.

"Baby, you just came three times," he said softly, his mouth close to my ear. "You think I'm flyin' across four states when you're topped up and tonight I get a chance to play?"

I felt my knees wobble.

"Tate," I breathed.

"And your ex is a fuckwad and until I know he's on a fuckin' plane on his way back to suburbia, I ain't goin' anywhere."

Oh.

My.

God.

"Tate," I whispered.

"And we don't know about your dad yet and until he's stable, I'm here."

I stared at him in the mirror.

Who *was* this man and what did I do with him?

"What about the bar?" I asked.

"I'll call Bubba, ream his ass and tell him about your situation. He'll dry out and go back."

I asked the all-important question, "What about Wood?"

His chin came up but his arms didn't leave me.

"That's later."

"I need to call him," I whispered.

"No, you don't need to call him. *I* need to call him. Wood and I need to have words. He's got more words for you afterwards, we'll see."

"We'll see?"

He nodded. "We'll see."

"I should—"

"Later."

"But—"

His arms gave a squeeze. "Jesus, Lauren. *Later.*"

We held each other's eyes in the mirror.

Then he said, "Breakfast, babe."

"Right," I whispered.

He dropped his head, kissed my shoulder, his beard tickling my skin and he left the bathroom.

I looked in the mirror at myself wearing my sexy undies. If I was honest, I didn't look half bad. It was all Tyler's "working the core." Weeks of my abs aching like crazy was paying off. There was even some definition at my midriff and the mini–Buddha belly was more like a soft pooch. I hadn't noticed. It was even kind of cute.

My eyes went from my pooch to my makeup bag. I dropped the blush brush in and pulled out some eye shadow.

CHAPTER TEN

Grape Kool-Aid

I WAS LYING in the rope hammock between the two elm trees that butted the front edge of my mom and dad's big, square, cement front porch, my eyes on Tate and Mack who were both standing at the raised bottom end of the huge pond that took up the side of our long front yard.

Mom was at the hospital with her best friend Norma.

We'd had breakfast. Tate had let Mom talk him into staying. Mom had let Tate pay for breakfast but not without a fight. She'd pulled the Dad card again. Tate's eyes had sliced to me and I knew he was about to blow. So I'd pulled the my-boyfriend-is-a-macho-man-bounty-hunter-and-if-you-don't-let-him-pay-my-life-will-be-a-living-hell card and Mom had spent a full minute assessing Tate's big, bearded badassness and what that might mean to me should he get miffed and wisely relented.

We'd gone to the hospital. I'd visited Dad for ten minutes. All of that time he was sleeping and I thought that he looked exactly like he'd had his chest cracked open and how that was the way wrong look for my big, tall, strong, farmer dad. Carrie had her visit and Mom had hers and then my mom's best friend Norma showed up and Mom talked Mack into taking us to the farm and out to lunch at The Station before we came back. Mack drove with Tate in the passenger seat and Carrie and I in the back. Mack talked. Tate didn't. Carrie and I looked out our windows. Both of us, I was sure, not seeing the landscape and instead seeing our dad in a hospital bed.

Now, Carrie was inside the house, Mack and Tate were inspecting the land, and I was freaking out and not just about my dad.

I heard Carrie approach and I looked up at her.

"Skooch over," she ordered and handed me one of Mom's Tupperware tumblers filled with purple liquid.

"No, is that—?" I started as I skooched.

"Grape Kool-Aid," she affirmed.

It was official. I *was* home.

With grace born of years of practice—Mom stretched that hammock out at the beginning of every May and rolled it up and took it in at the end of every September for as long as I could remember—Caroline got in the hammock while holding her tumbler.

Then, as if drawn by an invisible force, both of our eyes went to the men.

"Tate's hot," she whispered.

She had no idea.

I took a sip of ice cold Kool-Aid. Delicious, refreshing, and Tyler *and* Wendy's heads would explode if they knew I was drinking it, which made it perfect.

"Laurie, you look awesome," Carrie said to me and I looked from Tate to her.

"Thanks, honey."

"And more than just being tan and having cool hair. You look…" She studied me. "Happy."

This surprised me. "I do?"

"Well, outside of looking sad about Dad but, you know, deep down. Contentlike."

I looked toward Tate.

"Is it him?" she asked quietly and my eyes went back to her.

"Sorry?"

"Tate."

"Um…"

"See, 'cause, when you were with Brad…" She hesitated then shook her head. "I don't know. You were never yourself. You weren't our Laurie. Not when he was around. When you were alone, you were great. You were you. When he was around, there was something off. Like you were on eggshells. Like you had to be perfect and spent all your time in an effort to be that way."

I stared at her, both surprised at this and not surprised because her saying those words made me realize I *did* try to be perfect for Brad because I thought *he* was perfect and to keep him I had to match that.

Boy was I wrong about that.

Then I asked, "Really?"

"Yeah," she said, nodding. "Mom and I talked about it…" She paused. "A lot."

I was already surprised at what she said but this surprised me even more.

"You talked about it?"

She turned to me. "He wasn't all that and I'm glad you know that now. I'm sorry you went through what you did to find out. That totally sucks and I wish you hadn't had to go through that, but still, I'm glad you know. He was just a guy and not a very nice one. Brad's cute and all but he knows it. But you, it was like you didn't know how pretty you were. It was like you thought you were luckier to be with him than he was to be with you when that was the wrong way around. With Tate…" She trailed off and her eyes slid away.

"With Tate what?" I prompted.

Her eyes slid back. "You just seem…I don't know…*you*. Like you can be Laurie. You can be yourself and it's so cool that he's into that, into you just as you are because, well, he *is* all that."

I looked back at Tate. She was right. He was pretty much all that.

He was also other things.

"I have another man back at Carnal," I blurted and heard my sister gasp.

Then she asked on a whisper, "*What?*"

I shook my head and turned toward her. "Carrie, it's all messed up."

"What's messed up?"

I kept shaking my head while talking.

"I don't know, Tate and me, we met and we did *not* get along. Well, mostly, I didn't get along with him. He said some things about me and I overheard him and they hurt and, even though he apologized, I didn't accept and we bickered all the time and then, suddenly, *poof*." I threw out my hand with the tumbler and grape Kool-Aid almost sloshed on my jeans shorts. "Tonia gets raped and murdered and we find out about it together and we aren't bickering anymore. We're like, so far away from bickering it isn't funny. We're something else *completely*."

"Tonia gets raped and murdered?" she repeated, her eyes huge.

"Tonia," I told her, nodding. "She worked for Tate and he fired her *the night she got raped*. And he wasn't nice about it. He gets pissed and watch *out*. Stuff comes out of his mouth, that's why he said I was fat and sorry-ass, because he was pissed."

Her head jerked back and her eyes narrowed. "He said you were fat and sorry-ass?"

I nodded again. "He didn't mean it. He has a bad temper. He says a lot of things he doesn't mean when he's pissed. I've seen it happen three times and he's regretted it three times. He said those things to Tonia, right in front of everyone and she left the bar and that's the last anyone saw of her conscious. Then she was dead. Tate was a mess. I mean, in a badass, biker, bounty hunter kind of way. He freaked out and took off after her murderer and he was gone for *a month*. That's when Wood told me Tate was fucking his sister."

"Tate is fucking Wood's sister?" Caroline asked and I nodded.

"That's what Wood said."

"Wood?"

"The other guy I'm sleeping with," I informed her and her eyebrows shot up.

"You're sleeping with him?" she whispered, getting closer so, when she did, I got closer too.

"Not *sleeping* sleeping just, you know, sleeping and maybe fooling around a bit. He gets up early and I get home late—"

"Laurie!" she hissed. "How could you—?"

"I don't know!" I hissed back. "Tate went out of town and he took me for a ride on his bike and he kissed me before he left. But he didn't tell me he was going. He just said he wanted me on the back of his bike when he got back. But then he was gone. *For a month*. He didn't call. Nothing. He just vanished. Then I got my car from Wood and he said he'd seen me on Tate's bike and he didn't want to tell me what he had to tell me because *he* wanted me to be on the back of *his* bike. But then he told me Tate was with Neeta, Wood's sister, and she's *married*."

"The back of his bike?" she asked, looking confused.

I shook my head. "I don't know. I don't get it. I think it's biker slang for they want a date or something."

"What did Tate say about what Wood said?"

This was the tricky part therefore I mumbled, "Um…"

"What?" she asked.

"I didn't ask him," I admitted. "When he got back…" I moved even closer. "Carrie, when he got back I think he came straight to me, straight to the bar. He grabbed my hand and pulled me into the hall and kissed me and told me he didn't find Tonia's killer but it was good to be home then I threw the whole Neeta thing in his face. He got pissed, said some nasty stuff, and stormed off."

"You threw the whole Neeta thing in his face, a big, badass man with a bad temper?"

"Yes."

"Why on earth would you do that?" she whispered loudly.

"I don't know!" I whispered loudly right back, "I'm me. He's Tate. We haven't known each other for very long but that's what we *do*."

"When was that?" she asked.

"Two days ago."

My sister stared at me.

Then she said, "I don't get it. Did you make up?"

"No, he was just there when you called me. We'd just finished trading barbs and you phoned and…and…" I took in a breath then took a sip of Kool-Aid then finished, "Now he's here."

"Now he's here," she repeated, staring at me intently.

"Yeah," I said.

She kept staring at me.

Then she shook her head and muttered, "Some things never change."

"Sorry?" I asked.

"Honey," she whispered and that one word seemed to have grave meaning but she said no more.

"What?"

She lifted up several inches and looked down at me.

"Let me get this straight. You and Tate don't get on, then you do, more than likely because you *really* got on just one or the other of you didn't get that. And I'm guessing the one who didn't get that is you. Then he says he wants you on the back of his bike, which I think you don't get means more than a date. He takes off and doesn't call and some other guy talks trash about him to you behind his back. You listen to this trash and believe this guy. You don't call *Tate*. When he comes back you don't ask *him* what's up. You just listen to some guy with an ulterior motive talking trash. Tate gets home. You throw it in his face. He gets pissed like you know he's going to do, storms off but ends up a day later flying halfway across the country just to hold your hand because your dad is sick? Do I have that right?"

Uh-oh. I hadn't thought of it that way.

My eyes slid to Tate again to see he and Mack were walking up the yard toward us.

"So where is it now?" Carrie asked.

"We had sex for the first time this morning," I answered and I heard my sister gasp again.

I closed my eyes.

"Laurie," Carrie called and I didn't look at her. I just opened my eyes and stared at Tate getting closer.

"Mm?" I muttered.

"Big sister, I love you but you've always held a mean grudge and you've always, but always, leaped before you looked."

My eyes moved to hers. "What?" I whispered.

"Brad was a dick and you thought he was something special and he gave you attention so you grabbed hold, never seeing he was a dick. That wasn't good, not for years, and you followed him to Phoenix and lived a life you hated and did whatever you could to keep hold. That didn't work out and you sold everything you owned and took off in your car and wandered the country. Now you've set up a life in the middle of nowhere and you got a man who's into you and you listen to another man who's into you and you don't set the story straight. You just believe, shut down and, I'm guessing, intentionally piss him off to shut him out. A day later, he's at your side during an intense time in your life, what I'm guessing again is pretending to be your boyfriend to get in the face of your dickhead ex-husband and then you leap into bed with him. Laurie," she moved so her face was close to mine, "you're smart in a lot of ways but that doesn't mean you don't need to learn how *to think*."

Okay, I had to admit I'd heard that before, not only from Carrie but from Dad *and* Mom.

Still, I said, "Carrie—"

"Talk to him," she whispered as we heard the men approach. "Give him a chance to set the story straight."

"Right," I whispered back because the men were almost there, we needed to stop talking, and because she *was* right. She usually was. She was my baby sister and I knew I should be the smart and responsible one but I never was. I was always a good girl and I was always a nice person but I wasn't always smart and responsible. That had always been Caroline's role.

She got to within an inch of my face. "And *listen*," she finished.

"Right," I repeated still whispering.

"This doesn't look good," Mack remarked from close and Carrie moved back so we saw them both standing four feet from the hammock. Mack had his arms crossed on his chest. Tate had his hands resting on his hips. Mack's eyes were assessing and they were on Carrie. Tate's face was carefully blank and his eyes were on me.

Carrie ignored Mack's comment and asked, "You guys want grape Kool-Aid?"

"Jesus, is that what you're drinking?" Mack asked.

"Yes," Caroline answered.

"Little kids drink that," Mack noted.

"Laurie and me are always kids when we're home," Carrie replied. "You know that."

"God's honest truth," Mack muttered in a way that stated plainly this was not a good thing as he shook his head while glancing at Tate. Then he looked back at Carrie.

"You have a grape Kool-Aid mustache," he told Carrie and Carrie swiped the back of her wrist along her mouth at the same time she cried, "I do not!"

And she didn't. Mack was just teasing, which was why he grinned.

She stuck her purple tongue out at him and looked at Tate. "You want a Coke?"

"Yeah," Tate replied.

"I'll have a Coke too," Mack put in as Carrie and I swung the hammock back so she could get out.

"You can get it yourself," she muttered as she rolled out of the hammock to her feet. She rounded the hammock, jumped up on the patio and headed toward the door.

"I see the Grahame sisters have matching attitude," Tate murmured to Mack and my eyes narrowed on him but Mack chuckled.

"It's in the genes. Jeannie's shell-shocked 'cause Gavin's in ICU.

Just wait until he's fit. He'll be fakin' a heart attack to get some rest from the drama," Mack returned.

"Mack!" I snapped. "Mom's sweet as pie."

"Yeah, to *you*. You got balls, she'll bust 'em," Mack retorted and my eyes cut to Tate firstly because he'd accused me of busting his balls and secondly because he'd burst out laughing.

"Shit man, you're gonna catch it," Mack warned a still-chuckling Tate as he watched me glare at the still-chuckling Tate. "I'm gonna get a Coke."

Then Mack walked to the patio, jumped up on it and headed to the house.

Tate walked to me and smoothly entered the hammock to lie at my side like he slept in one nightly since he could walk.

Regardless of the fact that I was in no danger of spillage, I snapped, "Watch my Kool-Aid!"

"Babe," was his reply.

I glared at him.

He reached across his abs, wrapped an arm around my waist and curled me so I was on my side and resting the length of him. He also did this without endangering my Kool-Aid.

I decided to ignore him and take a sip.

Tate watched me doing this and remarked, "You grew up in heaven."

I swallowed, dropped my tumbler hand to rest on his chest, glanced at him, lifted up and looked. I saw sun dazzling lights on the pond, the long, green front yard Dad kept neat and trimmed, the lush, dense trees at the foot, the farmland beyond that, and Mom's tidy, flourishing garden on the opposite side of the pond where she planted strawberries, potatoes, tomatoes, regular corn, and popcorn every year.

I looked back at Tate and whispered, "Yeah."

"The first time I met you, you told me you grew up here, I'd call you a liar," Tate informed me.

I tipped my head to the side and asked, "Really?"

"Really."

"Why?"

"High-class," he replied.

"Sorry?"

"You looked high-class," he semi-repeated.

"I'm not," I stated.

"No, Ace, you're not. You're a different kind of class."

"Farmer class."

"Pure class."

That was so nice, and so unexpected, before I could stop myself, I melted into him, my face getting closer to his.

"Tate," I whispered.

His hand slid from my waist partly up my back.

"You get grape Kool-Aid on my tee, babe, it's gonna piss me off," he lied and I knew it was a lie from the look on his face, which was sweet and soft and more handsome than he ever looked.

"I'm not going to get Kool-Aid on your tee," I returned quietly.

He rolled into me and I had no choice but to lift the tumbler and hold it behind his back.

"Maybe it wouldn't be so bad," he said, his face in my neck, his beard tickling my throat. "You could lick it off."

"Captain, we can't fool around in the hammock at the front of my mom and dad's house with Mack and Carrie *in* the house," I informed him as his lips and beard slid up the underside of my chin.

When they reached my mouth, he whispered, "Yeah, sucks."

He was not wrong.

Suddenly his head came up and he looked over his shoulder.

I looked too, in time to see a police cruiser followed closely by a silver sedan coming around the bend and up my parents' curving, gravel lane.

"What the fuck?" Tate murmured then I knew he saw what I saw and that was Brad driving the silver sedan. I knew this because he bit out a repeated, "What *the fuck*?"

Before I knew it we were both rolling out of the hammock

and, with Tate firmly guiding our actions, I had a task of keeping my grape Kool-Aid safe. Tate grabbed my hand and dragged me around the tree and we both jumped up the two-foot-high side of the patio.

Caroline and Mack came out of the house. Carrie was still holding her tumbler, Mack had two cans of Coke in his hands. They both looked at Tate and me, then they looked to the side of the house where the cruiser and the sedan were parking. We all met up and walked toward the side together but stopped when a uniformed policeman entered the view and on his heels Brad followed.

Wonderful. Brad.

Again.

The policeman's eyes scanned us all but they jerked back to Tate, got wide, he stutter stepped and halted, staring bug-eyed at Tate like he would stare at a movie star he just happened to bump into on a farm in middle Indiana.

"You're Tatum Jackson," he whispered and I stared at him, then swung my head to look at Tate thinking he must be a really good bounty hunter if a policeman four states away knew who he was.

"I know you?" Tate asked.

"Tatum...," Mack started, trailing off and my eyes moved to him to see he was looking at Tate like he hadn't seen him before. "Shit," Mack muttered, "I knew there was something familiar..." He trailed off again as Brad spoke up.

"Yes, that's him!" He was pointing at Tate. "That's the man who assaulted me in the Marriott!"

My head twisted around and it did it fast so I could glare at Brad.

"He did not assault you!" I snapped.

"He put his hands on me," Brad leaned forward, "*twice!*"

I leaned forward too. "That's because you forced your way into our room and put your hands on *me* and wouldn't let me go even though I asked a *million times!*" I looked to the policeman and informed him, "And Tate didn't put his *hands* on Brad. He only needed to use *one* hand."

Caroline emitted a strangled giggle and Tate used one finger on one hand to hook one of my belt loops and pull me into his side.

I felt his lips at my ear when he ordered softly, "Quiet, Ace."

The policeman was still staring at Tate.

Then he spoke. "Dude, when I was a kid, me and my dad, shit, we were your biggest fans."

Tate's lips left my ear as he straightened and asked, "Come again?"

"My dad's Penn State alumni and he still says you were the best linebacker in the history of collegiate football," the policeman stated. "He was so devastated he didn't talk for a week when you blew out your knee that second game in for the Eagles." He shook his head. "Seriously. That sucked, man."

I felt my body go still.

"What's this?" Caroline asked the question in my head.

"Holy fuck, Jesus, shit, you're Tatum Jackson," Mack whispered, definitely now looking at Tate like he'd never seen him before.

"What's this about?" Brad clipped. "Why aren't you taking him to the station or something?"

"Can I have your autograph?" the policeman asked Tate.

"What?" I whispered.

"*What?*" Brad shouted.

"No," Tate said.

"It's not for me, it's for my dad," the policeman continued.

Brad threw up his hands. "This is *ridiculous*!"

Tate ignored Brad and spoke to the policeman. "Your dad live in town?"

"Yeah," the policeman answered.

"We're havin' lunch at The Station. Call him, tell him to come by, we'll have a beer," Tate offered.

"That would be *awesome*," the policeman breathed then said louder, "Dad'll freakin' *flip*!"

"Excuse me, would you mind if we talk about the assault

charge?" Brad asked sarcastically and the policeman's body jerked and he looked at Brad.

Then he looked at me. "You Jackson's woman?"

"Um...," I mumbled, uncertain of the appropriate response to that query.

"Yes," Tate answered, not sounding uncertain in the slightest.

"You married to this guy?" the policeman jerked a thumb at Brad.

"They're divorced," Tate shared.

The policeman looked at Brad. "Statement said she was your wife."

"Ex-wife, same thing," Brad muttered.

"No," Tate's rough voice put in and Brad scowled at him. "It ain't."

"She says you forced entry into her and Jackson's room, you do that?" the policeman asked Brad.

"She let me in," Brad replied.

"I did not!" I snapped. "I thought it was Tate back from running and he forgot his keycard so I opened the door. You just came right on in. I didn't invite you and you'd surprised me, considering at the hospital the day before I told you to go away. Not to mention I could not *believe* you were at my hotel room door at six thirty in the morning, knowing Tate was running because you saw him and you were taking advantage because he was gone."

I felt that scary energy start to emanate from Tate but before I could react or even process the even scarier look I saw Tate directing at Brad, Caroline spoke.

"She did say that, at the hospital," Carrie backed me up and then helpfully shared more information. "Dad had a heart attack and Brad just showed. We all tried to get rid of him seeing as he cheated on Lauren with her best friend then divorced her. Now he wants her back but she doesn't want him back because she's got a bounty hunter hot guy and Brad's a dick. He just wouldn't go."

The policeman looked at Tate with wide eyes. "You're a bounty hunter now?"

Tate didn't get to reply because something occurred to me and I spoke to Brad.

"How *did* you know about Dad?" I asked and Brad started to look uncomfortable. "Brad," I prompted.

"Tina heard from somewhere and she called me," Brad told me.

"Tina?" I asked softly knowing he meant Tina Blackstone, a woman I grew up with in that 'burg. She was a girl I didn't like and she grew up to be a woman I didn't like. She had her eyes on Brad from the minute I brought him to town on a visit and we'd bumped into her at a party. Then again, she always had her eyes on every guy she encountered if they were good-looking. Brad struck up a friendship with her that he said was totally innocent but it always made me uncomfortable. I had no idea they still talked. We'd been out of Indiana for years. Why would he stay in contact with Tina?

"Tina?" the policeman asked Brad. "You mean Tina Blackstone?"

Brad's back went straight and he looked at the policeman. "Yes, she's a friend."

"I bet," the policeman muttered, obviously knowing all about Tina Blackstone and I knew then too.

Tina wasn't just a friend and my ex wasn't just a dick. He was a screaming asshole dick.

Tate brought the matter back to hand by asking the cop, "He tell you he was accosting Lauren in our room?"

"Nope, didn't mention that," the policeman replied.

"I was hardly accosting her," Brad spat.

"Heard her shoutin' in the hall," Tate returned. "Got into the room and you had your hands on her, she was strugglin' and shoutin' for you to let her go. If that ain't accostin', what is it?"

"We were talking," Brad declared.

"Bud, a woman's strugglin' in your arms and shouting 'fuck you,' that ain't talkin'," Tate educated.

Brad gave up on Tate and looked at the cop. "He still put his hands on me, shoved me out of the room."

"He strike you?" the cop asked.

"Not exactly," Brad answered.

"Did he strike you?" the cop repeated.

"No," Brad snapped.

"You get injured?" the policeman went on.

"No, but that doesn't matter! He—"

"When I was a cop," Tate cut in, "we frowned on folks givin' false statements. Now that was in Colorado." Tate crossed his arms on his chest and leveled his eyes on the cop. "You might do things different here in Indiana."

The policeman looked at Tate. "You were a cop?"

"Jesus!" Brad shouted. "Stop acting like he's some kind of god! This is a serious situation! I was assaulted!"

The cop turned to Brad and he must have looked at him in a particular way because Brad clamped his mouth shut. Then the cop turned to me.

"You wanna make a deal outta him harassin' you?" he asked.

"This is insane!" Brad cried.

"No. I just want him to go away," I said to the cop.

"I can do that," the cop replied and turned to Brad.

"Are you serious?" Brad asked the cop.

"Deadly," the cop replied. "Jackson's right. I'm a cop in a small town but I got things to do. The IMPD got things to do. We don't got time to run around doin' errands for some guy who got his pride stung."

"I—" Brad started but the cop leaned in.

"You'd be advised to keep your trap shut," the policeman interrupted him. "They make a big deal outta this," he jerked a thumb at Tate and me, "trust me, way it sounds, you're not gonna come out on top."

Brad glared at the policeman then he glared at Tate. His angry eyes swept through Caroline, Mack, back to the policeman and then rested on me.

"You said we could work it out," he accused.

"Yeah, Brad, I said that *over a year ago,*" I reminded him.

"Bud, move on," Tate advised. "And clue in, Laurie already has. You're history."

"Piss off," Brad hissed.

Tate sighed.

Brad looked back to me and his eyes were squinty. "Be warned, Lauren, after this, you want back, you'll have to work hard for me to take you."

"Seriously?" Tate muttered.

"Jeez, Brad!" Carrie cried. "How far up your own butt are you? Look at her! Look at him!" She motioned to Tate and me with her arm. "You don't stand a chance. She's so far out of your league she can't even *see* you." She turned to me. "And, big sister, you always were."

"I'm uncertain why you're even talking," Brad snapped at Caroline. "You always had a mouth on you and it was always a mouth I did *not* like."

"Would I get arrested, say, if I assaulted him now, right in front of you?" Mack asked the cop but his eyes were on Brad.

"Probably," the policeman answered.

"*Probably?*" Brad shouted.

"That's too bad," Mack murmured.

Tate chuckled and Brad turned squinty eyes to him.

"This isn't over, Jackson," he warned.

Tate stopped chuckling and informed Brad in a dangerous voice, "Friendly heads-up, I don't respond well to threats."

"All right," the policeman got between the two of them, "let's not make this into a situation where I gotta do paperwork." He turned to Brad. "Best you go."

Brad skewered us all with a look, declaring, "You haven't seen the last of me."

"Might be wrong but that sounded like another threat," Tate noted.

"Fuck you!" Brad shouted and Tate looked down at me.

"He always need the last word?"

I considered this, realized it was true as I realized it always kind of annoyed me and nodded.

Tate grinned. "I get you naked in my bed and in the shower, he gets the last word." Tate's eyes sliced to Brad. "Works for me."

Brad lunged. "You son of a—"

Tate's finger, still in my belt loop, pulled me back. He stepped in front of me and the cop stepped in front of Brad, put a hand flat on his chest and cautiously pushed back.

"You don't wanna do that," the policeman warned.

Brad glared at Tate, then he looked at me.

"Mistake, Ree." He put a hand up, palm out in my direction. "Big fucking mistake."

Then he turned and stormed off the patio.

We all watched him as he tore down the lane, gravel spitting out from the tires of his rental car. The policeman turned back to us.

He stuck a hand out to Tate and said, "Marty Fink."

Tate took his hand, they shook and Tate muttered, "Marty."

They dropped hands and the cop glanced around us all. "Sorry about that, had to follow up."

"Your job. Not a problem," Tate said.

"Is it really cool Dad meets you for a beer at The Station?" Marty asked hopefully as Mack handed Tate a Coke and they both popped the tabs.

"Yeah, man, but we ain't hangin' out. We gotta get back to the hospital," Tate answered and then took a pull on his Coke.

"When you goin'?" Marty asked.

"Leavin' in fifteen, twenty," Mack answered.

"I'll call Dad," Marty muttered and then his eyes went to Tate. "You'll make his year."

Tate didn't reply. He just lifted his chin.

Marty raised his hand in a half wave. "Again, sorry folks." He looked at me. "Hope he burns out and realizes he's actin' like an ass and you can just keep on…" He paused and glanced at Tate before finishing, "Keepin' on."

"Thanks." I smiled at him.

Marty's eyes got serious and he stated, "Jackson was a cop, now a bounty hunter. I think he gets this but if you don't…that guy gets in your face again, you go to the police."

"It won't be an issue," Tate put in.

Marty nodded to Tate but repeated, "He gets in her face again, you get her to go to the police."

"Right," Tate replied.

Marty nodded again, looked at us all, gave another half wave, turned and walked away.

"Tatum fuckin' Jackson," Mack said and everyone turned to look at Tate who was studying Mack.

"What was that all about?" Caroline asked, getting close.

"First-round draft pick, Philadelphia Eagles, do I remember right?" Mack asked Tate and I felt my eyes get wide as I stared at Tate.

"Yeah," Tate answered.

"Star at Penn State, Eagles traded picks to get you, the whole fuckin' state adopted you as a native son," Mack went on.

Tate sighed then said, "Yeah."

"Holy cow," Carrie breathed.

Mack seemed not to hear Carrie as he put a big hand on Tate's shoulder and gave him a squeeze. "Bad shit, man. Remember it. Saw the game. Sucked."

"Long time ago," Tate muttered as Mack's hand dropped.

"What sucked?" I asked and Tate's eyes came to me but Mack spoke.

"End of his second game, pro ball, he got crushed after recovering a fumble he forced and ran back for a TD. Got nailed in the end zone. Late hit. Guy blew out his knee."

"Pro ball?" I whispered.

"Long time ago," Tate repeated.

"Pro ball?" I repeated back.

Tate turned to me. "Ace—"

I interrupted him. "You played professional football?"

"For two games," Tate replied.

I was unable to process this therefore kept repeating myself. "You played professional football?"

Tate's hand came to my waist and slid around to my back, guiding me closer to him as he did. "For two games a long time ago," he repeated quietly.

I was thinking I really did not know Tatum Jackson when I focused on his face and it hit my fogged brain I knew one thing about him. That one thing was how to read his face and his face said he didn't want to talk about this.

Then again, you're a first-round draft pick professional football player and your career is cut way short when some guy blows out your knee, you end up back in a nowhere town like Carnal working in a bar part-time, as a bounty hunter the rest of it, that wasn't a particular glory day you wished to spend a great deal of time reflecting upon.

I got closer and pressed my front to the side of Tate's long body.

Then I looked at Caroline and Mack and declared on a total lie, "I'm starved."

*   *   *

I was sitting cross-legged on the bed in our hotel room wearing one of my new pairs of pajamas. Little peach knit short shorts and a matching, tight, shelf-bra cami. The neckline of the cami had the same color lace threaded through with a thin, darker peach satin ribbon that tied in a tiny little bow at my cleavage.

I was also staring at my cell phone that Tate had given me before going into the bathroom. I'd totally forgotten about it. He'd had it all this time, turning it off to get on the plane and I'd just turned it back on for the first time since yesterday.

It was after we had lunch at The Station where Carrie and Mack spent some of the time happily reliving Tate getting in Brad's face yesterday, some of it interrogating us about the incident that morning, and then the rest of it regaling Tate with all the reasons Brad was an asshole.

It was after Tate (and the rest of us) shared a beer with John Fink, Officer Marty Fink's father and a man who seriously liked his Nittany Lions football but seemed to like Tate even better.

It was also after we went back to the hospital and got second ten-minute visits while Dad was awake and could talk a bit but was still scary weak.

And it was after we went out to dinner with Mom and Norma where this time Mom and Norma got in a fight with each other as to who would pay.

As they did, Mack excused himself on the fake errand of going to the bathroom and paid while they weren't paying attention. This meant, when they found out, both Mom and Norma busted his balls while Caroline and I rolled our eyes at each other and Tate grinned.

It was after Norma went home and after we got to the hotel.

It was after Mom went to her room to hit the hay and catch up on sleep seeing as they told her they were moving Dad out of the ICU tomorrow and it was all looking good. Not to mention, she was consistently tussling with the men in her daughters' lives about who was going to pay for what and she unrepentantly pulled the guilt card by explaining to both Tate and Mack it was flat tuckering her out.

And last, it was after Mack, Carrie, Tate and I had a couple of drinks in the hotel bar.

We'd come up to our room. I'd changed in the bathroom, washed my face, brushed my teeth and moisturized and, when I walked out, Tate was heading in and he handed me my phone.

"Forgot, babe," he muttered, then went into the bathroom and closed the door.

I sat on the bed and turned on my phone. I scrolled through missed calls. Then I froze and stared at my phone.

Tate came out of the bathroom with two buttons of his jeans undone, his belt hanging loose. Before I went into the bathroom, he'd taken off his boots and socks. Now he stood by the built-in luggage rack and lifted his arms, putting his hands between his shoulder blades, and tugged off his shirt.

I stared at the eagle. He dropped his shirt on the bag and turned.

"I got a bunch of calls," I informed him as he walked to me.

He stopped at the foot of the bed and leaned down, placing one fist on either side of my hips and his face within two inches of mine.

"Yeah?" he asked quietly.

I ignored his face being that close, his lips being that close, and his chest being bare (and that close).

"Two from Wendy, two from Betty, one from Sunny, one from Krys and...," my voice dropped to a whisper and I swallowed before finishing, "*five* from Wood."

Instantly Tate straightened and slid the phone from my fingers. Surprised at his quick movements, mutely I watched as his thumb slid across the screen then he put the phone to his ear. Still silent I watched as he stood there with a fist to his hip and waited.

Then he said, "No. Jackson." Pause then, "Yeah, I'm on her phone. I'm also in a hotel room in Indy with her sittin' on the bed and I'm callin' you on her phone. You get why that is?"

I blinked and started to come unstuck, mainly because Tate's aggressive tone was penetrating the exhausted, confused at life, freaked-out haze that had enshrouded me.

"No," I heard Tate say, "you can't talk to her but you can listen to me. That shit you pulled while I was away, not...fuckin'...cool. We got a problem. We had a worse problem yesterday but lucky for you, since then, I've had her, she's moaned sweet for me three times so I'm feelin' in a better mood."

At these words, the haze disintegrated. I came fully alert and I launched myself from the bed at him, exclaiming, "Tate!"

He caught me on the fly with an arm around my waist and held my front tight against his side, leaning his torso and head back to escape me reaching out to the phone, something he could do with his height, which ticked me right off.

"Oh yeah, Wood, when I get back, we're havin' words and you

better fuckin' believe it's gonna be face to face," Tate growled, pulled the phone from his ear, hit a button with his thumb and tossed it on the bed.

I watched it land then yanked free of his arm and squared off.

"I cannot *believe* you just did that," I snapped.

Tate's eyes stayed locked to mine. "Believe it, Ace."

"*I* was seeing him!" I retorted. "You think maybe *I* should have been the one to talk to him?"

"No, I fuckin' don't."

"Well I do!" My voice was rising. "You just told him—"

"I fucked you," Tate cut me off. "Yeah, I did. I wasn't so pissed, I'd have gone into detail at how you lit up for me, how hungry you get, how slick and tight your pussy is and how fuckin' hot you sound when you come. He ain't ever gonna have that but I know he has a good imagination. I'd be sure to give him enough to see him through."

I stared at him, mouth agape.

Then I breathed, "You didn't just say that."

"I did and I wasn't lyin'," Tate returned.

I leaned toward him and snapped, "What's your problem?"

"I was on the hunt and back home a man moved on what was mine. That's my problem," Tate declared.

"I wasn't yours!" I shot back.

Tate's eyes narrowed on me and he looked like he was getting even more pissed. "You were, babe. I told you, I got home, you were on the back of my bike."

There it was. Carrie was right. That back of his bike business obviously meant more than a date.

"I don't speak biker, Tate!" I snapped. "I had no idea what you were talking about."

He took a step toward me and whispered, "Bullshit, Ace, after that kiss you knew exactly what I was talkin' about and Wood knew exactly where I was at, which brings us to why the fuck I come home and you two are tight."

"I didn't know what you were talking about," I asserted. "What

I did know is that you left, you didn't tell me you were going and you didn't call me once while you were gone."

"Call you?" he asked as if the concept of telephones was foreign to him.

"Yes, Tate," I replied then went on sarcastically, "Ring ring, hello, I'm alive!"

I could tell right away that Tate wasn't a big fan of sarcasm.

"Tone it down, babe," he advised softly but dangerously. "You aren't the injured party in this scenario."

"I'm afraid I disagree seeing as you took off without a word, stayed gone for a month, again without a word, and thought you could come back and I'd be waiting for you even with all that."

"I remember that night pretty clearly, Lauren, and I remember I told you I had to focus," Tate reminded me.

"I remember that too but I still don't know what it *means*," I shot back.

"I got shit goin' down in my life," he bit out. "I needed to be in my truck, on the trail of a murderer at the same time not seein' to that shit and hemorrhaging *more* money seein' as I was workin' that on my own time and my own fuckin' dime like I needed a fuckin' hole in my head. You"—he jerked a finger in my face—"were a distraction."

"A distraction?" I whispered, not feeling happy about that word and really not feeling happy about his finger in my face.

"Life is choices, Ace. I went with the choice I wanted, I wouldn't have been on the road tryin' to hunt down a killer. I'd have been home explorin' shit with you. I call you, I lose focus, I forget what's the right thing to do and do what I wanna do," he told me and I felt a shiver slide through me and it was contradictory to the not feeling happy feeling I had moments before. "I told you I needed to focus. I told you I got back, you were on my bike. I made myself clear. In the end, it was all a fuckin' waste of time. I get home after a month of findin' a lot of nothin' that cost a lot of cake to find and you're mouthin' off to me about what fuckin' *Wood* told you."

"Maybe we should talk about that," I whispered but I did it hesitantly because he was making sense.

Though in my defense, I really *didn't* speak biker, so he actually didn't make himself clear but neither of us knew that at the time. I was realizing I might have made a big mistake and I wasn't eager to discover I'd made more mistakes but I felt perhaps the air should be cleared. That said, it should be noted I didn't relish the idea of clearing that air because I had the distinct feeling I'd made more mistakes and it was more than a feeling that Tate was angry.

"Neeta," he growled and I knew the way he did it Tate wasn't getting any happy shivers.

"Yes," I was still whispering.

"Neeta and I are history," he stated.

"That's what Bubba said," I told him quietly.

"Yeah? So why did you listen to Wood and you didn't listen to Bub?"

"Um…" I bit my lip and took a step back. "I was swimming. I saw you… with her… at the hotel."

"Yeah?"

"Tate…," I said softly and didn't carry on.

Tate stared at me and then asked bitingly, "Am I supposed to read your mind?"

"You were kissing her… you went into a hotel room."

"So?"

"Tate," I whispered. "That wasn't two weeks before we…"

"No, you're right, it wasn't," Tate confirmed. "Your point?"

"How can you be history if you were with her not even two months ago?" I asked. "That isn't exactly history."

"An hour after I walked into that hotel room, Lauren, we were history."

"You were… you both were… you seemed…," I stammered.

"We were, then an hour later we were *not*," Tate clipped.

"How can that be?" I asked, my voice pitching higher.

"The same way it can be that not two months ago you were

talkin' about how you loved that jackass of an ex of yours, how you stepped aside so you wouldn't prolong your sorrow at losin' him and yesterday and this mornin' you could barely stomach lookin' at him."

"That isn't the same," I whispered.

"Yeah, Wood tell you all about Neeta and me? You an expert now?" Tate asked scornfully.

"He told me about Bethany," I shared and took another step back as Tate's expression turned stormy.

"Good call, Ace, but you might wanna take another step back," Tate warned.

"Tate—"

"He tell you he had Bethany before me?" Tate bit out and my body jerked at discovering this news. News Wood had not shared.

"No," I whispered.

"He tell you she was nuts?" Tate asked.

I shook my head. "Nuts?"

"Fuckin' 'round the bend. Christ almighty, the bitch made Neeta look adjusted." His eyes swept me and he finished, "Seems I got a fuckin' type."

That made me take another step back but this time I did it like he landed a blow.

"Tate," I whispered.

"She was whacked, pure and simple. Didn't know it until I started it with her. Her dad knew it, lazy fuck, didn't do shit about it. Coulda got her help. Didn't. Didn't listen to Wood when he talked to him. Didn't listen to me talkin' to him after Wood. Total denial. She was high-strung, he said, but he knew better. She wasn't high-strung. She was fuckin' *cracked*."

I swallowed and stayed silent as Tate kept talking.

"I had Neeta jackin' up most of my life and then I had Bethany jackin' up the rest of it. I couldn't handle her. I didn't have the tools and I didn't have any help from her family. I couldn't do it so I had to scrape her off. She slit her wrists and almost bought it. Ten minutes later, Arnie showed ten minutes later, she'd be gone," Tate informed me. "She's in C Springs now, a live-in unit. Last time I visited her she was doin' a lot better. Half zombie on all the shit they gotta feed her but it's better than the strung out way she used to be."

That was sad.

It was also not exactly how Wood described it. He'd given me the bones of the story but he left out all of the meat.

I took in a breath and asked, "Is Neeta married?"

Tate answered immediately, "Yeah."

I closed my eyes and turned my face away, licking my lips.

"Look at me, Lauren," Tate demanded and I shook my head. "Babe, fuckin' look at me."

I looked at him.

"You hear other shit about Neeta?" he asked astutely and I nodded.

"Nothing much," I whispered. "People mention her name and yours. They sound...funny."

"Yeah," he agreed. "Fuckin' hilarious."

"Not funny like that," I told him softly.

"I know Lauren," he replied.

"Betty said she's the reason you're not a cop," I said.

"That ain't true though I bet she believes it like gospel. Neeta's bigger than life, likes it that way, works hard for that reputation. You ask about Neeta, people'll talk and you can believe about five percent of what they say and she likes it like that. It's exactly how she wants it. They mention me with her, you can believe about point five percent of what they say."

"Tate—"

He cut me off. "It's shit."

"But—"

"It's shit, Lauren," he clipped. "I quit the force because Arnie is a lazy fuck. Most of his officers were lazy fucks too. Shit happenin' in that town, you wouldn't believe. Still does 'cause he's still chief. Whacked. I didn't like the way he ran his station. I didn't like the way he played favorites with his boys. I didn't like the way he turned a blind eye when shit went down and I knew he did it because he'd had his palm greased. And I didn't like the way he didn't have the spine to admit his daughter was sick and get her help. I made detective because I worked fuckin' hard for it and I did it despite him because he never fuckin' liked me mostly because I didn't like him. That shit went down with Bethany, it was his gig. I knew I couldn't come to work and see his fuckin' face every day. So I quit and started huntin'. Make triple what I made then and don't have to deal with any fuckin' shit."

"Except Bubba," I reminded him, perhaps stupidly.

"Yeah, except Bubba," he agreed, luckily not getting even angrier being reminded of Bubba.

We stared at each other and I watched as Tate seemed prepared to hang on to his anger.

Therefore I told him, "Carrie says I leap before I look."

Tate didn't respond.

"And that I hold a mean grudge," I went on.

"Lived that nightmare," Tate muttered.

"I should have talked to you," I whispered.

"Yeah, Ace, you should have talked to me."

I watched some more as he continued to seem prepared to hang on to his anger.

"I'm sorry, honey," I kept whispering.

His brows went up and he crossed his arms on his chest.

"Should I forgive you?" he asked and I swallowed.

The tables were turned and now I knew what he felt like all those weeks ago and it really wasn't nice.

"Um…"

"I got home, Lauren, went straight to you. After a month of wantin' nothin' but that, to be home and have you on the back of my bike, I go straight to you and you throw attitude at me and shit in my face. I said somethin' that hurt your feelings and you busted my balls for two weeks. You treat me to that, what do you expect me to do?"

I gazed around in confusion, considering he'd been sweet to me for nearly two days: he got me safe to my family, got in Brad's face for me on more than one occasion, and gave me three orgasms. I'd already thought he'd forgiven me.

Perhaps I was wrong.

"Um...," I mumbled, not looking at him.

"Baby, get your ass over here," he ordered and my eyes flew to him.

"Sorry?" I whispered.

"Get your ass over here," he repeated.

"Are you going to throttle me?" I said it partially in jest, feeling the waters, partially seriously.

He moved fast. Stepping toward me in a lunge, he caught my hand and stepped back, taking me with him and yanking my hand at the same time so I crashed into his body.

His arms curved around me and he looked down at my face. "Lucky you're wearin' those shorts and that top, Ace. All that skin, those tits, those legs, can't stay pissed for long."

"Maybe I should go shopping again," I muttered.

"You plannin' on pissin' me off again?" he asked.

"Not intentionally," I answered.

"Not exactly what I wanted to hear," he murmured and started walking me backward toward the bed. "But it'll do."

"Tate?"

"What?"

"If Neeta's married—?" The back of my legs hit the bed and we both went down.

When we landed and Tate settled on top of me, his fingers slid into the hair at the side of my head but his eyes never left mine.

"It's over," he whispered.

"But—"

His lips touched mine and then he pulled back. "It's over, baby." He kept whispering. "It shoulda been over years ago but it's definitely over now."

"How could you—?"

"Because she's Neeta," he answered my not exactly asked question.

I shook my head and put my hands on his shoulders, not to push him away but also not to hold him to me. "I don't understand."

His hand left my hair and slid down to cup my jaw. His thumb moving out, the pad of it drifting across my lower lip as he watched and talked. "Years, she's been under my skin. Took me that long to work her out."

This was not the news any woman wanted to hear about another woman and I felt my body get stiff under his.

His eyes came to mine. "Laurie, it wouldn't be for a few days that I'd feel the difference."

"What difference?" I asked, my mouth moving under his thumb.

"Didn't know it then, know it now."

"What?"

"Two kinds of women get under your skin. The ones who do damage, they don't feel good there but once you're fuckin' stupid enough to let them in you got no choice but to take the time it takes to work them out. Then there are the ones who don't do damage, who feel good there, feed the muscle, the bone, the soul, not rip it or break it or burn it. The ones you don't wanna work out."

Was he saying what I thought he was saying?

"Tate—"

"You get me?" he asked.

"I don't know," I answered honestly but even I heard the hint of hope in those three words, probably because it was me who felt that hope.

"You will," he promised.

Wow.

"Tate—" I breathed.

"Quiet, Ace, done talkin'." And it appeared he was as his head was descending and his hand slid into my hair again.

"But—"

"Quiet," he muttered against my lips.

"I—"

He kissed me and my hands at his shoulders slid around his neck, definitely to hold him to me as he tuned me right out of my mind and right into the vibrations he was creating in my body.

His lips slid down my jaw to my ear as his hands slid down my sides to my hips and around to my behind where he pulled them up, fitting my soft ones into his hard ones.

The thin thread I was holding on to my mind with twinged.

We had a lot to talk about. I didn't know him, hardly at all.

He'd played professional football, for two games but still, that was huge and the fact that he played only that short time was heart-breaking. He had a bad knee and he didn't act like he had a bad knee so I wondered if he still did. And if he did, I wondered if he should be running. He had an eagle tattooed on his back and I wondered if that had something to do with the football team for which he'd played only two games. He had shit going on in his life but he didn't tell me what that was and I figured, since it seemed we were starting something, I should probably know. He'd just worked a woman out from under his skin and I needed to discuss that a bit further. Was she entirely gone? Was there a little bit of her left? What happened to make them history? Was I there now? How deep was I?

Not to mention, I needed a very long, thorough lesson in biker slang so I didn't accidently mess anything up again.

I held tight to that thin thread and I turned my lips to his ear.

"We should finish talking," I whispered.

"Fuckin' you now, baby," he whispered back. His tongue touched my earlobe and his hand slid from my bottom to between my legs where his fingers slid into the inside leg of my pajama shorts and drifted feather-light across my panties. "We'll finish talkin' later."

"Okay," I breathed, which was a lucky thing since his tongue and fingers snapped that thin thread that attached me to my mind and it was a miracle I could speak at all.

*   *   *

Laurie, it wouldn't be for a few days that I'd feel the difference.

My eyes opened and I saw the room was dark. We hadn't pulled the curtains again and I saw the outside lights shining in, illuminating Tate's painted shoulder in front of me. I was curled into his back, my arm resting on his waist.

I stayed where I was awhile, hoping sleep would come.

Seems I got a fuckin' type.

I closed my eyes tight in a flinch.

Boy, Tate could land a verbal blow.

Carefully, I rolled to my back and stared at the ceiling thinking of all Tate said, all Wood said, all Wood *didn't* say, and all I didn't know about Tate.

Then I thought about my dad, who still worked the farm even though he had a couple boys he'd hired to help him do it. Then I thought about if he could, or should, continue doing that and if he couldn't, or shouldn't, what would happen to our farm.

After I thought of all that, I thought about Tate more.

This took a while and included me attempting to get comfortable and find sleep in three different positions. After I tried the third, I knew sleep wasn't going to come.

Moving cautiously so as not to wake Tate, I slid the covers back and started toward the opposite side of the bed, trying to remember where Tate threw my pajamas.

I didn't even get close to the edge of the bed before an arm hooked around my belly and I was on my back in the bed.

"Where you goin'?" Tate muttered, his voice drowsy.

"Can't sleep or get comfortable," I whispered. "You go back to sleep. I'll—"

I stopped talking because Tate rolled me to face him then his hand slid over my bottom.

"Happen every night?" he murmured, still sounding sleepy.

"No, honey," I answered, pushing lightly against his chest. "Go back to sleep."

He lifted his head and then his face was in my neck.

"On the road," he said there, his hands moving on me, "at night, I'd lie awake wonderin' if you were sleepin' okay."

"That doesn't sound very focused," I whispered as his hand slid down my hip, my leg and then lifted my leg at the knee to hook it around his hip.

It didn't sound very focused but it sure sounded sweet.

"It wasn't," he whispered back and I felt his teeth nip my ear, his beard tickling my jaw and neck; his hand slid between my legs and his fingers moved whisper-soft against me.

"Tate," I breathed as I moved my hips to press into his hand.

"Like that, Laurie," he murmured.

"What?" I breathed again as his hand kept moving, still soft, so light.

God, such a beautiful tease.

He'd done that a lot earlier. It wasn't fast and hard like the first time. Tate was a man who knew how to take his time and make a woman's body sing.

"Those little hitches," he answered, lips still at my ear.

"Hitches?"

"In your breath," he explained. "You gettin' excited, like to hear that, baby."

His finger suddenly slid inside and my neck arched back as my back arced forward.

"Yes," I whispered, my arms moving around him to hold on tight as his finger moved in and out.

"Christ," he whispered. "Like that too."

"Not as much as me."

I felt his lips form a smile against my neck. His thumb trailed soft, teasing my clit.

My breath hitched again and my hips pressed into his hand.

"You like that too," he noted.

I didn't answer.

After more of his sweet torture, I called, "Tate, honey?"

"Yeah, baby," he answered.

"Am I under your skin?" I whispered as my hips moved with his hand.

He replied instantly, "Oh yeah." His thumb tweaked my clit harder, my hips jerked and a low mew slid out of my throat as the fingers of one of my hands slid into his hair and the other arm held on tighter. "Fuck yeah," he growled and his lips left my ear, his mouth found mine and he kissed me, wet and deep.

Then he stopped playing and started *playing,* which led to Tate fucking me so hard, when he was done, I couldn't move.

Luckily Tate could move. He rolled me so my back was pressed to his front, his arms both went around me tight, his knee bent, taking mine with it and his weight settled into me, pressing my front into the bed.

"Sleep, Ace," he muttered into my hair and I heard him but I heard him a nanosecond before I was out.

CHAPTER ELEVEN

I Ain't Fifteen

I WOKE BEFORE Tate and laid in bed listening to him breathe. I was again tucked to his back with my arm resting on his waist and I could see the eagle close up.

I stared at that eagle inked into Tate's skin and it hit me.

I was under that skin.

Me.

This beautiful man in front of me had me under his skin.

I smiled and lightly kissed the eagle's wing at his shoulder blade then carefully left the bed. I went to the bathroom, brushed and flossed my teeth, washed my face and grabbed my shampoo, conditioner, bath wash, shave gel, and razor. I got in the shower, did my business, got out, toweled off and wrung out my hair. Then I wrapped the towel around me, quietly left the bathroom and went to my suitcase.

I was pawing through it, thinking I'd go with the baby pink and ecru lace underwear when I heard movement in the bed.

I started to turn but didn't finish when a strong arm was locked around my belly, my feet were off the floor and my body was turned sharply toward the bed.

Automatically my knees came up, my hands went to his forearm and I shrieked a girlie, "Tate!"

He made no response because we were at the bed. He twisted and we were falling, Tate on his back, me on top of him. He let me go and I rolled off his body but didn't get very far when he tagged me and dragged me back so I was under his big, heavy frame.

"Took a shower without me, Ace," he growled, his deep voice rougher with lingering sleep, his handsome face soft with it but his eyes were intense in a way that was too sexy for words.

"You were asleep," I told him.

"Consequences," he muttered and before I could respond to that bizarre reply, his body shifted, he yanked the towel off me and my whole body jerked with the force he used.

"Tate!" I girlie shrieked again but his body rolled back over mine and he captured my mouth with his.

Then I found out that consequences for not waking Tate to take a shower with me were so divine. After he was done meting them out and I was lying facedown in bed unable to move while I listened to him shower, I decided I'd sneak a shower without him at any given chance.

The problem was, the shower I had with him was just as divine.

Lucky for me, these were my problems.

*   *   *

I walked into the hospital waiting room where Tate and Mack were sitting, Mack in a chair with his feet propped up on a low table, his eyes glued to a TV that had the sound down low, Tate in the same position but on a couch.

When I walked in, Tate's eyes moved to me.

"He's settled," I announced and lifted a knee high to maneuver over Tate's outstretched legs. I got to the other side and collapsed onto the couch beside him.

"He good?" Tate asked as his arm slid around my shoulders and he pulled me into his side.

I lifted my feet and put them on the table close to Tate's, nodding and relaxing into his heat.

"It okay for me to go in?" Mack asked. I looked over my shoulder at him and nodded again. Mack pulled his feet off the table, put his hands to the armrests and shoved up. "I won't tire him out," he muttered and strolled out of the room.

Dad had been moved out of the ICU. He was conscious a lot more that day and talking. This was all good.

He still was an alarming color and weak in a way that both freaked me out and made me so sad I didn't know what to do with the feeling. So I just let it happen and decided to process it later since there was nothing else I could do.

Tate's arm gave me a squeeze and I lifted my head from his shoulder where I'd rested it to look at him.

"You need to get outta here," he declared when my eyes caught his.

I shook my head and his arm curled me toward him so my front was pressed to his side and, to be comfortable, I was forced to uncross my feet and lift a knee until it was resting on his thighs. This was, by the way, *very* comfortable because I was wearing white shorts and the feel against my bare skin of his soft, faded denim and the hard muscle under it was really nice.

"Laurie, can't stay here all day, your mom either. She's barely left. We'll get her, check out of the hotel, take her back to the farm. She doesn't have to be this close anymore. He's good. She needs a break. She needs to connect with home and he needs to rest," Tate stated.

I nodded because he was right but said, "In a little while, maybe for lunch."

"Mack says he and Carrie need to get back to work," Tate told me and I knew this to be true. Mack owned his own construction firm. He was probably good but he also couldn't be away forever. Carrie was a paralegal and her boss was a jerk. From what I knew of him, he'd lay into her the minute she got back.

"I know," I said softly and dropped my cheek and rested it on his pectoral while my arm slid around his abs. "When they come out, we'll arrange things," I finished, settling into him.

Tate kept his arm tight around my shoulders and we fell silent.

I contemplated his boots thinking they were hot. I had no idea what he contemplated.

Then he told me.

"What'd you do?" he asked.

"Do?" I asked his boots.

"Before Carnal, where'd you work?"

I lifted my head, twisting my neck to look up at him, fear slithering through me because I was thinking this was dangerous ground with ex–football player, ex-cop, current bartender/bounty hunter Tatum Jackson.

"Where'd I work?" I asked in an effort to stall.

"Yeah," he answered.

I looked at his chest and mumbled, "Um…"

"Ace," he called and my eyes reluctantly went to his.

"Yes?" I asked and he stared at me for several long moments.

Four tawny flecks in his left eye, three in his right.

"Did you forget?" he asked and I focused on him and not the tawny flecks in his eyes. When I focused I noted he looked impatient.

"Forget?" I parroted.

"Jesus, babe, where'd you work before you left suburbia?"

I bit my lip. Then I realized this was it. Us starting out, getting along, learning about each other.

Therefore, I said on a rush, "I was an executive."

"An executive," he repeated slowly.

"For an airline," I told him.

"What airline?" he asked.

"Um…" His arm gave me a squeeze. "Kites?" I said it like a question, as if he could confirm its validity.

"Kites," he repeated.

"You heard of it?" I asked like it was a small airline that had a fleet of about twelve planes when it wasn't small. It wasn't international but it was national. Based in Phoenix. Flew mostly west of the Mississippi but also had flights all over the country and had so many planes sometimes Dean, the man in charge of keeping track of them, lost track. Though he only told me this but they figured it out. I knew that because one of the e-mails I read three days ago was from him telling me he got fired.

"Yeah, Ace, I've heard of it," Tate drawled. "Executive of what?"

"Um…"

"Babe."

"Senior vice president of Labor Relations," I said swiftly and then downplayed it, "Kind of the HR guru."

Tate stared at me.

Then he looked to the TV and muttered, "Jesus."

That fear started taking hold.

"Tate," I called and his eyes came to me.

"You make a lotta cake?" he asked.

"I did," I whispered.

"Now you're a waitress," he said.

"Now I'm a waitress," I confirmed.

"Livin' in a hotel," he remarked.

I bit my lip.

"Where'd you live before?" he asked.

"Horizon Summit."

"Suburb of Phoenix?"

"A housing development in Scottsdale."

"Scottsdale," he murmured.

"Um…"

"What's your ex do?" he asked.

"Executive vice president of Sheer Aeronauticals," I whispered.

Tate stared at me.

"He makes a lot of cake too." I was still whispering.

"Martinis and manicures," Tate mumbled.

"I don't miss it," I told him quickly but Tate didn't respond, didn't speak, didn't move. His face didn't even change. "I promise, I don't."

"Right," Tate muttered and his eyes went back to the TV.

I pulled myself up his chest so my face was in his line of vision.

"We lived in a gated community, our backyard butted a golf course," I said. "Every time I drove through that gate I wondered if it was there to keep people out or lock me in. I hated that gate. I hated living behind a gate and what that said. I hated golf and I still do. I had a girl who cleaned my house and I liked cleaning my house. It was a big house but I didn't do anything in my life where I saw the results unless they were on a graph in some report and what does that really *mean*?"

I planted a hand on his chest and kept going.

"I didn't even paint my own nails. I rarely cooked because Brad was never home and both our hours were crazed, not to mention he was carrying on an affair. If I wasn't cleaning my house, I didn't like it. It was too big, too shiny, too new. I didn't drink grape Kool-Aid there because Brad's not a Kool-Aid type of guy but I was scared I'd spill it on the furniture. Everything was so perfect. Nothing had personality."

I took a deep breath and kept babbling.

"I didn't like my job. I liked the people I worked with but I didn't like my job. It was all about rules, about policy. I'm all for rules and policy. I just don't want to be the one pushing them down people's throats. I don't know why I did it. I was lost after college and I got into human resources on a fluke. I liked it. It fascinated me, people fascinate me. And it just took off from there. My dad taught me to be a good employee, work hard and smart, be loyal. It just ballooned and there I was, where I didn't want to be, at work and at home. Sometimes I'd sit in my office and look at my computer and wonder how I got there and then I'd wonder why I stayed. But Brad liked the life we could live on our salaries and I loved him so I—"

"Ace."

I was so on a roll, I blinked when Tate spoke and asked, "What?"

"You can shut up now."

I studied his face and saw he was fighting a grin.

"What's funny?" I asked.

"I ain't a grape Kool-Aid type of guy either," he answered.

"That's funny?" I asked.

"But you want it, you shouldn't stop yourself from havin' it just because I ain't."

"Okay," I said softly.

"You spill it on my couch, babe, just sayin'..." He stopped.

"What?"

His neck bent and his face got close to mine. "I really don't give a fuck. My couch is shit."

It took me by surprise, starting in my belly then my body shook with it and finally I dropped my forehead to his chest and let the laughter escape my lips.

As I laughed I felt his arm give me a squeeze and his lips kiss the crown of my head.

I stopped laughing and turned my cheek to rest on his chest and my eyes to rest on the TV. We both watched the muted TV for a while and then Tate's arm dropped from my shoulders so his hand could pull my shirt up at the back. This done, his fingers trailed random patterns against the skin at its small. This felt nice and I relaxed deeper into him.

That was, I relaxed deeper into him until his legs and hips shifted and he muttered, "Fuck."

My head came up and I looked at him to see his eyes were beyond me, staring in the vicinity of our legs and there was an expression on his face I couldn't read.

"What?" I asked, pulling slightly away only to have his hand flatten on the skin of my back and hold me still. "Are you uncomfortable?"

His eyes went from our legs to my face.

"Yeah and no," he answered.

"Sorry?" I asked.

"Babe, sittin' here lookin' at your legs, thinkin' of this mornin', them wrapped tight around my back, I started gettin' hard. Just lookin' at your fuckin' legs. Christ." He bit off the last word.

That fear that went away came back. It was different and it was mostly about not understanding why he looked suddenly annoyed. To me, this was all good, really good, happy good. To him, it seemed the opposite.

"Um…isn't that kind of…" I hesitated. "Good?"

He stared at me then stated, "I ain't fifteen."

"No," I agreed because he wasn't. I still didn't know how old he was but he wasn't fifteen. I was sure of that.

"Fifteen-year-old kids get hard like that. Men…" He shook his head.

I tipped mine to the side, suddenly finding this conversation very interesting.

"They don't?" I asked.

"Nope," he answered.

"Really?" I asked and his eyes grew intense on my face.

"Okay, I've no fuckin' clue so let me rephrase. *I* don't."

He didn't.

So this meant Neeta, who could work her body and blow kisses to hotel clerks and laugh so loud it rang in the air, didn't make him start to get hard just looking at her legs.

But I did.

I dipped my chin but obviously didn't hide my smile because my face was captured with his hand at my jaw and forced back up.

He didn't speak when his eyes locked on my mouth but his face changed again and I couldn't read it but his eyes got dark in a way that was both sinister and exciting.

"Tate?" I called and his gaze lifted to my eyes.

"Now your fuckin' sexy little smile is makin' me hard," he growled, sounding more than slightly perturbed.

I felt my smile deepen, decided to change the subject and leaned my face close to his. "How old are you?"

"Forty-four."

I leaned back.

"What?" I asked.

"Forty-four," he answered.

"You are not," I stated and his head gave a small jerk.

"Babe, I am."

"Aren't."

His brows drew together. "You swipin' your dad's meds? What's the deal?"

"No forty-four-year-old man has your body," I informed him.

"Well, I do."

Light dawned. "You know how old I am," I stated.

"Yeah, Ace, read your application. Though, I'll point out, Kites wasn't on it."

I decided to ignore the fact that I fibbed by omission on my application so Krystal wouldn't eject me bodily from Bubba's and stayed on my chosen subject.

"So you're saying you're forty-four so you won't make me feel badly for being older than you."

"Lauren, I *am* older than you."

"You aren't."

He stared at me.

Then he burst out laughing, his head going back with it, his arms both came around me and pulled me to him, then up his chest and very close.

"I'm not seeing anything funny," I muttered into his neck.

"How old do you think I am?" he asked my ear.

I pulled my head back, examined his face and guessed, "Thirty-six?"

He grinned. "You want, you can go with that. I don't mind."

"Tate—"

He cut me off. "But I'm forty-four."

"Tate—"

"Though, it's okay with me my old lady looks older than me."

"Tate!" I snapped.

"Or thinks she does," he continued.

I glared at him. He kept grinning.

Mack, Caroline, and Mom entered the room. I heard them and slid off Tate's chest to look their way.

"Hey," I greeted when I saw them all looking at us, Mack's lips twitching, Mom out and out smiling and Carrie giving me a look that said she thought I was in the middle of full on leaping without checking first where I might land.

"Hey," Carrie replied as I felt Tate's body get tight against mine.

"Mack, turn that up," he ordered, straightening and taking his feet from the table effectively taking my feet and body with his.

"What?" Mack asked.

"TV, turn it up," Tate reiterated and he was pulling us both to our feet.

When I gained my feet, my head tipped back and I saw his eyes were glued to the television screen so my head turned and my eyes went there as well.

There was a male newsreader on the TV and I could barely hear him talking but I could see the words "May-December Murderer" in a graphic behind him.

"Oh my God," I breathed and Mack turned the TV volume up.

"…victim yesterday," the newsreader said. "The police of

Chantelle, Colorado, think this latest murder is the victim of what is known in police circles as the May-December Murderer."

"Chantelle," I whispered.

"Our fuckin' backyard," Tate growled and I felt that dark energy radiating from him but I couldn't tear my eyes away from the TV.

The newsreader kept talking. "However, this incident is outside the perpetrator's usual schedule and police and FBI are concerned these murders, now eight in total with the same modus operandi, are escalating." The newsreader turned to another camera. "We'll be back with more…"

I stopped listening because Tate's body moved and I turned to him to see he was digging his cell out of his back pocket.

"Tate," I whispered.

"A minute, Ace," he muttered.

"What?" Carrie asked as she, Mom, and Mack got closer.

I turned to them uncertain what to say. They wouldn't exactly want me flying back home when a serial killer was on the loose.

Tate moved away and he had his cell to his ear.

"What?" Carrie asked again as my family made it to me.

"That's um…," I started, bit my lip then finished, "the murderer Tate was hunting the last month."

"Oh my," Mom breathed, Mack looked over his shoulder at the TV but Carrie's eyes stayed locked on me.

"Tonia?" she asked and I nodded. "Holy cow," she finished on a breathy whisper.

I licked my lips.

Tate returned, got in my space and his hand came to my neck where it met my shoulder. His face was serious but his eyes were conflicted.

"Babe—" he began.

I interrupted him, "You have to go."

He used his hand at my neck to pull me closer and I put mine to his waist.

"Ace," he said softly.

I leaned closer. "It's okay, Tate."

"Your dad—"

"We're okay."

"I wouldn't—"

I pressed against him, my hands sliding up so my fingers could curl around his shoulders.

"Honey, it's okay," I said quietly. "Go."

He closed his eyes and when he opened them what I saw in them made my body automatically move closer.

"Baby," he muttered as his head dipped and then his mouth was on mine.

It wasn't a Tate kiss that took me out of mind and into my body but it was long and it was definitely sweet (and there was tongue, which made it sweeter).

He lifted his head but stayed in my space.

"Text me when you get up, when you get ready to go somewhere tellin' me where you're goin', when you get there, when you leave and when you go to sleep," he ordered.

"Okay," I whispered.

"Be smart, Laurie," he kept ordering.

"Okay," I kept whispering.

"Locked doors, in cars, houses—"

"Okay."

"Be aware of where you are, who you're with—"

"Tate—"

"Don't open any fuckin' doors unless you're sure who's behind them."

"I won't."

"Promise, Ace."

"I promise, Captain. I'll be safe."

Tate stared at me.

Then he whispered, "Fucker was in my backyard."

"Go, baby," I urged softly.

He touched his mouth to mine, his hand at my neck gave me a squeeze then he let me go and turned to Mack.

"Give me a ride to the hotel?" he asked.

"Absolutely, Tate," Mack replied.

I saw Carrie and Mom looking at me. Mom was smiling still; it was softer, knowing, with a hint of happiness mixed with the anxiety she'd worn the last few days and some confusion too.

Carrie was also smiling but it was in a way I figured she thought maybe me taking the plunge with Tate might not be such a bad thing.

Tate turned to Mom and kissed her cheek.

When he did she patted him on the back and breathed, "Oh my."

Tate did the same to Carrie and she gave him a hug.

He left the waiting room and Mack followed.

He didn't turn and look at me. I wanted to see his face but I got it this time.

He was focused.

CHAPTER TWELVE

Sweet Dreams, Baby

I WAS IN bed in my old room, which was now the guest bedroom at my family's farm.

I had my phone in my hand and I was punching out the words on the little keyboard.

Hey honey, going to bed.

I hit send but didn't put down the phone. I twisted, turned out the light, and settled in, all the while I kept the phone in my hand.

Over the past five days I learned Tate wasn't a big texter. At first, as ordered, I texted him as he asked me to, telling him my every move, to the hotel, farm, hospital, when I woke up, when I went to bed. He rarely texted back and when he did they were one of two words.

Good.

And.

OK.

So on day three I stopped telling him my every move because, in all honesty, he didn't seem all that interested.

This earned me a phone call in which, when I answered while pushing a cart through the grocery store at approximately ten thirty in the morning, Tate did not greet me.

Instead he said, "What the fuck?"

I was surprised at this opening so I non-greeted back, "What the fuck what?"

"Babe," was his reply.

I was silent because that wasn't much of a reply. He sounded slightly put out and I wasn't certain why.

"Is everything okay?" I asked.

"Where are you?" he asked back.

"The grocery store," I answered.

"You forget something?"

I looked in the cart. "No, it's just that Mom and I are at the farm and she hasn't had a home-cooked meal for a while and I haven't cooked at all for a while so tonight I'm going to cook…"

"Ace," he growled and I realized he did that a lot. Growl. He could, with that rough voice he could definitely growl. But he didn't have to do it so often and especially for reasons unknown.

"What?"

"Last I knew, you were goin' to sleep," he informed me.

He might not text but every night, from that first night, minutes after I texted him with the information that I was going to bed, he'd call. Our conversations weren't long, heartfelt, and soul-baring. They were short and informational but I thought they were sweet mainly because they were with Tate.

"Well, I'm awake," I pointed out the obvious.

"I'm gettin' that," he ground out. "We had a deal."

"A deal?"

"You *text,*" he clipped.

Well there it was. I was wrong. He was interested.

"Oh," I said.

"Oh," he repeated.

"I won't forget again," I promised.

"Yeah, Ace, don't forget again," he warned and it was definitely a warning.

I felt my back straighten as I stood in the grocery store aisle. I turned and stared at the shelves, feeling myself getting angry.

"Well, it's not like you're King Text," I snapped.

"Come again?"

"You don't reply," I told him. "I text and you don't reply. I mean—"

He interrupted me. "Deal wasn't that I was texting you."

"Yes, but—"

"I don't text," he informed me.

"But you expect me to?" I shot back.

"Yeah, Ace. Newsflash, I'm huntin' a raping serial killer. I think you get that he's tweaked me, that sick fuck takin' out Tonia. My old lady is four states away, not close, not in my control. You get that?"

"Um...," I mumbled because I partly did and the part I got felt nice. I also partly didn't because he referred to me as not in his control and I not only didn't get that I wasn't sure how to take it.

He kept talking. "And last time I left you on your own, you ended up with another guy."

Oh no he didn't. We'd talked about that. He didn't get to throw that in my face.

"I'm hardly going to pick up a man in Indiana," I snapped.

"Babe, *you* don't pick 'em up. Those fuckin' legs of yours, *they* pick *you*."

"Tate—"

"Text."

"Tate!"

"Askin' you to give me peace of mind here," he clipped. "Text."

"Oh all right," I relented because we were talking about peace of mind. We'd talk about me being in his "control" later.

"We done?" he asked.

"You called me," I reminded him.

"We're done," he muttered and then disconnected.

God, if he wasn't so handsome, strong, sometimes sweet, didn't have a Harley, that beard, a tendency to play with my hair, didn't look so good in jeans, and wasn't so danged good in bed, he would seriously not be worth it.

Of course he was, or had, all those things. Therefore unfortunately he was worth it.

I barely settled my head on the pillow when my phone rang.

Quickly, hoping it didn't wake my mother, I touched the button under the screen that said "Captain Calling" and put it to my ear.

"Hey," I whispered.

"Your mom asleep?" he asked.

"Yeah," I answered.

"Your dad?"

"Color's back, moving around, got more energy. It's all good."

"Good," he said softly.

"You?" I asked.

I had learned over the last several nights' conversations that due to Tate's past as a police officer and his present as a bounty hunter, he had relationships on Chantelle's police force. One of the FBI agents working the case was also, luckily for Tate, a huge football fan and the icing on the cake was he was an alumnus of Penn State and remembered Tate. Because of these two, unusually, they were letting Tate in on the investigation in a "consultative capacity." In other words, they were sharing information just as he was sharing what he knew with them.

The problem was neither side had much. In fact, nothing at all.

"Wind," Tate answered my question.

"Sorry?" I asked.

"He's in the wind. We got nothin'. No leads, no ideas and he's off script. Could strike at any time."

"Yes, but you said all the victims were like Tonia," I reminded him and he did say that. He'd told me that all the women were Tonia's age and reportedly dressed like her and acted like her prior to their deaths. Four, including Tonia and the woman just murdered, were waitresses in bars. Three were strippers. One was a prostitute.

"Yeah, they got people camped everywhere, got more people warnin' folks. But he wants the kill, he'll find it."

"Right," I whispered because this was creepy and scary and both in equal measure.

"What're your plans?" he asked and I sighed.

I was at a crossroads with my plans. I'd talked to Krystal and she said I could take all the time I needed.

This would have been very kind except she ended our conversation with, "No skin off my nose. Not payin' you to be home." Thus informing me I was on unpaid leave.

This was okay. I needed to be here, see to things, weed Mom's garden and mow the yard. It took me a whole day to do the front yard, the side yard across the lane by the grape arbor, and weed whack everything including around the pond. Tyler should take his boot camp out on a field trip to Indiana and force them to do that. It was killer. I was also cleaning the house, ferrying Mom around, and visiting with Dad.

But Dad was getting better, which meant he was getting antsy. He wanted out. He wasn't a staying confined type of person. In a day or two he'd be up the wall.

And I also felt the need to be home in Carnal. I'd started a life, I liked it, and I missed it. Betty and Ned, the pool, Bubba's, Jim-Billy, my visits to Sunny and Shambles, their treats, Wendy, Holly at the flower shop. I even missed Tyler's boot camps.

Then there was Tate.

I wanted to go home.

Mom wanted me to go home too.

"Need to get on with life, hon," Mom had said. "So do you."

"I can stay for a while," I'd told her.

"I know you can but that isn't my life and it isn't yours," she'd replied.

"But, you need—"

"To learn how to cope with what I got and what's happening next. You can't stay here forever."

This was true. I couldn't. I loved Mom and Dad, Caroline and Mack, Indiana and our farm and I'd spent ten years missing them and wishing I was back.

But my life was now in Carnal.

Mom had taken my hand and given it a squeeze. "We'll be fine, hon, and you can go home to Tate and bring him back when we can have a good visit. At Christmas. I can make Tate my chicken 'n' noodles and you all can go ice skating on the pond."

I tried to imagine Tate on ice skates. This vision didn't form in my brain likely because Tate's badassness reached across four states and halted such activity.

"Mom thinks I should go home," I told Tate.

"She'd be right, Ace," Tate told me.

"But I could stay a while. I think they need—"

"To get on with their life, babe, and it's a life you don't share with them. They need to learn to lead it without you there mowin' their lawn."

"These are my parents," I reminded him.

"You movin' home?"

"No."

"Then what good's it gonna do them gettin' used to you dealin' with all their shit only for you to up and leave? Then they'll have to learn to deal with all their shit. They might as well learn now."

"My dad just had a heart attack, Tate," I said softly.

"Yeah, and he survived it, Laurie," he said softly back. "And he's gonna recover and you won't be doin' him favors by fussin' over him. He needs to get back to life as it's gonna be, your mom too."

I considered this.

My father didn't like idle children and we had chores. We worked in Mom's garden. We cleaned the house. We helped him with his many "projects." But I'd never mowed the lawn. That was man's work (according to Dad). His head would explode if I tried to mow the lawn when he was in the house. Or do anything else that would even give a semblance of "fussin' over him." He'd rather the grass get hip high than one of his girls mowing it. Of course he would never allow the grass to get hip high. He'd call one of his buddies to do it, of which there were a million.

Instead of telling Tate he was right, I remained silent.

Tate knew my ploy. I knew he did when he asked, "So when you comin' home?"

"I'll talk to Mom tomorrow."

He was silent a moment then he said gently, "Good."

It *was* good. Home meant Tate and me being in his vicinity when he talked like that.

Tate kept speaking. "Though, I'm gonna be gone for a while."

All thoughts of home meaning Tate fled my head.

"Gone?"

"Had two files come in. High-bond skips, both of 'em. I been bleedin' money too long. I need to take 'em."

"Where are you going to be?" I asked.

"Wherever they lead me," he answered.

"How long are you going to be gone?"

"No tellin'."

Well this sucked!

"So I might as well stay here for a while," I decided.

"Babe, you ain't comin' back for me. You're comin' back because this is your life. Right?"

It was mostly that.

Okay, well, *partly* that.

"Though," he went on and his voice got a hint growly but the good kind, "good to know you wanna get back to your old man."

"Mostly I need to get back because I don't want Krystal to scare all my high-tipping customers away with her bad moods."

"Right," he said through a smile. I obviously couldn't see he was smiling. I just knew it.

"Are we done talking?" I asked because it freaked me out a little that he knew I liked him. Though he couldn't miss it, what with me snuggling up to him when he was awake and asleep, texting him constantly at his order and there was also the way I showed I liked him during our last night together and I did it with my mouth. Then again, he'd liked that too, a lot more than me and he'd proved it by using the part of him I was showing I liked and using it on me in a way that I *loved*.

"You tired?" he asked.

"Yes," and it wasn't a lie.

"Then sweet dreams, baby," he whispered.

I felt my stomach pitch.

I got that every night too. Tate telling me to have sweet dreams proving he liked me too.

"You too, Captain," I whispered back.

He waited to hear the words and then he disconnected. He didn't say good-bye. He never said good-bye. He just said "sweet dreams, baby" then he waited for me to say "you too" and he disconnected.

I touched a button. The screen went blank. I put the phone on my nightstand and stared at it in the shadows.

His voice came to me in my head.

Sweet dreams, baby.

I closed my eyes and, within minutes, I was asleep.

CHAPTER THIRTEEN

Buster

"WHAT? YOUR BRAIN in your boots? I said seven fifty," Twyla said to a customer.

Twyla was one of our two new waitresses. She was fifty-three, had the body of a pit bull, short, graying, very curly salt-and-pepper hair that was cut into a female mullet and she made Krystal look like she had the disposition of a happy fairy.

I heard her. Heck, everyone heard her and my eyes flew to Bubba behind the bar.

He was biting his lip and, being Bubba, this was because he was trying not to laugh out loud.

If it was Krystal, she'd be doing the same thing but only to stop herself from firing Twyla's ass.

"I gave you eight dollars," the tough guy, leather wearing, Harley boy customer returned.

Twyla's eyes narrowed and she leaned into him so she was leaning over him as he sat in his chair. "You're tellin' me you're givin' me a fifty-cent tip?"

He fidgeted in that chair. "Well, yeah."

Her loud voice got louder. "You think I bust my hump schleppin' drinks for fifty cents?"

"No, I think I'm givin' you a dollar and then movin' my ass to a table that other one waits on. The one who's got a great ass and *smiles* when she brings out a *fuckin' beer*," the Harley guy shot back, ceasing his fidgeting and jerking his thumb at me.

"Uh…gorgeous," Bubba stage-whispered to me where I was standing in front of him at the bar, "I think that's your cue."

I sighed.

I'd been home in Carnal for two weeks. After my conversation with Tate, I'd stayed in Indiana the three further days that it took to get Dad home and a nurse visiting morning and night.

Now I was back at the hotel with Ned and Betty. Back to my boot camps and the other camps I did, namely camping out by the pool or with a latte at La-La Land. And back at Bubba's.

Amber, one of our new waitresses, was twenty-two, five foot two with lots of wavy blonde hair and she was a baby biker babe in the making. She confided to me that she was saving for a boob job. This and her scant wardrobe in the face of a crazed serial killer who targeted scantily-clad waitresses were my evidence Amber was a biker babe in the making but maybe not a very smart one.

Twyla, our other new waitress, was an ex-marine and the antithesis of Amber, of Wendy, of me, and of most every female I knew.

I was on day shifts a lot considering that was what Twyla worked and both Bubba and Krystal were hoping I'd rub off on her.

So far, this hadn't worked.

I gave Bubba a look and moseyed hesitantly toward Twyla's table.

"Hey, Twyla," I called as I got close. She turned to me and her scowl was so ferocious it took a lot not to stop moving forward and start running backward.

"You gonna tell me that my tips'll be more if I smile at 'em and call 'em by name again?" she snapped.

No, I wasn't going to do that. I'd tried that one hundred and twelve times and it hadn't sunk in.

I actually didn't know what I was going to do, except try to stop her challenging the biker to an arm-wrestling match, the winner gets fifty dollars, a tactic Twyla had utilized on more than one occasion. I was guessing this was because she normally walked away with the fifty dollars and the biker walked out because a woman beat him at arm wrestling. Still this meant she didn't have to wait on them anymore and she had fifty dollars, which meant it wasn't exactly stupid. Then again, they didn't come back, which was bad for business.

"Um...," I replied.

"Common decency to give twenty percent," she went on. "Fifty cents on seven fifty ain't no twenty percent." Her eyes swung to the biker. "A *buck* fifty is twenty percent."

The biker's eyes came to me. "Can *you* wait our table?"

Twyla's back straightened so fast it looked like a steel rod had been jammed into it.

"You got a problem with the way I wait tables?" she asked the biker loudly.

"Well, yeah," he answered.

"What's your problem?" she demanded to know.

"Woman," he replied, "you're in my face. She don't get in a man's face. She serves the drink, takes her tip and walks away, an added bonus because it's a damn good view comin' *and* goin'."

Even though this was all unfolding in front of me, automatically I turned my head when the door opened. It was what I did in case someone I knew was coming in. I liked to greet them and they liked it too.

In this instance, I would have warned them.

Instead, when I saw who walked in I froze.

It was Tate, wearing a tight wine-colored T-shirt, belt, jeans, and boots. His hair was even longer and he still had his beard.

He looked beautiful.

I'd been doing the texting business for over three weeks. I'd been getting my sweet dreams phone calls every night for that same period of time. I got one last night and he didn't tell me he was heading home. I was surprised to see him.

Surprised and ecstatic.

So ecstatic I didn't even think. I just moved.

I darted across the bar, running full-tilt, my eyes locked to his. He had been moving into the bar but when he saw me running he stopped and, luckily, braced because I launched myself at him. Arms around his shoulders, I hopped up as he went back on a foot on impact and my legs went around his hips. I felt his hands move to hold me at my behind.

I stuffed my face in his neck and held on tight with all four of my limbs.

"You're home," I whispered.

"Yeah baby," he whispered back.

I lifted my head and smiled down at him.

His eyes touched mine briefly before they dropped to my mouth. Then one of his hands left my bottom, went up my back, and into my hair. He tipped my head down and then he was kissing me, a Tate out-of-mind, all-about-body kiss that tore straight through me in a good way.

I heard the catcalls and wolf whistles about two seconds after Tate released my mouth and started walking through the bar, holding me to him.

His head turned toward the bar as we got to its side.

"Laurie's on break," he said to a grinning Bubba.

"Guessed that," Bubba replied as the catcalls and wolf whistles reached zenith and were joined by some very raunchy words of encouragement.

"I'd pay a five hundred percent tip for *that*," I heard Twyla's biker nemesis shout.

Tate and I ignored him. Tate was busy carrying me down the hall. I was busy kissing his neck and feeling his beard rough on my cheek. One of his hands left me as he unlocked the door and I lifted my head to flip the light switch on when we entered. The door closed behind us as I noticed Tate's head tip back and then my mouth found his. We necked all the way across the office and my legs automatically accommodated a seating position, straddling him when he sat on the old, beat-up couch situated diagonally across the middle of the big office, my lips never leaving his.

We kept making out for a while, stopping only when Tate pulled the string of my apron and we separated when he tugged it from between us and we went back at it.

Finally, when his hands were roaming my skin under my T-shirt at the back and my hands were in his hair, his mouth disengaged from mine and his lips and beard trailed down my jaw to my neck as I shivered.

"Now that's a welcome home," he growled into my ear and I shivered again as I smiled against his hair. "Lot better than the last one, babe."

That didn't make me shiver. My head came up and my eyes went squinty when his head tipped back.

"How many times are you going to throw that in my face?" I asked when my squinty eyes caught his.

He grinned. "You strung out your grudge against me for nearly two weeks and I just said somethin' stupid. So I figure I get at least a month of throwin' that in your face since how you fucked up meant somethin'."

I put my hands to his shoulders and tilted my head to the side. "And how long are you going to throw my grudge in my face?"

"Until I get that you get that it was stupid and don't do it again."

I pressed against his shoulders and leaned back. "Would you like me to perform an altogether different kind of welcome home? The kind where the 'welcome' part doesn't factor into it?"

His grin turned into a smile, his hands flattened on my back and put pressure on, bringing me closer.

"No baby," he murmured, one of his hands coming out of my T-shirt to slide into my hair and bring my face closer to his too. "I like the 'welcome' part the best."

"Then maybe you'll let that stuff go so we can move on," I suggested but I didn't mean it as a suggestion. I meant it as a delicately worded warning.

He was smiling again when his face disappeared in my neck. "I'll let it go," he agreed, "since Deke told me you kept yourself out of trouble."

It was unfortunate he mentioned Deke.

Deke was kind of a new addition to my life. The "kind of" being that I didn't know much about him, didn't talk much to him, he rarely talked to me but he was around a lot.

Deke was a mountain of a man. Six foot eight and *big*. He made Bubba look like a slouch because Deke didn't have a belly. Deke was solid from head to toe. Solid as in *solid*.

Deke was also Tate's friend. Deke also met me at the airport even though I'd arranged it with Wendy that she would meet me. When I walked out of the terminal, Deke came straight up to me and I knew he was of my new people just looking at him. The hint was the motorcycle boots and the leather vest with patches on it but the jeans, black T-shirt, and multitude of tattoos helped.

His hazel eyes in his big, blond, ponytailed head looked right into mine as I stared up at him, mouth agape, and he asked, "You Tate's old lady?"

I nodded.

"I'm Deke. Tate and me are tight. I'm also your ride," he informed me then took my arm and marched me to the luggage carousel. Then, when I went for my bag, he thrust me aside, hefted up my bag, took my arm again and marched me to a dirty truck where he dumped my bag in the back and shoved me in the cab. And off we went to Carnal.

Deke wasn't much of a talker and I was busy marathon texting everyone in two states informing them of the fact that I was home as well as texting Tate, ascertaining that he was, indeed "tight" with a mountain of a man called Deke.

The next night, my first night back at the bar, Deke was there. He was also there the minute Wood walked in, his eyes on me (my eyes were on him too and I was pretty sure they were wide and a little panicked). Deke also planted a hand in Wood's chest and shoved him straight back out the door.

That was the last I saw of Wood but not the last I saw of Deke. He was a regular when I was on at night and he was a regular when normal day working hours were done for the rest of Carnal. He wasn't just my ride from the airport. He was my ride home too. This I found out when I left the bar that first night only to discover Deke leaning against his bike just outside the front door. The minute I exited, he came to me, grabbed my arm and marched me to his bike where he ordered simply, "On."

I got on. I might be able to trade words with Badass Tate but there was no way I was taking on Powerhouse Deke.

In other words, Deke was a regular when Wood wasn't working and also Deke was my bodyguard.

My hands slid to Tate's chest and I tried to push back. Tate's hand in my T-shirt became an arm wrapped tight around my back.

I gave up pushing and stated, "Let's talk about Deke."

"Ace—"

"That was unnecessary," I declared and watched the soft humor leave his face as it got deadly serious.

"All right, babe, I'll give this a minute. A, you talk to Wood after *I* talk to Wood and not before. And B, I'm not here, you're safe and I do what I gotta do to make that happen. Pull favors from friends and keep you outta Wood's path."

"It'll likely be uncomfortable for me but I *will* eventually need to talk to Wood to explain things."

"He doesn't need explanations."

"Tate—"

"Or, I should say, the only ones he's gonna get are gonna come from me."

"Tate!"

"Babe."

"It's rude for me to...," I hesitated, uncertain what word to use then I settled on, "*be* with someone and then the next day be with someone else without explaining to that first someone what happened. I owe him that."

Tate's arm tightened around my back and his hand cupping my head brought my face even closer.

"You don't get this because you don't know Wood. I know Wood. Trust me, you knew Wood, you'd get it and you'd know you don't owe him shit. I'll explain to you about Wood later. I ain't gonna do it when you're astride me, you're on a fuckin' break, and I just got home."

I stared at him and he held my stare.

Then he sighed before he muttered, "After bein' gone weeks at least I got your tongue down my throat and your legs wrapped around me before you showed me the edge of that tongue."

Although there were more than a few things we needed to discuss, he did just get home, we had been separated for weeks and since the beginning with him I'd been mostly shrew and partly stupid. He told me he "just got home," which meant, again, he'd come straight to me.

I decided I should probably stop being a shrew and I should definitely stop being stupid.

"We'll talk later," I said softly.

"Yeah," he said softly back, his hand left my hair and I lifted up a bit but kept my hands flat on his chest. "Gotta get home, clear out the truck. I'll be back to pick you up when you get off. We'll have dinner at my place."

I felt another shiver, this one internal, at the thought of having dinner at his place. I had no idea where he lived but I wanted to see it. I also wanted to have dinner with him. We'd never had dinner just the two of us. That would be nice.

"Okay," I agreed.

"We'll swing by the hotel first," he told me.

"Why?"

His brows drew together. "Get your shit."

"My shit?"

"Yeah."

"What shit?"

"Whatever shit you need."

I stared at him.

"Babe, your shit. You're spendin' the night."

"Oh," I breathed and the internal shiver went external. "Okay," I finished.

Tate's eyes roamed my face then he noted. "Figure you got about five minutes left on your break."

"Yes?"

He lifted up, his head slanted slightly to the side and his mouth got close to mine.

"What you gonna do with it?" he muttered, his eyes looking into mine, his words a dare.

My hands slid up his chest to curl around both sides of his neck, my head tilted the opposite way to his and, like any good employee, I used my five minutes with my boss wisely.

*   *   *

I was on the back of Tate's bike, my arms wrapped around him, my chin on his shoulder, the wind whipping through my hair.

It was after my shift, after we'd popped by the hotel to get my "shit," after I'd waved to Ned and Betty. We were heading into the hills, we were surrounded by pine and aspen and we were going to Tate's place.

After he left the bar, I had spent the rest of my shift contemplating my actions from the moment Tate arrived.

I wondered, this early in our relationship, if I should be running across the bar in front of our customers (and Bubba and Twyla), throwing myself in his arms and necking with him. That said a lot, maybe more than I wanted it to say. Granted, Tate seemed to appreciate it but I wondered if I should be playing it cooler. Running through a bar and launching yourself at your new boyfriend like he'd just returned from war, not like you'd been separated a few weeks, was far from cool.

I also wondered, since Tate brought that out in me, the desire to throw myself at him in front of an audience and the ability to do it without thinking, why, minutes later, I was, as Tate put it, showing him the edge of my tongue. Tate seemed to draw that out of me too.

This was, I decided, because he was not like any other man I'd met.

Brad got his way nearly all the time but he didn't do it like Tate did it. Brad controlled my emotions. I'd realized of late that Brad had insidiously planted that seed that I was less than him and lucky to have him and, for some fool reason, I nourished that seed. Brad had done what he wanted when he wanted and I fell in line because I was terrified of losing him or not living up to the false gloriousness that I had thought was him.

Tate did anything he wanted to and expected me to put up with it or give into it. This was annoying. I was all for Tate being a macho man, badass, bounty-hunting biker because all that was immensely attractive but I'd spent more than ten years being in the control of a man. I wasn't looking for that kind of thing again no matter what form it came in.

That said, as Caroline noted, Brad thought he was all that and wasn't but Tate *was*. No man liked a bitchy, nagging, argumentative shrew and, I would guess, definitely not a man like Tate. If I didn't cool that too maybe I'd turn him off and lose him.

So I was at a loss, thinking I should be both harder to get and easier to deal with. I needed to sort myself out, I just didn't know how. What I knew was Tate was who he was and that was unlikely to change and most of it I liked so I didn't want to do anything to mess it up.

I stopped chewing on this in my head when Tate turned into a long drive. This drive ran the length of a long house that was built into a hill. Its first floor was raised and its ground floor tucked into the hill, the windows only two or three feet from the ground. It fit cozily in a clearing of trees. It ended in a two-car garage and had a deck that ran high the length of its front at the first floor but it jutted out to a kind of balcony on the end.

Tate drove around the side and parked the bike. I hopped off and he swung his leg off, alighting in front of me. He opened the leather bag on the side of his bike where he'd stowed my stuff, tagged my small bag, grabbed my hand, and led me to the side door of the garage. He dropped my hand to unlock the door and then took it again to lead me through the garage, where his dusty Explorer was parked in the middle of the big space, to the side door of the house.

He pushed open the door and led me into a mudroom that was so big you could fit a couch and TV in there. There was a window through which I could see a patio out back and the hill had been terraced.

There were wildflowers, some perennials but those had been planted haphazardly. They obviously weren't tended and I doubted Tate planted them but wondered who did.

In the mudroom there were two big alcoves with hooks that were full of stuff. Jean jackets, leather jackets, canvas weatherproof parkas. On the floor I saw that Tate not only owned one pair of black motorcycle boots but around fifty. There were also muddy work boots, a pair of dusty cowboy boots shoved in a corner, and there was a mess of running shoes in different states of newness from totally battered and falling apart to brand spanking.

Tate didn't give me much of a chance to look around before he was pulling me through the room. I saw a doorway that led down some stairs and about three feet beside that we went through another opening. This one led to a hall.

As we walked through, to the left I saw a utility room that was the utility room to end all utility rooms. It was awesome. It was better than the utility room Brad and I'd had in Horizon Summit, which I thought was a danged fine utility room. I might not have liked my house but my utility room was the bomb. Tate's had a big washer and dryer, side by side. A long, deep counter opposite it. Hooks on the walls. Doors to a big built-in cupboard. A deep-bowled utility sink.

Tate tugged me farther down the hall and the space opened up into a kitchen and beyond that was even more open space, a dining area feeding to the side into a living room.

He dropped my hand when we entered a big, U-shaped kitchen with a middle island and I stopped but he kept moving into the dining area.

I looked around.

He needed new appliances. His range, fridge, and the front of his dishwasher were almond colored and probably worked fine but they were far from new. His cabinets were great, a glossy, lovely, warm honey-colored wood that I couldn't place and there were tons of them. The countertops, I noticed, were battered and needed to be replaced. But there was a big, wide, rectangular island in the middle that was covered with well-used butcher-block top and it was phenomenal.

I stopped looking around when I heard a soft "mew" and I

looked toward Tate to see he was crouching down. He straightened and turned to me.

I froze and stared.

Tatum Jackson, ex–pro football player, ex-cop, now bartender/bounty hunter, tall, beautiful, and more man than I'd ever experienced in my life was standing on the edge of his kitchen holding a cat.

And it wasn't just any cat and he wasn't just holding it. He was *cradling* it. It was white with big splotches of tiger-striped ginger. Its hair wasn't long or short but in between and it looked thick and soft. It was not small but not large, kind of petite and, no other word for it, *dainty*. What struck me most were the cat's eyes, which were just as ginger as its tiger splotches and downright striking.

Tatum Jackson owned a beautiful, dainty cat. He did not own a German shepherd or a rottweiler. He owned a dainty cat.

And he cradled it, the cat's lower body resting on his forearm, the cat's tail gliding across his biceps, the cat's front paws straddling Tate's wrist and the cat's head resting in Tate's big hand. It was purring loudly because Tate's fingers were giving it scratches and I understood that. I purred in my way too when Tate's fingers were in my hair.

My eyes went from the cat to Tate as he walked back into the kitchen, still holding the animal.

"You own a cat?" I asked.

"Yep," he answered and I moved farther into the room because he went to the fridge and I had to get out of the way. He opened it and looked inside. "You like BLTs?" he asked.

"Sorry?" I asked back, still processing the fact that Tate owned a cat.

He turned to look at me, the cat contentedly purring in his arm, the fridge door still open.

"Bacon, lettuce, and tomato," he said.

I pulled myself together and answered, "Yes," then pulled myself together more and amended, "without the L and the T and with ketchup." I stopped then remembered something and finished, "And the bread has to be toasted."

Tate grinned at me. "So, you're sayin' you like bacon and ketchup sandwiches."

"Um…yes," I affirmed.

"Right," he muttered, bent, dropped the dainty cat, straightened and reached into the fridge. The cat kept purring and started winding its way around Tate's ankles as Tate closed the fridge door and moved to the counter by the stove.

I dropped my purse on the top, leaned a hip against the island and watched the cat follow Tate, staying close and still winding and rubbing against his ankles. This was obviously a practiced dance because Tate moved naturally and the cat avoided his boots but remained close.

"What's your cat's name?" I asked.

"Buster," Tate answered, opening a drawer and pulling out a knife.

I looked at Buster. Buster was no Buster. He looked like a girl.

"He looks like a girl," I informed Tate.

"That's 'cause she is a girl," Tate informed me and my eyes went to his back.

"You named a girl cat Buster?"

He glanced over his shoulder at me as he slid the knife through the plastic on the bacon.

"Yeah," he answered.

I looked back at the cat who was now sitting by Tate's feet, sweeping her tail along the tiles of the kitchen floor and staring up at me with intelligent curiosity in her ginger eyes. She'd obviously just noticed my existence. Definitely female. Tate was around and showing you attention, all else in the world ceased to exist.

The cat and I stared at each other and I decided she was no Buster. She looked more like a Princess Fancy Pants.

"She doesn't look like a Buster," I declared. "More like a Princess Fancy Pants."

Tate was bent and pulling a skillet out of a cupboard.

His head tipped back and his eyes locked on mine. "You call my cat Princess Fancy Pants, Ace, we got problems."

Oh dear. Seemed Tate had bonded with his cat even more than it appeared he'd bonded with his cat and it was pretty clear he'd seriously bonded.

"Okay," I whispered.

Tate straightened with skillet in hand and his mouth moved while he did it. I noticed this and knew it was him fighting a smile. He turned to the stove and put the skillet on it. I crouched down and cooed to Buster. Without hesitation, she pranced to my outstretched hand, gave it the barest sniff then rubbed her head against it.

"She's friendly," I noted.

"Yeah," Tate agreed.

"Where'd you get her?" I asked.

Tate was yanking open the bacon packet and dumping its entire contents in the skillet without separating the strips. I bit my lip at witnessing these actions and rubbed Buster who was still rubbing back.

"Someone put a box with Buster's entire litter at the front door of Bubba's. Fuck knows why. Krystal brought them in and was gonna take them to the shelter. I got to the bar, Buster fought her way outta that big box, ran toward me and put her claws in my jeans. I was claimed. Nothin' I could do," Tate told the bacon.

He was wrong. There was something he could do. He could have put Buster back in the box. He could have let Krystal take Buster to the shelter. He wasn't claimed. You didn't claim a man like Tate. A man like Tate did the claiming.

Something about this story struck me and I really wanted to ignore the silken feeling of the blow. I didn't get it but I liked it and I didn't want to like it and I didn't get why I didn't want to. It said something about Tate that was unexpected and even astonishing. But it gave me a warm, sweet feeling knowing it. And that warm, sweet feeling terrified me.

To take my mind off this feeling, I scooped up Buster, doing it carefully just in case she only liked Tate cradling her. She relaxed instantly in my arms and I turned her to her back, holding her close to my chest as I gave her scratches and wandered farther into Tate's house.

There were lots of wide windows showing views of the trees surrounding his house. He had a six-seater dining room table, which sat by a sliding glass door that led to the deck, the door flanked by windows. The table was oval, U-shaped backs to the chairs, and somewhat beat-up.

I moved to the right into the huge living room. It had a long opening but was delineated from the kitchen by a counter of about four floor cabinets you could see over. More beat-up furniture, a couch, some comfortable-looking chairs, a TV, coffee table, end tables, all of it looking like it had been there for a while or been somewhere for a while.

I surveyed his couch. Tate was right. It was shit. It was beat-up to the point of tatty and needed to be replaced. You wouldn't think twice if you spilled grape Kool-Aid on it. Even so, it still looked comfortable in a cozy, sit down, stay awhile kind of way.

There was no décor, no candles, no knickknacks, no toss pillows, no pictures on the walls. The dining room table was covered with what looked like mail. Some envelopes open, their contents in disarray, some not, magazines, catalogs. There was a blanket on the couch, part of it scrunched up on the seat, a wide drape over the back. Someone had been resting under it and threw it wide when they got up and left it there.

I spied some frames on a wall, the only ones in the room, in the area tucked back behind the kitchen where the counters fed into a wall that on one side held the fridge and a big pantry unit, on the other side was Tate's living room. There were three of them, all the same size, stacked.

I walked to them, stopped, and Buster and I studied them. Well, perhaps Buster didn't. She'd probably seen them before and she was again purring loudly so I didn't think she was experiencing much but my cuddle.

When I saw what they contained, I stopped studying and started staring.

The top one had two boys, probably fifteen or so, standing next to dirt bikes. A younger, perhaps twelve-, thirteen-year-old girl was standing between them. They were all smiling. No, the boys were smiling. The girl was caught in midlaugh.

Tate, Wood, and Neeta.

Tate, *Wood, and Neeta.*

I looked down to the next one and saw the three kids, the two dirt bikes, and a man I didn't know. His arm was slung around Tate's shoulders and he resembled the man Tate was now. Tall, handsome but in a different way, less edgy, his face more open, his smile so warm I felt it coming from the picture.

The next one down again had the three kids and the dirt bikes but a younger Pop was standing between the boys, his arm wrapped around Neeta's chest, holding her back to his front. His smile was open and warm too.

Happy times.

Happy times with Tate, Wood, and Neeta.

What was *that* all about?

I heard and smelled bacon frying and dazedly meandered back to the kitchen.

There was a loaf of bread by the range and the toaster had been pulled out. Tate was at the skillet. Buster and I surveyed him.

"There's pictures of you and Wood on the wall in your living room," I stated.

Tate turned toward me. His gaze swept down to Buster, upside down in my arms, her feet dangling in the air, my fingers scratching her ruff. She was still purring but otherwise motionless in my arms. His gaze lifted and he caught my eyes.

"Yeah," he replied.

"You were young," I went on.

"Yeah," he repeated and turned back to the stove.

I saw there were low stools on the opposite end to the island from him and I walked to one, pulled it out, and sat on it.

"Um...Captain," I started, "you didn't mention—"

He twisted to me again. "Wood mention it?"

I shook my head.

He went back to the skillet and said no more.

"Tate—"

He sighed and the toast popped up in the toaster. He reached up, opened a cupboard, and brought down a plate.

"We grew up together," he said while he was doing this.

"Yeah?" I prompted when he said no more.

He put the toast on the plate and put more bread in the toaster, saying only, "Yeah."

"Were you friends?" I asked.

His eyes cut to me then he went back to the skillet.

"Yeah," he repeated.

"You aren't friends now," I noted.

"Nope," he agreed.

"Neeta?" I asked softly as to the reason they weren't friends now and Tate turned fully to me.

"Neeta, Bethany, and Wood bein' an asshole," Tate answered.

"Maybe you should explain about Wood," I suggested hesitantly, feeling some disquiet because he wasn't being very forthcoming.

He turned away from the skillet again and his eyes locked on mine. We both stayed that way for a while before he spoke.

"I get that you're curious, baby," he said quietly. "And I get why. But I just got back from bein' on the road, you been on your feet all day, shit has been intense and we've never had this." He lifted a hand to indicate "this" being us in his house doing normal stuff like having dinner and spending the night together. "Let's have this and not fuck it up. We'll talk about Wood later. Yeah?"

I wasn't certain if he was actually asking for my opinion, if he wanted me to agree that we shouldn't talk about it now, or if he was telling me and expecting me to agree we shouldn't talk about it now.

On the one hand, he was right. Since the minute we met it had been a rocky road and not just your normal, average rocky road but it included rape, murder, and parental heart attacks. We should have "this."

On the other hand, I just got out of a relationship where my husband lied to me, not only about Hayley but, I suspected, well before Hayley he'd lied about Tina Blackstone, which made me wonder how many Hayleys and Tinas there were for Brad. Tate wasn't being open. It seemed like he was guarding something, something he even said would fuck this up. After I went through what I went through with Brad I shouldn't put up with guarded. I should demand openness.

But I was sitting in the kitchen of Tate's house in the hills, a house which was kind of a mess but could be fabulous, snuggling and stroking his beautiful, dainty cat, and staring into eyes that were in the most handsome face I'd ever seen, the face of the most exciting man I'd ever met. I figured demanding openness at that juncture might be me messing things up. And I really didn't want to do that. As in, *really*.

So even though I wanted to know, had this niggling, somewhat alarming feeling that whatever it was I *needed* to know, I pushed that down and agreed with a soft, "Yeah."

My agreement was rewarded with a smile and an equally soft, "Come here, Laurie."

I got up, stooped, dropped Buster to her feet, and made my way to him.

He still had the bacon fork in his hand but, when I got close, he nabbed me with an arm curled around my neck and pulled me to him. I tipped my head back and the second I did I felt his lips brush mine, which was an even better reward.

He lifted away a scant inch and whispered, "Get your ketchup."

*　　*　　*

"Tate."

"Stay on your belly, baby."

"Please."

It was a whimper. I couldn't help it. I was naked, on my belly, in his big bed. I'd been this way awhile. Tate was at my side. His bearded lips were lazily traveling the skin of my back and his fingers were lazily whispering through the wet folds between my legs. Just when I thought I could take no more, they'd disappear and glide across the skin of my bottom. A worse tease because that felt nice, all the skin of my back from shoulders to behind was sensitized by what felt like years of his gentle play. But I wanted his hand back between my legs.

Where it was now.

I lifted my behind an inch and repeated, "Tate."

His thumb tweaked my clit, sheer, blissful sensations ripped through me, my breath audibly hitched, my hips jerked, and I felt his body move up.

"That's it, Laurie," he murmured into my ear. My head was turned away from him, my cheek to the pillow, my fingers clutching the case. "Lift your ass and spread your legs more for me."

I did as I was told. I thought I'd get rewarded but his touch stayed feather-light and it was driving me mad.

"Honey," I begged.

One of his fingers entered me and I held my breath but it didn't go very far before it moved out again. Another tease.

I squirmed. "Tate."

"Stay still," he ordered.

I stayed still. It was killing me. I thought I'd explode. But I stayed still.

Tate teased then his thumb flicked my clit again and my hips again jerked.

"Baby," I whispered my plea, nearly at my end but staying put.

"That's my good girl," he growled in my ear.

And there it was.

His good girl? Why did I always have to be the good girl?

Fuck that.

I whipped my head around, turned my body, dislodging his hand and I attacked.

I got him on his back, my hand pushing him down to the bed, my mouth in his neck, my tongue tasting his skin and my other hand wrapped around his hard cock as I moved astride him. I guided the tip inside and then I ground down, impaling myself. When I was filled with Tate, my upper body shot up, my back arched and my head flew back.

"Yes," I breathed as I ground down farther and then started to move, riding him hard.

He knifed up and one of his arms wound around me, his other hand slid into my hair, fisted and forced my head down.

I was still riding him and loving every stroke, so caught up in the feeling I didn't notice he was smiling huge before he forced my mouth to his and kissed me deep.

I was close, pounding down harder, faster, and losing my breath. His lips let mine go when my breath started coming in deep hitches but he didn't take his fist out of my hair or his mouth from mine.

"Fuck me, baby," he muttered as his arm came from around me and his hand went between us.

"Unh-hunh," I mumbled, incapable of speech, entirely focused on something else.

I felt his lips move under mine and didn't process his grin because his finger hit the spot. My hips bucked and I went faster, both my hands fisting in his hair as I breathed and whimpered in his mouth.

"Christ, Laurie, you're fuckin' magnificent," he growled and it started.

"I'm coming, baby," I whispered.

"I feel it," he muttered. "Let go, Ace."

I let go, grinding down, my back arching but I couldn't escape his fist in my hair and he forced my mouth back to his and absorbed my moan.

Midorgasm I found myself on my back and he was pounding into me, harder than I could ever manage while riding him and it felt brilliant. His hands behind my knees yanked them up high then swung my calves in to curve around his back. I tightened and held on with all my limbs as his hand slid down to my hips, lifted them up and he thrust harder and faster, his grunts vibrating against my mouth.

"Fuck me, baby," I whispered his words in the waning throes of my orgasm and as my teeth bit his bottom lip, he slammed into me and groaned low.

It took us both a while to recover and when Tate did, his head lifted and he took some of his weight on a forearm but he stayed rooted inside me. His hand came up and his fingers sifted into the hair at the side of my head while he watched. His fingers came out and glided aimlessly along my hairline as his eyes came to mine.

"It'll be interesting…," he said softly.

"What?" I asked when he didn't continue.

His lips twitched. "How you'll be after I give it to you regular."

"Tate," I warned. I was feeling supremely mellow, since he'd made bacon and ketchup sandwiches stuffed full of crisp bacon and loaded with ketchup, not to mention the after-dinner orgasm. I didn't need him to be annoying.

His mouth moved to touch mine when he spoke. "I find out you ignite like that normally, Laurie… *damn*. Gonna chain you to the bed, babe."

I felt his mouth smile against mine.

Arrogance.

"Tate."

"Can't blame it on a long abstinence this time."

"Tate—"

"You attacked me again," he informed me, his head moving away half an inch.

"Well *you* instigated it!" I shot back. "All that…" I hesitated, "before *stuff*."

"All that *before stuff*?" he repeated and I saw close up his eyes were dancing.

My eyes narrowed.

"You're a tease, Tatum Jackson," I accused.

He threw back his head and laughed at the same time he rolled us, his arms going around me, his shaft sliding out of me and he settled on his back, me at his side.

I got up on an elbow, put a hand to his chest and glared down at him.

"I think you just might be arrogant," I declared and he focused on me through his fading laughter, his hand coming up to sift in my hair, fingers curling around and putting pressure there to pull me closer to him.

"You light up like that for your asshole ex?" he asked.

"I don't wish to discuss my sex life with Brad while I'm naked in bed with *you,*" I snapped.

He grinned. "You didn't."

"Arrogant." I was still snapping but he started chuckling.

"Hard not to be when my old lady keeps attacking me. Jesus, Ace, no woman has ever fucked me that hard."

Oh God. I was not doing well with being cool and harder to get. I was also not doing well with not acting like a shrew.

I pulled away from his hand at my head and dropped to my back, reaching out to yank the sheet over my body.

Tate rolled into me and got up on an elbow, his hand sliding to become an arm wrapped around my be-sheeted belly.

I stared at the ceiling and tried to get my wits about me.

I heard his voice even though I was ignoring his presence (kind of, it was hard to ignore; I was really just not looking at him).

"I like it, baby."

"Unh-hunh," I said to the ceiling.

I felt his beard against my jaw, his nose flicking my ear. "It's hot."

"Mm," I mumbled.

"Never had better," he muttered in my ear; my head jerked from his and twisted so I could look at him.

"Never?" I whispered.

"Nope," he answered. His arm curving more fully around me,

he pulled me to my side and into his body. "Woman detonates like that for a man, fuck, Ace." His mouth touched mine before he pulled away. "That's how I know you didn't give it to that asshole the way you give it me. You did, no way in hell he'd ever…"

He stopped speaking, his head came up and it tilted.

"No way he'd ever what?" I prompted.

Tate's chin jerked and his eyes narrowed.

I wasn't paying much attention to what Tate was doing. I was intent. I wanted an answer because that answer was important. Almost as important as me finding out he'd never had better, not with Neeta, not with anyone.

"Tate, no way he'd ever what?"

"Shit," he clipped suddenly and rolled off the bed. "Stay there," he ordered as he grabbed his jeans and started dragging them on. I sat up, holding the sheet to my chest. "Don't move, I'll be back."

"What?" I asked, looking around the room. "Tate—"

But he was exiting the room still buttoning his jeans.

"What on earth?" I asked the door he'd shut behind him.

I sat there, staring at the door and wondering what just happened.

Then I heard the voices. Tate had company. He must have heard them approach the house. I'd only been to his house once. I didn't know the noises and I was focused on what he was saying. I hadn't heard a thing.

Then I heard the voices get louder. They were male, one Tate's and one…

I heard Wood shout, "*You are fuckin' shitting me!*"

Then I heard a loud crash.

Without thinking, I threw the sheet back and jumped from the bed. As alarming noises came from the living room, I searched frantically for anything to cover me. I grabbed Tate's T-shirt and pulled it on. I found my undies and stepped into them, hopping, skipping and running while I tugged them up on my way to the door.

I ran down the hall (three bedrooms, one bath, Tate's room had a master bath, none of which I'd had time to explore) and hit the living room to see Tate and Wood locked in mortal combat and the living room had been turned into a war zone.

Until that moment, I had never in my life seen two men fighting, not even pansy-assed ones.

But neither Tate nor Wood were pansy-assed and neither of them, from my unpracticed eye, were holding back.

There were grunts of effort and there was blood.

"*Stop it!*" I shrieked.

Tate connected with Wood's jaw and blood flew from his cut lip, turning my stomach with nausea at the same time my lungs froze.

I sucked in oxygen and repeated a screeched, "*Stop!*" when Wood connected with Tate's bared ribs, Tate's body jerking from the blow.

Again without thinking, I ran into the fray just as Wood swung wide, Tate ducked and Wood's blow landed on my temple.

I saw stars, the pain radiated throughout my skull and I fell straight to my hands and knees on the floor. My head was swimming so much, I had to go down to my forearms and I rested my head on the back of my hands, which were palms down on the floor.

"Laurie." I heard Wood say from far away, his voice barely penetrating the fog that formed around the acute pain.

"Get her ice," Tate ordered.

"Baby—" Wood said gently.

"Ice!" Tate bit out.

Then there was a hand on my back and I felt fingers pulling my hair away from my face, sweeping it across my neck.

"Ace," Tate called.

I didn't answer. I was busy blinking.

"Babe, sit up," Tate demanded quietly.

"Um...," I mumbled just to be nice and let him know I was alive.

"Laurie, baby, do me a favor and sit up," Tate insisted.

I pulled in breath and sat up, settling my behind on my calves as my left hand went up to cradle my temple.

I saw Tate's face in mine.

"Take your hand away."

"Um...," I mumbled again, confused even though the fog was lifting and the pain was dulling.

"Laurie, I gotta see."

I dropped my hand. His came to my cheek and carefully tilted my head to the side. His hand slid up and his thumb probed my temple gently.

I winced at his touch because it darn well hurt. Outside of the pain, all I could think was that those two taking repeated blows with that kind of power behind them and staying standing was a fucking *miracle*.

"Ice," I heard Wood say and I tilted my head back and blinked at him.

He looked both concerned and pissed. His lip was cut and still bleeding. There was redness around his cheekbone. He'd have a shiner the next day.

"Can you get to your feet?" Tate asked and my eyes turned to him.

He was crouched beside me. There were droplets of blood leaking from his nose into his beard. Other than that, he looked okay.

"Yeah," I whispered and got to my feet with Tate's hands at my arm and hip supporting me.

I got up and stood steady. Then I took in a deep breath.

Tate turned to Wood, tagged the ice from his hand, and came back to me, lifting it and pressing it gently to my temple.

"Laurie," Wood called; my eyes went to him and my mind snapped to sharp focus.

"You didn't tell me she was sick," I whispered, my hand going up to take over the ice from Tate. His hand let mine hold the ice as he moved to my side and slid an arm around my waist.

"Lauren, I—" Wood started.

"You what?" I interrupted, still whispering. "You didn't give me the full story, Wood."

"Baby, there's a reason."

"Really?" I asked. "I spent ten years with a man who kept things from me, Wood. I'm not going to start something with another man who'd do the same."

Wood's arms crossed on his chest, the gentleness went out of his face and he jerked his head to Tate. "*He* tell you everything?"

"We haven't had *time*," I reminded him. "My father being sick, Tate needing to work. You haven't told me everything either and you and me, Wood, we had *time*."

And we did. Me having dinner with him, sharing my breaks with him, necking on my bed. We'd had time.

I'd felt like a heel the last three weeks because I was a nice person and I found it hard to live with what I did to Wood. It hadn't occurred to me that what he did, with him knowing what it meant for me to be on the back of Tate's bike, wasn't nice either.

"I'm sorry it happened this way," I told him, still being nice. "I wish it didn't."

"I do too," he agreed instantly and walked straight away as I blinked at him, shocked by his sudden departure. I thought he'd get angry or at least have something to say like "Sorry I acted like a Neanderthal, fighting with Tate in his living room, and punched you in the head."

My body moved to watch him and Tate's moved with mine.

Wood stopped at the still-open sliding glass door and turned, his eyes leveling on me.

"You don't burden a good woman with that shit, baby. You find out, you'll know. You get a shot at her, you hook her deep, *then* you lay that shit on her," Wood stated and I felt my lungs freeze again but he wasn't done. He jerked his head at Tate and went on, "He'll tell you shit about me, if he hasn't already. And all of it's true. But none of it was true with you."

Then he disappeared into the night not even bothering to close the door.

I stood staring into the darkness even as I heard his bike roar. Tate let me go and walked to the door, sliding it closed.

When he turned and started back to me, my eyes went to his.

"What was he talking about?" I asked.

"Let's get you to bed," Tate replied.

"Tate," I said when he stopped in front of me.

"Bed, babe," he repeated. "You need to lie down and I need to clean up."

I didn't know what to do in this situation. I was losing patience with Tate being so cagey. He'd just had a no-holds-barred fight in his living room with my kind of ex-boyfriend. A man whose picture was on the wall in Tate's house. A man who used to be his friend. A man whose sister used to be under his skin. Now neither was true and Tate wasn't talking about it, wasn't sharing with me. And I'd told myself not to be a shrew. I'd made the decision I didn't want to fuck this up.

How on earth did I proceed?

"You just fought with Wood in your living room," I told him cautiously.

He came to my side and slid an arm along my waist, propelling me forward.

"Long time comin'," he muttered.

"That wasn't about me," I stated and Tate stopped us both at the mouth to the hall.

I looked up at him and held my breath at the fury I saw stamped into his features.

"Yeah, Lauren," he said and it sounded like a snarl. "It's all about you."

I braved the snarl and asked quietly, "How can that be? I haven't been around long enough for something like that to be a long time coming."

"You need to lie down," Tate reiterated and I could tell it was straining his patience to do so.

"Tate—"

Tate pulled in breath on a hiss and I stopped speaking.

"Put it together, Lauren, at least part of it," he demanded, definitely with strained patience.

"Sorry?" I asked, definitely with confusion.

"In my life, three women have been on the back of my bike. One was his sister, who fucked up my life. One was his ex, who fucked up my life. Now it's you, who's been in his bed."

All of that didn't pull together for me in any way mostly because, just like with Wood, I had the bones but none of the meat.

"Tate—"

"Babe, Christ," he clipped. "You just took a power punch to the fuckin' temple. I got blood leakin' outta my nose. Can we talk about this goddamned *later*?"

No strained patience now, he'd lost it. I could read it in the line of his body and in his face.

Even so, even though this was frightening, that scary energy emanating from Tate directed at me, I wanted to tell him we couldn't talk about it later. I wanted to tell him we were definitely going to talk about it *now*.

But something stopped me and instead I whispered, "Okay, Captain."

CHAPTER FOURTEEN

Your Own Brand of Trouble

And all of it's true. But none of it was true with you.

My eyes opened and I stared at the dark pillowcase.

I was in Tate's bed with Tate but he was far away. I could feel Buster's little body weighing the covers down between us.

We hadn't slept together very often but every time we'd done it either Tate held me close or I snuggled into his back.

Not that night.

After our exchange, he'd led me to the bed, made me get in it and ordered me to keep the ice on as long as I could. This was difficult since it was getting really cold but also I was uncomfortable because Tate still seemed really angry.

I'd lain there, holding the ice to my head while Tate cleaned up in the bathroom. Buster kept Tate company in the bathroom until he came out and then he left the bedroom without a word, Buster prancing after him. I heard Tate righting furniture and Buster came back, obviously not a big fan of hanging around while Tate was righting furniture. Buster leaped on the bed and curled up with me. I gave her scratches, saw the lights go out in the hall, and Tate came back.

He took off his jeans and climbed into his side of the bed. He turned out the light and didn't move to me, touch me, or speak to me. He settled on his back with one arm behind his head, Buster abandoned me, walked over my belly and curled up against Tate.

He took his hand from behind his head and started rubbing Buster.

Then he said in a low, menacing voice, "I tell you to stay where you are and not to move, Ace, next time, do what I fuckin' say."

I blinked in the dark, my eyelids the only things that moved. The rest of my body was statue-still.

There was a lot there I didn't like. Firstly, Tate again telling me what to do and expecting me to do it, even when he was in a fistfight in his living room! Secondly, the intimation that my getting hit was my fault because I didn't do what he told me to do when I was breaking up a fistfight in his living room! Lastly, Tate was again *telling me what to do* and he was clearly infuriated I didn't do it.

If I had my car, I would have gotten up, gotten dressed, and gone right to it.

Fuck that and fuck him!

I was better off at the hotel. It was below average but Ned and Betty never told me what to do *and* they had a pool.

But I was stuck in a house in the hills. It was night, it was dark, and I had no way home.

So instead, I got out of bed and walked to his bathroom, dumped the dripping ice into his sink, rinsed, and wrung out the kitchen towel Wood had put the ice in and hung it on a towel rail. Then I went back to bed and got in on my side, turned so my back was to Tate and closed my eyes.

He didn't say another word and neither did I. He fell asleep way before me and still didn't roll into me or reach out to me.

Apparently Tatum Jackson could be angry even in his sleep.

I eventually fell asleep and woke twice while words he'd said drifted through my head. I was able to get to sleep both times but this time, with Wood's words floating through, words I didn't understand but words I knew somewhere deep meant something huge, I knew I wouldn't.

I tried, adjusting my position to my back, then my belly, then my other side, and finally a combo of side and belly.

Nothing doing.

Instead of waking Tate with my fidgeting, I carefully got out of the bed and just as carefully walked through his bedroom, down the hall and into the living room. I went straight to the couch, stretched my legs out, pulled the blanket there over me but I twisted my upper body toward the window. I crossed my arms on the back of the couch, put my chin on them and looked out the window.

The moonlight made the trees and terraced plants silver.

You don't burden a good woman with that shit, baby. You find out, you'll know. You get a shot at her, you hook her deep, then you lay that shit on her.

I closed my eyes and the silver hillside turned to black.

Let's have this and not fuck it up. We'll talk about Wood later. Yeah?

I opened my eyes and stared at the plants and flowers, unruly, unkempt, but I knew not planted by Tate's hands.

You don't get this because you don't know Wood. I know Wood. Trust me, you knew Wood, you'd get it and you'd know you don't owe him shit.

I felt my lip tremble.

The thing you gotta know before you climb back on the back of his bike is that Tate Jackson is trash too.

I turned my head and looked at the six-seater dining room table.

Did a bachelor own a six-seater dining room table? I didn't think so. Tate didn't exactly strike me as a man who held dinner parties.

Maybe he played poker. Tate struck me as a man who *might* throw poker parties.

My eyes went back to the plants.

In my life, three women have been on the back of my bike. One was his sister, who fucked up my life. One was his ex, who fucked up my life. Now it's you, who's been in his bed.

I stared at the plants knowing it just by looking at them.

Neeta had lived there, or Bethany or, if not lived, then one of them was around long enough to put their stamp on it. Two women who fucked up his life.

Now, me.

His "type."

The type to fuck up his life?

Really, what was a man like Tatum Jackson doing with me? Miniskirt-wearing, hotel-assignation-exciting Neeta, yes. Crazy Bethany, I didn't know. Me, I didn't get.

In fact, what was handsome, gentle-talking Wood doing with me?

My mind moved to that morning in the forecourt of the garage.

You're on my bike, Tate had growled to me.

She's in the 'Stang, Wood had growled at Tate.

They were fighting over me because that was what they did. No matter what Tate said, it was not because of me.

I considered this.

Not being mean or anything but there wasn't a lot of female talent in Carnal. The best of the lot was Krystal and she was with Bubba, and also Wendy, but she was with Tyler and too young for Wood or Tate.

I'd been around a while. I'd seen what was available in Carnal and for men like that, I was pretty much it unless they wanted to go the Jonelle somewhat-skanky route and there was a lot of that. Even though some of them were very nice, they were still somewhat-skanky, which was probably why they weren't taken like, say, Krystal or Wendy or the rest of the cool-as-heck biker babes I'd met at the bar or in town that I knew were taken. And, clearly, neither of those men went for that.

I moved fully into the seat of the couch and curled up under the blanket, tugging it high over my shoulder and pulling my knees in my chest. Without any toss pillows, I used the armrest for my head. My temple throbbed but I ignored it as I searched for it, trying to call it up, to hear the whisper because I needed it.

Sweet dreams, baby.

The memory of Tate saying that to me came, my eyelids drooped, and I fell asleep.

*   *   *

I woke up when the blanket disappeared and my body was moved. My eyes opened as my body kept moving.

The sun was up but it was low, very early dawn, barely enough light to see.

I was cradled in Tate's arms.

"Tate?" I whispered, my hand moving to his chest, my arm that was dangling curling around his shoulders.

"Quiet," he growled.

Uh-oh.

"Tate," I whispered again.

"Shut it, Ace," he growled again.

I lifted my head to look at his angry, set profile and decided to stay silent at least until my brain fully came awake.

He took me to his bed and put me in it, following me in, yanking up the covers in an annoyed way and then pulling me under his body. Or, I should say, he *pinned* me under his body. I was on my back. He was mostly on me, his heavy thigh thrown over both of mine, his arm holding me tight about the waist, his face against my hair at the side of my head, his weight weighing me into the bed.

"Um...," I started.

He cut me off. "You curl into me."

"Sorry?" I asked.

"My back," he replied.

"Um…" I paused then repeated, "Sorry?"

"You curl into my goddamned back, Lauren," he ground out and his arm around my waist gave me a rough squeeze.

"I was…uh…"

"Pissed," he finished for me. "You can go to bed pissed just as long as you don't wake up that way," he informed me like this was a rule written in blood somewhere that all men and women must abide by under threat of certain torture although he seemed to have done just that. "You do not get up in the middle of the fuckin' night and crawl outta my bed to go be pissed somewhere else."

"I…um…" I took in a breath, "didn't actually do that. I couldn't sleep and I was restless, so—"

"You don't do that either," he declared.

"What?"

"You can't sleep, you can't sleep here. You don't go somewhere else."

"But I don't want to wake you."

"You wake me, I fuck you or we talk until you get back to sleep. You don't sneak outta the goddamned bed—"

"I didn't sneak," I interrupted him quietly.

He ignored me. "You sleep here or you lie here not sleepin'."

"Are you…?" I hesitated and started again, "Are you angry I didn't want to disturb you?"

"You're quick, babe," he muttered sarcastically and gave my waist another rough squeeze.

"Tate—"

"Three weeks, after fuckin' you, knowin' what you taste like, what you feel like, the sounds you make when you come, three weeks I'm on the road and all I got is a couple minutes of your voice on the phone every night. Fuckin' you, that's all I can think about, like a teenager, at night in the dark, it's the only thing in my goddamned head. So I jack off, hopin' to cut through it, but nothin' compares to you."

I stopped breathing at this admission and he kept talking.

"Then I know you can't sleep so I can't fuckin' sleep wonderin' if you're sleepin'. That shit's whacked and I come home, fuckin' beside myself it's over. First night you're in my house, you sneak outta my bed and sleep on the couch. What the fuck is that?"

"I was trying to be nice," I informed him.

"You failed, Ace," he informed me.

I felt a chill seep into my bloodstream.

"Which one are you?" I whispered.

"What?" he asked.

"Are you the good guy, the sweet guy who takes care of me or are you this guy who's kind of a jerk?"

His answer was instantaneous. "I'm both those guys, babe. Your job is to get used to it."

There it was. Another order. Not even an ultimatum. Just, "get used to it."

"Tate—" I started.

"It's simple, Lauren. You're in my bed or *any* fuckin' bed with me in it, you don't leave it."

"But—"

"That can't be hard to sink in."

"Tate—"

"Now can I get some goddamned sleep?" he asked on another squeeze and I could tell he was done with this conversation.

Therefore the conversation was done.

"Yes," I whispered.

And he could because he did. It was just me who couldn't.

Or, at least it would take a while.

*   *   *

I woke up to an empty bed.

I turned to my back, lifted up to sitting and pulled my hair out of my face. I saw movement at the window and sleepily watched Tate walk along the deck toward the balcony area.

Once he disappeared from sight, I stared out at the bright sunshine. Then I threw the covers back, got out of bed, and wandered to the window. I looked out and to the right to see Tate dressed in jeans and a tight, army green T-shirt, no belt, no shoes, sitting in a lawn chair pulled up to the railing. He was slouched in the chair, his feet up high resting on the railing, crossed at the ankles. He was staring out to the woods and drinking coffee.

His hair was wet but curling and drying fast in Colorado's arid climate.

Apparently I couldn't take a shower without Tate but he could take one without me.

Figures.

I walked as quietly as I could to the dining area and retrieved my bag where Tate dropped it, taking it with me back to Tate's bathroom. Buster came with me and glided around my ankles as I pulled my hair in a ponytail and surveyed my face in the mirror.

There was some purplish-blue bruising but hardly any swelling at my temple. There was a dull ache too but only when I thought about it.

I brushed and flossed my teeth and washed my face. Then I bent and picked up Buster and put her on the vanity counter so she could keep me company while I put on moisturizer, powder, blusher, and mascara. She watched me do this, her tail hanging off the edge of the counter and flicking, her eyes blinking but curious. This was new to Buster. Tate obviously didn't moisturize or apply makeup.

Then I got dressed in jeans and a girl-fit, faded aubergine-colored T-shirt that on the back had a set of black wings. It wasn't really me but Wendy found it, made me try it on and it fit really well, I liked the wings at the back, they screamed *Biker Babe!* so I bought it. Under this I wore my purple underwear with black lace.

I packed everything up, an activity Buster wanted nothing to do with and I knew that because she pranced out of the bathroom.

I went back into the bedroom and gathered my clothes from the floor and shoved those in my bag too. Normally I would make the bed but there was no point in Tate's room. The floor was littered with clothes and the surfaces of his nightstands and dresser were covered with the flotsam and jetsam from his life (likely from his pockets), change, receipts, slips of paper. There was no point tidying.

I walked out of the room, down the hall and all the way to the mudroom where I dropped my bag by the door to the garage. Then I went into the kitchen and searched the cupboards for mugs. We hadn't done the dishes last night. The bacon fat was still in the skillet. The plates in the sink.

I didn't tidy those either, mostly because I heard the sliding glass door open.

I didn't turn. I went to the coffeepot and started pouring.

My mug was mostly full when I felt bearded lips at my neck and an arm slid around my ribs.

"Mornin', babe," Tate muttered against my skin as he pulled my back into his front.

"Morning," I said to the coffee and put the pot back under the filter.

"Come out and sit with me on the deck," he ordered, his lips just under my ear, his soft words vibrating on the sensitive skin there in a way that would be delicious if I wasn't heartbroken.

Okay, maybe it was an invitation voiced as an order but I was in no mood mainly because I was heartbroken.

"Thanks but I need you to take me home," I told him. "Go for a swim."

I felt Tate's body go still.

He didn't speak so I asked the coffeemaker, "Can you let me go? I need milk."

He let me go but only so his hand could curl around my mug, pull the handle out of my fingers and put the mug on the counter. His mug joined it then his hands came to my hips and turned me around. He stepped in and I had no choice but to press my hips into the counter because of the limited space he allowed.

He put his hands on the counter on either side of me. I tilted my head back to look at him and saw he was studying me.

He did this for long moments so I repeated, "Tate, milk."

"What's up your ass, babe?"

Okay, now I was thinking maybe I was hallucinating during all those times Tate was supposedly sweet. He was most definitely a jerk.

"Nothing," I lied. "I just need caffeine."

His eyes moved over my face.

Then his voice changed to gentle when he asked, "You nap?"

"Sorry?" I asked back, confused at his tone and his question.

His hands on the counter came to my sides and slid around to my back, pulling me to him so he was holding me against his body. Because of this, I had no choice but to put my hands on his biceps.

"You don't get enough sleep, baby." His voice was still soft. "When do you catch up?"

"I don't," I told him and looked toward the fridge. "Now, if I can get some—"

"Ace," he cut me off and I looked back at him.

"Tate, I'd like some coffee."

He ignored me. "Everyone needs sleep."

"Like I keep telling you, I'm used to it."

"Yeah?" he asked as if he didn't believe me.

"Yes," I answered like I was getting impatient, which I was.

His eyes moved to my temple as his hand slid up my back and then wound my ponytail around it, coming to rest with fingers curled around the back of my head.

"Your head hurt?" he asked.

"Only if I think about it," I answered.

"Bruised," he muttered, his eyes still on my temple.

"It's not that bad," I pointed out and it wasn't. This was surprising, considering how much it hurt when it happened. But it was true.

His gaze moved to mine.

"What's wrong, Laurie?"

"Nothing *will* be wrong once I get my coffee."

"Why do you wanna go back to the hotel?"

"To swim before I have to go to work."

"Deck time now. I'll take you to the hotel and hang while you swim after work, before we come up here."

I shook my head.

"I'm not coming up here after work," I told him.

His fingers at my head tensed and his arm around my body tightened.

"Come again?" he asked.

"I'm not coming here after work," I repeated and his face changed from searching and gentle to a little bit scary.

"Why not?"

"I'll need to call Mom, Dad, Carrie. Check in. Make sure everything is still okay. I haven't called for a couple of days."

"You can do that here."

"It's long distance."

"So?"

"We talk a long time. It might be expensive."

"Been leakin' money awhile, babe, but just got two big paychecks and I wasn't destitute before that. Think I can cover a long-distance phone call."

I tried a different strategy. "I don't want you to watch me while I swim. It'll put me off."

"Then I'll hang with Ned while you swim." His face dipped closer and his tone dipped lower. "And then hang with you when you shower after you swim."

I pulled my head back.

"Tate, what I'm saying is, I need some alone time."

His head pulled back too but his arm grew tighter.

"What the fuck?" he whispered.

"Alone time," I reiterated.

"Just had three weeks of alone time, Ace," he reminded me, his voice back to a little bit scary.

"Tate—"

"Laurie, I'll repeat my earlier question: What's up your god-damned ass?"

At his words and tone, my hands reflexively clenched his biceps and I stared at him.

Then I told him, "This isn't working for me."

With a hint of alarm I watched his eyes narrow and I felt that dark, bad vibe energy start to spark from him.

"What isn't working?" he asked.

I took a hand from his biceps and motioned between him and me before putting it back and putting pressure on both.

"Us," I answered.

My hips went back into the counter because he pressed them there.

"Seemed to be workin' last night when you were fuckin' me so hard you couldn't breathe," he reminded me.

"Yes, well…"

"Yes, well what?"

"Um…"

His hand left my hair and became an arm wrapped around my upper back, jerking me tighter to his body.

"Jesus, Lauren, I'll ask one more fuckin' time. What's up your goddamned ass?"

At that, I lost hold of my temper, which was my only choice since the only other thing I could do was lose hold on the tears I'd been ignoring since my couch contemplations last night and our scene in the bed early that morning.

"You're a jerk!" I snapped.

"Yeah, I get pissed, I am. So?"

I felt my eyes get wide. "So?" I repeated.

"Not somethin' you don't know about me, Ace."

"I don't like it!"

"Yeah?" he asked and went on before I could answer. "And I don't like it when you lose hold of your attitude and turn into a bitch. But since most of the time you're sweet or hilarious or you make my dick get hard, I can put up with that."

"There it is," I pointed out, trying to slide away at the same time pushing against his biceps but his arms got super tight and I stopped.

"What?"

"You just called me a bitch!"

"Babe, honest to God?" he asked, his voice impatient.

"Honest to God!" I snapped, my voice rising.

"You don't know you can be a bitch?"

"No, I don't. Normally I'm not. *You* draw it out in me."

"So I'm not only a jerk, it's me who makes you a bitch," he stated.

"Yes," I replied.

His arms didn't loosen even as he tipped his head back and looked at the ceiling.

"Jesus," he muttered.

"Let me go," I demanded and his head tipped forward again.

"No," he replied.

"And there it is again!" I declared instantly.

"What?" he clipped, his arms giving me a minishake.

"I get that you're an alpha male, Captain, but bossing me around, making me do stuff I don't want to do? Not…liking…*that.*"

His face dipped close. "All right, Ace, get it all out. What else?"

I'd had enough, *more* than enough, so I got up on my toes and got close to his face too. "Okay, Captain, here goes," I started. "Neeta, Wood, Neeta, Wood and maybe a little bit more of *Neeta and Wood*!"

"You wanna expand on that?" he growled.

"Not me not expanding, Tate," I snapped.

Tate's head twitched then, immediately, he started his story.

"Knew her for as long as I can remember. Hooked up with her in high school. Partly 'cause she was gorgeous, mostly 'cause she put out. I was seventeen, she was fifteen and I wasn't her first."

I gasped at the knowledge that Neeta put out (and he wasn't her first) at the age of fifteen.

I lost my virginity at the age of twenty-one to my college sweetheart after his pregraduation fraternity dance. We'd been going together for two years and he'd taken me to a posh hotel and bought me roses and told me he'd love me until the day he died after we did it. We were still friends and he called me on my birthday every year and each time he did we laughed together about the good old days for at least an hour.

It was doubtful at fifteen Neeta held out for posh hotels and roses and equally doubtful her first still remembered her birthday, if he ever knew it at all.

Tate continued, "She was wild but I knew that about her and it was a fuckin' blast, always. She could have fun, Neeta. Always smilin', laughin', dancin'. She'd get up from watchin' TV and dance into the fuckin' kitchen to get a drink. The world was a dance for her. A party all in her head. But when I hooked up with her, spent that much time with her, something struck me, somethin' not right about it. It wasn't until later I realized she wasn't wild. She was desperate. For what, I still don't fuckin' know, spent years tryin' to figure it out same time I spent those years tryin' to give it to her. All I know is, back then, I was too young and too addicted to her mouth wrapped around my cock to think of much else."

This was *way* too much information.

"I—" I broke in but he shook his head.

"You wanted to know, babe, here it is," he told me. "I think you get I was a good football player. And I was *good*. So good, I had scouts comin' to games my junior year. Senior year I had six offers before I took the seventh and two came in the day after that. Neeta, she liked that, bein' with me, lookin' into *our* future, plannin' it all out. It wasn't about me, what I could do, what *I* earned. It was about what Neeta could get outta it."

I bit my lip.

Tate held my eyes and kept speaking.

"But Neeta, she's not like you. She isn't smart. She doesn't work hard. She thinks of the future with her head in the clouds. And she doesn't work for shit. Always, even when she was a little kid, expected everything to be handed to her on a silver platter. So she wants to party, have fun and she wants me with her. And I'm with her because I'll get

laid or get a blowjob but also because I'm not, there's no fuckin' tellin'
what she'll get herself into. And, fuck me, I love her. Not just her mouth
or her cunt, but *her*. The way she is, the way she dances through life."

"Tate—"

"So I gotta look after her. Problem with that is, she gets bored, she
wants somethin' new, new faces, new adventures, new ways to have fun.
And there I am, at her side one night when she finds that shit and the
party we're at gets busted. I know in my bones it ain't where we're supposed to be. These people are older than us, rough, no good. But she
wouldn't go, she was havin' fun. I could go, she told me, but she was
stayin' and I knew no way I could leave her there on her own. And I was
right, they were no good. So Neeta and I are there and we get busted
along with them. Drugs, not pot, not coke, not a little bit of it, they had
crack and they had lots of it because they *dealt* it. When I made the papers,
local football star busted at a party hangin' with drug dealers, Ace, let's
just say the football program at Penn State, they didn't like that much."

"My God," I whispered, horrified at what he was telling me.

"They almost pulled the scholarship. Dad and Pop didn't talk to
them, explain things, they would have. They were puttin' their money
down on a future All-American. Not some asshole who gets his shit
in the papers."

"Tate—"

He cut me off with a dare. "That's the first time she fucked up my
life, you wanna hear more?"

"But you went to Penn State," I reminded him quietly.

"Yeah, thanks to Dad and Pop," he returned. "I quit Neeta and
went to school."

"So, um…later you took her back?" I asked cautiously.

"More times than you got fingers, Ace. Each time, she fucked up
my life." His arms gave me a powerful squeeze that made my breath
catch and his voice got so low, I could feel it vibrating in my chest.
"So I find this woman, see. High-class, great fuckin' hair, legs that
go forever but I see her when I'm pissed. I'm pissed at Bubba and I'm
pissed at Krystal but most of all, I'm pissed at Neeta 'cause I let the

bitch play me again. Next day after Neeta plays me, the next fuckin' day, that's when I find this woman. She's workin' in my *goddamned bar*," he growled and my heart stopped. "And I do *not* need that shit. Had years of that shit. I need that woman and the trouble that's written all over her in my bar like I need a hole in my head. So I get pissed, say shit I don't mean and what happens? I walk out after sayin' that shit and she looks at me and I know she heard. Part of me, gotta tell you Laurie, is glad. Part of me can't take it. Which part wins?"

"Tate—"

I got another squeeze. "Which part?" he demanded to know.

"I don't—"

"You're right here, Ace."

"But I don't understand."

"What's that say about me?"

"Sorry?"

"What's that say about me?" he repeated.

"Honey, I don't understand the question," I whispered.

"Babe, honestly?" he asked.

"Yes." I was still whispering.

"You're standin' there wonderin' what the fuck you got yourself into after gettin' yourself outta that jacked-up situation with your asshole ex. After makin' two piss-poor choices in the women I let in my life, what do you think *I'm* thinkin'?"

I couldn't be sure but I *thought* I knew what he was thinking.

"I'm not Neeta," I said quietly.

"You're your own brand of trouble, I know that and you're still right here," he told me and I felt my heart start beating faster.

"But I'm a good girl," I whispered. "I've always been a good girl."

"Laurie, you strut up to a fuckin' garage, all tits, ass, and legs. Jesus, if you had a fishin' pole, you couldn't've hooked those boys faster."

"I needed my oil changed," I reminded him.

"Wood didn't come out first, babe, no fuckin' joke, the rest of those boys woulda fought to change your oil and bring you margaritas while they were doin' it."

"That's crazy," I breathed.

"Ace, hello?" he called. "I was fuckin' *there*."

"Tate," my voice was stronger, "I needed an oil change."

"Yeah, there it is," he shot back. "Your own brand of trouble."

"I don't understand what you mean!" My voice was definitely stronger since I was semishouting.

"What I mean is, two months ago I scraped off the bitch who's been ruinin' my goddamned life for over twenty years. The next day, the next *fuckin' day, you're* in it. You're totally clueless, wanderin' through a biker town like you're in Disneyland. And, I'll repeat, the day before I met you, I scraped off the woman who I spent two decades with, a different kinda clueless woman who lived in her own head."

I felt my head twitch.

"I'm not clueless," I whispered.

"You're clueless and you're lost," he returned.

"I'm not lost either," I told him.

"Lauren, you live in a *hotel*."

"So? It's home!"

"You can tell yourself that, babe, but a hotel is not home."

I switched topics because he kind of had me there.

"And I don't live in my own head."

His face changed, his voice changed, everything changed when he spoke again.

Everything.

The whole of Tate.

I watched it and it was so dazzling all I could do was stare.

"Honey," he whispered, using an endearment he'd never used on me in a voice he'd never used either. A voice that was quiet and sweet and the expression on his face was so tender it made my heart turn over. "You're so deep in your head you can't even sleep."

I felt my lips part and I kept staring at him.

Darn it all, he had me there too.

His arm left my back so his hand could curl around the side of my neck.

"This is what we got. You got burned by that asshole ex of yours and I got played by Neeta. We hooked up after that, for me *right* after that, and here we are. So what're we gonna do?" he asked.

"I…" I cleared my throat. "I don't know."

The pad of his thumb pressed my jaw up as his head tilted down and his face got close.

"I ain't Brad and you aren't Neeta," he said softly. "I also ain't perfect and neither are you."

He was right about that too.

"No," I agreed quietly.

"So we find out about each other and who we are together." His forehead dropped to touch mine. "I'm gonna piss you off 'cause I can be a dick. That's who I am. And you're gonna piss me off 'cause, babe, you got attitude. That's who you are. And that's who we're comin' out to be together. And I'm all right with that because, with what I had before, even when you're a bitch, I like it. But when you're not, it's a sweetness the like I've never tasted."

Oh.

My.

God.

I felt tears sting my eyes and my fingers curled around his biceps to hold on.

"Tate," I whispered.

"So, I'm not takin' you to the hotel. We're sittin' out on the deck and havin' coffee. Then I'll make you breakfast. Then we'll fuck in bed, then fuck again in the shower, then we'll go to work. I'll take you for your swim. We'll fuck in the shower at the hotel. Then I'll feed you and we'll probably fuck in my bed again."

"That's a lot of, um…"

"Maybe I should rephrase, some of it'll be fuckin', some of it'll be me makin' you come."

I felt and heard my breath snag as my hands moved of their own volition. They uncurled from his biceps and started to press under his arms to wrap around his back.

"I usually eat before I swim," I found my mouth informing him.

I watched his face relax and his fingers slid into my ponytail and twisted gently. "Works for me."

His mouth came a hairbreadth away from mine.

"Okay," I breathed as my eyes started closing.

"You over your snit?"

My eyes slowly opened and that disquiet I felt last night reminded me of its existence.

Then I whispered, "We should talk about Wood."

His lips touched mine. "You got Neeta today, baby. Wood can wait until later."

"But—"

His arms pulled me deep into his body. "Only so much of those two I can stomach in a day."

"Tate—"

"You gonna finally kiss me good mornin' or do I have to kiss you?"

I felt a flurry in my belly.

"I should probably kiss you," I said softly because I probably should. I'd been a bitch again and I needed to make it up to him.

"You got a second, Ace, then I'm takin' over."

"Tate—"

"Time's up," he said; his head slanted and Tate kissed me good morning.

CHAPTER FIFTEEN

Peace of Mind

THE PHONE RANG and my eyes opened.

Tate's painted shoulder and back were all I could see. I was curled into him and it was dark but the moonlight was shining in through the windows.

I felt his fingers wrap around my wrist that was dangling at his stomach, holding firm keeping my arm where it was as he lifted up. Once up, he let my hand go and reached for his cell on the nightstand.

I left my arm draped around his waist and snuggled closer. Lifting up a bit to rest on my elbow, I pressed my nose against his back then turned my head, so my cheek was there as my arm around his waist tightened and he answered the phone.

"Jackson," he growled, this growl due to sleep.

I listened to the silence. Tate listened to the phone.

"Who?" he asked, his voice no longer holding even a hint of sleep. "Right. Where?" he went on and then listened. "Right. Fax or e-mail?" He listened again. "Right," he repeated then said, "Next time, Thyne, do me a favor and let me in on this shit before it gets to this. Yeah?"

Hmm. He didn't sound sleepy anymore but he also *really* didn't sound happy.

"Yeah, I'll be there," Tate confirmed then flipped the phone closed.

He tossed it on the nightstand and turned toward me. I moved back to accommodate him and his arms slid around me, pulling me close again when he was facing me.

"Got a situation, Laurie," he muttered.

"Is everything okay?" I asked.

"Fugitive, probably armed, definitely dangerous. Why the fuck they let this guy out on bail is anyone's guess. He's serious shit."

For the first time it struck me that he hunted fugitives that could be armed and definitely dangerous. But then again, fugitives by definition of being fugitive were probably pretty dangerous, especially to the person who was hunting them in order to halt their fugitive status. I had no idea why this didn't sink in before but I figured it did it then because he'd received a middle-of-the-night phone call where they called him in during "a situation," thus giving his occupation a reality it never had before.

My arms around him got tight.

"Who's Thyne?" I asked.

"Bail bondsman in Denver. He's got two local guys he uses for the small-time shit. Calls me in when he has problems. He tried to find this guy usin' local talent, which was a mistake. Those boys take less of a percentage because they're part moron but not moron enough to know no one'll pay them for bein' part moron. Thyne is cheap and part moron too so he pays 'em. This guy is probably in Mexico by now."

My arms got tighter.

"Do you have to go to Mexico?"

"Fuck, I hope not," he muttered and I hoped not too. Mexico was a long way away and I had enough trouble thinking of Tate hunting a dangerous fugitive. I didn't want to think of him doing it a long way away. "He's faxin' me the particulars. I gotta get on the road."

My arms got even tighter though I whispered, "Okay."

His hand slid up my back and his fingers sifted into my hair to cup the back of my head.

"Kiss me, baby."

I used the moonlight on the angles of his face to aim and found his mouth. The minute my lips hit his, he rolled partially into me, forcing me to my back in the bed, and my mouth opened as did his. My tongue slid inside, he growled against it and when I absorbed that in my mouth, a small moan escaped my throat. His head slanted one way, mine tilted the other, and my kiss turned into a *kiss*.

I was breathing heavily and holding on tight when his mouth disengaged and his tongue slid along my lower lip.

Then he stated, "I want you to stay here. Look after Buster."

I blinked in the dark at his close up, shadowed face.

Then I asked, "Sorry?"

"I'll leave the keys to the Explorer and the house on the kitchen counter. Garage door opener is in the truck. Take the Explorer into town. I'll call Deke to bring it back. The alarm code is three five six one. To set it, you punch in the number and hit the red button and you got a minute to get into the garage. To disable it, hit three five six one and hit the green button. Once you enter, you got a minute to do that too. When you're goin' to sleep for the night, doors secured, windows stay closed and you hit three five six one and then the blue button."

"Um...," I mumbled, not keeping up with him. "Sorry?"

His arms tightened and he rolled to his back, pulling me with him so my torso was resting mostly on his chest.

"I want you stayin' here," he repeated.

"To watch your cat?"

"Yeah, to watch Buster. And 'cause I have an alarm."

This belatedly penetrated.

"You have an alarm?"

"Don't use it when I'm home. You'll use it when you're home without me."

I felt something silken slither through me.

"When I'm home?" I whispered.

"Yeah," he replied.

"But, my room at the hotel—"

"Want you stayin' here."

"But, the hotel—"

"Want you in my bed."

That slithered through me too.

"Tate—"

His fingers sifted in my hair, cupping my head again and bringing my face close to his.

"Could be gone a day, could be gone two weeks. I want you texting again and when I get my phone calls at night, I wanna know I'm talking to you while you're lyin' in my bed."

That silken thing started to wrap tight around me and it didn't feel bad at all.

Even so, I whispered, "Tate, I don't know."

"I do. You'll be safer here."

"The hotel's safe," I told him.

"Carnal Hotel ain't safe," he told me.

"Ned and Betty are right across the way."

"Ace, first, to find this place, you gotta know where it is. Second, to get to work from here, you gotta be in your car, a fact I like since it's a fuckuva lot safer than you walkin' to the hotel after your shift. Last, my alarm goes straight to dispatch. Boys'll know I'm gone, they'll also know you're stayin' here. They get the warnin', they won't fuck around. Carnal PD is mostly shit but I got some friends there that are good men. They know my woman is here and the alarm tells them you've been breached, they won't fuck around and they got trainin' and guns. Ned don't have that."

This was true. Still.

"Um…"

"And Buster likes you."

"She's friendly," I reminded him. "I think she'd probably like anyone."

"She is and she does and that's why I don't like leavin' her alone. She prefers company."

"You're out of town a lot, who looked after her before?"

"Krystal."

This surprised me so much I had to take a moment to let the thought sink in of Krystal coming up and taking care of a dainty cat as a favor to a friend. She didn't seem like a friendly-favor-doing type of person or a taking-care-of-a-dainty-cat type of person either.

"Babe, I gotta get the fax, get packed, and get on the road. You stayin' here or what?"

"I think—" I started hesitantly and he rolled me to my back again and pinned me to the bed with his big body.

Then he pulled out the big guns.

He did this by murmuring, "Peace of mind."

"I'll stay," I agreed instantly.

His head dropped but moved to the side and he flicked my ear with his nose.

Then he said in my ear, "That's my good girl."

And I was. I was his good girl. Even though this seemed like a big step, a step that was too big and too soon, a step that also didn't say "I'm a cool and hard-to-get biker babe" but said "I'm your good girl and you've already got me."

I was *such* an idiot.

His head came up and his mouth touched mine. Then he exited the bed.

I curled into myself and watched his shadow as he moved around. Then I listened as he took a shower. He came back, got dressed, and I lifted up to sitting cross-legged in the bed.

Buster joined me, sitting on her booty in my lap and since she was there, I gave her scratches. In that position, Buster and I watched as Tate packed mostly in the dark (he turned the light on in the walk-in closet and it partially shone in the bedroom). Buster knew the packing drill and I got the impression she wasn't a big fan. Then again, neither was I. Tate was going away for an unspecified period of time again and I was back to texts.

He turned the closet light out and came back into the bedroom. I heard the zip go on his bag that was sitting on the bed and watched his hand curl around the handle. My hand shot out and my fingers curled around his wrist.

"Tate," I called.

"Yeah, baby," he answered.

"Does this happen a lot?"

"It's my job, Laurie."

"No, I mean, phone calls in the middle of the night."

He paused. Then he answered, "A lot, no. Sometimes, yeah."

Without my mind willing my body to do it, I pulled on his arm as Buster daintily hopped off my lap. I was wearing a shelf-bra camisole and undies. I'd replaced these after cleaning up in the bathroom, after we'd made love before going to sleep.

When I got to my knees in front of him, my other hand flattened on his abs as my hand around his wrist tugged harder to bring him down to me. My hand at his abs slid up his chest to curl around his neck when he bent at the waist to get close. My hold at his wrist disengaged when both his arms wrapped around me.

I tilted my head back and his face got close.

"Please be careful, honey," I whispered and before he could answer, my arms tightened around his neck, I flattened my body against his, and I kissed him hard.

He crushed me to him with one arm, the other hand going into my hair, fisting and holding my mouth to his far longer than I'd intended.

He broke the kiss but didn't let me go nor did his mouth move very far away.

"I'll take care of Buster," I promised.

"Thanks, Ace," he murmured. "Don't get into trouble when I'm gone," he warned.

"I'm a good girl," I reminded him.

When his mouth hit mine I could tell it was smiling.

"Yeah," he said and that one word also held his smile.

His fist in my hair tipped my head down, he kissed the hair at the top, let me go, and he was gone.

CHAPTER SIXTEEN

Once We Were Brothers

IT WAS THREE days after Tate left to hunt a possibly armed, definitely dangerous fugitive.

Which was five days after the incident with Wood in Tate's living room.

It was midmorning and I was sitting out on his deck drinking coffee, my feet up on a lower railing, taking a break from what had become an ongoing three-day job of doing laundry and cleaning Tate's house.

I'd struggled with this decision. Cleaning his house was an intimacy he had not invited. Then again, he'd asked me to stay in it and I could (somewhat) ignore the state of it when Tate was there and most of the time we were eating or having sex. I couldn't ignore the state of it when I was staying there.

I was contemplating the trees that surrounded the house as my mind considered the fact that I might have taken things a bit too far. I hadn't only picked up his bedroom, done his laundry, and thoroughly cleaned out his kitchen, including a complete clear-out and wipe-down of the fridge and a full scouring of his baked-on, burnt-on oven that clearly hadn't been cleaned since the dawn of time. I'd also vacuumed and dusted the entire house, cleaned all the bathrooms, carried his boots in the mudroom to the closet in his bedroom, tidied his coats in the mudroom, organized his clothes in the walk-in closet, and cleared the dining room table, stacking his mail (without looking too much at it) on the kitchen counter (magazine piles, opened mail piles, unopened mail piles).

I'd also stripped his bed and noticed his sheets were old and, if not threadbare, they were getting there.

There were also no other sheets to replace them that I could find but I didn't look hard. The two bedrooms upstairs had their doors closed and I kept them like that. I found, on the ground level, the backstairs led into a big open space with a bunch of weight equipment in it and then there was a hall off which there were three rooms and a bathroom. The bathroom door was open (so I cleaned it) and another room was open.

This was obviously Tate's office with desk, computer, printer, fax machine, three filing cabinets, and a variety of files and paperwork (*not* in the filing cabinets) that were not only unorganized but looked in danger of forming a paper avalanche.

I didn't tidy his office because he probably knew where everything was and I didn't know what anything was so I couldn't organize it properly not knowing. The other two doors downstairs were not opened.

I didn't open the unopened doors because I didn't want him to think I was snooping. Though I found it slightly odd, with the upstairs and the down, that Tate Jackson had such a huge house. Essentially six bedrooms, three full baths, living room, dining room, family room. It was long and it was also large. Too large for one man and a dainty cat.

Unable to find sheets, I called Wendy, swung by to pick her up and we headed to the mall in order to buy some.

This was where I thought that perhaps I was stepping over the line.

Because I didn't only buy sheets. I bought Indian cotton, high thread count sheets and because Tate's comforter had seen better days, I bought a down one, a comforter cover, six new down pillows and shams.

I thought nothing of this until the clerk returned my credit card and Wendy giggled. Her giggle started slow, then gained in volume and hilarity.

Finally she shouted, "Love this!"

I turned to her. "Love what?"

"You and Tate buying sheets together." Then she laughed outright and grabbed me, giving me a big hug.

I hugged her back and looked over her shoulder at the clerk who was smiling at me like she knew what was going on. I didn't smile at her because I didn't.

"Tate and I aren't buying sheets together," I told Wendy.

She let me go and leaned back.

"You *so* are!"

I looked around to see if Tate was hiding somewhere and about to saunter out and surprise me. When I saw no Tate, I looked back at Wendy.

"It's just that he needs new sheets. His are old and he only has one set," I explained.

"He need a new comforter?" she returned.

"Yes, that's old too."

"A comforter cover?" she went on.

"You have a down comforter, Wendy, you have to have a cover," I explained patiently.

"Shams?" she asked.

Hmm. I could see her point on the shams. Tate wasn't exactly a man who needed two extra pillows, which were only there to sport decorative shams.

I bit my lip and looked at the huge plastic bags holding my purchases.

"And you're gonna sleep on those sheets," she reminded me. "You already are! And he isn't even *home*!"

"Um…," I mumbled.

"Love this!" Wendy shouted again then turned to the clerk and shared, "She's got a new man. He's a *good* man and he's *hot*. He's *totally* into her and they've known each other, like, two months and they're already *playing house*!"

"We're not playing house," I whispered.

"You *so* are," Wendy didn't whisper. She spoke so loud other people were staring (and smiling).

"Girlfriend, let me just say," the clerk butted in, "don't look so scared. He's a good man, he's hot, he's into you, go with the flow. He's used to bad sheets and an old comforter, you *go* girl and you buy him good sheets. A man appreciates good sheets. He ain't gonna say it but he's gonna think it and every time he slides between those sheets he's gonna be glad you gave that to him. We girls, we gotta look after our men. You tell him early on you're the type of woman who finds all sorts of ways to look after her man, it's gonna suck him in deep and he ain't even gonna know it."

"Unh-hunh," a woman in line behind us muttered. "You got *that* right."

I looked between the clerk and the nodding, smiling woman behind us in line and I wondered how a trip to the mall to purchase sheets had turned into a lecture from a clerk at a home wares store telling me how to suck Tate in deep. I didn't have the heart to tell her that Tate was such a badass he could probably sleep on a bed of nails. I didn't think he would even notice new sheets.

Or, at that point, I was kind of hoping he didn't.

Even though I thought what I thought, to be nice, I said to her, "Thanks for the advice."

"My pleasure," she said as Wendy shoved my purchases into the cart and started motoring toward the exit.

Even with my misgivings, I put the new sheets and the comforter (and the shams) on the bed. Standing at the foot surveying it, I had to admit, with the bedroom floor cleared and vacuumed, the dresser and nightstands cleaned off, the entire place dusted, it didn't look bad.

The room was painted a utilitarian cream. Considering Tate was a man and a biker, I bought a dark denim comforter cover and shams and sheets in what I thought was an awesome light clay that contrasted great with the indigo blue denim. They gave the room some color and made it look homier. Tate's house wasn't a bachelor pad, it was a crash pad. This meant it also wasn't a home. Those sheets gave it a stamp of "home." A little one but a definite one.

Studying my handiwork, I decided on the one hand it freaked me out. On the other hand, I liked it. Tate needed a home, everyone did.

Buster sashayed in, jumped up on the bed, and stopped dead. She gave the bed a look, gave me a look over her shoulder then she delicately dropped to her side, curled into a ball, and went to sleep.

Well, at least I had Buster's approval.

I let the sun shine down on me and sipped my coffee thinking about the sheets and the amount of stuff I brought up from the hotel, in other words, all of it. I'd checked out mainly because it was stupid to pay for a hotel room I wasn't using but also because Ned and Betty were at the height of the summer biker season and could use the room.

Lastly, I checked out because I liked to have choice and variability of wardrobe and I didn't know how long Tate would be gone. It would be annoying to have to keep carting stuff back and forth and it wasn't like I had a house full of stuff. I had a car full of stuff. I left my unused clothes in suitcases and my boxes in Tate's garage, the rest of it I lugged to his walk-in closet. I didn't go so far as unpacking (except bathroom stuff). I knew that was definitely crossing a line. A line I wasn't ready for and a line I didn't want to know if Tate didn't want me to cross.

I sighed and tipped my head back to the sun.

Weirdly enough, outside of fretting about cleaning Tate's house, buying him sheets and semimoving in, life felt normal. I hadn't felt normal, not in a long time. Not during my wandering, not during the separation and divorce from Brad, not even before that, when I knew something was not right.

But now I had work that I liked. I had friends I could trust who I could go to the mall with. I came home to a house ensconced in the quiet, wooded hills sandwiched among Colorado's mountains. I ate home-cooked dinners if I was working days. I made lunch in Tate's kitchen if I was working nights. Every morning, I made myself breakfast and a cup of coffee in a real coffeemaker that sat on a kitchen counter.

Normal, all of it … normal.

I was back in a rhythm of life.

Unfortunately that rhythm seemed surrounded by Tate but held no Tate.

That wasn't true. The two days we had together before Tate left obviously held Tate. He took me to work and worked my shifts with me, giving Bubba and Krystal a break.

Surprisingly, nothing dramatic happened during these days except for the fact that Tate took an instant dislike to Twyla. Then again Twyla was instantly dislikable and didn't mind that one bit considering she honed her instantly dislikable personality to a razor-sharp edge. I'd had to run interference but this wasn't difficult because Tate seemed in a good mood so, unusually, outside of scowling at her a couple of times, he didn't let Twyla's antics get to him.

And Tate and I working together was different when I wasn't holding a grudge. I had fun with him and he seemed to have fun with me. He liked being with me in the bar and I knew this because he laughed a lot and he smiled a lot too. In fact, I'd never seen him do either so much as in those two days after the Wood Incident.

As for me, I liked going to the bar and saying, "Need two Bud drafts," and hearing him say softly, "Right, baby," or, also softly, "You got it, Ace."

Because of these responses, I found myself hanging at the bar more often, Tate across from me, both of us leaning in and chatting. Me trying to be funny just to make him laugh or smile. Me getting a little curl of excitement when I succeeded.

I also found myself ending my orders with "honey." "A Jack and Coke and a Dewar's, honey," or "Four Coors bottles and a Keystone Light, honey." I found myself doing this because, when I did, I'd always get the smile so I went searching for it.

That smile didn't give me a curl of excitement. It made me feel something else, something comfortable and settled but very sweet. Even though, if Twyla heard me call Tate "honey," she'd give me a hard look or roll her eyes. I was guessing Twyla wasn't a big fan of a waitress sleeping with the boss. That said, as far as I could tell, Twyla wasn't a big fan of much.

After my shifts, Tate and I left work together and went to the hotel together where Tate would drop me off so I could have a swim and he'd go do stuff, like pick up groceries for dinner while I swam. Then he'd come back to get me. I'd pack more stuff and go to his house with him where he'd make me dinner and then we'd go to bed and make love and after we'd sleep somehow nuzzled together, him holding me or me curled into his back or, as the night progressed, both.

This felt good too. Comfortable. Settled. And definitely sweet.

On my day off, the day Tate had to go hunting, Tate had planned to take me for a ride. We were going to go out and stay out all day on the bike.

It was a bummer he'd been called away because I wanted to do that with him, have a day with him with nothing to do but ride. To be on the back of his bike and feel that freedom only Tate had given me, a freedom I'd only ever felt sitting on the back of his bike, letting go and thinking absolutely nothing at the same time feeling absolutely everything.

And I wanted to go back to work with him behind the bar.

I wanted him to come home.

I wanted him.

I heard the roar of pipes and my head righted and whipped to the end of the lane. A bike was coming up and I felt that curl of a thrill in my belly because Tate hadn't said he was coming home last night when we talked but he'd surprised me before.

Then I stared because it wasn't Tate. It was Wood.

"Damn," I whispered under my breath and watched Wood ride up the drive and stop at the front of the garage.

I got up and walked down the deck as he got off the bike. We met five feet into the deck from the stairs that led to it from the side of the garage.

"Wood," I greeted hesitantly.

"Laurie," he greeted back, his eyes hidden behind mirrored sunglasses so I couldn't read them.

"Um...," I mumbled, unsure what to say because I was unsure of why he was there.

Wood wasn't unsure.

"Neeta's in town."

I felt my body get tight.

"Sorry?"

He didn't repeat himself. Instead he asked, "Deke still playin' bodyguard?"

"No," I answered, finding this an odd question. "Why?"

Wood looked at the house then looked at me. "When's Tate due back?"

"Wood—"

He took a step toward me and, with effort, I held my ground.

He pulled his sunglasses off and shoved an arm of the glasses in the collar of his T-shirt. When I saw them, I noticed his eyes, as they normally were, were gentle on me.

"Know that ship has sailed, baby," he assured in his gentle voice. "Now, when's Tate due back?"

"It's uncertain," I replied. "Why?" I repeated.

"She's heard about you."

"What?"

"Neeta. That's why she's back. She's heard about you." He looked at the house again then at me. "You here alone?"

"Wood—"

His hand came up and curled around my neck. "Laurie, I asked, you here alone?"

"Yes, but why—?"

I stopped talking when he quickly dropped his hand from my neck and with somewhat urgent movements dug his phone out of his back pocket. He flipped it open, hit some buttons, and put it to his ear. His eyes locked on mine as he listened to it ring.

Then he said, "Wood," and he paused. "Don't be an ass and listen. I'm at your house with Laurie." Another pause then, "Fuck, Tate, goddamned relax. If you'd listen you'd know I'm doin' you a fuckin' favor here. Neeta's in town." Silence while Wood's face got hard then, "Yeah, she knows about Laurie, man. Why you think she's in town? She heard and hightailed it up from CB like a fuckin' rocket." He was quiet then, "Yeah, Tate, that's the gig. Same MO. She heard rumors, held tight, then heard Laurie was out of the hotel and in your house. Now she's here, same as always." More silence, then quietly, "No, man, Jonas isn't with her."

Jonas? Who was Jonas?

Same as always?

And what was with all the drama?

"What's with all the drama, Wood?" I asked.

He lifted a hand, one finger up and then dropped his hand and bent his neck, listening to Tate on the phone.

This went on for several moments before he said, "Deke's out?" Then a whispered, "Fuck."

I watched his mouth get tight as I watched him lift his hand to the back of his neck and squeeze.

Then he said into the phone in a way that sounded like the words were dragged out of him, "Seems like all you got is me." His neck straightened, his hand dropped, and his body got as tight as his mouth before he went on, "Bubba's useless and you and I know it. Deke's out. Neeta is what Neeta is because of Pop so I'm not fuckin' askin' him and you'd be a fuckin' fool to do it. So, way I see it, all you got is me."

He listened a moment then bit his lip in a scary way before he spoke again.

"Unlike you, *brother*, your woman's sleepin' in your bed, I ain't gonna make a move. I also ain't gonna stand aside 'cause you're in fuckin' Texas, Neeta's in town, and Laurie's un-fuckin'-protected. You don't like that, fuckin' tough. You know her, Christ, Tate, you know her better'n anyone. You shoulda planned for this eventuality. She's got that fuckin' posse here who keep tabs on you and always have so you knew this was gonna happen. Now, tables are turned, man, and I'm takin' care of *your* shit."

He flipped the phone shut and turned to me and all I could think to say was, "Unprotected?"

I heard my cell phone ring in the house but I was too busy staring at Wood and hearing his conversation replay in my head to move.

"Neeta's unpredictable," Wood stated and looked at the house again before his eyes came back to me. "Baby, that'll be Tate on the phone."

I ignored him and repeated on a prompt, "Unpredictable?"

"Tate explain about Neeta?" he asked.

"Um…a little bit," I answered as my phone stopped ringing.

"He explain about how she makes it clear he's her property?"

I licked my lips.

Then I said, "No."

"Well, she thinks he's her property."

"What does that mean?" I asked as my phone started ringing again.

Wood's eyes went to the house again then to me and he urged gently, "Baby, get your phone."

I turned on a foot and ran to the house. Tugging open the sliding glass door one-handed, I ran to the kitchen counter where my phone was. I put down my mug, touched the screen that said "Captain Calling" and put it to my ear.

"Tate?" I asked into the phone.

"Wood still there?" he asked back without saying hello.

"Yes, but he says—"

"Put him on the phone," Tate ordered.

"But, honey—"

"Lauren, put him on the *goddamned* phone."

Someone was *not* happy.

That was okay because I was not happy either.

"Maybe you might want to talk to *me* about what's happening," I suggested acidly.

Tate replied instantly, "What's happening, Ace, is Neeta's a fuckin' nut. I may have only had three women on the back of my bike, that doesn't mean I've only had three women. And one of the reasons I've only had three women that I put on my bike is because Neeta hears I got someone in my bed, and she hears I take them there more than once, she moves to stake her claim. She's been married to a man for seven years but, make no mistake, the bitch claims *me*. She might be forty-two years old but she never stopped actin' like a teenager. Not a lotta women like havin' threatening letters shoved in their mailboxes, crazy, screamin' women showin' up at their work shouting obscenities, or gettin' in hair-pulling catfights at the diner. She's in town it means she's in town for a showdown *with you*."

Oh my *God*!

"Tate—"

"And you grew up on a fuckin' farm in Indiana and spent the rest of your life in suburbia. You and your sister might know all about attitude but even your considerable attitude, babe, ain't gonna mean dick when you're up against Neeta. I like your face just like it is. I don't need her clawin' it with her fingernails. Firstly because, like I said, I like your face as it is. Secondly because, that bitch lays a fuckin' hand on you, I'm gonna take her ass down and I'm not big on takin' out a woman. Now give the phone *to Wood*."

I took the phone from my ear and held it out to Wood.

"He wants to talk to you," I whispered and wondered if Wood could hear me over the beating of my heart.

Wood gave me a look, took the phone and put it to his ear.

"You got me," he said into it, listened then said, "Yeah." A pause. "Yeah, man." And finally, "No shit? Remember who you're talkin' to, yeah?" He listened again and finished with, "Right." Then he held the phone to me.

Hesitantly, I took it and put it to my ear.

"Tate?"

"Wood takes you to work, he brings you home, and he sleeps on the couch. You with me?"

"Tate—"

"Yes or no, Lauren."

"Yes," I replied.

"I'm in Lubbock, sittin' outside a titty bar where my boy is havin' himself a good time. He's about to get a lap dance that isn't gonna end too good for him. Even though I'm takin' him down, time I get to Denver, get him processed, return Thyne's SUV I had to borrow, and get home, Neeta could wreak havoc. Deke's in South Dakota. Wood needs to cover you. I'll be home early tomorrow, latest."

"Okay," I said quietly, then asked curiously, "He's in a titty bar at ten thirty a.m.?"

"Ace, he ain't a member of the Rotary," Tate answered and I gave a short giggle.

Then I asked, "Titty bars are open at ten thirty?"

"This one is," Tate replied.

"Wow," I whispered.

"Question, babe," he stated.

"Yeah?"

"When I'm pissed as shit at Neeta, why am I sittin' in a borrowed SUV smilin' every time I hear you say the words 'titty bar'?"

"I don't know," I answered.

I listened to a moment of silence.

"Shoulda never started it with you," he muttered and I felt my breath stop coming.

I still managed to force out a "What?"

"Not feelin' happy vibes that my good girl is usin' the words 'titty bar' 'cause I'm sittin' outside one and that she's gotta count on Wood to keep her safe from my fuckin' ex when I'm not there. High-class good girl like you should live a life untouched by that kinda shit and a man like me should know better than to bring it on her."

"I lived a life untouched by that kinda shit, Tate, and I'd never been unhappier because there was worse shit in it and it had nothing to do with talking about titty bars," I whispered.

He was silent a moment as if contemplating this.

Then he demanded, "You sleep in one of my tees."

"Sorry?" I asked.

"Wood's in the house while you're in my bed. Only claim I can stake since I'm fuckin' three states away and I'm stakin' it. You sleep in one of my tees."

"Tate, that's unnecessary."

"Babe. Sleep. In. One. Of. My. *Tees*," he said slowly and with waning patience.

"Oh all right," I muttered.

More silence then a soft and sweet, "There's my good girl."

My breath caught and I opened my mouth to say something but he'd disconnected.

I touched the button and put my cell on the counter.

Then I turned to Wood and asked, "You want coffee?"

Wood crossed his arms on his chest and his eyes dropped to my bare, tan legs exposed by my cutoff jean shorts. I'd cut off the legs of some of my old, fat jeans so the shorts hung on my hips but even I thought they looked kind of sweet. However, now, I was considering changing them.

Wood's gaze came back to mine, he grinned slow—it was no less sexy than the times I'd seen it before—and he answered, "Yeah."

I went to get him coffee and I decided I was definitely wearing Tate's tee to bed.

*   *   *

At three thirty in the morning, I stood uncertainly in Tate's living room watching Wood nab the remote.

"Do you need more pillows?" I asked.

"I'm all right, Laurie," Wood answered, moving his body to lounge on the couch where I'd put the two sham-covered pillows from Tate's bed with the blanket from the couch.

"Um...I need to—" I started.

Wood flicked on the TV, turned the volume low, and his eyes came to me.

"Baby, go to bed," he said gently.

I nodded and his phone on the end table by the couch rang. He reached for it, looked at the display, grinned huge, flipped it open, and put it to his ear.

"Tate," he said, his voice vibrating with the chuckle he was suffocating and I bit my lip and decided to listen to the conversation.

"Yeah, she's home safe and sound. No Neeta. Though, some guy named Brad turned up at Bubba's."

I could swear I heard Tate roar, "*What the fuck?*"

Or maybe that was in my head.

Wood burst out laughing.

Nope. It wasn't in my head.

I closed my eyes but opened them again when Wood started talking.

"Yeah man, you meet this fuckin' guy?" he asked, his voice amused. "I know. Total dick," Wood agreed. "Bar was jammed. Saturday night but more. Word was out Neeta was in town. Half the folks came to see the face-off. Other half came to take Laurie's back. Ned and Betty were there, both of 'em. All the waitresses were there, even the ones who weren't on including fuckin' Jonelle. Krystal, Bubba, *and* Dalton were all mannin' the bar. Stella, Holly, that trainer Tyler, and that gay guy who owns the salon showed. Even those two fuckin' hippies were there, the guy still wearin' those fuckin' glasses even though it was night, purple this time."

This was true. Everyone I knew or even spoke to in Carnal was at the bar. Twyla even turned up. Apparently Neeta was a big draw. Also apparently I'd made some good friends.

At first Krystal, Bubba, Jim-Billy, Wendy (who was on with me), and Wood seemed a little stunned at this show of support. Then they all thought it was hilarious. Then they all talked about it, *loudly,* sometimes yelling about it across the bar.

My "posse" as Wood started to refer to them, joined in the yelling conversation and everyone thought this was the height of comedy, especially the more liquor they got down them. Even Krystal joined in the fun, not only making acid comments about Neeta (who it didn't take a psychologist to read she did *not* like) but also ending the night doing shots with Twyla. I'd stood at the bar waiting for Dalton to fill an order and stared at her like I'd never met her. Dalton was right there with me. Then he turned to me, smiled, and put my drinks on my tray.

My mind came back into Tate's living room when Wood started talking again. He was warming to his story and enjoying telling it, if the massive grin on his face was anything to go by.

"Then this fuckin' guy walks in...to Bubba's...," Wood started choking because he was laughing so hard he was having trouble speaking but he forced out, "in a fuckin' *golf shirt*. Man, I think he had girl shit in his hair."

Wood lost his battle with his hilarity and burst out laughing.

I wondered if Tate was laughing or if he was looking for something to throw.

Wood controlled his mirth and, still chuckling, stated, "No wonder Laurie got in a car and fled suburbia. The prospect of that guy the rest of her life...Christ."

I sighed and crossed my arms on my chest.

Wood kept talking. "Trouble? No man, he came in ready to bring it on but Laurie's posse saw him walk in, eyes on her, they clocked him immediately, and he didn't make it within five feet of her. The whole lot of them closed in, except the hippies but they kept goin' outside to their van so I think they were stoned outta their minds by this time. They were in their own world, they missed the whole thing. Anyway, he started to throw 'tude and fuckin' Jim-Billy, of all people, sucker punched him in the gut. Then that butch chick, the new waitress, she got him by the scruff and frog-marched him out the door." Wood shook his head. "Wish I had that shit on tape."

I didn't. Experiencing it once was enough.

Though seeing Twyla frog-march Brad out the door *was* kind of funny and Carrie and Mack would get a kick out of seeing it on tape.

"No, Tate, not a problem. Bubba jumped on his bike and followed him to the town line. The guy got frog-marched out the door by a chick. She's solid and her chick status is questionable but I'm pretty certain she's still a chick. That kinda hit to his manhood? He ain't comin' back."

Wood was wrong. Tate, Wood, Bubba, Jim-Billy, Dalton, they took that kind of hit to their manhood, they wouldn't come back.

Brad was another story. Brad got something in his head, even Twyla delivering a hit to his manhood wouldn't get it out.

Which meant I had the unpredictable Neeta and the stupid, stubborn, idiot Brad to worry about. Not to mention a night with me in Tate's bed and Wood on Tate's couch.

I was beginning to wish I was back in Horizon Summit, locked behind the gates.

Though I was wishing for the time when Brad was gone and I was there alone. I could have made it. I made good money. I'd have to fire Griselle, the cleaner and Juan-Carlos, the gardener, and maybe forgo my monthly pedicure and bimonthly manicures but I could have eked by.

"Yeah?" Wood asked. "Okay, I'll hang until you get here."

I stared at Wood and wondered if my luck was changing and realized it was when his eyes came to me and he said into the phone, "Yeah, she's awake." And then he held it out to me. "Wants to talk to you, baby."

I walked to him, took the phone, and put it to my ear.

"Hi," I said.

"You okay?" Tate asked and I heard in his tone that he wasn't looking for something to throw but that he had found the whole story amusing.

"Yes," I said shortly, not finding anything amusing.

"Goin' to bed?"

"Yes."

"Wearin' my tee?"

"I haven't changed yet."

"Right, then change of plans. I'm in Denver. I'll be home in less than two hours. Wear nothin' to bed."

I blinked at Wood's feet on the couch.

Then I turned with a jerk and walked toward the kitchen.

"Tate—"

"Naked, babe."

"Tate, I can't—"

He cut me off. "Buck."

I stopped in the kitchen.

"Sorry?"

"Buck naked."

"Wood's here," I whispered.

"He'll be gone in two hours and I'll be there."

"I just got done working the night shift," I reminded him.

"And I just got done apprehending a man out on bail on a murder charge and drivin' over six hundred miles."

"So you'll be tired and I'll be tired—"

"You're naked, I'll find a way to revive you."

"Captain—" I whispered.

"You're not naked, I'll still find a way to revive you."

"Tate, it's three thirty in the morning, you've had a long day. You shouldn't even make that drive."

"Baby, you're naked in my bed, no way I'm not."

"Tate," I said to dead air. He was gone.

I took the phone from my ear and stared at it. It slid from my fingers, my head came up, and I watched Wood flip it closed.

"Go to bed, Laurie," he said quietly, his eyes soft on me.

I swallowed. He was really handsome, almost as beautiful as Tate but in a different way. There was an edge to both men but I got the sense that Tate's was sharper and closer to the surface. Wood's was just as sharp but it ran deeper.

"Okay," I replied then I pulled in breath. "You…today…what you did, looking out for me." I paused. "It was really kind, Wood," I finished on a whisper.

His body moved slightly toward me but he locked it down and I saw his jaw tense.

Then he repeated, "Go to bed, baby."

I nodded, thinking exiting his presence immediately was probably a good idea. I walked by him and headed down the hall.

"Lauren," he called and I stopped and turned back to him. He was leaning into a fist on the kitchen counter and his eyes were on me. "Once we were brothers," he told me and I held my breath. "I'd do anything for him."

I didn't know what this meant and I stayed frozen, staring at him, waiting for him to go on.

When he didn't, I chanced my guess on a whisper. "You miss him."

Wood held my eyes and didn't speak. Then he turned away,

walked across the kitchen, and hit the light switch. The kitchen went dark but I watched Wood in the light coming from the living room walk back to the couch. He dropped down to lounge there, his eyes on the TV, his face blank.

I'd known that whatever had happened, the history and bad blood between Tate and Wood was big.

Now I knew it wasn't big. Whatever it was was colossal.

I wanted to go to him, stretch out beside him, hold him close in my arms, and watch television. Not in a lover-ly way, in a way I sensed he needed.

But that would be bad.

So I turned and walked to Tate's room.

CHAPTER SEVENTEEN

What Do You See?

MY BODY JOLTED awake when I heard the loud bang on the window, a sound like the strong, angry crack of knuckles.

"Bitch! Get out here!"

After the shrieking female's words, the bang came again and I sat up in Tate's bed, holding the covers to my naked chest, looking toward the window and staring in shock at a ghostly face framed with a mass of dark hair staring into the window.

She lifted a fist and banged again, so hard it was a wonder her hand didn't go through the glass. My body jumped with the sound.

"I said, get the fuck out here!" she screeched.

The outside light went on and she was illuminated.

I'd never seen her up close and her face was twisted with fury, making her not at all attractive. Even so, I knew when it untwisted, she'd be a knockout.

"Yeah," she shouted, "I see you, bitch!"

It dawned on me Tate needed curtains. Badly.

"Jesus Christ, Neeta, what the fuck?" I heard Wood's angry clip.

Neeta's head twisted to the side, it jolted with surprise and then she glared.

Then she screamed, "*Traitor!*"

"Get away from Laurie's goddamned window," Wood ordered.

"Fuck you!" Neeta shouted back.

I sat there immobile, shocked at what was happening and unable to move considering she could see me and, as Tate had demanded, I was buck naked between his new, high thread count sheets.

"What's the matter with you?" Wood asked loudly, with anger and frustration clear in his tone. "Honest to God, Neeta, I wanna know."

"And what's the matter with you?" she shot back. "Honest to God, Wood, I wanna know," she mocked, threw out an arm and her knuckles cracked alarmingly against the window also making equally alarming clinking noises because she was wearing rings. "I thought she was yours."

"Get away from her goddamned window!" Wood shouted.

"Just like you," she snarled. "Got no fuckin' balls. Never had any fuckin' *balls*. Word is, Tate nailed her *right under your nose*."

This wasn't exactly true. This also pissed me off.

Not thinking, I left the bed, dragging the sheet with me. I wrapped it around me, rushed to the dresser, pulled open the second drawer down, grabbed the first T-shirt of Tate's on top (one I'd laundered, folded, and replaced just that day), yanked it out and then pulled it over my head as I clutched the sheet to me. Once I got it on, I dropped the sheet, hurried to the closet, pawed through my open suitcase on the floor, grabbed some panties and yanked them on. Then I dashed out of the room.

Buster was close at my heels. She'd been sleeping with me and now she was sticking with me. This was probably because there was more shouting, more hurling of abuse and a fair amount of obscenities coming from outside. I guessed Buster probably had met Neeta but I figured Buster wasn't a big fan of shouting and obscenities and I knew she wasn't a big fan of having her sleep disturbed.

I hit the sliding glass door, which was open, slid through it and tugged it closed, using my foot gentle on Buster to keep her back so she wouldn't get out. I turned to the left and saw Wood was dragging a fighting, hissing Neeta by her upper arm down the deck toward the end where her convertible was parked, top down.

Of course. Neeta drove through the night with the top down.

Neeta saw me, jerked free of Wood and came at me, launching herself my way with such velocity, she nearly bent double when Wood's arm wrapped around her stomach, halting her progress.

She yanked up her torso, her eyes slashed the length of me and she threatened, "I'll rip that shirt off you, you fuckin' bitch."

My eyes went the length of her too. Another very short miniskirt. Another tight tank. A pair of flip-flops. Full makeup even though it was the wee hours of the morning, dawn only a promise.

Taking her in, standing on Tate's deck, facing off against the Dread Neeta, for some reason I was completely composed. I'd never been in a catfight and would have been glad never to get in one in my life. But at that moment I didn't care. It was likely she could kick my ass but maybe I could get a few licks in and I was kind of looking forward to it.

"What did I do to you?" I asked her.

She struggled against her brother's hold, eyes fixed to me. "Take it off right now or I'll rip it off," she hissed.

"I don't even know you," I informed her.

"Laurie, get inside," Wood ordered, his other arm wrapping around Neeta's chest and he was dragging her back.

Neeta threw out a hand and grabbed the railing, successfully stopping Wood from retreating.

"You know me," she snapped.

"I've never met you," I pointed out the obvious.

"You live in Carnal, you *know* me," she repeated. "You also know you're tryin' to take what's *mine*."

"He isn't yours," I stated calmly.

"He's mine," she shot back and threw out an arm indicating the house. "This house is mine." She jabbed a finger at me. "That shirt is mine." She strained against Wood's hold and her eyes got squinty. "His *cock* is mine. He's…fuckin'…*mine*."

I looked to Wood and told him, "She needs medication."

"*Fuck you!*" she shrieked, letting go of the railing and struggling against Wood's grip.

"You can't really believe you can behave like this and think you're going to scare me away. I know about you and I also know Tate wants not one thing to do with you," I declared.

She stopped struggling and looked me straight in the eye.

"Yeah?" she asked. "He tell you that?"

"Yes, he did," I answered.

"That's what he says, bitch, then I whisper in his ear and open my legs and he likes the smell, the taste, and he's right back in there."

"Maybe so," I replied. "But that was before me and he told me I was the best he ever had. He also told me, after two decades of you leaving nothing but bitter in his mouth, I was a sweet the like he never tasted."

I was making some of that up but I thought the situation merited it.

At my words, she quieted in her brother's arms. I watched her stare at me for a second then, when she had no response, I kept going.

"He admitted you were under his skin. He admitted he loved you. But he told me I'm under his skin now, he's worked you out. Or, the way it sounds, you treated him so poorly you worked your own way out." I shook my head and said quietly, "Stupid, honey, you should have done everything to stay where you were. I'm there now and, you have to know, it's a good place to be."

"Shut your fuckin' mouth," she whispered, the words shaking with fury.

I ignored her.

"So, this house isn't mine and this shirt isn't mine, they're Tate's. But *he's* mine."

"*Shut your fuckin' mouth,*" she screeched and started struggling against Wood's hold again but we all heard the roar of the pipes and saw the headlight shine on the house.

I turned and watched Tate ride up the drive and park beside the convertible. There were lots of outside lights shining on the deck, the drive, the area around the garage. He was illuminated fully but he moved so quickly I didn't see him swing off the bike and walk to the deck. It was just that he was suddenly there.

Wood and Neeta had separated but Wood had only moved a few feet away from her. They were facing each other but both of their heads were turned to Tate.

Tate stood there and he wasn't that close to me but I still felt that scary energy sparking as his angry eyes took in the scene.

"Familiar," I heard him mutter, "you two standin' between me and somethin' I want."

I felt a chill enter my bloodstream.

"Send her away," Neeta demanded in a way that it sounded like all she had to do was make the demand and it would be hers.

Tate shook his head. "I'll ask once: Get in your car and go. You don't, Neeta, you can stand out here shoutin' the house down for a month and I won't hear you. You won't exist. Fuck, woman, you already don't."

"I exist," she spat.

"Nope," Tate replied.

"Right," she drawled, leaning back and crossing her arms on her chest. "Baby, I roll my tongue around the tip of your cock, you'll remember I exist."

"Oh yeah, I remember that," Tate returned. "Though, since, I've had a woman who knows how to use her mouth and doesn't forget to check her fuckin' teeth."

Quick as a flash, she leaned forward and planted her hands on her hips.

"You love my teeth!" she hurled at him.

"Told you once, told you a million times, Neet, no man likes a woman's teeth scrapin' his dick. Christ, agony, somethin' you're good at dishin' out in a variety of ways."

"You never complained," she retorted.

"I did, woman, you just never listened," Tate fired back. "Gotta say, never knew what it'd be like to tag a piece I didn't have to give instruction. And, damn babe, trust me, it's fuckin'... *sweet*."

He stopped speaking and I bit my lip, wondering how I felt about being referred to as "a piece" that Tate had "tagged," considering I was guessing he meant me.

Neeta changed tactics and when she did, the deck rocked under my feet.

"You fuck with me, you *never* see Jonas again."

She barely got out the word "again" when Tate took four swift, long, angry strides, all of them right at her.

Her face visibly paling, she retreated on an angle at the last minute but Tate kept bearing down on her until he had her pinned against the railing, his body in her space, the line of it outright hostile. She stared up at him, mouth wide, eyes huge, body braced. She was staggered.

I watched this frozen with morbid fascination.

She'd fucked up his life but he'd never done that before.

Never.

He bent his neck so his face was in hers.

"Warning," he growled. "You use my boy against me, Neeta, I swear to God, you'll regret it."

His boy?

I felt the blood drain from my own face and my head got light.

"And," Tate went on, "I see you within hearing distance of Laurie, I'll fuck with your life so much you'll wish you lived on the goddamned moon."

Neeta recovered and her back went straight.

"I got the papers, Tate, and you can tell your lawyers to go fuck themselves. After this shit, Jonas no longer exists for you."

"He's here next weekend or I swear to Christ—"

"You're a joke!" she cut him off. "Do you think that any judge is gonna give custody of a ten-year-old kid to a bounty hunter who's home two days a month?"

Oh my God.

Tate had a son. Tate and Neeta shared a child. And Tate was going for custody of his son.

I got shit goin' down in my life. I needed to be in my truck, on the trail of a murderer at the same time not seein' to that shit and hemorrhaging more money seein' as I was workin' that on my own time and my own fuckin' dime like I needed a fuckin' hole in my head. You were a distraction.

Here it was.

This was the shit going down in his life. This had something to do with why that night in the hotel, that night before he met me, was the night it finally ended between these two.

Jonas. Tate's ten-year-old boy. A son he never, not once, mentioned.

A son, it was likely Neeta was right, no judge would give to a bounty hunter who was home two days a month.

Unless he had someone in his home to help out. Say, a high-class, good girl who was smart, worked hard, and grew up on a farm. A woman he ran into the day after whatever happened, happened.

I took a step back and noticed Wood make a slight movement. My eyes slid to him and I saw he wasn't watching Tate and Neeta. He was watching me and he was doing it closely.

"Right," Tate bit out and my gaze went back to him. "And do you think any judge is gonna think that what I can give him here isn't better than stayin' with *you*. A woman with a record and a husband with no fuckin' job who drinks himself sick every night? You promised you'd leave that fuckwad and get my boy outta that mess you call a home. You didn't. I told you, you didn't, I'd get him out. And, make no mistake, Neeta," he got closer to her face, "I'll stop at fuckin' *nothin'* to get Jonas out."

"I'll fight you 'til I'm dead, Tate," she retorted, then her eyes slid to me as her arm lifted and she pointed at me. "No way I'm gonna let your whore raise my kid."

Tate's hand shot out and his fingers wrapped around her wrist, twisting it behind her back as she emitted a small cry. I did too just because I was surprised at the vicious way he handled her. But Tate didn't hesitate. He stepped back, turned, moving her with him, and pushed her off. She went back two feet and righted herself.

"Perfect, Tate, thanks," she snapped acidly. "Got witnesses to *that* tender act from my kid's dad."

"Get in your car and go," Tate clipped, holding his body completely still.

"You carry on like this, with her, we'll be free and clear for Blake to adopt the kid and you'll never see him again," she threatened.

"Get in your car and go," Tate repeated.

She ignored him. "I'll parade all your trash for the court." Her eyes came to me. "You aren't the first, darlin', and, trust me, you won't be the last."

"Go," Tate growled, "now."

She looked at Tate and hissed, "Trash."

"Yeah," he replied, still growling. "I've fucked trash. Gotta tell you, Neet, after all those years fuckin' you, you cannot imagine how good it feels to thrust my cock into somethin' sweet and clean."

I pulled in both my lips and bit them, my eyes going to Wood. His eyes were fastened to the show that was happening not three feet in front of him.

Neeta glared at Tate and Tate's back was to me but I suspected he held her glare. Then her eyes went to Wood.

"He's talkin' to your sister, you got nothin' to say?" she snapped.

"Kills me," Wood whispered and I felt my heart stutter because the tone of those two words elegantly underlined that what he was going to say next did, in a way, kill him. "But I know, I've known for a long time but with this fuckin' mess you orchestrated tonight, Neet, I know nothin's changed."

"What?" she hissed.

"You," Wood replied and then he was whispering again, "Jonas? Neeta, seriously?"

"I'll not—" she started.

"Keep custody, you keep actin' like a goddamned lunatic," Wood cut in. "And, I gotta say, Neet, I fuckin' hope you don't. I just hope you and Blake haven't fucked that kid up so much he ends up like one of you."

"You asshole," she whispered.

Wood looked at Tate.

Then he stated firmly, "Anything you need, man. Anything you fuckin' need."

Then he turned, walked right to me, lifted a hand and curled it around the side of my neck. His fingers squeezed while his eyes searched mine in a way I thought he was communicating something but I was too stunned by what had happened, what I'd learned, to understand what it might mean. He gave my neck another squeeze, released me, and walked down the deck, right by Neeta and Tate and right to his bike. He got on, started it up, and roared down the drive.

When he turned into the road, I heard Neeta warn, "You just bought the fight of your life."

My eyes went back to her to see she was glaring up at Tate. He didn't move but I heard him sigh. It was deep and it was heavy and I knew exactly what it communicated. He was done. He was angry. He was over this. And he was going to take her on, no matter what she brought.

Not getting a reaction, she tore her eyes from Tate and they cut to me.

"Watch your back, bitch," she snapped, turned, and ran gracefully on her flip-flops to her convertible. She started it up with an alarming rev of her engine, backed out, and sped down the drive so fast, gravel flew.

My body had turned to watch her go. I was so intent on doing this, I jumped when I felt Tate's hand settle on the space where my neck hit my shoulder.

"Baby," he whispered and my eyes moved to him.

God, he was beautiful.

He was also a liar, a playing, hideous *liar.*

I swallowed then jerked away from his hold, turned and ran to the sliding glass door. I tugged it open, ran inside and down the hall, straight to his room. I flipped on the light switch then ran to the closet and flipped on the light switch there. I was on my knees, zipping one of my suitcases closed when Tate was there.

"What are you doing?" he asked and I looked up briefly to see him standing at the doorway, then I looked back down at my case.

"Leaving," I whispered.

"Laurie," he said quietly and my head jerked back and I glared at him.

"Fuck you!" I shouted, surged up, and took two wide steps toward him, planted my hands on his chest, and shoved. He went back on a foot, his fingers wrapped around both of my wrists and held strong. "Fuck you!" I repeated.

"Ace, calm down." He was still talking quietly.

"Jonas?" I asked.

"Babe—" he started but I ripped my wrists from his hold and went back to my bag, dropping to my knees in front of it.

"Fuck you, Tate," I snapped, yanking the zip on my bag even though it was caught in a T-shirt I hadn't tucked in. "God!" I cried, shaking my head. "What is the *matter* with me? How do I get messed up with this kind of *shit?*"

"Lauren, calm down and come into the bedroom so we can talk," Tate ordered.

I shook my head, still struggling with the zip. "Oh no. No way. You've had your chance to talk. You've had plenty of opportunity to tell me you have *a son.* A son with that…that…," my head whipped back and I looked him in the eye, "that *woman.*"

"Ace, listen to me—"

I shot up to my feet and rounded on him. "I went to bed *naked,* Tate. I *never* sleep naked. I don't like to sleep naked. It isn't comfortable. And I did that *for you*." I stabbed a finger toward him then threw up both my hands. "God, what a fool! I should have known. You," I thrust a finger at him again, "want me? What the fuck was I thinking?"

"Lauren—"

"An old, fat, sorry-assed bitch." I hurled his words at him. "That'd work, Tate. Good call, honey. At least that old, fat, sorry-assed bitch would work when paraded in front of a judge as a show you could give a stable home to Jonas!"

One second he was standing in the door, the next second I was pinned against the back wall of the closet. He'd moved so fast, and I'd retreated so automatically, I didn't even know how I got there. I just felt the wall against my back and Tate was deep in my space. I felt that energy coming from him, so strong it was a flood and it enveloped me so tight it felt like there was no oxygen in the air to breathe. His body wasn't hostile, not like he was with Neeta, but it was aggressive in a way that I had absolutely no choice but to pay attention.

"That's the last time you get to throw that in my face," he whispered and even his voice scared the shit out of me.

I sucked in breath and, in doing so, tried to suck in courage. "Step back, Tate. I'm leaving."

"You have nothin' to do with Jonas." He was still whispering.

"Step back," I demanded.

His face came to within an inch of mine. "Not one fuckin' thing."

"Right," I shot back, my tone filled with sarcasm.

"She promised me she was leavin' him," he said. "She promised me she'd come home, bring my boy home, we'd start over, she'd get her shit together, we'd have a life, a family."

I made no response but that didn't matter, Tate kept talking.

"But she showed and she was supposed to bring Jonas. She didn't. She just wanted to get off. She likes to get off. She likes to suck cock. Her man, he drinks so much, his dick is so limp, it's been so long since he used it for more than to take a piss it's a wonder it hasn't fallen off. She came back not to make a family. She promised that shit just to get *my cock*. Just to *get off*. Christ, Lauren, this woman is raising *my son*."

"Tate, step—"

"I was through with her before. We'd been fightin' this battle for ten years. Broken promises from her which led to us bein' in and outta court for control of Jonas. Her asshole of a husband would lose another job or lose another game of cards and back in court we'd go. Not for custody, for more support so I could prop up her and that dickless husband of hers. Jonas can't suffer so what do I do, Lauren? What do I do?"

"Tate—"

"I give more. He drinks it or gambles it. She snorts it or smokes it. Christ, who knows?" Tate bit out. "I gotta juggle everything so I don't miss a weekend with him. Twice a month I get to see him. That is, twice a month until that night, when she showed up at the hotel room, I got inside and my son wasn't there and I knew her game. I knew, no matter how sweet she could tell her lies, she'd played me again and used my kid to do it. So that was it and she knew it. We didn't fight. I told her to get her shit sorted because my attorney would be in touch. She tried to play me again but I was done. You don't use my kid against me, not for a fuckin' orgasm, for fuck's sake."

"Tate, I—"

"I haven't seen him in two months, Lauren. Your shit, Tonia's shit, needin' to work so I can pay my bills and keep my kid fed because neither of those two do jack. I haven't seen my boy."

"I'm sorry, but—"

"I get home, that scene goes down and you...what? I don't even know what the fuck you're on about."

"I know why you're with me," I told him.

"Yeah, babe? And why's that?"

"I..." I took in a breath then started again. "I don't have any kids but that sounds awful, Tate. I'm sorry about that, it sounds... I'm sorry about it. And I can understand why you'd do anything you

could to get Jonas but you can't act like Neeta. You can't play someone else to take care of your son."

His head tipped to the side. "Act like Neeta?"

"To make a home for your son. Make a family. Make something a
judge would look at favorably and use me to do it."

His brows snapped together under narrowed eyes.

"Use you to do it?" he repeated.

"Yes," I stated. "That's why you're with me. A man like you...a
woman like me." I shook my head and whispered, "I didn't get it but
I get it now."

"Tell me you're shittin' me," he demanded.

"Sorry?" I asked.

He moved quickly and he did this to pound the side of his fist on
the wall by my head.

He got in my face and shouted, "*Tell me you're shittin' me!*"

I jumped with the fist action and went still at his shouting in
my face. Then I shouted back, "No Tate! I am *not* shitting you! I get
it! You can stop...," I got up on my toes and got into his face too,
"fucking...*playing* me!"

He took a step back and then I was in the air. I blinked at his
back in surprise and realized I was over his shoulder as he turned and
stalked to the door of the closet.

"What on—?"

"Shut it," he growled.

"Tate, put me down!" I shouted, putting my hands to his waist
and pushing as my feet kicked and he rounded the bed.

I felt his palm smack my ass. It wasn't light, it wasn't harsh, but it
made a point.

"Shut it, Lauren."

I shut it. I'd never been spanked before. Not in my life. My dad
wasn't afraid of discipline but he dished it out verbally.

Tate carried me to the bathroom. The light went on. He bent and
put me on my feet. Then he jerked my body to facing the vanity and
mirror and he moved in, pinning me to the edge of the basin counter.

"Look," he ordered.

"What?" I whispered, still recovering from being hauled bodily into the bathroom and pinned to the counter against my will.

One of his arms locked around my ribcage, his other hand curled under my jaw and he leaned in, forcing me forward over the basin.

"Look," he demanded. "What do you see?"

"Tate—"

"What do you see?" he repeated on a growl.

With no choice and more than a little scared, I looked at him in the mirror and answered. "I see me."

"What do you see?" he reiterated.

"Tate, I see me," I whispered.

"Lauren, look at you, not me. What the fuck do you see?"

I stared at him in the mirror and then my eyes went to my reflection.

"I see me," I said softly and I did.

"Who did it to you?" Tate asked, releasing my jaw and he bent farther forward, his hand covering mine on the counter.

"Did what?" I asked.

"Twisted what you see," he answered. "'Cause, babe, I'm guessin', with that shit you just fed me, what you see ain't what I see."

My breath caught and I remained silent.

"I know it ain't your folks. They see what I see, so who did it?"

"Tate," I breathed but said no more. My heart was beating wildly. I could feel it in my chest, my neck, my wrists and my legs felt like jelly. If he wasn't pressing me into the counter and holding me up, I was certain I'd fall.

His hand left mine at the counter and his arm at my ribs moved us slightly back so he could pull up the tee, exposing my panties and bunching the shirt under his arm. Then both of his arms locked tight around me and he pressed me into the counter again.

"Baby," he whispered, "I don't fuckin' get it. Is it easier for you to see what he made you think was there? And if that's it, why? What the fuck are you protecting yourself from?"

"I…" I swallowed. "I don't understand."

"No, babe, you don't. He twisted it in so deep, you can't straighten it out but look, look at you." My eyes stayed locked to his in the mirror and he urged softly, "Laurie, baby, look at you."

I forced my eyes to my reflection and I took it in, all of it. Not only me, my hips, undies, and belly exposed, my breasts resting on his forearm, my hair a mess around my makeup-free face, and Tate behind me, tall, dark, broad, and beautiful.

"You said you were waitin' for something special and he took away your chance to figure out that you were carryin' it with you all this time. *You* are special, Laurie."

No.

No.

I closed my eyes and clenched my teeth, tilting my head down and to the side, automatically trying to block out his words.

Tate's mouth came to my ear. "That gay guy, those hippies, even fuckin' Twyla showed up to have your back tonight. They did it because they see what your folks see, what I see. They did it because somethin' special hit Carnal two months ago and they did it because you go all out to protect beauty like that."

His words hit me like a silken blow and my breath hitched as I swallowed a sob.

His mouth went to my neck and he spoke there. "You're right, baby. I like the idea of Jonas knowin' you, learnin' from you, how to work hard and be smart and treat people. But you're wrong. You're in my bed because I've never had beauty like that and I got a shot at it and you think you can twist our shit in your head into something ugly, fuck that. I won't stop until I set it straight."

My eyes opened. I looked at him in the mirror and his head came up to look at me.

"Why didn't you tell me you had a son?"

"Because Wood was right," Tate answered instantly.

"Sorry?" I asked.

"Because, shit like that—not Jonas but what I got in my future to beat that bitch and get him safe—you don't lay on a good woman when you and her are just startin' out. Especially not when another woman's been brutally murdered and your old lady's dad had a heart attack. You stick close, you stand strong and you work to hook her deep and *then* you lay it on her. I want you where you are." His arms gave me a squeeze. "So yeah, I played you and I'd do it again, no joke, I'd do it. And I'd do it with no hesitation. I needed to know you were what the promise of you seemed to be because I haven't been good with that shit in the past and, if you were, I needed to make certain you stayed where I wanted you to be."

"Keeping the existence of a son from me—"

He interrupted me, "I'd do it again."

"Well, I don't like that. I can't ignore that I don't like it and I can't forgive it."

"Same old shit, Laurie," he muttered.

"No, it isn't. We're talking about you having *a child* with *Neeta*."

"Yeah, babe. Was that a pleasant scene? Did you like what happened outside?"

"What?" I snapped and answered, "Of course not."

"Twenty years of that," he told me. "Twenty fuckin' years. She's got a filthy mouth and shit for brains and she's spoiled rotten and thinks she can do anything she wants. No man who's had a woman like that in his life jumps back in without testin' the waters and no father who's goin' for full custody brings a woman in his son's life without makin' sure she's fit to be there. No, I didn't tell you about Jonas because I needed to be certain you were who you are and, since you are, I needed to keep you safe from that shit you just experienced outside because I didn't want you jumpin' in your goddamned car again and findin' yourself a new Carnal."

God, I *hated* it when he made sense, *especially* when I was furious at him.

"Let me go, Tate," I demanded.

"Not gonna happen," he replied.

I strained backward. "Let…me…*go*."

"Nope, baby, you're gonna watch in the mirror as I fuck you and I'm gonna do it until you see what I see."

I stopped straining and stared into his eyes in the mirror.

"No," I whispered as one of his hands slid down my belly and the other one ducked under my shirt and curled around my breast.

"Yes," he whispered back.

"Tate—"

His hand cupped me between my legs and his other thumb slid across my nipple. I bit my lip and watched his eyes drop to his hand at my sex.

"Wood's a player," he whispered bizarrely as his fingers pressed in between my legs, his middle one hitting the spot; my hands moved to curl around the edge of the counter and his thumb did another swipe at my nipple. "He's hit every decent piece in three counties."

His middle finger pressed deeper and made a lazy circle.

"Tate, please—"

Tate's head dropped and his bearded lips tickled my neck.

"Saw him come outta the garage at you, I knew," he muttered against my skin. "I was strugglin' with it but I knew then. I knew you were my girl."

My breath stuck in my throat as his finger did another lazy circle, his tongue touched my neck, and his finger and thumb rolled my nipple.

Oh *God,* but it was beautiful.

My hands grasped the counter and I tried to stay strong.

"Tate—"

His finger stopped pressing and his hand slid up and then down, this time in my panties and the pressure came back, skin to skin, another lazy circle.

Delicious.

My body trembled and Tate's mouth moved to my ear.

"He didn't fuck you while I was gone. A miracle. Respect. He knew what he had in his bed."

"Please," I whispered and his finger and thumb gently tugged my nipple and my breath snagged.

"Even if he fucked you, I woulda still won you back. Mad as I was when I left you that night in the hall at the bar, I was half over it by the time I got to my bike. By the time I saw you at the pool the next day, mostly just nursin' it 'cause I'm a dick."

"Stop," I breathed and I meant him talking. My body was too far gone to want him to stop doing what he was doing to it.

His finger slid back and I opened my legs to allow it access.

"That's my girl," he murmured in my ear and reached even deeper, his finger sliding inside.

My head fell back on his shoulder. "Tate."

His teeth nipped my ear and his finger started moving in and out.

"Wet, baby," he whispered in my ear.

"Yes," I whispered back and turned my head toward him.

His came up. He knew what I wanted and, thank God, he gave it to me. He kissed me, deep and hard as he finger fucked me, the fingers of his other hand rolling my nipple, his thumb tweaking my clit. He kept kissing me while his hands moved on me until my breath started coming in gasps. I was so close, my hips were moving with his hand between my legs, reaching for it.

His head came up, my eyes fluttered open and saw his on me.

"Look, baby," he urged.

I ground down on his hand and it stopped moving, his finger deep inside and his eyes went to the mirror.

"Jesus, Laurie, baby, look at you."

My eyes followed his, mainly because I wanted him to keep at me and I'd do just about anything he told me to do to get it.

But what I saw made my heart skip and my legs fail.

Tate, dark, tall, behind me, his hands on me. Me, blonde, my face flushed, my eyes hooded, tucked tight against him. A perfect fit, made to be there. A perfect match, made to be together.

Made to be there.

Made to be together.

We looked great.

We looked hot.

We looked beautiful.

My eyes went to his in the mirror.

"Fuck me," I whispered.

His eyes locked on mine, then he shoved his face in my neck. His arm fastened around my ribcage again but his finger slid out of me. Then my panties were yanked down past my hips and I felt him working his jeans at my backside.

"Tilt your ass for me, Laurie," he muttered into my neck and I did as asked. I felt the tip of his cock and then he thrust inside.

My head flew back.

He started moving and I watched in the mirror as Tate fucked me, one arm wrapped around my ribcage, his torso bent over mine, his other hand between my legs, finger at my clit, his eyes on mine in the mirror.

"Do you see it?" he demanded, his thrusts building in power, his finger circling faster.

"I see it," I breathed, the urge building inside me, my hips rearing back to meet his thrusts.

He drove in, burying himself to the root and stayed planted.

"Why do I want you here, Laurie?" he growled.

"Don't stop, baby," I pleaded.

He ground his cock deeper. "Why do I want you here?"

"Tate—"

"Why, baby?"

"We're perfect," I whispered. "We fit," I kept whispering and pressed back into his hips. "Honey, I'm made to be here."

He pulled out so fast I gasped and then I was over his shoulder again and he walked out of the bathroom into the bedroom. With a bump of his shoulder he tossed me on the bed, straightened and yanked his T-shirt off. Then he reached down and tore my undies down my legs. He spread them wide and he was covering me, back inside, thrusting harder, faster, pounding. God, ecstasy.

His mouth took mine in a deep, wet kiss then I tore it away.

"Tate," I moaned as it hit me, my nails scored a path up his back and my spine arched, pressing my torso into his.

It took me a while to ride the wave and come down and, when I did, he wasn't done.

"Wrap me up, Laurie," he groaned between grunts and I folded my limbs tight around him. His mouth came to mine. "There it is," he muttered then growled deep and plunged deeper as he came.

I felt it and listened and held him tight and when he was done his teeth tagged my lower lip, giving it a gentle tug before he let it go, and his tongue slid along it.

I closed my eyes, my mind completely clear and just let myself feel the sweet path of his tongue.

It went away and stayed away and I noticed I didn't even feel his breath against my lips so I opened my eyes again.

Tate's head was tipped back and he was staring beyond me, a hint of surprised puzzlement in his face.

"What—?" he started, stopped, a slow, lazy smile spreading on his face and his eyes moved to mine.

I was so busy watching his lips, framed by his beard smiling, it took a while to feel his body's gentle tremors and a while longer to realize it was silent laughter.

My gaze flew from his mouth to his eyes.

"Tate?"

"Baby," he whispered, "you bought a new comforter." My breath caught, his head twisted and he looked at the head of the bed then at me, his body shuddering less gently now, it was full on quakes. "And sheets."

Oh God, he noticed. He'd been on the bed for approximately two seconds after fucking me and he noticed I bought a new comforter and sheets.

Why was I such an idiot?

"Um…," I mumbled.

He burst out laughing, his hips pressing deep into mine making me gasp as his hands tagged the back of my knees, pulled them up, and tucked my legs tight to his sides.

"You bought me sheets," he repeated, his voice clogged with laughter.

"Um...actually," I started timidly, "I bought them for me, seeing as I was sleeping in them."

His head came up. "Yeah? And the comforter?"

Yes, *such* an idiot!

"I was sleeping under that too."

"And you didn't think about me sleepin' under it?"

"No," I lied.

"So, you go back to the hotel, you take them with you?"

"Um...," I hesitated. "No," I whispered.

He grinned. "Right."

"Yours were a little...well..."

His head moved so he could look back at the sheets at the head of the bed then over mine at the comforter, then his eyes came back to mine.

"Yeah, Ace, I can see these are a whole lot better than mine."

"Um..."

"High-class girl, nice fancy sheets."

I felt my body get tense.

"They aren't fancy."

"Babe, in comparison, they are."

They were, darn it all.

I made no reply. Tate's face got closer.

"Ace, you wanna tell me why, half the time after I finish fuckin' you, I'm still inside you and I'm laughing?"

"I've no idea," I replied haughtily.

His face changed, his eyes warmed, his hand came up, fingers sliding into the hair at the side my head and his mouth came to mine.

Then he whispered, "I do."

I fought back my more than pleasant response to all of that but I only won the fight in my head. My traitorous body melted under his.

"You weren't supposed to notice them," I informed him and he burst out laughing again, going so far as to throw his head back to do it, such was the hilarity of my comment.

He slid out of me, rolled off, gained his feet by the side of the bed, and then tugged me to standing in front of him.

I stood there while he shifted around me, pivoting me with him with hands at my hips and he sat down on the bed in front of me.

He bent and tugged off his boots and socks while asking, "How did you think I wasn't gonna notice?"

"You're a man. Men don't notice sheets."

He dropped his second boot and went after the sock, tilting his head back to look at me as he did. "Babe, we do."

"Well...," I muttered, feeling stupid standing in front of him, so I crossed my arms on my chest. "Whatever," I finished lamely.

He chuckled as he stood up and his arms wrapped around me. He kissed my neck, still chuckling, then let me go and tugged his jeans down.

"Any other surprises? New towels? Bath mat? Did you order a new grape-Kool-Aid-free-zone couch?"

"No," I snapped, again haughty even though he was being kind of funny.

"What happened? Not enough time?" he teased.

"Tate, I'm not finding this funny," I informed him, somewhat lying.

He sat again, pulled me between his legs with an arm around my waist, then fell back, taking me with him and twisting us so we were lying right in the bed. He twitched the comforter over us then came up on his forearm and looked across the room.

"What's the top sheet doin' on the floor?"

I got up on my elbows and looked where he was looking. Then my head turned to him.

"Neeta was banging at the window and looking in. I was naked so I had to use the sheet to...um..." I stopped talking because he didn't look amused and content anymore.

His eyes moved to the windows.

Then he muttered, "Fuckin' bitch."

"Tate," I called and his eyes came back to me.

"Tomorrow, you buy curtains," he ground out.

"Um...," I looked at the clock on his nightstand to see it was nearly six in the morning, "it *is* tomorrow."

"What shift you got?"

"I'm off."

He grinned, came off his forearm and rested his weight mostly on me so I was forced to slide off my elbows.

He shoved his face in my neck and stated, "Good, then *we'll* buy curtains," and he kissed my neck.

"Tate," I called again as he moved off me, settled on his side and pulled me into his arms, front to front, face to face.

"Sleep, Ace," he ordered, his voice suddenly sounding tired. "Then shoppin'."

"Um...," I said to him, thinking about shopping with Tate and liking those thoughts, rather than thinking about Tate having a son, that scene with Neeta and all the other things I should be thinking about and I noticed his eyes were closed. "Are we done talking?"

"For now, yeah," he answered.

"Um...," I mumbled again. "Perhaps we should—"

His eyes opened and with one look into them, I quit talking.

Then I whispered, "The lights are on."

His head came up and then he turned, rolled out of bed and, naked, he went to the bathroom, switched out the light, went to the closet and switched out the light, went to the bedroom door, and switched out the light.

I watched as he came back to bed, got in, and rolled back to me. His arm came around me and he pulled me close again, front to front.

"Tate—"

"Babe, bad guy, titty bar, lots of road, Neeta, dealin' with you, and a really sweet orgasm. Honest to God, I don't have a lot more in me."

"Okay," I whispered instantly.

Yes, his good girl. Always a good girl, now his.

Such.

An.

Idiot.

His head bent, he touched his mouth to mine then his hands rolled me so my back was to him. He leaned in, hitching my leg with his knee in the back of mine, his arm curled around my belly, his face burrowed into my hair and I took the rest of his weight which pinned me to the bed.

"Sweet dreams, baby," he whispered into my hair, his arm giving me a squeeze. "See you on the other side."

"You too, Captain," I whispered back and stared at the light clay–colored pillowcase in front of me, the water-colored brushstrokes of sun hitting it.

He'd noticed the sheets.

I felt Buster jump up on the bed. She walked up Tate's and my legs to our hips and then back down and her weight disappeared. She tucked herself into the crook of our knees, likely curled and ready to resume her Crazy Neeta disturbed sleep.

It didn't take her or her master long. Both of them were out within minutes.

I didn't know it but it took me precisely two minutes longer to join them.

CHAPTER EIGHTEEN

Curtains

"ACE," I HEARD Tate call and my eyes fluttered open.

My neck twisted and I saw he was sitting on the bed but was leaning down, forearm in the mattress, other hand on my waist, his face close to mine.

"What?" I asked, mind fogged with sleep.

"Curtains," he answered and I closed my eyes.

"You can get them. That big home store outside the mall. They have a wide variety," I informed him and snuggled my head into the pillow.

"Laurie," he called.

"Mm?" I answered.

"Babe, wake up," he ordered and my eyes opened again.

I looked at the clock. It was just after eleven. Way too early. No way I was getting up.

I closed my eyes again.

His hand slid from my waist, to my hip, and back to my behind as I felt his presence invade the space around me.

"Baby, you did my laundry." I heard him whisper in my ear.

His words tugged forcefully at the sleep that had hold of me and my body tensed.

"And cleaned my house," he went on whispering.

I turned my face partially into the pillow and pressed in as the edges of sleep started to separate with jagged little tears that I knew, from experience, would never mend.

"And the fridge," he continued.

"Quiet," I muttered, the word muffled in the pillow.

"Fridge is jammed, babe, more food than it's ever seen."

This was true. Seeing as I had a full, clean fridge for the first time in months, not to mention a kitchen, a couple of days before I went a little nuts at the grocery store.

"Go away," I mumbled.

"We got grape Kool-Aid."

"Go. Away."

"In a new pitcher."

I turned my face fully into the pillow and groaned.

His beard tickled my shoulder and then his lips kissed me there.

"Sweet pitcher, babe. Never owned one of those."

In the window of the little country shop (that happened to be two doors down from the grocery store) they had these adorable, big, old-fashioned glass pitchers with a beautiful shape, dimpled glass, and they were tinted pink. Now Tate had this pitcher.

They also had matching glasses. Tate probably didn't look but the glasses were in the cupboard.

I lifted my head, his body jerked back a foot, and I glared at his grinning, arrogant, beautiful face.

"Go! Away!" I snapped and suddenly I was on my feet by the bed and just as suddenly I was in front of Tate, his hands at my hips, and I was moving toward the bathroom. "Tate!"

"Seein' as you're up, time to shower," he stated, shoving me into the bathroom.

I twisted my head around and gave him a look.

"You think you're funny but you…are…*not*."

He whipped my body around, his arm went around my waist and held me close to his T-shirted, jeaned front and he reached beyond me, opening the door to the shower. He turned on the taps, the water shot down and he looked down at me.

"Curtains," he muttered.

I glared up at him then muttered back, "Whatever," turned to the shower, stuck my hand in, found it was hot, yanked off his tee that I was wearing and stepped in, firmly closing the door behind me.

* * *

I was still nursing my grudge at all things Tate (primarily his waking me up, being arrogant, and finding his morning amusing after I had *the* worst night of my life, a night that contained Brad, Neeta, and the unexpected knowledge of ten-year-old Jonas) when Tate, me beside him, drove his Explorer into Carnal on our way to the mall.

I had been silent all morning as I got ready, something Tate found funny if the amount of times I saw him grin, smile, or heard him chuckle was any indication as he came in and out of the bedroom or stood at the counter in the kitchen sifting through his piles of post while I was preparing for my day, making the bed, replacing the be-shammed pillows, and getting myself coffee.

I spied the coffee shop and fairly shouted, "La-La Land!"

Tate's head turned to me. "Come again?"

"Stop. Park. Coffee. Orgasmic bread. Now," I demanded.

"Orgasmic bread?" Tate asked.

"Tate, you're passing it!" I cried desperately as we went past, my head turning to watch the shop through the window. "Park!"

Tate braked and swung into a parking spot three doors down from La-La Land. He barely had the ignition switched off before I had the door open, hopped down, slammed the door shut, and was motoring.

I was nearly there when I was hooked with an arm across my chest and pulled back into the solidness that was all Tate.

"Hang on there, Ace, the shop isn't gonna go up in a puff of smoke," he said into my hair as I forced us forward even though we were locked together.

"Unh-hunh," I said back, pushed open the door to La-La Land and entered, pulling Tate with me.

"Flower Petal!" Shambles cried upon seeing me, his face lighting up behind his round blue-tinted sunglasses. Then his eyes went to Tate and his face froze.

Sunny's head popped up down the counter.

"Petal," she said, smiling at me and her smile didn't waver when her eyes went to Tate. She watched as, still locked together, he moved us to the counter.

"Hey guys, what's today's theme?" I asked.

"Who's that?" Shambles asked, stealthily moving away from the front counter toward the back.

"Ignore him, I am," I stated audaciously, seeing as Tate still had his arm around me, and I looked in the display case. "Let me guess, chocolate?"

That wasn't so much a guess as a dream.

Tate's other arm joined his first wrapped around my chest.

"Lemon," Sunny answered and came to stand in front of Tate and I at the counter. "Hey, dude, I'm Sunny," she said to Tate.

"Tate," Tate replied.

"Awesome, Tate. This is my man, Shambles." She gestured to Shambles.

"Dude," Shambles muttered, eyeing up Tate and me in a way I didn't really notice but if I had I would have seen it was like a brother would eye up his sister's new boyfriend. Uncertain, tentative, holding back, and ready to pass resoundingly negative judgment if the new boyfriend gave even a hint of being a jerk.

I ignored this, focused on processing my disappointment that Shambles had yet to hit on a chocolate theme at the same time surveying the case seeing lemon drizzle cake, lemon squares, and lemon curd–filled cupcakes and wondering what I was going to order.

I looked at Shambles. "What do you recommend?"

"Um...," Shambles mumbled, still eyeing Tate, still not quite certain how his judgment would come down.

"That's hard," Sunny put in. "Shambles is a master with lemon."

After she imparted this knowledge, I stared at her. Then, knowing what it meant, I ordered, "I'll take one of anything with lemon in it."

Tate burst out laughing behind me, his arms going tight. His head moved so he could shove his face into my neck where I felt his beard tickle me and his lips kissing me.

Shambles looked at me then he looked at Tate's head bent to my neck. Then he took two steps forward.

"Dude," he called and Tate's head came up.

"Yeah?"

Shambles swallowed and his Adam's apple bobbed when he did.

"You look like you like her but Petal doesn't look like she likes you. What gives?"

"Petal?" Tate whispered in my ear.

"She's flowery," Sunny answered him. "See? At her ears and her wrists and her neck. Flowers. Petal. Get it?"

Tate curved me around to face him and his eyes went from my ears to my neck to my eyes.

"Flowery," he muttered and something about his deep, rough voice saying that word slid through me in a way that felt *really* nice.

Even so, I demanded, "Do you mind letting me go so I can have something lemon chased by coffee?"

Tate didn't answer verbally but him not letting me go was his answer physically. His fingers came to my neck and I felt one twist a chain there, tightening it. His eyes watched his movements then they came to my face.

"That dick buy you these?" he asked.

"No," I answered truthfully wondering, if I said yes, if Tate would rip it off, which he seemed like he was preparing to do.

Then I realized, outside my wedding and engagement rings, Brad had never bought me jewelry. In fact, he'd not bought me many presents. In fact, even though my college boyfriend remembered my birthday every year, Brad normally forgot it, even though I always made a big to-do about his and spent weeks prior dropping hints about mine. Ditto with our anniversary. At first, I used to remind him. The last two years of our marriage, I didn't bother.

"You got anything he gave you?" Tate asked as his finger released the chain at my neck.

My eyes slid to the side and I thought about it.

They slid back and I answered, "No, except a lot of really bad memories and the knowledge that I was stupid enough to put up with him for ten years."

"Right," Tate said then asked, "You done bein' pissed at me, again for no reason?"

I felt my body get tight.

Then I whispered, "No reason?"

"Babe," was his response.

"You have a child!" I shouted, trying to pull back but both his arms went around me and he yanked me forward.

"Yeah and you get to meet him next weekend."

Oh no. I hadn't thought of that.

I wasn't exactly good with children. I wasn't bad with them, as such. I just wasn't around them much and, because of that, when I was, they freaked me out because I didn't know what to do with them.

"Oh my God," I breathed.

"He lives with those idiots but he's a good kid, takes care of his mom, puts up with that jackass. Patient. Smart. Loyal. Funny. You'll like him. He'll like you."

"Oh my God," I breathed again, not even hearing his words. Instead, thinking of a ten-year-old Tate and wondering what on earth I'd do with him. I didn't even know what to do with a forty-four-year-old Tate and I was used to dealing with adults!

"Petal, you okay?" Shambles asked and I turned woodenly in Tate's arms.

"Tate has a ten-year-old son," I told Shambles and Shambles's eyes shot to Tate.

"Cool!" Sunny shouted. "I like! Kids are *awesome*!"

I stared at her.

"Kids *are* awesome, Petal," Shambles said quietly.

"Unh-hunh," I mumbled. "Coffee. Multiple lemon treats. Stat."

"I'll get the treats, you get the coffee, Shams," Sunny said on a grin and looked at Tate. "You?"

"Dazzle me," Tate invited and Sunny's grin spread to a smile.

"I can do that!" she cried and turned to get a bag.

Shambles leaned toward me and, with a jerk of the thumb toward Tate, he whispered as if Tate weren't right there, "Petal, dude's into you."

"Coffee, Shambles," I prompted.

"I'm a dude and even as a dude I can see this dude is *all* dude. That isn't a bad thing, especially with the rumors I hear around town. *All* of them. You get what I'm sayin'?"

"Shambles, honey, coffee," I repeated.

"You guys havin' a tiff?" he asked.

"His ex is a nightmare," I shared.

"I missed it last night but word on the street is your ex isn't too groovin' either."

This was true. I didn't admit that because I heard Tate chuckle.

I leaned into Shambles. "His ex is a nightmare's nightmare. You know, the kind where you wake up and you think you're safe but then you realize you're still asleep and you're still in the nightmare but this one is way worse and finally you wake up with a jolt and your skin is all tingly and you know, you *just know* someone is in the room and you're going to be brutally attacked and killed." I leaned back. "That's Tate's ex."

"She isn't wrong," Tate agreed.

"Bummer," Shambles muttered.

"Unh-hunh," I mumbled. "She visited last night at about five o'clock in the morning. She woke me up by shouting through the window and banging on it, calling me a bitch. I'd never met her before in my life. There was a lot of shouting and obscenities and then there was more shouting and obscenities but these were liberally mixed with threats. The last thing she told me was to watch my back. And she told Tate she would fight him until she died so he'd never see his son again. Now, I've had about five hours of sleep and I need coffee. Can you do that for me, Shambles?"

"Your life is pretty wild, Petal," Shambles observed.

"Thus my need for lemon treats and really, really good coffee, Shambles," I replied. "You're keeping me standing."

Shambles smiled. "I better get you coffee then."

"That would be good."

Shambles shuffled to the espresso machine and Sunny filled his spot.

"Here we go," she announced, proffering a big bag. "Two lemon squares. Two lemon-curd cupcakes. Two slices of lemon gingerbread with pistachios. And two pieces of lemon drizzle cake."

I reached forward, took the bag, opened it, yanked out the first thing my fingers touched (lemon drizzle cake) and I took a huge bite.

"Jesus, Ace," Tate mumbled and I knew by his voice he was smiling.

I twisted to him, lifted the cake to his mouth, he looked at it, looked in my eyes, leaned forward, and took a big bite.

Then he chewed.

Then he swallowed.

Then he said, "Gotcha."

"Unh-hunh," I muttered and turned back to Sunny. "Two more of each, please."

Tate burst out laughing.

Shambles cried in Tate's direction, "Dude! Give me a chance, I'll rock your world."

I twisted to Tate again, looked up and suggested, "Take him up on that."

Tate looked at Shambles. "Rock my world," he invited, then he looked at me, his fingers curled around my wrist. He lifted my hand to his mouth and he took another huge bite of my cake.

"Hey!" I exclaimed, pulling my hand back. "That's my cake."

"Yeah," Tate muttered, mouth full, his hand moved to my neck, his thumb at my jaw tilting my head back and his head bent. He swallowed, then he kissed me, a kiss that was short but included a sweep of his lemony tongue.

Beautiful.

His mouth left mine and he asked, "You still pissed?"

"I don't think so," I answered, still tasting lemon and Tate so it was debatable, but it might be physically impossible to be pissed.

He grinned. "Give it time, somethin'll come up."

I turned and rolled my eyes to Sunny who was grinning at the both of us.

Then I took another bite of cake.

Heaven.

*   *   *

We were in the home store and Tate was pushing the cart as only men do. That was to say, he was bent at the waist, his forearms crossed on the handle, his chest leaning into them, the look on his face part glazed, part blank indicating clearly any question I could ask him would receive the answer, "Hunh?"

I was leading the way to the curtain section while realizing Tate's rabid need to go shopping for curtains was because, with Neeta on the loose, he needed curtains. Not because he needed to shop. Shopping was the necessary evil that came with owning curtains.

He'd seemed game until I commandeered a cart at the entrance.

"We're buying curtains, babe, that activity hardly requires a cart," he noted.

"We're in a home store, Tate," I replied, thinking my answer said all.

"And?" he returned, stating plainly my answer did not say all.

"A mega home store," I added.

"And?"

"And, I came here a few days ago to buy you sheets. I ended up buying you two sets of sheets, six new pillows, a down comforter, a comforter cover and shams. That happens in a home store," I educated him. "You come in needing a spatula and you go out with a spatula, new kitchen towels, candles, candle holders, cool things to seal open chip bags, a variety of frames, a soap dispenser, and a new vacuum cleaner."

After I delivered this lesson was when Tate's face went blank and, shortly after that, his eyes glazed over. He hijacked the cart so he could lean on it in order to remain standing, even as he fell asleep while walking the aisles, and we headed to curtains.

"Tate?" we heard and I turned around to see Tate had stopped but hadn't straightened and was looking over his shoulder at an advancing Stella, the Queen Biker Babe from Wood's garage. She approached and took us both in, a grin spreading on her face. "Lauren," she greeted when she arrived.

"Hi, Stella," I returned, walking back to stand beside the handle of the cart Tate had straightened from.

"You're at a Deluxe Home Store," she stated the obvious since we were, indeed, standing in a store called Deluxe Home Store.

"Um…," I mumbled. Tate's arm slid around my shoulders and he hauled me into his side.

"Yeah," Tate replied. "How's things, Stell?"

"Hoppin'," she answered and her eyes moved between the both of us and settled on me. "You okay?"

"Um…," I repeated. "Yeah?" I answered in a question because I was uncertain of her question.

Her eyes went to Tate. "Neeta?"

"Visited Laurie last night," Tate shared.

"Shit," Stella hissed.

"She got the papers," Tate kept sharing.

"Yeah?" Stella asked.

"She's gonna fight it," Tate answered.

"Stupid bitch," Stella muttered.

"Um…," I put in and Tate looked down at me.

"You ever meet Pop?" he asked and I nodded. "Stell is his little sister. I grew up with her too."

"Practically raised the three of 'em," she told me. "Even though I was a kid myself."

"Oh," I whispered, wondering about this but not having much time to do so.

Stella looked at Tate. "I'll track down Neet, see if she's receptive to a chat."

"Mighta been, if I was livin' a life where I wasn't in a fuckin' home store buyin' curtains with Laurie. Now, no way."

"That girl," Stella whispered. "She never gave away any of her toys." Her eyes came to me. "And she never shared."

"I got that from her last night," I said quietly and cautiously considering Stella might have called Neeta a bitch but she was still Neeta's aunt.

She read my tone because she stated, "Darlin', no love lost, trust me. Not a lot of bridges Neeta hasn't burned."

"Oh," I repeated and Stella looked back at Tate.

"Curtains?"

"Don't have any and Neeta called Lauren out last night through my bedroom window."

"Christ," Stella muttered. "How could she be Kyle and Brenda's?"

Tate made no response so I asked, "Kyle and Brenda?"

"Pop and his wife, Ace. Brenda died when Wood and I were eight, Neet was six. Diabetes," Tate answered.

"That's horrible," I whispered.

"Yeah, horrible normally, more horrible because Brenda was a beauty, inside and out. Pure through and through. Pure goodness. Pure kindness. Pure love. The real deal. A good girl. Everyone loved her," Stella added and Tate's arm tightened around my shoulders when she said "a good girl."

"I'm sorry," I said to Stella.

"Long time ago, darlin'. Sucks to say but one thing good about it, she didn't live to see Neeta turn out the way she did and she didn't live a life like Kyle, puttin' up with Neeta's shit," Stella remarked.

Before I could stop myself, I turned to Tate and started, "But Wood said—"

"Wood blames Pop 'cause that's Wood," Tate interrupted me. "He's gotta have someone to blame."

"A trait you two share," Stella put in smoothly.

Tate's eyes cut to her and his mouth got tight.

My whole body got tight.

They held each other's eyes and I stood there, supremely uncomfortable while they did it. Something was happening there and I didn't get it.

Stella proved herself the Queen Biker Babe by not backing down from Tate's dark look and instead saying, "You two share a lot, Buck." Her eyes slid to me and then back. "And not just taste in women."

"That'll do, Stell," Tate warned in a low voice.

"You let it go, he finally might be able to," she went on.

"What'd I say?" Tate asked.

"He took your old lady's back, Tate," she reminded him of a fresh memory. "Goes without sayin' that was big, seein' as he was thinkin' Lauren would be on the back of *his* bike."

"Stella," Tate's tone had degenerated from scary to ominous.

In return, her voice got soft. "Cut him some slack, Buck, all I'm sayin'."

Tate didn't speak but a muscle in his jaw jumped.

Stella kept at him. "You get Jonas, and you'll get Jonas, Tate. Neeta'll make it a pain in your ass but you'll get him, what with her history, her record and that ass in her house not to mention Pop and me at your back. Then when you get him, you'll need all the family you can find. Wood loves that kid. He'd do anything for him. And you'd be a fool to harbor bad blood when you can let it go and build a family for Jonas."

"You done?" Tate asked.

"Never," Stella answered.

"You are for now," Tate replied and then turned us away from her, tagging the cart with a hand and moving the cart and me unavoidably forward without saying good-bye.

I twisted my head to look over my shoulder at Stella.

"Um...see you later?" I called.

"Yeah, darlin', you take care," she called back.

"You too," I replied, smiled an embarrassed smile, and looked forward again. "What was that all about?" I asked Tate under my breath.

"Curtains, Ace," was Tate's nonanswer.

"Tate, honey, I think you get I'm not big on you keeping stuff from me," I reminded him gently.

He stopped the cart and looked down at me.

Then he stated bluntly, "Wood killed my dad."

I blinked.

Then I whispered, "Sorry?"

"Car wreck. Wood was drivin'. Wood walked away. Dad died at the scene. Now you know. Can we buy curtains?"

I didn't hesitate even a second in my response.

"Yes, baby." I was still whispering but my arm had moved to slide around his waist both to support him and also to keep myself standing.

I had questions. Lots of them. But they weren't for a home wares store.

I led Tate to the curtains.

*   *   *

I wasn't paying attention when we walked up to the cash registers.

This was because they always put the good stuff around the cash registers and therefore my attention was turned and I was wondering if Tate had a cool spoon/bowl scraper in the awesome color of teal. Then I wondered if he should have two, one teal and one purple. Anyone could easily use two spoon/bowl scrapers in their house. You could use them for *everything*.

"Ace!" Tate called.

I jumped, looked to see he was at the head of the line at a register, and I grabbed both the teal and purple ones because, from the look on his face, he was pretty much done with Deluxe Home Store. I obviously didn't have time to make a considered decision about the spoon/bowl scrapers.

I rushed to the cart and started unloading. Curtains for the bedroom (denim). New curtain rods (awesome). New kitchen towels (bright and cheery). New bathroom towels (thick and lush). And one of those shelf things for the shower because Tate really needed one.

Our cart was so full because Tate had been distracted by brooding over his conversation with Stella. I wasn't proud of my behavior but I couldn't deny I took advantage.

"Girlfriend!" our cashier cried.

I straightened and looked at her.

It was my cashier from when Wendy and I were there a few days before. Her eyes were fastened on Tate in a way it looked like it might cause bodily damage if she was forced to tear them away.

"Hey," I greeted. Her body jolted and her eyes came to me.

She asked with a tilt of her head to Tate, "This your hot guy?"

Tate looked at me.

I bit my lip. Then I said, "Yeah."

The clerk's head shot around and she shouted, "Hey, Maybelline! This is the sheet chick and her hot guy."

A rotund, older black lady four registers down turned to us, gave Tate a once-over, and shouted, "Ooh doggies. That boy's hot all right!"

Wow. Conversation in the staff room at Deluxe Home Stores must be relatively limited for my sheet purchases to make the agenda.

"Uh…Ace," Tate called and my head swung in his direction to see his eyebrows were up but his mouth was twitching.

"Don't," I warned.

"What'd she get this time?" Maybelline called.

The clerk at our register was scanning as she called out our purchases across the register lanes, "Curtains! Kitchen towels! Bath towels! Rods! A shower shelf! Ooh! And a teal *and* purple spoon/bowl scraper." She looked at me. "Good choice, I got the purple first and came back for the teal. These things are *great*! They don't even melt. You can use them making cakes *and* cookin' scrambled eggs. You got two, you can do both at the same time."

"Great," I muttered.

"Sounds to me like someone's settin' up house," Maybelline remarked loudly.

"Me too," our clerk called back.

Tate's hand came to my hip and slid around to my belly as he pushed the cart through to the end and then his mouth was at my ear.

"Uh…Lauren, you wanna tell me why—"

I twisted my head to look at him.

"Don't," I whispered.

He grinned down at me. "Babe."

I looked at the clerk and asked, "What's your name?"

"Wanda," she answered.

"I'm Lauren."

"Hey, Lauren." Her eyes slid to Tate then back to me. "You gonna be in lots?"

"No," I answered.

"Probably," Tate answered at the same time.

Wanda leaned toward me. "Sorry, girlfriend, but I'm gonna go with his answer, you know, just 'cause it gives me hope. We girls, we need hope, even if we're hopin' for someone else."

"By all means," I invited and she smiled and looked at Tate.

"Next week, we're havin' a sale," she informed him.

"I'll put that in my calendar," he replied on a grin.

"You do that," she muttered and gave us our total.

I dug in my purse and came out with my wallet just in time to see Tate hand Wanda his credit card.

"I thought I'd—" I started. Tate's eyes came to me, and I pressed my lips together and shoved my wallet back in my purse.

"Good call," Wanda whispered to me and swiped Tate's credit card.

We'd left Wanda and Maybelline behind with fond (loud) farewells and were walking through the parking lot to the Explorer, Tate guiding the loaded cart with one hand, his other arm around my shoulders, my arm curled around his waist, when Tate spoke.

"You wanna explain about Wanda?"

"No," I replied.

"You know her?"

"Not exactly, except she gave me a minicounseling session when I came here with Wendy."

"Come again?"

"Doesn't matter," I murmured.

Luckily, Tate let that go.

"You wanna tell me why you know everyone every place we go?" he asked.

"No," I answered.

"How long you been in Colorado?" he went on.

"Um…"

"Babe," he muttered and I knew he was smiling.

"I'm nice," I explained and he didn't respond so I continued, "And to be nice you have to be friendly so even if someone you don't know butts into your conversation and gives you advice, you stay friendly. Wanda's kind of nosy and somewhat inappropriate but she means well. And anyway, I'm nice and I'm friendly and I don't know how else to be."

He stopped the cart and me at the back of the Explorer and looked down at me.

"We get home, maybe you can be friendly to me."

I felt a twinge in three places.

Regardless, I informed him, "You have to install curtain rods when we get home."

"Right, then after I install the curtain rods, we can close the curtains and then you can be friendly to me."

"No," I replied. "I'm making a Moist Factor Five Hundred Cake, I'll be busy."

"A Moist Factor Five Hundred Cake?"

"Shambala told me one of his secrets. I've been dying to test it out."

"Ace, we got five pounds of lemon shit in the truck. Do we need a cake?"

"Everyone needs a cake and I haven't had a kitchen for months, except when I was home and then I didn't get to enjoy it because my dad was in the hospital after having a serious heart attack."

"You a good cook?"

I shrugged. "Passable."

Tate stared at me.

"I'm a passable cook but I'm a hell-on-wheels baker," I bragged truthfully.

"So you like bakin'," he noted.

"Love it."

"Miss it?" he asked.

I nodded.

He stared at me again. Then he cupped my jaw with his hand, tilted my head back, bent his head, and touched his lips to mine.

"Then you can make your cake," he whispered.

"Thanks," I whispered back.

He grinned. "After that, you can be friendly to me."

The twinges came back double strength. He let me go, beeped the locks, and pulled open the back of the SUV. We loaded our bags. Tate let me in the cab, returned the cart, came back, climbed behind the wheel, and we went home.

*   *   *

I was in Tate's kitchen chopping cucumbers and tossing them in the bowl with the rest of the veggies I'd prepared for the salad we were having with dinner.

The Moist Factor Five Hundred Cake was in the oven and the bowl of my grandfather's famous mustard glaze I'd mixed together was fermenting in the fridge ready to put on the pork tenderloin, which would go into the oven after the cakes came out.

I sensed movement and my head came up from chopping to see Tate walking through the dining room toward the kitchen, a drill in one hand, the handle of a toolbox in the other. I was so busy chopping, I hadn't noticed I wasn't hearing the drill anymore. His eyes came to me. I smiled at him, his face got soft in a warm way when he caught my smile and he walked right through the kitchen to the hallway leading to the garage.

I stared after him long after he disappeared.

I didn't think I'd ever seen his face get soft like that. I figured I hadn't because it was definitely a look I'd never forget seeing.

I pulled myself together, dropped the knife, wiped my hands on a towel and walked to the bedroom.

The curtains were up. They were to the floor, dark denim with loops at the top that were hooked over rusty-looking thin, square rods that had killer jagged ends. Tate had two big windows in his bedroom, one facing the front of the house, one the side; the bathroom and walk-in closet took the back of the room. The curtains transformed it. The new sheets and comforter were one thing but the curtains offered a big slash of color, giving the room personality, making it homier and making the big room seem almost cozy.

All the room needed now was a paint job (the walls were a little tired and I thought a nice, warm, pale blue would be awesome, maybe with a terra-cotta accent wall), blinds (because with those dark curtains closed, it would be a blackout situation), and some pictures on the walls.

And I knew exactly what picture would be perfect.

I'd seen it through the window of one of the biker shops in town. A large frame around which was a sepia photo of two bikers riding side by side into town. There was no one on the straight road for as far as the eye could see except those bikers. They had their backs to the camera and to their side was the sign that was still there that read "Welcome to Carnal." Even though the bikes were older, the picture taken probably decades ago, the long Main Street of Carnal lay in front of the bikers and it didn't look much different. When I'd spied it, I'd stopped and studied it through the shop window. It was awesome and it would be perfect over Tate's bed.

Buster pranced in and jumped up on the bed. She stood there, blinking at me, her tail swishing. Then she blinked at the curtains at the window facing the bed that had a view out the front of the house. She collapsed on a flank, stretched out her other flank and delicately licked her foot.

I decided to take that as approval.

Tate sauntered in.

"They look great," I told him.

"Yeah," he agreed, coming to stand by me.

I twisted my head to look up at him. "Now you need some venetian blinds," I informed him. "Just in case you don't want blackout conditions but still want to mute the light."

He looked down at me, then he curved an arm around my shoulders and began to curl my body to his.

When my front was pressed to his, he stated, "I'll get right on that, Ace, soon's I pay off the million-dollar lawyer's bills I'll be accumulatin' in order to get Jonas."

I bit my lip because I hadn't thought of that. He'd spoken several times about his money situation. He had a son to win. He didn't need to be buying home wares.

"Captain—" I started but Tate had turned me and was moving forward, pushing me back toward the bed. I felt my legs hit it. Buster jumped away, I went down, and Tate came down on top of me.

His face went into my neck and he declared, "Curtains are up. Time for you to be friendly." Then I felt his tongue slide along my neck.

My arms circled him, the fingers of one hand going into his hair as I turned my head to say in his ear, "Cake's in the oven, honey."

His head came up and he looked at me. "How long we got?"

I shrugged, my shoulders moving on the bed. "Ten minutes?"

His mouth came to mine. "Time enough to start bein' friendly."

"Tate—"

"Then you can finish bein' friendly later."

"Tate—"

He kissed me and I instantly got friendly. So did he. I thought he was friendlier than me but he might have been able to argue that.

We got so friendly, we were both shirtless by the time the buzzer on the oven interrupted our friendliness.

"Cake's done," I breathed against his mouth as I shivered when his hands slid lazily along the skin of my sides.

"Yeah," he whispered and then knifed up.

I'd moved on top and therefore automatically straddled him. He lifted us both up from the bed, putting me on my feet. I started to pull away to bend and get my shirt but his hands at my hips turned me and they guided me to the door.

"Tate, my shirt," I protested.

"Takin' cakes outta the oven doesn't require you bein' fully clothed," he replied and I didn't exactly agree but we were out the door. He was moving me down the hall and I was wearing nothing but a pair of khaki shorts and my bra.

I decided not to fight it. I was into being friendly and as soon as the cakes were out of the oven, I could go back to that.

We went to the kitchen and I opened the oven. The cakes smelled amazing, the house reeked of it and I forgot how much I loved that smell. I stuck my hand in, did the press test, the cake bounced back so I grabbed a kitchen towel and took them out, putting them on the burners of the stove.

I turned the oven off and looked up at Tate to see he was staring down at the cakes.

His eyes came to me. "Looks good, babe."

I grinned. "Yeah."

Then he moved and I was over his shoulder. I let out a little, surprised scream and grabbed on to his waist.

"Tate!" I shouted when we were going through the dining room.

"Friendly," he returned.

He wanted to carry me to his bed? All right, well, whatever.

He threw me on the bed, came down on top of me, and we started getting friendly again.

We were redefining friendly in a very good way when something strange happened. Something mammothly strange. Something so strange it tilted the foundations of all that I'd come to be.

Tate's fingers were curled around my breast, my hand cupping his behind, his lips were trailing down my throat and I was out of mind and in my body when I came back to my mind with a vicious snap.

So you forgive him for bein' a cheatin' asshole and a liar and a dickhead who's so fuckin' dumb he throws away a good thing but you can't forgive me for sayin' somethin' stupid?

My eyes opened and my body stilled. Tate's mouth moved down my chest.

You want sweet dreams, lose the attitude and you might find I'll give you reason to have them.

I closed my eyes and my arms around Tate flexed.

Laurie, baby, wake up. You're gonna fry out here.

Tate's lips moved along the lacy edge of my bra.

You were sleepin' in the sun, babe, not goin' to the mall to get a phone. So I got you a phone.

I turned my head to the side and closed my eyes tighter trying to focus on what his mouth was doing and block out his voice in my head.

Yeah, Ace, fucked you so hard you couldn't move, couldn't do anything but sleep. Exhausted you. You were in my bed, couldn't sleep, that's what I'd do.

I bit my lip and felt the tears sting my nose.

I get back, Lauren, you're on the back of my bike.

My hands lifted and slid into his hair.

Sucks, but fuck, Laurie, it's good to be home.

My fingers curled into his hair.

Then you shouldn't have thrown her away when she was your wife. Now she ain't. Now she's somethin' to me and I don't let men I don't like get close to her and I gotta tell you, man, I do not like you.

Tate's head came up.

No way you can look like all the rest.

"Laurie," Tate called.

Pure class.

"Lauren," he called again, his body moving up, his hand coming to my jaw.

Two kinds of women get under your skin. The ones who do damage, they don't feel good there but once you're fuckin' stupid enough to let them in you got no choice but to take the time it takes to work them out. Then there are the ones who don't do damage, who feel good there, feed the muscle, the bone, the soul, not rip it or break it or burn it. The ones you don't wanna work out.

I righted my head, opened my eyes and looked in his handsome face.

It was then my mind filled with him, with Tate, all things *Tate*. It filled so full, it felt like my head would explode.

Never had better.

That's how I know you didn't give it to that asshole the way you give it to me. You did, no way in hell he'd ever…

Three weeks, after fuckin' you, knowin' what you taste like, what you feel like, the sounds you make when you come, three weeks I'm on the road and all I got is a couple minutes of your voice on the phone every night. Fuckin' you, that's all I can think about, like a teenager, at night in the dark, it's the only thing in my goddamned head. So I jack off, hopin' to cut through it, but nothin' compares to you. Then I know you can't sleep so I can't fuckin' sleep wonderin' if you're sleepin'. That shit's whacked and I come home, fuckin' beside myself it's over.

But Neeta, she's not like you. She isn't smart. She doesn't work hard.

So I find this woman, see. High-class, great fuckin' hair, legs that go forever . . .

So we find out about each other and who we are together. I'm gonna piss you off 'cause I can be a dick. That's who I am. And you're gonna piss me off 'cause, babe, you got attitude. That's who you are. And that's who we're comin' out to be together. And I'm all right with that because, with what I had before, even when you're a bitch, I like it. But when you're not, it's a sweetness the like I've never tasted.

You said you were waitin' for something special and he took away your chance to figure out that you were carryin' it with you all this time. You are special, Laurie.

. . . they did it because you go all out to protect beauty like that.

And last, *Sweet dreams, baby.*

"Jesus, Lauren, baby, what the fuck?" Tate whispered and I realized tears had pooled in my eyes and were sliding down the sides into my hair.

"You like me," I whispered back and his head gave a small jerk.

"What?" he asked.

"You were right." I was still whispering. A sob moved up my throat, I swallowed it down but my voice was thick when I kept whispering, "You were right." I gulped back another sob as I felt more wet trail from my eyes. "I . . . I'm lost."

I couldn't hold it back any longer. I burst into tears and tried to slide out from under him but he held strong.

"Baby," he muttered.

Without any other way to escape him, I lifted my head and shoved my face into his neck as my arms wrapped around him and I held on tight.

"I'm l-l-lost," I choked as my body bucked when a powerful sob tore through me.

Suddenly Tate rolled off and I was moving. He went up the bed, pulling me with him, arranging the pillows behind his back and he rested against them, settling me tight to his side. I wrapped an arm around his abs, pressed my forehead into his neck and held on as my body shook with my tears.

One of his arms was wrapped around my waist, the other came across his chest to sift through my hair and he was quiet while he held me as I wept.

This lasted a while and when it subsided I tilted my head down so my temple was at his collarbone and I saw my bare, tanned legs tangled with his long, jeans-clad ones.

It came to me again. *You said you were waitin' for something special and he took away your chance to figure out that you were carryin' it with you all this time. You are special, Laurie.*

"Talk to me," Tate urged gently.

It was time. It was time to let him in but more, it was time to let me out.

I took in a shuddering breath and my arm gave him a squeeze.

"My first was my college boyfriend," I whispered. "His name was Matt. He was lovely. When we did it, he took me to a fancy hotel and he'd arranged it so there was a bouquet of red roses by the bed when we got to the room. After he made love to me, he told me he'd love me forever. A year later, he got a job where he had to move to Tennessee and he asked me to go with him. I was young and I couldn't even think of leaving Indiana, leaving my family. It scared me so I let him go. We tried the long-distance thing but it didn't work. He's married now to a nice woman named Ellen. They have three kids. He calls me every year on my birthday, though. He never forgets. I call him on his. We talk forever and we laugh like crazy."

My breath hitched as new tears threatened but I gulped them down and held Tate tighter. In return his arm pulled me closer but he didn't speak.

"He loved me," I said softly.

"Yeah," Tate agreed.

"I think, in a way, he still does," I went on.

"Yeah," Tate repeated.

"I don't know when it happened," I whispered.

When I said no more, Tate prompted, "What, honey?"

"When he took me away. How he got me. How he did it," I answered, referring to Brad and when I did Tate's arm squeezed tight, and I shook my head against his chest. "I didn't even feel it happen. I didn't know it. I don't know…" My voice broke. I swallowed again and Tate's hand still sifting through my hair dropped to my neck and his fingers curled there, giving me a squeeze and I forged on, "I don't know why I *let* him."

"He say shit?" Tate asked and I shook my head against his chest again.

"No, it was just that…just that…he was so convinced he was all that, somehow he convinced me and for him to be all that, I had to be less. Not me having to be less, Brad needing to make me less and he just…just…made me feel that way and I just…I…" I pulled in breath and finished, "I just faded away."

Tate didn't respond and I lifted up, taking my arm from around his stomach and swiping at my face. I turned to him and looked in his eyes.

"I wasn't running from him hurting me with Hayley," I told him softly. "That's not why I got out of Horizon Summit, why I fled my life." My voice dropped to a whisper. "I lied to Krystal when I asked for that job but I didn't know it then. I know it now. She was right. I got lost and I was trying to find me."

His hand slid up my neck to my jaw and his thumb glided along my lower lip.

"You just find you, baby?" Tate asked.

"Not exactly," I answered.

"Then what exactly?" he pressed.

"I…" My teeth bit my lip, tagging the pad of his thumb, which he didn't move so I released it. "My brain just suddenly started paying attention."

"To what?"

"To you."

His brows went up and his thumb swept along my cheekbone. "Wanna explain that?"

"You're beautiful," I whispered and watched his face change. Surprise was there but it was soft, not astonished ... moved.

"Ace," he whispered back.

"I saw you," I kept whispering, "at the hotel, meeting Neeta—"

Tate cut me off. "Know that, babe."

"I know," I replied. "But you don't know that I hated Neeta instantly when I saw her throw herself in your arms. Pure jealousy. I didn't know you, I didn't know her. I just took one look at you and I ..." I stopped speaking, suddenly embarrassed and more than a little scared and my eyes slid away. I would have moved my face but his hand tensed against my jaw.

"Keep talkin'," he urged.

"I can't," I said softly.

"Baby, I think you don't get this but you're safe here." His hand left my jaw and both arms wrapped tight around me, giving me a squeeze, at the same time pulling me up so my face was level with his. "You're safe, Lauren," he murmured and my eyes came back to his. "You weren't safe with him but, honey, swear to God, you're safe with me."

I felt the tears smart in my eyes and my lower lip quivered so I pressed them together.

"Keep talkin'," he repeated. I took a breath in through my nose and nodded.

"You were far away," I whispered. "It was night. I could barely see you..." I hesitated. "But you still took my breath away."

His eyes closed and his hand slid up my neck into my hair and he put pressure there so our foreheads were touching.

"Christ, Laurie," he muttered.

"The next day," I went on, "I saw you walk into the bar and you were so beautiful…"

His eyes opened and his fingers tensed against my scalp. "All right, maybe you can quit talking."

I ignored him.

"That's why it hurt so much." My voice was so quiet it was barely audible. "What you said. You being you, looking like you, breathtaking…"

"Stop, Lauren." His voice was a growl.

"I'm not throwing it in your face. I'm just saying—"

He interrupted me again. "I know what you're sayin'."

I put my hand on his chest and told him softly, "Tate, you're all that."

"Baby—"

"And you like me."

"Shut it, Laurie."

I moved my head, sliding my cheek against his beard so my lips were at his ear, my arms went around him and I whispered, "So maybe I'm a little bit of all that too."

I found myself moved suddenly, landing on my back with Tate's body covering mine, his head up and his hand back at my jaw.

"You were all that before me," he declared, his voice again a growl.

"Tate—"

"My guess? You been all that for a while."

"Captain—"

"Shitty luck, stupid decisions…I lost a lot in my life. My mom left when I was a kid. Thought I'd live life high, playin' football and that dream was dead almost the second it began. Then my dad died. Mixed up with Neeta, with Bethany, havin' Jonas and thinkin' I finally got a hint of sweet only to have it come along with a lot of fightin' and headache and broken promises I was fuckin' stupid enough to believe. I haven't had much of all that. All I ever had I had to fight for, pay for, or do penance for because I jacked up. Then *you* walk into my goddamned bar lookin' for a job."

"Tate—"

His thumb came to my lips and put pressure on.

"Shut it," he whispered.

"Okay," I said against his thumb.

"I don't define you," he told me.

"I know, but I—" I started and his thumb, still against my lips, pressed gently so I shut up.

"You're not found because you found me," he went on. "You think that you're still lost."

I didn't speak.

Tate did. "I wasn't here, you cuttin' ties and gettin' out from under him, you woulda found your way."

He stopped talking so I chanced speaking.

"Can I say something now?" I asked against his thumb and he moved it away, rolled to his side and brought me to facing him.

Then he said, "Yeah."

"You're right," I agreed. "But—"

"No buts about it, Ace."

I put my fingers to his lips and asked quietly, "Can I say what I need to say, Tate?"

He didn't speak or nod, he just waited.

So I spoke. "I would have come back to me, eventually. It's just that, it so happens I found myself with you leading the way."

"Laurie—"

I moved my hand and replaced it with my lips.

"Thank you," I whispered and then I kissed him, doing it hard and putting feeling into it, a lot of it, as much as I felt for him and what he'd given me. And what he'd given me was huge.

He'd given me *me*.

I pushed him to his back, slid on top, and kept kissing him with Tate kissing me back.

Eventually, I lifted my head to look at him and Tate's hands slid into my hair, pulling it away from my face and holding it behind my head.

His eyes were on the fall of hair that escaped his hands and curtained my left eye then they came to mine.

"You got great hair, babe," he muttered.

I lifted a hand so my finger could slide along his hairline, then all of them glided in.

"You do too," I replied.

One of his hands left my hair and became an arm wrapped around my upper back, his other hand cupping my head and both brought me back down to him.

"I have to frost the cake," I whispered.

"In a little while," he whispered back.

"And make dinner," I continued.

"Later."

"Captain—"

He cut me off with, "Ace."

I studied his beautiful face.

She's mine, he'd said to Wood.

I was his. And he was mine.

I smiled and my mouth went to his. "All right, honey. Later."

His head slanted one way, mine tilted the other, and it was a lot later when I was able to get up, frost the cake and make dinner.

*   *   *

We had pork tenderloin with Gramps's famous glaze, boiled new potatoes, salad, and delicious rolls with sunflower seeds crusting the top, eating it at the wrought-iron table on Tate's back patio.

My eyes were on his terraced yard and my mind was filled.

It was filled with what I would say to Tate if I spent a day weeding the plants and adding more. It was filled with if I cared anymore about Tate reading into what that said (and I figured I didn't). It was filled with Tate telling me his mom left and his dad was dead and how little I knew about him. It was filled with how strong the feeling was that I wanted to know more and the fact the power behind that feeling didn't scare me.

It was filled with the knowledge that Wood "killed" Tate's dad in a car accident. With Stella telling Tate to cut Wood slack. With Stella saying, if Tate let it go, Wood would be able to. And with Wood telling me they once were brothers. It was filled with Wood coming to take my back when Neeta was in town, for me but also for Tate, even after what passed between the three of us. And it was filled with Wood telling Tate he'd do anything he could to help Tate get Jonas from Wood's sister.

Wood missed Tate and you only hold on to anger that long if the person you're angry at meant something to you so I was guessing Tate missed Wood too.

"Ace," Tate called and I looked from his plants to him. "You lied."

Taken from my thoughts and surprised at his words, I felt my eyebrows draw together. "Sorry?"

He slid his fork on his plate and his brows went up. "Passable?"

I looked at his clean plate then back to him. "My cooking's okay, not much to write home about. This was good because of my grandfather's famous mustard sauce, not me."

"Your grandfather come for a visit while I was puttin' up the curtain rods?" he asked.

"No, he's dead," I answered.

"Babe," Tate replied on a grin.

I felt the sudden, intense need for Tate to know about me. I'd let him in, I'd let me out. I wanted this and I wanted him and I wanted him to have me.

Therefore, I shared, "All my grandparents are dead."

He sat back in his chair, his eyes never leaving mine. "Yeah?"

"Gramps, that's Mom's father, he's the mustard glaze guru," I informed him. Tate didn't reply so I went on. "It was his farm that became Dad's. He had only girls. Three of them. Dad studied agriculture at school. His folks owned a farm too but it was smaller and he was the second of two sons. My uncle George got that farm." Tate remained silent so I went on. "Dad took over Gramps's farm. We all lived there together, all my life, until I left and, after that, Grams and Gramps passed away. It was okay though, us being together, because it was a big house and it made us a big family."

Tate still didn't speak, didn't start sharing his own stories so I continued.

"Mom's mom, Grams, she made great chocolate chip cookies. The best," I stated. "She used to refrigerate the dough between making it and baking it. I don't know what this did but it made her cookies *killer*."

Tate watched me and made not a noise.

"Dad's dad, he was a master at the grill. He could grill an *amazing* steak," I continued.

Tate's lips twitched but he remained quiet.

"Dad's mom," I blathered on. "She was Polish and she could cook. I mean she could *cook*. She made these cookies, like crescent rolls but in cookie form with lots of cinnamon and sugar and butter and the dough was made with sour cream so they were rich and she sifted powdered sugar on them. She made them every Christmas and I always went over to help. She let me brush the melted butter on the rolled out dough and sprinkle the cinnamon and sugar on and she let me sift the powdered sugar on top."

Finally, Tate spoke.

"All your memories come with food?" he asked.

"Dad makes the best cocktail sauce for shrimp you ever tasted. Carrie concocted this homemade macaroni and cheese that's out of this world. And Mom got all the good of Grams and Gramma and put her own spin on it. Everything she makes will knock your socks off but her chocolate pecan pie is *unbelievable*."

"I'll take that as a yes," Tate mumbled.

"Food is love," I replied.

"No, babe, it ain't. But makin' it for the ones you love so they can brag about it is," Tate returned.

He had a point.

"You have a point," I told him.

His arm shot out, his hand tagged me at the neck and he leaned forward as he pulled me to him. Then he touched his mouth to mine.

When his head moved away two inches, I asked softly, "Do you want cake?"

A smile spread on his face, a face that, at my question, grew soft and warm like earlier. Since he was so close, all I could do was stare.

Finally, he answered, "Yeah," and let me go.

I grabbed my plate and beer bottle, Tate grabbed his, and we took them into the house going through the back door into the mudroom. As we walked through the mudroom, I heard Tate's cell phone ring on the kitchen counter.

When we hit the kitchen, I took his plate from him and walked to the sink while he walked to his phone.

I heard him answer, "Pop?"

I started to rinse the dishes.

"Yeah?" Tate asked and then there was a long silence. So long I had the plates and cutlery rinsed and in the dishwasher, I'd grabbed a knife and was cutting into the cake that was sitting on a plate on the island (homemade yellow cake, homemade chocolate buttercream frosting) when Tate spoke again. "Tell her, when I show, I don't see that jackass."

My eyes went from the cake to Tate. He had a hand on his hip, the other one holding his phone to his ear, his bottle of beer was on the counter and his head was bent, eyes studying his boots.

"Right…and Pop?" he said, then finished with a quiet but intense, "Thanks. Owe you big."

I stopped cutting and Tate flipped his phone closed, set it on the counter, and started to me.

"Um…" I hesitated. "What was that?"

I held my breath for his response because his face was as intense as his voice had been and I didn't get it. He also was coming to me in a way that was strangely purposeful and aggressive and I didn't get that either. I let go of the knife still stuck in the cake and started to take a step back when he caught me and yanked me forward so hard I collided with his body.

I looked up at him as his arms wound around me. "Tate—"

"Pop ran interference with Neeta. Wood told him that I told her I was gettin' Jonas this weekend and Pop stepped in, had a few words, calmed her ass down and I get him Friday at noon, takin' him back Sunday by five."

I still didn't get why this made him look and act like he was.

"That's…good," I said searchingly.

"It's fuckin' great." His arms around me gave me a squeeze. "Miss my kid, babe."

Finally, I kind of got it. My body automatically melted into his and my arms went around his neck.

"Then that's great," I said quietly. "But, you haven't seen him in a while. I know that scene last night was intense but don't you have visitation rights? Was it in question that you'd get a visit?"

"No tellin' how they'd jack me over. Even when things are steady, I'm not on the road and need to change a visit, she fucks with me. I get him after school on my Fridays but sometimes he's not at home when I come to pick him up. She's made me wait an hour, two, once they dragged in at ten at night."

"You're joking," I whispered, stunned at this news.

I had not come from a broken home. My parents stayed married and in love and my grandparents had stayed married and in love. Even my aunts and uncles all stayed married and in love. None of them left town so I grew up with all of them and all of my cousins and they were—*we* were—always together. A big family in each other's business. Thanksgiving was a madhouse and, whoever's house we had it in, it took hours to do the dishes because of the amount of food that needed to be cooked.

I'd always had family, a together family. I couldn't fathom the consequences of a broken home but I really couldn't wrap my head around the concept of using a child to screw with that child's father.

He shook his head. "Nope. And when I gotta make a change 'cause of work, she makes me pay. She likes her chance to fuck with me so she makes it tough, gives me shit, tells me I gotta renege and not make up a weekend."

I remained silent and this was because I was expending a great deal of effort at keeping my body still and my mouth from screeching.

"So," Tate continued, "goes without sayin', us breakin' it off permanent, me bein' gone a while then you bein' here, she's chompin' at the bit to fuck with me."

"Will Jonas be there on Friday?" I asked and he shrugged but grinned.

"Lucky for me, I'm a bounty hunter and I'm done with her shit. He isn't, I'll find him."

"You put up with it before?" I asked and his grin turned into a smile.

"Babe, have you not got that I've put up with a lot of her shit before?"

"Why?" I blurted a very important question that I realized just then I'd wanted to ask for ages. Then I snapped my mouth shut because I didn't want my question to come out as questioning *him*.

Tate didn't have a problem with my question and I knew this because he answered it immediately.

"She was Neet. She was close to her mom, I knew that. Everyone did. Thick as thieves. When Brenda died, Neeta unraveled. I was eight and I still remember it, still felt it, her pain was so absolute, it was physical. You got anywhere near her, you felt it. We were family, my dad and Pop best friends since they were kids. Neeta feeling that kind of pain, losin' Brenda myself, the only mom I knew, Kyle losin' her, Wood...it marked me. We all recovered but Neeta never did. And we all spent years puttin' up with her shit in a variety of ways because we hoped she eventually would." He took in a heavy breath and finished, "I told you she was always like she is 'cause that was most of what I remember. But when she was a kid, before Brenda died, she wasn't like that, Laurie. Sweet kid, the image of Brenda in every way. All of us hoped she'd come back to her. She just never did."

"Brenda was the only mom you knew?" I asked softly, cautiously, not wanting to push.

"Yeah," he replied instantly. "My mom left us when I was three. She'd come back, still does. Not often, though, and not long. Not then, not now. She doesn't come back to stay, she comes back to visit. Even when I was a kid, it was like she was distant family, checking in, touching base, then she was gone again."

My hand slid into his hair and I whispered, "I'm so sorry, Tate."

His arms gave me a squeeze. "Babe, don't be. Dad was a good dad, the best. She was no loss."

My body jerked in surprise at his words. "But—"

"Flighty," he cut me off, "fuck, she was flighty, self-absorbed. Not like Neeta. Different. She wasn't lookin' right at you, swear to God, she'd forget you existed."

"That's terrible." I was still whispering.

"That's my mom. She ain't a bitch, she's just her."

"So it was just you and your dad?" I asked carefully.

"Yeah, and Pop, Wood, Neeta, Brenda, then Stella. Stella's about ten years younger than Pop. She was a kid but she pitched in when Brenda died. We were tight."

"You still tight with Pop and Stella?"

"Yep."

"Just not Wood and Neeta," I murmured.

He moved, twisting so his hips were resting against the counter, I was in front of him and my body was resting against his. My hands slid to his chest and he spoke.

"Neeta, you get. Wood…" He stopped. I waited and he started again. "Wood and Dad were fishin'. Not like Bubba, they fished. Liked it. Did it together all the time. Pop and me, we weren't into it but Wood and Dad would go out as often as they could. They were comin' home, it was late, fuck knows what was in his head 'cause it was too late. Wood fell asleep at the wheel, veered, truck hit somethin', it rolled. He musta been goin' fast, wantin' to get home. The roll was bad. They came to rest against a tree. They were both belted, both of them shoulda made it but they went through a barricade. Jagged edge of the barricade cut through the truck and cut through Dad."

Tears instantly filled my eyes. "No," I breathed while working to keep the tears at bay.

Tate's eyes held mine. "Yeah, baby," he said quietly.

"Oh honey."

He didn't reply at first.

Then he said, still speaking quietly, "Stell's right. I should let it go. But I can't. Dad was all I had and Wood actin' stupid took that all away. It was about a year after that tackle took out my knee. I was fit, but the knee... it healed right but it didn't heal right enough for me to play pro ball. My life was fucked. I had no clue where I was goin' because I was certain where my life was leadin' me and it sure as fuck wasn't back to Carnal. I was back with Neeta and those times were good 'cause I was on her road. I could see the good in bein' aimless, not givin' a shit. We had a fuckin' blast. Not proud of it because it was stupid but at the time, I didn't care. Gettin' drunk, gettin' laid, doin' whatever the fuck I wanted when I wanted and screw the consequences, that was the place I needed to be. That's the last my dad ever knew of me."

"Tate—" I murmured.

"He didn't see me get my shit together. Go into the academy," Tate said. "He didn't see Neeta and me do one thing good together, makin' Jonas."

"Tate—"

"He was worried about me. Died worried about me. He was thinkin' I'd end up like Blake, Neeta's old man. Sittin' in front of the TV with a beer in my hand gettin' smashed every night and the only gumption I'd get was to cart my ass to a poker game."

"Tate—"

"He was tryin' to get me to get my shit together. He was also failing."

"Captain, honey, listen to—"

"Took him dyin' for me to sort my shit out."

"Honey—"

"Still, didn't manage it until years after that."

"Tate, honey—"

"I wanted to play ball," he stated in a way that my body got very still and my eyes, already locked to his, became glued there. "It wasn't the money. It wasn't the fame. It was the game. The goddamned game. I didn't feel like I was breathin' right if I wasn't playin' or practicin'. Felt like life was still, someone hit pause, then I'd put on my pads and jersey and walk on the field and then everything would come alive. Dad and I were Eagles fans since I could remember. Puttin' that fuckin' jersey on, Christ, Laurie... *Christ*."

His last word seemed ripped from his throat and when he released it and it went through the air, its razor-sharp edge cut clean through me.

My hands went to his neck and I held on. "Baby—"

"Can you imagine, babe, can you fuckin' imagine what it feels like, gettin' a taste of your dream then losin' it?" His hand came up and his fingers made a loud snap. "Gone."

"The eagle on your back," I said gently.

"Got it my junior year at Penn State, the first year I made the All-America Team. When I knew I had a shot at it. When I knew I'd be wearin' green."

I dropped my head, my forehead falling to his chest and my arms slid around, ducking under his to wrap him tight. I turned my head, pressed my cheek in, and held him even tighter.

"Can't absorb the pain, babe," he whispered, his lips at the hair on top of my head, "lives in me."

"You haven't let it go?" I asked.

"Don't know how," he answered.

"You had a taste of something special," I stated. "But you lost it."

"No babe, that's the problem. I haven't lost it. Even after all these years, I can still taste it."

Oh *God*.

"I don't know how to help," I whispered and his body started moving.

It took me several moments to realize that, bizarrely, he was laughing.

I left my arms where they were and tipped my head up to look at him.

"Are you laughing?" I asked, even though I could tell by his face that he was.

"Babe," he said, his deep voice also trembling with laughter, "you did my laundry."

"Sorry?"

"You vacuumed," he went on.

My head jerked and I asked, "What?"

"You bought me sheets."

"I don't—"

His arms gave me a squeeze.

"Ace, I never had a mom."

"A mom?" I asked, confused.

"Neeta sure as fuck never cleaned. She made more of a mess than me; one reason, when she'd make a promise she didn't intend to keep, I started meetin' her at the hotel. Not a big fan of cleanin' up my own shit, much less when Neeta'd tear through. And she never gave me one thing. Not a birthday gift, not a Christmas gift, not somethin' just because. Only thing she ever gave me was an orgasm."

"She gave you a son," I told him.

"I kinda had a hand in that, babe. Didn't do the term or push him out but been fightin' for him to have a decent life ever since."

He was right about that.

"What does vacuuming have to do with—?" I started.

"My memories don't come attached with shit like makin' cookies with my grandma, Ace. My father was a man and he expected his son to be a man. I've never worn a piece of clothing in my goddamned life that I haven't washed myself."

"Oh," I breathed.

Apparently Wanda at Deluxe Home Store was right. You tell a man early on you're going to take care of him, it's going to suck him in deep.

Tate carried on, "Don't even know when I learned to do laundry, just knew, I wanted clean clothes, I had to do it."

"Tate—"

"Leave you in my house once, babe, come home and the whole fuckin' place is cleaned, the fridge is packed full, a sweet, girlie pitcher in the fridge filled with Kool-Aid and I got soft, fancy sheets on my bed."

"I was worried that I—"

His head bent and his lips touched mine, stopping my words.

When his face moved away he replied in a very firm way to my unanswered statement, "Nope."

"Then who planted those plants in your yard?"

"Mom," he replied. "Came home, don't know, five years ago. Stayed awhile. Got a wild hair, did some gardening. Unlike Mom, the plants took root."

"Who bought your dining room table?" I asked.

"What?" he asked back.

"Your dining room table. It's—"

"It's Dad's. I grew up in this house, Laurie. Bought a new bed when I took over Dad's room, made Jonas some space. Other than that, everything here is what he left me."

"Oh," I whispered, my mind turning all of this over, all he'd said and all it meant.

"Yeah." He grinned. "Oh."

"You're stuck," I blurted. His grin died and he blinked.

"Come again?"

I swallowed, sucked in breath and forged ahead.

"I was lost but you...Tate, you got stuck," I told him.

He stared at me and it took a lot but I braved his stare.

Then he asked, "You up for the job of pullin' me out?"

"I…" I swallowed again. "No," I answered truthfully.

"No?" he asked, his eyebrows lifting, his face getting dark, his arms growing tighter.

"I…" I pulled in breath then whispered, "I kinda like it here."

With a sudden change that made me jump, he threw his head back and burst out laughing, pulling me into a close hug when he did it.

My cheek was smushed to his chest and it was going to stay where it was since his big hand was crushing my head there, so I mumbled a smothered, "Tate—"

"Keepin' you stuck with me," he said over my head.

"Okay," I replied.

"Okay?" he asked and his tone had changed again, now sounding slightly surprised.

My arms gave him a squeeze and I answered, "Yeah, honey. Okay."

He was silent for a while then I felt his lips against the hair at the top of my head.

Then he stated, "Baby, you know the worst about me."

I tried to pull my head from his chest but he kept it pressed there so I gave up and whispered, "Tate."

"Keepin' you stuck with me, Ace," he repeated in a murmur against my hair and I shivered because his tone had changed.

This wasn't just a statement. It was a vow.

"Honey—"

"Bet Jonas likes grape Kool-Aid," he whispered and I shivered again.

"He doesn't, I'll get him the flavor he likes," I promised.

He let my head go and I tilted it back as his hand slid to my cheek.

"I know you will, baby," he said gently.

I felt a nervous flutter in my belly.

"You're sure he'll like me?"

"Yeah," Tate answered immediately.

"How can you be sure? Maybe he'll—"

Tate cut me off. "He's just like his old man."

"How like his old man?" I asked and his hand moved to my jaw, his thumb tipping my head farther back as his head bent forward.

"*Exactly* like his old man," he said softly.

"I'm in trouble," I whispered.

His mouth came to mine and I felt his lips smile.

"Oh yeah," he muttered, then he kissed me.

The knife stayed stuck in the cake for a while and Tate and I didn't test out Moist Factor Five Hundred until it was dark. Tate sat on the island wearing nothing but his jeans only half buttoned up. I stood between his legs wearing nothing but his T-shirt. We ate a huge slice he held in his big hand, using our fingers to feed each other. This meant frosting got all over our fingers but cleaning it up was just a bonus to an already delicious activity.

Shambles was right. Moist Factor Five Hundred was a hit. But it wasn't Shambles's secret cake ingredient that made it a hit.

It was my very own chocolate buttercream frosting.

CHAPTER NINETEEN

Jonas

THE DOOR TO the bar opened, most of my body locked but my eyes flew to it.

Nadine walked in.

I heaved a sigh of relief.

"Laurie, honey, you okay?" Jim-Billy asked and I looked at him.

It was Friday. I was on the day shift. Tate was gone, picking up Jonas. I'd been on tenterhooks since noon, like Tate could step on Scottie's beaming pad and beam himself and Jonas back and right outside the bar. But now it was nearly three and they could be here at any minute.

I was not ready for this.

Tate had told me before he left that morning that he'd bring Jonas by the bar to meet me then they'd go off and do their thing then they'd pick me up and we'd all go to dinner. I'd wanted to make Jonas a welcome-home dinner and maybe buy my way into his heart through his ten-year-old-boy's stomach because I didn't figure Neeta was a master chef. Though, if I waited until after my shift, they wouldn't eat until late so going out it was. The diner could cook faster than what I had planned.

I bought all the stuff for dinner anyway because I had Saturday off so I decided I'd make it then. I didn't find out until I got in the bar that day that Krystal and Wendy had conspired against me. It was Wendy's day off but she was coming in to take over for me at three thirty and Krystal had made last-minute schedule changes so I had the whole weekend off.

I didn't want the whole weekend off. I just wanted Saturday. I told myself that this was so I could give Tate and Jonas time together. It was really because Jonas scared me half to death.

The dinner I picked was a specialty of mine. My family loved it but Brad hated it, said it was over the top, said it was so many calories and fat it was impossible to count so I only made it when I went home to Indiana. Pork chops stuffed with Rice-A-Roni accompanied by real bread stuffing like you make for Thanksgiving and green bean casserole (the gooey kind with the crispy onions in it and on top). This would be followed by red cake with that creamy white frosting that took a powerful hold on my willpower not to eat it all before I frosted the cake.

I made the cake the night before using nervous energy to do it. Tate had been gone, called away for a few days to round up a bad guy. Luckily, this only lasted a few days. Unfortunately, we'd fought when he'd returned, which was the night before, approximately three minutes after I put the final flourishes on the frosting on the cake.

We fought because, until that day, I'd worked nights so I spent the days while he was gone painting his room as a surprise.

It wasn't me painting the room that pissed Tate off. When Tate came home and saw it, he liked it. A lot if the kiss he gave me was any indication.

It was the invoice for the blinds that Tate saw on the counter after we'd walked out of the bedroom and into the kitchen that pissed him off. I'd had a local man come in and measure and I ordered venetian blinds. Really cool ones made of a rich, dark wood. They cost a fortune but they would be awesome with the curtains.

Tate picked up the invoice, gave it a glance, looked at me and asked, "What's this?"

"Um…surprise part two?" I answered in a question because the look on his face was a little scary.

"Lauren, fuck, did you *not* hear me when I said the blinds were gonna have to wait?" He spoke at the same time he agitatedly threw the invoice down on the counter.

"Yes, I heard you. You said that you couldn't afford them. So, really, you kind of need them…um…in a way…" I was talking stiltedly because his face wasn't getting any less scary and because he actually didn't *need* them in *any* way. "So…um…I bought them."

"Yeah, you bought them and I can't afford them."

I didn't understand so I asked, "You can't afford them?"

"Gonna be another hit to pay you back, Ace. Don't need any more hits. My balance needs to start goin' *up,* not sinkin' *down.*"

"No, I mean, I bought them, *for you.*"

I thought this would go over well since no one ever took care of him and Neeta had never given him anything but an orgasm. I'd given him those too and I was on a mission to suck him in as deep as I could get him so I had to pull ahead of all his history with Neeta and any other woman for that matter.

This, however, did not go over well.

"You bought them for me," he repeated quietly but his voice was hard.

"Yes, I thought—"

He interrupted me. "No, babe, you didn't."

"Sorry?"

"You didn't think," he explained.

"I—"

"Got money," he cut me off again, leaning a bit toward me. "Yeah, I know. It wasn't in my face every time you put on clothes or spray on your fancy-ass perfume in my goddamned bedroom, I'd still know after you told me about your life with that fuckwad."

"Yes, I have money, but—"

He broke in again. "No woman takes care of me."

"I'm not taking care of you. I'm—"

"Takin' care of me."

I lost a bit of hold on my temper and therefore snapped, "Would you let me finish?"

"No," he answered.

"No?"

"Actually, fuck no," he amended.

"Sorry?" I whispered and he leaned forward further.

"I got a dick, babe," he clipped.

"I know that, *babe*," I snapped back.

"No woman takes care of me," he repeated. "I make a home for me and my kid."

"I was trying to do something nice!" My voice was rising. "It's just blinds, Tate."

"It's you shovin' your money in my face, Lauren."

I reared back. "It is not."

He leaned back. "You buy me sheets. You paint my room. What's next? You gonna wash my balls?"

It was at that I sucked in breath and lifted a hand palm up between us. Then I took my purse from the counter, snatching my car keys from there. I walked out to the car in the garage and used the garage door opener that Tate had given me that was in my car. I walked the opener to his Explorer, opened the driver side door, tossed it on his seat, went back to my car, started it up, backed it out and went right to Carnal Hotel.

I checked in with Ned. Betty came out and we played Harry Potter Clue. They didn't ask questions and I didn't share. When Betty went to bed, I went to my room and crashed, wearing my makeup, taking off my jeans but keeping on the T-shirt I'd worn that day.

This sucked because Tate had been gone for days and I missed him. And I missed being in bed with him most of all. I didn't sleep great because I never slept great but also because I missed him and I was angry with him, both in equal measure.

After a fitful night's sleep, I got up, pulled on my jeans, slid on my flip-flops and dragged myself to the reception desk. Betty let me into her house, she gave me face wash, an extra toothbrush and toothpaste. I washed my face, brushed my teeth, had a cup of coffee with her and told her I'd be back while she stared at me with an open face and kind eyes, inviting a talk if I needed it, ready to keep her mouth shut if I didn't.

I might have mentioned before, I really liked Betty.

I went out to my car and drove to Tate's. He was sitting on his deck, feet up on the railing, coffee cup in his hand when I pulled up his drive. I parked where Neeta parked, walked up the deck steps, keeping my eyes averted from him, went in through the sliding glass door and headed straight to the bedroom to get my bags.

I didn't make it to the closet.

Halfway across the bedroom, Tate tagged me with an arm around my stomach and he pulled me back into his body.

"Not fun sleepin' alone," he muttered into my ear as I pulled against his hold but he was stronger than me and he switched our direction so we were heading to the bed.

"Let me go, Tate," I demanded, my hands shoving at his arm.

"Gotta learn to get over it, Ace," he told me.

"Let...me...*go,*" I repeated.

We made it to the bed. He twisted, going down on his back, me landing on top of him. I struggled, slid off his body, but he rolled over me, pinning me to the bed.

I pushed at his shoulders but his hands came up my sides, sliding over my armpits, my triceps, my elbows, my forearms, and then my hands. His fingers forcing themselves to lace between mine, he pushed my arms and hands to the bed over my head, all the while his mouth was working at my neck.

"Tate!" I snapped.

His knee came up, parting my legs.

"Bet, way you catch fire, make-up sex'll be hot," he muttered.

"We are not making up and we are *not* having sex."

His head came up, I saw he was grinning and through his grin he said, "Babe."

"Babe yourself!" I spat.

He burst out laughing and while still doing it, he kissed me.

Thus started the struggle and I did pretty well, considering Tate was bigger than me, heavier than me, and stronger than me.

Unfortunately, along the line, I caught fire and we had make-up sex and Tate was right, it was hot.

I was on my knees in front of him, my torso to the bed, my cheek pressed against the comforter, my arms straight out in front of me and my hands clenching the sheets when Tate encouraged roughly, "That's it, baby, fuck yourself."

And I was. He was on his knees behind me but I was rearing back into him, doing all the work.

"Tate," I breathed. I was about to come but before I could, he pulled out so I cried, "Tate!"

"Not yet," he muttered, flipped me over, spread my legs and then his mouth was on me.

He was good at this because he had a variety of speeds and levels. He could go slow and be gentle or he could go fast and be hungry. It usually started with one and then moved gradually (and never fast enough but definitely good enough) through the rest.

The beard helped. Loads.

He was at his top speed, his most voracious, his hands cupping my behind, holding me to him when I gasped, "Tate."

He knew what that meant and his mouth was gone.

"Baby," I begged as his body came over mine, his hands lifting my legs to throw them over his shoulders.

"Wanna watch," he murmured and then he was inside me, his hands in the bed giving him leverage to pound deep.

"Oh my God," I whispered as it came over me and I watched his head tip so he was looking at our connected bodies.

"Your pussy, baby, Jesus, so fuckin' sweet," he whispered back.

"Oh my God," I repeated as it washed in on a tidal wave. His head came back up and his eyes locked with mine.

"That's it, Laurie," he muttered but I closed my eyes, my head arched back, my back arched up, my legs tensed, my calves digging into his shoulders and he kept thrusting, hard and deep.

"Don't stop, Tate," I pleaded, still coming.

"Fuckin' hell, baby."

"Don't stop," I whispered and he didn't, not until I finished and he did too.

He slid my legs off his shoulders, wrapped them around his waist, and then gave me his weight.

His mouth was at my ear, his hand curled around my breast when he stated, "Oh yeah, Ace, make-up sex with you is hot."

I'd had a very, *very* good orgasm but, nevertheless, that was when I belatedly remembered he was a very, *very* big *jerk*.

"That was good-bye sex," I announced. "I'm moving back to Carnal Hotel."

His head came up and he looked at me.

"No you aren't."

"Yes I am."

"No. You aren't."

"I am!" I snapped.

"Told you, Lauren, you keep igniting for me like that, I was gonna chain you to the bed. You try to check back in that fuckin' hotel, I'll do it right now."

"That's against the law," I informed him acidly.

"How you gonna tell someone when you're chained to my bed?" he asked.

"You aren't chaining me to the bed!" I cried loudly.

"You aren't moving back to the hotel."

"It's home. You're back in your house, Buster doesn't need me anymore. And, might I add, you're a jerk so I don't want to *be* here anymore."

"You wanna be here."

"Do not."

"Babe, when you were on your knees, took everything I had not to go back on my calves you were fucking me so hard. You wanna be here."

"See!" I cried. "Jerk!"

He smiled. "Babe."

"Get off."

"You're not goin' back to the hotel."

"Off!" I shouted and bucked.

His mouth came to mine, his teeth nipped my lower lip and my body stilled because this was a surprise move, it felt good and, I was so angry, I didn't want it to feel good.

"I was a dick," he stated.

"Yes, you were."

"I admitted it. Now stop bein' pissed."

"And what?" I asked. "You just get to be a dick and then admit it and I have to get over it?"

He grinned and answered, "Yeah."

"Tate—"

"Ace."

"I'm going back to the hotel."

His good mood fled from his face and he said, "No, Lauren, you aren't."

"But—"

"You need your own space for a while, get an apartment in town. But you aren't movin' back into that hotel."

"But I—"

"Jesus, we've had this conversation before," he muttered.

"So?" I asked.

Tate tried a different tactic. "You want, I'll take you down, you go into a room and I'll show you how easy it is to pop a lock or pick one."

"The doors have chains," I reminded him.

"Then once I pick the lock then pop it, you chain it and I'll show you how easy it is to pop that."

"Ned and Betty will be right next door."

"You're here, I'll be right beside you. I'm bigger than Ned, I got more than one gun, I keep one close and I know how to use them. That compare?"

I hated it when he was right.

I didn't tell him he was right. I changed the subject.

"You keep a gun close?"

He reached beyond me, opened a nightstand and came back with a gun, the butt of it resting against his palm, his ring and index fingers curled around it, the other three fingers splayed wide. The natural, casual way he held it made my breath catch because, firstly, I wasn't certain I'd ever seen a gun except my father's hunting rifles and secondly, the natural, casual way he held a weapon freaked me out.

"Oh my God," I breathed.

He reached beyond me again, I heard the thud of the gun hitting the nightstand and then he was back.

"No hotel," he declared.

"I—"

"And stop bein' pissed," he went on.

"Tate, you were a *jerk*."

His hand came to the side of my head and his face got close.

"Yeah, I was, baby, and I'm sorry. I gotta go get my kid, done nothin' but talk to him on the phone for over two months. And he's meetin' you. Got a lot on my mind and blinds were just one thing too many. You're in my house and it ain't in a gated community. It doesn't have a pool and it doesn't butt a golf course. You grew up on a farm but you became a woman that doesn't belong here and right now, it fuckin' kills me to admit it, I gotta focus on Jonas and I can't afford to get you the goddamned blinds you want." His words made me blink but he kept talking. "So, yeah, all that built up, I lost it, and I was a dick."

"I don't belong here?" I whispered.

"No, babe, clue in," he answered. "High-class." His thumb slid across my cheekbone. "Look around you. *Not* high-class."

"I grew up on a farm."

"And ended up an executive."

"I'm a waitress."

"Yeah, *now*. You think I don't lose sleep wonderin' what you gave up and wonderin' when you'll want it back and knowin' I can't give it to you?"

"Tate—"

"I got those demons in my head already, Ace, don't need you throwin' them in my face."

"I—"

"In this town, people prioritize and the shit they gotta prioritize is not should they go to Paris for vacation or invest and buy themselves a condo in Vail. It's a fuckuva lot different."

"Tate…" He opened his mouth to speak and my hand clamped over it. "Let me *talk*."

I could tell by his eyes he wasn't a big fan of my hand over his mouth but I also could tell he was going to let me talk. How I could tell this, I had no clue. I just could. So I took my hand away and put it to the side of his face as he had his at mine.

"You haven't had a lot," I told him.

"Babe—"

"Please, honey," I whispered. He shut his mouth and I went on, "Wanda, at the home store, when she was advising me, she told me to take care of my man. I was trying to take care of you *not*," I said sharply when he looked like he was going to speak again, "to take care of you take care of you but to take care of you like a woman should." My hand left his face, slid down his chest and around his back. "Baby, you live in a crash pad. Maybe it was stupid and maybe too soon but I was trying to give you a home. I just wanted to give you something because…" I paused. "Because…I don't know, but I'm guessing, not a lot of people have done that for you and I wanted you to be able to count on me to do it."

"So you're tellin' me you're takin' advice on how to deal with me from some random, nosy chick at a home store?"

That didn't sound good.

"Um…"

"Ace, your ex, not a man," he informed me. "I know men who got jobs like him, dress like him who are men, but Brad?" He shook his head. "No man has to make anyone feel less than him to be a man. That makes *him* less of a man, less of a goddamned person. What you wanted to do was sweet, but, babe, no offense, you don't know dick about dealin' with a man."

"Okay," I whispered.

"It isn't that it's too soon. You're on the back of my bike, it ain't too soon. You can buy sheets. You *cannot* install blinds."

"Um…," I mumbled. "Can you explain the difference?"

"Sheets are chick territory," he said without delay. "You gotta use tools, that's dick territory."

"Oh," I whispered.

"Don't tread on dick territory," he advised.

"So, um…is a paintbrush a tool?" I asked cautiously.

"If you're paintin' the side of the house, yeah. If you're painting mud-colored paint in a room, no."

"It's terra-cotta," I said softly.

"Whatever," he muttered, his mouth twitching.

"Or, the paint chip called it Mexican Horizon. The blue is Dawn Sky."

"Definitely chick territory," Tate replied, losing the fight with his grin.

"What about...pictures for the walls?" I asked.

"Chick," he answered instantly.

"Um...could I ask that, instead of you getting angry and being a jerk, maybe you give me a heads-up when I'm doing something stupid?"

"Yeah, you can ask that and I'll promise to do what I can do. But, Ace, since I was a kid, I had a temper. Tellin' you that don't mean I can't compromise, just means I am who I am, I know who I am, and you gotta take me as I am and learn to get over it."

"Okay, then, can I ask, while I'm learning to be a biker babe, you try to be a bit more patient?"

The grin hit smile level and he let out a low chuckle before asking, "A biker babe?"

"I'm kind of in training, as you can tell."

He burst out laughing so hard his body collapsed on mine but he rolled almost immediately so I was on top.

My face ended up in his neck, my hair in his face and he moved it away, sweeping it over my shoulders as my head came up.

Then, his eyes scanning my face, he murmured, "Martinis and manicures."

"Dominic at Carnal Spa does manicures," I told him. "He does really good hair. If his manicures are half as good, I'm covered."

"Babe—"

"And I think Ned and Betty'll let me use their pool whenever I want. They like me."

"Laurie—"

"And martinis are bad for me. I get drunk on one and a half and I mean *drunk*."

He smiled at me. "Then we're hittin' the home store sale."

"We are?"

"Martini glasses. Fuckin' you normal is hot. Make-up sex is un-fuckin'-believable. Drunk sex might just kill me."

"Tate—"

"Though, won't mind dyin' that way."

"Tate!"

His face went soft and his hand slid into my hair.

"As cute as you are, tryin' to be a biker babe and all, honey, I gotta pick up my boy," he murmured.

I relaxed against him. "Okay."

"I get him to Carnal, I'll bring him by the bar so you can meet him."

"Oh no," I stated quickly. "You two be together. I'll see you when I get home. Or, do you want more time? Maybe I should—"

"I'll bring him by the bar to meet you. We'll pick you up after shift and go out to dinner."

"Really, I can—"

"Babe."

"What?"

He didn't speak and neither did I. It was a standoff.

Finally, I gave in, "Okay."

"He's gonna like you."

"Okay."

"Lauren, honey, swear to God, he's gonna love you."

I bit my lip and nodded.

He watched my teeth bite my lip, then his eyes came to mine.

"You wanna know why I know?" he asked.

I nodded again.

"Because you want him to like you and you're worried he won't and you care about me. Jonas spends a lot of time with people who don't give a shit about anything but themselves. He'll respond to someone who isn't like that."

I relaxed against him again and repeated a hopeful, "Okay."

"Get off me, baby, gotta shower."

I rolled off but he rolled right on top of me.

"I thought you had to shower," I asked when I caught his eyes.

He held my gaze for a moment and I couldn't read his face before his head dipped and I felt his nose tweak my ear.

"I'm sorry I was a dick," he whispered there.

There it was. That was all he had to do and I knew at that moment there would be times when he'd be a jerk and that was all he'd ever have to do.

My arms slid around him. "Honey," I whispered back.

He gave my shoulder a bristly kiss and then he was gone.

I rolled into the unmade bed so the covers were over me and listened to the shower.

Then Buster came up on the bed and gave me a look that communicated, "Where were you last night?"

I cooed to her. She moved to me and flopped gracefully into the crook of my bent hips. I petted and she purred.

Tate left me after getting dressed and leaning into the bed to give me a kiss and Buster a stroke. Then I took a shower, got ready, and went to work, calling Betty after I got there to tell her that I wasn't moving back to the hotel.

"Didn't think so, hon."

"I'm sorry," I said and I heard a surprised burst of laughter.

"Why?" she asked.

"Well, I told you I was coming home and I miss you guys, I didn't…"

"Laurie, honey, you and Tate are right up the way. You didn't move to Fiji."

"Yes, but…"

"You're still home. You're just sleepin' in a different place."

That shut my mouth.

"Tell Tatum Jackson to let you loose every once in a while. I miss my coffee time with Laurie," she finished.

"Okay," I replied. "I should get back to work."

"See you later, hon."

"Bye, Betty."

We hung up and I stared at my phone thinking dang, but I liked Betty.

I went back to work and did my job for hours jumpy as a cat.

"Laurie, I asked, you okay?" Jim-Billy repeated.

My eyes had glazed over so I focused on him.

"Tate's bringing Jonas to the bar," I told him.

"I know," he told me.

"I'm not good with kids," I shared and he blinked.

"You ain't good with kids?"

I shook my head as Krystal wandered to our end of the bar.

"You ain't good with kids?" she repeated Jim-Billy's question.

"No, they freak me out," I answered.

"They freak you out," Jim-Billy said.

"Laurie," Krystal called me. "Two nights ago two boys were drunk and lookin' for a fight. A beer bottle was thrown, which means broken furniture is about two seconds away. You waded into that and, with a smile and a flip of your hair, you talked them down and had them laughin'. You can handle drunk, angry bikers bent on blood with a flip of your hair, how can kids freak you out?"

"I didn't flip my hair," I told her.

"Darlin'," Jim-Billy put in, "you did."

I looked at him. "I did?"

"Who cares?" Krystal asked impatiently. "I asked, you can deal with that, wadin' in without thought, how can kids freak you out?"

"Those are adults," I explained.

"Yeah. So?"

"Adults aren't kids," I finished.

"No, darlin', they aren't," Jim-Billy agreed and I looked at him again to see he was smiling at Krystal.

"This isn't funny," I whispered and then, desperate, I leaned toward Krystal. "Am I dressed okay?"

She gave me a once-over and I took two steps back to give her the full view.

I had on a pale pink blouse with a mandarin collar, little ruffles on the edges of the little poofed sleeves and darts up my ribs, molding the top close to my midriff. I had some cleavage going, for tip purposes (upon research, I'd found this was an excellent motivator for higher tips). My hair was down and styled. I had maximum makeup, for me, when it wasn't evening makeup of course. And I was wearing jeans, a dark brown belt with little, round silver rivets at the edges and a pair of hot pink, high-heeled, strappy sandals. I had on my flowery jewelry at ears and throat and a bunch of stretchy, beaded bracelets in hot pink, baby pink, clear, and blue.

"Well," Krystal drawled, "you wanna catapult him straight into puberty and discovering alternate uses of socks, you picked a winner."

"What?" I breathed as Jim-Billy guffawed.

Krystal grinned and I stared at her because she rarely did that as in, never.

"You're fine," she assured me but I felt far from assured.

"I should go home and change," I declared and turned toward the door.

Jim-Billy got up off his barstool, a virtual miracle in itself, and headed me off.

"Darlin', she was jokin'. You look sweet," he told me.

"Krystal doesn't joke," I reminded him.

"I got a computer in my stockroom with a spreadsheet you made that makes stock takes a piece of cake. I got a full stable of waitresses and only one of 'em gives me fits. Business is up so much I'm thinkin' about lettin' Dominic turn me into a redhead. So, even though Bubba is fishin', I'm in the mood to joke," Krystal stated and I forgot my nerves and walked back to the bar.

"Bubba's fishing?" I asked as Jim-Billy settled back onto his stool.

"Didn't come home last night, don't 'spect him home tonight, tomorrow, or God knows when," she answered.

I looked at Jim-Billy and Jim-Billy lifted his brows, his mouth a grimace as his ear tipped toward his shoulder.

I looked back at Krystal. "I'm sorry, Krys."

Her face changed and I felt a knife in my gut because she let me see pain before she wiped it clean.

"No offense, honey, you know I like you but the worst thing a woman can hear is another woman, a woman who has a good man, sayin' she's sorry about your man."

Then Krystal walked away and I grabbed on to the edge of the bar to hold myself up because my legs were trembling. This was with both sadness and anger, sadness for Krystal, but mostly anger at Bubba for making her feel that way.

I looked at Jim-Billy. "She was joking," I whispered. "Then I messed it up."

"She'll be okay, darlin'," Jim-Billy whispered back.

"I'm gonna get Tate to call Bubba and get his ass home," I declared and Jim-Billy shook his head.

"Jonas is home, which means Tate is home, which means Bubba is g-o-n-e, *gone*. Even if Tate calls him, Bubba won't be back until Sunday night."

I felt my eyes get wide. "Always?"

"Yup."

"But, Tate can't come down to help if Jonas is here."

"No, but he can if there's trouble."

I felt my lips thin.

I liked Bubba. He was funny and he was sweet and he called me gorgeous in a way that I knew he thought that was true. He wasn't as good a bartender as Krystal, Dalton, and Tate but he knew his way around the back of the bar. He was slow because he saw no reason in life to go fast.

But I didn't like him taking advantage of Tate or causing Krystal pain.

"Uh…Laurie?" Jim-Billy called and I focused on him. "It is what it is and has been goin' on a long while. Leave it be."

"But—"

"Darlin', listen to Jim-Billy. Leave it be."

"I—"

"Ace!" I heard, jumped and turned to the door.

Tate stood there. I'd been so caught up in Krystal and Bubba I hadn't been paying attention. My legs started trembling again and I didn't move a muscle.

"Babe, you gonna stand there starin' at me or you gonna come meet Jonas?" Tate called.

"Go get 'im, tiger," Jim-Billy encouraged.

I licked my lips, looked at him, nodded, and walked on jellied legs toward Tate.

"Um...," I started when I got close. "Did everything go okay?"

"No," he answered.

"What happened?" I asked as I made it to him.

His hand came up and curled around the side of my neck. "Tell you later."

"Hey, Tate!" Krystal called and Tate's head swung to her. "Laurie's off. Wendy'll be in in half an hour to finish her shift. She's got the weekend."

I stared at Krystal, then I looked at Tate to find he was grinning down at me.

"Good news, Ace," he said.

"I can always, you know, paint another room or something while you do boy stuff," I offered.

"How 'bout we do boy-girl stuff, the clean kind durin' the day, the dirty kind at night?"

I did *not* need him talking nasty prior to me meeting his son and therefore hissed, "Tate!"

He grinned, slung an arm around my shoulders, and propelled me to the door. "Come meet Jonas."

It was the time of judgment. I couldn't delay and I couldn't run, so I wrapped my arm around his waist and let Tate take me to his son.

He was standing, shoulders leaned against the passenger side of the Explorer, a video game in his hands, his dark head bent to it.

"Good news, Bub," Tate called, "Lauren's got the rest of the day off."

That was when his head came up and my step stuttered.

He was the spitting image of Tate. There wasn't a hint of Neeta to be found.

He was the most beautiful child I'd ever seen in my life.

Then he smiled at me and my heart turned over.

"Hey, Lauren," he said.

"Um…hi, Jonas," I replied and Tate stopped me in front of his son.

"Dad said you made me a cake," he told me.

"Red cake, white frosting," I replied and his head tipped to the side.

"Red cake?" he asked.

"Um…it's really chocolate but I dye it red. I don't know why, it's just, that's what the recipe says so that's what I do."

"It got Moist Factor Five Hundred?" he asked and I knew they'd been talking about me, more than a little, more than likely a lot.

My heart started beating very fast and very *hard*.

"Yes," I answered.

"Dad said that's the bomb," Jonas informed me.

"The, um…master of Moist Factor Five Hundred works over there," I pointed to La-La Land, "at the coffee shop. He shared the secret of his success with me."

Jonas took a step forward and twisted his torso to see beyond the truck to where I was pointing. Then he straightened and looked back at me.

"Cool," he replied.

"Yeah, um…cool," I reiterated.

He grinned.

My heart turned over again.

"You look just like your dad," I whispered and his back went straighter, giving him at least another inch.

"Be just like him when I grow up," he stated proudly.

"A football star?" I asked.

"Nah, a bounty hunter," he told me.

"They carry guns and hunt dangerous fugitives." I informed him of something he probably knew and I probably shouldn't remind him of, therefore I clamped my mouth shut after speaking.

"Yeah, why you think I wanna be like my dad?" Jonas asked.

"Perhaps you can consider alternate future employment," I suggested. "Maybe an accountant."

Father and son burst out laughing.

I looked up at Tate. "I wasn't being funny."

"I know, babe," he replied, still chuckling. "That's why it was hilarious."

I looked back to Jonas and stated somewhat haughtily, "An accountant would not make his girlfriend worry while he was away at work."

"Yeah," Jonas shot back with a smile. "But he also wouldn't have a MILF girlfriend either."

I felt my eyes round as Tate said in a father's warning tone but still I could tell from his voice he was smiling huge, "Bub."

"Dad, seriously, she's a MILF," Jonas returned.

"Think it, boy, don't say it," Tate replied.

"Right," Jonas muttered but he was still smiling at me and his smile was unrepentant.

Jonas had called me a MILF. I knew what that meant and I didn't know what to do with it.

Seriously, Tate from head to toe.

"I think I need a latte. Does anyone need a latte?" I asked, then didn't wait for them to answer. "No? Okay, you boys go on and do father-and-son stuff, toss a baseball, build a barn, whatever. I'll get a latte and meet you home for dinner."

Jonas looked at Tate. "They have smoothies?"

"We'll find out," Tate answered and my eyes darted to him because he was moving me toward the sidewalk and, I knew, La-La Land.

Jonas fell in step beside me.

Not Tate.

Me.

I looked down at him and I knew in a couple of years if I was still around I wouldn't be looking down anymore.

"Are you tall for your age?" I asked.

"Yep," he replied.

"Tallest kid in his class," Tate put in.

"Do you play sports?" I asked Jonas.

"Yep," he answered then he observed, "You're tall. Did you?"

"I was a cheerleader," I shared and both father and son laughed again. "What's funny?" I asked into their laughter.

"MILF," Jonas said under his breath and Tate chuckled anew.

"Cheerleading is considered a sport," I informed them snootily.

"You flip around in a short skirt with your panties showing," Jonas informed me back.

My eyes narrowed on his grinning face. "How old are you again?"

"Ten," he answered.

"You act fifteen."

"Thanks," he replied.

"That wasn't a compliment," I explained and his smile got broader telling me he took it as one anyway.

We crossed the street and were a door away from La-La Land when I clarified, "Just because the subject has come up," I looked down at Jonas, *"repeatedly,* a MILF refers to a mother and I'm not a mother therefore I cannot be a MILF."

"You're Dad's girlfriend. If a dad's girlfriend is hot, she's always a MILF," Jonas told me.

"Is that a rule?" I asked.

"Yeah, one I just made up," he returned.

"You can't just make things up," I told him.

"Sure you can," he retorted. "Anyway, a girlfriend could turn into a stepmom and a stepmom is a kinda mom so she can also be a MILF."

Tate pushed the door open, held it for Jonas and me to precede him and he muttered as I went by, "He's got you there, Ace."

"Tate, we're talking about *MILFs*," I shot back.

"He's still got you," Tate said on a grin.

"MILF? What? Where? Who?" Shambles called from under the counter. He popped up and he looked at me, then Tate. "Petal! Dude!" Then he looked at Jonas and shouted, "Groovintude! Is this Little Dude?"

"Shambles, meet Tate's son, Jonas," I introduced.

"Hey," Jonas greeted.

"Little Dude! Hey back, you want a smoothie?"

Of course, Shambles had smoothies.

I sighed. Tate chuckled again. I turned and glared up at him.

"Yeah, can I have—" Jonas started and Shambles lifted a hand.

"Let me rock your world," Shambles requested.

"Cool." Jonas smiled.

I walked to the counter. "When you're done with Jonas's smoothie, rock my world too."

"Got it," Shambles said and then his eyes moved from Tate to Jonas. He leaned into me and advised in a stage whisper, "Petal, talkin' about MILFs in front of kids…" He trailed off and shook his head.

I pointed at Jonas and exclaimed, "He brought it up!"

Shambles leaned back, his eyebrows up. "He did?"

I tipped my head back and asked the ceiling, "Can we stop talking about MILFs?"

Jonas ignored me by declaring, "She is one."

I tipped my head down to glare at Jonas.

"Big Dude is right, he's got you there," Shambles muttered and went to the blender.

"Where's Sunny?" I asked in an effort to change the subject.

"Bringin' down the sun. We had a quiet afternoon so she headed out," Shambles answered.

"Lauren said you're the master of Moist Factor Five Hundred," Jonas put in.

"Little Dude! I *so* am!" Shambles fairly shouted and looked at me.

"Did you try it?" I nodded. "Was I wrong?" I shook my head. He looked at Tate. "You?"

Tate's arm slid along my shoulders and he tucked me into his side. "Outstanding."

I was pretty sure he meant the frosting, or, more like the mess created by the frosting and the way we cleaned it up.

I didn't inform Shambles of this.

"You wanna try Moist Factor Five Hundred?" Shambles offered Jonas. "I got plenty."

Jonas didn't even look at his father before he replied, "Nah, thanks. Lauren made me a cake and I don't wanna ruin it."

My heart turned over again and my eyes flew to Shambles who was midscoop of something he was putting in Jonas's smoothie and his eyes were on me.

I didn't know many children but I'd never known a child to turn down a treat, not even when their accepting it might ruin something nice someone had done for them.

Shambles tore his eyes from mine and went on scooping, muttering, "Good call."

I curled closer to Tate but my eyes moved to Jonas who was watching Shambles make his smoothie.

Then in my ear, I heard Tate ask softly, "What'd I say?"

I looked at him and nodded. "Just like you."

His arm gave me a squeeze and his hand lifted so his finger could slide along my jaw.

"Yeah, baby," he whispered. "Just like me."

I melted deeper into Tate and Shambles broke the moment when he called, "What about you, Big Dude? Am I rockin' your world too?"

Tate dropped his hand and looked at Shambles. "Knock yourself out."

I felt something funny and I looked down at Jonas. When I did, his eyes darted away. I could only see his profile but, even so, I saw he was biting his lip to hide a smile.

He'd seen Tate touch me. He'd probably even heard what we said.

And he liked it.

I relaxed into Tate and bit my lip to hide my own smile.

*   *   *

I was making Rice-A-Roni when my cell rang. I went to the opposite counter, grabbed my phone, saw it said "Krys Calling," touched the button, and put it to my ear.

"Everything okay, Krys?"

"It's Jim-Billy," I heard. "And that's what we wanna know about you."

"Sorry?"

"Is everything okay?"

"Who's we?"

"Krystal, Wendy, Dalton, Nadine, Amber, Jonelle, *everybody*. So?"

"Jonelle?"

"Yeah, and...*so*?"

"Jonas called me a MILF."

Silence. Then a loud cackle of laughter.

Then, not into the phone, I heard Jim-Billy saying through a voice suffocated with mirth, "Jonas called her a MILF."

I heard more laughter in the background and Jim-Billy back at my ear.

"Everything's okay," he declared.

Then he disconnected.

I rolled my eyes, touched the button, and put the phone down. Then I smiled at it on the counter.

Tate and Jonas walked in from outside and Jonas went right to the cake and stuck his finger in it, swiping off frosting and putting his finger in his mouth.

This was the third time he'd done this.

"Keep doing that, honey, you'll get cake and no frosting and what good is that?" I warned also for the third time.

"Maybe you can make more frosting?" Jonas suggested.

"No, but I can cut the cake so you get the nonfrosting bits and Tate and I get the yummy-with-frosting bits."

"Yummy?" Jonas asked, his eyes dancing.

"You've tasted the frosting," my head tilted to the cake, "and you've come back for more. You know it's yummy."

"No one says yummy," Jonas informed me.

"I do," I informed him back.

"You're hot but you're also a little goofy," he returned and grinned.

I looked at Tate. "Can you ask your son to stop calling me hot?"

"Calls 'em as he see 'em, babe," Tate replied, grinning like his son.

"He's *ten*," I reminded Tate.

Tate shrugged.

I looked between them both and I did this twice.

Then I went back to the Rice-A-Roni, and I did this wondering if Tate fathered a child or he'd been cloned.

*   *   *

Dinner consumed, we were eating cake and ice cream (and I hadn't given Jonas the nonfrosting bits because I was a pushover) at the dining room table when Tate's phone rang.

I noticed Jonas's head twist quickly when it did and I also noticed his body get tight.

My eyes moved slowly to Tate to see he was looking at the display on his phone, his face hard. Then he looked at me.

"A minute, babe," he said, pushing his chair back. He tousled Jonas's hair and walked to the sliding glass door, flipping his phone open, putting it to his ear, and answering with an impatient, "Yeah?"

He slid the door open, closed it behind him, turned right, and disappeared.

I looked to Jonas to see he was no longer eating his cake like it was the best thing he'd ever tasted as he'd done his entire dinner. He was shoving it around and slopping melted ice cream on it.

"You okay, Jonas?" I asked. His head came up and he straightened.

"Yup," he answered, the lightness of his tone forced.

"You sure?" I asked.

"Sure I'm sure," he answered.

"You want more cake?"

"Nah."

"You want to help me with the dishes?"

He looked at the kitchen as if it and any activity you could do in it was foreign to him, then at me. "All right," he agreed uncertainly.

We got up and took the plates to the kitchen. I rinsed, Jonas loaded the dishwasher. I did this while looking out the window to the deck about seven hundred times. I couldn't see Tate and I also couldn't hear him.

"She does this," Jonas stated and my eyes went from the window to him.

"Sorry, honey?"

"Mom, she calls Dad when I'm here. Rags on him."

Oh.

My.

God.

He knew that? How?

The only way was for her to tell him because I knew Tate wouldn't. Or for him to figure it out, which I knew Jonas could. He was a smart kid and kids noticed a lot more than adults gave them credit for, or at least that was what I heard.

"Um...," I mumbled.

"It's okay, he's used to it."

It was *not* okay. Of course, this was not my place to say so I kept my mouth shut.

"I'll tell the judge I wanna live here," Jonas announced unexpectedly and my eyes shot to him.

"Sorry?"

"Can you tell Dad that?" he asked.

I took in a breath and wondered what to do in this situation.

Then I decided most parents probably wondered what to do in a variety of situations that occurred daily and they went with their gut. So I decided to go with my gut, grabbed a kitchen towel, wiped my hands, tossed the towel on the counter, leaned down and shoved the drawer into the dishwasher then closed the door. Then I curled my fingers around his shoulder and moved us both so we were leaning sideways against the counter.

"Do you know—?" I started.

"About the papers?" he asked and I nodded. "Yeah, she talks about it all the time. She's pretty pi—I mean, upset."

I bit my lip.

Then I went with my gut again and cupped the underside of his jaw with my hand, tipping his head up to me and leaning slightly down to get close to him.

"Yes, baby, I'll tell him," I spoke gently. "What I'd like to know is, why won't you?"

Jonas stared up at me, his eyes wide, his lips parted and something about his astonished look set me on edge. He acted old for his age, held intelligent conversations (when he wasn't talking about MILFs that was). He was young but he wasn't stupid or childlike.

He looked like a child right then, vulnerable with a hint of innocent wonder.

Then I figured out what set me on edge.

I guessed that Neeta didn't talk gently to her son and she didn't touch him gently either. He'd never felt it, at least not from a woman or, at least, not on any kind of normal basis. The other night, when she referred to him, she called him her "kid." I'd thought nothing of it at the time but now it seemed detached. She didn't call him "my son" or "my boy." Just "my kid."

This beautiful child was just her kid.

My heart turned over again as my stomach clenched and I had to take a cautious breath so he wouldn't hear it and I could still control the tears that threatened.

He recovered and whispered, "She finds out, she'll freak."

"Finds out you want to live with your dad?"

He nodded.

Of its own accord, though I didn't do a thing to stop it, my hand slid from his jaw, across his soft cheek, over his thick hair, and then down to curve around the side of his neck.

"And she'll freak if she knows you're willing to talk to the judge?"

"That and that I told Dad. But if she finds out and I say I didn't say it to him, she'll believe me."

"She will?"

"I don't lie to her."

I thought this was likely because she lit into him if he did.

Still, I asked, "You don't?"

"No. She's not…she's…Blake…She's used to getting lied to. She knows when someone's lyin'. She told me that Dad and me, Grandpop, Uncle Wood, we were the only ones never lied to her. She always believes me. I just gotta let Dad know and I gotta do it so I don't hafta lie to her."

I studied him.

Then I nodded. "Okay, honey, I'll tell your dad."

He looked visibly relieved and I instantly wished I'd gotten into a catfight with his mother so I had a chance to get my licks in.

"Thanks, Lauren," he said quietly.

"Laurie," I corrected.

"Laurie?"

"What your dad and my friends call me."

He smiled a small smile. "Okay. Laurie."

"All right, baby," I whispered. "And Jonas?"

"Yeah?"

"Before you leave, I'll give you my number. You have anything you need, any time, call me. And if you have anything you need to keep from your mom but you need your dad to know and you feel you can't tell him, you let me know and I'll tell him for you. We got a deal?"

His smile got a bit bigger. It wasn't his normal, broad, confident smile but it was better.

"Yeah," he answered.

"Now, one more chance, you want more cake?"

The smile came back full force.

"Yeah."

"I rinsed your plate, honey, get me another one."

I was cutting Jonas's second slice of cake when Tate came in. Both Jonas and I looked at him and I noted his face wasn't hard anymore but he didn't look happy.

"Jonas is having more cake, honey. You want another piece?"

"No, Ace. Thanks," Tate answered and I lifted my brows to him. His answer was to close his eyes slowly, tilt his chin in a subtle negative, then open them and look at Jonas.

I wouldn't find out what had happened on the deck until after Jonas ate his cake, after Jonas and I finished the dishes, and after we watched a movie that was so gory, I spent the vast majority of it with my face in Tate's chest, which Jonas thought was amusing, considering he'd seen that movie *a gazillion* (his words) times and he thought the gore factor was average (again his words). It was also after Jonas went downstairs to his bedroom (one of the rooms to which I didn't open the door when Tate first went away but had since seen and cleaned).

When Jonas was off, Tate went straight to the fridge and got a beer. I followed him to the kitchen, his hand came out of the fridge and he lifted up a bottle in silent question. I shook my head. He twisted off the cap, tossed it into the garbage and led me out to the back patio where we sat in wrought-iron chairs. I suspected he took me here because the front deck was just over Jonas's room and, if he had his windows open, he could hear.

"Well?" I asked when we'd settled.

"She's off on one," he told me, taking a pull of his beer.

"What does that mean?"

"Said she was comin' tomorrow to get him."

"Why?"

In the dark, I saw his head turned to me. "You."

"Me?"

"You're here. She's got one of her posse spyin' and they said you're still here. So she says she doesn't want him here if you're here."

"I'll go to the hotel," I offered. "I'll do it tonight."

"The fuck you will, babe."

"Tate—"

"She doesn't control your life. She doesn't control my life. And, when my son is with me, she doesn't control *his* life."

He sounded pretty angry, in fact, his voice was vibrating so I said softly, "Okay, honey."

"You went to the hotel last night, Laurie, and one of those bitches saw you with Ned and Betty. She thought you were out."

Darn, darn, and double darn.

How could Neeta have a posse? Who could even like her? And why did I lose it and walk out on Tate?

So *stupid*.

I stopped mentally kicking myself and asked, "Would she have given him to you if she knew I was still here?"

"Nope," he replied then took another pull of his beer. "She wasn't home when I got there anyway. Neither was Jonas. But Blake sure was. She rolled in half an hour late. That whole time I sat in my truck at the curb."

"Oh Tate," I whispered.

He shook his head and said, "I called Pop after I hung up on her. He's gonna see what he can do."

"What if she comes?"

"Don't know, don't care."

"You can't have Jonas see a scene like last week."

He sighed. Then he tilted his head back and took in more beer.

"Jonas and I talked," I told him and his head turned to me.

"Yeah?"

"He knows about the papers," I started but stopped when that scary energy started to flash off Tate.

"Christ," he whispered then repeated, "Christ." He shook his head. "Can she once act like a goddamned mom and shield him from shit? He's fuckin' ten. We started this shit when he was born and since he could understand words, she told him we were battlin' every time we were doin' it. Is it that hard to let him be a kid and let his parents deal with their own shit?"

I thought this was a good question but I didn't have an answer to it.

"Sympathy?" I guessed.

"Damn straight, Ace. She's been tryin' to turn him since I could remember. Hell, she probably talked trash about me when he was in the womb."

"You weren't together then?"

"Fuck no," he answered.

This surprised me. "You weren't?"

"No, babe," he answered firmly.

"But, don't you kind of have to be together to *make* a baby?"

"Yeah, and you have to be together to *trap* a man into marrying you."

I gasped. Tate nodded.

"She pushed the marriage card the minute after she skipped her first period. The bitch has been on the pill since she was fourteen. Not even a scare. Religious about it. All of a sudden, she's knocked up. All of a sudden, that is, after she'd been naggin' me about gettin' hitched."

"Why didn't you?" I asked gently.

"Unconscious self-preservation," he muttered, took a sip of his beer, swallowed, and finished, "Thank fuck."

I drew in a soft breath, sat back, looked into the night, and let it go.

Then I told Tate, "Jonas wants to live with you."

I felt rather than saw Tate's head turn and his eyes lock on me.

"He tell you that?"

"Says he wants you to know but he can't tell you. Says he'll talk to the judge."

"She finds out, she'll give him shit. He can deny it technically without lyin'," Tate mumbled.

"That's what he said," I affirmed.

"Throwin' you under the bus."

My head turned to him. "Sorry?"

"Someone's gotta have told me. He said it, he meant it, he'd do it, it gets to that. She'll know it, she'll know he didn't tell *me* but he told *someone* who told me and she'll be pissed at me and that someone who told me. You've seen her pissed, Ace. So has Jonas. There it is. That's you under the bus."

"He didn't mean—"

Tate leaned into me and the movement was sharp and angry. "I know he didn't, Laurie, but that's what she made him do. My ten-year-old son is playin' people. At ten...years...old. This is what she does to people. He didn't like it but he needed me to know and he knew he was throwin' you under the bus and he had to make that play. Fuck." He sat back and repeated, "Fuck."

"Tate, you're doing what you can do," I assured him.

"Right," he bit off.

I reached out a hand and wrapped it around his forearm. "It's all you can do. Do it. Get him home. He wants to be here. That says a lot. You have support. You just have to be patient."

Tate looked at me and I knew he was going to mouth off. Then he turned away, took a sip of his beer, swallowed, pulled in an audible breath, and on the exhale repeated, "Right."

I stood and bent over him, my fingers sliding into his hair, and he tipped his head back to look up at me.

"I'm going to go take my makeup off. You want me to come back out?"

"I'll be in in a second."

"You okay?"

"No."

I aimed at his mouth in the dark and hit it, brushing my lips against his.

"I'll be in bed when you get there," I whispered when I was done.

His voice was less harsh when he said, "That makes me feel better, Ace."

"What does Jonas like for breakfast?"

"Considering his breakfast is usually sugar-clogged cereal or fast food, you make him a home-cooked breakfast, he'll like anything."

"French toast it is," I whispered, brushed his mouth again, then lifted up and kissed him on the forehead.

I had straightened and started to move away when he caught my wrist, detaining me.

I looked back.

"You let on you knew he was playin' you?" he asked.

"No. I told him I'd give him my number and if he ever had anything he needed you to know, he could tell me and I'd let you know."

"Threw yourself under the bus," he muttered.

"I didn't think he was playing me, Captain," I replied. "But even if I did, I'd do it again."

He didn't speak but he also didn't let go of my wrist. Then he lifted it, turned it inward, and kissed the inside. His beard tickled the sensitive skin there. The gesture and how he did it touched a sensitive part of me you couldn't see because it was deep on the inside.

He let my wrist go and said softly, "Meet you in bed, baby."

"Okay," I whispered and left him to finish his beer.

CHAPTER TWENTY

Rollin' in Her Grave

THE NEXT MORNING, Tate and I were out on the deck drinking coffee.

My chair was close beside his, his legs were up on the railing and he'd reached down and wrapped an arm around the backs of my knees and pulled my legs up on his. As we sat, silent and sipping our coffee, bathed in the morning sun, my legs naturally and comfortably tangled with his.

As the time slid by I was thinking I could start every day for the rest of my life like this. I didn't know what Tate was thinking but I hoped it was much the same.

I heard the sliding glass door open and I craned my neck back to look beyond Tate to the door.

Jonas was closing the door and he turned toward us. He was wearing a pair of loose-fitting knit shorts and a T-shirt, both wrinkled with sleep. His hair was adorably tousled. And, I was alarmed to note, he was stumbling somewhat drunkenly down the deck toward us.

I felt my body tense, wondering if he was sick or something when Tate moved. I looked to him to see he'd stretched an arm toward his boy. Then I watched as Jonas walked straight into it, not stopping at Tate, instead colliding sleepily with him and then leaning into his side as Tate curled his arm around his son.

My heart turned over yet again.

Tate and Jonas stayed this way for several long minutes without speaking.

Finally, Tate asked quietly, "You sleep okay, Bub?"

Jonas nodded, staring blankly into the trees, his body still heavy against his father.

"Bed all right?" Tate asked.

"Like it better than home," Jonas mumbled. "Bigger."

Jonas's bed downstairs was a double. It was covered in light gray sheets and a forest green comforter both of which were far newer and better quality than Tate's had been before I replaced them. There was a lamp on the nightstand, its base a football, its shade covered with Philadelphia Eagles emblems. The walls had posters of Eagles players on them. The dresser had T-shirts, shorts and underwear in it, the closet had jackets and jeans on hangers, some shoes on the floor. There was a TV with some video game player attached to it, a mess of controls and cords.

There was a boom box with CDs scattered around. There was boy stuff lying here and there, on the nightstand, dresser, on top of the TV.

When I'd discovered and cleaned it, the bed was unmade, some clothes on the floor. I'd noticed that Jonas's room wasn't where he slept when he was here. He had clothes, he had things. It wasn't his room at Tate's house. It was his room in his home.

"You want Laurie to make you breakfast?" Tate asked.

Jonas's eyes didn't move from the trees when he muttered, "Unh-hunh."

I leaned across Tate. "What do you want, baby?" I asked. "French toast? Pancakes? Eggs?"

"Eggs," Jonas said.

"Scrambled? Fried? Poached?" I went on.

"Fried," Jonas answered.

"Gotcha," I said softly, untangled my legs from Tate's and stood. He looked up at me when I did. "You want a warm-up?" I asked, tipping my head to his mug.

"Yeah, honey," he answered.

I took his mug and looked into his beautiful eyes. That was when the spirit moved me and I didn't know if it was right but I also didn't care. A biker babe would act when the spirit moved her so I did.

I leaned down and touched my mouth to Tate's. When I did, his hand came up and curled at my upper hip, his fingers pressing in firmly.

I lifted my head and saw his face soft and warm. Then I looked at Jonas to see he was not looking at the trees anymore. He was watching me with his father. His face was still sleepy but I knew he'd seen the kiss and he'd seen his father's face after.

The spirit moved me again and I leaned into Jonas and touched my lips to his forehead, pulled slightly away and looked into *his* beautiful eyes.

"Eggs," I whispered, straightened, skirted Tate's chair, and walked away.

*   *   *

"Do it again!" Jonas shouted.

I lounged in the lounge chair watching father and son playing in Ned and Betty's pool.

"Again" meant Tate grasping Jonas by the waist and tossing him bodily through the air to splash in the deep end. This had been going on awhile and I, and two twentysomething girls in bikinis across the way from me, had been watching it avidly.

This was because Tate, slicked with wet, his eagle tattoo on show, his powerful muscles bunching when he tossed his son around the pool, was a sight to see.

It was late afternoon but the day was still hot. Tate and Jonas had dropped me off at boot camp and picked me up afterward. I'd packed our bags for the pool visit before boot camp and changed at Ned and Betty's house while Tate and Jonas hit the pool.

Jonas had swim trunks.

Tate didn't. Tate hit the pool in a pair of faded, cutoff jean shorts. Another reason to watch him avidly for he might pull himself out of the pool, his whole body slick and those shorts plastered on him was not a sight to see. It was a sight to prove there was a god and that god might just be Tate.

I watched Tate throw Jonas again and watched Jonas land with a splash. He surfaced laughing and shaking his head. As beautiful a child as Jonas was, and he was more beautiful when he was laughing, I noted the twentysomething girls kept their eyes glued to Tate who had lifted a hand to run his fingers over his wet hair, his eyes on Jonas, his lips smiling. All of this was fascinating and I was sleeping with the man. Those two girls probably thought they'd died and gone to biker babe heaven.

I should have been worried about the twentysomethings. They were thinner than me, prettier than me, younger than me, their bathing suits were a lot dinkier than mine and they were making it obvious that Tate could have one, the other, or both of them at the same time if he just crooked a finger.

Instead, I was wiped from boot camp and as much fun as it was to watch a wet Tate in cutoff jean shorts horse around with his son in Ned and Betty's pool, I decided I was going to take a nap. I decided this firstly because I was pretty certain Tate was into me. Secondly, because Tyler's program that day had nearly killed me and if one, the other or both of them made a play, I didn't have it in me to fight for my man or do anything with him for that matter.

I readjusted the back of my lounge, flipped to my belly and closed my eyes.

I was deep in a boot camp, hot sun–induced snooze when I was torn from my catnap by a multitude of fat, cold water droplets raining on my back.

I lifted and twisted to see Jonas standing beside me shaking the wet in his hair on me.

"Stop, Jonas, you rat!" I girlie screeched.

He stopped and grinned at me. "Quit bein' lazy, Laurie, and come into the pool with us," he demanded.

"I am *not* being lazy. I spent an hour sweating and wheezing and panting, running around a hot gym. I'm giving my body the break it needs," I returned.

"You're bein' lazy," Jonas retorted.

"Am not!" I shot back.

Then, in a sneak attack coming from the other side, I was suddenly rolled to my back, curled into Tate's arms and lifted.

"Tate!" I shrieked. "Put me down!"

He didn't put me down. He walked to the edge of the pool.

"Don't you dare," I warned and then let out a shrill screech when I found myself flying through the air. I had the chance to close my eyes and pinch my nose with my fingers before I hit.

I surfaced gasping, the water freezing cold against my heated skin.

"You jerk!" I yelled and saw both father and son were standing side by side, staring at me and grinning identical grins. "And *you* are a rascal!" I said to Jonas.

Tate's knees bent and then he propelled himself off the side, his body in dive position knifing into the water. Jonas followed him much less gracefully by doing a cannonball.

Stupidly, I kept treading water and glaring at their forms under it instead of making my escape. Tate's hand wrapped around my ankle, yanked, and I went under. I kicked at him under the water and he let me go but came up, grasping me at the waist and we both surfaced together, face to face.

"You dunked me," I accused but that was all I got out. I had a hand on the top of my head and one on my shoulder. Tate let go of my waist and I was down again, Jonas dunking me this time.

Thus it started. I was able to get Jonas under the water, not Tate, and the horseplay lasted awhile before Tate wrapped an arm around my waist and pulled my back to his front, taking me with him as he did an underwater back flip. We surfaced, Tate still holding me close.

"Do me! Do me!" Jonas shouted.

Tate let me go and then he flipped with Jonas.

He let Jonas go and as both of them shook the water from their hair, I wrapped one of my arms around Jonas's middle.

"We're going front this time," I said in his ear and then I tucked us into a ball and propelled us forward in a front flip. When we surfaced, I let him go and he drifted away.

"See, it's better in the water," he told me with a big know-it-all smile.

I agreed by challenging, "Bet I could beat you by doing the longest handstand."

"No way!" Jonas shouted, already striking out for the shallow end.

"So way," I replied following him.

We got on our hands and I poked him in the ribs underwater. He poked me in the belly. I could have stayed down longer but I let him win. I did this five times.

"Told you no way," Jonas stated after his fifth win.

"Whatever," I mumbled with fake disgruntlement and that bought me another smile.

Jonas turned to his dad and declared, "Bet I could beat you too."

"Yeah?" Tate, who was now sitting on the edge of the pool, his feet in the water, his eyes on us, asked.

"Definitely," Jonas declared.

Tate used his hands to shove himself into the water and I drifted away, alternately treading water, crawling, and floating. Sometimes watching. Sometimes trying not to gloat in front of the twentysome-thing girls. Tate let Jonas win twice and beat him the third go.

They surfaced and Tate was done with handstands. I knew this because he ordered, "Get the ball, Bub."

"Cool!" Jonas shouted and headed to the steps that led out of the pool.

I did a slow crawl to the side, happy with handstands, back flips, and dunking contests but not about to participate in anything that required dexterity, which any activity with a ball would suggest. I put my hands on the side of the pool, prepared to let the boys play boy games and ready to get back to my lounger.

I didn't make it.

I was mostly out when two big hands gripped my hips and pulled me back in. Before I knew it, those hands became arms wrapped around me tight and my front was plastered to Tate's.

I tipped my head back, opened my mouth to say something but his head was already coming down. Then he was kissing me.

We were mostly to the deep end but Tate was tall enough that he was standing, his neck above the water lapping gently against us. He held me close and kissed me deep. It was a hot kiss but getting it after horsing around in a pool with him and his son, it was also sweet. Very sweet. In fact, it was sweetest kiss I'd ever had.

Which might have been why, once his mouth released mine, I looked into his handsome face, his spiky-with-wet-lashed eyes and, without thought, dipped my face to his, veering to the right at the last minute and sliding my smooth cheek against his rough one.

When my lips were at his ear, I whispered, "Love you, Tate."

The instant the words came out of my mouth, his body went solid against mine and his arms around me tightened to the point I found it hard to breathe.

Not that I was breathing. I was staring at the water beyond him, wondering what on earth I'd just done and why on earth I'd done it.

My arms moved from around his neck so I could plant my hands in his chest and I pushed off, gaining about three inches before he hauled me back in.

"Ace," he called softly when I kept my eyes averted.

I was saved from having to answer when Jonas shouted, "Dad, quit making out with Laurie! Go deep!"

I turned my head to look up at Jonas standing at the side of the pool, avoiding Tate's eyes as I did so.

"Go deep, Dad!" Jonas repeated.

"Laurie," Tate called.

My head turned again, my eyes flitted across his and I pushed at his chest as I stared over his shoulder at the sun sparkling off the water.

"Go deep, Captain," I whispered.

He squeezed me with his arms. "Baby—"

"Dad!" Jonas shouted.

"Go deep," I said again when Tate didn't let me go.

His wet hand came to my jaw and he forced me to look at his face. It was soft, it was warm and his eyes were searching.

Then he bent his head, touched his mouth to mine and let me go. I immediately twisted and put my hands on the side of the pool. Hefting myself up, I bent my knee, placed it on the edge and dragged myself out.

I heard a strong surge of water as I got to my feet, my entire body trembling and not from cold. I turned and watched Tate power backward through the water thinking how stupid I was. How very, very stupid.

I'd told him I loved him.

I did, of course, love him. Though I'd only just figured that out and then *blurted* it out, but it was true.

I was in a pool in a Nowheresville town with a man who preferred to watch me doing handstands with his son than check out twentysomething girls. A man who called his son Bub and held him in the curve of his arm as he shook off sleep. A man who called me Ace and talked to me or made love to me when I woke up in the middle of the night, even if he was sleepy. A man who flew home with me to make sure I got to my sick dad. A man who noticed new sheets, spoke his mind, put me on the back of his bike, was nothing but himself, and was great in the shower.

After years of searching, years of longing, years of hoping and then giving up, I'd found special in Carnal and in Tate. Special wasn't exactly perfect but, even so, it was pretty fucking spectacular and it was finally, *finally* mine.

So I loved him.

But I shouldn't have *told* him. It was way too soon. It was way too open. And it put me way too out there.

Because he didn't say it back.

Stupid!

I looked down at Jonas and saw his arm was up then he threw a minisized Nerf ball at Tate. I watched it sail through the air with astonishing accuracy straight at Tate's raised hand. As Tate tagged it and brought his arm down, my eyes went beyond him and my body stilled.

Neeta's Chrysler convertible, the top down, a sunglassed, big-haired Neeta behind the wheel, was turning into the hotel.

My body stilled.

"Oh shit," Jonas muttered and I looked down at him. Then automatically my arm darted out, fingers curling around his shoulder. I yanked him to me, my arm going around his chest, and holding him close.

Neeta parked in the open area by the pool and barely stopped her car before she was flying out of it. She didn't even close the door before she was marching quickly toward us on high-heeled, strappy sandals, her legs bared almost to indecent levels due to her ultrashort miniskirt.

"Get in the car, Jonas!" she shouted.

I held on tighter.

"Car!" she shrieked, bearing down on us. "Now!"

I noticed both Ned and Betty heading our way. Betty had been deadheading her now abundantly filled window boxes at her house. Ned had been inside at reception.

I also noticed Shambles's VW van round its way into the lot.

"What'd I say?" Neeta demanded sharply, coming to a halt in front of us. She was talking to Jonas but her narrowed eyes were glued to me.

Jonas didn't move. I heard a rush of water and I knew Tate was there but I didn't tear my eyes from Neeta.

"Let him go, bitch," she ordered.

"That's enough, Neeta," Tate's deep voice came from close behind me.

"I said, let him *go*!" she screamed at me.

Ned and Betty both joined our group, not close but not far away.

"Jonas, get our stuff," Tate instructed. "Help Laurie get packed up and get to the truck."

"He's not going anywhere with you!" Neeta shouted at Tate.

"He'll be home tomorrow at five," Tate stated.

"He's comin' with me and he ain't comin' back 'til that bitch is outta your house!" she returned on a yell.

"Petal!" Shambles cried and my eyes went to him to see his van parked behind the Chrysler and he was rushing toward us, his long hair flying behind him.

I took two steps back from Neeta, dragging Jonas with me. She took a step forward, Betty going with her but both Neeta and Betty stopped when Tate stepped between us.

"Petal!" Shambles repeated.

"Shambles, honey, now is not—" I stopped speaking when he skidded to a halt in front of us and I caught a look at his face.

Ignoring Neeta, he looked from me to Tate, face pale, obviously panicked and asked, "You find people?"

I watched the line of Tate's body go alert, every inch of it and I did this while my own body tensed.

"You got a problem, Shambles?" Tate asked.

"Get in the fuckin' car, Jonas, *now*!" Neeta ordered.

"They say you find people," Shambles stated.

"Yeah, I find people," Tate replied.

"Sunny's missing," Shambles told him. My body went solid and I saw Shambles was shaking.

"Jonas—" Neeta started but Tate's hand came up, palm in her face and her mouth clamped shut.

"Bitch, shut your mouth right fuckin' *now*." Tate growled, then without hesitation, he dropped his arm, looked at Shambles, and ordered, "Talk to me."

"She didn't come home last night," Shambles explained without delay. "We've been together for six years, we've never slept apart. Not once. Not even once and she didn't come home. Last night, when it was getting late and she hadn't come home, hadn't answered her phone, I went out to find her. She told me where she was going to draw down the sun. I went there and she wasn't there, her bike wasn't there, nothing. I thought maybe she might have gone to one of our other places but I went to those too and she wasn't at any of those either. I called her friends, the hospital, the police, nothing. So I went home and waited for her. It's not like her. It just isn't like her. She says where she's going to be and she's there. I waited all night. Called her phone, called the hospital again. I went to the police this morning, first thing. They said she had to be gone for forty-eight hours before they could do anything even though I told them this was not like her. I went around town, asking anyone if they'd seen her and I went to Bubba's. Lady there said you find people. Do you find people?"

"I find people," Tate replied.

"We need to find her," Shambles whispered.

"Jonas, I'm not gonna say it again," Neeta broke in to warn her son and I belatedly felt his body was trembling against mine.

Betty stepped forward and got between Tate and Neeta.

"Neeta, get in your car and go," she demanded.

Neeta turned squinty eyes to Betty. "What's this got to do with you?"

Betty didn't answer. She turned her back on Neeta and she looked at Tate, Jonas, and me. "Use the house to get changed. Go on. Ned'll let you in." When none of us moved, she urged softly, "Get now. This boy here needs Tate."

I came unstuck and started to shuffle Jonas to the loungers that had our stuff scattered around and it happened.

Neeta lunged for Jonas, grasping his arm and tugging him violently out of mine. So violently, I watched his shoulder wrench in an unnatural way and he let out a surprised but agonized cry of pain.

When this happened, everyone flew into motion.

Ned jumped in front of Tate. I bent and grabbed Jonas's hand, my head filled with visions of Neeta and me playing tug-of-war with poor Jonas as the rope. I was about to let go and go after Neeta when Betty's hand came up sharply and then down sharper, smacking Neeta's forearm so hard the crack of it filled the air and she let Jonas go, emitting her own surprised, pained cry.

I carefully pulled him to me and once I had him, I wrapped my arm around him again and stepped out of reach, twisting my body to shield Jonas as Neeta made another lunge but Betty got in her way.

"Step back, bitch!" Neeta shrieked at Betty.

"Honestly, Neeta? Is *this* how you want your son to remember you? Behavin' like this?" Betty shook her head and continued, "Your mother must be rollin' in her grave," she said softly. Neeta's face went slack and she stepped back as if she'd been struck. "Thank the good Lord, praise thank Him, she never lived to see what you've become."

"I can't believe you'd say that to me," Neeta whispered.

"And I can't believe I just watched you handle your boy like that," Betty returned. "Brenda was a good girl. She loved her babies. She'd do anything for them. She'd do anything *for you*. One thing I know sure as certain, she'd never touch you like that and she'd fight to the death if she knew anyone had done that to you. Right now, I just know, she's rollin' in her grave."

Betty didn't wait for Neeta to reply. She turned to me.

"Get him inside, hon," she prompted.

Far faster than before, I scuttled Jonas and me around Neeta and Betty, placing my body in a way that I was using it to shield Jonas from Neeta. Once clear, I rushed the both of us to our loungers. Jonas and I shoved our stuff in the bags as I heard Tate talking to both Shambles and Ned. I was hefting a bag over my shoulder when the bag was caught at the handles. I whirled, ready to do battle if it was Neeta, only to see Tate had taken it from me. He grabbed my hand but his eyes were on Jonas. He jerked his head toward Ned and Betty's. Jonas took off on a dash and Tate dragged me with him as we followed.

Ned was there before us and he let us in. We took turns in their bathroom, me first. I peeled off my suit and tugged on my underwear, jean shorts, and T-shirt, even though my body was still clammy with wet. I yanked out my flip-flops, shoved my feet in them and exited the bathroom only to have Tate, a hand gentle in his back, shove Jonas in.

"Quick, Bub," he muttered, his hand on the doorknob.

Jonas nodded and Tate shut the door.

I looked up at him. "You okay?"

"Forget me," he said, his hand coming to curl around the side of my neck. "Get out to Shambles."

I nodded. He gave me a squeeze and let me go.

I rushed to Shambles.

*   *   *

Tate, Jonas, and I in the Explorer, Shambles following in his VW van, Neeta following Shambles in her Chrysler, pulled into the forecourt of the garage.

Tate stopped close to the office door, Shambles pulled in beside Tate on the driver's side and Neeta pulled in beside Jonas and me.

Jonas and I hopped down just as Wood and Pop exited one of the bays and Stella walked out of the office.

I quickly moved Jonas to the hood of Tate's SUV as Tate rounded it, his eyes on Stella.

"Need you to look after Jonas," he stated and Stella must have read the mood for she asked not one question. She simply nodded, her eyes on Neeta.

"That won't be necessary since I'm takin' him home with me," Neeta announced.

"What's up, Buck?" Pop asked, ignoring Neeta, as Wood and Pop made it to our group and Shambles hit Tate's side. Shambles looked impatient. Pop had his eyes glued to Tate. Wood had his gaze on Neeta.

"Man here's woman is missin'," Tate told Pop, jerking a thumb at Shambles. "She's been gone since yesterday. I need to get out and see if I can help."

"Did you call the cops, bud?" Stella asked Shambles, walking down the steps that led to the office.

"They say forty-eight hours," Shambles answered her and turned directly to Tate. "Can we go?"

"Yeah," Tate murmured and said to Stella, "Stell?"

"Don't worry, Tate," she answered his unasked question.

"Shee-it," Pop muttered. "What's happenin' 'round here and they say forty-eight hours? Got their heads in their asses."

"I'll come with you," Wood offered and Tate looked at him, his eyes slicing to Neeta, then back to Wood.

"Maybe you can see to that situation," he suggested and I held my breath because suddenly everybody was tense and I suspected this was because Tate hadn't asked Wood for anything, not for a long time and not something as important as dealing with Neeta.

"Jonas is safe with me," Stella stated. "Many eyes…" She trailed off.

"My kid's goin' home with me," Neeta put in, a dog with a bone.

"Girl," Pop turned to her, "it's Buck's weekend."

"He's comin' home with me," Neeta repeated.

"He's not," Tate declared in a way that everyone's eyes went to him. "And he ain't comin' home tomorrow." He looked at Jonas and ordered, "Go, Bub, into the office."

"What do you mean he ain't comin' home tomorrow?" Neeta snapped.

"Go into the office, Bub, now," Tate reiterated.

Jonas nodded and moved quickly toward the office.

"Tate, goddamn it, what in the fuck do you—?" Neeta started but she stopped and I figured this was because Tate speared her with a look that was so hostile it took her breath away. I figured this because it took mine.

We all waited, the door closed behind Jonas and finally Tate spoke and he did this with his eyes still locked on Neeta.

"I gotta do this with Shambles so I don't got a lot of time but I'll tell you this: You think for one fuckin' second after you handled my boy that way that he's goin' anywhere near you, you're a bigger fuckin' lunatic than I thought."

"What's this?" Pop whispered.

"You wanna tell your dad what you did?" Tate dared.

Neeta raised a hand and jabbed a finger at me. "She wouldn't let him go."

"Which was good, since you were actin' like the whacked-out bitch everyone here knows you to be; he was shakin' so hard, he wouldn't have been able to keep his feet," Tate shot back. "And nothin', and you know it Neet, there is not one damn thing in this fuckin' world that excuses you handlin' my boy so rough he cries out in pain."

"Good God," Stella whispered, her tone filled with horror.

"Neet," Pop whispered, his tone filled with pain.

Neeta turned and whined to her father, "She wouldn't let him go, Pop."

Pop didn't even look at me when he asked, "That's your excuse?"

"She—" Neeta began.

Pop cut her off. "Lauren's got not one thing to do with this. It's all you, Neeta. It's always you."

"Pop—" Neeta started but he lifted a hand.

"Get outta my sight, girl. I don't wanna see you." He whispered words that seemed dragged out of him.

I heard Neeta draw in breath in a way that I knew she'd never heard them before, not after anything she'd done and there clearly had been a lot.

"I don't think I ever wanna see you again," he went on and then he stared at her as if he'd never seen her in his life and wished he still hadn't. Finally his eyes moved to Tate. "Do me a favor, just one, Buck, take Wood. Find this man's woman. He can help." He waited for Tate's nod. Tate gave it to him and he concluded, "I'm gonna go be with my grandson." Then he moved to and up the steps, disappearing behind the office door.

"I can take you, Neet, you know it so don't even try," Stella warned and my eyes moved from the office door to her to see she was giving a hard look to Neeta.

Neeta gave up on her family and looked at Tate.

"We'll see what the judge says about this," she threatened.

"Yeah, we will, with Ned, Betty, and Lauren all there to witness what you did, Neet, and Jonas wantin' to live with me anyway, we'll fuckin' see," Tate returned, his eyes shifted to Wood and he clipped, "You're in the Explorer with me." He looked at me. "You're ridin' with Shambles, babe." His eyes sliced to Shambles. "You lead. Take us to where she told you she would be," he ordered. Shambles nodded and Tate finished, "Let's roll."

*   *   *

We hit the clearing in the woods, Shambles was leading and speaking, "There," he pointed to the clearing, "that's where we—"

We were at the edge of a glade and he stopped speaking and walking because Wood reached up and grasped his shoulder, pulling him to a halt.

"Hang there, pal," he said softly, his eyes coming to me. "Hang with him, yeah, Laurie?" I nodded and he looked at Tate.

Then Wood moved forward, Tate rounded me, they separated and skirted the clearing, both of their eyes pointed inward, to the dirt floor. They only did this for five, six steps before they stopped and looked across the glade to each other. When they did, I saw both men's faces were set and both of their mouths were tight.

I reached out, grabbed Shambles's hand and squeezed.

Something must have been communicated nonverbally because Wood nodded once, turned and kept moving but this time he did it into the trees. Tate came back to Shambles and me.

"Do me a favor, Shambles. I left my cell in my truck. Can you get it for me?" Tate asked.

"Is something—?" Shambles started.

"My cell, Shambles," Tate said firmly.

Shambles stared at him, swallowed, and then turned and rushed through the woods to the cars parked a short distance away.

I looked up at Tate. "What—?"

Tate interrupted me, "See that ground?" He pointed to the floor of the glade and my eyes followed his hand.

"Yes," I said.

"All those marks," Tate whispered and I saw a lot of marks in the dirt but Tate didn't wait for me to say anything. His hand came to wrap around the back of my neck, my gaze went to his face and he finished, "Struggle, Ace."

I felt tears fill my eyes as I breathed, "Oh God, no."

"I need you to get him home. Get Jonas. Get Stell. Get Pop. Go out to dinner. Keep Shambles occupied. I'm callin' the cops. We gotta sweep this whole area."

I moved closer to him and put my hands on his stomach.

"Do you think—?"

"I don't ever think. I just go where the trail leads me. But in this case, I'll hope."

"Tate, Sunny's not his style," I told him.

"Get him home. Keep him occupied."

"She doesn't... she's not like Tonia," I pressed.

His fingers gave my neck a squeeze. "Baby, I've given you a job. It's an important one. Focus. Yeah?"

I stared into his eyes. Then my head turned and I looked at the glade, then past it to where I could see Wood, no longer close, walking through the trees, eyes to the ground.

I looked back at Tate and whispered, "Okay."

He reached to his back pocket. "My cell's not in my truck," he stated. His arm came around and he showed me his cell. Then he urged, "Go."

I understood what he was saying and told him so by nodding. He put pressure on my neck. I got up on my toes and his head came down. We touched lips briefly. He let me go and turned instantly toward the wood, flipping his phone open.

I didn't delay further. I turned and ran through the woods to the cars.

CHAPTER TWENTY-ONE

Safe

SHAMBLES, JONAS, STELLA, Pop, and I were sitting in the diner. Everyone had ordered food but no one had eaten much of it. We'd been there ages but the waitress hadn't cleared our table. Our vibe was not conducive to approach. We were given a wide berth but that didn't mean employees and customers alike weren't giving us curious glances.

I was busy trying to take the mental temperature of both Jonas and Shambles, though it wasn't tough.

Shambles was a wreck, jumping visibly at every noise, his eyes flying to the door whenever it was opened.

Jonas seemed focused on Shambles and, probably due to his age and what Shambles had seen his mother do to him, he was the only one who could break through. Jonas wasn't being playful and funny. He was just trying to keep Shambles's mind occupied by chattering about smoothies, school, his friends, video games, and locking on to any conversational gambit that seemed to draw Shambles out, even minutely.

I was sucking back my third refill of diet through a straw in my mammoth, red hard plastic cup when the door opened. Shambles's eyes flew to it and his body locked.

I looked over my shoulder to see Tate, Wood, and Frank, the uniformed officer who came to tell Tate about Tonia, entering the diner. They stopped just inside the door and, one look at their faces and the fact they didn't walk to our table, my heart stopped with them.

I heard chair legs scraping the floor and twisted back to see Shambles was up. I rose with him.

"Bub, you stay here," I heard Pop order gently.

"Goin' with Shambles," Jonas muttered.

They were on the move so Pop said no more and I glanced at Pop and Stella, then followed them.

Tate turned and opened the door, holding it for all of us to walk through. Shambles moved down the sidewalk several paces, stopped, and turned. Jonas stopped close to his side. The rest of us formed a huddle. All eyes were on Tate but Tate was looking at Jonas.

"Bub, think you should—" he started.

"Stayin' with Shambles," Jonas cut him off.

Tate's eyes stayed on his son half a second, then they went to Shambles.

"We found her, man," he said softly. "She's alive, at the hospital—"

Shambles's body appeared to melt and I moved quickly to him and slid an arm around his waist.

He gave me his weight and whispered, "Alive."

"It's not good, pal," Wood told him gently. "She's been attacked."

I lost his weight as Shambles's body went rigid against mine.

"Found her in the woods, 'bout half a mile from the clearing. She's been out in the elements all night. Stabbed, looks like five times, lost a lot of blood," Frank added and my eyes shot to Tate.

He shook his head. "Stabbed, her hair shorn, but not like Tonia."

This didn't make sense but I didn't care. Tonia had lived too for a while. But she'd been so brutally attacked, she didn't make it. This sounded different. It sounded better. It was hideous but it was still better.

"We need to get you to the hospital, Shambles," Tate went on. "Wood's gonna drive your van. You come with Laurie and me."

Shambles nodded but Jonas piped up.

"And me," he stated.

"No, Bub, you stay with Pop tonight," Tate replied quietly.

"I gotta stay with Shambles," Jonas insisted and Tate opened his mouth to speak but Shambles spoke first.

"No, Little Dude, you stay with your granddad."

Jonas looked up at Shambles. "But—"

Shambles put a hand on top of his head. "Stay with your granddad."

Jonas stared at him a second, then he nodded.

"I'll get my bag," I whispered and gave Shambles a squeeze. "Be right back."

I let him go and dashed into the diner. I went straight to the table and Stella and Pop watched me from the minute I entered the diner to making it to the table.

"They found her. Stabbed. She's alive, at the hospital. Not like Tonia. We're going there now." I looked at Pop. "Tate needs you to look after Jonas."

"Sure thing, sweetheart," he muttered, his eyes going beyond me.

I grabbed my bag and turned to see Tate and Jonas walking in, Tate's arm around Jonas, hand on his shoulder.

"Laurie tell you?" Tate asked Pop when they hit the table.

"Yeah," Pop answered.

"We'll pick him up in the morning," Tate finished.

"Right," Pop said.

Tate turned his son into him, removed his arm but curled his fingers around Jonas's shoulder.

"We'll get you first thing," Tate stated. "Bring you home, then Laurie'll make you French toast."

Jonas nodded, then he swallowed and he did a face-plant in his father's midriff, wrapping his arms around Tate's waist. Tate's arms circled his son and he gave him a squeeze.

He bent at the waist and I heard him whisper, "Who's my big man?"

"Me," Jonas whispered back.

"That's right," Tate replied, gave him another squeeze, and let go.

Jonas took a step back and his head tipped to look up at his father. He swallowed again and turned to me. I lifted a hand and cupped the side of his face.

"See you tomorrow, honey."

He nodded, hesitated and then did a face-plant in me. My arms went around him and held him tight. I bent to press my cheek against his hair then I kissed the top of his head and he let go.

"Tomorrow, baby," I whispered.

"Tomorrow, Laurie," Jonas whispered back.

I touched his cheek again, dropped my hand and looked at Tate. He lifted an arm toward the door. I nodded and moved toward it, looking back over my shoulder at Jonas, Pop and Stella at the table. Stella had risen and was giving Jonas a sideways hug. I gave them a small smile.

I turned forward, Tate opened the door for me and we walked into the falling night.

*   *   *

It was dark. We were driving through Carnal on our way home, Tate at the wheel by my side.

Sunny was stable. I spent my hours at the hospital with Shambles. Tate spent his with the police and FBI. Wood took Shambles home in Shambles's van, Frank following in his cruiser to drop Wood back at the garage to get his bike.

Shambles got to see Sunny after she got out of surgery but she was sleeping and, after he visited with her, I urged him to go home, telling him I'd see him the next day. It took a while to urge him to do this, explaining he needed his sleep, to rest and be strong for Sunny because she needed him. I finally broke through and he agreed, taking off with Wood and Frank.

I watched the hotel slide by, the pool lit, the parking lot lit, the hotel below average but the whole place kept neat and tidy, a riot of flowers blooming everywhere, the pool clean and bright, the waters tranquil, beckoning. It might not be the greatest hotel ever but just one look at it and you knew you'd be welcome there.

Staring at the pool as we passed, suddenly in my head I saw Neeta wrench Jonas's arm and the memory of his wounded cry rang in my ears.

"Maybe we should stop by Pop's, get Jonas," I said softly.

"Hopefully he's sleepin'," Tate replied.

"But—"

"He's had a tough day. Needs his sleep, Laurie," Tate interrupted me. "We'll get him first thing."

I pressed my lips together, then I sighed.

Then I agreed, "Okay."

Tate flipped on his blinker and turned right into the hills.

"Tell me about Sunny," I whispered.

"Ace—"

"Tell me."

It was Tate's turn to sigh, which he did, heavily.

Then he said, "Wood found her bike about ten minutes after you two left, before the cops got there. It was tossed into the trees. I found her clothes thrown not too far from the bike. He moved around a lot in those woods but the trail wasn't hard to follow, footprints, depressed grass, broken twigs. They sent two officers and we followed the trail. Found her, called the ambulance. Left her with the paramedics, I followed more trail. He took a different route to get back, came out at the clearing. Lost the trail at the road, he had a car."

This wasn't enough information. It *was,* on one hand. It wasn't on the other.

"I don't get it," I said. "It doesn't make sense."

"I don't either," Tate replied.

"It's not the same. Is this someone else?" I asked.

"Don't know. Could be two things," Tate answered and said no more.

"Those are?" I prompted.

Tate hesitated for long moments before going on, "Copycat who got started then figured out he doesn't have a taste for it or doesn't know the full MO or our boy is..." He trailed off.

"Tate," I whispered.

"You wanna hear this shit?" he asked.

"No," I answered. "But I have to."

"Why?"

"I don't know."

"And I'm thinkin' it's better you keep not knowin', Ace."

I looked at him. "I don't know why I have to know but I have to know."

"Babe—"

"Tate, he's hurting women, two of them I know. Please, honey, I have to know."

Tate was silent for several beats then he asked, "Do you know what drawin' down the sun means?"

"No," I answered.

"Sunbathing nude. Shambles and Sunny are naturists."

"Oh," I mumbled. "So?"

"I think our boy is local. I think this was an incident of opportunity. He's got a problem with women who show skin, don't follow convention. He sees Sunny in the nude, whatever fucked-up shit in his head that drives him kicks in but he knows Sunny ain't like all the rest. He can't follow through. He follows his impulses but he can't take it to climax."

"He stabbed her five times," I reminded Tate.

"Stabbed Tonia sixteen times and raped her with that knife," Tate told me.

I sucked in breath then on the exhale breathed, "Sixteen? Really?"

"Yeah, babe," Tate said softly. "Also took all her hair he could get with that knife. Only cut Sunny's. Like he bunched it in his hand and sheared it off in one slice. But he didn't take it all."

"What does that mean?"

"The whole show is fucked, all over the place. Part of it is an effort at humiliation. Takin' the hair, leavin' 'em naked and exposed. Part of it is sexual. All the victims had semen on them. Not *in* them, *on* them."

"Oh God," I whispered, torn between sick disgust and horror.

"Yeah, fucked-up shit. It's brutal but every single one of them is left positioned the same. On their side, knees to their chest, hands tucked under their cheek. Gentle, almost respectful. Remorse. Remorse after he uses that knife instead of his dick and gets off on it. Remorse after he jacks off on them during or after."

"Sunny?" I whispered.

"Didn't violate her or come on her. Another change, he left a blanket with her. My guess, it was hers. She'd crawled, blood trail shows she got about fifteen feet, took the blanket with her but then she lost consciousness. The blanket, at least, offered some protection from exposure."

I closed my eyes. "Thank God."

"So we got DNA from the semen, we just got no matches. And that's all we got. It's like this guy doesn't exist. Now we got boot prints and maybe more DNA on the blanket. They find somethin', they'll know if it's the same guy."

"You think he's local?"

"Yeah."

"Do you know anything about him?"

"Profilers think he's able to assimilate. He's one of us."

I turned my head and stared at Tate, whispering, "What?"

"Not one victim, outside of Sunny, showed signs of struggle. We don't know how he got them we just know he didn't kidnap them, it wasn't violent. He either knew them or he doesn't pose a threat. He comes off as friendly. He might even be attractive. A good flirt. Turn a woman's eye. Thinks she's gonna get her some, not havin' any clue."

"So why did he struggle with Sunny?"

"He doesn't act on instinct. He hunts. She was not planned. The urge hit him and he acted. Maybe she didn't know him so she fought him. Shambles and Sunny picked that place because it's off the beaten track. Not a lot of people come around there unless they live up the way. Even if they did, they'd have to be lookin', the clearing is far enough from the road. He probably surprised her."

"They didn't question her," I told him something he knew.

"She's been out. They will soon's they can."

"Then it's done? They'll find him?"

"Unless I'm wrong, he didn't come prepared. She'll have seen him or somethin' that identifies him. He fucked up. They always fuck up and he fucked up. Cops're hopefully keepin' an eye out. He knows he fucked up and he's probably gone."

"But he had a knife," I pointed out.

"He uses a hunting knife. Probably keeps it clipped to his belt."

"I still don't get it. Why would he—?"

"Sometimes even monsters can feel the touch of a good soul," Tate said gently. "Sunny's a good soul. He's convinced he's doin' right, teachin' bad girls a lesson. He knew he had a good girl. He knew he was doin' wrong. He did her there, right where we found her, left her bike, left her clothes, left the evidence of the struggle, left a trail. He's smarter than that. Maybe he was freaked out or maybe, after what he did to Sunny, knowin' she wasn't his usual prey, that he hurt a good girl, he wants to get caught."

I looked out the windshield as Tate turned into his drive. The entire time he drove down it and swung into the garage he opened with the remote, I thought about Sunny being a good soul but still finding herself attacked by a monster.

Tate switched off the truck. I grabbed my purse, hopped out, and then opened the back door to reach in and grab one of our bags. Tate had the other one. He waited for me to precede him. I skirted my car in the garage and went to the mudroom. I dumped my purse and the bag on the floor the instant I got in.

"Toss that there, honey. I'll worry about them tomorrow. I need a shower," I murmured, not looking back as I walked into the hall. I kept going, flipping on the light switch by the dining room table.

Buster came out of the bedroom and stretched in the hall, booty in the air, paws straight out in front of her. She righted when I got close and asked a questioning "Meow?"

I cooed nonsensically at her, leaving her for Tate, whom she preferred anyway. She liked me well enough but she definitely knew who her daddy was. I went into the bedroom, right to the nightstand where I switched on the light.

I started for the bathroom but got waylaid with an arm around my belly. I was pulled back, turned into Tate's body and his arms curved around me.

"Tate," I said looking up at him and putting my hands on his pectorals, "my hair is straggly. I still have chlorine on me. I need a—"

"You love me."

My breath caught and my fingers automatically curled into fists against his chest.

"I—"

"Love me."

"Tate," I whispered.

"You said it, Ace."

"It was the moment," I quickly (and somewhat desperately) half-lied. It was the moment but it was also the truth. "I was having a good time with you and Jonas and I—"

"You protected him."

I blinked then asked, "What?"

"When Neeta was there, fuck, before she even got there you had hold of him, but after she did what she did, you got hold of him again and used your body to shield him."

"That was messed up," I said softly. "Anyone would do that."

"Wasn't anyone doin' it. It was you. It was you doing handstands with him in the pool and you makin' him eggs too."

"Tate."

"And bringin' me coffee." He paused, his face changed, shifted, that tender look came into it, not the soft and warm one, the tender one that was so sweet it made my heart stop beating and he kept talking quietly, "Long's I can remember, he wakes rough. Takes him a while to shake it off. You brought me coffee and left so I could be with him."

"I didn't know that. I just…I'm a waitress," I explained lamely. "I bring people drinks. It's instinct."

He pressed his lips together.

Then he muttered, "Babe."

"Tate," I whispered. "I need a shower."

Very unfortunately, he returned to his earlier subject. "You told me you love me."

"Can we talk about that tomorrow?" I asked. "Or, um…the day after that?"

"No," he answered.

"Captain, I was just…it was just…the moment."

His brows drew together.

"So you don't love me?"

My eyes slid to the side. "Well…"

"Lauren, eyes on me," he ordered and of their own accord my eyes moved back to him and, with one look at him, my heart slid straight up into my throat.

His face was still tender but his eyes were intense, burning into mine.

His head bent and his face got close to mine.

"Say it again," he demanded gently.

I felt the pulse in my throat beating. I licked my lips and stared into his eyes.

"Baby, say it again," he repeated.

"I don't want—"

His arms gave me a squeeze.

"What'd I tell you?" he asked.

"About what?" I asked back, not following.

"About bein' safe here," he answered.

"This isn't safe," I whispered.

"Why not?"

"I'm out there," I found my mouth admitting, unable to hold it back and then it kept talking. "You... I'm out there and it doesn't feel safe."

"Babe, you aren't out there." His arms gave me another squeeze. "You're right here."

"You know what I mean," I said quietly.

"I need you to say it again," he told me.

"Why?" I asked, my voice pitching higher.

"So I can say it back, Ace."

My body locked and I stared up at him.

"You—?" I breathed.

"Yeah," he cut me off.

Oh.

My.

God.

My body unlocked and melted into his.

"Really?" I whispered.

"Oh yeah," he whispered back, starting to move, taking me with him, shuffling us toward the bathroom.

My eyes filled with tears.

His hands went into my T-shirt.

"Tate—"

"Time to shower."

"Tate—"

I said no more because he kissed me. I kissed him back. Somehow he got us naked and in the shower. I wasn't paying much attention because of what his hands and mouth were doing and because I was assisting in the getting-us-naked part. Once in the shower there was soap and shampoo, on both of us, but I didn't pay much attention to that either.

My mind honed into my body around the time he lifted me with his hands at my behind, my legs went around his hips, he pressed me to the tiled wall and, with the water raining down on us, he slid inside.

I pressed my head against the tiles, held on tight with all my limbs, and he moved in and out of me, gentle, slow.

"Work with me," he said against my neck. "Touch your clit, baby."

I did what he asked.

Brilliant. So brilliant, I moaned.

"That's my girl," he muttered, his head coming up, his cock sliding in and out, his mouth touching mine. "You'd do anything for me, wouldn't you, Laurie?"

"Anything," I whispered and it was the truth.

"Put up with my shit."

"Yes," I breathed, rolling my finger.

"Take care of my kid."

"Yes."

"Take care of my house."

"Yes, Captain."

"Eat you how I want, fuck you how I want, sweet, hard, dirty."

"Yes."

"You'll get dirty for me?" he asked.

It was building and I wasn't paying attention to what I was saying. Therefore I promised, "Anything, Tate."

But that wasn't a lie either.

He started moving faster, going deeper.

"Then you're gonna come for me, Laurie."

He was right. I was.

"Yes," I breathed.

"Say it," he demanded, going faster, beginning to pound.

"I'm going to come for you, baby."

"No, honey, say it."

My eyes opened, looked directly into his, and I knew what he meant.

"I love you, Tate," I whispered against his mouth.

Definitely pounding now, his hands pulling my hips in to meet his thrusts and I heard the whimper slide out of me as it built higher.

"Say it again," he growled.

"I love you," I repeated.

"Again," he demanded but I couldn't. It was happening.

"Baby—" I moaned.

"Fuckin' say it," he commanded, pounding hard now, exquisite, and it hit me.

"I love you," I whispered on a hitched breath and he knew what that meant, he'd heard it enough times, and his mouth opened over mine, taking my cry.

I was still coming when his teeth bit my bottom lip, his hips drove into mine and he growled, "Love you too, baby. Christ," he clipped, the power behind his thrusts building even higher. "Fuck, but I love you."

His mouth opened over mine, his tongue invaded and then he groaned deep into my throat, his hips bucking hard, pounding me into the tile as he came.

He held me aloft as we both came down but his mouth left mine to trail down to my neck and his cock moved slow again, gliding in and out. I wrapped both my arms tight around him and held on.

He loved me. Tatum Jackson, ex-football star, ex-cop, and current badass bounty hunter hot guy loved me.

He loved me.

I closed my eyes and smiled.

"Feel safe, baby?" he asked my neck.

"Yeah, Captain," I answered, holding tighter with all my limbs.

He slid in and stayed there. I opened my eyes and his head came up so he could look into them.

"So my good girl's gonna get dirty for me?" he asked, his lips slightly turned up at the ends.

I pulled back, stupidly, since I was tight to the wall and had nowhere to go. He felt and it and pressed deeper into me, his lips turning up more.

I bit my lip, let it go and mumbled, "Um…"

"Don't worry, Ace, I'll break you in easy."

I'd thought about the stuff we'd already done. None of it was dirty, exactly, but a lot of it was wild and out of control, so I wondered what dirty would entail.

"Maybe you should explain dirty," I suggested.

"More fun to show you."

"Tate—"

He stopped me speaking by touching his mouth to mine.

Then he said, "You can trust me, Laurie." His voice got deeper, that growl vibrating through it. "Swear to God, baby, there will never be a time when you can't. Yeah?"

I looked at his face. He wasn't smiling anymore, not even a hint of it. This was important. He was serious.

"Yes," I answered softly, which earned me another light kiss.

He slid out and dropped me to my feet. Then he turned me to the spray, my back to him, his face went into my neck and his arms went around me, one going south, his fingers gently invading to wash me clean.

We got out, toweled off, and I lotioned because I was in Colorado and as exhausted and sated as I was, there was no way I was missing lotioning. Tate ran his hands through his hair. I combed mine. We brushed our teeth standing together at the sink. Tate left the bathroom while I moisturized. I walked into the bedroom, around the bed to the closet. I grabbed undies and a shelf-bra camisole, pulled the towel from around me, tugged them on and met him in bed.

"My hair's going to be a rat's nest tomorrow, sleeping on it wet," I stated inanely because what did you do after you had fantastic sex in the shower all the while sharing avowals of love with a badass biker?

Tate turned out the light and then turned to me, pulling me face to face.

"Lucky that's an easy fix, Ace."

"It means you can't look at me first thing in the morning," I informed him and he burst out laughing and pulled me deeper into his arms.

I snuggled into his chest. Tate kissed the top of my head.

"Wiped, Ace," he muttered.

"Okay," I muttered back.

"Sweet dreams, baby," he whispered.

"You too, Captain," I whispered back.

And for the first time, even after what had transpired that day and that night and three refills of diet pop, I fell asleep before Tate.

*   *   *

My body jolted and I came awake when I heard the noise.

My eyes opened and I saw Tate's back in the moonlight. I was snuggled up to him, my arm draped around his waist.

I came up on an elbow at the same time Tate did. We both looked over our shoulders to the window.

Another rap sounded on it and I could see the pale knuckles and the ghostly pale face surrounded by dark hair that almost, but not quite, faded with the night.

Neeta.

"You have got to be…fuckin'…shittin'…me," Tate whispered slowly as we both lay there, looking over our shoulders at the window.

"I think, since we have curtains," I whispered back, "we might want to remember to use them."

"Tate!" She shouted my man's name in the middle of the night while she was standing out on his deck, after she'd made his life a living hell because he'd believed in her, he'd wanted to guide her back to herself and she didn't let him. After she touched Jonas the way she did. After guessing that she didn't touch him much better his whole life either physically or emotionally. After the night we had, Sunny in the hospital, Shambles in shambles. After the last few months of topsy-turvy road guiding us to each other.

I lost it.

I crawled over Tate and out of the bed. I felt his fingers try to grasp hold of my hips but I was on the move and on a mission and they slid right off.

"Ace, let me deal with this," Tate said and I heard him moving but I went right to the closet, my mind buzzing with Brad, with Neeta, with my dad's heart attack, with Tonia dead, with Bubba off fishing—I was focused. That focus was on the fact that I could not take one more thing and I was absolutely not going to allow Tate to take anymore.

My hands searched through my clothes in the dark closet. I felt a pair of shorts and I dragged them on, then exited the closet buttoning and zipping them.

"Damn it, Lauren," Tate clipped. I heard him behind me but I was on the move, going faster, darting down the hall.

I stopped at the sliding glass door to switch on the light and I saw Neeta outside by the door. My hand went to the lock on the door and I slid it down.

"I said, let me deal with it." Tate was right behind me.

I whirled, my shoulder glancing off his bare chest, the deep recesses of my mind noticing he was wearing jeans, but I was intent and nothing, not even big, bad Tate was going to stop me.

"You are not going to deal with one more thing from *that woman*!" I declared rather loudly.

I turned back and threw open the door.

"You want this?" I announced to Neeta the second my foot hit the wood of the deck. "You got it!"

Her upper body listed forward. "Bring it on, bitch," she slurred and I was pulled up short taking my second step toward her because

Tate's open hand planted itself on my chest and his other arm came up and hit the advancing Neeta in hers.

She fell back a step, then two, then hit the railing and stopped. When she did she looked to her left and right with confusion as if she didn't know where she was.

I stilled and stared.

Tate sensed my stillness, dropped his hand and studied Neeta.

"You blitzed?" he asked in disbelief and her head tilted back but it took it a long time to do this. Once it did, it took even longer for her to focus on him.

Then she said, "Whas it to you?"

Tate's head turned to look at the drive. I followed the direction of his gaze and noted that Neeta's car, top still down, headlights still on, driver's side door open, interior lights on and beeping because she'd left the keys in the ignition. She'd also parked with her bumper butting a tree across Tate's drive.

"Oh my God," I whispered.

She'd driven there hammered.

My eyes went back to her and before I could speak, Tate did.

"You drove here drunk?" he asked.

"Got things to say to you," she answered.

"You drove here *drunk*?" Tate repeated, his voice lowering to a growl.

"Gimme Jonas," she slurred.

Tate had his side to her but he turned fully to face her and I felt those sparks of fury flash off him.

"Let's forget for a second you coulda hurt someone else, you coulda hurt *you*. What's Jonas gonna do without a mom?" Tate asked.

She waved a hand in the air and said breezily, "Relax, I'm fine."

"You're plastered," Tate returned.

She dropped her hand, her eyes narrowed, she leaned forward clumsily and stated, "I'm *fine*."

Tate leaned forward too. "And I asked a fuckin' question. You're not much of a mom but you're still his goddamned mom. He loses you, no matter you're shit at bein' a mother, it'd mark him. *Fuck,*" he hissed. "Neeta, you know that better than anyone."

She leaned back too far, hitting the railing again and she snapped, "Fuck you!"

I was done and therefore I stepped forward to stand by Tate.

"It's been too long," I started.

"Ace, let me fuckin'—"

I talked over him. "You don't get that excuse anymore. Your mom's been gone too long. You can't use losing her to behave this way."

"Wad d'you know 'bout it?" she sneered.

"Not one thing," I replied. "My mom's still alive so I grew up with her around to teach me how to be a good person. So let me educate you on how to be a good person, Neeta, something I suspect from what people say about her, your mother taught you before she passed but you forgot."

"Don't choo talk about my mom!" she yelled.

I ignored her. "You don't take your pain out on anyone but especially not the people you love. Never do that. Not ever."

"Piss off."

"You lost the world," I shot back. "I can't imagine. I don't want to and I dread the day I will. But she left you with gifts and you squandered every one of them."

"She left me with *shit,*" Neeta hissed.

"She left you with your looks, you're beautiful. She left you with a good dad, a gentle brother, a kind aunt who stepped up—"

"Lauren the good." She leaned forward again and spat, "You think you can win them? Take them all away from me? *My* friends? *My* family? *My* man? No fuckin' way." She shook her head, suddenly grinning drunkenly. "They'll be back. They always come back."

"Not this time, Neet," Tate stated and she swiveled her head to look up at him.

"Yeah," she was still grinning, sure of herself in her inebriation, "right."

"I'm in love with Laurie," Tate announced and the smile dissolved

from her face. It seemed to take a long time to do it, almost as if she
didn't comprehend, she couldn't wrap her mind around this concept.
As the smile evaporated, her face went slack.

"The fuck you say," she whispered.

"Her car's in my garage, her clothes in my closet, and they're gonna
stay there. Jonas digs her. You don't shape your shit up, I'll make it so
you're a bad memory and the only mom he knows is Laurie."

"The *fuck* you say," she whispered again.

Tate's arm slid around my shoulders and he pulled me into his
side. I wrapped my arm around his waist, turned my front into his
side and then wrapped my other arm around his stomach, holding
him close but loose, natural, casual, exactly how I fit at his side.

"You had him so he could be a tool to manipulate me," Tate
stated. "Fought with that knowledge for a while, couldn't believe it,
even of you. But today you proved it. You don't get your head outta
your ass, you'll lose him."

She wasn't listening. Her eyes had glued on our stance, our close-
ness, moving slowly from my arms around his middle to his around
my shoulders.

Then her eyes went to him. "You love her?"

"Outside Jonas, she's the best goddamned thing to ever happen
to me."

I held my breath at this announcement, my stomach doing a little
flip, but Neeta slid slightly to the side along the railing as if inching
toward escape.

"No," she breathed.

"Oh yeah," he returned.

"I gave you Jonas," she reminded him softly.

"Yeah, woulda thanked you, minute I saw him bawlin' in the
nursery. Since then you used him to make life a livin' hell so now,
knowin' you have no good in you and knowin' he's all about good, I
take total credit."

"He's ours." She reached an arm out to him. "We made him."

"You carried him but, lucky for Jonas, he's all about Brenda, about Pop, about Dad, and about me and he didn't get even a trace of you. He's all that but I brought out the good in him. He puts up with you and that's it."

"We made him," she repeated, dropping her arm but leaning toward Tate.

"For you he was the result of an orgasm. For me, he jump-started my world. We made him, yeah, but I claim him."

She closed her eyes tight and when she opened them, I knew her tactics had changed.

"You could show me—" she entreated.

"Tried to do that, Neet, never took hold."

"I could be—" she went on.

"Tried to find out what you could be too. You never let go of who you are and I want nothin' to do with that."

Her eyes slid to me then back to Tate. "But you love *me*."

"Never loved you, Neet. Thought I did. Now I know what it feels like, know I didn't."

She winced, her eyes closing again, her head moving to the side and down. She lifted a hand to the railing as if to hold herself up.

"Callin' Wood to come get you, take your ass wherever he wants but you're leavin' here and you're not comin' back. You come back, I call the cops. I'm not steppin' out on this deck again when your feet are on it," Tate finished with her and looked down at me. "Babe, go to her car, she left her keys in the ignition. Get 'em, yeah?"

I nodded, let him go, and moved away.

Neeta didn't move a muscle to stop me. By the time I got to her car, pulled the key out of the ignition, figured out how to turn off the head-lights, closed the door and returned to the deck, Tate was there, his phone to his ear. Neeta was now sitting on the deck, her knees curled into her chest, her arms wrapped around, the picture of pathetic. But, studying her, I could call up not even a hint of compassion.

"Wood?" Tate said into the phone. "Sorry, bud, but Neeta's at my place. She's smashed and drove her car up here. I want her gone. Either you get her or I call the station. You comin'?" He paused and held his hand out to me for the keys. I dropped them in his hand as he said, "Right. Later." He flipped his phone closed, his arm curled around me again, bringing my front to his side but his eyes went down to Neeta. "Wood'll be here to take care of your shit…again."

"Don't got nothin'," she told her knees, beginning to rock.

I wanted to feel sorry for her, even tried to call it up, but after what she did that day, the other night, and the fact that Tate and I were standing out in the dark on his deck dealing with her *again,* I couldn't.

Therefore, I said to her, "That's because you threw it all away."

She didn't even look up at me when she repeated, "Don't got nothin'."

I opened my mouth to repeat myself too but Tate's arm gave me a squeeze.

"Gonna be a bit before Wood gets here, Ace, and seen this before. Save yourself the hassle of watchin' her feel sorry for herself. Go to bed. I'll be in after Wood gets here."

I looked up at him, my arms around him getting tighter.

"I'll stay with you," I said.

"Ace, she's gonna sit there, whine and convince herself life just sucks rather than her doin' shit to make it suck. Trust me, it ain't interesting."

"I'll stay with you," I repeated.

"Baby—"

"Captain," I cut him off and then used words he used on me, "Shut it."

His mouth twitched then his arm curled me closer, he bent his head and he kissed me lightly.

"See you're comin' into your inner biker babe," he muttered.

I smiled up at him. "Yes, well…I'm learning."

"Then I'm fucked," he muttered teasingly.

"Mm. Maybe tomorrow," I muttered back and he chuckled.

"That's what I wanted from you," Neeta whispered and both Tate and I looked down at her. "That's all I ever wanted from you. Why couldn't you be that way with me?"

"You missed it, Neet. Too focused on latchin' on to my dick to lead me around by it, you missed it."

"You never gave me that. It was always Tate and Neet, the wild ones," she replied. "I thought you wanted it like that."

"Like I said, you weren't payin' attention," Tate returned.

Her eyes stayed locked on him, then she turned her head away, pressed her cheek to her knee and kept rocking.

Tate and I stood quiet and holding each other. Wood showed and got his stumbling sister to his truck. He came back for the keys to her car, which Tate gave to him.

He gave us both a chin lift, obviously a bit more than a little annoyed he was collecting Neeta in the middle of the night and not feeling in the mood to socialize.

He was walking away when Tate called him.

"Wood."

Wood turned back.

"I shoulda let it go a long time ago and I didn't," Tate began. I pulled in a breath because I knew where he was leading with that introduction and I was happy he was doing it but I couldn't believe he was doing it *now*. "Had to blame someone 'cause I couldn't blame myself for Dad leavin' me the way he left me. Placed that shit on you. It was a dick thing to do."

Wood stared at Tate and said not a word.

I held Tate tighter and Tate kept talking.

"Dad thought you were the shit. He wouldn't have blamed you and he would be pissed as hell knowin' I did."

Without a word, Wood looked away and started to turn.

"Wood," Tate called and Wood stopped moving, hesitated, and turned back. "Thanks for your help today, bud."

Wood stared at him. His eyes flashed to me and then back to Tate.

"She a miracle worker?" he asked and I blinked, not understanding the question.

"Yeah," Tate answered immediately, clearly understanding it.

Wood stayed silent a moment, then suggested, "Maybe you'll give it a coupla weeks before you two invite me over to a barbecue."

"We can do that," Tate replied and my eyes were on Wood but I could tell by Tate's voice he was smiling.

"Right," Wood muttered and turned again but was stopped again when Tate spoke.

"Jonas'll be here. We have a barbecue—"

Wood started walking but he looked over his shoulder. "Then I'll be here." He faced forward again and I heard him say quietly, "Not just for Jonas."

"Laurie?" Tate called to his back. It was a question for Wood, not Tate addressing me.

"She's got great fuckin' legs, man," Wood called back. "Not havin' 'em wrapped around my back don't mean I can't appreciate 'em as close as I can get."

Tate chuckled. Wood jogged down the steps and swung into his truck. I was still confused.

We watched Wood turn around in the drive and pull out. When his brake lights faded to normal and he took the turn out of the drive, I looked up at Tate.

"What was that all about?"

Tate turned me to the door. "Don't worry about it."

"Are things okay with Wood?" I asked as he pulled open the door.

"Yeah," he answered.

"So that was it? Years of bad blood and you two talk about my legs?"

He'd guided me through the door, closed it, locked it, and switched off the outside lights.

"It's a guy thing," he stated.

"It's a crazy thing," I mumbled.

He headed us toward the hall. "Speakin' of your legs wrapped around my back..."

"We weren't."

I saw his head tilt down to look at me through the dark as we hit the mouth to the hall.

"We are now."

"Tate, it's the middle of the night. We just survived another drama."

"I'll go fast," he assured me.

"Right," I muttered.

"Baby, trust me, I can go fast."

"*I* can go fast. *You* take your time *until* I go fast."

We were at the foot of the bed and he stopped me, turned me to him and his hands settled on my hips.

"Okay, babe, let me introduce you to fast," he invited.

I rolled my eyes.

His mouth came to mine where he didn't kiss me, he murmured, "And dirty."

My heart skipped a beat, his hands gripped my hips and he threw me on the bed much like he threw Jonas through the air in the pool but except without the distance or elevation.

I bounced, he landed on top of me, and then he showed me he could, indeed, do fast.

And he did it dirty.

And it was so fantastic, I wished he'd gone slow.

CHAPTER TWENTY-TWO

My Job Was Done

I woke up confused. It had to be morning but the room was way dark and I wasn't snuggled into Tate nor was he curled into me.

I got up on an elbow and noticed I was alone in the bed and the dark denim curtains were closed. I'd never been in the room when the curtains were closed but I was right in my estimation of what it would be like when they were pulled, the room was nearly pitch.

I threw back the covers, wandered to the windows facing the front of the house and pulled back a side, looking to the right to see if Tate was having coffee on the deck.

The chairs were empty.

I pulled open the other side of the curtains and let the sunshine in. Then I turned to the bed, seeing the note on Tate's nightstand. I walked to it, picked it up and read it.

Ace,
Getting Bub.

That was all it said but, then again, that said it all.

I dropped the note and went into the bathroom, looked into the mirror and that was when I saw my hair out to there. I stared at myself in frozen horror for several long seconds, thinking about all who saw me with wild rat's nest hair three times the volume of my normal hair. Then I allowed myself an inner *and* outer cringe that the three people who saw me thus were the three people I would never want to see me thus until the day I died. Then, considering I couldn't travel back in time to find some way to change this, I stopped staring at myself in horror and did my morning routine, adding wetting down my hair and digging through my bottles and jars to find the leave-in conditioner Dominic sold me after I told him about my swimming.

I found it, worked some through my hair, walked out of the bathroom, made the bed, and wandered into the closet. There I stood staring at my suitcases laid open on the floor, my clothes part folded and tidy, part exploded and a mess.

Her car's in my garage, her clothes in my closet and they're gonna stay there.

Tate's words to Neeta last night slid through my head and I wondered if that meant he wanted me to move in. If he wanted me to paint more rooms. If this gave me the all-clear to weed his garden and take him couch shopping.

I bit my lip and stared at the suitcases, uncertain.

If I unpacked and he wasn't ready for that yet, I'd feel like an idiot.

I *wanted* to unpack because I loved him and he said he loved me and I liked his son and his house and I wanted my clothes to stay in his closet, my car in his garage.

But he hadn't asked me.

I bit my lip harder. Then I heard the sounds of Tate and Jonas coming home.

I grabbed a pair of jean shorts, the bra that matched the undies I had on, and the first T-shirt my hand could find. I had the bra and shorts on and was pulling the T-shirt over my head when I heard Tate close.

I yanked the T-shirt down and turned to the door. He was standing in it and staring at my suitcases.

I bit my lip again, wondering if his thoughts were similar to mine when looking at my suitcases, or if they were (hopefully not) vastly different.

Then I said, "You went to get Jonas without me."

His eyes came to mine. "Mornin' to you too, babe."

"Um…," I mumbled and tucked some hair behind my ear. "Mornin'."

His eyes followed my hand, then roamed my head before they came back to mine. "You tamed your hair."

He *would* comment on my hair.

"Uh…yeah," I muttered realizing I felt self-conscious and even shy. Why, I had no earthly clue, I just was.

"Why?" he asked.

"Why?" I repeated.

"Yeah, Ace," he said coming into the closet. "Why?"

As he got close, I tipped my head back to look at him. "It was a rat's nest."

His hand came up, his fingers sliding into the wet hair at the side of my head then through it, down the length pulling it over my shoulder. The tips of his fingers fiddled with the ends of my hair at my breast as he watched, then his gaze came to my face.

"It was you," he stated.

"Me?" I asked.

He got closer. "Yeah, babe, you." His fingers left my hair so his hand could go to where my head met my neck and he tilted my head back farther with the pad of his thumb against the underside of my jaw, doing this while his other hand came to rest at my waist. "Wild," he said softly. "Hot. I liked it."

"You liked my hair in a rat's nest?" I asked it like I couldn't believe it mainly because I couldn't. I had a lot of hair normally, it was hard enough to tame with beaucoup products, wielding a roller brush and an industrial-strength hair dryer. When untamed, there was so much of it, no other word for it, it was *huge*.

His thumb slid along my jaw and the touch, the warmth coming from his body, his proximity and the look in his eyes made my nipples tingle.

"I liked it wild," he said.

"Oh," I replied because there was no other response to that and I liked that he liked my hair wild. That said, I pretty much liked that he liked anything about me.

He grinned.

I stared at his mouth as it started to get closer.

"Is Jonas here?" I asked against his lips.

"Kiss me good mornin'," he demanded against mine, ignoring my question.

"Tate."

Both his hands tightened. "Babe."

I gave in, put my hands to his abs, and pressed my mouth to his.

Then I pulled back and reiterated, "Is Jonas here?"

Tate's hand slid back to wrap around my neck. "He's here. He's still half asleep, which means we got about ten minutes to make out in the closet. So, like I said, kiss me good mornin'."

"I just did," I reminded him.

"You love me?" he asked suddenly and, at his question, my stomach flipped then twisted.

I stared up at him unsure of myself and back to shy.

Then, without me telling it to do so, my mouth whispered, "Yes."

"Then fuckin' kiss me good morning, Ace," he demanded softly but firmly.

"Oh all right," I grumbled because he was being bossy and also because he didn't return the sentiment.

My hands moved to curl around the sides of his waist. I went up on my toes and pressed my lips to his, harder this time, my mouth opening under his. His hand slid to the small of my back, pressing in, the fingers of his other hand slid into my hair and his head slanted as his tongue glided into my mouth.

At the taste of him, I melted into him, my arms locking around him and we kissed good morning.

When his mouth detached from mine, he muttered, "Now that's good morning."

He wasn't wrong about that.

"You went to get Jonas without me." I took us full circle.

"You don't get enough sleep, babe," he replied. "You were out. You need to sleep when you actually can sleep so I let you sleep. I was gone twenty minutes."

This was nice. I liked it when Tate was nice. I liked Tate all the time, even when he was a jerk, which made me slightly insane, but it was Tate and I had to admit, I liked all things Tate, even when he was a jerk. But I liked it when he was nice the best. So, since he was being nice, I pressed deeper into him.

"Is he okay?" I asked softly.

"No tellin'. He's a zombie," Tate answered. "We'll know more when he pulls out of it."

I looked over his shoulder toward the door. "I need coffee, honey, and I need to make Jonas French toast."

"Ace," Tate called and my eyes went back to see his were looking over my shoulder and down, toward my suitcases.

He didn't speak for several seconds so I asked, "Tate, what?"

He looked at me and he muttered, "Nothin'," let me go and moved to my side. "Coffee," he finished.

I nodded and we walked out of the room, down the hall and I saw Jonas on a stool at the island, slouched into an elbow, head in his hand, staring blankly at Buster who was sitting on the floor in front of him looking up at him.

"Hey, Jonas," I called when I hit the dining area.

He didn't lift his head from his hand but his body shifted so he could see me.

He blinked then mumbled, "Hey."

I went to the coffeepot and saw Tate had already made coffee so I grabbed a mug from the cupboard over the pot.

"You need coffee, honey?" I asked Tate and turned to him to see he had his hips to the counter, his eyes on Jonas, and his phone to his ear. He looked at me and nodded.

I prepared coffee as I asked Jonas, "French toast or pancakes today?"

"French toast," he mumbled, again staring at Buster who was now rubbing against Tate's ankles.

"Right," I replied, grinning because Jonas was cute when he was sleepy.

I walked toward Tate to take him his mug.

"Bubba," I heard Tate say and I looked at his face to see he was speaking into his phone. "This is the fifth time I've called you. Comes a sixth, we got problems."

He pulled his phone from his ear, flipped it closed, dropped it on the counter and took the mug from me.

"No answer?" I asked.

"Nope," he replied and our eyes locked.

He didn't look happy. I scrunched my nose. He watched my nose, the unhappiness slid out of his face, the ends of his lips tipped up, then he shook his head once and lifted his mug to take a sip. I went to the fridge to get milk and eggs.

I had milk in my coffee, had taken a sip and I had a bowl out, the bread beside it and was cracking eggs into the bowl when Jonas spoke.

"After breakfast, can we go to the hospital?"

I was working at the island and my head came up from my task to look at Jonas. He was still slouched into the island but now looking at his dad.

"Yeah, Bub," Tate answered. "Not long, though. Shambles needs space."

"Okay," Jonas replied then went on. "After the hospital can we go back to the pool?"

"Maybe," Tate said. "We'll see."

I figured this meant no because when my mom or dad said that, it meant no. I also figured that was why Jonas straightened from his slouch, because he was preparing to fight for his trip to the pool.

I walked the eggshells to the trash bin, dumped them in, rinsed my hands, dried them and went to the cupboard where I'd started to store the spices and baking ingredients I'd been buying. Tate didn't have much in his cupboards and therefore I had plenty of choice as to where to store my cooking supplies.

During this time, there was surprising silence not filled with Jonas talking his father into a trip to the pool.

This silence lasted until Tate asked his son, "You want juice, Bub?"

"Why's Mom's car outside?" Jonas asked back and I stopped, my fingers around the little brown bottle of vanilla and I turned slowly around, closing the cupboard as I moved.

I saw Jonas's back was straight, both of his hands were flat against the top of the island, and his eyes were glued to Tate. He didn't look sleepy at all anymore and this was a strange position for him to be in so I knew something was about to go down. Something between father and son. Something the MILF girlfriend needed to absent herself from so they could talk it through.

I put the vanilla by the bowl, muttering, "I'll just—"

Jonas talked over me. "She come over last night?"

"Bub, we'll have breakfast and we'll—"

Jonas talked over Tate, "She came over, why'd she leave her car?"

"After breakfast," Tate stated.

"Was she smashed?" Jonas kept at it.

I pulled in a soft breath. Tate stared at his son.

Then Tate asked, "She get smashed a lot, Jonas?"

Jonas didn't tear his eyes from his father but it looked like he was pressing his hands into the counter. His body was visibly tight and his throat was working. His mind was working too, I could see it in the activity behind his eyes, and he was scared.

Then he said quietly, "All the time."

Tate was silent. So was I, though I figured everyone in the room could hear my heart beating. Even Buster had stopped moving and stood by Tate's feet, her pretty face staring up at Jonas.

Jonas kept his eyes on his father and his hands pressed to the counter as if he was preparing at any moment to push up and run away.

"She drive like that?" Tate asked softly.

"Yeah," Jonas answered just as softly.

"You ever in the car with her when she's like that?" Tate continued.

Jonas pulled in an audible breath, let it out slowly, then he swallowed.

"Yeah," Jonas whispered and instantly Tate's dark energy invaded. So huge, it filled the house and assaulted its inhabitants.

I edged toward Tate, saying gently, "Tate, honey—"

"She jerks me around too," Jonas announced, the words a rush. My body stilled and my eyes shot to him, seeing him still staring at his father but he wasn't scared anymore.

No, he looked downright terrified.

"She jerks you around," Tate repeated slow, low and dangerous.

"Yesterday wasn't the first time." Jonas was still speaking swiftly. "It wasn't even the worst."

Oh no.

No, no, no.

This wasn't happening. That didn't happen to Jonas.

No.

I stared at him staring at his father, looking frightened out of his brain, knowing his father, knowing what imparting this knowledge would mean, knowing he wouldn't lie. I knew it happened. I was right. Neeta wasn't gentle with her son.

I stood, uncertain, not knowing which one to go to. Tate was visibly struggling with fury, Jonas the same with fear.

"I wanna live here," Jonas whispered, his voice sounding clogged, his eyes filling with tears. "Laurie tell you?"

Tate didn't answer and I wasn't certain he heard his son speak. He was stuck in time hearing his son telling him his mom drove drunk with him in the car and jerked him around.

Jonas pushed up so he was squatting over the stool, his hands still on the island, his feet on the edge of the stool, panic edging into his fear.

"I wanna live here," he repeated.

Tate scowled at his son, immobile but still somehow hyperalert and he did this for so long, waiting for him to answer, listening for the words to come out and doing it so intensely, I felt like I was going to faint.

"You already fuckin' do," Tate finally returned, his voice an infuriated growl. Then he tagged his phone from the counter, turned on his boot and prowled down the hall to the garage.

I looked at Jonas to see his face had gone white as a sheet and I watched a tear slide down his cheek.

Seeing that lone tear, three words sprung to mind.

That.

Fucking.

Bitch!

"Dad!" Jonas shouted, coming off the stool and my mind jerked into the moment.

"Stay here," I ordered.

"But—"

"Here!" I said it unintentionally sharply, waited only for him to nod. I gave him what I hoped was a reassuring smile, and then I ran after Tate.

I caught him at the side of the garage. He was already astride his bike and I knew from his movements the bike was about to roar, he was going to take off, and Neeta was going to get what she deserved.

Even if she deserved it, I couldn't let it happen.

"Tate!" I shouted.

He ignored me.

"Tate!" I yelled, making it to him, my hands going to his body, one to his back, one to his chest.

"Back up," he growled.

"Come inside," I urged.

His eyes came to me and it took everything I had not to turn and flee at the rage I saw in them.

"Back the fuck up, Ace."

"Come inside, baby."

"*Back up!*" he roared.

In the face of his wrath, I didn't know how I found the courage but I called it up and moved closer.

"Don't, Captain," I begged. "Don't make him sorry he told you."

"Back up," he repeated.

"Lock it down, Tate."

"Lauren, not gonna say it again."

"Please, *please.*" I got as close as I could, my hands moving to his bearded cheeks and my face getting into his so I was all he could see. "I know you're angry. You have a right. If you need to work that out, then be a jerk. Say something mean to me. But don't make Jonas sorry he told you."

"Lauren—"

"You made this place safe for me. I spent ten years in a place that was unsafe. Jonas has too. Make this place safe for him too, baby. Please."

His eyes closed and he jerked his head away, tearing it from my hands.

I bent my neck so my forehead was resting against the side of his head and I whispered in his ear, "Please, Tate. You can do it, I know you can. You did it for me. Please."

He didn't speak and I wrapped my hands around his neck, keeping my forehead pressed to him.

Finally, he growled, "She coulda killed him."

"She didn't," I whispered.

"She hurt him."

My nose stung with the tears but I had too much going on. I needed to get him off the bike, I needed to get back to Jonas, and I needed to get him back to Jonas. I didn't have it in me to hold them back so I let the tears go.

Feeling them slide down my face, my voice was a croak when I said, "Yes."

"Bub," he whispered, his voice rough.

My hands tightened. "Yes."

"My boy."

"Tate, please come inside."

He fell silent, then his neck moved, not forcefully, and I lifted up as his torso twisted to me. I put my hands on his shoulders and stared down at him.

"How do I make that right?" he asked, his beautiful eyes bleak, and I vowed I'd hate Neeta until the day she died for making my man look that way.

I swallowed a sob-induced hiccup and shook my head. "I don't know. I just know you will."

It was his turn to shake his head. "You believe that?"

"I believe you can do anything."

The minute I said it his face changed and, I swear to God, he looked just like his son did two nights before. He stared up at me with astonished marvel.

"Christ, you actually think that," he whispered, his eyes studying my face.

"No," I replied and my fingers gave him a squeeze. "I know it."

"Dad." We heard and we both turned, Tate twisting farther to look at Jonas who was standing just outside the side garage door. Jonas rubbed a hand jerkily along his cheek to wipe away tears and

I saw his hand was shaking. "Dad," he repeated like he didn't know what to say.

"You get a shower at your grandpop's last night?" Tate asked, his voice low and even.

Jonas blinked, openly surprised at Tate's even tone delivering a normal, everyday question. I turned to look at Tate and saw him start to swing off the bike.

And I knew from watching him he'd done it. He'd locked down the fury. He'd found a way to control it even with what caused it and even being justified having it.

I was right. He could do anything.

I moved out of his way and Jonas answered as Tate stopped moving at my side.

"Yeah."

I looked back at Jonas and heard Tate order gently, "Then go change your clothes, Bub, while Laurie makes breakfast."

Jonas swallowed again but otherwise didn't move.

Then he asked, "You mad?"

"Yeah," Tate answered instantly.

"At Mom?" Jonas went on.

"Yeah," Tate repeated.

"She's—" Jonas started.

I knew he was going to defend her. I opened my mouth to speak in order to intervene should that set Tate off again but Tate got there before me.

"She's Neeta, Jonas. I know what she is. Go change."

"It's just how she is," Jonas said quietly.

"Yeah," Tate answered. "Change your clothes, Bub."

"She can't help it. It's just how she is." Jonas kept at it.

Tate walked to his son, I held back and watched Jonas brace.

Tate put his hand on his son's shoulder.

"I know. I know it's how she is. Don't make it right. That shit isn't right, Jonas. All I can say now is, it's over. Yeah?"

Jonas, his head tipped way back to look up at his father, nodded. Then he whispered, "She'll be alone, without me."

He was struggling with his decision.

I closed my eyes, fresh tears forced themselves out and I clenched my teeth against the whimper gurgling in my throat.

I opened my eyes when Tate spoke. "Her turn. I get you now."

"Blake isn't—" Jonas started.

"He was her choice. You're young, Bub, but I'm tellin' you this because you gotta know. She coulda had me. I made that clear more times than years you been alive. She chose him. Bein' free, that means I got to choose Laurie so now she'll never get another shot at me. You live with your life's choices. Your mom, she's an adult, she's made choices, she's gotta live with 'em. You're smart, you fuck up, you learn from that. She doesn't learn. That's her choice too. I spent years tryin' to shield her from her choices, didn't work. I'm not gonna let you do it and I'm not gonna teach you that someone's gonna shield you from shit. You gotta learn too. You make choices, they're yours and you gotta take responsibility for them."

He jerked his head to the house and his voice got quiet when he went on.

"You made a choice in there, Bub. I know you struggled with it, probably been strugglin' with it for a while, but it was the right one." Tate's hand gave Jonas's shoulder a gentle tug. "Trust me, it was the right one."

Jonas stared up at his father for several long, agonizing moments before he nodded again.

"Now, Bub, do what I asked. Go get changed. Okay?"

"Okay," Jonas whispered then continued. "You're not gonna go—"

Tate squatted in front of his boy.

"No. I'm here with you and Laurie. We're gonna have breakfast. We're gonna go to the hospital to see Shambles. And, if you're lucky, we're gonna talk Laurie into makin' you chocolate chip cookies like her gram used to make."

"We still have cake," Jonas said, like having chocolate chip cookies *and* cake in the house was a treasure trove of goodies that was too good to believe was real.

"I could do with a cookie," I put in and both Jackson boys turned their eyes to me. "Or two," I finished.

"Are they good?" Jonas asked me.

"She refrigerated the dough before she made them," I answered like this would make any sense to him, which, from his small, confused grin, it didn't.

The confusion left his face and he asked, "Can I have some dough?"

"No," I lied and communicated that it was a lie by smiling at him.

Jonas looked at his dad, who was watching me. Tate's head slowly turned to his son when Jonas spoke.

"She's full of it. She's *so* gonna let me eat dough."

"Laurie's full of it a lot," Tate shared.

"I am not!" I snapped, only partly annoyed by this blasphemy. Mostly I was just glad that the latest drama appeared to be over and I wasn't crying anymore.

Tate straightened from the crouch, ignored my snap, and commanded, "Babe, get your ass in the house and make breakfast."

I crossed my arms on my chest and glared at him. "First, *babe,* don't say 'ass' in front of Jonas and second, don't tell me to make breakfast."

Tate's eyebrows went up. "You intend to starve my boy?"

"No, I'll make breakfast for me and Jonas. *You* can make yourself a bowl of cereal."

Tate burst out laughing, his hand snaking out to hook his son around the neck and pull him into his side. When he did, Jonas's arms slid around Tate's middle and he pressed himself to his dad's frame.

Tate was still chuckling when he looked down at Jonas and stated, "See? Full of it."

I glared at them both but gave up glaring because this had no effect whatsoever on either of them and they looked sweet standing like that. As sweet as it was, I still stomped toward them, then by them, then into the house.

I made French toast.

Yes, for Tate too.

But I also made certain that, after I plonked Tate's plate in front of him, it was clear I did it under protest.

This made both of them burst out laughing.

Tate was bossy and that was annoying but, after that scene, both my boys were laughing.

Therefore, my job was done.

*   *   *

"She ain't talkin'," Special Agent Garth Tambo said to Tate in the hall just down from Sunny's hospital room.

I looked down the hall to see Shambles in a crouch in front of Jonas. Jonas was speaking and Shambles, looking like he had exactly three seconds of sleep, was nodding.

Tate, myself, FBI Special Agent Tambo and Arnie Fuller, Carnal chief of police, father to Tate's crazy ex-girlfriend, and Tate's mortal enemy (and a man I did not like because he had beady eyes, a serious beer gut, which was wrong in his uniform, and a penchant for glowering ferociously at Tate) were standing about ten feet from Shambles and Jonas.

"Not talkin'?" Tate asked Tambo and Tambo shook his head.

"Not a peep." He jerked his head at Shambles. "Not even to her man."

"Man, right, that's what he is," Chief Fuller muttered with disdain and I caught both Tate and Special Agent Tambo's eyes cutting to him before mine went to him. I noted Tate's gaze was annoyed, Tambo's was frustrated.

As for myself, I was angry.

"They've been together for six years," I said to Chief Fuller. "And in those six years they spent two nights apart. One of those nights

Sunny spent naked in the forest oozing blood from stab wounds while Shambles nearly lost his mind with worry looking for her and the other she was in a hospital bed. Six years together, six years of every night but two sleeping in the same bed. If I was Sunny, that'd be the definition of Shambles being my man. Knowing what he went through and how he feels about her, that's *my* definition of Shambles being a *man*."

Chief Fuller turned his glower to me but Tate spoke.

"Ace—"

I lifted a hand palm up in Tate's direction and kept my eyes on Fuller.

"They live in your town. You don't like hippies, that's your choice. But that personal choice gets put in a box the minute you put on that uniform."

"Don't need you to tell me my job, Miz Grahame," Fuller said to me.

"I don't know. I'm new to these parts but, word around town, someone needs to do it," I shot back. Tate's arm curved around my shoulders and he pulled and twisted me so my front was against his side.

"That's right, Jackson, rein her in," Fuller warned.

"Arnie," Tate replied, "she's close to the two of 'em. Cut her some slack."

"I'll cut her some slack when she ain't mouthin' off at me," Fuller returned.

"You'll earn some slack when you aren't confronted by a friend of a victim after you got a report of a missing person, a female, a report you didn't act on when you know you got a monster huntin' your patch. And you don't mutter slurs," Tambo put in. "Oh, and, I'll add that you might wanna leash that shit about the partner. Miss Grahame is right. He's your citizen. You're wearin' that uniform, you don't get to pick which ones you protect."

Fuller was now glowering at Tambo, then he switched it to me, then it moved to Tate and I braced because he looked ready to spit.

Then he moved away, thankfully leaving us and doing it without another word.

"That guy's a jackass," Tambo muttered.

Tate didn't respond to his comment, instead, shockingly, he said, "Wire up Lauren and send her in."

"What?" Tambo asked, his eyebrows going up.

"*What?*" I cried, my body going tight.

Tate talked to Tambo. "Wire up Lauren, send her in. She'll get Sunny talking."

I stared at Tate in horrified disbelief.

I decided to take this opportunity to remind Tate I wasn't good in a crisis. This wasn't a crisis, as such, but I still knew I'd be no good at it.

Therefore, I started, "Tate—"

Tate looked down at me. "She'll talk to you."

"No she won't. If she won't talk to Shambles—"

"Ace, the woman at the home store gives you relationship advice. Sunny'll talk to you," Tate replied.

"Wanda is nosy, Tate. Sunny's different. She's been attacked."

"Stood in that line a while, babe, saw three customers cash through. She was nice enough but she didn't babble at any of 'em like she was their best friend."

I wasn't there but I reckoned this was true. People talked to me. It had always been the way.

Then again, I talked to people. It had always been my way.

Tate kept speaking. "Jonas trusted you within hours of meetin' you. He sized you up and gave you his burden. She'll talk to you."

This was definitely true.

Still.

"It's not the same," I stated.

"It was today," Tate replied.

"Sorry?" I asked.

Tate turned so we were front to front and both his arms were around me. "Babe, he didn't wait until he and I were alone. He didn't ask you to leave. And he didn't wait for you to leave when you were offerin' it. He said what he had to say when you were there *because* you were there. Don't you get that?"

"No," I said.

"He trusted you to deal with the consequences he created."

"But, he—"

"And you did, you dealt with me."

"I don't think he thought it out that much, Tate. He's just ten," I pointed out.

"You don't think he hasn't learned to scheme the best way to do shit livin' on eggshells with a coupla drunks, Ace, you're wrong. That shit with Neet? It's been goin' on a while and he didn't tell me until *you* were there."

This was probably true too.

Tate kept pushing. "She'll trust you."

"I don't know," I whispered.

"Can't know, unless you try."

I bit my lip. His arms gave me a squeeze.

Then his face got close to mine and he whispered, "Babe, we *need* this."

I stared into his face knowing he was right. We needed this. For Tonia and those seven other girls and the girls who were out there, marked by this lunatic and unsafe. We needed this, even for Sunny.

I just didn't want it to be me who got this.

So I asked softly, "Do I have to be wired?"

Tate's arms gave me another squeeze, this one reassuring and maybe a little proud (yes, I could read that in an arm squeeze). "They'll need to hear everything she said, and she won't even talk to Shambles. I reckon they can't be in there."

"But, a wire?"

"You need to be you. You need to pose no threat. You can tell her you're wired but you need to look like you. Not holding a recorder. Not with someone with a notepad at your back. She's gonna talk, it's gotta be just you."

I wasn't sure Tate was right about Sunny talking to me and, even if he was, I still wasn't sure I wanted to do it.

What I was sure of was someone killed Tonia and seven other women and the same someone may have attacked Sunny. Even if it wasn't the same someone, still, someone had attacked Sunny.

And whoever it was, they had to be stopped.

I looked at Tambo standing silently at our side, then I looked at Tate.

"Can we ask Shambles first if it's okay?" I whispered.

Tambo turned immediately and walked toward another agent while Tate's arms gave me yet another squeeze.

Then he answered, "Yeah."

*   *   *

I thought I'd not be able to take my mind off the microphone taped to my chest but the minute I walked into Sunny's hospital room that thought flew away.

Her ash blonde hair was cut blunt. Her skin was pale under her tan. She had some bruising and swelling on the left side of her face. There were a bunch of tubes sticking in her. And her eyes were dead.

Those eyes came to me the minute I walked in and that was all I could think, her bright, shining, usually smiling, always friendly eyes were dead.

I swallowed back tears and looked across the room to see two women, an older one, dressed conservatively, a younger one, dressed a lot like me but in jeans rather than shorts. I knew, because Shambles told me, they were Sunny's mom and sister.

"Hi," I said softly. "I'm Lauren, a friend of Sunny's."

The mom nodded and looked at Sunny.

The sister said, "Hey."

"I…" I looked at Sunny before I looked back at her family. "Can I talk to her?"

They both stared at me without speaking.

Shambles, who had come in behind me, said quietly, "Mom, Moonbeam, she means alone."

They looked at me again. They looked at Sunny. I tried to look reassuring. Sunny just looked blank and Shambles took control, herding Sunny's family out the door.

He stood in the doorway, nodded to me, then closed the door.

I walked to Sunny and sat at the very edge of the seat of a chair that was pulled close to her side. I looked to her and she was staring at the ceiling.

I took her hand in mine. It was limp. I leaned forward and pressed it against my face, my eyes smarting and I felt the wetness escape and glide down my cheeks. I knew she had to feel it too.

My eyes closed.

"I'm sorry, baby," I whispered to her hand. "I had magic, I'd take this away."

I opened my eyes, kept her hand to my face and looked toward her head, which had turned and her gaze was on me.

Still dead.

"I can't do that." I was still whispering.

She didn't reply.

"You and me," I kept whispering, "honey...," I pulled in a breath and let it out, "we have to do the next best thing."

Nothing about her face changed. Not a thing.

"You don't think you're strong enough but we'll find your strength together."

She looked back at the ceiling.

"He has to be stopped, Sunny."

Suddenly, she yanked her hand forcefully from mine.

Too fast, I went too fast. Darn.

I gave it a minute then got up and sat on the side of her bed but she turned her head away.

I leaned toward her, not too close, not threatening and I laid it out.

"I'm wired. They're listening, the police, the FBI, you need to know that."

She swallowed.

"They can hear but this is just you and me, baby. Right now it's just you and me."

No response.

I closed my eyes and bit my lip, opened them, and urged, "Please, talk to me."

Sunny remained silent.

I wiped my face and looked out the window not seeing the landscape there, only thinking of finding some way through.

Then it came to me. I should tell her the truth.

"I stayed in Carnal because of you," I whispered.

I heard movement and I looked back down at her to see she was looking up at me.

I nodded. "It's true. You and Shambles. Betty and Ned too. Banana bread and Middle Eastern night and knowing I was going to have friends, good ones, ones who genuinely cared. Didn't just say it but acted it…when I met you guys, I knew I was home."

Her lip quivered.

"I'd been far from home a long time, Sunny, lost and wandering. It's scary to be in that place alone." My voice dropped to a whisper. "Thank you for bringing me back home."

"Petal," she croaked, her voice thick.

"Talk to me, baby,"

She shook her head.

"You're safe here. You're safe with me," I promised her.

She kept shaking her head so I grabbed her hand, leaned deeper and pulled her hand to my chest, encasing it in both of mine and holding strong.

"You're safe with me," I repeated and squeezed her hand. "You can't wander, lost and alone in your head forever. You can't." I squeezed her hand again. "Give me the chance to return the favor, honey. Let me give you a little of what you gave me. Let me bring you back home."

She stared in my eyes for a long time.

Then she opened her mouth and talked to me.

And I realized, even after Tate and Special Agent Tambo's coaching before I went in her room, I wasn't prepared.

They didn't warn me that words could burn straight into your brain.

Sunny's did in a way that I knew it would take years for those burns to heal.

And when they did, they'd leave scars.

But I'd got her to say the words.

My job was done.

*   *   *

When I walked out of Sunny's room the door didn't even close behind me before I felt Tate's arms close around me.

I shoved my face in his chest and held on tight.

"You did good," he whispered into my hair.

I nodded against his chest.

He held me a while then kept me close as his hand went under my T-shirt. I felt his fingers move on me, taking the kit that was attached to my waistband, then going up, his big body shielding mine from onlookers as his fingers followed the thin cord. He carefully ripped the taped microphone off my chest and his hand moved out of my shirt.

Tucking me to his side, he turned to Tambo and handed him the wire.

"Don't know how to thank you, Miss Grahame," Tambo said gently to me. "That had to be tough."

I nodded and said quietly, "It's okay."

But it wasn't okay, my brain was burning and dang, but it *hurt*.

Tambo nodded back.

"Bub, let's get Laurie home," Tate called to Jonas and didn't wait for a response. He started walking us down the hall.

"I'll see you tomorrow, Shambles," I said as we made it to him and Tate stopped when I spoke.

Shambles looked toward Sunny's door then back to me. "You think she'll talk to me now?"

"Go and see, honey," I prompted.

He nodded, leaned in, and kissed my cheek then hurried down the hall.

Tate started us moving again. We were stopped at the elevators when I felt a hand take mine.

Tate tagged the elevator button and I looked down to see Jonas looking up, studiously avoiding my gaze and staring at the red digital display over the elevator telling us what floors it was moving through like this display might communicate to him straight from God that week's winning lottery numbers.

And he did this holding my hand.

*   *   *

I didn't pay much attention as we walked through the grocery store. I was focused on getting ingredients for chocolate chip cookies and the pasta-Dijon-mustard-mayo-pickle salad that was another one of my specialties Brad had hated due to its abundance of calories and fat. Tate was going to grill burgers for dinner that night and my pasta-Dijon-mustard-mayo-pickle salad went perfectly with hamburgers.

I didn't pay much attention when we loaded the groceries in the back of the Explorer and I didn't pay much attention as we started to head home.

I only paid attention when Tate parked outside La-La Land and Jonas jumped out.

I focused on Jonas as he ran to La-La Land and I watched him lean a store-arranged bouquet of flowers against a long, thick line of flower bouquets that had already been laid there.

I turned to Tate.

"He saw 'em when we drove through earlier," Tate answered my unspoken question. "He asked me at the store while you were takin' a

year to pick between spiral pasta and macaroni. He wanted our flowers to be there."

Our flowers.

Our.

I looked back out the windshield to see Jonas jogging toward the
SUV. He hefted himself in and closed the door.

I stared at the flowers the folks of Carnal had laid out to show
Sunny and Shambles they had the town's support.

Carnal was a good town. It was home.

I licked my lips as Tate pulled out of the parking spot.

Then I said, "I didn't take a year to pick out pasta."

Jonas chuckled.

All Tate said was, "Babe."

*   *   *

Petal, it hurt.

My eyes opened.

The room was pitch. No moonlight because Tate had closed the
curtains.

It was the middle of the night and I couldn't sleep. This was
the fourth time Sunny's voice woke me up and her saying *hurt* in
the tone that told me exactly how much it hurt, exactly how it felt
when the blade sunk in her flesh, exactly how exquisite the pain was,
exactly, I knew I wouldn't get back to sleep again.

Carefully extricating my arm from around his waist, I rolled away
from Tate's back to rest on my opposite side.

Earlier that day, we'd come home to find Neeta's car gone. Tate
discovered through a phone call to Pop that Wood and Stella had
come to collect it.

We'd had lunch. I made cookies while Tate and Jonas cleared
the gutters of leaves and yes, I'd let Jonas have some dough, a lot of
it. This took them a while so I sorted our pool bags, did laundry,
changed sheets, and ran the vacuum cleaner in random rooms, all

this intermingled with sitting out on the deck and listening to them work and talk.

When they were done they played multiple games of horse at the basketball hoop that was mounted over the garage door. Sometimes I watched (okay, mostly I watched) while I sipped grape Kool-Aid.

The Kool-Aid reminded me of Carrie and Mom and Dad and home so I went into the house, got my phone, went back out to the deck and called them while I watched Tate and his son play basketball. I told my family about Jonas and about Neeta. I told my sister about Tate loving me and me loving him. She was cautiously happy for me, still thinking it was too soon but also liking Tate so she didn't give me much guff. And I told them all about Sunny. I didn't want to worry them but I also didn't want to keep it from them. They didn't like hearing it but they also made it clear they'd prefer it that way rather than me keeping it buried like I did with Brad and when I wandered the country looking for Carnal.

As for me, it felt good telling them. I needed to do it. To give it to them and they took it, as families do.

After basketball, I was off the phone and Tate and Jonas came to me. Tate took my retro pink glass, newly refilled with Kool-Aid, and downed a huge gulp.

When his hand dropped, his eyes narrowed on the glass then came to me.

"Jesus, Ace, that's like suckin' back a mouthful of sugar."

He said this like it was a bad thing.

"I know," I replied. "Isn't it yummy?"

"Yummy," Jonas muttered, his voice filled with humor. "Goofy."

"Do you want some?" I asked Jonas.

"He knows where it is," Tate answered for his son and then looked at the boy. "Get me a water while you're in there, Bub."

Jonas nodded and raced to the house, his arm still curved around the basketball.

I knew why Tate sent Jonas on his errand when he put the glass on the table beside me and leaned into me, a hand to either arm of my chair. He was sweaty, his hair around his neck and ears was wet and curling and there were more wet bits plastered to his forehead, as his T-shirt was mostly plastered to his chest.

Another kind of yummy.

"How you doin'?" he asked softly.

I took in a breath and on the exhale shared, "How I'm doing is, I keep thinking about it and she told me all of it but I still think we didn't get much."

"We got more than we had," Tate replied.

"That's true but it's not enough," I said. "He was wearing a ski mask."

"Bad luck," Tate muttered. "He came prepared."

"She was too scared to notice the color of his eyes and he didn't barely speak," I reminded Tate of what he already knew since he'd been listening in with the Feds.

"She's talkin' now and they'll get someone in to work with her, get more. But now we know he's built, strong, not a wimp, and we know he's white. We also know it wasn't opportunity. He'd seen her before."

"How do we know that?" I asked and, unfortunately, Tate moved away but pulled another chair close to mine and sat down.

"He came prepared," Tate repeated as he leaned down, wrapped an arm around the backs of my knees and then lifted his legs, feet to the railing, pulling mine up, twisting me in my chair and throwing my legs over his.

"The ski mask," I guessed.

"Yeah, it's July," Tate stated. "He was also wearin' gloves. Left no prints on her bike, left nothin'."

"But it's him, the one who killed Tonia," I stated.

"It's the same kind of knife so that's a good assumption."

"I don't get it."

"Shambles was with her before," Tate told me. "Tambo talked to him. She'd go out and draw down the sun on her own but not at that spot. At that spot, Shambles was always with her."

"So this time, alone..."

"He'd seen them together. She was alone this time, he took his shot."

"So, planned but not planned, exactly."

"Not planned exactly but planned, yeah."

I looked to the trees.

"He lives up there, Laurie," Tate muttered and my eyes shot to him.

"What?" I breathed.

"Bet my fuckin' life on it, he lives up there," Tate reiterated. "He knows that spot. He knows those woods. Bet my fuckin' life he lives up there. He hunts up there. That's his space. It's his."

With what he said and the way he said it, I felt my blood run cold.

"Is Tambo going to check?" I asked.

"Runnin' everyone now."

"How stupid would that be, that close to home, to—?"

"Pretty fuckin' stupid," Tate cut me off.

"But why?"

He shook his head, staring at the conifers at the front of his home, his mind somewhere else.

"It's jacked," he whispered. "Can't get my head around it. Nothin' fits but it all fits. Eight identical murders and now this, all the same MO, but all wrong."

We heard the sliding glass door at the same time as I heard Jonas saying, "No, Buster, you stay inside."

Quickly, I leaned close and whispered to Tate, "She said he said 'sorry.'"

His arm slid around my shoulders and pulled me closer so my side dug into the arm of the chair but I didn't care because the rest of me was resting against him.

"Yeah," Tate whispered back.

"That's creepy, Tate." I was still whispering.

"It's all creepy, Laurie." He was also still whispering.

He was right about that.

Jonas made it to us and he handed Tate a bottled water. Then he dragged a chair close to his dad and sat down with his own glass (not pink, one of Tate's old ones) of grape Kool-Aid and a handful of cookies that he proceeded to start eating.

"You like grape Kool-Aid, Jonas?" I asked him.

"Cherry's better," he muttered, mouth full and then turned to face me and grinned a chocolate chip cookie crumble grin. "But it'll do."

"I could do cherry," I stated and then finished on a mumble to myself, "Or I'll buy another pitcher. They had green ones too."

"Dad, Laurie's fillin' the house with girlie crap," Jonas told on me while I was sitting right there.

Tate was staring at the trees and I watched him smile at them while he murmured, "Yeah."

Clearly Tate didn't mind me filling the house with "girlie crap." I gave Jonas a "so there" look and Jonas rolled his eyes.

Then he asked, "We gonna eat hamburgers or what?"

"Soon's Lauren makes 'em," Tate answered.

"I thought you were grilling them," I said to Tate and he looked down at me.

"Yeah, I'm grillin' 'em, not *makin'* 'em."

"So I have to do the icky, squishy part?" I demanded to know.

Tate smiled at me. "Yeah."

Before I could protest, Jonas spoke.

"I'll do the icky, squishy part," he offered. "I like icky and squishy."

"It's all yours," I muttered.

"Cool!" Jonas cried.

"After a shower, Bub," Tate stated.

"Right," Jonas replied, shoved the last cookie in his mouth, jumped up and ran to the house.

Tate looked back at the trees. I rested my head on his shoulder. We sat together silent for a while before Tate broke the silence.

"He thinks you're the shit, Ace."

He meant Jonas.

"That's good since I feel the same way," I replied.

We were quiet again, then, for some reason, he asked softly, "You love me?"

My heart skipped and my body got tight.

But again my mouth answered for me, "Yes."

His arm gave me a squeeze and he muttered, "Good."

He fell silent and I focused on getting my heart rate normal even as I worried about the fact that he kept asking me that question, and getting his answer, and seeming content with that but not returning the sentiment.

Because I was worried about it, I couldn't get my heart rate normal and my mouth formed more words.

"Do you…uh…," I got out before my brain shut my mouth down.

His arm squeezed again, differently this time, curling in and I lifted my head up to find his had turned and he was looking down at me and, witnessing the look on his face, I found my heart rate accelerating startlingly.

"Never doubt it, Ace," he declared on a growl.

"Okay," I whispered and then asked, "Why do you keep asking me?"

"'Cause I like hearin' you say yes."

I lifted my hand and placed it on his bearded jaw as his head tipped down and he kissed me. It wasn't hard and demanding. It was soft, sweet, wet and deliciously long.

After Tate and I made out on the deck, I supervised Jonas's hamburger making at the same time making my pasta salad and we did this while Tate showered. Then Tate grilled. We ate out on the back patio while Jonas and I chattered and Tate infrequently interjected since Jonas and I chattered so much. We had cake after hamburgers. Then Jonas and I did dishes while Tate called Krys to make sure everything was okay. Then we camped out in the living room and watched comedies.

"No blood, no gore, Bub," Tate commanded when Jonas was picking our viewing fodder.

Tate was laid full out on the couch, his head on the headrest and I was tucked between him and the back of the couch, my head on his chest, his hand playing with my hair. We were on film number two and I was struggling to keep my eyes open. Therefore, I sleepily announced I was going to bed, pulled up Tate's body, kissed his lips, climbed over him and off the couch and went to Jonas where I touched his hair and then I went to bed.

The first time Sunny's words woke me up, Tate wasn't there. The second time, his big body was curled into mine. The third through fifth times, I was snuggled into his back.

Which brought me to now, very awake in the dead of night and facing a night shift the next day. I'd survive it, I had before, but it wouldn't be fun.

I rolled to my back and when I did, Tate rolled into me.

His hand slid along my belly as his face buried itself in the hair at the side of my head.

"You're havin' a rough night." His voice was scratchy with sleep.

"I'm okay."

His arm gave me a squeeze.

"Had to send you in there, babe."

He meant to talk to Sunny.

"I know," I whispered.

He was silent a moment then he said, "Knew it'd do this to you but had to send you in there."

"I know, Tate."

"I did it knowin' she'd give it to you and it'd mark you."

"Tate—"

"Also did it knowin' I'd be here when you dealt with it."

I rolled into him, wrapped my arm around him and he pulled me close.

"I know," I repeated, then whispered, "It's okay, Tate."

He felt guilt. I knew he did. He didn't like me losing sleep and he didn't like knowing he did something to exacerbate that.

But he had to do it and so did I. We both knew it but these were the consequences. He was right, he was here to help me deal with it and I was right too, I had him with me so it would be okay.

"Why didn't you have kids?" he asked and I blinked at his change of subject before I realized he changed it to take my mind off Sunny.

"Unconscious self-preservation." I used his words and he chuckled, his hand sliding up my back and into my hair where his fingers started to play with it.

"Knew, deep down, he was a dick," he guessed.

"Yes," I answered.

"Didn't want to bring a kid into that," he went on.

I sighed then said, "Yeah, but I wanted kids, so did Brad. I put it off, made excuses and he didn't push it. Then I felt him pull away, he didn't talk about it anymore and I buried it."

"Regret it?"

"Not having kids with Brad?"

Tate amended my statement. "Not havin' kids."

I thought about it and thinking about it made my stomach hurt.

And that hurt sounded in my word when I said, "Yeah."

Tate's hand cupped the back of my head and he tucked my face in his throat while he said, "Baby."

"It's okay," I whispered into his throat.

"Right," he replied and I knew he didn't believe me. Then again, he was right not to believe me since I was lying.

I changed the subject. "Tell me about your dad."

"Show you," he offered and I tipped my head back to look at him even though I couldn't see him in the dark.

"Show me?"

I heard his head move on the pillow as he looked down at me.

"Dad was big on video cameras, huge. Minute they were on the market, he bought one. The thing was mammoth, had to put it on his shoulder. It cost a fuckin' fortune, but he got one. Traded up every time a new camera came out. He even did edits. Put shit to music. Was always fuckin' around with it. My games. Parties. Holidays. Barbecues. When Wood and I went out on our bikes. Pop would get hold of the camera. Stella, Neet, Wood, me and we got footage of him. So, I'll show you."

"He was a good guy," I stated.

"The best," he replied.

"Proud of you."

I felt his body go solid for a moment before he relaxed.

"Yeah," he whispered.

"He still would be," I told him.

His body went solid again.

"Babe—"

"He would, Tate. You're a good man, a good dad."

He didn't respond and he kept quiet for so long, I let it go.

Then he relaxed against me and the feel of his hard, big body, his warmth, his scent hit me as his hand lazily traveled the skin of my back.

So my hand lazily traveled the skin of his side, his hip, then between us where my fingers wrapped around his cock and started stroking.

A low, sexy noise came out of his throat and he did the impossible, his teeth found my bottom lip in the dark and nipped it.

My legs moved restlessly as I felt a swell between them.

I kept stroking.

"Funny," Tate muttered, his lips still so close to mine I could feel his escalating breath.

"What?" I asked when he said no more.

"When I played ball, at Penn State, one thing I liked about it, outside the game, it got me great pussy."

My fingers squeezed his cock as a startled giggle escaped my throat.

"It got you great—?"

His hips pressed into my hand and I started stroking again.

"High-class college girls," he said, his voice getting thick. "Sorority."

He moved, his hands on me and his head so his lips were drifting light on the skin of my shoulder, my neck, but he didn't move in a way where I lost purchase on his cock. I knew what this meant so I kept stroking.

"Sorority," I whispered.

"Oh yeah," he whispered back, lips at my ear. "Liked that idea. Knew, when I made the pros, that was laid out before me."

"I might take that part back…," I stated, my hand stopping but not moving from its position, "about you being a good man."

His head came up and his hips pushed into my hand. "I was early twenties, Ace."

"Right," I muttered.

His hips thrust again and my hand started moving.

"Knew I'd find one, though," he whispered, his lips back to traveling my skin as he spoke. "With that amount of choice, I'd settle on a good one. Gorgeous, sweet, high-class pussy in my bed every night, goin' to my games, watchin' me play, helpin' me make babies and I could take care of her."

I liked what he was saying, my mind liked it, and my body liked it so I started stroking faster.

"Tate."

His mouth came to mine but he didn't kiss me.

Instead, he said, "Sucked when I lost that. I lost the game and I lost that future and that fucked with my head."

"Tate," I breathed against his lips.

"Came home, hooked up with Neet and knew that would be my life. Neet or someone like her and, havin' that taste of the good life, knowin' it was gone, that fuckin' sucked."

"Honey—"

"Didn't have any fuckin' clue, I waited twenty years, here I'd be, a gorgeous, sweet, high-class piece in my bed givin' me a hand job."

My heart stuttered, my breath caught, my nipples got hard and I felt a rush of wet between my legs.

"I'm not a piece," I told him, trying to sound offended but not really offended at all.

His hips started moving with my hand.

"Nope, babe, you're a *high-class* piece."

I felt another rush between my legs and I pressed against him as I stroked harder.

"That's it, baby," he muttered, his voice almost a groan.

"This high-class piece is done giving you a hand job, Captain."

"No you aren't," he growled.

My hand wrapped tight. I pressed even closer. I aimed with more hope than certainty and, luckily, my teeth succeeded in nipping *his* lip.

Then I whispered, "She wants to give you a different kind of job, honey."

I felt his lips smile before his mouth took mine in a deep, hot kiss.

He rolled to his back, pulling me on top of him and he stopped kissing me to invite on a murmur, "Knock yourself out, Ace."

I grinned in the dark. Then I took my time moving down his chest. Then I took my time doing other things to him.

I'd stopped sucking and started licking when I heard Tate growl, "Stop fuckin' around, babe."

"Mm," I mumbled against the head of his cock and his hands, already in my hair to pull it away from my face, fisted.

"Ace," he called as I kept licking.

I didn't reply. I took him in my mouth, his hips bucked up, I pulled him deep, heard his groan and then slid him out and glided my tongue from tip to base.

"Babe, seriously," Tate warned.

My hand was wrapped around him, holding him so my mouth could work him, I swirled the tip and then stated, "I'm enjoying myself."

"You're makin' a point," he returned.

I opened my mouth over him and sucked him deep again. His

big hands cupped my head and held it down so I gave him what he wanted until I heard him groan again then I pulled him out.

"Damn it, Laurie," he growled.

"Patience, Tate," I told him but he was done.

I knew this because he knifed up, I found my body pulled from between his legs and positioned at his side, my head still facing his lap. My knees were in the bed, he pushed them apart, yanked my panties down my behind and his hand was between my legs. He didn't tease. He wasn't playing. He was serious and it was my turn to groan, which I did, pushing my hips into his hand.

"Suck me off, babe," he demanded.

"Okay, baby," I gave in and immediately did as I was told.

It took some concentrated effort, considering he was working me, fast and hard while I was working him, fast and hard. But he kept giving it to me while I gave it to him so I had to return the favor.

Luckily, we both succeeded in bringing it home and it was unbelievably hot.

Tate righted my panties on my hips and my body in his bed and threw the covers over me before he went to the bathroom to clean up. When he came back, he took me in his arms and held me close.

Then he said, "We'll talk about that shit in the morning."

He didn't sound angry. He sounded tired, satisfied but mildly disgruntled.

"What shit?" I asked, sounding much the same, except the disgruntled part.

"I get to play, babe," he answered and my head came up.

"I don't?"

"Nope."

"Why?"

"You just don't."

I felt my chest seize and I whispered, "You didn't like it?"

His body went still a moment, then he burst out laughing and rolled into me so he was mostly on me.

"Tate—"

He cut me off. "It seem like I didn't like it?"

"Well...no, you were, um...groaning and—"

"Clue in, Laurie, I'm gonna tease you and I'm not just gonna tease you in bed."

"You were teasing?"

"Partly, yeah," he answered.

"What's the other part?"

"No woman has taken that kinda time with me."

"So you liked it," I stated hopefully.

His lips touched mine, then slid to my ear where he said, "Yeah, baby, I liked it. And you can do it again. But, I'm just sayin', I like to be the one who plays."

"Oh...kay," I said hesitantly because I didn't get it.

"I like making you catch fire," he went on.

"Okay."

"And I like control."

"Okay."

"And I don't like losin' it."

"So you didn't like it."

"Babe, I liked it."

"But Tate, I don't get it."

He rolled us to our sides again and stated decisively, "You will."

"I will?"

"Once you come fully into your biker babe, Ace, you'll get it."

I still didn't get it but now he sounded amused so I knew he wasn't angry and I was too sleepy to try.

I snuggled into him and muttered, "Well, *I* liked it."

"I got that," he muttered back.

I felt my brows draw together, "You did?"

"Babe, you were drippin' wet when I got my hand between your legs."

"Oh." Well that explained that.

His hand slid into my hair and he gently ordered, "Sleep for me, Laurie."

"Okay, Tate."

"Sweet dreams, baby."

I closed my eyes and snuggled closer. "You too, Captain."

For some reason, his hand suddenly twisted in my hair. It didn't hurt at all but there was something intense about it and my eyes opened.

"You'll have sweet dreams?" he asked quietly and sounding like he cared, a lot.

God but I loved this man.

I felt my mouth smile and I pressed even closer.

"I'm a good girl. I always do what I'm told."

His hand left my hair so both his arms could wrap tight around me.

"Love you, Ace," he murmured and my stomach melted.

He said it. Right out.

He said it.

"Love you too, Captain."

He kissed the top of my head and, in return, I kissed his chest.

Then I fell asleep and had sweet dreams.

Just like I was told.

CHAPTER TWENTY-THREE

Unpack

FOR A MONTH and a half, nothing big happened.

Well, big things happened. I should say nothing *mammoth* happened.

*   *   *

The first big thing to happen was that Tate didn't take Jonas back to Neeta.

This pissed Neeta off. She also blamed me for it. I knew it three days later when Tate had been called to go round up a fugitive from justice and therefore was out of town.

Even with more information, nothing had moved in the May-December case. Tambo told Tate that all the residents in the neck of the woods where Sunny was attacked didn't fit the profile and every last one (not that there were many) had alibis.

This didn't make Tate feel elated he had to go out and hunt down a fugitive. He didn't like leaving me and his son when a murderer was on the loose. But he also had bills to pay and mouths to feed so he set up a posse of semibodyguards who drove me to work, took me home, stayed with Jonas when I wasn't around and only left when they knew that I'd set the alarm. This posse included Pop, Dalton, Jim-Billy, Ned, and even Wood. Once Tate set this up, away he went.

It was the very day he left when they came to Bubba's when I was at work.

Three skanks, only one of them mildly attractive and one of them was overweight but dressed like a skank showing lots of skin. I tried not to be judgmental, to each their own, but really, exposing that amount of flesh when there was that amount of flesh to show was just plain wrong.

I knew they'd lived hard and rough and I could tell that by their faces *and* their attitude.

Twyla had squelched her own attitude enough to have been released from day duty (but only if I was working with her) so she and I were on nights and it was closing in on eleven. Dalton was behind the bar and Krys was back in the office when they came through the door.

I was standing at the bar in front of Dalton and he was completing an order when he looked over my shoulder, clocked them, and muttered, "Fuck, Laurie, get behind the bar."

I looked over my shoulder at them too, then at Dalton and asked, "Sorry?"

"Behind the bar," Dalton repeated.

"You! Bitch!" I heard shouted and I looked back at the women to see they were advancing on me.

Like she had magic, Twyla appeared at my side.

The three stopped in front of me and the heavy one looked me up and down and stated, "What's the big deal? She ain't all that."

Then the somewhat attractive one declared, "We're here for Neet."

"Oh my God," I whispered, staring at them and figuring out who they were. "You're Neeta's posse."

"Damn straight," the nondescript skank confirmed like she was proud of this insane fact.

"You got a problem?" Twyla asked, moving slightly in front of me.

"Not your business, dyke," the somewhat attractive one returned.

Oh no.

As Twyla's entire body puffed up in affront, I quickly moved in front of her as Dalton made it to my side.

"Maybe you should just go," I suggested.

"And maybe you should just leave Tate, bitch," the somewhat attractive one ordered, definitely the voice of Neeta's Crew. "He's personal property. You get what I'm sayin'?"

"Are you serious?" I asked, thinking the whole thing was funny. Personal property? Had I been hurtled back through time to junior high?

"Deadly," the somewhat attractive one leaned in and hissed and she looked serious.

"I'm not leaving Tate," I replied only because they seemed to be waiting for my response. "And you all coming in here for Neeta is absolutely ridiculous. I mean, really?"

"You're tryin' to turn her boy from her," the nondescript one alleged.

"Hardly," I retorted.

"Carmen, maybe you should—" Dalton started to say to the mildly attractive one.

"Not your concern either, Dalton," she cut him off then her head turned and she glared at Jim-Billy, a new arrival at our group. She looked him up and down, her lip curled and she sneered, "What you gonna do, Pops?"

"I'm just positionin' so's I can watch Twyla kick your ass up close," Jim-Billy replied.

"Right," she stated and turned her sneer to Twyla. "Like we can't take this bitch and her lesbo bodyguard."

Quick as lightning, Twyla moved, jumping in front of me, her arm shooting out and she jabbed Carmen right in the nose. It took Carmen by surprise but it also wasn't a light tap either. Her head jerked back, hair flying, she went back on a foot and her hands came up to her face. When they came down they were covered in blood, as was the lower half of her face.

"You *cunt*!" she shouted and, without delay, they all pounced as one on Twyla.

And Twyla took on the lot.

The second it started, Dalton turned to me, put both hands to my waist and lifted me straight up, planting my booty on the bar.

Then he tried to wade in but it was a whirl of hands and legs, big hair and fingernails so he could find no opening and eventually had to give up, step back and let the catfight reach its natural conclusion. Steg and Wings, two regulars, came to the bar to flank me. Jim-Billy got close and we all were trying to watch, leaning this way and that so as not to miss anything as Twyla beat the crap out of three skanks at once.

I decided, watching, they probably shouldn't have come to a showdown in miniskirts and high heels. Twyla was definitely no pushover but I figured miniskirts and high heels put them at a further disadvantage. Not to mention, some of the unintentional crotch shots . . . seriously unattractive.

This went on for a while, long enough for a standing crowd of bikers and locals to form around the ruckus. Then it was stopped by the chilling sound of a shotgun ratchet.

The combatants all froze. Twyla had hold of Carmen's skintight camisole in one fist and had her other arm cocked to deliver another blow. The nondescript one was on her knees, trying to get to her feet. The heavy one was rolling to her side. And all of them looked up at Krys who was aiming a sawed-off shotgun at Carmen.

"What'd I tell you, Carmen?" Krys demanded to know.

Twyla pushed Carmen off and stepped away as they all got to their feet and rounded on Krys.

"I'm lookin' out for my girl," Carmen said to Krys, wiping blood from her mouth. "You know how it is and you know nothin'll stop me."

"I know you're gonna get a taste of buckshot, you ever come into my bar again," Krys shot back. "Told you the last time, you ain't welcome here. I'll tell you one more time, you ain't welcome here. I'm warnin' you, there won't be a third time."

Carmen locked eyes with Krys and Krystal didn't flinch. She just held her gaze and held the shotgun steady, aimed at Carmen.

Finally, Carmen's eyes cut to me.

"Watch your back," she threatened, jabbing a finger at me.

That's when the shotgun blasted. Buckshot imbedded in the ceiling, dust, bits and buckshot that didn't find purchase raining down. I couldn't stop my short scream or my knees from automatically curling up to my chest as my head snapped around to look at Krys. Everyone around the bar had ducked and mine wasn't the only cry.

"You get near Laurie, in this bar or out of it, you answer to me," Krys warned.

"Can't carry that gun with you everywhere, Krystal," Carmen returned.

"You touch Krys or Laurie, you answer to me too," Steg, standing in front of me, stated. "Any of ya'll," he finished, his hand lifted high, his finger pointed down and twirling to indicate the entire crew.

"Neeta's bullshit and your bullshit, it's done," another voice called and I turned to see Stoney, the owner of one of the biker paraphernalia shops on Main Street, chipping in.

"Yeah, grow up. What ya'll think? You're still in high school?" another voice yelled out.

"That bitch is tryin' to take Neeta's man and her boy," the nonde-script one defended, pointing at me.

"Far's I can see, she's already got Neet's man and good for Tate," Stoney put in. "Finally Tate's got himself a woman who don't cause no headaches and we all know Tate comes with his boy."

"I wouldn't say I don't give Tate headaches, Stoney," I clarified. "Seeing as I'm a biker babe in training, sometimes I mess up and make him mad."

I heard chuckles, Wings turned toward me and grinned before saying, "You need lessons, darlin', Tate's gone, I'll do what I can."

"Thanks Wings, I'll…um, consider that," I lied on a smile. I felt eyes and I looked to see Carmen's gaze narrowed on me.

"I don't find you funny," she said softly.

"I don't care," I replied.

"You're still here," Krystal prompted.

Neeta's crew liberally handed out glares as they made their way to the door. I figured this was mostly to save face but I didn't think too much about it. They were leaving, that was all I cared about.

Steg helped me down from the bar and Twyla got close.

"You good?" she asked as her eyes looked me up and down and then she answered her own question. "You're good." She turned and shouted, "Who needs a fuckin' beer?"

I looked at Krystal and smiled. She looked at me and shook her head.

Then she moved to return the shotgun to its hidey-hole (wher-ever that was) and I went back to work.

*   *   *

That night, on the phone with Tate (even though it was after three in the morning, I was still on orders to call him the minute I hit his bed), I told him the whole thing.

His amused-sounding reply?

"Babe."

*   *   *

The second and third things that happened came as a one-two punch.

*   *   *

See, before Tate left, Ned, Betty, Shambles, and I all went to Tate's attorney's office in Gnaw Bone and swore out depositions. Ned, Betty, and Shambles's were about what happened at the pool, mine also included what I witnessed when Neeta came for her nocturnal visits and what Jonas shared before French toast.

These depositions were needed as Tate was outside the visitation arrangement, essentially having kidnapped his son (but not really) and he needed to make his case urgently to get custody awarded to him considering the state of play at Neeta's house.

While Tate was gone, he received word that the judge had read the depositions and found them concerning enough to award temporary custody to Tate and find a slot for Tate's case.

Tate was under the gun to hunt down the bad guy and get back home for the hearing. This he managed to do, with no time to spare, arriving home the night before the morning hearing.

I was on tenterhooks.

I was on tenterhooks because I needed to be at the courthouse. They were going to call me, Ned, Betty and Shambles as witnesses.

I felt bad for Shambles being dragged into this though he said, repeatedly, he didn't mind at all.

Sunny was home and recovering, physically, but she wasn't yet fit to go back to La-La Land and wouldn't be for some time. Jonas and I would visit both Sunny at their house and Shambles at La-La Land but things were not good in their world and it didn't seem they were recovering as quickly as Sunny's body was.

I was also nervous about appearing in court. I was Tate's MILF girlfriend, an ex-executive, current waitress, and divorcée who wandered around like an idiot in her car for months before finding Carnal and, once I did, I'd lived in a hotel. If Neeta's attorneys got hold of that, I didn't think it would sound too good to the judge.

So I needed an outfit that said I was smart, respectable, kind, and motherly but not overly motherly as in, I was out to wrest Neeta's child from her and would stop at nothing to do so. I couldn't wear one of the suits I used to wear to work because they said smart and respectable but not kind or motherly. I didn't have anything else that would do either and I'd tried on practically everything that wasn't shorts, jeans, or T-shirts.

So Wendy and I took Jonas to the mall and spent three hours torturing poor Jonas (who didn't mind the mall, for, say, the first five minutes, then, just like his father, he found it not so fun) until I found something. I bought it because Wendy swore it was perfect. She swore it was me and she advised I had to be me because the judge would see through anything else. And I bought it even though I thought it made me look more MILF than mother and I bought it because Jonas looked ready to beg the next woman he saw to adopt him immediately.

I also bought Tate the picture of the bikers driving into Carnal. I bought this from Stoney who didn't want to sell it. As in, he *really* didn't want to sell it. This meant I had to go all the way up to $1,500 to buy it in the haggle with a biker to end all haggles with a biker, one I obviously lost. This was a little insane but it was also how badly I wanted Tate to have it. Pop went to go get it and he and Jim-Billy fixed it to the wall over Tate's bed.

Seeing it there, I didn't mind that it cost an absolute fortune. I was right. It was perfect. It made the room.

And it was Tate. The minute I walked into Stoney's and saw it up close, I knew he had to have it. I made it mine to give; I gave it to him and it was worth every penny.

But I worried Tate would find out how much I spent and lose his mind, even though I swore Stoney to secrecy.

Tate didn't get a chance to see the surprise in his bedroom to get pissed off about it.

No, he was pissed the minute he walked into the house.

I knew this because I was standing in the kitchen, Jonas was in the living room playing a video game on the TV and Tate walked in, his eyes locked on mine. I didn't even get my mouth open to say hello before he growled, "Bedroom."

Then he prowled toward the hall, only his head turning toward Jonas to whom he said, "A minute, Bub." Then he disappeared down the hall.

I thought he'd heard about the picture and I followed him, taking my time, not wishing to rush to my punishment, and I threw a curious-looking but grinning Jonas a nervous smile before I hit the hall.

I cleared the door to the bedroom and Tate, standing in the middle of the room, his back to the bed and the picture, his arms crossed on his chest, ordered, "Close it."

I took in a breath, turned, and closed the door.

Then I leaned against it and started, "Tate, I know you're—"

He cut me off on a snarled, "What the fuck, Ace?"

"I wanted—"

He interrupted me again. "I thought we had this straight."

"We did, I just wanted—"

"Space?"

I blinked, confused. "Sorry?"

"Christ almighty, Lauren, I'm gone half the time."

I shook my head, not following. "Gone half the time?"

"You and Amber went to look at apartments. Stella saw you and told me."

Oh, that.

He couldn't be angry about that. He hadn't asked me to move in, not officially, and he didn't seem bothered that I was living out of suitcases. Obviously, he wasn't ready for me to move in and it was too soon to be living together, *living together*. He had plenty of help with Jonas. I would even help out when I got a place. But I needed to get settled and not in a hotel and not crashing at his place to take care of his cat and his son while living out of a suitcase. He loved me. He couldn't want that for me. I needed to call someplace home, the time had come. And he loved me. He'd want that for me.

"I need to settle, Captain. I'm tired of living out of a suitcase," I said softly.

"So fuckin' unpack," he returned, as if it was as simple as that.

I blinked again. "What?"

He threw his hands out impatiently. "Unpack."

"Here?" I asked disbelievingly.

I watched his face go hard. "Why the fuck not? You need space, babe, I'm on the road half the time. You want a fancy couch, fuckin' buy it."

"I…" I shook my head. "Um…"

"You, um, what?" he shot at me. "What do you need to make this good enough?"

"Good enough?" I whispered.

He took five long strides to me and they were so fast suddenly his face was all I could see.

"Get your damned blinds, buy a fuckin' couch, recarpet, I don't care, just unpack your fuckin' bags," he growled.

"Are you…" My head jerked spasmodically and I tried again. "Are you asking me to move in with you?"

"Sharp as a tack, Lauren," he bit out, one of his barbs that stung.

"No," I whispered as the point of the scene dawned on me, "you're *telling* me to move in with you."

"Unpack your…fuckin'…bags," he clipped.

I stared up at him.

Then I glared up at him.

Then I planted my hands on my hips and leaned in, getting even closer to his face.

"You know, Captain," I whispered in a voice that sounded more like a hiss. "I've been waiting for you to ask me for weeks, *weeks,* to make it official and move in and you do it like *this*." I flipped a hand out and then returned it right back to my hip.

I was too angry to notice the change in his face, I just kept right on hissing.

"Every time I walked into that closet, I looked at those bags and I worried. Was I staying too long? Did *you* need your space? Did you want time with Jonas? Or did you want me to stay? Should I unpack? Should I leave it as it was? I thought that was safest, so I did. But you didn't say anything. You didn't *care* I was living out of *suitcases* on the *floor* of your *closet*."

His hand came to my neck and he murmured, "Baby," but I was too far gone to stop so I didn't.

"So I figured you not saying anything meant it was too soon and yes, Amber and I looked at apartments." I threw out my arms in exasperation. "What was I supposed to do? Read your mind?"

His fingers at my neck gave me a squeeze, his body moved closer and his other arm started to wind around my waist.

"Laurie—"

"And now this, you hear it from Stella and you come home after being gone over a week and you don't even say hi to Jonas. You don't ask me about it. You don't even kiss me. You just start—"

I stopped talking because I couldn't speak with his mouth on mine and his tongue in my mouth. I tried to tamp down my reaction but he'd been gone over a week, I missed him and lastly, but most importantly, it finally sunk in he wanted me to move in.

So it might have been weak, but I didn't gosh darned care.

I kissed him back.

My arms were around his neck, my body plastered to his when his lips unlocked from mine and trailed to my ear.

"See you came into your biker babe," he whispered there, his hands moving on me, making me shiver. "The escalation of attitude's impressive, Ace."

"You're a jerk, Tate," I replied but it came out kind of breathy mainly because I was breathless.

His head came up and his eyes found mine.

"Unpack your bags."

I felt my short-lived happy vibe flee at the same time I felt my eyes go squinty.

"You're very bossy."

"Unpack your bags."

"Those apartments are sweet. The one they have available has a view of the—"

His hands stopped roaming at the sides of my ribcage and they squeezed.

"Unpack. Your. Bags."

I glared at him.

Then I announced, "Tatum Jackson, you're lucky you're a smokin' hot, badass, biker, bounty hunter who looks good in jeans and is a good dad and I love you or you would *seriously not* be worth it."

I thought this was a well-delivered line but he clearly thought it was amusing and I knew this because his face dipped close to mine and I felt the side of his nose brush the side of mine before he moved back again and I saw he was smiling.

Then, his brows up, he asked, "Smokin' hot?"

"Shut it," I snapped.

Tate burst out laughing at the same time his arms went super tight around me and he gave me a big hug.

"You know," I told him, "this latest tirade bought me new carpet *and* a new couch."

His jaw was pressed to the side of my head. He moved back, looked down at me and declared, "Chick territory, babe, I don't care."

"You should care," I went on. "There's a snag in the rug in Jonas's room and if that starts unraveling, he might trip on it and crack his head on the nightstand or something."

Tate's head descended again, this time to brush my mouth with his and when he pulled back, he invited softly, "Make things safe for my boy, baby."

I liked his soft voice and he'd been gone awhile so I missed it being live and in person but I still felt it necessary to hold a grudge.

"I would have done it anyway, just because it's a hazard," I grumbled, my eyes targeted to his ear. "Wrath of Tate be damned."

"Babe," he called.

"What?" I snapped, my eyes moving back to his.

"Unpack," he whispered, kissed me lightly, let me go and pulled me from the door, turning me. I knew he was going to go talk to Jonas but his eyes went beyond me to the wall over the bed and then he went completely still.

Then he muttered, "Christ."

Uh-oh.

"Um...," I mumbled and his gaze moved to me.

"I don't wanna know," he said.

"Stoney was—"

"I don't wanna know," he repeated.

"Stoney understood you needed it in your—"

He yanked my body to his, his head came down and he gave me a hard, bruising but thorough and delicious kiss and then his head came back up.

"I love it, babe, loved that picture all my life," he whispered, my stomach flipped, my heart turned over and he went on. "And I know Stoney loved it too so, you gettin' it from him...I don't...wanna... know. Yeah?"

I felt it prudent at that juncture to agree so I nodded.

"Good girl," he muttered, let me go, left the room and went to say hello to his son.

I stood there and stared at the picture, smiling to myself. Then I stared at the closet and I wondered if I unpacked right then, if Tate would think I was too eager.

So I decided not to unpack right then.

Instead, I walked out of the bedroom, down the hall, to the kitchen and finished pouring myself a Kool-Aid, which was what I had started doing when Tate arrived home. I offered Tate and Jonas drinks and brought Tate a beer and Jonas an iced Kool-Aid.

Then I went back to the bedroom, taking my Kool-Aid with me, and unpacked.

*   *   *

I would figure it out later, in bed, when it woke me up.

Tate was going to court the next day to battle for his son.

He had been hunting a fugitive and he'd lose time and money if he had to abandon that hunt so he was under the gun and lucky he found his prey before he needed to come home.

And he loved me and wanted me to move in with him, he heard I was looking at apartments and, like usual, when it all came at him at once, he got angry.

I'd have to see what I could do to shield him from that.

"Baby, you awake?" Tate's drowsy, rough voice called.

I rubbed my nose against his back and pressed deeper, my arm going tight around his stomach.

"No," I answered against his skin.

"Bullshit," he muttered.

"Go back to sleep, Tate."

"Laurie—"

I pressed in and held on tight.

"For me, baby?" I whispered.

His hand found mine at his stomach and covered it. His fingers lacing through mine, he rolled slightly forward, pulling my arm up so our hands were tucked to the bed and I was resting mostly on his back.

I liked this position, a lot, so I tangled my legs with his and settled in.

"Laurie," he called but I didn't answer even though I heard him.

I didn't answer because, a second later, I really settled in, giving him all my weight when I fell asleep.

* * *

Ned, Betty, Shambles, and I stood in the courtroom. Tate was at the desk with his attorney, a very pretty yet very pregnant blonde named Nina Maxwell. Neeta's attorney was at the other desk with no Neeta. I was jittery as a cat but Tate looked hot, wearing a well-cut suit and looking unbelievably gorgeous in it, and completely calm.

I was fidgeting, rubbing my hands together and moving from foot to foot when Tate's eyes came to me. They dropped to my hands, then they came back to my face and that tender look was there. He gave me a barely there grin and then his attention turned back to Nina. I took in a breath, my mind imprinted with Tate's tender look and I settled.

I was wearing a pale pink blouse with cap sleeves, a skintight pencil skirt in cream linen, and a pair of rose colored, high-heeled slingbacks. I had pearl studs at my ears and my watch but no other jewelry. I'd pulled my hair back in a ponytail at my nape.

I found out earlier I was correct in thinking I was more MILF than motherly when I walked into the living room. Tate, Stella, and Jonas all looked at me in my outfit. Tate smiled sexy slow and declared, "Jesus, you look like a sex kitten school marm."

I turned instantly on my heel and headed back to the bedroom while I heard Jonas cackle loudly and effusively, which almost, but not quite, drowned out Stella's laughter.

Tate caught me before I made it to the bedroom and led me firmly to the Explorer.

The doors to the courtroom opened, I jumped, and Wood walked in.

His eyes moved through me to Tate and he walked right to the front where the little, shiny wooden partition separated the onlookers from the opponents.

Tate stared at Wood as did Nina.

"I said anything," Wood murmured to Tate and then turned his attention to Tate's attorney. "I was there both nights Neeta showed at Tate's, includin' the night she drove there drunk."

"And you are?" Nina asked.

"Neeta's brother," Tate answered.

Nina Maxwell grinned.

*　　*　　*

We were all seated, me between Wood and Shambles. It was ten minutes after the time court was supposed to be in session, the courtroom personnel were looking impatient and Neeta's attorney was looking harassed.

He was about to be more harassed for the doors opened and Neeta came in and it didn't take a waitress at a biker bar to know instantly she was drunk off her ass.

"Lordy be." I heard Betty murmur as I stared at Neeta making her intoxicated way down the aisle.

She was dressed about two steps up from usual. Short skirt (wrinkled), see-through blouse (no camisole, black bra, blouse also wrinkled), and high-heeled, strappy sandals (with scuffs).

She was followed by a dark-haired man in an ill-fitting suit, the suit clearly purchased in a time when beer wasn't the main component of his nutritional intake. I found myself even more fascinated by him than I was the inebriated Neeta because I knew, I knew just looking at him, he once was beautiful. He could have been as beautiful as Tate but I'd need picture proof of that, but the indicators were all there.

Tate was forty-four and looked in his thirties.

Neeta's man was likely close to Tate's age but looked in his fifties.

Boy, she wasn't just dumb, the woman was stupid.

It was bad manners to gloat so I didn't and anyway, I was too startled by Neeta showing up drunk to her son's custody hearing to gloat.

My eyes moved away from the spectacle of Neeta's man attempting to guide her to the front and I saw Wood watching his sister.

I reached out and wrapped my fingers around his biceps. At my touch, he turned to me and showed me his pain.

"Honey," I whispered.

"Stupid," he whispered back. "Fuck me. So fuckin' stupid."

I squeezed his arm and my eyes went to Tate who was still standing, his gaze glued to Neeta. His jaw was tight and his eyes were cold.

He looked to me and shook his head in disgust. I shook mine back and squeezed Wood's arm again before I dropped my hand in my lap.

Neeta's man got her to her attorney and she didn't look at anyone as she passed us. This was likely because she was concentrating on walking. Blake retraced his steps and sat across the aisle from Wood. He didn't look at Tate. He didn't look at Wood. He didn't look at anyone. He just sat down and faced forward.

"Are you finally ready?" the bailiff asked Neeta's attorney.

"If my client and I could have—" Neeta's attorney started.

"You're ready," the bailiff cut him off and disappeared behind a door.

I looked back at Tate to see he was seating himself.

Five seconds later we were all standing after we heard, "All rise…"

When we were given the all-clear to sit again, I did and held my breath.

*   *   *

Five minutes later, the judge cut off Neeta's attorney midsentence and, eyes narrowed on Neeta, he asked her directly, "Mrs. Daniels, are you intoxicated?"

"Your honor, if we could—" Neeta's attorney started.

The judge cut him off by saying sharply and impatiently to the bailiff, "Get a Breathalyzer in here."

Then he abruptly stood, the bailiff called out, "All rise…" We all rose and the judge stormed out.

*   *   *

"I bought this outfit for nothing," I groused in the Explorer on the way home.

"Baby, it's sweet," Tate replied.

I turned to Tate. "The judge talked to me for five seconds. I told him about the snag in Jonas's carpet and how I was going to fix it and he just said, 'Good thinking, Miss Grahame, those can be dangerous, send the hotel people in here on your way out, would you?' That's it!" I ended on a cry.

"Laurie—"

I crossed my arms on my chest and interrupted him. "I don't think he's a very good judge. How does he know if I'm a good person to have around Jonas?"

"Lauren—"

"He had Ned and Betty in there for fifteen whole minutes. I timed it and I heard them *laughing*. Fifteen minutes and they don't even *live* with Jonas. He just goes to their pool. He had me in there less than *five* and he sent me out and I *live* with Jonas! I could be anyone. I could be a crazy woman who feeds him only cat food!"

"Honey—"

"I think you should ask for another judge," I declared and Tate emitted a startled bark of laughter so I turned to him. "What?"

"Babe, I got full custody. I'm not asking for another judge just so you can convince him you'll be a good stepmom and knock him out with your sex kitten school marm getup."

He was, of course, right and I was acting like a lunatic.

I took in a deep breath and looked out the side window.

"I got wound up for nothing," I whispered. "Stupid."

"What's stupid is showin' trashed out of your fuckin' brain to a custody hearing. That's stupid. Givin' a shit enough to buy a new outfit, do your hair, look presentable and responsible even though you're nervous as all hell and knowin' there's a snag in your kid's carpet and worryin' about it ain't stupid. It's the kind of person a judge can trust around a ten-year-old kid. You think he doesn't see that?"

Tate was, again, right.

I turned to him and asked quietly, "Do you think she was nervous too?"

"Scared outta her brain," Tate answered.

"But nervous to lose Jonas?"

"Don't know about that but scared, fuck yeah. Scared of losin' child support, which is pretty much all they got. Scared of lookin' bad because everyone in Carnal's gonna know the outcome and she knew it wasn't lookin' good. And scared because she knew you'd come in there lookin' like you look and makin' her look even worse. Neeta's the master of self-fulfilled prophesies and today she topped even her best efforts and there've been some really fuckin' good ones."

"But not scared of losing Jonas," I whispered.

"Don't know but if she was, she fulfilled that prophesy too."

I looked out the windshield and murmured, "She's beginning to make me sad."

His hand reached out and took mine. "Yeah, baby, you spent time with Jonas. A mom losin' that? It's sad."

I turned my hand in his and held tight.

Then I said, "She doesn't get anything but supervised visits for a day every two weeks so you don't have to worry anymore."

"Yeah."

"And you don't have to pay child support anymore."

"Nope."

"We should celebrate," I decided and his hand squeezed mine.

"We are. We got reservations at The Rooster."

I turned to him.

I'd heard of The Rooster. It was a fancy steak place in the mountains about half an hour away. It was supposed to be fabulous.

"We do?" I asked.

"Yeah, babe, we do."

He'd made those reservations while on the road, thinking about his son and hoping there would be something to celebrate.

I leaned across the seat and kissed his bearded jaw.

Then, in his ear I whispered, "I'm so happy for you, Tate."

His hand tightened in mine. Mine tightened in his.

I sat back and looked out the windshield.

"At least, going to The Rooster, I have a decent reason to have spent money on my outfit," I noted.

Tate chuckled and I listened contentedly while I watched the landscape roll by and Tate took us home to Jonas.

*   *   *

After the judge's decision, Tate and I kept a close watch on Jonas.

He tried to hide it but he struggled with conflicting emotions of relief, guilt, and worry about his mother.

In an attempt to counteract that and create a new routine for his son, Tate encouraged him to call her frequently.

Jonas didn't call her frequently but he called her.

The conversations were brief, clearly confusing, and equally clearly hurtful.

Therefore Tate stopped encouraging his son to call his mother.

*   *   *

It was around three o'clock four days after Tate got Jonas. I was on day shift, Tate was behind the bar, when Krystal and Bubba walked in.

I hadn't seen Bubba in ages and, in that time, I didn't bring him up to either Krys or Tate because I knew both of them were feeling intensely unhappy feelings about Bubba. So intense, I steered clear from unleashing those feelings, not for Bubba's sake, or my own, but for theirs.

Bubba looked rough, straggly hair, eyes red rimmed and blood-shot, face hangdog.

Krystal looked far more than her usual angry at the world. She looked fit to be tied.

My eyes moved to Tate to see his were on Bubba and his face was granite.

"Got it at home, Tate, don't need it here," Bubba muttered, his hand lifted, palm out, toward Tate. I pressed my lips together as I felt my belly start to burn.

"Laurie, darlin', keep cool," Jim-Billy whispered to me, sitting beside where I was standing at the bar.

Krystal didn't say a word. She just disappeared down the back hall.

Tate headed down the bar our way as Bubba slid onto a stool beside Jim-Billy opposite from where I was standing.

"Hey gorgeous," Bubba called quietly to me, avoiding my eyes.

I opened my mouth to speak but Tate had arrived.

"I want out," Tate declared without preamble and Bubba looked up at him.

"What?" Bubba asked Tate.

"Out," Tate replied. "You and Krys need to get it together and buy me out. You also need to put up the sign in the window. Laurie's givin' notice. She's gonna work for me."

My wide eyes moved to Tate.

I was?

"What?" Bubba repeated.

"You heard me," Tate answered.

"You can't—" Bubba started.

"I can," Tate cut him off. "Sick of this shit, Bubba. Didn't buy into this. You made me promises, a fuckload of 'em, and you broke every fuckin' one of 'em."

"Tate, man, you can't—"

"I can and Laurie can. We got Jonas at home. We're needed there," Tate stated.

"I heard about that but Pop and Stell—"

"Can't count on them all the time, that's not cool. They got lives and I got work. I don't need to be on the road, worried about Jonas, Lauren, *and* the bar. Gotta scrape somethin' off and it's the bar."

"But Krys—" Bubba began.

"Krys knows what's good for her, she'll scrape somethin' off too," Tate returned.

We all knew what that meant, Bubba, Jim-Billy, and me. Bubba's back went up and his face got tight. I looked at Jim-Billy. He felt my gaze and he looked at me, his eyes wide.

It was then Krystal joined our group.

"What's goin' on?" she asked, instantly feeling the bad vibe.

Everyone looked her way.

"Tate wants us to buy him out," Bubba answered and Krystal's gaze shot to Tate.

"What?" she whispered.

"We'll get the accountant to look at the books, decide what's fair," Tate answered and I watched Krystal's face pale.

At that, I thought it was time to intervene so I said softly, "Captain—"

Tate spoke over me to Krystal. "Lauren's givin' notice. Got work,

Jonas, and Laurie. Don't need to be on the road half the time, in the bar the other half, and havin' to deal with paperwork. Lauren's gonna take care of that for me and the half of my life I free from the bar, I spend with my family."

Krystal's eyes then shot to me and I saw instantly her guard was down. There was pain in her face, and betrayal.

"Krys—" I whispered.

She tore her gaze from me and looked back at Tate. "We had a good summer but part a' that is because Laurie's here. The boys love her. She goes, they ain't gonna come in and hang with Twyla."

"Not my problem," Tate stated.

"Captain—" I tried again.

"I lose Laurie, I lose the drinks she sells. I buy you out, I'll be hurtin'," Krystal pointed out.

"Again, not my problem," Tate reiterated.

"Tate, honey—" I tried yet again.

"I don't believe this shit," Bubba muttered and Tate's gaze sliced to him.

"You don't?" he asked curtly. "How? Christ almighty, Bubba, I told you once, I told you a thousand times, you don't pull your shit together, I'm gone. Now I'm done tellin' you. I'm gone."

"I know shit's whacked around here and heard about Neet and Jonas, Tate. I shoulda sorted my shit out and it was a crap thing to do, leavin' while you all were in the middle a' that but, bud, that's done. Krys and I talked and—" Bubba explained.

Tate interrupted him, "Heard this before, don't believe it anymore."

"But, Tate, swear to God—"

"Don't believe it."

"But—" Bubba pushed it.

"He's gone," Krystal whispered and everyone looked at her to see her gaze pinned to Bubba.

"What?" Tate asked and slowly her head turned toward him.

"Bubba, he's gone," Krystal said.

"*What?*" Bubba shouted, coming off his stool but Krystal didn't tear her eyes from Tate.

"Would you help me buy him out?" Krystal asked and my belly stopped burning but I felt my heart start beating wildly.

"What're you talkin' 'bout, woman?" Bubba demanded to know.

Krystal ignored Bubba. "Whatever you want, Tate, I'll sort the bar, I'll make the deal you need, but Bubba's gone."

Bubba started rounding Jim-Billy and me to get to Krystal but Tate also ignored him and spoke to Krystal.

"We buy him out, you find another bartender, we make Lauren a manager and she gets a pay hike. She handles the schedule, she handles stock, she handles payroll, personnel, and orders. You hate that shit anyway and she's good at it. Frees your time to be front of bar. She works the floor, only days, shorter shifts, ten to five. Office work before opening, five days a week, every other weekend off."

I stared at Tate in shock because he seemed to have this all thought out and hadn't mentioned a word to me. Bubba had made it to Krystal and lifted a hand to latch on to her arm.

Tate's eyes cut to him and his voice was an angry growl when he warned, "Touch her, Bubba, I won't fuckin' like it."

Bubba glared at Tate then threw up both his hands and shouted, "This is whacked!"

"This is consequences," Tate shot back. "You live your life not worryin' about 'em and everyone else deals with 'em for you. I'm done with that." He looked at Krystal and demanded, "Well?"

"Deal," she replied instantly and turned to Bubba. "Go home, pack your shit. I want you out by tonight."

"Have you lost your mind?" Bubba was still shouting, now at Krystal.

"Yeah," she answered. "Ten years ago."

Bubba scowled at her, then sucked in breath, shook his head, and his tone was much quieter when he said, "Darlin'—"

"Gotta hold on to what's real," Krystal cut him off. "This bar is real. I lose Tate and Lauren, I won't be able to hold on to the only thing in my life that's real."

"We—" Bubba started.

"There is no we, never was. You fooled me into thinkin' there was a we, then I fooled myself into thinkin' it. But now I know, there is no we and never was."

Bubba pushed close to her. "Darlin', we gotta talk. Let's go to the office."

"Not talkin', go home, get your shit out."

"We gotta talk," Bubba pressed and that was when I watched Krystal change.

She turned fully to face Bubba and her body got visibly tight but her face went soft, not with tenderness, not with love, but with anguish.

"It isn't about the bar," she whispered and shook her head. "It isn't about the bar," she repeated and sucked in breath through her nose. "There's a maniac out there, Bub. Laurie doesn't make a move without someone takin' her back. She doesn't step a foot out that door unless she's got a man at her side. She doesn't walk in that door unless someone who's lookin' out for her brought her here. She's never alone because these days, in Carnal, alone can get a woman hurt. Alone can leave her vulnerable. She didn't arrange that, Tate did. But you? What'd you do? Tonia's sliced up and raped and that hippie coffee girl gets attacked, a killer is on the loose in your town and you're out gettin' drunk, gettin' laid, havin' a good ole time and I'm here, alone, no one at my back. That's what it's about, Bub. I'm already alone. I'm just makin' it official."

Bubba got closer to her, lifted a hand to touch her and she jerked away so his hand fell.

"But, baby, you can take care of yourself. I know that," he whispered.

"So could Tonia," she replied.

"Tonia was young and stupid, you ain't that," Bubba returned.

"No, what I am and have been for months is scared outta my fuckin' brain," Krystal said softly. "Alone and scared outta my fuckin' brain."

"Baby," Bubba whispered.

"Go," she whispered back.

"All you had to do is tell me," Bubba kept trying.

"No, see, that's what you don't get. I shouldn't *have* to tell you," Krystal retorted. "You should want me to be safe and do what you gotta do to make that so *without* me tellin' you."

"Krys—"

"Go."

"Darlin'—"

"*Go.*"

They stared at each other and I held my breath.

Bubba opened his mouth to speak but Tate got there before him.

"Bubba, two choices, man. You go or I make you go."

Bubba's head turned toward Tate and his face got hard. I braced and Jim-Billy slid off his stool.

"Bub, buddy, I'll help you at home," Jim-Billy offered.

Bubba crossed his arms on his chest and declared, "My house, my bar, not leavin' either. Fuck this."

That was when I knew the laid-back biker Bubba was digging in to save face.

And that was when I knew I was done.

"Honestly?" I asked and his eyes came to me. "You put them both through what you did and now, when it comes down to it and you can finally be a man, you're gonna put them through more?"

"Don't know what this has got to do with you, Laurie," Bubba retorted.

"You wouldn't, since you've been gone so long, you don't know that I love Tate and I love Krys and, since you go fishin' so often, you haven't cottoned on to the fact that so does everyone else. If they're done with you then the rest of us are too." Bubba glared at me and I kept talking. "We put up with you because we care about them. Now they're done, so are we."

Bubba uncrossed his arms and declared, "I don't need this shit."

"There it is," I replied immediately. "That's your problem. All you think about is *you*. What you don't understand is *they* don't need this shit and they haven't needed it for a long, long time."

I watched a muscle jump in Bubba's cheek, then he looked at Jim-Billy. "Don't need your help, old man," he announced, then strode right out of the bar.

We all watched the door close behind him and then I looked at Jim-Billy to see he was looking at Krystal. My eyes moved to Tate to see he was watching me and looking far from happy. Then both Tate and I looked at Krys.

"Krys, honey—" I started.

She cut me off, "Tomorrow mornin', I'll show you the office work."

"Why don't you and I have a drink now?" I suggested.

"Case you missed this, darlin', I ain't like your other girls. I don't process over girl talk. Life happens and I move on," she returned. "Life just happened and I'm movin' on."

After she finished speaking she turned and again disappeared down the hall.

I looked to Tate. "You okay out here alone?"

"Yeah, babe," Tate answered.

I nodded, my eyes went to Jim-Billy who nodded at me. Then I went behind the bar, grabbed a bottle of vodka (Krystal's preference), two glasses that I filled with ice and I followed Krystal.

It took fifteen minutes to talk her into a drink.

It took half a bottle to talk her into talking.

Dalton, Wendy, and Jonelle came on at seven and Tate rode his bike back to the house and got the Explorer.

A mostly drunk, very exhausted, girl-talked-out Krys came home with us and slept on the couch.

*   *   *

With Krys snoring on the couch, Jonas asleep in his bed, I sat cross-legged on Tate's bed in a pair of panties and a shelf-bra camisole while Tate brushed his teeth.

He came out of the bathroom naked, which was a hit to my

resolve to have a serious chat with him, one that got my point across but didn't make him mad, but I sucked it up and looked from his body to his eyes.

"Can I ask…," I started, speaking softly, "that you discuss my future with me before you decide what I'm going to be doing, where, and for whom and then announce it to the world?"

Tate held my gaze then he bent, pulled back the covers and got in bed. He lay back against the headboard and his eyes came to me.

"I didn't announce it to the world."

"You did."

"I said it to Bubba, Krys, and Billy. That's not the world, Ace."

"It's most of *my* world."

He sighed then his hand shot out, wrapping around my wrist and he tugged. I came forward on my knees, my free arm moving out automatically to control my fall. My hand landed on his chest about two seconds before he curled up slightly, both his arms went around me and then my torso landed on his chest.

I pulled back, snapping, "Tate—"

"You missed it, babe."

I glared at him and asked, "Missed what?"

"I don't give a shit about the bar."

"Sorry?"

He didn't answer me, instead he stated, "I give a shit about Krys and I give a shit about you. I don't want outta that bar. It's turnin' a damn good profit now with you and a stable of decent waitresses who sell booze instead of socialize. Boys'll be puttin' their bikes away for the winter soon but the mountains come alive when the snow falls. We got three slopes within an hour's drive. Be stupid to get bought out now that we got decent help."

"So, what—?"

His arms gave me a squeeze before he whispered, "She needed motivation."

His intent dawned on me and I relaxed against his body.

"You wanted her to get rid of Bubba," I whispered back.

"She's a good woman, deserves more than that," he muttered. "Can't find it, then she still deserves a life without that."

God, but I loved this man.

I lifted a hand and laid it on his bearded jaw.

"Tate."

"And you like it there but you also like it here. I knew you wouldn't ask for special treatment and you wouldn't put Krys out. So, I made it so you could keep workin' there, share the load with Krystal, and feel good about that but be home for me and Jonas."

I relaxed more against him and my face came closer to his.

"Tate," I repeated softly.

"And I wasn't lyin'. The office is a fuckin' mess. I know you got the skills to sort that out. I don't have the patience, the time, or the inclination for that shit so I could use your help too."

He could use my help. I liked that.

My face got closer.

"Captain," I whispered.

"To fix what Neet broke in Jonas, I need to build a family. I'm guessin' you wanna be a part of that."

"I do," I replied quietly.

"Then I gotta do what I gotta do to build that for Jonas. I played Krys, for her, for you, for Jonas, and, yeah, for me."

"Okay," I agreed.

"You still pissed?"

"No," I answered, though he had to know I wasn't considering I'd all but melted into him, but I went on. "Though, you could have spoken to me first."

"Didn't know I was gonna do it until Bub walked in."

My head tipped to the side, I decided our current conversation was over since I liked his responses so much and therefore I changed the subject. "Why do you call Jonas 'Bub'? Is it because of Bubba?"

One of his hands slid up my back into my hair, the other one slid down, then up into my camisole.

"Yeah, Bubba's real name is Jonas. I talked Neeta into namin' him after Bubba, and then I gave him Bubba's nickname. When he was younger, called him Bubba. Shortened it to Bub later."

This surprised me. "Bubba's that good a friend?"

"We played ball together in high school. Him, Wood, and me were tight." His hand slid through my hair and the fingers of his other hand drew patterns on the skin of my back as he finished quietly, "He was a great friend, Ace, just a shit business partner. Shoulda known but I got a habit of thinkin' the best'll come outta people when it won't."

"Sometimes it does," I replied.

His hands stopped moving when he muttered, "Right."

I pressed into him by giving him all my weight. "It does."

His eyes locked on mine. "You know, part of me was hopin', faced with the prospect of losin' her son, Neeta'd get her head outta her ass."

"Tate—"

"She didn't and in the end it was worse than I thought."

"She isn't a good example," I told him.

"Bubba is?" he asked.

"I am," I answered.

His brows drew together. "What?"

"You bring the best out of me."

He stared at me a second then both his arms wrapped tight around me and he gave me a hug as he chuckled.

"What's funny?" I asked.

"Babe," he replied and said no more.

"Babe what?" I pushed.

His hand slid back into my hair, he cupped the back of my head and brought my lips to his for a light kiss.

Letting me pull slightly away, he murmured, "I was thinkin' it was the other way around."

My heart turned over; I liked that he thought that so I stroked my thumb along his bristly beard and smiled but said, "No."

He grinned back and replied, "Ace."

"The way I see it," I told him, "you haven't changed at all, just your focus has. For me, I'm completely different."

"No, Lauren, you aren't."

"Yes, I am."

"How you figure that?"

"Never," I said then dipped my head so my lips were at his ear. "Never has sex been so good for me."

His fingers fisted in my hair, his head turned and his lips slid along my neck until his mouth was at my ear. "All right, Ace, I'll give you that."

Arrogant, but...whatever.

I lifted my head and looked down at him. "And never, never, not even with my boyfriends who were nice to me, did I feel safe enough with them, safe enough with how they felt about me, to throw attitude."

His body went still but his face registered surprise and I continued.

"I was scared of losing them. I was scared of them not thinking I was good enough." I bent and touched my lips to his and then said there, "See? You bring out the best in me."

He rolled us so I was on my back, he was on top and he was looking down at me.

"Not sure I'm big on the best in you bein' attitude," he said but I knew he was teasing. I knew it because his face was warm and his eyes were dancing.

"I am since it's the real me and I feel safe being just that with you." My hand went to the side of his head and my fingers slid into his thick hair. "It was exhausting, trying to be perfect. It feels good being able to be just me."

"Laurie—"

"Kiss me, Tate," I demanded softly.

"Baby—"

I lifted my head and put my lips to his, encouraging on a whisper, "I wanna catch fire, honey, and only you can bring that out for me."

I watched up close as Tate's eyes went intense then his head slanted and he muttered, "You got it, Ace."

Then he kissed me.

Then he made me catch fire.

*   *   *

Two days after that, Tate was back out on the road, the blinds guys were up in our bedroom installing Tate's new, cool as heck, dark wood venetian blinds and I was in his office sorting through his stuff.

I was coming to the realization that I could spend four, sixteen-hour days organizing his office and I still wouldn't have it in hand when a thought occurred to me. It involved the computer and the computer was right there so I followed through with that thought.

I turned on the computer, typed in the password Tate had given me, pulled up the search engine, and typed "Tatum Jackson."

Then I hit enter.

A listing of sites with Tate's name in them instantly appeared.

The top listing was an online encyclopedia entry. I held my breath and clicked on it.

At the right top side was a photo of Tate, surprisingly not from his football days, relatively recent. It was torso and up, mostly his side, his neck was twisted and he was looking in the direction of the camera. In shot, but turned away, his back to the camera, Tate's hand wrapped around his biceps, was a blond man in handcuffs. Under this photo was a caption that said, "Jackson, after apprehending now convicted murderer Cleeg Johansson" and under that were Tate's stats.

The rest of the site contained a good deal of description mostly of Tate's short-lived football career but also Tate's accomplishments as a police officer and bounty hunter with some alarming information about the fugitives he'd found, a goodly number of them being very high on the armed-and-dangerous scale.

There were photos of him playing football but they were small so I clicked backward to the search results and randomly chose a site farther down the list.

It came up with a black background, "Tatum Jackson, God" in green writing at the top with blue footballs dancing on the left side of his name and red hearts dancing to the right by the word "God."

I stared at the page and the two side-by-side photos of Tate prominent on the front of it. One was of him walking from the field at what appeared to be halftime or after a game, helmet held by the faceguard dangling from his fingers, hair wet with sweat, eyes still intense with residual focus on "the game," body lean and fit and spectacular in his Penn State jersey and football pads. The other was a black-and-white, taken from the back, a football field with a bunch of equipment in front of him. Tate was standing on the sidelines wearing a pair of loose-fitting athletic shorts that hung down his thighs and he held a T-shirt bunched loosely in his hand. His muscled back was bared and the eagle tattoo was on prominent, glorious display. His neck was twisted, his head slightly tipped down, you could see his profile and he was grinning at someone out of shot.

Wow, but he was something.

"Cool!" I heard Jonas cry from behind me. I jumped and turned to see him rush into the room. "You found Loretta's site."

It was way too late for me to hide the fact that I'd Internet searched his father and I knew this because Jonas had pushed my hand away and was clicking through "Loretta's site" with what looked to be great familiarity of what it held.

"Loretta?" I asked him.

"This page is my favorite," Jonas said and looked at me as I looked at the page and he went on, "Yeah, Loretta. She's Dad's stalker."

I knew my mouth was hanging open but I couldn't close it because I was staring at a page that was a mélange of photos of Tate from what appeared to be high school, through Penn State (not just playing football but also walking to class and sitting on barstools and the like).

I shoved Jonas's hand out of the way, commandeered the mouse, and scrolled down.

The photos also went through Tate at awards ceremonies and his short-lived career with the Eagles (mostly shots during practice).

I scrolled down farther.

And shots of him in Carnal and doing bounty hunter things, like dragging fugitives into police stations or standing over them with their bellies to the pavement and their arms cuffed behind their backs.

"Oh my God," I breathed.

"She's harmless," Jonas told me.

"Oh my God," I repeated.

"Dad's talked to her. She's agreed not to put pictures of me on there but I think that sucks, since the kids at school thought it would be cool. Hey, wait!" he cried. "She's got a new page."

He pushed my hand away, clicked on the "3" at the bottom of the page, which was next to the "Pages 1, 2," and a new page came up with one picture.

Tate and me on his bike.

We were waiting to pull out of Bubba's parking lot, Tate's booted foot was to the ground, his head was turned to look down the street and I was tucked close to his back, my arms around him, my thigh against his, my chin to his shoulder.

The caption under it said, "Tate's flame, love her or hate her (and I hate her), she's got great legs."

I shot from the chair and squealed, "Oh my *God*!"

Jonas grinned up at me. "You're famous, Laurie."

I didn't hear him. I was too focused on my horrified panic.

I tore my eyes from the screen, reached out to where my cell phone was on top of a pile of scattered papers on Tate's desk, snatched it up and called Tate.

"Laurie, it's cool. Loretta's awesome. She went to school with Dad at Penn State. They had some class together. He knew her. Dad says she's harmless," Jonas, reading the atmosphere, assured me.

I looked down at him and didn't answer because Tate said into my ear, "Everything okay, babe?"

"You've got a stalker!" I shouted into the phone.

"She found Loretta's page, Dad!" Jonas yelled to be heard by his father.

"Ace—" I heard Tate say in my ear.

I interrupted him. "There's a picture of me."

"Fuck," he muttered. "There is?"

"She said she *hated me*!" My voice got shrill on the last two words.

"Honey—"

"Oh my *God*!" I shouted.

"Babe, calm down and listen to me. I'll talk to Loretta—"

"No," I cut him off. "I can't deal with this. Too much. I have officially had too much. There's a serial killer on the loose! I don't need to deal with your *stalker*!"

"Lauren, quiet down and listen, all right? There's bad stalkers and then there's stalkers like Loretta."

"She's taking pictures of me! And saying she hates me! On the Internet!" I screeched.

"She would say that 'cause you're with me. She hated Neeta too."

"Oh my God," I whispered and then looked down at Jonas. "Jonas, go to the alarm panel and activate it," I ordered, too frenzied to notice Jonas didn't move a muscle and I said into the phone, "Where do you keep your guns?"

"Babe—"

"What if she's out there?"

"Lauren—"

"What if Loretta *and* her camera are out there?"

"Laurie, Loretta and I have a deal. She doesn't come to the house."

I didn't hear him. I kept panicking.

"What if she snaps? What if she snaps when Jonas is here? Oh my *God*!"

"Lauren, shut it, take a deep breath and fuckin' listen to me." Tate's voice was firm and unyielding in my ear. "Loretta is harmless."

"Right," I snapped.

"She lives in Pennsylvania. She works there too. She's married and has three kids. She takes her vacations in Carnal or wherever she finds out I'm gonna be. Sometimes, she even brings her husband and kids with her."

"That's crazy," I breathed.

"I'm her hobby," he told me.

"That's crazy," I repeated.

"Some women get hung up on movie stars, some on sports stars, Loretta's stuck on me. She lives her life normal. I've met her husband and her fuckin' kids. She's completely harmless."

"She tracks you down!"

"She likes me."

"She's devoted a website to you and she says on it she hates me!" I reminded him.

"She doesn't mean it. Other people devote websites and blogs to shit they get off on. She started puttin' pictures of Jonas on there, I called her and told her I didn't like that, they were gone in an hour. She's got a good life but that don't mean she can't fantasize and she does, usin' me. There's nothin' wrong with that."

"I fantasize too, Tate, but I don't stalk hot guys, take pictures of them when they don't know I'm around and spend my free time building websites devoted to them."

"You fantasize?"

Uh-oh.

I had the feeling from his tone that our conversation just took a drastic turn.

"Tate—"

"Who do you fantasize about?"

"It doesn't matter. This matters. This freaks me out."

"Who do you fantasize about, Lauren?"

"It doesn't matter!" I shouted.

"I got shit to do and I know Loretta's website matters to you so I'm takin' my time talkin' to you about it. I'll call her, tell her to knock it off with pictures of you and comments about you. She'll probably call you and apologize. That's the kind of person she is. Now, who you fantasize about matters to me so you're talkin' to me about it."

I looked down at Jonas and informed Tate, "Jonas is in the room."

"Tell him to get out, close the fuckin' door then you answer my question."

"I'm not going to tell Jonas to get out!" I snapped.

"I'm gone, Dad!" Jonas, the little traitor, yelled into the room, smiled at me and then left, closing the door loudly behind him.

Tate heard the door close. I knew this because he ordered instantly, "Answer my question."

"Why does this matter to you?"

"I got my cock in you, Ace, you're moanin' sweet for me, you close your eyes, I *still* wanna know I'm all you see."

"Are you nuts?" I asked.

"Answer my fuckin' question."

Oh no. He was mad. Really mad. I knew it and I also knew I had to stop it before it got out of hand.

Therefore, I whispered, "You."

"Come again?"

"You. I fantasize about you."

Silence.

For some stupid reason, I kept talking, "Before we were together and um... when I... when you're gone, I..."

He cut me off, muttering, "Fuck me."

"Though I wouldn't build a website devoted to you," I added idiotically.

"Our nighttime telephone conversations just changed," he announced.

"Sorry?"

"You've been holdin' out on me. You touch yourself thinkin' about me when I'm gone, babe, you're not so high-class and too good a girl not to let me listen."

Pretty much every erogenous zone in my body started to hum.

"Tate—" I breathed.

"Startin' tonight."

Oh my God.

"Tate, I'm not—"

"And you're gonna describe to me everything you're seein' in your head."

Oh my *God*.

"Captain—"

"In detail."

"Tate—"

"While I listen to you makin' yourself come."

"Um…"

"I'll call Loretta, tell her to get in touch with you. She'll apologize. You call me tonight I want you ready to put your hand between your legs."

"Uh…"

"We done?"

"I don't think so."

"We're done."

Then he hung up.

I stared blankly at nothing. Then I stared at my photo on the screen of his computer. Then I took my phone from my ear and dropped it on the desk.

An hour later, Loretta called and apologized. I checked the website as she invited me to do and saw my photo was gone. She chattered to me for another twenty minutes about life in general, hers, mine, and a little bit of Tate's. Not in a stalker-esque way, in a normal-esque way. I'd long since realized she was nice when she said she'd call next time she was in Carnal and we'd have coffee "at that place where that hippie makes great lemon-poppyseed bread." I got the courage to ask if she would e-mail me the photo she'd taken of Tate and me. She agreed, sounding delighted to do so. Then she rang off.

An hour after that, I checked my e-mail to see that Loretta not only sent me the picture of Tate and I on his bike, she sent me another one of us standing by his bike, his hand to my jaw, my hands were at his waist and we were kissing. Her hilarious commentary was, "Girl, you are so lucky! Isn't he hot?"

She'd never know just how hot he was.

Poor Loretta.

A number of hours after that, part anxious, part scared and part turned on, I climbed into bed, called Tate and five seconds later I had my hand between my legs.

The anxiety and fear melted a second after that.

I melted ten minutes later.

*　　*　　*

Four days after that, I was dead asleep when Tate came home.

He woke me and this was the first part of the first fantasy I described to him over the phone.

He then proceeded to help me live out the rest of it.

In detail.

After we were both done, Tate pressed his hips into mine, I came off my knees, he came off his. I went down to my belly, his body covered my back and he rested his forearms in the bed on either side of me.

"You like that, baby?" he whispered in my ear.

"Yeah, Captain," I whispered my understatement back.

He kissed my shoulder and muttered against my skin, "Fuck, it's good to be home."

I didn't get a chance to reply. He righted us in bed, pulled the covers over us and tucked me close.

"Go back to sleep, Laurie," he murmured.

"Okay, honey."

His arms gave me a squeeze. "Sweet dreams, baby."

"You too, Captain."

I settled into him and fell asleep before he did.

I didn't wake up once.

*　　*　　*

It wouldn't be for weeks when I would realize I'd stopped waking up at all when Tate was home with me. It was only when he was away that I was restless.

It was Tate who made me realize this and he did it when he walked into the bathroom one morning while I was brushing my teeth wearing nothing but my undies. He stopped behind me, slid an arm around my stomach and pressed into my back.

My eyes went to his in the mirror and I noted instantly he had something on his mind.

He didn't make me wait.

"You keepin' somethin' from me?" he asked.

I blinked, pulled the toothbrush out of my mouth then answered, "No."

His arm gave me a squeeze, a physical warning, and he gave me a verbal warning through the way he said, "Babe."

I stared in his eyes, finished brushing, spit, rinsed, wiped and tried to turn but Tate kept me where I was, facing the mirror with his arm wrapped around my waist.

"Tate—" I said into the mirror.

"I don't like you doin' it alone."

"What?"

"The night."

I shook my head and asked, "Sorry?"

"I don't like you facin' the night alone. You wake up, I don't, I'm tellin you now, babe, you wake me."

That was when it hit me and I stared at him in the mirror, silently.

I did this for a while, long enough for him to get impatient, give me a squeeze and prompt, "Got me?"

"I'm not waking up," I whispered, stunned, still staring at him.

There hadn't been a time I could remember when I didn't wake up, not since I was a kid. Maybe for a night or two but not regularly. My mind had tortured me, and my sleep, since forever.

"Come again?" he asked.

My hands went to the basin and I held on.

"I'm not…" I shook my head in disbelief. "Tate, baby," I was still whispering, "when you're here, I don't wake up." I felt the sting of tears in my eyes and kept whispering, "It's only when you're gone that I—"

His arm went loose, his hands came to my hips, he stepped back and turned me to face him then stepped back in, his arm going back around me, his other hand coming to my jaw.

I tipped my head back to look at him.

"Honey—" he started and a tear slid down my cheek.

"All my life," I interrupted him, "since I could remember. And now I'm not. Not while you're around."

"Laurie—" he whispered, his thumb moving to wipe away my tear.

"You're . . . ," I swallowed, "you're it."

"I know, baby," he murmured, his forehead dropping to mine. "You're it for me too."

"No," I told him. "You don't get it. You're the something special I've been looking for. And what I was looking for was what I needed to put my mind at ease."

"Ace—" he started but I fitted myself to him and slid my arms tight around him.

"I knew it but I didn't *know* it. Now I *know* it."

For some reason, suddenly his head came up and he stared down at me with such concentration and for so long, I couldn't take it anymore.

"What?" I asked.

"You aren't goin' anywhere," he stated and I blinked again.

"What?"

"This is good enough for you."

I shook my head and squeezed him with my arms. "Tate, you aren't making—"

"You don't just believe I can do anything, I *can* do anything, for you."

I stopped breathing.

"Fix your sleep," he stated.

I stared.

"Fucked up my whole life, made shitty decisions, almost fucked up my son's life, but not you. I can do anything when I'm with you."

"You could before," I told him.

"Not until you."

"Tate, you—"

"The day you rolled into town, babe, you saw me with Neeta. The next day, the day I met you, that's when it began."

"It isn't."

"Fuck," he hissed, his voice so intense it was nearly physical. "Wish Dad coulda met you."

I stared at him, stunned speechless when it hit me my beautiful, badass biker had been broken.

And I'd fixed him too.

"It broke you," I whispered.

"What?"

"When you lost the game, it broke you. You were on your way to self-fulfilled prophesies too."

He stared down at me and I held my breath for his reaction.

Then he said softly, "Yeah."

"You didn't think, without the game defining you, that you could find a good life."

"No."

"And, for whatever reason, I didn't think I was worthy of something special so I never found it, until you."

His bizarre response to that admission was, "Thank Christ."

"Sorry?"

"Babe, you let your college boyfriend show you you were somethin' special all along, right about now, I wouldn't be standin' in my bathroom with you in my arms. I'd be fucked."

"Well—"

"Jonas would too."

"Um…"

His forehead came back to mine but his chin moved down half an inch so his nose was alongside mine. "Makes me a dick, you lived with it for so long, but I don't care. You still gotta know, I'm pleased as fuck I'm the only one can give you sweet dreams."

The tears came back and instantly spilled over.

"Me too, Tate," I whispered.

"Waited a long time to be somethin' special again, baby," he whispered back.

"I'm glad it's me who gets it."

I watched through wet eyes as he smiled.

"All right, Ace, this is done," he announced quietly.

"What?"

"These heart-to-hearts."

"Oh," I whispered, disappointed because I kind of liked them. "Okay."

"We get it now," he explained. "We don't need 'em."

"Oh," I repeated, not disappointed anymore because he was right. "Okay." Then I asked, "Is Jonas still asleep?"

"Yeah," he answered.

My hand trailed to his abs.

"Good," I murmured.

"Baby?"

The fingers of my other hand slid into his hair as my hand at his stomach dipped down to cup his crotch.

"Feel like playing," I whispered.

He grinned.

"Can I?" I asked.

"I'm ready for you to stop playin' and get serious, I tell you, you get serious."

"Deal," I agreed and his eyes grew dark.

"On your knees, Ace," he growled.

That was when I grinned.

Then I got down on my knees.

*   *   *

Life got pretty sweet after Tate and my final heart-to-heart in the bathroom that ended in him getting a blowjob from me followed by me getting an orgasm sitting with my behind on the edge of the basin, my legs wrapped around his shoulders and his mouth between my legs.

This didn't mean we didn't have dramas.

But all of our dramas revolved around Jonas.

One included Jonas having a ten-year-old-boy fit at the mall, a fit which was backed up by Tate when Tate and I took him back to school clothes shopping. I felt his closet and drawers should be far fuller. Tate and Jonas didn't agree and felt after we bought two pairs of jeans, a few T-shirts and a pair of gym shoes that cost nearly as much as the picture I bought Tate (slight exaggeration), it was time to go see a movie.

I gave in and, since I knew his sizes, I took Amber, Betty, and Wendy to the mall the next day and we augmented Jonas's wardrobe.

We also augmented Tate's.

We also augmented Amber's, Betty's, Wendy's, and mine.

We also visited Wanda at the home store because Jonas got new towels for his bathroom and Tate and I got a new soap dispenser and toothbrush holder for ours.

We also got new canisters for the kitchen and a new set of earthenware bowls that were heavy, gorgeous, fit snug in each other for easy storage but since they were painted a muted, dusty green, pink, and blue, I set them out on the island because they looked cool there.

Jonas, on the other hand, thought they looked girlie.

Tate just looked at them, looked at me, his lips twitched then he walked away so I decided to take that as approval, or at least not objection.

The other drama included Tate registering Jonas for junior league football, something he excelled at and something Tate tried very hard not to miss, either practices or games. However, seeing as fugitives didn't take your call and wait for you to meet them at the local police station so you could turn them in, this didn't happen as much as Tate or Jonas would like. I, however, didn't miss a game, though if Tate was home to pick him up for practice, I let them have their boy time and only picked him up when Tate was gone.

Luckily, the first game Jonas's team lost, Tate was there. This was lucky because Jonas didn't like losing. As in, he didn't like it *a lot*.

This manifested itself in another ten-year-old-boy fit. One during which Tate ordered Jonas to go to his room. Tate followed. I heard Jonas hollering for a while, then I heard nothing.

I was in the garden yanking weeds when Tate came out after dealing with Jonas.

"He okay?" I asked.

"Still pissed," he answered.

"It's just a game," I muttered.

"It's never just a game," Tate replied and I looked at him.

"You can't win at everything in life, Tate," I said softly. "He should learn that."

"You're right, Ace, you can't. But you can learn from losin' how not to lose again. Or at least not make the same mistakes."

This was true.

"Still, honey, he should learn not to pitch a fit," I said carefully.

"That intensity is good, he's just gotta focus it."

"Did you teach him that?"

"No, but I will."

I felt my face go soft and I smiled at him.

Tate smiled back.

Then he said, "Probably help, you give him some of your grandma's chocolate chip cookies."

"I'm making Mom's chocolate pecan pie."

His smile got bigger.

"That'll work too."

"Food isn't love, Tate," I teased him with his own words.

He bent over where I was sitting on the ledge, wrapped his hand around the back of my neck and kissed my forehead.

He didn't let me go but he looked me in the eyes when he whispered, "I was wrong about that, Ace. I get it now. The way you make it, it is."

He let me go and I stared at him as he walked away.

Then I shouted at the door he disappeared behind, "I could make better pie-type love with a new stove!"

I heard his disembodied voice shout back, "Dick territory, babe. Don't even think about it unless I'm there."

"Chick territory," I kept shouting. "A stove's in the kitchen!"

"It's got a plug and weighs over fifty pounds. Totally dick," he shot back on his own shout.

I gave in, turning to the plants while giggling.

Totally dick.

My old man was funny.

* * *

And that was it. Some of it big, some of it bigger.

But nothing mammoth.

And I liked nothing mammoth.

I especially liked it after the mammoth, life-altering, heartbreaking, soul-shattering day at Bubba's, and, worse, after Tate and I went home to share what had happened with Jonas.

CHAPTER TWENTY-FOUR

Hold On

"THREE BUDWEISER BOTTLES, honey," I said to Tate, looking down at my pad.

"Babe," Tate called.

"Yeah?" I answered, pulling my pencil from behind my ear.

"Ace," he called.

"Yeah?" I answered again, scratching on my pad.

"Baby, look at me," Tate said softly and I looked at my clean-shaven man.

We'd had a fight that morning mainly because he'd shaved. Perhaps my reaction was a wee bit over the top but he was now in no doubt how I felt about his beard considering I'd threatened him with zero access to certain parts of my body unless he grew it back. Tate had found this amusing, not annoying, and I knew this because he burst out laughing and continued to do so even after I repeatedly told him I didn't think anything was funny. Then he proved to me I would not be able to carry out my threat of zero access to certain parts of my body and he did this by gaining access to those very specific parts.

Even so, I was pretty certain my point was made, but if it wasn't, I also didn't much care. Truth be told, he was hot with or without the beard. I just liked the beard.

"What?" I asked when my eyes met his.

"Come here," he ordered and I noted he had his arms wide and he was leaning into both fists to the bar. I'd seen him like that before and the last time he was angry.

"Um...," I mumbled. "I *am* here."

"Closer," he demanded.

I got closer, putting a hand to the bar.

"Closer," he repeated.

"Tate, what on—"

"Now, babe."

I sighed and leaned into him, putting both forearms on the bar.

He leaned in too, put a forearm beside mine, hooked me behind the back of my neck, pulled me closer, and his head slanted right before he laid a long, wet, very hot kiss on me.

I had one hand curled around his forearm, one hand curled around his neck—I was using both to hold me up—when his lips moved from mine.

"That should do it," he muttered, his face still super close.

"Do what?"

He didn't answer, instead he stated, "Need to put a fuckin' ring on your finger, Ace."

I quit breathing and my legs wobbled.

"What?" I breathed.

"Those boys you been servin' ain't from around these parts. They stare at your ass or tits when you're comin' or goin' one more fuckin' time, we got problems. I figure I just made my point you're mine. They do it again, I know they want problems so I'll give 'em to 'em."

I didn't hear a word he said. I was back at his earlier statement, therefore repeated, "What?"

"Lauren?" I heard from behind me and I knew that voice. I knew it and I couldn't believe it. It was so shocking to hear it, Tate's throwaway comment, which was anything but throwaway to me, flew out of my head and my entire body froze as I stared into Tate's eyes.

He looked into mine, his brows knitted and he didn't let my neck go or move away as his eyes went over my shoulder. I saw them move down, then up, then he grinned huge, like something was tremendously funny before he whispered, "Fuck me," and let me go.

I turned woodenly and stared at my nemesis from Horizon Summit, the woman who pretended to be my best friend while she was fucking my husband, the dreaded Hayley.

"Hayley?" I whispered and stared at her.

She looked just as good as ever. What she didn't look, in her designer jeans, complicated designer blouse, seven-hundred-dollar shoes, and two-hundred-dollar haircut, was like she belonged in a biker bar.

I, on the other hand, was wearing a Harley T-shirt that Deke brought back for me from Sturgis. It fit snug, was pale blush and super cool with Harley-Davidson written in burgundy and silver on the front and a pair of wide silver and burgundy wings on the back. I was also wearing jeans (that were designer) and silver strappy sandals that didn't cost seven hundred dollars, not even close, but they were hot.

My hair was down, I'd just had it touched up by Dominic (at the same time I gently forced Sunny out of her house and into the salon so Dom could work his magic on Sunny too, and he did, and even she liked the result), and I'd let it dry somewhat wild because Tate liked it that way.

Hayley looked like an upper-middle-class suburban housewife who had a personal trainer and a standing appointment for monthly visits to the salon.

I looked like a biker babe.

And she'd just seen me kissing the beautiful, badass Tatum Jackson. I knew it by the astonished, yet envious look on her face. A look that I suspected I sported the first time I saw him with Neeta.

This was why I smiled.

"Hayley, girl, what're you doin' here?" I asked, loud and friendly, didn't wait for an answer and turned to Tate. "Honey, this is Hayley. You know, the woman who pretended to be my friend while she fucked my husband, Brad?"

Tate, standing again with arms wide, fists to the bar, tried not to smile, failed when his lips twitched up and then he muttered in his rough, sexy voice, "Yeah, babe, I know who Hayley is."

I turned back to Hayley to see she was staring at Tate, her eyes wide, shocked, and openly covetous. Her lips were parted and her face pale.

"Come on, I owe you a drink," I announced, moving to her and shuffling her toward the bar as I saw Jim-Billy, Nadine, Steg and Wings all watching, all smiling, and I helped Hayley onto a stool then I turned to Tate, "Honey, can you get Hayley a martini?"

"No," Tate replied.

"Oh," I said and then turned to Hayley. "We don't do sissy-ass drinks here. Will you drink vodka straight?"

She blinked up at me and then she blinked up at Tate. What she didn't do was answer.

"Maybe we'll start you with a diet pop," I suggested.

"I...you...," she struggled then asked, "Why do you owe me a drink?"

I leaned back, crossed my arms on my chest and grinned. "To thank you because you freed me from Brad."

"What?" she whispered.

"You freed me from Brad so I could get out of that hellhole of a life and that cesspit that was Horizon Summit and find Carnal and Tate." I uncrossed an arm and motioned to Tate, leaning forward and informing her conspiratorially, "He's my old man."

"Your old man?" she asked.

"Biker slang for he's my um…man," I explained. "We're together."

Her eyes went back to Tate and she observed, "He isn't much like Brad."

"Thank fuck," Tate muttered and I swallowed a giggle.

Then I asked, "Tate, honey, would you get Hayley here a diet and I'll go serve those Buds?" I looked back at Hayley. "I have to serve a few beers. Be right back."

Tate popped the caps of three Buds. I rushed them to the customers, they paid, tipped big, and then I rushed back to see that Tate had served Hayley a diet and was leaning with his hips against the back of the bar, arms crossed on his chest, watching me. I also saw that Jim-Billy, Nadine, Steg, and Wings had moved down to stools closer to Hayley and she was eyeing them and Tate uncertainly.

I slid on a stool beside her and asked, "So, what're you doing here?"

She looked at me. "I…erm…"

"Yeah?" I prompted.

"I heard Brad's here," she answered quickly. "Hasn't he been in?"

At her words, Tate pushed away from the back of the bar and got close, saying in an unhappy growl, "You are fuckin' shittin' me."

Hayley swallowed as she stared up at Tate. Then she looked at Jim-Billy, Nadine, Steg, and Wings and her head turned so swiftly to me I was certain she had to have wrenched her neck.

"They say he's in town. He wants you back. So much, he won't take *me* back," she said quietly, like this was unfathomable, like some-one was trying to convince her the sky was fuchsia.

"Take you back?" I asked.

"Nathan left me," she whispered.

"Went back to his wife you mean," I suggested and she swallowed again, which I decided to take as an affirmative.

"Ace," Tate called and I looked at him. "Tell this one"—he jerked his head to Hayley—"to call that fuckwad and tell him, he doesn't want to know what assault actually is, I don't see his ass in my bar."

I nodded, looked at Hayley and advised soberly, "You should do that, call Brad."

Hayley's eyes were wide. "You mean he'd assault Brad?"

"Probably," I replied. "Actually, I'm not sure but I wouldn't test him."

She stared up at Tate then nodded and opened her purse.

"You...," she muttered as she dug through her purse. "You..." She pulled out her phone and then looked at me, her phone in her hand. Her eyes moved to my lap and back up. "You fell apart when Brad left."

"Tate put me back together." I leaned into an elbow on the bar and looked at Tate. "Didn't you, baby?"

I could tell with just a glance Tate wasn't having near as much fun as me.

I knew this for certain when he ordered, "Get her to call him."

"All right, Captain, calm down," I muttered and then to Hayley I said, "You better hurry up and call him."

"Hayley?" I heard Brad call. My eyes went beyond her as she twisted on her stool to look and we saw Brad in another golf shirt, a pair of chinos, and his eyes were glued to Hayley. "What the fuck are you doing here?"

"Out," Tate growled. Brad's eyes flicked to him but he still walked to Hayley and me.

"I asked, what the fuck are you doing here?" he asked Hayley.

She stared up at him, her fear gone, her face getting hard, and she stated, "You said you wanted her back and I couldn't believe it. I heard you were on your way up here and I had to come see for myself and I still don't believe it." She leaned forward and finished with, "You can't honestly want her. She's a waitress!"

Well, there you go. Nothing had changed with Hayley.

"And you can't honestly believe you could fuck around on me and think I'd want *you,*" Brad shot back.

Hmm. It appeared something had changed with Brad.

I settled back to watch the show as Hayley crossed her arms on her chest and snapped, "You told me you loved me and always would."

I leaned in and shared, "He said that to me too."

Jim-Billy guffawed. Brad glared at Jim-Billy. Out of the corner of my eye I saw Tate move and I turned to him.

"Don't, honey, please?" I asked. "This is fun."

Tate stopped moving, stared at me a second, his eyes roaming my face, then he muttered, "You get five minutes of fun, Ace, then you get both their asses out of here."

Hayley was focused. My exchange with Tate was lost on her. She got up from her stool and repeated to Brad, "You told me you loved me and always would."

Brad ignored Hayley and looked at me. He did a top-to-toe and back again, then his gaze moved to Tate.

"I'm here to tell you I'm suing you," he announced.

Jim-Billy, Nadine, Steg, Wing, and my eyes moved to Tate.

Tate stared at Brad then he said, "Come again?"

"I'm suing you," Brad repeated.

"For what?" Tate asked.

"Alienation of affection," Brad answered.

Without hesitation, Tate threw his head back and burst out laughing.

Then he looked at me and remarked, "You're right, babe, this *is* fun."

Ignoring Tate's comment, Brad declared, "You stole my wife."

Tate looked back at Brad. "Yeah, bud, I did."

Brad pointed at Tate and his voice was raised when he proclaimed, "See? You admit it." He threw his arm out. "I have witnesses."

"Not that any judge'll hear your case, seein' as Lauren divorced your ass before I alienated her affection, but you manage it, I'll pay the fine. In the meantime, I'll keep alienating her affection. You should know, and feel free to share it with your lawyers," Tate continued magnanimously, "schedule's comin' out mornin' and night. Usually, in the mornin', she sucks me off or I make her come in the shower. Night, man...shit, that's even better. Definitely worth the fine."

I rolled my eyes (mostly in an effort to ignore the fact that Jim-Billy, Nadine, Steg, and Wings were all grinning at me, the men somewhat lasciviously, Nadine just happily) but Brad glowered at Tate then his eyes moved to me.

"Honest, Ree? Is that filth what you like?"

"Oh yeah," I muttered the God's honest truth and heard Nadine, Steg, and Wings all chuckle but Jim-Billy guffawed.

Brad glared at me and then looked at Tate. "I'm moving to have the divorce declared null and void."

I felt my body tense, unsure if this was even possible and hoping to God it wasn't, but Tate didn't seem concerned.

I knew this when he replied, "Good luck with that."

"Ree didn't want the divorce until she came up here and met you," Brad went on.

"Maybe not but you should know before you drop a shitload of cake on this crap, she's glad she's got it now," Tate returned.

"You've brainwashed her," Brad shot back. Jim-Billy guffawed again. I stared at Brad in stupefied disbelief at the mind-boggling extent of his conceit and he continued, "I get her away from you, we'll find our way back, she said so."

"Yeah, that was before. Since..." Tate paused, leaned in, fists again wide to his sides, and in the bar. "Since, she's tasted the good life and she knows you'll never give her that."

Brad's lip curled up, he looked around the bar, back at Tate and sneered, "*This* is the good life?"

"Part of it," Tate replied instantly, taking his fists from the bar, leaning into his forearms and asking softly, in a tone meant both to challenge and provoke, "She ever ignite, lose so much control she'd attack you? Climb on top and fuck you so hard she can't breathe?"

I watched Brad suffer that blow because I hadn't, not even close. We'd had good sex but not *that* good and Brad was extremely proud of his sexual prowess. He was convinced he was the best. And he knew, with Tate's words, he was wrong.

"Jesus, you're disgusting," Brad muttered, calling up revulsion to save face.

"She does that to me," Tate continued.

"Fuck off," Brad snapped.

"All the fuckin' time," Tate pushed.

"Fuck *off*," Brad repeated.

"It's fuckin' magnificent," Tate declared.

"Thanks, honey," I whispered and grinned at him when his eyes came to me.

I was actually expressing gratitude, although embarrassed by his conversation, but I was also kind of joking to get in Brad's face.

Tate wasn't. His expression was serious when he said, "You are, Ace. Fuckin' magnificent."

He meant that and he meant it about more than me fucking him so hard I couldn't breathe. And this meant so much to me, I stopped breathing as I looked into his dark, tawny-flecked eyes.

"I suggest you find an attorney," Brad butted into our mostly nonverbal exchange.

Tate's dark, tawny-flecked eyes cut back to him. "Got one, bud. You're stupid enough to bring it, bring it."

Brad looked at me but insulted Tate, "Jesus, Ree, he can't even speak proper English."

That was when I stopped thinking this was fun. And I stopped thinking this was fun because no one insulted my man.

"I'm in love with him," I announced and Brad's lip curled again.

"He's twisted your—" Brad started.

"No, he hasn't," I cut him off. "*You* did. You fucked Tina, you fucked Hayley, you've never been faithful to me and you made me feel unworthy. You did it on purpose. You're even doing it right now with the way you're looking down on me, on Tate, and on this bar. You're an asshole and I regret every minute I spent with you. Every… single…minute."

"Ree, you—" Brad started and I advanced on him a step and leaned into his face.

"Don't you tell me what I think," I hissed. "You don't know what I think." I leaned back. "Do it, Brad," I invited. "Make the divorce null and void. I *want* you to. I want you to because I want to divorce your ass again and take you to the cleaners. I'll get a private detective and dig out all your dirt. Tina, Hayley, and all the ones in between. I'll take everything you have. Do it. I can't *wait*. Tate and I need new countertops and carpet and I like the idea of walking on *you* and slicing vegetables on *you*. Go ahead, Brad, *do it*."

"That would not be good," Hayley whispered and my eyes swung to her.

And for the first time, I saw her, straight into her black soul.

And seeing that, I told her, "You're a joke."

"What?" she was still whispering.

"You're a vulture but the thing is, you aren't very good at it."

Her back straightened, her eyes narrowed, and she came right out and showed her true colors when she stated, "Good enough to get your man."

"Right, good enough to get *that*," I pointed at Brad. "But, see, *I'm* good enough to get *that*." And I pointed at Tate. "And that, darlin', is something you'll *never* have because a good man will see straight through you and want nothing to do with that and that's just plain, old *sad*."

Hayley stared at me, then she looked at Brad and asked incredulously, "Is she really what you want when you can have me?"

"He only wants me *because* he can't have me," I educated Hayley. "And he no longer wants you because he knows he can have you and he knows someone better than him doesn't want you. Jeez, Hayley," I muttered impatiently, "wake up and get a clue."

She opened her mouth to speak but Tate got there before her.

"Five minutes are up, Ace," Tate cut in.

I looked at him then I saw Steg, Wings, and Jim-Billy come off their stools like soldiers who had just been given orders.

I nodded to Tate and looked at Brad, deciding to sum up.

"I don't hate you. I hate her." I pointed to Hayley and my eyes went to her. "Women have it hard enough. We don't need our sisters behaving like you. It was up to me, we'd take away your membership card."

Nadine laughed softly at this but I looked back to Brad.

"But you, I don't feel anything for you. I just want you to get out of my life so I can live it. And you, you're so full of yourself, after taking so much from me for so long and not giving anything in return, not love, not attention, not affection, not understanding, not even birthday presents, you won't give me even this. So you want to take more so you can try to save face? Do it. I don't care. It's all the same to me because while you're making a fool of yourself, I get to go home to Jonas and Tate and make them dinner and watch TV and climb into bed with my old man and you don't exist until you make your presence known and then you're just a nuisance and a reason for Tate and me to share a laugh because just like her"—I jerked my head at Hayley—"in the end, you're just a joke."

"You can't make me believe you honestly want this life," Brad returned.

"Brad, it's so beautiful, I not only want it, I'd fight and die to keep it," I shot back.

Not just unwilling but completely unable to believe I'd pick a life without him, Brad kept going. "You know I can give you more than he ever can."

"You're wrong," I whispered, looked him straight in the eye, and kept whispering when I pulled out the big guns. "I sleep."

Brad's face got pale.

"What?" he asked, but he knew what. He knew exactly what. I'd aimed, I'd fired, and I'd hit the bull's-eye.

"Like a baby, straight through. Tate's in bed with me, I don't wake up."

Brad stared at me, his face blanched of color, his expression stuck in a flinch. "Ree—"

"Straight through," I repeated quietly. "He gives me peace."

"Darling—"

"Peace, Brad, which means he gives me everything and you never, *never* gave me that." I shook my head. "Not even close."

"Honey—"

"Please give me one thing, just one thing. Leave me to my peace," I whispered.

Brad held my gaze and I saw his throat working and I remembered, a long time ago, when my insomnia bothered Brad like it bothered Tate. I remembered a time when he wanted to make me better. I remembered a long, long time ago when he thought he too could fix me and give me peace and he wanted that for me and he wanted to be the one who gave it to me.

And I remembered that it didn't take long for him to stop wanting that.

And I knew Brad remembered too because a miracle occurred in the instant he did.

Bradford Whitaker finally became human.

I knew when he asked, "Who's Jonas?"

"Tate's son," I answered and Brad closed his eyes, pain, fleeting but real, sliced through his features because, a long time ago, he'd wanted to give me that too and then he didn't.

He opened his eyes again.

"We should have had children," he whispered.

"We didn't," I replied.

His throat worked again but his eyes didn't leave mine when he admitted quietly, "I miss you, Ree."

"I'm sorry, Brad, but I can't do anything about that."

He stared at me for long moments, his face still pale, his eyes wounded before he finally nodded.

"You done?" Tate impatiently demanded to know and Brad looked at him.

"One thing." He was still talking quietly.

"You got one thing then you get out," Tate allowed and Brad's gaze came back to me.

"I loved you," he stated.

I sensed Tate moving but I didn't look from Brad. "Brad—"

"I did, Ree, swear to God. I just don't know where I lost my way."

Tate was suddenly there, at my side and partially in front of me.

"You're done," Tate declared and Brad looked up at him and you could have knocked me over with a feather because another miracle was happening.

Now Brad was looking at Tate like he was a god.

"She sleeps," he whispered, visibly swallowed, and repeated almost inaudibly, "She sleeps." He looked at me and finished, "I wanted to give you that."

I felt tears prick my eyes as I watched Brad, my ex-husband and a man I once loved, it was without reason but I loved him, have his epiphany. But the tears didn't form and Brad said not another word, he just turned and walked straight out of the bar.

"Get out," Tate ordered, my body jerked, and I looked up at him to see he was scowling at Hayley.

"I—" she began.

Tate leaned forward and bit off, "Bitch...get...*out*."

Hayley stared at him, eyes wide. Then she looked at me, ducked her head, and quickly scuttled out.

The door barely closed on her before Tate's arm was around my shoulders and he curled me to his front. His other arm wrapped around my waist as my arms went to hold him loosely at the waist and I tipped my head back to look at him.

"You okay?" he asked.

"No," I answered and his arms gave me a squeeze.

"Think it's over, Ace," he said softly.

"That's not what I'm not okay about," I replied. His brows went up. I got on my toes and whispered, "Captain, you told everyone I go down on you in the morning."

His face relaxed into a grin. "You do."

"And about the shower."

"I get to do that."

"And about me...um, until I can't breathe."

"It's the truth, Ace."

"I know but—"

"Needed to make my point, babe."

"Did you need to make it like that?"

"Well, yeah," he said like that was a given and I should know it.

"Why?" I asked, because it was *not* a given in any way, shape, or form.

"It's a guy thing," he explained.

"Just so you know, it's a girl thing *not* to have private time shared in her place of work," I replied. "Or anywhere, for that matter."

"Why not?" Tate asked.

"Why not?" I repeated.

He grinned again. "Babe, I just made you a legend."

"But—"

"You think those boys don't wish you were in their beds suckin' them off every mornin'?"

I glared at him and pointed out, "I don't do it *every* morning."

Tate grinned yet again.

I tried a different strategy. "That's between you and me."

Tate was still grinning when he noted, "Not anymore."

I was realizing he not only thought this was funny, he didn't think anything was wrong with sharing private moments with our bar regulars. And this made me forget the scene we just had and it made me get very, *very* angry...at Tate.

"Captain," I started, sounding as angry as I was, "I understand that drama was a drama and you sometimes don't guard your words, but you should know, I didn't like what you shared."

Tate was unaffected by my obvious anger and I knew this because he returned, "And you should know, Ace, I could hire a sky writer to share the way you light up for me, I'd do it."

I felt my eyes get wide and my body stiffen. "Are you nuts?"

"Nope."

"You are."

"Babe, again, guy thing."

"No it is not."

He started chuckling and I kept glaring.

"Oh yeah, it definitely is," he stated.

"So, essentially, you're pissing in your corner and not just doing it to claim your territory with Brad but with everyone."

His arms tightened, bringing me deeper into his body. "I wouldn't put it like that, but, yeah. Essentially."

"The alpha male," I muttered irritably.

"Absolutely," Tate muttered back with total unconcern.

"You just lost my mouth in the morning," I hissed and he burst out laughing. "I'm not joking," I warned into his laughter and he dipped his face close to mine.

"Right, baby, I'll believe that when it happens."

"It will," I snapped.

He shook his head then dipped it farther so his nose could tweak my ear.

Then he spoke there. "You're addicted to my cock, Ace. You like suckin' me off more than I like you doin' it."

I jerked my head back and stated, "That is just not true."

Though, I had to admit, maybe it was.

I knew he was teasing by the way his eyes were dancing.

"Just you wait and see," I threatened.

His eyes danced more, showing he clearly didn't believe me. Then I watched them sober.

"It's over, baby," he whispered.

I glared at him some more and then I looked at the door. When I did that, I sighed and relaxed in his arms.

"Yeah," I whispered back.

"You love me?" he asked softly and my eyes went to his.

"Yes," I replied, then shared, "Though, I will state, I do so despite you sometimes being a jerk."

His grin came back. "I can live with that."

While he was speaking, I heard the door open and I looked that way to see Frank, in uniform, walk in.

One look at him and I felt my body get tight again. I knew Tate had seen Frank because I felt his body do the same.

"Christ almighty," Tate muttered and looked down at me. "Fall break, you and Jonas and me are goin' to a beach."

I wanted to go to a beach with Jonas and Tate and I wanted to share that fact with Tate but I couldn't tear my eyes off Frank who was approaching us.

"Tate—" I whispered.

"In Australia," Tate went on.

"Tate—"

"We might not come back," Tate concluded.

"Tate, buddy, gotta talk to you, private, in the office," Frank said and I gave Tate a squeeze.

"You got the bar?" Tate asked and I looked up to see he was addressing me.

I started to answer but Frank spoke.

"Lauren should come with."

My arms gave Tate another squeeze, this was automatic as my eyes shot to Frank.

Frank didn't meet my eyes. He looked at Jim-Billy. "Billy, do me a favor, call Krystal in, yeah?"

"Oh my God," I whispered because something wasn't right and whatever that something was, it *really* wasn't right.

"Frank, what—?" Tate started.

"Do it," Frank ordered.

Jim-Billy nodded and Nadine started digging in her purse.

"I got a phone, Jim-Billy, I got her number," Nadine said quietly.

Frank wasted no time. He moved to the hall and Tate's arm dropped from my shoulders but his hand curled tight around mine and we followed. Frank stopped at the office door and waited. Tate dug his keys out of his pocket and opened the door, holding it for me to precede him. I switched on the lights before I took four steps in and turned. Tate was at my side in a second. Frank closed the door and turned to us.

"I don't even know…," Frank started then trailed off.

"Just fuckin' say it," Tate growled and Frank's eyes latched on Tate's.

"May-December Murderer, Tate, buddy, fuck…" Frank yanked his fingers through his hair before his next, heinous words came out. "Buddy, he got Neeta."

My body jerked like I'd suffered a blow and, at that moment, I could swear that it had as the pain sliced through my innards.

But Tate didn't move, not a muscle.

"Come again?" he whispered.

Frank's eyes came to me, then went straight back to Tate and he said gently, "She's dead, buddy."

"Oh my God," I whispered, my stomach tightening, my heart constricting, my head filling so full of thoughts about Tate, Jonas, Pop, Wood, Stella, even Neeta and Blake, my head so full, it instantly began to pound.

Frank took a step forward, saying, "Tate—"

Tate lifted a hand, palm toward Frank, and Frank stopped moving.

"Buddy—" Frank muttered.

"Does Pop know?" Tate asked.

"Only you," Frank answered.

"Fuck," Tate whispered, his voice tortured.

I turned to him and started to put my hands on him. "Baby—"

"*Fuck!*" he roared and walked past me, my hands glancing off his body as he did and he picked up the desk lamp and tossed it, side armed. It flew across the room and crashed against the wall.

I rushed to him when he swept up the laptop Krys had bought after I presented my stock spreadsheet to her. He barely missed me when that followed the lamp, flying to pieces after it hurtled across the room and smashed against the wall.

I put my hands on him, one at his abs, the fingers of the other one curling around his wrist as I whispered urgently, "Tate, honey, stop."

Surprisingly he stopped, looked down at me and I winced when the burning power of emotion coming out of his eyes seared right through me.

"Baby." I breathed the only thing my brain could think to say.

His arms came around me, one at my neck, one at my waist and he pulled me to him so violently, my head snapped back and my body slammed into his. He shoved his face in my neck. I slid my arms around him and held on.

"Hold on," I urged.

"Fuck," he whispered into my neck and his arms got tighter.

"Hold on, baby," I whispered back as my arms got tighter around him and the tears welled over, spilling down my cheeks.

"Jonas," he whispered.

"I know," I said quickly.

"Fuck," Tate repeated.

"Hold on," I begged.

He held on and I held him while he was doing it.

After a while, I pulled in breath and advised using the word, "Band-Aid."

His head came up and he looked down at me, his eyes carrying anguish.

"Like a Band-Aid," I said gently. "We have to tell them quick, inflict the pain, make it fast, so we can start to deal with it."

"Right," he said.

"Call everyone to the house," I ordered softly.

"Right," he repeated.

"Baby?" I called and he didn't answer, didn't let me go, he just looked at me. I lifted a hand, put it to his jaw and whispered, "Love you."

His eyes closed slowly, he opened them and they were no less bleak. He let me go, stepped back, and his hand went to his back pocket.

Then he pulled out his phone.

*   *   *

Wood came to the house first because Tate arranged it that way.

Tate told Wood on the deck while I made coffee.

Then the sliding glass door opened, Tate came through, and his eyes came to me.

"Go to him," he ordered on a growl.

I nodded and moved immediately to do as Tate said.

Wood was leaning into his hands on the railing at the end of the deck, his eyes pointed to the trees.

I walked up to him and stopped a few feet away.

"Wood," I called.

"Get the fuck away, Laurie."

My head twisted to the side and I pulled in a breath.

Then I walked to him and placed a hand gently on his back.

"Wood," I whispered.

"Laurie, fuckin' leave me be."

My other hand went to his hip and I rested my forehead against my hand on his back.

"Wood," I whispered.

Wood didn't reply and I didn't move.

This lasted a long time.

Then Wood said, "She was a goddamned mess."

"I know."

"For fuckin' decades."

"I know, honey."

"Walked all over people, fucked with people's lives, didn't give a shit about anyone."

"Don't," I whispered.

"She didn't deserve that," he whispered back.

"No," I agreed.

"She didn't deserve that," he repeated and my head came up.

"No, honey, she didn't."

"My sister," he whispered and I watched his head drop like he couldn't hold it up anymore.

My arms went around him and I hugged him from behind. His hand left the railing and found mine at his belly, his fingers lacing through and he held on.

So did I.

And we did this until I felt his body tighten.

"They're here," he stated, letting my hand go. I let him go and stepped away.

I stood by him and Tate joined us when Stella's car pulled into the drive.

When Tate and I were working, or I was working and Tate was hunting, the deal was that Stella or Pop picked Jonas up from school and he hung with one or the other of them at the office at the garage until Tate or I could come and get him.

Today was no different.

Tate, Wood, and I watched, our bodies turning slowly as the car made its way up the drive, Pop sitting up front by Stella, who was at the wheel, Jonas in the back.

"I'll finish coffee," I muttered and quickly went into the house.

They didn't need me there, not now. There was a time when I'd be needed, but it wasn't now.

I went to the cupboard, pulled down mugs, went to the fridge, got the milk, slid the sugar across the counter away from the wall.

Then I heard it and I stopped. My hands pressed into the counter, my teeth clenched, and my eyes closed tight.

It kept coming at me and the sound was so monstrous it felt like it was tearing away my flesh. If I felt like that, removed, how did Tate feel, being right there while Jonas was making that hideous noise?

The door slid open and I whirled around, opening my eyes and

I watched Jonas dash through. He kept going but caught sight of me and skidded to a halt.

I stared at him, his face red, his eyes and cheeks wet, his breath coming fast and uneven and I didn't know what to do. He stared right back at me but I couldn't read anything in his eyes, nothing but pain.

Finally, I could take no more and I whispered, "Baby," and the minute I did, he moved, straight at me. His head down, he crashed into me, forcing my breath out and pain in. I went back with Jonas propelling me until I hit the counter, the small of my back slamming into it, throbbing pain radiating instantly out.

I thought, at first, he meant to hurt me, to take his pain out on me. And then I felt his hands grabbing at my clothes, tugging at my T-shirt, his face still buried in my ribcage.

"Laurie," he groaned as his legs gave out and I felt him falling, his hands grasping my shirt. I went down with him, to my knees, Jonas to his and I wrapped him tight in my arms. His face was in my chest and he was burrowing there, like a kitten into his mother, shoving his face this way and that as he kept grabbing at my clothes.

"Baby, I'm right here," I whispered, holding him tighter, my hand coming up to grasp his head and press his cheek into my chest.

"Laurie." His voice was a croak.

"I'm right here," I whispered.

"Laurie," he repeated, his hands twisting in my shirt, holding on.

I bent and rested my cheek against his head. "Right here, Bub," I murmured and started rocking him. "Right here, baby. Hold on."

"Laurie." I could hear his tears and mine came too, my breath hitching with them so violently, my body shuddered.

"Hold on, baby."

He held on, his fists still twisted in my shirt and I gently moved to my behind, pulling him down with me so he was mostly in my lap and I kept rocking him like a baby as we sat on the floor and both of us sobbed.

This went on for a while, how long, I didn't know, but it went on until I felt Tate get close. I lifted my cheek from Jonas's thick, soft hair and looked through my wet eyes at Jonas's father crouched beside us.

"Let go of Laurie, Bub," Tate said softly.

Jonas didn't move.

"Let go, Bub," Tate repeated.

Jonas sucked in a broken breath and looked up at his dad. Then he let go, Tate's hands went to his son and he lifted up, swinging Jonas's body in front of him. Jonas circled Tate's hips with his legs, his shoulders with his arms and Tate, his son in his arms, walked out of the room and down the hall toward the mudroom.

I sat on the floor and watched the space I last saw them in.

Then a hand filled my vision, I looked up and saw it was attached to an arm attached to Wood.

"Let's get you up, baby," he said gently. He squatted, grabbed my hand, his other arm going around my waist and he pulled me up to my feet.

He kept my hand in his and his arm around me as I wiped my cheeks.

"Do you…," I said to him and then my eyes went to Stella and Pop—Stella looking shell-shocked, Pop's eyes rimmed with red—and my gaze went back to Wood. "Do you want coffee?"

"Yeah, baby, coffee'd be good," Wood said in his gentle voice.

I nodded but Wood didn't let me go.

I sucked in breath, closed my eyes, opened them, and looked at Pop.

"I'm so sorry," I whispered.

"Me too, sweetheart," he whispered back.

I nodded again and bit my lip.

"I don't want coffee," Stella stated. My eyes went to her and she finished, "Bourbon."

"We have that," I said.

"Good," she replied.

I looked at Wood. "Coffee or bourbon?"

"Both," Wood answered.

I looked at Pop and didn't get a chance to speak before he said, "Same as Wood, sweetheart."

I nodded, sucked in breath through my nose, and looked up at Wood. He leaned in and kissed my forehead then he let me go.

I got Neeta's grieving family their drinks.

*   *   *

She's dead, buddy.

My eyes opened.

I was pressed into Tate's back and I heard it.

A television.

The house was big but the night was quiet and I could hear it, even from far away.

Jonas's room.

I slid carefully away from Tate trying not to disturb the covers or him and I got out of bed. I went to the closet, blindly grabbed off a hanger the first of Tate's shirts that I found. It was a soft flannel that had been washed a gazillion times. I shrugged it on over my camisole and pajama bottoms and I stealthily left the room.

I walked through the dark house, down the backstairs and down the hall guided by the flickering light coming from Jonas's partially opened door.

I knocked once and pushed it open.

Jonas was lying in bed, his back against the headboard, the remote held loosely in his hand resting on his lap, Buster stretched the length of his hip down his thigh. His eyes were blank on the screen and just as blank when they came to me.

"Can't sleep?" I whispered.

He shrugged.

"Want company?" I asked.

He shrugged again.

I decided to take this as a yes and I walked forward, crawled into bed with him and rested my back against the headboard.

It took me a while before I got the courage to slide my arm around his shoulders and pull the side of his body into mine.

I should have known, with my sweet Jonas, I didn't have to find the courage.

He immediately curled into a ball and slid down so his head was resting on my belly and his arm was wrapped around my hips.

I carefully pulled in breath, slid my fingers through his hair and I kept doing that as we watched TV.

I knew Jonas had long since fallen asleep but was loath to disturb him so I kept my place and mindlessly watched TV until I saw Tate standing in the door wearing nothing but jeans.

"He couldn't sleep," I whispered and I watched Tate's eyes, illuminated by the light from the TV screen, look to my belly and back to me.

"He's out now, Ace," he whispered back.

"I'm scared to move," I told him.

Without hesitation, Tate walked into the room and he carefully slid his son off me and into bed. Jonas didn't stir through this or while Tate pulled the covers over his shoulders and tucked them in.

Then he straightened and looked at me. "Bed, babe."

"What if he wakes up again?"

"Bed."

"Tate—"

"He knows where we are."

"I don't want him to be alone."

"He isn't."

"Captain—"

"Bed."

"But—"

"Lauren. Bed."

I looked at Tate and then I looked at Jonas. I leaned down and kissed his hair, carefully exited the bed, and walked to the door. Tate flicked off the TV. I saw dark, then felt his arm slide along my shoulders. When we were in the hall my arm slid along his waist.

Connected, we walked all the way back to our room. I pulled off Tate's shirt and got into bed as Tate took off his jeans and, when he joined me, he pulled me right into him, my front to his.

"What woke you up?" he asked.

"I heard Frank's voice," I answered.

"Right," he whispered.

"Then I heard Jonas's TV."

Tate didn't reply.

I snuggled closer and Tate's fingers sifted into my hair.

"Reckon it'll be a while before you'll have sweet dreams," he remarked.

"Probably," I replied, hesitated and started, "Tate—"

He cut me off. "I'm okay."

"You and..." I stopped. "There's history."

"Know that, babe."

"Sorry," I whispered. His hand fisted and he rolled into me so I was on my back, his body was the length of mine and his face was in the side of my hair.

"History is just that, history. I can't say this hasn't rocked me but what I'm feelin' is about Jonas," he told me.

"Okay." I was still whispering and I was also not believing him.

History was history but Neeta was Neeta. You didn't spend your whole life knowing a girl, then the woman, sharing part of your life with her, making a child with her, and feeling nothing but worry for your son after she was brutally murdered.

"Trust me, Ace."

"Okay," I repeated.

Tate was silent.

"I just want you to know, I'm here or..." I hesitated and then said, "I could be gone if that's what you and Jonas need."

His arms got tight and his voice was a growl when he stated, "Lauren, you even think of leavin' me and Jonas, I swear to God—"

"Just for a while," I said quickly, "I don't want—"

"Shut it." He was still growling.

"Seriously, Tate, you need to know, I want for you and Jonas—"

"Babe. Fuckin'. *Shut it.*"

"Okay," I whispered.

"Christ," he bit off.

"Sorry."

"Say you're sorry with your mouth, babe."

Confused, I told him, "I just did, Tate."

"With your mouth," he repeated and I understood what he meant.

"What if—?" I started.

"Need your mouth, babe."

"Tate—"

His arms gave me a squeeze and he whispered, "Need you, Laurie."

He needed me.

Therefore, I rolled into him, then rolled on top of him and I gave him what he needed. Before he came he pulled me up and to his side, yanked off my pajama bottoms and underwear and positioned me straddling him.

"Fuck me, baby, I want my cock inside you," he growled.

I wrapped my hand around him and slid him inside.

"Fuck me," he groaned and I moved.

His thumb went to my clit and circled, so I moved faster.

"That's it, Christ, that's it, baby," Tate encouraged.

"Hurry, Captain, faster," I whispered.

"Come here."

I bent to him, still riding him and his fingers pulled down my camisole, his hand cupped my breast, he fed my nipple between his lips and pulled hard.

That felt so unbelievably good, my hips bucked.

Tate kept sucking and his thumb kept circling. Then his tongue rolled my nipple and his hand left my breast, slid into my hair, and pulled my mouth to his.

"You close?" he grunted.

"Yeah," I whispered.

"Harder baby."

I fucked him harder, felt it coming, and breathed, "Yes."

"There you go."

My hand circled his wrist as it hit me and his thumb became too much.

"Tate."

"Fuck me harder."

"Oh God, baby," I moaned, my back and neck arching and I came hard and rode him harder as his thumb kept at me.

"Keep ridin' me, Ace."

"Tate—" I breathed, pushing at his hand, still coming. God it felt amazing, overwhelming, it felt like I would shatter but his thumb circled faster.

"You're gonna come again," he ordered.

"No," I whispered.

His hips started bucking to meet my strokes and his hand in my hair went to my hip to yank me down.

"Tate, God, baby," I whimpered as the second wave hit.

"Fuck yeah," he groaned, his hips surging up, his thumb left my clit and both his hands slammed me down so he was buried inside me and, through my second orgasm, I listened to his grunting moan.

I collapsed on top of him, my face in his neck and I listened to his breathing even as I struggled to even my own.

Then he reached out and, still connected, he yanked the covers over us.

I started to move off him but his arms wrapped around me.

"Want you to fall asleep on my cock," he growled in my ear.

"Tate, I'm too heavy—"

"Don't move." He was still growling.

"Baby—"

His arms tensed. "Want you close as you can be."

I closed my eyes tight.

Then I whispered, "Anything you want, Captain."

"That's right, baby."

I settled into him, shifting my hips, causing a low noise to come from his throat.

"I love you, Tate," I said softly into his ear.

"I know, baby," he said back. "Sleep."

"Okay."

And if you'd have asked me, after all that happened that day, and what could assault my mind in the night, if I could fall asleep on top of Tate with his cock still hard inside me, I would have said no, definitely not.

But I did.

CHAPTER TWENTY-FIVE

After Neeta

"ACE!" I HEARD Tate bellow and my eyes went from the mirror, to Buster sitting on the vanity watching me arrange my hair in a bun at the nape, to Jonas, who was sitting on the lowered toilet lid wearing his black suit, the collar of his white shirt open, his little kid's tie unknotted and hanging loose.

For the last five days, Jonas had stuck to me like glue.

I found this surprising. I didn't know what he'd do but sticking to me like glue wasn't one of my top-ten guesses.

But I wasn't complaining.

"Ace!" Tate bellowed again and I whispered to Jonas, "Oh dear."

Tate, like his son, had also stuck to me like glue. As the days passed, I realized both Jackson boys were behaving, as usual, just the same. One of their women had been brought low—no matter how they felt about her, Neeta was still one of their women—and they weren't taking any chances.

Jonas gave me a smile that didn't reach his eyes. I returned it but hoped mine reached my eyes and I hurried out of the bathroom, hearing Buster drop down to follow me with Jonas. I grabbed my black pumps from the bed and stopped twice in the hall to lift up a foot in turn and shove them on. We all arrived in the dining area in time to see Tate, wearing charcoal gray suit pants and a midnight blue shirt open at the collar, slide the glass door open and walk through.

I looked down at Jonas and we followed Tate, me stopping for Jonas to precede me. I pushed Buster back with my foot and slid the door closed. I turned toward the deck steps just in time to see my father, my mother, my sister, and Mack climbing the steps. Dad was going slowly but he looked fit, if much thinner, and he had a tan. All of them were wearing funeral black.

I stared at them a second, in shock. They knew, of course; I'd called them the day after we found out about Neeta. They'd called every day since and they knew the funeral was today.

I just didn't know they were planning on coming.

I stopped staring and started running. I slowed my progress so when my arms closed around my dad, I didn't hurt him.

"Daddy," I whispered.

"Honey," he whispered back as his arms went around me strong and tight.

I was holding on to my dad, feeling his healing arms around me but I heard Mom say, "Tate, hon, give Jeannie some sugar."

I smiled over Dad's shoulder at Carrie who smiled back. If Mom was talking in third person and asking for sugar, she was back.

Dad kissed my cheek and let me go in time for Mack to give me a bear hug then, while I was hugging Carrie, I heard Dad say, "You must be Tatum."

"Tate," Tate replied and I pulled away from Carrie but kept an arm around her to watch Dad shake Tate's hand.

When they released hands, Dad looked at Jonas but asked Tate, "This your boy?"

"Of course it's his boy, he's the spittin' image," Mom declared and bustled up to Jonas. "Hi, Jonas, I'm Gramma," she announced, then demanded, "Give me some sugar."

Jonas stared up at her, clearly uncertain what to do with a self-appointed Gramma since, between Tate and Neeta, he'd never had one.

"She means she wants a kiss, honey," I informed Jonas and Mom bent down and pointed her index finger at her cheek.

"Right there, hon, a big smackeroo," Mom instructed and Jonas's eyes shot to his father. Tate nodded and Jonas leaned in and swiftly kissed her cheek.

"Ooh!" Mom shouted and shot upright, smacking her hand on her cheek. "Keeping that one *forever.*"

"Oh God," I whispered and Mom turned to me.

"Neither of you girls gave me grandkids, I'm claiming Tate's," she declared.

"Jeannie, you might wanna tone it down before you scare the kid silly," Dad cautioned.

"Baloney, he's not scared," Mom said to Dad and then looked down at Jonas. "Are you, hon?"

"Um...," Jonas mumbled, which meant yes.

"Let's get coffee," I suggested in an effort to save Jonas.

"Great idea, I'm three quarts low," Mack put in and walked to Tate, taking his hand, giving it a firm shake at the same time clapping him on the shoulder. "Tate, man, shit reason but still good to see you."

"Same here, Mack," Tate replied and Carrie moved in for a hug from Tate.

"Hey there, honey," she whispered, giving him a good squeeze then leaning back, leaving her hands on his shoulders. "You doing okay?"

"We're hangin' in there, Carrie," Tate murmured.

"Well, I'm not. We flew in late last night, stayed at a hotel by the airport, been on the road all mornin'. Then Gavin got lost—" Mom stated, forging toward the house.

"I did not get lost," Dad declared.

"Hon." Mom stopped at the sliding glass door and turned to him, "you...*did*." She looked at Tate. "Sat nav who? Sat nav what? I don't need a sat nav. Acting like he drove through the Colorado mountains for a living!" Then she threw open the door and disappeared into the house but we heard her shout, "Good God, look at that *cat*!" Then we heard her coo, "Who's a pretty kitty? Come to Gramma, pretty kitty."

"I'm feeling nostalgic for my hospital bed," Dad muttered to Tate and moved to follow Mom, tousling Jonas's hair as he went by.

I got close to Jonas, bent down, and whispered, "My family's a little goofy."

"I can tell," he whispered back.

I winked at him and straightened.

Then I introduced, "Jonas, baby, this is my sister, Carrie and her partner, Mack."

"Hey," he said on a barely there wave.

"Hey, big man," Mack said back.

Carrie smiled at him and Jonas looked at me.

"Your sister is as hot as you," he announced.

Carrie let out a startled giggle and Mack straight out laughed.

"He thinks I'm a MILF," I whispered to Mack.

"Darlin', you are," Mack whispered back.

"Whatever," I muttered.

"Let's get inside," Tate said brusquely. I looked at him, Mack and Carrie looked at me but Jonas led the way and Mack and Carrie followed.

I hung back, caught Tate's hand, and spoke when he looked down at me.

"Is it okay they're here?" I asked quietly.

"Yeah," he answered, then started to move away but I tugged his hand and he looked back at me.

"They just want to—"

He cut me off, "I know."

"This is what families do, or, it's what my family does," I told him and he turned to me, his hand coming to my neck, his head dipping toward mine.

"Babe, I know," he repeated firmly.

"You sure you're okay?" I asked, searching his features.

He closed his eyes and his forehead came to mine before he whispered, "I'll be better once she's in the ground."

I nodded my head, my forehead rolling against his and watched his eyes open as he lifted his head from mine. My hand went to his neck too and my thumb swept his clean-shaven jaw as my eyes watched.

"You miss the beard," he muttered.

"I fell in love with you when you had a beard," I replied.

Suddenly his arms closed around me tight and, lips at my temple, he said, "Fuck, I love you."

I gave him a squeeze and whispered, "Me too. Well, I mean, I love *you,* I don't mean I love me too," I blathered stupidly and felt his arms give me a squeeze back as I heard his soft chuckle.

I held him, he held me, and then he let me go, took my hand and led me inside.

Mom had clearly taken control, for everyone but Jonas had coffee and Mom was at the island, squirting chocolate syrup into a glass at the same time she was stirring it into milk that was so far from the color of milk and so close to the color of chocolate that the milk was in danger of *becoming* chocolate.

"Mom, what are you doing?" I asked as I hit the island.

"Making Jonas chocolate milk," Mom answered.

"You can quit putting in chocolate now," I informed her.

"It's not quite there," Mom informed me back.

"It's there," I stated.

"Not quite," she returned.

"Mom," I warned.

She splodged in a thick, last squirt, and announced, "There!"

I rolled my eyes, pulled in breath, and when I rolled them back I looked at Jonas. He was grinning at Mom.

"Shit, Laurie!" Mack exclaimed, sounding like his mouth was full and I looked at him to see he was eating one of the fudge-filled chocolate cupcakes with chocolate fudge icing I'd made for Jonas the day before.

"Mack!" Carrie snapped. "Don't help yourself!" But Mack was ignoring Carrie and looking at Jonas.

"Big man, she made you Grandma Grahame's chocolate fudge cupcakes. Awesome," Mack stated.

"She makes me chocolate chip cookies too," Jonas shared.

"Awe . . . *some*," Mack reiterated.

"And chocolate pecan pie," Jonas went on.

"Did I say awesome?" Mack asked.

"And this red cake stuff that's chocolate too but it's red," Jonas continued.

"She must love you, big man," Mack proclaimed, throwing an arm around Carrie with the hand not holding his cupcake and yanking her close to his side. "Trust me, those are heavy artillery in a Grahame woman's arsenal."

Mack had been trying to take Jonas's mind off the day's events but his words had an effect even I wouldn't have guessed and I pretty much knew Jonas liked me. I watched, heck we all watched his body stiffen. Then he turned to me and his head tilted back so his eyes could lock on mine.

But he didn't speak, he just stared at me and the look on his face made my heart skip.

"Bub," Tate called, seeing the look.

"Mom never made me pie," Jonas told me.

I heard Mack mutter an expletive under his breath but I crouched down and lifted an arm to Jonas.

"Come here, baby," I urged.

"She never made me cookies," Jonas said.

"That's all right, come here," I repeated.

"She never made me a cake, not once, even on my birthday. She'd buy 'em," Jonas went on.

"Honey," I whispered, "please, come here."

"You make me that stuff." He told me something I already knew.

"I know," I replied.

"You make me that stuff because you love me?" he asked.

"Yes, Bub, of course," I answered.

"You love me," he whispered.

"Yes, Bub," I whispered back.

"Does that mean she didn't love me?" he asked and tears instantly filled my eyes.

"No," I answered firmly.

"Do you..." He swallowed. "Do you know I love you?"

I swallowed too and lied, "Yes," because I didn't know until just then.

"Do you think she knew I loved her?" he asked.

"Absolutely, baby," I whispered. "She knew. She definitely knew."

He didn't move, but his throat did and I knew he was fighting back tears.

"Baby—" I was still whispering but before I could move or Tate could, Dad did.

"All right, son, you don't know me and I don't know you but I'm thinkin' it's time we changed that." Dad put his hand on Jonas's shoulder, Jonas looked up at him, and Dad handed him the glass of brown milk. "Take that. We'll walk. You'll drink and we'll get to know one another. You all right with that?"

Dad didn't wait for Jonas to answer. He just guided him to the door, slid it open, and pushed him through. His eyes went to Tate before he closed it. They communicated something I didn't get since they were using male telepathy. Dad slid the door to and put his hand back to Jonas's shoulder to lead him away.

"Sorry, Tate," Mack muttered.

"Not a problem," Tate replied. "This shit's bound to come out."

"Yeah, but not by me actin' like a jackass," Mack murmured, clearly kicking himself.

"He didn't have a good mom, Mack," Tate shared and this so surprised me my eyes swiftly went to him. "She was a drunk and she didn't give much of a shit about him. She's dead but he's in a better place with a woman who sits up at night and watches TV with him until he gets to sleep and makes him cupcakes. He's strugglin' with that, knowin' his life is better without her in it, feelin' guilt that that's how he felt when it became permanent. He's gonna struggle with it for a while. It's good you made it come out, he's gotta let it come out and it's best it comes out when people are around who'll handle him with care."

Mom, Carrie, Mack, and I all stared at Tate. Then I moved to him, pressed my front to his side and wrapped my arms around him.

"Dad'll handle him with care, Captain," I whispered, my head tipped back to look at his profile and he twisted his neck to look down at me.

"I know that," he whispered back and then his eyes went to Mom. "I'm pleased you're here, Jeannie."

"Family looks after family," Mom replied softly. Her eyes went to me and then went back to Tate. "But you already know that, don't you, Tate?"

"Yeah," Tate answered.

"You want coffee?" Mom asked, wisely changing the subject.

"Yeah," Tate repeated.

"You take it black," she muttered and walked to the cupboard.

I pressed into Tate, my body relaxing.

"Wow!" Carrie exclaimed and my body got tense again as I looked at my sister. "That *is* a pretty kitty."

"Her name's Princess Fancy Pants," I blurted. Tate's arm gave me a warning squeeze. I ignored it and finished, "She's Tate's."

Carrie's eyes flew to Tate and she giggled. "You named your cat Princess Fancy Pants?"

"Holy fuck," Mack muttered.

"Her name is Buster," Tate declared.

"*Her* name is Buster?" Mom asked, handing Tate a coffee.

"I like Princess Fancy Pants better," Carrie decided.

"Tell your sister, she calls my cat that, she's ejected," Tate said to me as he took the coffee from Mom and I tried not to laugh.

"Um...Carrie, I was just joking," I clarified. "Tate and Buster are tight. He's protective and he *really* doesn't like Princess Fancy Pants."

Carrie watched Buster wind her way through our ankles, and her lips were twitching when her eyes went to Tate then came to me, and she murmured, "Right."

"It's going to be a long day," Mom noted, her eyes on Mack. "Mack, pass me a cupcake."

Mack grabbed a cupcake and handed it to Mom and I slid away from Tate and went to the sliding glass door. I looked until I found them, Dad and Jonas standing out in Tate's drive, Jonas's arm lifted to point at something.

I felt Tate move in behind me, then I felt his arm around my chest pulling me into his body. I knew he was watching too and I knew he saw it when Dad said something to Jonas that made Jonas tip his head back and grin at Dad like he was exceptionally funny, something my dad could be. I knew this because Tate's arm tightened reflexively.

Tate's lips came to my ear.

"Special," he muttered.

I lifted my hand to curl my fingers around his forearm and I held on as I fought back tears.

*   *   *

Tate parked the Explorer in the parking lot of the funeral home, my family following us in their rental and parking on Tate's side.

I undid my seatbelt, opened the door and jumped down, then stilled when I saw Jonas had also jumped down and was instantly accosted by an older woman with lots of blond hair. She was wearing a brightly colored gypsy skirt with sequins stitched in a pattern around the hem and little bells jingling at the bottom, a hot pink gypsy top that had flowing sleeves gathered at the wrists and a tie that gathered at the neckline, scuffed, fawn suede cowboy boots, and lots and lots of silver and turquoise jewelry at ears, neck, fingers, and wrists.

"Bubby baby," she whispered and latched on to Jonas so that Jonas's face was stuffed into her ample cleavage. His hands were at her waist in a way I couldn't tell if he was trying to push away or hold on and she was rocking him roughly back and forth.

I got close. "Um, can I help you?"

She lifted her head to look at me with dark brown eyes flecked with tawny. Eyes I knew very well.

Tate's mother.

Wow.

Something washed over her face as she stared at me and I didn't know her but I knew that something was not good.

I felt Tate round the hood of the SUV as I saw my family round the back.

"Mom?" Tate asked and she tore her eyes from me to look at Tate.

She unceremoniously let Jonas go so swiftly he listed to the side and she said, "Buck, baby." Then she threw herself in Tate's arms.

I moved to Jonas, pulling him carefully to my side with an arm around his shoulders. His arm slid along my waist and I looked at Tate to see he was holding his mother but his eyes were aimed over her head at me.

"I can't believe it, baby, I can't. I heard and I couldn't believe it." Her voice was heavy with tears. She tipped her head back and Tate looked down at her when she finished. "You must be devastated."

"Mom—" Tate started.

"I mean *Neeta*," she went on.

"Mom—"

"*Your* Neeta," she continued.

"Mom, you wanna—"

"I never thought I'd see it. It's like the end of an era. You were born two halves of a whole," Tate's mom proclaimed, then wailed, "Buck, baby, how're you gonna live without your other half?" And she collapsed in Tate's arms, her sobs clearly audible because they were *loud*.

I watched Tate's jaw get tight as his eyes went over his mother's head to find mine.

"Babe, take Jonas inside," he ordered.

I nodded because he looked pissed. And because of that, I tried not to let it show that his mother's words affected me. I glanced at my family and then led Jonas toward the building.

We'd taken five steps when I heard her say in a loud whisper, "Buck, darlin', who on earth is *she*?"

Jonas's arm convulsed at my waist. I avoided my family's eyes and I hurried him forward.

* * *

Jonas didn't stay glued to me during the run-up to the memorial service because Tate's mom commandeered him, acting like she was a staple in his life even though he looked confused and uncomfortable as she pulled him this way and that, keeping her hands on him nearly all the time.

Stella shared her name with me, Shania. Stella also shared that wasn't her real name. Her real name was Bernadette but it was the name she changed it to when she was forty and having her *first* (Stella reported there were three that she knew of) midlife crisis.

Shania also spent a great deal of time sobbing, exclaiming about what a loss wild, crazy, full-of-life Neeta was to the world and generally sucking all the attention she could get.

I hung back with my family who stayed close and quiet. What made matters worse was the fact that Tate was clearly incensed by his mother's behavior and he wasn't the only one. Pop, Wood, Stella, Krystal, Jim-Billy, Betty, Ned, and practically everyone else glared at her openly but her shields were solid and these glares glanced off her with no visible effect.

Tate stayed close to Shania but I figured this was because of Jonas rather than any need to be near his mother. In fact, he seemed to be struggling with his desire to say something. But the events of the day forced him to behave with decorum and I knew this was taking a lot out of him because my man pretty much let it rip whenever the mood came over him and I could tell the mood was most definitely over him.

It was when the service was about to start and I'd shifted with my family and sat in the back when it happened.

Shania led Tate and Jonas to the front row and made a show of declaring the seating arrangements, herself between "my two boys" (her loud words). Neither Tate nor Jonas sat, however, even when she pushed at the both of them. The Jackson boys' eyes searched the large congregation and found me. When they did, I shook my head and smiled that it was okay and it was. It wasn't for me to sit with them in the front row at Neeta's funeral.

I was looking at *my* boys, therefore I was startled when I heard Pop say from beside me, "Sweetheart."

I looked to the side and up to see he had his arm extended in front of my dad, his hand toward me.

"Pop, it's okay," I whispered.

"Family sits in front," Pop stated.

"It's okay. I think—"

"Family sits in front, Laurie."

"Pop, you should—"

"Front," he rumbled.

"Go, hon," Dad whispered. I looked at him. He nodded to me. I bit my lip, looked at Pop, and took his hand.

He led me to the front.

"Move along, Shania," Stella demanded quietly when Pop and I got there.

"What?" Shania asked Stella but her eyes were on me.

"Down the row," Stella stated.

Shania twisted her neck to look at Stella. "I'm sittin' with my boys."

"Fine, you can do that but down the row," Stella returned.

"But—" Shania started and Tate moved.

He leaned in, grabbed my hand, and looked down at Jonas. "Sit, Bub."

Instantly, Jonas sat. Tate used my hand to pull me in front of Shania and he pushed me in the seat beside Jonas, then he sat down beside me.

He looked up at his mother and jerked his head down the row. "Sit, Mom."

Quickly, Stella sat at the beginning of the aisle. Wood sat by her, Wood's pretty, dark-haired six-year-old daughter crawling into his lap. Pop sat between Wood and Jonas, Tate sat by me, and Shania had no choice but to sit at the end.

Blake, Neeta's man, sat opposite the aisle with what looked like his parents beside him and Neeta's posse led by Carmen plopped down in seats by the parents. I glanced in Blake's direction but Tate didn't, nor did any of Neeta's family, nor Jonas, and Blake didn't look our way. But I could see, even from his profile, he was lost and suffering. It might have gone bad along the way but once it had been good and that was what Blake Daniels was remembering while he stared at the closed casket.

"This is bullshit," I heard Shania mutter, taking my mind off Blake, and then I felt Tate's angry, dark energy flash.

He turned to her and whispered, "One more word, I swear to God..."

He let that hang and I felt Jonas get stiff. I slid my arm around his shoulders and he didn't hesitate before he fell sideways into me. I felt Tate's arm go around my shoulders and I pulled Jonas with me as I fell sideways into Tate. Then I felt Tate's lips come to my ear.

"I know why you did it, Ace," Tate said quietly in my ear and I knew he was still angry when he finished. "But don't you fuckin' leave us again."

I didn't look at him when I nodded. His arm squeezed my shoulders. I squeezed Jonas's then I leaned down to whisper into the top of his head, "Relax, baby, this'll be over soon."

"Okay, Laurie," Jonas whispered back.

I held him tighter. Tate held me tighter.

Then Guns N' Roses' "Sweet Child o' Mine" started playing and out of the corner of my eye I saw Wood move. I looked at him to see he'd turned his head toward Tate.

The lone guitar strains tore through the quiet space. They were joined by more guitar, then drums. The beat throbbed loud and pounded into our chests, the tempo increasing and finally Axl Rose's voice rocked out words so sweet they tore at your soul.

Wood grinned at Tate.

I twisted my neck and looked up to see that Tate grinned back.

*   *   *

Later, at the graveside, opposite where Jonas and Tate were sitting by the casket, me behind them, I saw Bubba walk up to the mourners moments before the minister started speaking.

The minute the service was done, Tate got up, pulled his chair out of the row, grabbed my hand, and tugged me through. With one hand in mine, the other hand on Jonas's shoulder, he led us straight to Bubba.

Bubba watched as we walked up to him, his eyes locked on Tate.

Tate stopped in front of Bubba and I held my breath.

"Tate—" Bubba started then Tate moved, letting my hand go, one of his arms wrapped around Bubba and I watched Bubba's eyes close as one of his arms wrapped around Tate.

They stood that way for long moments before Tate pounded Bubba's back and stepped away.

Bubba looked down at Jonas. "Hey, little man," he whispered and Jonas moved forward and hugged Bubba's waist.

When he moved back, I moved in, fitting myself to his front and giving him a squeeze.

"Hey, gorgeous." He was still whispering and doing it into the top of my hair.

"Hey," I whispered back.

When I stepped away, Tate claimed me with an arm around my shoulders but his eyes were on Bubba.

"You comin' to Pop's?" he asked.

"I don't know," Bubba answered. "You want me at Pop's?"

Tate didn't respond, just gave Bubba a look.

Bubba dropped his head and said to the grass, "I'm comin' to Pop's."

Tate nodded, lifted a hand, and clapped Bubba on the shoulder. Then he moved Jonas and me toward the Explorer.

Then we went to Pop's.

*   *   *

It took approximately twenty minutes for the pall to lift and the backyard at Pop's became less a postfuneral gathering and more a party. This had a lot to do with the keg that was out there sitting by a cooler that was full of bottles of beer, as well as the fact that a lot of people brought their own bottles of hard liquor from which they imbibed liberally, some of them not even using glasses to do it.

I stuck close to Jonas and Tate and my family stuck close to me, thus us. It wasn't until half an hour later that the beer and partaking of the food covering the table in Pop's dining room and the counters of his kitchen that we loosened up.

I noticed that Dad and Mack had Jonas and they were standing talking with Stella and Wood and Wood's two kids. Wood's ex-wife, Maggie, a pretty, petite, curvy brunette was there (Tate pointed her out to me with a jerk of his head and a mumbled, "Wood's old lady, Maggie") but she was giving them a wide berth.

It was after I spent some time studying Maggie, thinking she was very pretty and also that she looked somewhat sad and adrift when I realized I'd lost sight of Tate so I quit studying Maggie and went to find him. Not finding him in the house, I went to the backyard and didn't see him there either. I rounded the house and stopped when I saw him, his back to me, the bright colors of a gypsy skirt all I could see of his mother standing in front of him.

"…since he was five years old. That sure as fuck doesn't give you the right to act like that," I heard him say and I knew, just by his voice, he was seriously angry.

"Tatum—" she started.

"He doesn't even fuckin' *know* you. This shit's hard on him and you come in and…" He hesitated. "Fuck, I don't even know what that shit was about."

"I'm his grandmother," she snapped.

"He met his gramma today, Lauren's mom, and she's the only one he's ever gonna have if you don't fuckin' cool it."

"*Lauren's* mom?" she hissed and I stared, the words I was going to say to intervene lodging in my throat when I watched Tate's body get tight from head to foot and he leaned forward threateningly.

"Yeah, *Lauren's* mom," Tate shot back and continued angrily, "You know, I always thought it was okay, you bein' you 'cause it was the only thing I knew. And because of that, I thought it was okay for Jonas, Neet bein' Neet. Better he have somethin' than nothin' 'cause what I knew was, nothin' made you like Neet and somethin' was a fuckuva lot better than that. Now I know that shit's not right. *Your* shit's not right."

"Did *Lauren* teach you that?" Shania snapped her question.

"This isn't about Lauren," Tate returned.

"Seems to me it is. Seems to me someone got himself a little swanky somethin' somethin' and now he thinks his shit don't stink like he thought when he was Mr. Hotshot Football Player."

I gasped and Shania leaned to the side, saw me and her eyes narrowed but Tate stayed on point.

"You been gone for five years, Jonas doesn't even remember you, and you think you can roll into town and make this day, the second shittiest day in his life after the day he found out his mom's dead, all about you. Woman, that shit's whacked."

"You wanna join our conversation?" Shania asked, ignoring Tate, her eyes on me. "Seein' as you seem so interested in it."

Tate turned to the side and his eyes came to me but I kept my eyes to Shania when I replied, "No, I'm good with just listening."

"Well, maybe you'll do me a favor, darlin', and give me a second alone with my boy," she demanded through suggestion.

"And maybe I won't," I replied and Shania looked at Tate.

"Neeta's fresh in her grave and she's already rollin' in it, knowin' this one's here, wearin' her fancy-ass outfit and her fancy-ass shoes, lookin' down her nose at the rest of us," she remarked.

Tate stared at his mother for long moments, then looked to the heavens and sighed.

He righted his head but shook it and muttered, "We're done."

"We aren't," Shania stated and Tate leveled his gaze at her.

"We are and I mean that in every way it can be meant, you get me?"

She looked like he'd slapped her before she began, "I—"

Tate cut her off. "Jonas has had enough of your brand of dysfunctional bullshit in his life and I didn't shield him from it. The way I see it, I got eight years to keep him safe from that shit before he finds his own way and I'm doin' it."

"I can't believe you," she hissed. "Sayin' this to me, *today*. Neeta was my girl and we just laid her in the ground."

"*We* didn't do *shit*." Tate leaned toward her to say, "You paraded in, as usual, makin' a big scene and makin' it all about you. Pop, Stell, Wood, and Jonas laid her to rest today. You just showed up and turned it all to shit." He leaned back and drawled sarcastically, "Congratulations, Mom, I would figure that was an impossibility, makin' shit even shittier, but you managed it."

"I loved her!" she snapped, her voice rising.

"If you did, then why'd you let her down when she lost her mom and needed another one? I was young but I remember Neet turnin' to you and you doin' what you do best, turnin' away." Shania's face paled but Tate kept at her. "For that matter, why'd you let *me* down seein' as *you* made it so I never had a mother at all?"

Her voice was barely a whisper when she said, "You know me, Tate. You know I gotta be free."

"Yeah, so the good news is, you can be as free as you want. Rest easy, Mom, we got it covered," Tate retorted.

Shania's eyes slid to me and she accused, "This is about her."

"Damn straight," Tate shot back, then reiterated, "Damn fuckin' straight."

Then he turned away from her and came right at me. He hooked an arm around my neck, turned me and propelled me forward as he prowled to the backyard, through it, and to the backdoor.

Once we were inside, I whispered, "You okay?"

"Fuck no," he replied, not whispering at all.

"Is there something I can do?" I asked and he stopped us in Pop's living room, turned, and looked down at me.

"You're doin' it," he stated.

"I am?" I asked.

He looked over my head and shook his, then he looked back down at me.

"You love me?" he asked.

"Yes," I answered instantly.

"That's it. You're doin' it," he finished.

His arm staying around my neck, he guided us to Jonas.

*   *   *

It was getting late.

I was sitting on Pop's couch, sipping at a bottle of beer, leaning a bit into my dad at my side while my fingers slid through Jonas's hair, his head on my thigh, his body curled into the couch beside me. He was asleep.

"Like your boy," Dad muttered and I looked at him.

"Which one?" I asked and Dad smiled at me.

"Both of 'em," he answered and I smiled back.

I looked across the room to see people pecking at the remainder of the food on the table, Tate and Stella standing among them, slightly removed. Tate had his arm around Stella's shoulders. She was leaning her head on his and what appeared to be the rest of her weight into his side with her arms loose around his waist. Carrie and Mack were standing with them. From my vantage point I could see Mom in the kitchen with Pop. He had his hips to the counter, arm lifted, pulling at a bottle of beer at his lips. Mom was chattering at him while bustling around, moving leftover food from one plate to another, condensing at the same time she tidied. There was music coming from outside and the party was getting rowdy if the noise from the people out there was anything to go by.

"You feeling okay?" I asked Dad, not looking at him.

"Better," he answered. "Got a new diet and exercises I do every day. Food stinks. I'd kill for some fried mushrooms but if I even looked at 'em your mother'd have a conniption. She doesn't even keep shortening in the house. She *steams* everything. Vegetables, fish, swear the woman would steam steak if she could do it," Dad replied.

"You have to stay fit, get your cholesterol level down," I told him.

"Your mom keeps at it, my body'll forget what cholesterol is," Dad muttered.

I grinned and looked down at Jonas's head on my thigh as my fingers slid through his hair.

"Your mom told me about him," Dad said softly. "Tate."

"Yes?" I asked softly back, my fingers moving again through Jonas's hair.

"Said he took care of you when you found out about me bein' sick. Brought you all the way to Indiana, laid it out for that idiot ex of yours," Dad went on.

"Yeah." I was still speaking softly.

"Gotta say, hon, years I been worried. Years, you were with that man. Never trusted him to take care of my girl. Never. Never thought he'd look after you, keep you safe. And, in the end, I was right."

I turned and looked at my father.

"Dad," I whispered.

"Can't tell you, Lauren." His voice got lower and thicker, his eyes slid toward Tate before coming back to me. "Can't say...beside myself knowin' I can quit worryin' about my girl."

"Daddy," I whispered again but said no more because Jonas's body moved, like a flinch, and I knew he wasn't asleep.

Before I could say anything to Jonas, Dad, who obviously hadn't felt Jonas move, kept talking. "He's a good man, I can tell. It's stamped all over him but the best part is the way he looks at you and his boy."

Jonas's body got tighter.

"Dad—" I started.

"He'd die before he let anything hurt you," Dad continued.

"Dad," I said urgently as I felt Jonas's body get even tighter.

Dad talked over me. "You or his boy, he'd lay his life down, wouldn't blink, wouldn't think."

"Dad, Jonas is—" I started. Jonas rolled to his back and Dad's eyes went to Tate.

"That's the kind of man who's good enough for my girl," Dad concluded but I looked down to see Jonas looking up at me.

"What man were you with, Laurie?" Jonas whispered and out of the corner of my eye I saw Dad's head jerk down to look at him but I kept my gaze on Jonas.

"You playing possum, Bub?" I asked on a grin, trying to change the subject.

"What man were you with?" Jonas repeated, not feeling like a subject change.

I slid my hand along his cheek and then rested it at the top of his chest. "I was married before I met your dad," I told him gently.

Jonas lifted up to sitting and twisted his torso toward me and Dad, his eyes on Dad.

"He wasn't as good as Dad?" Jonas asked my father.

"Not by a long shot," Dad answered firmly and Jonas looked at me. Then he grinned, which was when I relaxed.

"Dad's a catch," he remarked.

"Um...yeah." I grinned back.

"Girls think he's hot," Jonas noted.

I looked at Tate then back at his son.

"Yeah." I was still grinning.

Jonas's grin turned mischievous. "Everyone says I look just like him."

I heard Dad chuckle and I swallowed a giggle before nodding. "Yes, baby, you do."

"Means I'm hot too," Jonas stated.

"Well—" I began.

"Girls're already all over me, want me to kiss 'em at recess," Jonas informed me audaciously.

"Do you kiss them?" Dad asked.

"Only the pretty ones," Jonas answered.

Dad laughed right out but my eyes narrowed on Jonas.

"Jonas Jackson, are you telling me you kiss pretty girls at recess?"

"Well, yeah," Jonas answered.

"Bub, you're *ten*," I reminded him.

"So?" he asked.

"You're not supposed to be into girls for at least five more years," I proclaimed.

Jonas's head tilted to the side. "Is that a rule?"

"Yes, I just made it up. It's Lauren's rule for when Jonas can be into girls."

"You can't make up rules, Laurie," Jonas told me.

"I just did," I replied. Jonas looked at Dad and rolled his eyes but I looked at Tate and shouted across the room, "Tate! Jonas is kissing pretty girls at recess!"

Tate's eyes cut to me but Jonas threw himself at me and cupped his hand over my mouth.

"Laurie!" he yelled.

I struggled with his lean, too strong for a ten-year-old kid's body, one arm wrapped around his waist, my other hand at his wrist, trying to pull his hand from my mouth.

I succeeded and yelled to Tate, "Jonas is ten and already breaking girls' hearts!"

"Laurie!" Jonas repeated, sounding mortified and exasperated and I looked from Jonas's father's face, his mouth twitching, to Jonas.

"Well, you are," I said.

"You don't have to shout it across the room!" He was still yelling.

"Your father should know," I informed him. "Seeing as you're moving so fast, you'll probably start going on dates next week and Tate'll have to drive you and I'll have to make more cupcakes, all your women showing up at the house to study with you."

Jonas slouched back and crossed his arms on his chest, telling me, "I'm not goin' on dates. I'm playin' the field."

Dad burst out laughing but I glared and snapped, "Jonas!"

Jonas looked at Dad. "I gotta keep my options open, make sure I get a good one."

I looked at the ceiling. "Lord, deliver me," I implored and looked back at Jonas when he poked me in the ribs.

"Laurie, I'm *ten*." He used my words against me, then grinned cheekily again. "Like I said, gotta keep my options open."

"You're grounded," I announced.

"Why!" Jonas shouted.

I didn't answer, instead I went on, "And you're staying grounded until you're sixteen."

Jonas's head whipped around and he yelled, "Dad! Laurie grounded me until I'm sixteen!"

I looked to Tate to see Mom and Pop had joined Tate, Stella, Mack, and Carrie and they all had eyes to the couch.

"Sure I can talk her outta that, Bub," Tate called back.

Jonas looked at me and grinned smugly.

I glared at Jonas, rolled my eyes, and then muttered, "I need another beer." I looked back at Jonas, lifted my brows, and asked, "Since you're growing up so fast, do you want a beer?"

"Yep," he answered instantly.

"Tough," I replied, caught him by the neck, pulled him to me, and kissed his forehead.

Then I let him go, pushed off the couch, gave Tate a "we're going to talk later" look, which only made him shake his head, still fighting his grin and I headed to the cooler outside.

When I got outside, I saw, through the sea of people, Bubba sitting on top of a picnic table at the bottom end of the yard.

I gave up on the beer, threw my bottle in an overflowing garbage bin and wended my way through bodies. When I got to him, I started to climb up carefully (my skirt was tight and I still had on my pumps), then Bubba's hand came out and grabbed mine, holding firm and steadying me until I sat down next to him, hip to hip and he let my hand go.

He'd looked at me when I arrived and kept looking at me as I sat down but he didn't say a word. I let this go on for a while before I bumped him with my shoulder.

"You okay?" I asked quietly.

Bubba didn't answer so I turned to him.

"Bubba?"

"Miss my cloud," he muttered, then sat back. He lifted a can of Coke to his lips and took a deep slug.

I stared at the Coke, a Coke that was not a beer and it was not a bottle of bourbon, vodka, or gin, then I stared at Bubba.

"You miss your cloud?" I asked.

He leaned into his elbows at his knees and didn't reply.

I leaned into mine but twisted to him.

"Bubba, honey, talk to me," I whispered.

"Motherfucker got Neeta," he whispered back.

I put my hand to his back. "I know."

"Krys was right, Laurie." He was still whispering. "Coulda been anyone. Coulda been her and that would be on me."

"Bubba," I said gently.

His head twisted so he could look at me. "See her man?"

"Sorry?"

His eyes went over my back and he looked into the yard. My eyes followed his and I saw he was looking at Blake, standing apart from the crowd, a mostly empty bottle of bourbon in his hand, his face desolate, his manner removed, his eyes on the people in the backyard like he didn't know who they were, even *what* they were, as if he'd been beamed to another planet to study aliens.

"Blake, her man," Bubba replied, shook his head, looked away, and muttered, "Fuck."

"Honey—"

"He feels it, that fucker, written all over him, and he should," Bubba told me.

"Bubba—"

"Actually thought, long time ago, he'd be good for her. She wasn't any good for Tate, too much shit between them, too much shit. But Blake, he was a good guy and he loved her. No shit there. He was solid, had a good job, had a strong hand with her. Don't know what went wrong, don't care. He fell down and she got raped with a—"

I leaned into him and said quickly, "Bubba, don't."

He looked to me and stated, "Coulda been Krys."

"It wasn't."

"Still could be," he went on like I didn't speak. "Fucker's still out there. And here I am," he threw a hand out, "I'm fuckin' *Blake*. Whatever went wrong along the way, he ain't even a man anymore, proved it true when his woman got murdered and that's me." He shook his head, looking away again. "That's me."

"Honey—"

"Miss my cloud," he whispered and his head dropped.

"She's not dead, Bubba, and neither are you," I told him. He didn't reply and I kept going. "Nothing's happened you can't change."

"Got the check and paperwork two weeks ago, gorgeous," he told his lap. "Signed it. It's done. I'm out. The bar is called Bubba's but I'm out."

"Then get back in," I urged and his head twisted to look at me again.

"What?"

"You aren't Blake," I told him.

"Laurie—"

I jerked my head at his Coke. "Get yourself sorted out and get back in."

"She don't want me," he replied.

"She wanted you once," I reminded him.

"She don't want me now."

"Then remind her of why she wanted you then." I got close to his face. "I don't know him but I know this, I knew it the minute you walked up to the graveside today. You aren't Blake."

"Laurie—"

"You're a good man, Bubba."

"Gorgeous—"

"You're a good friend, Tate said so."

"He did?"

"Yes." I smiled at him. "Shit business partner, he said, but a great friend."

Bubba shook his head and looked away.

"He named his son after you," I whispered and felt Bubba's body stiffen at my side.

He didn't speak and I let the silence go for a while.

Then I kept whispering, "You don't have to sleep by her side to be certain she's safe." My arm slid around his bulk and I gave him a squeeze. "Think about that, Bubba. She might not care, she might be done, but it wouldn't be about what you could get out of it. It would be about keeping her safe. Find a way to do that until they find this guy. Then whatever happens happens. But in the meantime, keep her safe. Yes?"

Bubba didn't answer, just stared at the grass then tipped his head back and took another slug of Coke. I leaned into him for a second then moved away and hopped off the table.

"Getting late," I told him.

"Yeah," he replied.

"See you later?" I asked.

"Sure, Laurie," he answered halfheartedly.

"Bye, honey," I whispered.

"Later," he returned, not looking at me.

I moved away from Bubba, wending my way back through the crowd and feeling eyes on me when I did. My head turned left and I saw Blake staring at me, not studying me like I was a martian, but staring at me with his face tight, his eyes sharp. There was something about it that sent a chill through me but I didn't get to process why when I ran into something solid, something that put two hands to my hips.

"Babe," Tate said when I looked up at him.

"Hey," I replied.

"We gotta go, get Jonas home," he told me and I nodded. "Can't find his jacket," Tate went on.

"I know where it is. I'll run and get it."

He nodded back but his head turned to the right and my eyes followed his.

"Tate," I said gently when I saw he was looking at Blake.

They seemed to be locked in optical combat until I pressed up to his front and my hands curled on his biceps.

"Baby," I whispered and he looked down at me. "We have to go. Jonas."

"Right," he muttered, his hands left my hips and he guided me in front of him toward the door.

To keep it out of the way, I'd taken Jonas's jacket to an upstairs bedroom and I headed straight there, Tate at my heels. We walked up the stairs, down the hall, and I opened the door. I walked right in then stopped dead, Tate coming to a halt behind me, his hand coming to my waist as I stared at Wood who had Maggie pressed against the wall, his hands at her bottom, his tongue obviously in her mouth, one of her arms was tight around his waist, the other hand cupping the back of his head.

Tate made a grunting noise that sounded like a swallowed bark of laughter and my body jerked at the sound at the same time Maggie and Wood separated, their heads swinging toward us.

"Sorry, sorry…um, sorry!" I muttered, rushing to the bed and blathering. "Jonas's jacket. I put it up here to get it out of the way. He was getting hot and you know kids, he just threw it anywhere and I was worried someone would get beer on it or something."

"Ace." Tate cut off my chatter as I pushed aside some purses and other jackets and grabbed Jonas's.

I straightened and looked at them. "I don't know how to clean a jacket like this, so it'd have to go to the dry cleaner," I informed them stupidly. "Not that it would, really, since he doesn't wear suits on a regular basis and he's growing so fast, he'll be out of it in, like, a week, but, you know, it would."

"Ace," Tate repeated, his hand closing around mine and he yanked me toward the door.

"Right," I mumbled, dipping my chin and avoiding Maggie and Wood's eyes as Tate moved us to the door.

"I'll just," Maggie whispered. Tate stopped moving us and my head came up to see her running her hand through her hair, her other smoothing her skirt down at the hip, her cheeks flushed bright pink. "Just…um…" She looked at Wood then Tate and me and finished, "Go check on the kids."

Then she ran, actually *ran* out the door.

Tate and I watched her then Tate and my heads swung to look at Wood.

Wood's eyes were locked on Tate.

"Don't," he warned low.

"Brother, I told you—" Tate started.

Wood cut him off, repeating, "Don't."

"She's a sweet piece," Tate remarked casually but his voice held a tremor of humor and at his words my head jerked back to look up at him.

"Man, like I said, *don't*," Wood growled and I looked back at him.

"Never shoulda let her go," Tate returned.

"I'm tellin' you—" Wood started.

"Wasn't speakin' to you when you jacked that shit up," Tate said, jerking his head toward the door. "Glad I got the chance to say it now."

"Jackson, seriously," Wood bit off.

"She's a sweet piece?" I asked, butting in, and Tate looked down at me and grinned.

"Yeah," he answered.

"A sweet piece?" I repeated.

"Yeah, babe," Tate replied.

"She's the mother of Wood's children!" I snapped.

"She's still a sweet piece," Tate, undaunted by my tone, reiterated.

I yanked my hand out of his and crossed my arms on my chest.

Tate's arm hooked around my neck, he hauled me forward into his body and burst out laughing.

With Jonas's jacket bunched in one hand, I kept my arms crossed and turned my head to look at Wood.

"I'm thinking nothing's funny," I told Wood.

Wood took in my stance as well as Tate and he grinned.

"I wasn't, but I am now," he stated.

"Whatever," I muttered.

Wood walked up to us, put a hand right to my face, his thumb sliding across my cheekbone. Then his hand dropped, he glanced at Tate, shook his head, and walked out.

I kept myself stiff as Tate moved to my side and guided me to the door.

"Let's hope that shit takes," he muttered when we were in the hall.

"What shit?" I asked as we made it to the mouth of the stairs.

"Wood back with Maggie," Tate told me.

"Wood said she was a bitch," I told him.

Tate looked down at me as we descended the stairs. "He would say that, babe. He was tryin' to get in your pants."

"But—"

"He's not gonna say he acted like a dick, which meant she acted like a bitch in return and that shit escalated because they didn't talk about it and work it out and then it got so bad, neither of them could deal so they called it quits."

"What do you mean, acted like a dick?" I asked when we reached the bottom of the stairs.

Tate stopped me and explained, "He was workin' through some shit, primarily him killin' my dad and his sister bein' a pain in the ass. Maggie tried to help with the first, had trouble puttin' up with the last, seein' as she didn't like Neet around her kids. Neither of them handled it well and they split. It was stupid. She's a good woman, great ass, sweet as hell, and she loved him."

I looked beyond him, searched the room, couldn't find Maggie or Wood and looked back at Tate.

"She's very pretty," I noted.

"She is," he agreed.

"Did he love her?" I asked.

"Oh yeah," he answered.

"Do you think—?"

"He gets his head outta his ass, yeah."

I sighed then informed him, "I sat with Bubba outside for a while. He misses Krys."

"He would. She's a good woman too. He had it all and lost it by bein' a dick, same as Wood."

"Do you think—?" I repeated and Tate cut me off again, shaking his head.

"Crapshoot, Ace. Krystal can hold a grudge."

I nodded, then started to move around him but he caught me with an arm along my belly and pulled me back in front of him, his arm wrapping around my waist.

"You pissed?" he asked, his eyes studying me closely.

"No," I answered and his head tipped to the side.

"You're not?"

"I was . . . *ish*. I'm over it," I informed him and he grinned.

"That easy?" he asked and I shrugged.

"You are who you are, Tate, and part of who you are is a guy who'd call a woman a sweet piece. Life's too short to get pissed about stupid shit like that. And anyway, you're right. I mean, I'm not a guy but even I can see Maggie's a sweet piece."

His body shook with the force of his low laughter and I knew he would have burst out with it if we weren't at Neeta's postfuneral bash.

I slid my arms around his waist as he burned out his humor.

"You seem better," I whispered when he was done.

"She's in the ground," he whispered back.

I nodded. "That gives you peace."

He shook his head. "What it does, watchin' her search all her life, desperate for somethin' she never found, is makes me feel *she's* at peace."

I melted deeper into him, muttering, "Right."

His arms gave me a squeeze. "Gotta get my boy home."

"Right," I repeated.

He let me go. We went to Jonas, rounded up my family. Stella and Pop followed us out to the Explorer (Wood and Maggie both had disappeared) and we gave out long hugs. Jonas, Tate, and I climbed into the SUV and Mom, Dad, Carrie, and Mack climbed into their rental.

They went to Ned and Betty's hotel.

Tate and Jonas and I went home.

*   *   *

Amber called while we were in the SUV on the way home; Ned and Betty phoning five minutes after we walked in. I hadn't even taken my shoes off.

I was barely off the phone when Sunny and Shambles came by. They didn't know Neeta so they didn't go to the funeral but they wanted to check we were okay. Jonas talked them into staying for a cupcake. Shambles was Shambles, seeming a little less buoyant but mostly his regular self. Sunny was timid around Tate, avoiding his eyes and getting too close to his body. Clearly big, masculine men frightened her and Tate read this instantly, talking in a softer voice and making it easy to avoid him by giving her a good deal of space.

They took off and weren't gone a minute when Wendy phoned on her break at Bubba's and talked the whole way through it. When she was off break, she handed the phone to Twyla, who I was surprised to discover could jabber on the phone like a total girl and she only handed the phone off to Jim-Billy when I informed her of that fact. Jim-Billy had left the funeral bash earlier to go to Bubba's. Since Neeta, I'd noticed that Jim-Billy drank less and stayed a lot more alert. He also walked the waitresses to their cars after shift and had taken to following Amber, Krystal, or Jonelle home, even if it was three thirty in the morning.

By the time I got off the phone with Jim-Billy, Tate had long since taken Jonas downstairs to watch TV with him in his bed. I was still in my funeral black and I decided it was time to take off the black at the same time I decided I might never wear black again.

I was in the closet, having taken off my black blouse and thrown it in the direction of my wicker hamper when Tate came in. I was wearing nothing but my skirt, a lacy black demibra, and the black, lace-topped thigh-highs.

"Hey," I said softly and pulled down the zip at the back of my skirt then bent to shimmy out of it. I stepped clear, twisted my torso, and tossed it toward the hamper.

My hands were at one of my thigh-highs when Tate's finger wrapped around one of my wrists and I heard him mutter, "Unh-unh."

My head came up so I could look at him and I saw he had his suit pants on but he'd taken off his shirt.

"Sorry?" I asked.

His hand slid to fold around mine and then he tugged it, and me, out of the closet.

"Tate—"

He flipped off the switch in the closet and headed to the bed.

"Honey, Jonas—"

"He's out," Tate said, sat on the bed, his hands went to my hips and he pulled me toward him in a way I had no choice but to straddle him so I did.

"He's not sleeping too well," I reminded Tate as my bottom came to rest on his thighs and my hands went to rest on his shoulders.

"He comes up, I'll hear him," Tate muttered and his hands didn't rest, they slid up the sides of my back.

I looked down at his face, which I couldn't really see since he was looking at my breasts in my bra, watching his hands move forward along my bra line and cup them.

One could say that our sex life was regular, healthy, and active but since Neeta died Tate gave new meaning to regular, healthy, and active. If we weren't looking after Jonas or I wasn't working, Tate had me as close as he could get me, literally.

I didn't know if he was proving to himself I was alive, he was alive, or he was determined to suck as much out of life in general as he could get but I didn't question it or him. If that was what he needed, which it obviously was, that was what I'd give to him.

Therefore, I whispered, "Okay," but I did it beginning to get worried about his state of mind. He'd stayed strong for Jonas and he seemed okay but this behavior concerned me. I didn't mind the intimacy. I was just troubled at his driving need for it.

His hands moved back, pushed in so my back arched and his lips trailed the lace at the cup of my bra.

One of my hands slid into his hair while the other one glided down his neck.

"Mom and Dad are staying a week," I told him.

"Yeah," he said against my skin, his lips moving between my cleavage, then mounting the swell of my other breast.

"Carrie and Mack have to leave Sunday," I went on.

"Yeah," Tate repeated, one hand moving down my back so his fingers could trail the lace that rode high on the cheek of my bottom, the other hand slid forward, his thumb under his lips gliding across my nipple.

This felt good so I sucked in breath and fidgeted in his lap.

"Tate, baby, you okay?" I whispered.

"Yeah," he said yet again, his thumb catching the lace at my breast and pulling it down.

"Baby—" I started and stopped, my breath hitching when he drew my nipple in deep. My hips rolled against his lap and my head fell back.

His mouth detached from my nipple and traced up my chest, his hand at my bottom drifting up to glide into my hair and pull my head down so he could kiss me, wet, slow and sweet, while the pad of his thumb tormented my hard nipple.

When his mouth detached from mine, my lips moved along his cheek to his ear. I tried to pull it together and asked softly, "What's on your mind?"

"Tryin' to figure out how to fuck you while you're wearin' these panties," he answered.

I was pretty certain that was what was actually on his mind but still, my head came up, both my hands went to his jaws and I whispered, "Baby, talk to me."

His eyes looked into mine and his hand in my hair pulled me down to touch his lips to mine. Then he let me move away half an inch before he said, "Laurie, I'm good."

"I'm worried about you." I was still whispering.

"Baby, I'm good," he repeated.

"You've changed," I told him and quickly went on. "It isn't a bad change. I'm just…concerned."

"Yeah, babe, I've changed," he surprisingly agreed.

I dropped my forehead to his. "Talk to me about it."

He sighed and fell to his back. I followed him down, planting my forearms in his chest, my hands flattening there as his hands cupped my behind.

His eyes caught mine and he announced, "I'm over it."

My head tipped to the side. "Sorry?"

"I'm over it," he repeated.

"But—"

"This sucks, all of it. But I was way over her when I started it with you. I don't like Pop, Stell, Wood, and definitely Jonas bein' on their path but, Ace, I ain't suffering."

"But earlier—"

"Today was shit, babe, and I can't say it doesn't hit me, that ugly end to her livin' an ugly life but, outside of keepin' an eye on Jonas and my mom actin' whacked, today, mostly I was struggling with the fact that I'm *not* suffering."

One of my hands slid up to curl around his neck and I whispered, "But Tate, you...with me...we—"

"Life hands you lessons, Ace. This one taught me to enjoy what I got. My dad died and I didn't learn shit from that at the time, didn't learn until it was almost too late. This time, Neet dyin', 'specially like that, I learned quick." His hand slid up my spine and into my hair. "I'm happy, Laurie. This is good, what we got, and I'm gonna fuckin' enjoy it."

"So you don't want me close, um...sex close to be, uh...*super* close to prove to yourself that I'm here and I'm okay?"

His brows knitted while I spoke and when I was done he asked, "Sex close?

"We're having a lot of sex, Captain."

"We have a lot of sex all the time, Ace."

"You said, the day she died, you needed me and you wanted me close," I reminded him.

"It was fresh then," he told me.

I tipped my head to the side. "So you're okay now?"

"Yeah."

"You're not, um...dealing with death in a macho-man, badass, alpha-male kind of way?"

He pressed his lips together, his expression softening and then he said, "No."

"You're sure?" I pushed.

"Ace, I'm okay."

"Yeah?"

He tipped his chin up and then he rolled me to my back, getting on top and he shoved his face in my neck.

That's when I heard him laughing.

"Tate?"

"Give me a sec, Laurie," he rumbled into my neck, still laughing.

I lay under him for a while, hearing and feeling his laughter. Then I muttered, "I can't believe you're laughing."

His head came up, his mouth still curved into a smile, he looked at me and said, "Dealing with death in a macho-man, badass, alpha-male kind of way?"

"Well I don't know!" I snapped. "I was worried!"

His head dipped, his nose sliding along mine and he whispered, "Yeah." Then he pulled back and looked at me. "You good?"

"I guess so," I answered snippily.

"Can I fuck you now or you wanna process somethin' else?" he teased.

"I suppose we can have sex but, I'll warn you, I like these panties so don't tear them or anything in your quest to fuck me while wearing them."

"I tear 'em, I'll buy you new ones," he said, his mouth coming toward mine.

"Tate—" I started when his lips hit mine.

"Shut it, Laurie," he growled.

"Oh all right," I mumbled but I didn't shut it since he kissed me, with tongue, so I couldn't.

Then he fucked me and Tate could do just about anything for me, but he couldn't figure out how to fuck me wearing the panties.

But he did manage to do it without tearing them when he whipped them off.

CHAPTER TWENTY-SIX

Birthday

AFTER MY SHIFT at the bar, I went to the office, opened it with my new key, stepped inside, turned on the light, walked to the couch and sat down. Then I pulled my cell phone out of my jeans.

I scrolled down my contacts, hit the button, put the phone to my ear, and listened to it ring.

"Derriford." I heard my college boyfriend answer.

"Hey, Matt," I said softly.

"Laurie?" Matt asked.

"Yeah," I answered.

"Shit, Laurie, been callin' all day. Your number was disconnected, your cell, at home and they said you quit work over a year ago. I've been fuckin' worried sick. What's up?"

"I've got a new phone," I told him. "Moved from Phoenix, living in Colorado now."

"Brad moved you guys from Phoenix?" His voice was incredulous. He knew Brad liked his golf. "What? He get a better job?"

I had not shared anything with Matt during our birthday calls, not on my last birthday, when I was in the throes of a postdivorce wander, his birthday, or the ones the year before when I knew in my soul it was going bad. My calls with Matt on our birthdays were about laughing and reminiscing about good times, not getting into anything heavy.

That day was my birthday and the time had come to tell him.

So I did. I told him everything.

When I was done, he was silent.

"Matt?" I called.

"I'm here," he said quietly.

I misread his quiet mood. "I'm okay, honey. I'm . . . well," I smiled to myself, "I'm really good."

"Yeah, I can hear," he replied but he didn't sound happy for me.

"Are *you* okay?" I asked.

"Left Ellen," he announced. I pulled in a breath and he went on, "'Bout a year ago, now."

This shocked me. I thought he and Ellen were solid.

"Matt," I whispered, "what hap—?"

He cut me off. "Shoulda called me, Laurie."

"What?"

"Shoulda called me."

"Why?"

"Wished you'd've called me," he stated softly.

It was my turn to go quiet because I knew what he was saying.

Then I whispered, "Matt."

No answer.

Then, "His name's Tate?"

I swallowed, then nodded even though he couldn't see me. "Yes, Tate Jackson."

"And he's a bounty hunter?"

"Yeah."

Nothing.

I waited.

Then, "Jesus, Laurie, only you could go from a pansy-assed dick-head to a badass bounty hunter in the space of a year."

He was teasing me and I knew it was going to be okay. So, he'd just rocked my world, letting on he'd been carrying a torch for me for decades and making me feel a hint of regret that I hadn't told him about Brad because he'd been a great boyfriend and I knew he was a good man. A year ago, I wouldn't have minded exploring that.

Now, no way in hell.

"So," I returned, "you knew I had an inner biker babe all these years?"

"Biker babe?"

"Tate's a Harley man," I explained.

"Goody Two-shoes Lauren Grahame on the back of a bike," he hooted. "Fuck me."

"Tate's bike is hot," I retorted.

"Honey," he replied, a thread of amusement in his voice.

"He part owns a biker bar. I'm a waitress there. I wear high heels, tight jeans, and Harley shirts and break up fights, when I'm not running checks on the skips he's tracking down. I'm the woman behind the info, Matt. He's got bounty hunter databases on his computer. He needs it, I run the checks and feed him the data. You should be nice to me, I can find out anything about you."

"Then I better stay on your good side."

"You got that right."

We slid into our comfortable banter after that, laughing and reminiscing and only going serious when he told me about Ellen, who he spent the last three years falling out of love with because she sounded kind of like a nagging bitch. Suffice it to say, Matt definitely couldn't drink grape Kool-Aid on his couch because Ellen would have a conniption and Matt was not down with that, at least not fifteen years of it with Ellen growing more and more uptight rather than less and less.

"Glad to hear you sounding so happy, honey," Matt said quietly when I told him I had to go home and make dinner for Jonas.

"I'm glad to be so happy, honey," I said quietly back, then whispered, "Hope you find this, Matt."

"Had it, Laurie, lost it," Matt replied, also whispering.

Cut. Right to the quick.

"Matt—"

He cut me off, "Next year, Lauren."

"Next year."

"Later."

"Bye."

I hit the button to turn off my phone and stared at it. Then I sighed and pushed up from the couch to get my purse and head home.

*　　*　　*

Sitting beside Jim-Billy in his beat-up truck I watched the dark landscape slide by.

It was early November and the May–December Murderer still hadn't been found. He also had not committed another act of violence since Neeta.

Neeta had been in the ground awhile and Jonas was beginning to move on from those frequent moments where his eyes would go lost or pained and I knew his thoughts had grown dark. They were still there, they'd probably always be there, but they were less frequent.

This was why I hadn't told him, Tate, or anyone about my birthday. Christmas was around the corner and we were going to Indiana for two weeks to celebrate it. That was soon enough for fun and laughter. If the pond froze, Jonas could skate on it. My mother would spoil him rotten and we'd all probably come back needing a new wardrobe because we'd gained so much weight from her cooking.

But right now, things didn't need to be about me. They needed to be about Jonas.

Tate had even gone off that morning to hunt down a bad guy. It sucked that he wouldn't be around for my birthday, even if he didn't know it *was* my birthday. But, though we both kept close watch over Jonas, our lives were settling and I noticed he liked to work. He hadn't been able to do it for a while without a lot of stuff hanging over his head but with Jonas sorted, me in his house, the bar ticking over well, and Neeta not making his life a misery (in the usual ways), he was able to do his job with more focus and I realized he liked doing it. He either got off on the hunt or he got off on making the world a little safer, or both. Therefore, I didn't make excuses to try and keep him home when he said he had to go that morning. He arranged for Pop to take me to work and Jim-Billy to bring me home and I didn't breathe a word.

I thought, when the dust had settled after Neeta's funeral, that Tate would again go after Tonia and Neeta's murderer.

He didn't.

I asked him about this and he explained simply, "Feds got their job, cops got theirs. Mine is to keep my family safe."

There was nothing to say to that so I didn't say anything. That didn't mean I didn't *do* anything and what I did was kiss him, hard and long.

I noticed Jim-Billy's truck stop and I saw we were in Tate's drive. I also saw Stella's car in the drive, which wasn't a surprise. She was tasked with bringing Jonas home after my shift. I'd called and told her I'd be a little late due to my phone call to Matt though I didn't tell her about my phone call to Matt. Tate and I had settled but Tate was a badass alpha male. Brad wasn't concerned in the slightest that I gabbed and laughed with my ex-boyfriend for an hour on my birthday. Tate, I didn't think, would like that. And Stella, I'd learned, had a big mouth.

I turned to Jim-Billy. "Want to come in for dinner? I'm making roast chicken and mashed potatoes."

Jim-Billy grinned at me. "Don't mind if I do."

I grinned back and jumped down from the truck. Jim-Billy followed me up the steps to the deck, along the deck, and through the sliding glass door. The lights were off and the television wasn't on, which surprised me. If he wasn't doing his homework or playing video games in his room, Jonas was always camped out in front of the television. And with Stella there, and Jonas being a polite kid who liked company, I thought for sure he'd be camped out in front of the television.

I flipped on the lights, turned right, and froze.

Then my mouth dropped open.

The battered countertops were gone. Fabulous, gleaming granite ones were in their place (except the butcher block island, that was just the same). The old fridge, stove, and dishwasher were also gone. Where they once stood, there was a brand-new, glossy black fridge, a matching dishwasher, and a beautiful stainless-steel restaurant quality stove. Above the stove, the old microwave had been pulled out and a fancy new one matching the stove was there.

It looked fantastic.

I just *knew* Tate's kitchen could be fabulous!

There was a beautiful, old-fashioned, pink glass cake stand sitting on the island, the edges of its top polka dots of glass. On the stand was a delicious-looking cake with generous swirls of creamy chocolate frosting and it was topped with an abundance of pink candles. A huge bouquet of balloons in every color of the rainbow festooned the middle of the island, their multicolored strings held down under one of my heavy stoneware bowls.

"Happy birthday, Laurie!" I heard Jonas shout and my body jolted as I watched him run from the mudroom followed in a stream by Wendy, Tyler, Shambles, Sunny, Ned, Betty, Pop, Holly, Twyla, Amber, Krystal, Bubba, Dominic, Nadine, Steg, Wings, Stoney, Stella, Wood, and, bringing up the rear, Tate.

Jonas's body hit me, his arms going around me for a tight hug as I went back on a foot on impact.

His hug was fast and he let go, jumping back a step and announcing, "Dad and Uncle Wood spent all day putting in the counters. He ordered them *forever ago*! The guys who brought the fridge and stuff from the store just left, like, a second before you and Jim-Billy drove up. It was good you were late because Dad was *freaking out*! Totally pi…I mean mad as all get out because he didn't think they'd be done before you got home. Uncle Wood had to hide Dad's guns!"

I looked from Jonas's smiling face to his father who was standing at the end of the counter, his hip to it, his arms crossed on his chest, his eyes on me.

Then I looked into the kitchen at the new countertops, the new appliances, the cake, the balloons, and, most of all, my friends.

Then I burst out crying.

These were not delicate, quiet, ladylike tears. No. They were loud, out-of-control, eyes- and nose-streaming sobs.

I was in Tate's arms in an instant and I heard through my bawling a muttered, "Jesus, Ace."

I yanked back, succeeding in only moving my head and shoulders because his arms were tight. I focused on Tate through the wetness in my eyes and I yelled, "You're supposed to be after a fugitive from justice!"

"I lied, babe," Tate replied. "There was no skip."

"You *lied* to me?" I screeched hysterically because I was hysterically happy and I had absolutely no clue how to deal with that.

"Couldn't tell you I couldn't take you to work because I had to go pick up countertops, Ace, that would spoil the surprise," Tate answered.

My head jerked and I asked, "How did you know it was my birthday? You weren't supposed to know it was my birthday."

"It's on your job application, Laurie," Krys called and I heard her but I watched Tate's face dip close at the same time it got serious.

"Yeah, and we're gonna talk about that," he murmured and I had the distinct feeling he wasn't too hot on me keeping my birthday from him.

"I thought—" I started.

"I know what you thought," he cut me off, "and we're gonna talk about that."

I swallowed back tears, wiped my face, and sniffed loudly.

Then I changed the subject. "Did you make the cake?"

Tate grinned. "Fuck no. Shambles made it."

"Moist Factor Five Hundred, babeeeee!" Shambles shouted from somewhere behind Tate.

I giggled softly.

Then I whispered to Tate, "You bought me a new stove."

"Yeah," he whispered back.

"And a new fridge."

"Yeah."

I moved to fit myself to his front and wrap my arms around him, tipping my head back further to hold his eyes.

"And a new dishwasher," I continued.

"Yeah, babe."

"That's a lot of appliances, Tate."

"Yeah," he agreed.

"And a lot of cake," I observed because I knew from just glancing at them that the appliances and countertops were top of the line and they had to cost a whack.

"No shit," he replied.

I smiled at him and kept whispering, "I think you like me."

"I like how you cook, probably like it better, now you got better tools to do the job."

My smile got bigger. "You like more than how I cook."

His arms gave me a squeeze and he whispered, "Yeah."

I moved my arms from around his back, wound them around his neck and got up on my toes to touch my mouth to his. Then my lips went to his ear.

"Do you love me?"

His lips at my ear, he answered, "Oh yeah."

I smiled and stuffed my face in his neck.

"Sick!" Jonas shouted. "Jeez, can we have cake or what?"

"I'll go fire up the grill," I heard Pop say as I shifted back and Tate's arms around me became only one as he tucked me into his side and turned us to face our audience. "Stell, sweetheart, bring out the chops," Pop finished.

"You got it, Kyle," Stella replied, heading to the fridge.

"Chops first, Bub, then cake," Tate told Jonas.

"Tyler and me are giving you a week of boot camps, free of charge!" Wendy called.

"Great," I muttered, uncertain if a week's worth of physical torture was a good birthday present but I still muttered this smiling at them.

Sunny came forward, holding out a card while saying, "Free coffee for your birthday month."

"Oh Sunny, I couldn't," I told her, taking the card.

"All November, Petal." Shambles walked up and slid an arm around Sunny's chest from behind, his grin pinned to me, "on the house."

"Thanks," I whispered.

Krystal came forward with a package wrapped in birthday wrap but no ribbon or bow.

She handed it to me and stated, "It's a Harley tee and it's sweet. They only had that one left in our size. You don't like it, give it back. I want it."

I didn't think Krystal was the same size as me and I figured she bought her own size so I'd have to give the T-shirt back. I laughed softly and shook my head while she avoided my eyes, turned and also avoided Bubba on her way back into the kitchen.

Tate let me go and drifted away as others came forward with cards and gifts. A huge bouquet of flowers from Holly. A smokin' hot biker babe belt that Stoney had noticed me checking out at his store. A gift certificate for a mani and pedi from Dominic. A white ribbed tank with a black, silver, gray, and orange design of skulls, hearts and flowers around the words "Carnal, Colorado, Harley Heaven" from Amber and Jonelle. Two gift certificates for the home store, one from Ned and Betty, one from Pop, Stella, and Wood. A bottle of very good vodka from Steg, Wings, and Nadine. A neck choker I would never have considered buying for myself (but it was hot and I couldn't wait to wear it) made out of a thin strip of black leather with silver rivets on it from Bubba.

And a can of Mace with a mumbled, "Can't be too careful," from Twyla.

Once I'd opened all my gifts, read my cards and set them on their sides on the counter that separated the kitchen from the living room, everyone had a beer and Stella, Krys, Wendy, and Amber had put out bowls of chips, macaroni, potato salad, and fluffy dinner rolls, Tate returned to me.

And he did it carrying a martini, with olive, in a fantastic, long-stemmed, elegant martini glass.

When I took the martini all the while my eyes never leaving his, he murmured, "Wanda says happy birthday."

Tate had braved Wanda and Deluxe Home Store for me.

I felt tears sting my eyes.

"Tate," I breathed.

His hand slid along my waist as he muttered, "Shit, babe, are you gonna cry again?"

"No," I lied as a tear ran down my cheek.

Tate watched it fall then his free hand lifted and he used his thumb to swipe it away. He left his hand cupping my cheek when he was done and I'd gotten control of myself.

Then I whispered, "Thank you, baby."

His face got soft, tender and his head dropped so he could run his nose along mine.

He moved an inch away, his eyes locked on mine and he whispered back, "You're welcome, Ace."

My parents were good at giving birthdays. My mom was a birthday freak and she made every one more special than the last.

But I stood in my new-ish kitchen, looking into Tatum Jackson's brown, tawny-flecked eyes, and I loved my mom and all the hard work she'd put into giving me great birthdays...but Tate had given me the best.

And it wasn't over yet.

*   *   *

I returned to the house after waving good-bye to Bubba, Wendy, Tyler, and Amber, the last of the lot to go.

Jonas had left earlier with Pop. He was spending the night with him. I suspected this was because Tate had another birthday treat for me, one I was *seriously* looking forward to because I'd had more than one martini and I was *seriously* drunk.

I slid the sliding glass door shut and cooed nonsensically at Buster who was weaving around my ankles as I weaved my way toward Tate who was standing at the debris-filled, brand-new, shit-hot kitchen counter, something in his hand, his neck bent to look at it.

I sidled up to him and then plastered myself against his side.

His neck twisted to look down at me and I whispered what I hoped was a suggestive, "everyone's gone now, we can have wild, crazy, biker on biker babe sex," "Hey."

"Who's Matt Derriford?"

I blinked drunkenly.

"What?"

He lifted my phone, pointed at me, and I saw my call history: Mom and Dad and Carrie were on it but at the top was Matt's name.

"Um…" I muttered, trying to think fast, however I was inebriated so thinking fast was an impossibility.

"College boyfriend?" Tate surmised.

"Um…," I muttered again, trying to read his face, however I was inebriated so reading his face was an impossibility considering it was carefully blank.

Tate looked back down at my phone. "When'd you talk to him?"

"Um…," I repeated. "At the bar, after my shift."

Tate looked back at me. "Tryin' to hide it, Ace?"

I bit my lip as my mind screamed, *Yes!* considering he didn't seem too happy. Hiding it was a moral imperative and I decided next year to do a heck of a lot better with that.

I didn't answer and Tate put my phone on the counter and turned into my arms. His hands came up and settled where my neck met my shoulders.

"You drunk?" he asked.

"Yes." I thought it safe to answer.

"How drunk?" he asked.

"Very drunk?" I answered with a question even though it should have been said firmly as I was, indeed, *very* drunk.

"Too drunk to hold on, I take you for a ride?"

My belly fluttered at the thought of being on the back of his bike but my eyes slid to the new microwave over the new stove and then back to him.

"Tate, it's nearly one in the morning."

"Too drunk to hold on, Ace," Tate repeated.

"I'm never too drunk to hold on," I replied.

"Get your jacket," he ordered.

I stared at him and I couldn't decide if he was pissed or if he was something else. Since he loved me and he loved me lots and he'd proved that over and over again, most recently with a bunch of expensive, brand-spanking-new stuff in the kitchen, I figured I was safe even if he was pissed about my call to Matt.

I got my jacket and he led me out to the garage, threw a leg over his bike, backed it out and I got on behind him.

Then we rode. It was cold, the wind whipped my face and hair and bit through my jeans.

And I didn't care.

Because I had Tate's back tight to my front, my arms wrapped around his belly, and my cheek to his shoulder. I was drunk on martinis he'd made me and I'd drunk them in delicate glasses he'd bought me. And my mind was free, clear and free and I was, for the first time in my life, deliriously happy. Content, settled, safe, and happy with my family of three, me, Jonas, and Tate.

It was late and it was cold but Tate and I rode for a long time. Finally, he stopped at a ridge, Carnal spread out before us, its lights blinking in the utter darkness of the hills and mountains surrounding it, covered in a blanket of midnight blue that was the sky.

Tate thrust down the stand, turned off the bike, and I hopped off the back, Tate coming off after me. I walked to the edge of the ridge and stopped. He moved in behind me and circled me with his arms, one at my chest, one at my ribs.

"Next year, babe, you call him when I'm there," he said in my ear.

My mind had been filled with nothing during the ride. Tate's mind had been filled with Matt.

"Okay," I whispered. "But, Tate, it isn't a big deal," I assured him, even though this year it was. I didn't share that. "We've been doing it for—"

His arms gave me a squeeze and I shut up. "You do it when I'm there."

"You have nothing to worry about," I told him.

"I know," he replied.

"So why—?"

"Don't want you hidin' anything from me."

"It wasn't like that."

He was done with this topic, I knew that when he muttered, "Simple request, Ace."

I was beginning to realize that, although some of the ways of a badass, biker, bounty hunting, alpha male would become clear to me, others would forever remain a mystery.

My hands came up and my fingers curled around his forearm at my chest. "Okay, Captain. Next year, I'll talk to Matt when you're there."

His arm at my chest tightened and he kept muttering when he said, "Seal the deal."

I blinked at the vista.

"What?"

His arm around my ribs stole away. Then his hand came back, prying my left one from his forearm at my chest. I felt something cold at my ring finger and Tate slid its coldness to rest at the base.

"Seal the deal," he repeated, his hand curling mine back on his arm and his lips went to my neck to give me a kiss.

That neck was bent and I was staring at a diamond glittering dimly in the night.

I simply stared at it, mind blank, stomach hollow, heart stopped as Tate kept talking.

"Seal the deal," he said yet again. "You talk to him next year, another ring's gonna be sittin' at the base of that one."

I felt my throat get tight.

Tate went on, "We'll get married in April, anniversary we met."

I swallowed and couldn't tear my eyes from the ring.

Tate continued, "You want a big thing, we can do that, but, babe, I'd prefer it small."

I stood statue-still, fingers frozen clutching his arm, eyes still locked on the ring.

Tate carried on, "Same people there as tonight, 'cept your family too."

I finally pulled my eyes from the ring and looked at the lights of Carnal but I still didn't speak.

This went on for a while and Tate's arms, now both wrapped around me again, gave me a tight squeeze.

"Laurie?" he called.

"You spent thousands of dollars on me for my birthday," I said, my voice rough, abrasive, sounding weird.

His arms squeezed me tight again but they stayed tight this time.

"Yeah, babe, and I get why you didn't want to make a big thing about it but that shit's whacked. That isn't a lesson to Jonas. The lesson he needs to learn is life goes on and we're lucky enough to be livin' it so we should do it, as much as we can, while we got the chance."

It was like he didn't speak.

"You spent thousands of dollars on me for my birthday," I reiterated.

He sighed then replied, "Overhead's reduced, Ace, shit's not tight. It ain't even comfortable. We're good, more than good."

"Martinis and top-of-the-line appliances," I whispered.

I felt Tate's body shift into hardness when he muttered, "Somethin' like that."

I stared at Carnal and Tate's arms remained around me, his body solid behind me.

"Lauren," he called again but I didn't answer. I stared at Carnal, a Nowheresville town that looked magical after midnight. "Shit, baby, give me something," Tate growled in my ear.

"Brad never remembered my birthday," I told him.

Tate made a move as if to shift me, turn me toward him, but my fingers curled deeper into his arm and he stilled.

"When he asked me to marry him, the first thing I felt was fear," I went on.

"Ace—"

"Fear because I wanted him and I knew, eventually, I'd make it so he didn't want me."

"Lauren—"

"And I did," I continued.

"Christ almighty, Laurie, I thought we were past—"

"Not once, not once in all the years I was with him did I feel happy."

Tate was silent.

"Not even a little," I said.

Tate remained silent and so did I and we both stayed this way for a long time.

Finally, Tate asked, "You happy now, baby?"

"Yes," I answered instantly and felt his face in my neck. "A small wedding," I whispered. "Maybe Ned and Betty will let us have a pool party after."

His head lifted and his voice was a thick growl when he said, "Sounds good."

"You fucked up, Captain," I told him and his arms got even tighter.

"Come again?"

"I'm not drunk anymore. You could have had Drunk Lauren Sex."

I felt his body moving behind me and I knew it was with laughter.

"I was in the mood to attack," I informed him. "You could definitely have had it dirty. You could have had anything you wanted."

"I don't get that now?" he asked, his voice still thick and now rumbly but with humor.

"Oh yeah, you still get it," I started to turn. His arms loosened, I faced him and mine went around his neck as I pressed deep into him. "But it's my birthday and I'm not drunk anymore so now you have to do all the work."

His mouth came to mine and he muttered, "I'm up for that."

I pressed my lips to his, opened my mouth and slid my tongue inside. Tate's head slanted and his hand sifted into my hair, tilting mine the other way as he took the kiss far deeper and made it much, much better.

When his lips broke from mine, he whispered, "Happy birthday, baby."

To which, I whispered back, "Love you, Tate."

His neck bent, his lips brushed mine and then slid to my ear, where he kept whispering. "Love you too, babe."

I melted completely into my old man, thinking how could I ever have not wanted him to call me babe?

CHAPTER TWENTY-SEVEN

December

THE GARAGE DOOR was going up, Tate was turning the key in the ignition and I was strapping in when I remembered to ask Jonas, "Did you get the gift for your teacher?"

"Where was that again?" Jonas asked from the backseat.

I twisted to look at him. "On the kitchen island."

His eyes hit mine and he muttered, "Whoops."

"Go get it, Bub," Tate said from behind the wheel.

I twisted forward as I heard Jonas unbuckle his seatbelt, open his door, and jump from the SUV. As he ran in the front of the truck, I remembered something else, unbuckled my own seatbelt, leaned clean across Tate, hit his electric window opener and shouted as the window rolled down, "Did you get your secret Santa gift?" right before Jonas hit the door to the mudroom.

"It's in my backpack," he yelled back.

"And the cookies for your class party?" I bellowed.

Jonas was inside and his disembodied voice could be heard hollering back, "Backpack!"

I closed the window and sat back. I'd buckled my seatbelt again when I felt eyes on me and I looked at Tate to see he was staring at me, a strange look on his face.

"What?" I asked.

"Christ almighty, Ace, you're like the Christmas Beast."

My eyes narrowed, Tate watched them and his lips twitched so they narrowed further.

The Christmas Beast, easy for him to say.

He didn't buy Christmas cards. Write and festively design a witty Christmas letter with pictures, which I sent to all my old friends in Phoenix because any picture with Tate in it, and I included *loads* of them, would make them all green-eyed with jealousy. Print out dozens of letters. Sign the cards. Address them and send them.

He didn't buy presents for everyone we knew, wrap them and deliver them, packing up the ones to send to Indiana because, with baggage restrictions, we couldn't carry them with us. This meant I had to memorize the post office's schedule and rush around so I was sure the packages were away on time.

He didn't bake twelve dozen Christmas cookies to sell at the Junior Football League's table at the Christmas Fair in Carnal in an effort to help the moms raise a bunch of money because the boys needed new jerseys and equipment for the next season. *He* also didn't man that booth for five hours in the Colorado mountain cold.

He didn't organize, put together party trays, coordinate the staff secret Santa gift exchange and throw the Christmas party at Bubba's. This was for staff, regulars, and whoever was around. It included a big bowl of spiked eggnog, another big bowl of spiked, spiced Christmas punch on the bar, with trays of cheeses, cold cuts, veggies, varied Christmas treats and bowls of chips in the office for the staff (as well as Jim-Billy, Nadine, Steg, Wings, Stoney, and select other regulars) to munch on through shift. *He* also didn't decorate Bubba's. Me, Wendy, Jim-Billy, Amber, and Krys did.

Further, *he* didn't have many Christmas decorations at his house but even so, *he* didn't run around Carnal, Chantelle, Gnaw Bone, and the mall finding decorations, lights, Christmas cookie jars (for the personal cookies I made us), Christmas dishtowels and bathroom hand towels (because even bathrooms needed Christmas cheer). Okay, so he set up the tree and he and Jonas did a really good job on the outside lights and they both helped decorate the tree, but the rest of the house was *all me*. We were going to Indiana for Christmas, leaving the next day, but that didn't mean we didn't need a little bit of Christmas at home on the lead up to it.

He also didn't pack for the three of us to be away for two weeks, which I'd already done, mainly because there was a lot to do between now and leaving and I didn't want to pack in a rush but also because I was excited to go home for Christmas.

And lastly, *he* wasn't helping to plan the wedding, which I'd already started doing. Sure, it was a small wedding but it was still *a wedding,* which required *planning* and a lot of it.

He went after a skip and was gone for two weeks. Sure, that skip was a high bond and the payoff was mammoth. So mammoth Tate didn't really have to work for months if he didn't want to. And it meant I could double the flower and catering budgets for the wedding, which Holly, who was doing our flowers, and Shambles, who was doing the catering, were ecstatic about. But still!

"The Christmas Beast?" I asked on a warning whisper.

"Yeah, babe, seriously, half the shit you been doin' you don't need to do," Tate answered.

I felt pressure in my head indicating it was about to explode.

"I'm sorry?" I was still whispering. "Which part would you leave out? Do you *want* the boys in Junior Football League to have tatty jerseys? Do you *think* we shouldn't have decorated and given Jonas a festive house, especially *this* Christmas, his first one with us and without his mom? Do you *think* I should bypass the opportunity to shove my smokin' hot, badass biker fiancé down the throats of my ex-friends in Horizon Summit? Do you *think* Jonas shouldn't give his teacher a present when all the other kids are going to do it which will make her think we're bad parents or Jonas is a shit kid? Hunh? Which part would you leave out, Tate?"

He studied me then deduced on a mutter, "I see the shit you been doin' is shit you need to do."

"Damn straight," I muttered back, straightening in my seat.

"Next year, Laurie, we're goin' to a beach," he told me and I twisted to him.

"*We can't go to a beach!*" I screeched. "My mother would have a stroke! Christmas is about family!"

He again studied me and I was thinking that he was thinking much what I thought the night he asked me to marry him (or, more accurately, gave me a ring and told me we were getting married next April, which I decided to think was the same thing). That was, there were many of my ways that had or would become clear to him. There were others that would remain a mystery.

"So, you're sayin', every year you're gonna go Christmas crazy?" he asked when Jonas hit the garage carrying the shiny red and green Christmas bag with a big gold glitter star on it, satin ribbon handles and big tufts of gold glittered tissue paper spiking out of it.

"Yes," I answered.

He grinned then murmured, "Good to know." Jonas jumped into the cab, slammed the door and Tate announced, "Just had the talk with Laurie, Bub. She gets this way at Christmas. Get ready, every December we're gonna be neck deep in Christmas until the day we die. But, good news is, next year we'll know to brace."

Jonas chuckled then said, "Gotcha."

I jabbed a finger at Tate and snapped, "Scrooge One!" And then twisted in my seat and snapped, "Scrooge Two!"

Jonas burst out laughing.

Tate put the SUV in reverse and backed out of the garage. He was turned in his seat to look out the back window and his smile was wide.

I crossed my arms on my chest, looked out the front window and harrumphed.

*   *   *

I walked out of the office at Bubba's, turned, and locked the door.

I'd just finished the schedule for the next three weeks and I'd finished payroll as well as written out the Christmas bonus checks that

I'd talked Tate and Krys into giving the staff. They weren't huge but anything at Christmas was welcome.

A Christmas miracle had happened and Tate had talked Krys into letting Bubba take shifts while we were away. Krys had hired Izzy, a new bartender, and he was good but she also stayed open throughout Christmas, every day just like normal, and with Tate and me both gone, and ski season upon the mountains, she needed an extra pair of hands.

Not to mention, for Tate's peace of mind, he wanted that extra pair of hands to be the big, bad Bubba.

Bubba had got a job working for Tate's attorney, Nina Maxwell's husband Holden Maxwell. It was construction, the job they were doing just finished and Maxwell was giving his crew until the new year off.

Bubba was already burning the candle at both ends, working construction during the day, sitting on his Harley at three thirty waiting to follow Krys home at night if it wasn't snowing, that was. If it was snowing or the roads weren't clear, Bubba sat in a pickup truck that was more beat-up even than Jim-Billy's. But he sat in it every night Krys was on. Still, taking shifts through Christmas would probably seem like a break after the schedule he was keeping.

I walked down the hall and into the bar to see Krys standing inside the bar, bent over it, head close to Jim-Billy who looked, even though it wasn't even two in the afternoon, like he was drunk as a skunk. She was murmuring to him and Jim-Billy was staring into his beer. This was the third day in a row this had happened.

This was also surprising. Jim-Billy liked his beer and he drank a lot of it but he was no drunk.

The bar was pretty empty, too early for people to be off the slopes and looking for a different kind of fun. It was also a weekday prior to a Christmas where the bar would not close. This meant, to give them some kind of break, I scheduled lots of time off for our staff and only Tate, Krys, and me were on and Tate, I suspected, was only there because I was.

I walked around the bar to where Tate was standing, his hips against the back bar, his eyes on Krys and Jim-Billy.

I stopped where he was, got close and put my forearms on the bar. Tate saw me, pushed away and came in close, putting his forearms on either side of mine.

"What's that all about?" I whispered with a barely there tilt of my head toward Krys and Jim-Billy.

"Christmas," Tate replied.

"What?"

Tate's eyes got funny and not in a good way before he explained, "Jim-Billy used to be married to a woman named Elise. Pretty thing, reminded me of Betty. Lots of energy, fuckin' sweet. They were tight, always tight. Jim-Billy was a trucker but, he was in town, you wouldn't see them apart."

"And?" I prompted when he stopped and I did this even though I wasn't certain, with the way his story had started, that I wanted to know.

"Christmas, 'bout seven years back, faulty lights on the tree, tree caught fire, house caught fire, smoke detector didn't go off and Elise was burned alive."

Even though I wasn't guessing Tate's story was a jolly one full of Christmas cheer, this wasn't what I expected to hear or *wanted* to hear. Not about anybody but especially not about Jim-Billy's wife. Jim-Billy was a barfly but he was also a good guy straight to the core.

I closed my eyes tight and whispered, "Oh my God."

"Yeah, babe," Tate whispered back and I opened my eyes.

"Was Jim-Billy on the road?"

"Yep, Billy was on the road. Billy was also the guy who didn't change the batteries in his smoke detector." Tate shook his head and glanced at Jim-Billy before his eyes came back to me. "Blamed himself and then unraveled. Remember it. It was difficult to witness."

Feeling my heart break, I peeked at Jim-Billy and Krys then looked back at Tate and said, "I bet."

"He went off the rails. Took him a few years to get it out of his system. A few more to clean up his shit. He never went back to work. Managed somehow to get disability and lives off that and the insurance payout."

"Poor Jim-Billy," I whispered and I did this with feeling.

"For obvious reasons, he ain't good at Christmas. Krys takes care of him and I'm thinkin' she agreed to Bubba takin' shifts because Bubba is good with him. They'll see him through."

I looked at Jim-Billy and said, "Maybe I can, I don't know..." My mind was shifting through all my fix-it strategies and coming up with zilch when my eyes went back to Tate and I tossed out a long shot. "Captain, I think maybe Nadine's sweet on him."

Tate shook his head. "Don't go there."

"Well, I don't know if she is but she comes in a lot and she almost always sits with him. I can talk to her first, feel her out, see if—"

"Yeah, Ace, she's into him. He ain't much to look at but he's a good guy and she saw his devotion to Elise. Her first husband was an asshole, her second one a drunk and an asshole, and her third one a drunk asshole who beat her. She knows Jim-Billy likes his beer but he can also hold it and he's so far from an asshole, it ain't funny."

"So—" I started but stopped when Tate's face changed, went from serious to deadly serious and he leaned in super close.

And when he spoke, his voice was near to a growl. "A woman gets under your skin, the kind of woman that feeds the muscle, the bone, the soul, no replacing that. Jim-Billy knows it. Nadine's a good woman but once you have that, there's no replacing it."

I stared at him and he stared back.

Then I whispered, "Tate—" but stopped speaking when his hand moved and his thumb tweaked the diamond he'd slid on my finger six weeks before.

"No replacing it," he repeated on his own whisper.

He was right. I knew it because he was under my skin too. He was feeding the muscle, the bone, but mostly my soul. And if I ever lost him, there'd be no replacing him. I didn't know if I'd give up and drink beer in a biker bar for the rest of my days. What I did know was a life without Tate didn't bear thinking about.

"I want to make out with you right now," I blurted, but I did it quietly.

His head jerked almost imperceptibly at my words and he asked, "Come again?"

"You're being sweet and when you're being sweet, I always want to make out with you. So, I want to make out with you."

He grinned then he said, "Have at it, Ace."

"Not in front of Jim-Billy," I whispered.

His grin became a smile.

Then he said, "Office, in five."

I smiled back and said, "Gotcha."

I peeled away, checked on my very few customers, none of whom needed drinks and, after five minutes, I met Tate in the office where I participated in a heated and highly enjoyable make-out session on the couch with my boss.

* * *

I had Christmas music playing softly something Tate and Jonas could take, in small measures, then they couldn't take any more so I was enjoying it while I could. And I was standing in the opened door of the fridge, staring at its contents, determined to make a good dinner out of whatever was in there in order to eat up all the food prior to us going off for two weeks when I heard a knock on the sliding glass door.

Tate and Jonas were in town running an errand the purpose of which they did not share. I didn't pry. It was Christmas and when someone ran an unexplained errand at Christmas you didn't ask questions.

Tate had been right that night six weeks ago, we were more than comfortable. We were good. I knew this because I'd taken over dealing with our bank accounts. Mine was still hefty because Tate didn't let me pay for anything but food, clothing, and the variety of household items I'd been buying to make his house a home. Tate's was hefty because the bar was doing an excellent turnover and the skips he brought in earned him a whack and he (or, now, me as I prepared, sent, and processed his invoices) charged expenses.

Considering the fact that Tate seemed dedicated to the cause of making certain I never regretted my move from a life of martinis and manicures in the gated community of Horizon Summit to a family life in a house on a hill in Colorado, I suspected that my Christmas was going to be good that year. I didn't want him to worry about this because it didn't matter to me. It also didn't penetrate the many times I shared this fact with him. Therefore, I'd come to terms with the fact that it was something he was driven to do so I was going to let him do it. Really, who was I to complain?

I turned to the door and walked to it, seeing Dalton standing outside. This was a surprise and a worry. Outside of coming to get me or taking me home when he'd been called into Lauren Duty by Tate, Dalton didn't hang out at my house and he'd never stopped by unannounced. He wasn't on that night at Bubba's but that didn't mean that he hadn't popped by for a drink, something he did, if not regularly, then regularly enough. That meant he might be there about Jim-Billy.

I smiled at him tentatively through the glass and flipped down the door to the security panel on the wall, tapping in the code. Tate was adamant about the alarm being set when he was away, even if he was away for an errand. I left the door down to the panel, unlocked the sliding glass door and slid it open for Dalton.

"Hey, Dalton, what are you…?"

For some reason, Tate's long ago words sifted into my head.

Profilers think he's able to assimilate. He's one of us.

Tonia. Neeta. The girl in Chantelle.

He either knew them or he doesn't pose a threat. He comes off as friendly. He might even be attractive. A good flirt. Turn a woman's eye. Thinks she's gonna get her some, not havin' any clue.

"Laurie," Dalton said, coming into the house, the look on his face funny, tortured, his eyes shining with a light I'd never seen in my life. An unnatural light. A light lit from a deep inner madness and I knew.

I jumped forward and to the side, my finger extended to hit the red panic button on the alarm panel.

I had no idea if I touched it before the jolt hit me and everything went black.

Tate

Tate Jackson's cell rang and, driving home to Lauren with his son in the seat at his side, he leaned forward and pulled it from the back pocket of his jeans.

He flipped it open, put it to his ear and said, "Jackson."

"Tate," Frank replied. "You at your house?"

Those four words coming from a cop hit him like a sucker punch to the gut.

"No, on my way home with Jonas, why?"

"Weird," Frank muttered.

"Why?" Tate bit out.

"Laurie with you?" Frank asked.

"No, Frank, damn it. *Why?*"

"Somethin's up with your alarm, buddy. Dispatch got the alert that your panic button's been hit."

Tate's gut dropped and his foot pressed down on the accelerator.

"Get units to the house," he ordered.

"What?"

"Get units to the house!" Tate barked.

"Fuck, Laurie there on her own?"

"Frank—" Tate growled and Frank interrupted him.

"On it," he stated and disconnected.

Tate flipped his phone closed, then opened, then he went to favorites to find Laurie's number, accelerating faster.

"Dad," Jonas whispered, hearing his father's words, feeling his father's vibe.

"It'll be okay, Bub," Tate told his son.

"Is something—?"

Tate glanced at his son to see his face pale in the lights of the dash and his eyes glued to his father.

"Everything'll be okay," he assured Jonas but Tate's chest was tight, so fucking tight he was finding it hard to breathe. He hit the button for Laurie, looked to the road, put the phone to his ear and repeated, "Everything'll be okay."

*   *   *

"Stand right there, Jonas, don't move, yeah?" Tate ordered his son.

Jonas nodded and Tate turned away and stood a moment, taking in every nuance of the house.

Lights on in the kitchen, the living room, on the Christmas tree, the Christmas lights lit outside. Candles burning, the scent of pine. Christmas music playing. Laurie had loads of Christmas CDs, some compilations she'd burned. Now it was Bing Crosby and David Bowie, "Peace on Earth." One of Laurie's favorites, he'd noted she always teared up when that song played. She loved it. When he'd asked, she said it reminded her of home. It was her sister and mother's favorite Christmas song too.

The kitchen was empty.

Laurie was almost always in the kitchen. Making herself a drink, getting one for him or Jonas. Cooking. Baking. Sitting at the island and scratching out a grocery list. Tapping on her laptop e-mails to friends and family or checking her Facebook page. Talking with her mother, sister, Betty, Sunny, Wendy, Amber, Twyla, Krys; even though she spent hours with them working she could talk for hours with them on the phone, a cup of peppermint tea in front of her, cackling like a lunatic (even with Krys).

It was her zone and not only because she used it to take care of her family but it was the center of the house. She used it as her vantage point to keep her finger on her boys. No matter where they were, from the kitchen, she could hear them or see them. That was why he spent a fucking fortune fixing it up for her. If she was going to spend that amount of time in it, she was going to have the best fucking kitchen money could buy. So he'd made that so.

But she wasn't there now and her cell phone sat on the island.

She never went anywhere without her cell.

He moved through the house. The rest of it was dark and he didn't light any lights, just looked for her even though he knew she wasn't there. She'd call a greeting if she heard them come in, no matter where she was in the house. She always did.

He knew she wasn't in any of those rooms because she also always turned the lights out when she left a room. Said it was because she was an environmentalist but admitted later it was because her dad had a rule when she was growing up, lights out if you weren't in a room. They were farmers, not rolling in it. They needed to keep the electricity bill down and, even though she'd moved on to a life where that wasn't a worry, she'd kept doing it. Habit.

He stood in their darkened bedroom.

The blinds down but opened. The Christmas lights outside illuminating the room and the picture she'd bought him hanging over the bed. The walls painted in paint she'd chosen. The bed made, the floor tidy and recently vacuumed.

New framed photos on his chest of drawers. One of him and her at her birthday party; she was drunk and plastered to his side, her arms around his middle, her cheek pressed to his shoulder, his arm around her waist. He was smiling down at her. She was smiling at the camera. Another one of him and Jonas captured after one of Jonas's football games. It was a candid. Tate had his hand on Jonas's shoulder pad, he was looking down at him. Jonas had his helmet dangling by the faceguard from his fingertips, he was looking up at his dad. They were both smiling. And another frame, on Tate's nightstand, the three of them at Thanksgiving. Pop took it, Laurie in his lap, Jonas tucked to his side, Tate smiling at the camera but Jonas and Laurie were looking at each other, their faces awash with laughter.

He could smell her perfume.

She was everywhere, her presence filled every damned centimeter of the room.

"*Fuck,*" he whispered.

He walked back down the hall, tipping his chin up to Jonas when he saw his son's face wore so much concern, it had already turned haggard. Tipping his chin was the only thing he could do to communicate to his son as the fear clawed at his gut. He walked down the back hall to the mudroom, down the stairs. He saw his weight equipment and remembered, just the week before, working out when she was doing something in his office. He noticed she'd come out and leaned against the door frame at the mouth of the hall. She'd been sipping coffee and watching him.

"Sissy," she'd teased when she caught his attention. "You should come to boot camps with me. Tyler'd kick your ass."

Jonas had been at school so Tate had made the decision to end his workout a different way, right in the hall. She didn't complain. She liked him sweaty.

She liked him any way she could get him.

That fear clawed deeper and his calm slipped, his eyes got blurry, his mouth got dry.

"Focus, Jackson, fuckin' focus," he muttered to himself, his vision cleared and he moved through the dark, silent rooms and then came back to the weight room and stood still.

No forced entry. No signs of struggle. She wasn't out on a quick, secret errand. She'd left the candles burning.

She'd opened the door to someone she knew. She wouldn't disarm the alarm, unlock the door, and open it to someone she didn't know. She'd learned that lesson. She'd be cautious. Unless she knew who was on the other side.

Trusted them.

There were a lot of people Laurie trusted and they all centered around one place.

As he heard the sirens approaching, he pulled his cell phone out of his back pocket, flipped it open, and called Krys.

"Hey, Tate," she answered.

"Who's there?" he asked without a greeting.

"What?"

"Who's at the bar?" he asked.

"Why?"

"Who's at the fuckin' bar, Krys?" he demanded.

"Um…" She hesitated, "Izzy, Bub, Jonelle, Jim-Billy, Nadine, Steg, Stoney—"

He'd asked the wrong fucking question.

He interrupted her. "Who's *not* there?"

Another brief hesitation then, "You, Laurie…um…" She paused. "Tate, I wanna get you what you need but I don't know what—"

"One of us, who's not there, someone Lauren would trust."

"Dad!" Jonas shouted from upstairs, his voice strong and scared at the same time. "The cops are here!"

Krystal heard him. "The cops are there?"

"Lauren hit the panic button. Jonas and I were out pickin' up her Christmas present. We're back. She's gone."

Silence and Tate felt her terror coming through the line.

"No, Tate, no," she whispered and he heard the tremor in her voice.

"What's goin' on?" Tate heard Bubba ask, his voice firm but distant, coming through Krys's phone.

"Who's not there, Krys?" Tate repeated.

"Tate—" she started.

"*Who's not fuckin' there!*" he roared.

He heard her phone jostling as he heard footsteps coming down the back steps.

"Tate?" Bubba was on the phone.

"Lauren's been nabbed. It's someone she knew. Look around, Bub, who's not there?"

"Fuck, fuck, *fuckin' shit*!" Bubba shouted. "Hold on, I'm doin' a scan."

"Jackson," Frank said as he approached Tate.

"Give me a minute," Tate said to Frank.

"Tate, buddy, no forced entry," Frank said quietly.

Tate speared Frank with a look.

"Give me a *fucking* minute, Frank," Tate ground out.

"Dalton," Bubba said in his ear.

Dalton. Dalton was on when he'd fired Tonia but she was local, he had the rest of the night after the bar closed to pick her up and play with her.

Dalton was one of them. Good-looking. Easy smile. Not tall, not built but still lean and strong. Definitely bigger than the petite Sunny and what she was used to with Shambles. Lived local but not all his life. Moved there a few years ago. But outside of the fact he was a good bartender and dependable employee, Tate didn't know one fucking thing about him.

Totally fit the fucking profile.

"Go to the office, check the back schedules, time cards. Find out if he was on the night Neet was murdered and if he was on the night that girl got done in Chantelle."

"You remember dates?" Bubba asked and Tate knew he was on the move.

"Check the Internet. Get Krys on it," Tate ordered.

"Don't have broadband to the bar, bud," Bubba said quietly. He was in the hall.

"Someone in that bar has got to have a phone with Internet access and if they don't, we got a fuckin' phone. Make calls. Find the dates. Check the schedules. I want info in ten minutes, Bubba, faster, you can do it. And pull his application, fax it to me."

"Got it," Bubba replied and Tate heard the disconnect so he flipped his phone closed.

"Dalton?" Frank asked.

"Jonas!" Tate bellowed. "Come down here!"

"Tate, Dalton?" Frank repeated.

"Call the Feds," Tate demanded instead of answering as his son ran down the stairs.

"Dad?" Jonas asked.

"Computer, Bub. Go fire it up. Now," Tate ordered and Jonas took off toward his office.

A couple more officers were coming down the stairs as Frank kept talking.

"Tate, buddy, now think about this. This might not be what you think. It might not be May-December. It's Christmas. Laurie could be doing anything. I get you're tweaked, Neeta, Tonia. But Lauren isn't his type and you cast suspicion on someone in something like this—"

His vision got blurry again and his hands clenched into fists as his body leaned into Frank.

"You hesitate one more fuckin' time when I tell you to do something, I swear to fuckin' *Christ*, I'll rip your goddamned heart out. Call the *fucking Feds*!"

Frank stared at him for half a second, then lifted his hand to the radio at his shoulder, pressed the button and muttered, "Dispatch, we need a 10-18 call to Special Agent Tambo. Suspected May-December activity at Jackson residence. Out."

Tate heard Jacinda in dispatch reply with a shocked, "Jackson residence? Out," but he wasn't listening. He was walking to his office.

Lauren

"You shouldn't have fought me, Laurie," Dalton whispered. "Why'd you fight me?"

I tasted my cloth gag and blood.

This was because I'd woken up in Dalton's truck, sorted out my head, realized I wasn't bound and then opened the door, rolling out to the earth even though the truck was speeding through the hills. This did not feel good and I suspected I did myself damage but I still got up and did my best to make a run for it, straight through the spiky pine and leafless aspen of the hills surrounding where Sunny had been attacked.

Dalton had caught me. He knew those woods. I didn't.

Then he'd beaten the shit out of me no matter how hard I tried to fight back. He bested me and dragged me back to his truck. He cuffed my wrist to the door and then he'd driven me here.

Here.

I closed my eyes and turned my head away because, in a line, their hair was in plastic baggies nailed to the walls.

I saw Tonia's gleaming black locks, Sunny's shorn, frizzy, ash blonde hair.

And Neeta's thick, lush dark brown.

I felt the sick slide up the back of my throat.

He lives up there Laurie…bet my fuckin' life on it, he lives up there. He knows that spot. He knows those woods. Bet my fuckin' life he lives up there. He hunts up there. That's his space. It's his.

Tate knew where I was, he had to know. He'd find me. He could do anything for me. He'd find me.

Please, God, let him find me.

"I didn't want it to be you," Dalton told me. "I didn't. Fought it, Laurie. But you should have married him before you moved in. Good girls get married, Laurie. They get married before they move in and let men touch them. I could handle it but then you let *Jonas* live with you. You and Tate, fuckin' each other constantly, right when his boy was there. *His boy.* I see it. See the way you two are together. Barely able to keep your hands off each other. Your tongues down each other's throats every chance you get. And I heard about it. You goin' down on him in the mornin'." He sucked in a breath. "Jonas could see you, he could *hear* you. And I know he did. He did. Hedid-hedidhedid."

I swallowed back the bile, then yelped behind my gag as I heard the fabric tearing and my head snapped around to look at him.

I was on a dirty mattress on the floor, the mattress covered in brown stains. Blood. Old blood. Tonia all but died here. Neeta *did* die there. And God knew who else.

I was bound and I was gagged, my hands tied over my head to an old, rusty radiator, my legs, opened wide, tied to huge, wide screws fixed to the floor.

"You shouldn't have let him hear you, Laurie," Dalton whispered and then the blade sunk into my side and my cry of pain was muted by the gag.

His mouth came to my ear as the blade slid out.

"I'm sorry," he whispered.

Tate

"I'm gettin' nothin'," Tate said to Bubba who was standing at his back.

Bubba and Krystal had shown up five minutes ago. Bubba had had to drive like a wild man to get up there as fast as he did, all the while talking to Tate on his phone, giving Tate the info he had.

Dalton was off for two days when Neeta was done, he was off when Sunny was attacked, and he was off when the girl in Chantelle was brutalized.

Krys had brought the application with them but Bubba had given him the details on his way up the hill, Krystal reading the data to him in the truck and Tate had been running the info through his databases for the last fifteen minutes.

Dalton Caulfield McIntyre didn't exist. His address was in town but it was a fucking warehouse. He didn't own a car. He didn't own property. He didn't have a record. He didn't pay taxes. He didn't have a fucking driver's license. He didn't even have any credit history.

Tate knew Dalton had a truck and a bike and Tate knew Krys,

and now Laurie, withheld taxes on Dalton's wages but for some fucking reason none of this showed anywhere.

Dalton McIntyre was a black hole.

He only had a bank account into which they transferred his pay and how the fuck he got that without any apparent ID was anyone's fucking guess.

Except it had a second name on the account, not McIntyre, first name Michael, last name Simpson, middle name, eerily, *Caulfield*.

So Tate ran Simpson and got shit. Same thing all around. No taxes, no license, no credit, no car, no property. Nothing. Not one fucking thing. Except a birth date, born in County Hospital, the same hospital where Tate was born, a hospital twenty minutes away. Simpson's birth date was nearly thirty years ago. His birthday July eighth and Dalton's birth date on his application stated August seventh.

Transposed.

So who the fuck was Michael Simpson?

No wonder the Feds never got close. Both of them, Dalton and Simpson, totally off the grid.

Tate swiveled in his chair and leaned forward, putting his elbows to his knees and his head in his hands.

"Think, Jackson," he muttered to himself, "think."

He felt movement and looked up to see that Deke's mammoth frame was filling the door. Then Tate's eyes went to Bubba.

"I made some calls," Bubba mumbled.

"Came by to see if we had to lock you down," Deke announced.

"No one's fuckin' lockin' me down," Tate returned.

"You holdin' your shit?" Deke asked.

"Yes, I'm fuckin' holdin' my shit," Tate clipped in answer.

This was true. The part he didn't share was that he was barely fucking holding his shit.

Deke surveyed Tate, then looked at Bubba. "Wood's organizing search parties at the garage. You comin'?"

Bubba glanced at Tate then he looked to Deke and said, "Yeah."

Deke's eyes moved to Tate. "You?"

Tate stood up. "We're combin' the hills where Sunny was attacked."

Deke nodded. "Wood's already got boys headin' that way. They even got fuckin' quadrants. He's all over it."

"Feds didn't find anything up there," Bubba noted.

"That don't mean there's nothin' to be found," Deke replied.

"Krys got Jonas?" Tate asked Bubba and Bubba nodded.

"Stella's on her way up," Deke added.

"Let's go," Tate muttered and headed out the door.

Krys and Jonas were in the living room when they arrived. Both sets of eyes flew to the three men as they hit the dining area.

Jonas shot off his chair and ran to Tate, slamming into him head-long and throwing his arms around Tate's middle.

Jonas was holding his shit too, but that hold was slipping.

"Dad," Jonas whispered, his voice small and scared and Tate allowed himself in that instant to acknowledge what he'd known since he'd heard Frank's voice on the phone and that was the fact that tonight someone was going to die and Tatum Jackson was going to fucking kill him.

"Goin' out, Bub, lookin' for Laurie," Tate muttered, his hand moving along his son's hair and down to curl around his neck.

Jonas's head shot back. "Can I—?"

"No," Tate cut him off.

"But—"

"I gotta go, Bub," Tate told him.

"But Dad—"

Tate grasped him by his biceps, pulled him firmly but gently away and held on as he bent double and looked in his son's eyes. His eyes. Eyes Laurie had told him, in the dark when they were in bed after he'd made love to her weeks ago, that she thought were the most beautiful eyes she'd ever seen, both sets of them.

"Who's my big man?" Tate whispered.

Jonas's lip trembled.

Then he whispered back, "Me."

"Look out for Krys," Tate directed.

"Okay." Jonas was still whispering.

Tate let him go but hooked him with an arm around his shoulders, yanking his son into his body and squeezing tight. Then he let him go again and his eyes swept Krys. She was standing and he saw her eyes were bright but her jaw was clenched. Gritting her teeth to keep back the tears.

"Be back with Laurie," Tate told her.

She swallowed.

"Right, Tate," she said.

They were out the door, Deke peeling off to his truck, Bubba to his, Tate to the Explorer when they saw lights coming up the lane. They stopped to see Shambles and Sunny's VW van park off to the side. Both got out, Shambles ran to them, Sunny coming slower.

"Word?" Shambles demanded.

"We're goin' to look for her," Bubba answered.

"I'm coming," he turned to Tate. "Jonas?"

"In the house," Tate answered and looked at Sunny. "He could use you."

She didn't even nod. She ran to the house.

Shambles ran to the passenger side of Bubba's truck.

They all climbed in and went down the mountain.

Jim-Billy

He should have bought one of those cell phones.

He really should have.

But he didn't and there was no time to spare.

He also shouldn't drink so goddamned much.

But it was Christmas and every twinkling light, every swaying garland, every Christmas tree blinking in every goddamned window reminded him.

So he drank too much.

But not too much not to remember gabbing with Dalton ages

ago, it had to be over a year, and Dalton telling him about his place. Jim-Billy hadn't even thought about it, not then, not later when all that shit with the girls was going down. It was a nothing conversation he put out of his mind.

But Dalton had told him he didn't have an apartment in town or a house. He lived in the hills, the hills where the hippie chick was attacked.

"My ma's old place," he'd muttered.

And drunken Jim-Billy, hearing about Laurie when everyone at the bar was murmuring about it, panicking, the men heading to the garage, fear threaded its way through the alcohol drenching his system and he'd remembered pretty Jane Simpson who'd gotten knocked up in high school and had a boy. She'd lived up there with her folks until she got herself a man and she'd moved to Ouray to be with that man. And he remembered vaguely hearing word that she'd been killed, knifed to death by her boyfriend who swore he didn't do it, swore he loved her, swore she was the love of his life even though he was charged and found guilty and went to prison for it. Everyone they knew, Jim-Billy remembered the talk filtering from Ouray, had been stunned. All those folks said Jane and her man were tight. They were in love. They meant the world to each other. And with Jane's folks both dead by then, Jim-Billy remembered hearing her son had gone into foster care.

No one had lived up at that house for years.

Or at least they thought no one had.

Dalton was a good kid. Everyone liked him, especially Tonia. Jim-Billy spent a lot of time in that bar and he'd noticed the way she'd looked at him. She'd crushed on him huge, always trying to catch his eye. Jim-Billy figured her clothing got scantier and her flirting got flirtier as she got more desperate to make an impression or make him jealous.

But Dalton wasn't interested, not in her, not in any of the girls. He'd flirt but that was it. Hell, Izzy had been working there less than three months and that kid got laid practically every night. Jim-Billy knew all about it. Izzy was young but he wasn't as good-looking as Dalton so he bragged, *a lot.*

Not Dalton.

Young, good-looking guy like that? That wasn't right.

Jim-Billy had never thought anything of it.

Never.

Until now.

Now he had Laurie and he was going to hurt her. Hurt her like he hurt Tonia. Like he hurt Neeta. Like he hurt that pretty, sweet hippie chick.

And Laurie was Tate's Elise. He had Jonas, so she wasn't his everything, but that didn't mean she didn't make up half his world.

Once half of your world was torn from you, you could live to be a hundred and never build it back up.

Never.

And Tatum Jackson was a good man. He didn't deserve Jim-Billy's life, going home alone to a cold bed every night and staying awake remembering what it felt like when his bed wasn't cold when he slipped into it. When he never felt alone, even when he wasn't with her.

And he was going to do something about it.

He knew he should call the cops, or even call Tate, but he didn't have a cell phone.

And he didn't have time.

Someone had to get to Laurie.

Tate

"It's a federal investigation, Jackson," Chief Arnie Fuller said through the phone.

"Yeah, it is, Arnie, that don't mean you can't send your boys out to look for her while you wait for Tambo to get his ass here from Denver," Tate growled back.

"We fuck that shit up, we got federal heat. We don't need federal heat," Arnie shot back.

"No, Arnie, *you* don't need federal heat. *You* don't need the Feds gettin' more in your business than they already are. You don't think Tambo's already got your fuckin' ticket?" Tate returned.

"Fuck you, Jackson, you were always a pain in my ass," Arnie retorted.

"You aren't fuckin' *me*, you wait two hours for Tambo to get here. You're fuckin' *Laurie.* In two hours she could bleed out of multiple stab wounds, some of 'em in places I swear to God, you sit on this, you'll feel 'cause I'll make certain you see jail time, you asshole. A cop in lockdown will get all sorts shoved up his ass," Tate promised.

"Go to hell, Jackson," Arnie snapped then disconnected.

"*Fuck!*" Tate barked.

"I take it we got no support from the Carnal PD," Wood noted, his voice vibrating with anger.

Tate's eyes went to his friend.

"Got your .38?" Tate asked Wood and Wood's eyes narrowed on him.

"Tate," he said, his voice gentling.

"Didn't want to leave the house armed, Jonas would see. Need a gun, Wood," Tate stated.

"You think—?"

"I asked," Tate cut him off. "Do you got your .38?"

Wood sucked in breath. Then he jogged to his office. By the time he jogged out of the office to Tate's Explorer, Tate was behind the wheel, the SUV was idling.

Tate's head turned to him when he swung in.

"Got it?" he asked.

Wood handed over the .38 and Tate noted Wood had a 9mm. Tate took the .38, released the clip, studied it a split second, jammed it back in and then leaned forward so he could slide the gun in the back waistband of his jeans.

Then he put the truck into reverse and sped backward out of his parking spot in front of the garage.

Lauren

He'd cleaned the knife of my blood on the mattress and then cut the length of my hair off with it, cutting it at my shoulders, getting started, the rest would go later, I knew. He was shoving my hair into a new baggie when it happened.

The door flew open and Jim-Billy was there.

I was so shocked, and thrilled, and hopeful, thinking Tate would come in next, my whole body bucked, apparently violently because, surprisingly, the rusty pipe my hands were tied to at the radiator pulled clean away from the wall.

"What the—?" Dalton gritted out, getting up, whirling, armed with the knife.

It hurt like hell, pain slicing through the wound at my side, but I had to get up. I had to *get out of there*. I sat up, yanked the gag from my mouth, leaned double and went for the ropes at my right foot.

"He's got a knife!" I shouted but I did this over a gun blast.

I looked up and saw Dalton go back, blood pouring from a wound in his middle.

Then Jim-Billy was skidding on his knees, stopping at my left foot, he put the gun down clumsily and then his fingers were on the ropes.

"We gotta get you outta here, Laurie," Jim-Billy said, slurring only slightly, calling my attention from Dalton, who had his back to the wall and his hand to his middle, blood seeping through his fingers, his face pale, his eyes blank, his body beginning to slide down the wall. "Get your other foot free, darlin'."

I went back to work on my foot as Jim-Billy got the left one untied. Then he shuffled over to my right one, pushed my awkward hands away and worked that one.

I was free and Jim-Billy grabbed my hand, straightening and beginning to pull me up with him, when Dalton was suddenly there. Dalton hit Jim-Billy in a flying tackle, Jim-Billy and Dalton went careening to the side and I fought through the pain and instead of falling back, I pushed to a crouch, one of my hands going to the wetness at my side. The other one reaching out toward Jim-Billy's gun.

"Go! Go! *Go!*" The last "go" Jim-Billy uttered ended in a grunt. Dalton rolled off of him and I saw his knife jutting out of Jim-Billy's belly.

"*No!*" I screamed.

"Go," Jim-Billy whispered.

I stared into his pain-filled eyes and hesitated.

I looked at Dalton whose eyes came to me.

I was in no shape to help Jim-Billy. I had to *find* help.

I had to get to Tate.

I stopped reaching for the gun, found my feet and *ran*.

Tate

"Simpson," Tate muttered into the cab.

"What?" Wood asked.

"Jane Simpson," Tate kept muttering.

"Tate... *what*?" Wood bit out.

"Jesus, fuck, Wood, you remember that girl? She was ahead of us in school, two, three years. Whole town was talking about it. She got knocked up. Then she started dating that guy from Ouray, he was here, forget, working on an oil rigger or somethin'. She moved back to his town with him, then she got killed and he got life for doin' it."

"Oh fuck. Yeah," Wood replied.

"She was blonde. Blue eyes. Like her kid. Remember her kid?" Tate asked.

He felt Wood's head turn to him in the dark. "The Simpson place."

"Old one-lane track. Not paved. Remember it only 'cause Amelia's kid went missin'. Cops formed search parties, we went through these hills. I found him by that track, wondered what it was, stayed curious and looked it up when I got back to the station. The Simpsons left it to their daughter and it went to the kid when she was murdered. He never paid taxes on it and the government seized it but never did anything with it. They let it sit. Fuck, no one would know it was even there, they didn't know to look for it."

"You remember where it is?" Wood asked.

"Yeah, call Deke, Bub, get everyone headed there," Tate ordered and Wood moved to pull out his phone.

Even so, he asked, "You that sure, Buck? Pullin' the boys, focusin' in one direction?"

Tate had lived by his gut a long time, not only on the hunt or as a cop but also on the football field. You looked at someone running at you, you needed to take them down, or you were following a receiver running a play, you had to go with your gut about which way they'd bolt to avoid you or which way they'd turn to catch a pass because you sure as fuck didn't want to go the other way. Tate couldn't say he picked the right direction every time but he didn't make the All-America Team two years in a row picking the wrong direction.

"Get everyone headed there, Wood."

"Gotcha," Wood muttered, then said in the phone, "Bub, Tate's thinkin' it's Jane Simpson's son. The Simpson place. Get the word out..."

And Wood talked as Tate drove.

Fast.

Lauren

I was running down the hill, my entire side had gone past pain and felt like a ball of flame and I knew he was after me. I could hear him crashing through the wood behind me. We both were injured but he knew these woods. He'd already caught me once. He knew them.

And I didn't.

But they were Sunny's hills and Tate found people for a living.

He'd know.

He'd know.

He'd know to look for me here.

Pray God, he'd know.

"*Help!*" I shouted, hoping they were out looking for me and someone would hear. "*Help! Help! Please, please, please help me!*"

I looked behind me to see him closing in. I looked forward, came out at a clearing and saw the headlights to my left. They shocked me so much my body shuddered to a halt but the truck was right there and I threw out an arm as it skidded across the mud, its brake lights illuminating its tail in a flash of red.

Before it stopped, it came so close to me, my palm came to rest on the hot hood. It did this for only a second before I looked through the windscreen and saw Tate.

Relief flooded through me and I mouthed the word, "Baby."

Then Dalton hit me in the back in a tackle, pain seared through me and I went down full frontal on the mud in front of Tate's Explorer. The double blow of pain from being hit and landing, not to mention my head landing on a rock, meant I was out like a light.

Wood

"Buck!" Wood shouted but Tate wasn't listening. Tate was gone. Tate was gripped tight in a fury so extreme nothing was going to break through.

Wood had to break through. Wood had checked Laurie after Tate had yanked Dalton off her and she was breathing and coming to but she was bleeding from a stab wound and beaten. She didn't need to survive this only to spend the next five-to-ten visiting Tate in the penitentiary.

Wood got close to Tate who was holding Dalton up by the neck of his T-shirt and beating his already bloodied-to-a-pulp face into a bloodier pulp. He wrapped both his arms around Tate, taking Tate's arms down to his sides so Dalton crumpled to the ground and Wood yanked Tate back, shouting again, "Buck! We gotta get Laurie down the hill."

Tate jerked violently to the side, focused, wanting to get back to his target and Wood's body went with him but he held on with everything he had.

Then Wood heard trucks arriving.

Thank, fucking, God, Wood thought.

"It's over, get her to the hospital," he said.

Tate's body jerked again and Wood again went with it, his eyes on Tate's profile, Tate's eyes looking down on the moaning, crawling body of Dalton.

"She's injured, Buck, take her to the hospital," Wood whispered, using the only thing he had to break through.

More trucks arrived, headlights everywhere, rushing feet.

"Got her, got her, goin' down the hill," Wood heard Deke shout and then men were all around.

Wood felt it safe to let Tate go and turned to see Deke's back departing on a jog, Laurie held in his arms.

"I'm with him!" the hippie guy, Shambles, yelled and then took off after Deke.

"*Motherfucker!*" Bubba bellowed, yanked back a foot and then landed a kick so savage in Dalton's bleeding side, Dalton howled with pain even as he rolled twice.

Bubba stalked the step it took to get back to Dalton and landed another kick before Wings, Stoney, and Pop were on him, pulling him back.

"Where are the fuckin' cops, this is what I wanna fuckin' know!" Steg shouted, standing in the grass, staring down at Dalton.

Wood had no answer to that. It occurred to him that Tate had not moved nor spoken in the last two minutes so his eyes moved to his friend to see Tate still staring at the ground, even though Dalton was no longer in his line of sight.

Pop saw it too because he called, "Buck?"

"Two sets of tracks," Tate muttered.

"What?" Wood asked, getting close to his side as Pop got close to the other.

"Warm winter, ground not frozen solid," Tate was still muttering, his eyes pinned to the dirt. "Two sets of tracks. One back and forth. One just forward."

Wood looked to the ground and stared but he couldn't see it. Then again, he wasn't a tracker like Tate was.

"What are you thinkin'?" Wood asked the ground, then looked at Tate to see his head was up and he was staring into the distance.

"She was on the run," Tate whispered. "He'd been shot."

"Tate, son, let us in on what's goin on up there," Pop urged, his finger jabbing impatiently toward Tate's head, but Tate turned abruptly and headed back to the Explorer. Sirens could be heard in the distance but Tate had opened the driver's side door.

Wood wasted only the second it took to catch his father's eyes then he sprinted to the passenger side door. He was still swinging himself in when Tate accelerated so fast, the tires skidded, spewing mud, which was good because it gave Wings the second he needed to yank Dalton's body clear of the track as the Explorer barreled forward.

Wood got his ass in the seat, slammed the door and turned to Tate. "Talk to me."

"Someone else is up there," Tate said.

"Who? A partner?" Wood asked.

"No," Tate answered. "A hero."

Lauren

I opened my eyes. It was dark. I smelled hospital. I felt no pain.

I turned my head to the side and saw Tate.

He was awake, sitting in a chair pulled close to the side of my bed, his elbows to his knees, his eyes bloodshot. He looked wiped.

"Hey," I whispered and I felt my lips form a small smile.

His eyes dropped to my mouth then they closed, so slowly it felt like it took ten minutes watching him do it.

Then his head dropped and he muttered to his knees, "Jesus fucking Christ. Jesus *fucking* Christ."

"Honey," I whispered and his head shot up. And then he filled my vision because his mouth was on mine, gentle but firm and his big hands had spanned either side of my head, holding me still.

He broke the connection of our lips and he rested his forehead against mine.

"Baby," he whispered.

"Jim-Billy?" I asked.

"Okay, knife did more damage on him than you, went through his stomach, but they patched him up."

I closed my eyes this time then opened them to have the only thing I saw be his.

"Thank God," I breathed then asked, "Jonas?"

"Outside sleepin' on a couch with Krys and Stella and Sunny and Wendy and half of Carnal."

"Half of Carnal?"

He nodded, his forehead rolling against mine. "Half of Carnal."

"Must be a big waiting room," I whispered, realizing this was taking it out of me, my eyelids were getting heavy and I fought it. It was the first time I didn't want to sleep.

Tate saw it and his head came up a couple of inches but both of his hands slid down to my jaws.

"Go to sleep, honey," he urged gently, both his thumbs lifting up, stroking my cheekbones, "I'll be here when you get to the other side."

"Don't wanna," I muttered, my lids lowering and, with effort, I pulled them open again.

"Go to sleep, Laurie."

"Tate," I whispered, my eyelids falling again and I couldn't pull them open.

But before sleep swept me away, I felt his lips on mine form the words, "Sweet dreams, baby."

Jim-Billy

Jim-Billy woke feeling something he hadn't felt in seven years.

A soft, warm female pressed to his side, her hand under her cheek at his shoulder.

With effort, he looked down to see the top of Laurie's blonde head, her shoulder covered in a hospital gown, the rest of her body covered in a thin hospital blanket.

He sensed movement, his head settled back on the pillow and his eyes turned to the bright, Colorado sunshine coming through the window where Tate stood, Tate's eyes on the two people in the bed.

"She asleep?" Jim-Billy asked, his voice a soft rasp.

Tate nodded.

"Made me bring her in here, wanted to be with you," Tate whispered, his voice barely audible.

Jim-Billy nodded.

"She okay?" Jim-Billy asked.

"Better than you," Tate answered.

Jim-Billy nodded again.

He didn't feel much pain but then again, he wasn't moving and he had a soft, warm female body pressed to his side. She was Tate's but she was still a soft, warm female *and* she was Laurie, alive and breathing. It was a gift and life was too short, you get a gift, especially one as precious as the one squeezed next to him in a damned hospital bed, you accept it.

Tate walked from the window to the bed, the entirety of this short trip his eyes never leaving Jim-Billy's.

Once he made it to the bed, though, they flicked down to Laurie then back to Jim-Billy.

Then he said in a fierce whisper, "Owe you, Billy. Owe you *huge*."

Jim-Billy nodded again.

"I know."

And he did know, not because Jim-Billy suffered whatever was behind the complete numbness of his gut, made that way from whatever was feeding into his bloodstream from the drip in his arm, but because Jim-Billy suffered it to do his bit to keep what was squeezed in bed beside him alive and breathing.

Jim-Billy grinned his semitoothless grin at Tate.

Then he said, "Merry Christmas."

Tate stared at him for a second and he did this hard.

Then Tate's face relaxed and Jim-Billy heard his low, amused chuckle.

CHAPTER TWENTY-EIGHT

Where Are They Now?

"IN ONE OF the most remarkable where-are-they-nows, Tatum Jackson, All-American linebacker for Penn State and first-round draft pick for the Philadelphia Eagles, is back in the news after a twenty-two-year absence."

The minute they said Tate's name, I pushed a bit up Tate's chest where we were lying on the couch.

Me and my whole family were watching the football commentators doing their bit during halftime of the Sunday game the day after Christmas.

Pop had called my folks the minute he had a chance after they found me. They decided not to wait for the next flight out, which was late the next morning, because by that time, my dad said, they could be halfway across Nebraska (and were). So they packed up their stuff and all the presents and took turns driving all night to get to Colorado.

"Turn that shit off," Tate growled, as he would, since he was in a very bad mood even though it was the day after Christmas.

I'd been let out of the hospital on Christmas Eve.

I'd talked to the cops in the hospital. Dalton was in bad shape from a gunshot wound and the beating Tate had given him. He'd also confessed after Special Agent Tambo explained the extent of the evidence against him, which was a lot, considering he'd abducted me, cut my hair, kept trophies, didn't dispose of his mattress that was covered in DNA and used the same knife on us all, leaving that knife in Jim-Billy's gut.

Not to mention, Sunny had given a partial ID.

He'd also confessed to murdering his mom and pinning it on her boyfriend. He was, as Tate would call him, seriously whacked. Not appreciative of the fact that his mom had found the love of her life and especially not appreciative of the fact that she didn't mind hiding it.

She was, Tambo told Tate that Dalton told him, meant to be only his.

They'd released Dalton's mom's boyfriend after he spent nearly twenty years in prison for a murder he didn't commit against a woman he adored. The State gave him restitution but, I figured, losing the woman he loved and nearly half of his life to prison, no restitution would heal those wounds.

Tambo had also told Tate that I'd gotten loose, in a way, partially thanks to Tonia, Neeta, and the other girls. They'd struggled, weakening the pipe of the radiator.

I hated this fact, hated knowing their torture helped to save my life, but I was thankful all the same.

And lastly Tambo told Tate that Dalton did all the girls there, at that old house, then took them home even if that meant Nevada or Utah. Dalton said they needed to go home, needed to be with their families, needed to be at rest someplace familiar. Dalton was contrite, driven to his behavior but he struggled against it. He killed in May, his mother's birth month, and December, her boyfriend's. That he would allow. Knowing he could give in those months kept the urge at bay the rest of the time. But, when I got to the bar and Dalton watched Tate and me falling in love, that triggered something, flipped the switch, and he lost control.

I hated this fact too but I didn't dwell. Tate had taught me—with what I allowed Brad to do to me, with what he felt after his dad died, with how he acted after Neeta's murder—that life was too short to dwell, to twist special in your head and make it go bad. Tate and I falling in love was just that, a biker and his biker babe falling in love. It was something else for Dalton and that was on Dalton. After searching my whole life, I wasn't going to finally find special and let some psychopath twist it and make it go bad.

No, I was going to hold it precious.

Forever.

As for my family, we'd had a pretty good Christmas, considering I was still banged up and in some pain. As I suspected, Mom had spoiled Jonas but she'd also spoiled Tate and me. Jonas definitely had a good Christmas, what with Mom, Carrie, Pop, Stella, Wood, and me giving him his every heart's desire (and some of them he didn't even know he wanted). It had taken us hours to unwrap presents.

Tate had left me to spoil Jonas and he'd just spoiled me. He'd had a silver necklace custom-made, a fall of five exquisite silver flowers in a pendant hanging from it, the links in the chain were unusual and beautiful. He'd also had a set of five silver bangles made, two had flower pendants dangling, three had been inset all around with peridot and rose quartz. He'd also had a wide silver band made, it fit my index finger, went from base to knuckle and it was also inset with peridot and rose quartz. He'd given them to me telling me, right in front of everyone, "From now on, babe, you only wear my silver." This, I figured, was healthy indication that he intended to add to my new silver collection and since Tate had good taste, the jewelry so gorgeous, I didn't mind that at all.

Even with Mom and Carrie's great cooking, family and friends all around (because practically everyone in Carnal trooped through our house the last few days), and almost constant Christmas music being played (because I might give in to Tate and Jonas not liking it much but Mom was a Christmas Music Freak and she knew I loved it too and I'd been abducted, beaten and stabbed so she was going to play my beloved Christmas music even if Tate was a badass) things hadn't been good.

We'd had to unplug the phone so many people were calling and not just friends and family. My ex-friends from Horizon Summit had all phoned and Tate was not very diplomatic when he'd answered these calls, usually saying something like, "You one of those who hung Laurie out to dry when her fuckwad husband was cheating on her?" Pause for answer then, "Bullshit, go fuck yourself," then disconnect (when Carrie heard this, she burst out laughing, every time).

We also had calls from journalists for print and television and even a production company that wanted to pitch a reality program, starring Tate.

Not joking. A reality program starring Tate.

"No, Dad!" Jonas shouted from the floor, taking my mind off my thoughts. Jonas was nearly bouncing in excitement and not taking his eyes from the TV screen.

"Nittany Lions fans still feel the pain remembering Jackson's professional football career being cut short when he was hit with an illegal tackle in the end zone after forcing a fumble, recovering it and entering the end zone in a monumental touchdown in the last seconds that won the Eagles the game against their rivals the Giants," the commentator continued.

"After leaving football," the other commentator took up the story, "Jackson became a decorated police officer and is now one of the most sought after, and successful, fugitive apprehension agents in the country." He grinned devilishly at the camera. "That's *bounty hunters* to those of us not in the game."

"But, little would he know," the other commentator butted in, his voice had gone grave, "that two days before Christmas Eve, Jackson would be hunting a serial killer who'd murdered his ex-girlfriend, an employee, and a string of other young, innocent females over a four-year period and who had, that very night, abducted Jackson's fiancée."

The commentators switched. "Even with the murderer on the loose for four years, the Federal Bureau of Investigation failed to crack the case. But Jackson cornered the killer within an hour and handed him over to the local authorities, saving the life of a local, who'd been stabbed, and his fiancée, who had been stabbed and beaten but luckily otherwise unharmed."

"Bullshit," Tate muttered. "Total bullshit."

"Tate," I whispered. "Shush."

"Let's take a look at Tatum Jackson's career," the commentator invited with a warm smile and then we were treated to a montage with a prerecorded voiceover and sappy music playing over a variety of live action and still pictures of Tate's short football career with some still frames of Tate's longer bounty hunter career.

These were pictures I recognized from Loretta's stalker site, pictures I knew would mean about seven thousand new Tate Stalker Sites were going to spring up. The football footage included the tackle that took out Tate's knee. A late tackle and dirty, made by an offensive lineman who was unbelievably huge, and, worst of all, it looked like it freaking *hurt* and I could have done without seeing *that*.

The montage done, with a photo in the top, left corner of the screen of Tate, looking tired, but definitely still smokin' hot, striding purposefully toward the hospital, his eyes straight, his hand on Jonas's shoulder, Jonas's face blurred out, the camera closed in on one of the sports commentators as he looked soberly straight into the camera.

"They blurred out my face!" Jonas shouted, clearly aggrieved.

"Every Sunday," the commentator's voice was low and serious, "we report to you about the heroes of the gridiron. Many of those men do good deeds but not many of them save lives. Tatum Jackson, a promising recruit for the Eagles, had his football career cut tragically short. But the real tragedy would have been if Jackson had not gone on to protect the people of the town of Carnal, Colorado, and the future victims of the vicious May-December Murderer. Our hats off to you, Jackson. You are a *true* hero."

"Fucking hell," Tate muttered and I giggled, which was bad since it hurt my side.

"I liked it," Mack declared, lying on the floor with Jonas and Carrie. He rolled to his back and looked up at Tate and me. "Pure drama, absolute class."

Tate scowled at the screen and ignored Mack. "They didn't mention Jim-Billy."

"We all love Jim-Billy but, it must be said, Jim-Billy isn't as hot as you, Tate," Carrie noted, also turning but lifting up with her forearms in Mack's chest. "And, as far as I know, he didn't make the All-American Team." She hesitated before finishing, "Twice."

"I think we should do the reality show," Jonas chimed in. "That would be *so cool*!"

"We?" I asked Jonas.

"Bub, get that outta your head. Not gonna happen," Tate said over me.

"We!" Jonas ignored Tate. "You, me, and Dad. You and me will be, like, the brains behind the action, doin' searches on Dad's computer and, I don't know, other stuff."

"The brains behind the action," Dad murmured through a chuckle.

"Laurie would look hot on TV." Jonas thought this was enticement but it was not.

"Reason one not to do it," Tate said to Jonas.

"Why is that reason one?" Jonas asked his father.

"Bub, it isn't gonna happen," Tate repeated.

"She'd be hot, you'd be cool, and I'd be famous!" Jonas shouted.

That's when Tate got mad, so mad, he didn't weigh his words.

"You think Dalton McIntyre is the only cracked fuckwad out there? You want Laurie on TV so any sick fuck can fixate on her? Bub. It. Is. *Not*. Gonna. *Happen*."

Jonas's face got pale and my body got tight. Then Jonas shot up from the floor and ran from the room.

I started to make a move, mumbling, "I'll go—"

"I'll go," Mom said over me, didn't look at anyone, and swept from the room.

Dad got up from the armchair announcing, "We're out of beer."

"We aren't, Dad, there's—" Carrie started but Dad interrupted her.

"We're out of beer," Dad stated firmly. "Mack, Carrie, you comin' to town with me?"

Carrie looked down at Mack and Mack looked up at Carrie. Then without glancing in any direction but the door, Dad, Mack, and Carrie walked out of it.

Carefully, because my stab wound miraculously didn't hit anything vital, but it still hurt like a mother, I twisted to look up at Tate.

"Baby, you should go talk to Jonas."

Tate was staring at the TV screen, a commercial now on, he lifted the remote and I heard it go mute. Then he looked down at me and I held my breath at the anger still darkening his features.

"What happened to you isn't exciting. The aftermath of it, with those fuckin' buzzards circling, isn't cool. It's fucked. He needs to get that."

"He's coping," I said softly, "the only way he knows how."

"And you?" Tate shot back a question that confused me.

"Me, what?" I asked.

"I was in that house, Lauren. When we went after Jim-Billy, I saw where he had you. I saw what you saw. I saw your blood on that mattress. Are *you* coping?"

"Well…," I said. "Yeah."

He stared at me, his jaw went hard and a muscle ticked there.

Then he bit out, "Bullshit."

I turned fully to him. I was lying partly on him, partly on the couch but my movements brought me fully on him. They also hurt but I fought back the pain and put my hand to his heavily stubbled jaw. He hadn't shaved, not since that night. He was growing back the beard, for me.

"Honey," I whispered. "I'm okay."

"I saw what you saw and I wasn't tied to a mattress," Tate repeated.

"I'm okay," I repeated.

Then Tate glared at me, his entire frame tensed the length of mine and he roared, "He cut off your goddamned *hair*!"

I stilled and stared at him as Tate shifted out from under me and stalked out of the room. I lay on the couch continuing to stare at where I last saw him. I knew something like this was going to happen eventually. Tate had been nursing a slow burn for days and Tate wasn't the kind of man to let it smolder and then burn out. He was the kind of man who let it explode.

Gingerly, I got to my feet and followed him.

As I did, my hands went to my hair, which Dominic had come to the hospital to do an emergency cut and style on the day I was released, making it seriously nice, Dom showing up like that. But he'd said reporters were outside and "no girlie of mine is gonna face the media with bad hair."

Dalton hadn't got the chance to take it all. It now brushed my shoulders and it looked good because Dominic was a master. That said, I liked it better longer and, apparently, so did Tate.

I hit the bedroom and saw Tate standing, staring out the side window to which he'd yanked up the blinds.

"Tate—" I started the minute I hit the room.

He turned sharply toward me and I stopped talking *and* moving when I caught the look on his face.

"Neet's hair was there, and Tonia's, and Sunny's and yours was in a bag, ready for his trophy wall. Jim-Billy hadn't shown up, you'd have been on that wall, Lauren."

"But I wasn't," I whispered.

"We would have been too late," Tate ground out.

"You don't know that."

"He didn't hit anything important with his first thrust. He had enough time to get in a second, a third, he could have cut you places, babe, places that only I—"

"Stop it, Tate." I was still whispering.

"I should have killed him."

"Stop it."

"He cut your *hair*. He cut *you*. You didn't see Jonas, babe, you were livin' your nightmare and me and my boy were livin' an entirely different one but, trust me, Ace, it was a fuckin' nightmare."

"I know," I whispered.

"I don't need that shit from the TV to remember it. I don't need it on the phone. I don't need it in town. I don't need it shoved down my throat everywhere I turn which means I don't need it from my *son*."

I moved as swiftly across the room as I could and put my hands to his abs.

"Lower your voice, Captain," I hissed.

"He took you from me," Tate bit back.

"He didn't, Tate, I'm right here," I reminded him.

"He took you from me, right from my goddamned house."

"He didn't. I'm right here."

"I called him to take you to work, bring you home. I trusted that sick fuck to keep you safe and he took you from me."

There it was, the crux of his anger. Tate was blaming himself.

I pressed into him, lifting my hands to hold each side of his head and I shook it, repeating, "Baby, *I'm right here*."

Tate closed his eyes.

"You didn't do anything wrong," I whispered and Tate opened his eyes.

"I trusted that sick fuck to keep you safe," he repeated.

"I trusted him too," I told him. "I opened the door to him. So did Tonia. So did Neeta." I fitted myself into his front and slid the fingers of both of my hands into his hair, pulling his neck to bent and his face closer to mine. "And I didn't do anything wrong either. He's crazy and now he's incarcerated."

"It's gonna haunt you," he informed me.

"It's not me who's not sleeping," I reminded him and his whole body jerked.

This was true. I'd only been home three days but every night I knew he woke because, when he did, he woke me. And when I was in the hospital, he stayed with me all day, all night, the last night climbing into my hospital bed with me and holding me close. I woke twice because hospitals were noisy and both times I saw Tate awake, eyes open, staring at the ceiling.

I pushed up on my toes so my face was an inch from his and I whispered, "You're beside me, baby, I'm sleeping just fine."

Both his hands came up to cup the back of my head as he murmured, "Laurie."

"I lay on that mattress and I knew you'd find me. I ran through those woods, Tate, and I knew you'd be looking for me. I was shouting because I knew you'd hear me. And I ran right into you because you were coming for me."

His mouth lowered to mine. "Baby."

"Mack's right, that was pure drama on TV but what they said was true. You might have made a lot of money playing football but you make this world a safer place doing what you do and you didn't even know the faceless people whose futures you changed by putting bad guys behind bars. But now one of them isn't faceless, Captain. She's standing right here."

"Jim-Billy—"

"Got there first," I cut him off. "But you were not even ten minutes behind. Dalton was taking his time, he had all night. Even if Jim-Billy didn't get there, you would have."

"Lauren—"

"And you think, knowing that, knowing that four years they've been looking for him, four years and ten women before me, he only had an hour with me before you got to me, you think after that, I lay my head on a pillow by yours and I relive it? You think I can't cope? You think I don't know I'm safe, right here, beside you?"

His hands at my head lifted me up a centimeter and his head slanted, his mouth taking mine in a wet, thorough kiss that would have been fantastic if it hadn't made my breathing erratic, which made my wound hurt.

When his mouth let mine go, I whispered, "I love you kissing me, honey, but—"

"Right," he muttered, cutting me off. Then he let me go, stepped back, bent and lifted me in his arms. He carried me to the living room, set me gently on the couch, threw the blanket over my legs and then put his fists in the couch on either side of my hips, his torso bent, his face in mine.

"I'm gonna go talk to Jonas," he said softly.

"Good idea," I replied and smiled but he didn't move away. Instead his eyes did a scan of my face.

His hand lifted and cupped my jaw.

Then he whispered, "You humble me."

I blinked then breathed, "What?"

"Your strength, Ace, it's got nothin' to do with boot camp."

I somehow managed to swallow and smile at the same time even while fighting back tears.

"Tate—"

"You gonna help me have sweet dreams again, baby?" he asked softly.

"I'll try," I answered.

"It's fresh and it ain't gettin' any less fresh," he shared.

"We'll settle," I promised him.

He didn't look like he believed me and I'd know why when he spoke again.

"That hour, Lauren, that hour he had you, that's an hour I'll never forget in my whole fuckin' life."

My hands came up to frame his face. "I'll help you."

"I know you'll try but I'm tellin' you, I'll never forget it, not in my life."

"Baby, don't let him do that to you."

"He took your hair, he took your blood, and that's what he took from me."

"My hair will grow back and my wound will heal," I told him. "And we'll get back what he took from you, Captain. I swear, we'll get it back."

"Ace—"

"You gave me sweet dreams, Tate, now I get to return the favor."

Tate stared at me and I held his handsome face in my hands as I stared back.

Then he whispered, "Love you, Ace."

"Love you too, Captain."

He touched his lips to mine, ran his nose along mine, then he pulled away and went to his son.

I looked to the TV and then grabbed the remote to switch channels. On my third press of the button, I saw Tate's picture on another halftime show and I hit the button to turn off mute.

Then I turned the volume down so Tate wouldn't hear as I listened to the commentators bragging about my old man.

EPILOGUE

Special

I WALKED OUT of our bedroom wearing a robe, my long, wet hair combed back, a wide headband pulling it away from my face, my cell phone in my hand.

Jonas and Tate were camped out on the new furniture in the living room watching Saturday morning, collegiate football preshows.

I was pretty pleased with the results of my seven-month search for the perfect living room furniture. The couch and armchairs were wide-seated, comfy and inviting and nearly brand-spanking new but not in a way where you didn't feel like you could eat spaghetti or drink Kool-Aid on them. The new tables were rustic and sturdy so you didn't hesitate putting your drink on them. Though I bought coasters and nagged my boys to use them, something I had to do often considering they were clearly deaf to my explanations of the importance of coasters. The new carpet was thick pile, wool, and cost a mint but looked freaking fabulous.

The newly painted walls were studded with pictures, not paintings or prints, of family and friends. Some small frames, some large, some multi. There were photos of us on the beach in Saint Thomas last spring break. There were photos of our trip to Indiana last summer. There were photos of the New Year's party Krys threw at Bubba's because Jim-Billy was out of the hospital and getting around. Photos of barbecues at our house, Pop's house, Wood's house. Photos of us horsing around in Ned and Betty's pool. Photos inside Bubba's of the staff and the regulars, some of them just our friends, some of them me or Tate or both of us with our friends.

The biggest was the photo of Tate, Jonas and me and it hung on the wall over the TV. In it, Tate wearing his dark suit, Jonas wearing his dark suit, me wearing a form-fitting, cream silk, boat-necked dress, the hem hitting above my knee, sexy, pink strappy sandals on my feet and a massive bouquet of delicate, pale pink peonies and roses in my hand. Tate had his arm around my shoulders, my front was to his side, my arm was around his waist, my other arm, hand holding my bouquet, around Jonas's chest. You couldn't see it for the flowers but Tate's fingers were curled around Jonas's shoulder. Jonas was standing in front of us, his back pressed tight to our bodies. Jonas and I were smiling straight into the camera but Tate's head was tipped slightly back and to the side because he'd just burst out laughing.

Our wedding day.

I poured myself a cup of coffee and Tate's eyes came to me as I pulled out the stool to the island and sat at it. I smiled at him and I knew it was a soft smile, barely there. I felt my eyes get soft too, just from seeing my old man lounging on our new couch.

Then I looked down at my phone and went to my contacts, found who I was looking for, hit the button to call and I put my phone to my ear.

"Hey, honey." I heard in my ear.

"Hi, Matt," I said back.

It was my birthday.

"How you doin'?" Matt asked.

"Peachy. You?" I asked back.

"Good. This is early, something up?"

"Got big plans for the day," I told him.

"Yeah? What're you doin'?"

I told him and we talked and laughed and about fifteen minutes in I saw Tate move. He got up off the couch and I heard him say, "Bub, shower, we gotta go soon."

Then he came to me, pulled my wet hair off my shoulder, bent and kissed my neck. His hand came out to mine lying on the island. When it did, his thumb tweaked the two rings there, my engagement diamond and a very wide gold wedding band.

Then he pulled away and turned to the living room to see Jonas hadn't moved.

"Bub, I said shower," he repeated and Jonas sighed, got up and started to slink out of the living room.

"That your man?" Matt asked in my ear.

I twisted my neck and watched Tate walk down the hall toward our bedroom.

"Yeah," I replied and I knew it sounded breathy and I figured that was uncool, considering Matt still hadn't moved on from Ellen.

But I couldn't help myself.

*   *   *

I was standing in my undies in the bathroom, putting the finishing touches on my hair.

Buster was sitting on the bathroom counter, her ginger eyes watching my hands in my hair.

Tate was standing in the doorway, wearing his suit pants and a dress shirt not done up, leaning against the doorjamb, arms crossed on his chest, watching my hands in my hair.

"You should wear it down, babe," he noted for the fifth time.

"Krys wants it up," I replied.

"Looks better down," he told me.

"Okay, but Krys wants it up," I repeated.

He didn't answer. I finished my hair and then reached across the basin to the shelves where I kept my hairspray. This meant Buster scampered. I didn't often use hairspray but Buster had made a habit of hanging with me in the bathroom. She'd been there when I'd given my hair a good shot and she was a smart cat. She learned quick she wanted to be nowhere near the bathroom when I was wielding a can of hairspray.

I was about to give my hair a good dose when Tate's body hit my back, his hands sliding along the skin at my belly.

His mouth dropped to my bare shoulder and he muttered there, "Like this underwear, Ace."

He would. It was pale yellow and all lace, a strapless bra and barely there panties.

"Captain—"

His big hand roamed up from my belly to cup my breast.

"I like it a lot," he murmured, his lips moving up to my neck.

"Tate, we're already going to be late."

I watched in the mirror as his head lifted and his eyes caught mine.

"Right," he muttered but the tips of his fingers trailed the lace at the edge of my bra and I shivered.

Tate felt the shiver. I knew this because he grinned then he let me go and walked out of the bathroom.

I dosed my hair with hairspray. Then I walked into the bedroom and dosed my body with perfume.

Then I went to the closet to put on my bridesmaid dress.

*   *   *

"How many kinds of fool am I?" Krystal, standing at the back of the church about to walk down the aisle, asked. "I'm marrying *Bubba* in a *church*."

I stared at her in shock.

And this was not because somewhere between seeing her yesterday at the bar and seeing her today she'd dyed her hair a deep auburn red (that looked fantastic, by the way).

No, it was because Krystal was nervous.

I looked over her shoulder at Jim-Billy who looked hilarious wearing a suit with a yellow rose in his lapel. I'd never seen him in anything but jeans, T-shirts, ball caps, and hospital gowns.

He was giving Krystal away. Krys didn't have a good relationship with her parents. So not good, they weren't even invited. Several months ago, right in the bar, Krys had asked Jim-Billy to walk her down the aisle and she'd done it in her usual Krys, no-nonsense type of way. Even so, when she did, Jim-Billy had stared at her, then he'd burst into tears and he'd sobbed huge man sobs in his beer for at least five minutes.

Then he said yes.

I got close to Krys. "You're not a fool, this is good," I assured her.

And it was.

Bubba was still working construction. Bubba was also still devoted to making certain Krystal felt safe and loved at all times. Bubba didn't drink at all anymore, even when he did shifts at the bar occasionally or when he hung there not occasionally. He never went fishing. Ever. Krys was his world and he'd devoted himself for over a year showing her that.

It took a while but she cracked. Then she let him back in and a week after she did, he wasted no time and tried to put a ring on her finger.

She didn't wear it for three weeks but eventually she gave in.

Now, today was the big day.

"It's good, honey, but I don't trust it," she told me.

"Krys—"

"He's Bubba. I know—"

I interrupted her. "He's Bubba and *I* know he's had a taste of a world without you and he wants no part of that."

"Right," she whispered, not believing me.

"I know something else," I went on. "I know what it's like to give up thinking there's something special out there and I know what it's like to have it walk into your life and I also know what it's like not to believe. But, honey, now I know what it's like to live something special every *freaking* day."

"Tate is—"

"Lucky," I cut her off again. "'Cause the something special I have is in *me* and I give it to him so he gives it right back. And that's what you've got. *You're* special, Krystal, and you deserve this and you deserve to know that Bubba finally gets it and he's going to do everything he can to give it back."

She shook her head. "Darlin', I ain't special. I—"

I got even closer and broke in yet again. "Took a chance on me and, doing it, gave me a shot at a beautiful life. Took a chance on Twyla when no one else would hire her because she's crazy. Took a chance on taking back Bubba even though you were scared. And you take care of everyone around you. You aren't sweet about it, but, honey, that doesn't mean you don't still do it." Krystal stared up at me and I finished, "Now, walk up that aisle with Jim-Billy and grab on to a bit of your something special."

"Okay," she whispered.

I looked in her eyes, saw she was settled and wasn't going to bolt. Then I looked at Jim-Billy and he smiled at me so I smiled back. I walked to the door of the church and saw Bubba, looking far more nervous than Krystal, Tate at his side at the front of the church. I grinned at Tate then nodded my head at the organist. She started playing Pachelbel's Canon.

I darted away and grabbed Krystal's bouquet from Holly and handed it to her then Holly handed me mine and dashed down the hall to enter the sanctuary by a side door.

I went to stand in the doorway and held my flowers in front of me. In my strapless, to-the-knee, skintight, way-too-sexy-for-a-church-wedding pale green dress (but Krystal insisted), I walked down the aisle smiling at Bubba then smiling at Tate.

After I arrived at the front, the organist trailed off and started playing the wedding march.

Everyone stood. Krystal and Jim-Billy walked down the aisle. I felt tears sting my eyes.

After the pastor declared them husband and wife and told Bubba he could kiss his bride, Twyla shot straight up from her pew and shouted very, very loudly, "*Yee-haw!*"

I burst out laughing but Bubba and Krys made out through Jim-Billy jumping up and adding, "About time!" Then Nadine jumped up and yelled, "Woo-hoo!" And others shot up, catcalling and shouting encouragement and screaming out cheers.

Bubba quit kissing Krys and they turned to face the congregation and, to be heard over the clapping and shouting, the pastor had to yell his introduction to the new husband and his wife.

Krys and Bubba walked down the aisle, having to stop to shake hands, receive tight hugs and weather hearty back slaps.

Tate came to my side and grabbed my hand. I leaned into him, grinned up at him, and we followed.

We had to stop too as Krystal and Bubba accepted a variety of biker-type congratulations and I felt Tate's mouth at my ear.

"Ace, have I told you how much I fuckin' love you in that dress?"

I kept my eyes glued to Krystal and Bubba's backs as my breasts swelled and my mouth murmured, "Um...no."

"Minute we're home, that skirt's around your waist, baby," Tate whispered, mouth still at my ear.

My nipples got hard and my neck twisted. "Tate, we're in *a church*," I hissed and his brows shot up.

"You sign the marriage certificate?" he asked.

"Yeah," I answered.

"So did I so I figure God doesn't mind. Fuck, babe, He made you that hot."

I glared at my old man.

Then I burst out laughing.

*   *   *

I was naked, straddling Tate, his cock still hard inside me and he'd just come, though I'd come earlier, twice.

I bent and pressed my torso to his, tilting my head back to kiss the underside of his bearded jaw.

"Jesus, Ace," he muttered, his arms going tight around me.

"What?" I asked.

"Danced all night, drank yourself stupid, and you still rode me hard."

I lifted up to look down at him. "I didn't drink myself stupid," I objected.

"Baby," he whispered, his eyes dancing. "You're hammered. You just let me do things to you that—"

I smiled because I had and the things he'd done were *fabulous*.

"It's my birthday and all day I've been at *someone else's* party. What? I don't get my own party?" I asked.

"Yeah, baby, you can have your own party every fuckin' night, you wanna party like *that*."

"*Excellent*," I breathed and heard him chuckle.

Then he rolled, pulling out of me, taking me to my back, him mostly on top of me, and he reached out toward the nightstand. He pulled open the drawer and came back with a square box wrapped in pale blue paper and tied with a wide, see-through, darker blue ribbon.

"Happy birthday, Ace," Tate whispered and I looked from the box to him. Then I grabbed the box and pushed up so my shoulders were to the headboard. Tate pulled up too, so he was resting on his elbow in the pillow. I ripped off the bow and paper.

The box said bangles and I couldn't wait to see them. Tate more than occasionally brought me custom-made silver jewelry he got in Gnaw Bone from a talented jewelry designer by the name of Jenna. Since Christmas, he'd added so many pieces to my stash that I'd lost count. They were all one-of-a-kind and they were all *fabulous*.

The paper fell away and I opened the top of the glossy cardboard jewelry box and in it I found a big, black key fob and on the key fob was an unmistakable insignia.

I blinked at it then I hooked the ring with my forefinger, pulled it out of the box and tossed the box to the floor beside the bed to join the paper and ribbon.

"What is this?" I asked.

"Escalade hybrid. It's parked at Wood's garage. We'll go down tomorrow to get it."

I blinked again and stared at him.

"You bought me an SUV for my birthday?" I asked.

"Yeah," he answered.

"You spent tens of thousands of dollars on a *Cadillac* SUV for my *birthday*?"

"Uh...," he mumbled. "Yeah."

"*Tate!*" I screeched.

"Babe," he whispered, his eyes going to the door before coming back to me. "Keep it down."

"Are you nuts?" I hissed and watched his face go hard.

"No," he answered.

"You are. That's…a Cadillac…it's…*insane*!"

"Your fuckwad ex buy you that Lexus?" he asked and I stared hard at him.

Then I answered, "Yes."

"Then that's it. It's gone. I'm puttin' you in a Caddy that's far safer on mountain roads than that fuckin' Lexus that dickhead bought you. We get rid of it and there's nothin' left of him and your old life. It's just us. You, me, Jonas—"

I cut in, "And a Cadillac."

His face went soft and he grinned. "And a Cadillac."

"Tate, you don't even drive that fine of a ride."

"Yeah, babe, but I put scum in my truck," he informed me and then went on firmly, "You'll be puttin' you and my kid in yours and you'll be drivin' with Jonas around Carnal in a fuckin' Caddy."

Jesus, I loved this man.

"Okay," I gave in and it was his turn to blink.

"Okay?" he asked.

I curled my fingers around the key fob and said, "Yeah, okay, cool. When can we go get it? First thing?"

He stared at me and he grinned. Then his hand came to mine, his thumb forcing my fingers open, he took the key fob and tossed it on his nightstand.

His arms curved around me and he pulled me down into the bed, his lips coming to mine where he said, "Yeah, first thing, after you go down on me."

"Unh-unh," I shook my head slightly, my lips brushing his, "I get your fingers in the shower."

"Ace, you rode my fingers not thirty minutes ago."

I tipped my head to the side, again brushing my lips against his. "So?"

"So, tomorrow I get your mouth," he replied.

My hand slid from his back around to his front, where I wrapped it around his cock.

"How about you get my mouth now?" I whispered and I felt his mouth smile.

"Jesus, babe, I knew drunk sex with you would kill me."

I bent a knee, planted a foot in the bed and rolled him, my lips sliding through his beard and down his neck where I mumbled, "Thought you said you wouldn't mind dying this way."

My lips kept sliding down his chest and his fingers glided into my hair.

"Why don't we see," he growled because my hand was still wrapped around his cock and it was stroking.

"You got it," I whispered, then slid down farther.

Tate

Tate slid out of Laurie, kissing her gently as he did so. Then he rolled off and to his side where he reached to turn out the lamp on the nightstand.

Lauren rolled into him, fitting her body down the length of his back, her arm tight around his middle. He settled into the bed, he felt her lips kiss the eagle at his shoulder blade and then she settled, fitting her body deeper into his. His hand found hers and his fingers linked through, pulling her even closer as he lifted their arms to bent and pressed their hands to his chest.

"You good?" he muttered into the dark room.

"Oh yeah," she muttered back and he felt his lips smile.

"Sweet dreams, baby."

"You too, Captain."

He waited, like he always waited, for her body to grow heavy with sleep. It took about thirty seconds.

Then Tate followed her into sweet dreams.

About the Author

Kristen Ashley grew up in Brownsburg, Indiana, and has lived in Denver, Colorado, and the West Country of England. Thus she has been blessed to have friends and family around the globe. Her posse is loopy (to say the least), but loopy is good when you want to write.

Kristen was raised in a house with a large and multigenerational family. They lived on a very small farm in a small town in the heartland, and Kristen grew up listening to the strains of Glenn Miller, the Everly Brothers, REO Speedwagon, and Whitesnake.

Needless to say, growing up in a house full of music and love was a good way to grow up.

And as she keeps growing up, it keeps getting better.

You can learn more at:

KristenAshley.net
Twitter @KristenAshley68
Facebook.com/KristenAshleyBooks